OXFORD WORLD'S CLASSICS

THE WELL OF LONELINESS

RADCLYFFE HALL was born in Bournemouth in 1880. After an unhappy childhood, an inheritance from her paternal grandfather at 21 allowed Hall to pursue a life of leisure and romantic pleasure. In 1907, she fell in love with Mabel 'Ladye' Batten, whose cousin Una Troubridge would become Hall's lifelong partner. Though Hall published volumes of poetry in her twenties, her career as a writer of fiction began at 40, when she started work on *The Unlit Lamp* (1924). Other works would include *The Forge* (1924), *A Saturday Life* (1925), *Adam's Breed* (1926)—which won the Prix Femina Vie Heureuse and the James Tait Black Memorial Prize—*The Master of the House* (1932), and *The Sixth Beatitude* (1936). Hall's fifth novel, *The Well of Loneliness* (1928), was banned in one of the most well-publicized obscenity trials in British history. In 1934, Hall met Evguenia Souline, a Belarusian nurse with whom she would sustain an affair for the rest of her life. Hall died in 1943 and was buried at Highgate Cemetery, London, in a catacomb with Batten. Troubridge's biography, *The Life and Death of Radclyffe Hall*, was published in 1961.

JANA FUNKE is Associate Professor of English Literature and Sexuality Studies at the University of Exeter. Among other volumes, she has edited *The World and Other Unpublished Works by Radclyffe Hall* (2016) and, with Elizabeth English and Sarah Parker, *Interrogating Lesbian Modernism: Histories, Forms, Genres* (2023). She is the author of *Sexological Modernism: Queer Feminism and Sexual Science* (2025).

HANNAH ROCHE is Senior Lecturer in Twentieth-Century Literature and Culture at the University of York. She is the author of *The Outside Thing: Modernist Lesbian Romance* (2019) along with articles on queer modernism in *Textual Practice*, *Essays in Criticism*, *Modernist Cultures*, and *Modernism/modernity*. She is currently at work on a second book, *Houseproud: A Literary History of Lesbian Homemaking*.

OXFORD WORLD'S CLASSICS

For over 100 years Oxford World's Classics have brought readers closer to the world's great literature. Now with over 700 titles—from the 4,000-year-old myths of Mesopotamia to the twentieth century's greatest novels—the series makes available lesser-known as well as celebrated writing.

The pocket-sized hardbacks of the early years contained introductions by Virginia Woolf, T. S. Eliot, Graham Greene, and other literary figures which enriched the experience of reading. Today the series is recognized for its fine scholarship and reliability in texts that span world literature, drama and poetry, religion, philosophy, and politics. Each edition includes perceptive commentary and essential background information to meet the changing needs of readers.

OXFORD WORLD'S CLASSICS

RADCLYFFE HALL

The Well of Loneliness

With an Introduction and Notes by
JANA FUNKE AND HANNAH ROCHE

OXFORD
UNIVERSITY PRESS

Great Clarendon Street, Oxford, OX2 6DP,
United Kingdom

Oxford University Press is a department of the University of Oxford.
It furthers the University's objective of excellence in research, scholarship, and education by publishing worldwide. Oxford is a registered trade mark of Oxford University Press in the UK and in certain other countries

Published in the United States of America by Oxford University Press
198 Madison Avenue, New York, NY 10016, United States of America

British Library Cataloguing in Publication Data
Data available

Library of Congress Control Number: 2023951615

ISBN 978–0–19–289445–8

Printed and bound in the UK by
Clays Ltd, Elcograf S.p.A.

CONTENTS

Biographical Preface vii

Introduction xi

Note on the Text xxxiv

Select Bibliography xxxv

A Chronology of Radclyffe Hall xl

THE WELL OF LONELINESS 1

Appendix 429

Explanatory Notes 441

BIOGRAPHICAL PREFACE

MARGUERITE ANTONIA RADCLYFFE-HALL, later known as John Radclyffe Hall, was born in Bournemouth on 12 August 1880, the second daughter of Radclyffe (Rat) Radclyffe-Hall and Mary Jane Sager, née Diehl, a widow from Philadelphia. Her sister Florence's death at a year old, only a few weeks after Hall's birth, was swiftly followed by her father's desertion and her parents' divorce. From the age of 3, Hall scarcely saw her philandering father. Her mother's third marriage, to her singing master Albert Visetti, a professor at the Royal College of Music, brought further misery: Hall's 'disgusting old stepfather' made sexual advances from her early teens. Her education was perfunctory but varied: governesses and Mrs Cole's day school were followed by some months at King's College London and a year studying literature in Dresden. Intensely musical and introspective, she began to write poems under the tutelage of her first love, the singer Agnes Nicholls, three years Hall's senior. Their relationship was an overture to the twin themes of Hall's later fame: writing and what she would come to understand as sexual inversion.

At 21, Hall inherited a fortune from her paternal grandfather, Dr Charles Radclyffe Hall, liberating her from the family home and enabling her to divide her leisure between a Kensington town house and her country retreat at Malvern Wells. A life of cigarette smoking, hunting, occasional poetry, travel, and romantic intrigue followed: Hall's early loves were American cousins Jane and Dolly, courted while on extended trips to the United States, and her literary mentor Violet Hunt, eighteen years her senior. But it was not until 1907, while taking the waters in the German spa town of Homburg, that Hall met her first significant partner, Mabel Batten, a noted amateur lieder singer whom she had admired across the dining room of an Edinburgh hotel a year earlier, married with a daughter, and 51 to Hall's 27. Hall fell 'head and heart and soul in love with her', and Batten—or 'Ladye', as she was known—directed her reading and cultural education, introduced her to a sophisticated circle of women writers and artists, and encouraged her to publish three volumes of poetry. After the death of Ladye's husband George in 1910, the two set up home together, Hall adopting the name John along with masculine tailoring.

She converted to Roman Catholicism and established a vibrant home life with Ladye, including a menagerie of dogs, horses, and their 'beloved parrot Cocky'.

Ladye's death after a sudden stroke in May 1916 followed a period of domestic unrest. John had pursued affairs with two young married women: her friend Phoebe Hoare and Ladye's cousin, the sculptor Una Troubridge, whom she met in August 1915. John and Una would become life partners, well-known 'first-nighters' at London theatres, and celebrated breeders of champion dachshunds with the pedigree prefix 'Fitz-John'. But the first years of their relationship were shadowed by remorse. The guilty couple's quest for Ladye's forgiveness from beyond the grave led to their involvement in the Society for Psychical Research (SPR), and to legal action when prominent SPR Council member St George Lane Fox-Pitt denounced Hall as a 'grossly immoral woman' who had separated Una from her husband Ernest Troubridge and their young daughter. The widely reported slander suit against Fox-Pitt was won in November 1920, a few weeks before Una cut John's waist-length plaits into the Eton crop that would become her signature style.

At 39, Hall began her writing career in earnest with her first novel, *The Unlit Lamp*, initially titled *Octopi* and concerning the wasted life of a *démodée* New Woman heroine Joan Ogden, emotionally manipulated by her controlling mother. Although begun in late 1919 it was not published until 1924, shortly after *The Forge* (1924) and months before *A Saturday Life* (1925). Her fourth novel, *Adam's Breed* (1926), was her triumph, winning two prestigious literary awards: the Prix Femina Vie Heureuse and the James Tait Black Memorial Prize. All four novels were subliminally queer, through autobiographical undertones, same-sex attractions, gender-nonconforming characters, and unconventional family bonds, but the critical and commercial success of the bestselling *Adam's Breed* emboldened Hall to greater daring.

The Well of Loneliness (1928) was the first attempt to treat 'congenital sexual inversion' seriously in fiction. Issued by Jonathan Cape in plain covers and priced highly at fifteen shillings to deter casual readers, it was introduced by sexologist Havelock Ellis as a work of both 'accomplished art' and 'notable psychological and sociological significance'. Nonetheless, it caused such a furore that Cape felt obliged to withdraw the novel, and it was subsequently banned in its home country, Chief Magistrate Sir Chartres Biron ordering that all copies be destroyed. Although Biron's judgement was upheld on appeal, the controversy around its suppression, and the Bloomsbury intelligentsia who rallied in its defence, helped to further Hall's reputation on the global literary stage.

The Well of Loneliness was published across the world, appearing in a US 'Victory Edition' in 1929 after a ban was overturned on appeal, and in French translation by Troubridge in 1930. It established Hall as exemplar of and authority on sexual inversion and introduced the feelings of martyrdom and sacrifice that she would explore in her next novel *The Master of the House* (1932), based on the life of Christ. Hall's sense of herself as outlaw was evident in her restlessness and rootlessness as she moved between the South of France, Italy, and England, buying and selling homes in London and Rye. Restlessness marked her emotional life, too: in 1934 she began an affair with Evguenia Souline, a White Russian nurse who had been hired when Troubridge suffered a bout of enteritis in Bagnoles, France. Almost two decades after falling for Troubridge while living with Ladye, Hall entered into another uneasy ménage à trois that she would sustain for the rest of her life.

Hall's next major publication was *Miss Ogilvy Finds Herself*, a collection of five short stories of queer anguish and displacement, issued weeks before she met Souline in July 1934. By then, poor health, including a series of eye infections, colitis, pneumonia, and lung complaints, had disrupted her ability to write. *The Sixth Beatitude*, her final published novel, appeared in 1936, but *Emblem Hurlstone*, written in the mid-1930s, was never published, and *The Merano Shoemaker* was destroyed in manuscript. The onset of war necessitated another move to Lynton in Devon, where she was sustained by her Roman Catholic faith but beleaguered by both her health and the emotional turbulence of parallel relationships with Troubridge and Souline. In April 1943, she returned to London for treatment for an illness that would ultimately be diagnosed as inoperable cancer. She died on 7 October 1943 and was buried in Highgate Cemetery. Una, named as her sole executrix and beneficiary after a late change of will, took responsibility for her legacy, issuing *The Life and Death of Radclyffe Hall* in 1961. Una continued to write letters to John for as long as she lived.

INTRODUCTION

Readers unfamiliar with the plot may prefer to treat the Introduction as an Afterword.

'I would rather give a healthy boy or a healthy girl a phial of prussic acid than this novel,' wrote editor James Douglas in the 19 August 1928 edition of the *Sunday Express*. 'Poison kills the body, but moral poison kills the soul.'[1] The novel in question, published by Jonathan Cape on 27 July, had circulated safely and without scandal for three weeks, enjoying remarkably healthy sales and satisfying a robust (largely adult) readership. Vera Brittain had described it as both an 'important, sincere, and very moving study' and 'a plea, passionately restrained and never offensive', while L. P. Hartley had noted its 'earnestness and sincerity' and 'passages of great force and beauty'.[2] The novel's author, pictured alongside Douglas's article in a smoking jacket and bow tie, cigarette and monocle in hand, was already a literary celebrity: her fourth novel, *Adam's Breed* (1926), had won both the Prix Femina Vie Heureuse and the James Tait Black Memorial Prize in 1927, and her unusual appearance had raised both eyebrows and smiles across the world. 'Her flaxen Eton crop, monocle, and masculine style of dress make her a notable figure in any assembly', the *Westminster Gazette* had observed, while the *Houston Chronicle* had been more blunt: 'YOU ARE WRONG—IT'S NOT A MAN.'[3] Yet for Douglas, the writer and her novel posed a toxic threat not only to child readers but also to public decency, the Christian Church, and the very institution of English fiction. Radclyffe Hall's *The Well of Loneliness* was a book that must be suppressed.

Few expected Douglas to be taken seriously. As the *Wembley News* put it, he 'has achieved little except in making himself a laughing stock to every intelligent reader of his paper. To our minds there is

[1] James Douglas, 'A Book That Must Be Suppressed', *Sunday Express*, 19 Aug. 1928, 10.

[2] Vera Brittain, 'New Fiction: Facing Facts', *Time and Tide*, 9/32 (10 Aug. 1928), 765–6; L. P. Hartley, 'New Fiction', *Saturday Review of Politics, Literature, Science, and Art*, 28 July 1928, 126–7.

[3] 'Year's Best Novel: Award to Monocled Woman Writer', *Westminster Gazette*, 12 Apr. 1927, 7; *Houston Chronicle*, 8 May 1927.

not the least likelihood of this book being suppressed'.[4] Douglas's opinion piece had appeared in the August 'silly season', when real news stories and political updates are scarce, and its overblown style had placed it firmly in the category of stunt journalism. But against the odds, the combination of a publisher's apparent panic and a notoriously puritanical Home Secretary—Jonathan Cape quickly sent a copy of the novel, along with Douglas's article and a selection of positive reviews, to the infamous 'Jix', Sir William Joynson-Hicks—led to one of the most well-publicized obscenity trials in history. The vaguely defined law on censorship was, like Douglas's tone, a Victorian hangover. While the 1857 Obscene Publications Act had applied 'exclusively to works written for the single purpose of corrupting the morals of youth', the introduction of the 'Hicklin test' in 1868 shifted legal focus away from intention and towards impact: a book could be deemed obscene if it displayed a 'tendency [. . .] to deprave or corrupt those whose minds are open to such immoral influences, and into whose hands a publication of this sort may fall'.[5] But if the law was cloudy, the verdict, delivered by Chief Magistrate Sir Chartres Biron on 16 November 1928, could not have been clearer: *The Well of Loneliness* 'is an offence against public decency, an obscene libel, and I shall order it to be destroyed'.[6]

Though Biron admitted that *The Well of Loneliness* had 'some literary merit' that intensified its danger—'The more palatable the poison the more insidious'—the quality of Hall's book was, like her intention in writing it, largely immaterial. Jix later claimed that it was the duty of the Home Secretary to 'read such books or have them read', but he is unlikely to have read the novel in the two days between receipt of Cape's parcel and his hand-delivered reply.[7] When the verdict was appealed and upheld on 14 December 1928, Hall complained that 'the bench of magistrates [. . .] presumedly should have read the

[4] *Wembley News*, 24 Aug. 1928.

[5] Hansard, HL vol. 146, col. 329 (25 June 1857); Regina v. Hicklin, *Law Reports 3: Queen's Bench Division* (1868), 371.

[6] Sir Chartres Biron, 'Judgment', repr. in Laura Doan and Jay Prosser (eds.), *Palatable Poison: Critical Perspectives on The Well of Loneliness* (New York: Columbia University Press, 2001), 39–49 (49).

[7] Viscount Brentford (William Joynson-Hicks), *Do We Need a Censor?* (London: Faber and Faber, 1929), 15. Joynson-Hicks received the novel on 20 August, and his reply was delivered on 22 August.

novel before sitting in judgement upon it'.[8] *The Well of Loneliness* had reached a diverse range of readers, including such unlikely allies as 'a married coal-miner' from Doncaster, a London clergyman, and an Illinoisian 'woman past middle age, hating all things indecent and obscene', whose expressions of gratitude and respect Hall had compiled in its defence.[9] Yet the Home Secretary responsible for the novel's trial and the magistrates who supported its ban had presumably not read it. In the words of E. M. Forster and Virginia Woolf, Hall's 'restrained and perfectly decent' novel had 'obviously been suppressed because of the theme itself'.[10] The theme in question—'congenital sexual inversion', or inborn homosexuality—had, as indicated by the novel's 'Commentary' from leading sexologist Havelock Ellis (p. 7), long been the preserve of medical men. To quote Doncaster's married coal-miner, the subject of sex was 'that which we least understand'. But Hall's treatment of her theme, and her sensitive, straightforward, striking portrayal of her 'inverted' protagonist, would lead to Hall's recognition as one of the boldest queer pioneers of the twentieth century. When Douglas claimed that *The Well of Loneliness* would be 'read by people of all ages, by young women and young men as well as by older women and older men', he could not have imagined the novel's extraordinary impact, legacy, and identity-shaping power.[11]

Censorship, Sacrifices, Silences

The Well of Loneliness charts the development of its aristocratic protagonist, Stephen Gordon, who from childhood feels an innate sense of masculinity and desire for women. She eventually discovers her own identity as a sexual invert when she finds her recently deceased father's copies of key sexological works in his 'special book-case' and feels that she has been betrayed ('All the time you knew this thing, but because of your pity you wouldn't tell me', p. 203). After relocating

[8] Hall, unaddressed and undated letter (multiple printed copies), in the Radclyffe Hall and Una Vincenzo, Lady Troubridge Papers, Harry Ransom Center, University of Texas at Austin, 17.3; hereafter cited as Hall–Troubridge Papers. Copies of the letter were sent to Lytton Strachey and Sheila Kaye-Smith.

[9] Hall–Troubridge Papers, 17.3.

[10] E. M. Forster and Virginia Woolf, 'The New Censorship', *Nation and Athenaeum*, 8 Sept. 1928, 726.

[11] Douglas, 'A Book That Must Be Suppressed', 10.

first to London and then to Paris, and establishing a career as a novelist, Stephen encounters queer characters from all walks of life, from the sapphic salon hostess Valérie Seymour to the 'miserable army' (p. 344) of outcasts that frequents the 'merciless, drug-dealing, death-dealing' bars of Montmartre (p. 377). Stephen serves valiantly in an ambulance unit at the front in the First World War, where she meets and falls in love with a younger woman, Mary Llewellyn. Tormented by the knowledge that the world will not tolerate their love, Stephen engineers Mary's relationship with a man, Martin Hallam, who will provide marital stability and social protection. Stephen is left without a romantic partner, pleading to God (and to Hall's readers) for 'the right to our existence' (p. 428) and preparing to fight for the acceptance of sexual inverts through her written work.

At the time of the novel's publication and trial, Hall was no stranger to either the headlines or the courtroom. In 1920, she had successfully charged St George Lane Fox-Pitt, fellow member of the Society for Psychical Research (SPR), with slander. She and her partner Una, Lady Troubridge, had produced a 'research paper' detailing their contact with Hall's recently departed partner Mabel 'Ladye' Batten, Troubridge's cousin, via a spiritualist medium. When Hall delivered the paper to members of the SPR's Council, Fox-Pitt—a friend of Admiral Sir Ernest Troubridge, from whom Una had recently separated, and son-in-law of the Marquess of Queensberry, unsuccessfully sued for libel by Oscar Wilde—informed the SPR's secretary that Hall was a 'grossly immoral woman' who had 'come between [Una] and her husband and wrecked Troubridge's home'.[12] The trial that followed, haunted by the unspeakable spectre of lesbianism, went in Hall's favour: she was awarded damages of £500 (which were never paid), and Fox-Pitt resigned from the council. Though Hall's confidence and courage—some may say audacity—in taking Fox-Pitt to court cannot be denied, Una Troubridge does not once mention the slander trial in her hagiographic biography of Hall (1961). As Troubridge tells it, the conviction required to write and publish *The Well of Loneliness* was granted by the success of *Adam's Breed*. Hall had long wanted to write a book on sexual inversion, a term she used affirmatively, but 'her instinct had told her that [. . .] she must postpone such a book until her name was made'; while she understood

[12] 'Psychical Research: The Spirits of the Dead', *The Times*, 19 Nov. 1920, 4.

that 'the publication of such a book might mean the shipwreck of her whole career', she was prepared to lay her reputation on the line in the name of truth.[13]

It would be inaccurate to present Stephen Gordon as a fictional incarnation of her creator, but themes of martyrdom and self-sacrifice are central to the novel. The Christlike Stephen, born on Christmas Eve 1886, is named after the first martyr of Christianity (because her father 'admired the pluck of that Saint', p. 10), and she effectively martyrs herself by giving up Mary to Martin in Montmartre, the French capital's 'mountain of the martyr'. While Hall's alliterative patterning clearly suggests a certain inescapability—Stephen is trapped in a narrative of martyrdom from her earliest days at Morton—suffering saints make their presence felt in less obvious ways. Mademoiselle Duphot's blind and benevolent sister Julie, for instance, puts her faith in 'our little Thérèse' (p. 258), the Carmelite nun Marie Françoise-Thérèse Martin, who idolized the martyred Joan of Arc[14] and whose name brings together Mary and Martin. Hall, a devout Catholic, would later play up the narrative of her own martyrdom to maximum effect, publicly championing 'fearless' propaganda novels written 'in defence of the unpopular lost cause' and apparently developing stigmata when writing her next novel, *The Master of the House* (1932).[15] But even before *The Well*'s ban and her saturation in the spiritual, Hall was evidently driven by the idea of persecution for the greater good. Stephen must 'stand or fall by the courage of [her] love to proclaim its right to toleration' (p. 200).

If martyrdom is stitched into the very fabric of *The Well of Loneliness*, so too are themes of censorship and suppression. Douglas's 'healthy girl' is present in the form of Violet Antrim, Stephen's performatively feminine neighbour, who must be protected from the pages of a racy sporting newspaper (p. 108). We learn that Violet's henpecked father's 'taste in art was heavily censored, even on the walls of his own water-closet' (p. 108), while the unfaithful Angela Crossby must censor herself: 'Angela's caution was a very strict censor' (p. 159). Stephen's

[13] Una, Lady Troubridge, *The Life and Death of Radclyffe Hall* (London: Hammond, Hammond and Co., 1961), 81–2.

[14] See Explanatory Notes, note to p. 258.

[15] Radclyffe Hall, 'The Writing of Novels' (Hall–Troubridge Papers, 22.3), read for the English Club, Oxford, 24 Feb. 1933, and the Literary Society, University College, University of London, 2 Mar. 1933; Troubridge, *Life and Death*, 104–5.

father, Sir Philip, keeps his copies of sexological publications behind a row of books in a locked cabinet (p. 203); as an adult in Paris, Stephen will admire the 'splendid display of yellow bindings' (p. 253)—books wrapped in yellow paper to warn readers of their lascivious content.[16] Stephen's sexual otherness is difficult for some characters, including Stephen herself, to define or diagnose—'What in the Lord's name are you?', asks Angela (p. 143)—and Hall maintains a distinction between those who can identify inversion and others who, like Julie, are 'blind'. At Morton, characters with the knowledge or experience to recognize 'this thing' (p. 199) cannot discuss it freely: Philip favours 'absolute silence' (p. 27) with both Stephen and Lady Anna, and the queer-coded governess Puddle is bound by the 'tyranny of silence' (p. 121) that makes sexual difference taboo. Later, the kindly countryfolk of the Tenerife town of La Orotava, where Stephen and Mary enjoy 'enchanted' days and nights (p. 308) before making a home together in Paris, choose not to acknowledge the couple's relationship for what it is, considering it 'better to suppose that there is nothing to see' (p. 307). At a time when the very idea of love between women was hazy for some and unimaginable to others—an attempt to criminalize 'gross indecency between female persons' had failed in 1921—what is spoken and not spoken, seen and not seen, shapes the novel's plot and its characters' interactions.[17]

Hall's drafts of *The Well of Loneliness*, key extracts from which are included in the Appendix, show that the novel was not initially as 'restrained' as Brittain, Forster, and Woolf observed. A comparative reading reveals Hall's decision to censor her own work, softening discussions of sex and sexuality and removing or diluting moments of intimacy. A particularly direct conversation between Stephen and 'young Humphrey Brock the playwrite [*sic*]', an early Jonathan Brockett, was omitted from Chapter 30: Brock 'suddenly asked ~~an impertinent outrageous~~ her a blatant question: "Are you a Lesbian?" he had enquired. "No—I'm English on my father[']s side and Irish on my mother[']s." Stephen had told him, smiling' (Appendix, p. 433 (3.3)). Different in tone but similarly illuminating is a wartime embrace between Stephen and Mary. In the published version of events at Compiègne, affection develops through conversations and the gentle

[16] See Explanatory Notes, note to p. 252.

[17] Hansard, HL vol. 43, col. 567 (15 Aug. 1921).

stroking of a shoulder (p. 278), but the handwritten draft describes a night spent clinging together in a dark cellar, finding 'each other[']s lips there in that shell wracked darkness', with death coming near 'as though fascinated by such strange lovers' (Appendix, p. 435 (4.1)). Explicit instances of erotic intimacy in *The Well* are famously few and far between—'she kissed her full on the lips, as a lover' (p. 144) and 'that night they were not divided' (p. 304)—but the drafts are much more daring, lingering on risky themes (including menstruation, Appendix, p. 429 (1.1)). Though Douglas's outburst in the *Sunday Express* was exaggerated and, for many, unexpected, and while the strength of Stephen and Mary's sexual connection is plain to see in the published novel, Hall was clearly careful to share only the most palatable version of *The Well of Loneliness* with the reading public.

Style and Sincerity

High modernists, meanwhile, were having fun with fiction. Among 1928's array of sapphic-centred texts were Woolf's fantastical faux-biography *Orlando*, published just a month before the trial of *The Well of Loneliness*, and Djuna Barnes's 'slight satiric wigging' of Parisian salon culture, *Ladies Almanack*, which took a playful swipe at Hall and Troubridge.[18] As writers were subverting expectations of literary fiction, experimenting with narrative style, disrupting linearity, and bending and blending genres, the sincerity and stylistic conservatism of *The Well of Loneliness* appeared embarrassingly out of touch. While members of the Bloomsbury Group leapt to Hall's defence, they were quite clear that their support was for Hall's political cause rather than her creative prowess. Forster and Woolf's letter to the editor of the *Nation and Athenaeum*—where Leonard Woolf had reviewed the novel as 'formless and therefore chaotic', arguing that it 'fails completely as a work of art'—focused not on *The Well of Loneliness* but on the future of literary freedom: 'What of the other subjects known to be more or less unpopular in Whitehall, such as birth-control, suicide, and pacifism? May we mention these? We await our instructions!'[19]

[18] Djuna Barnes, 'Foreword', *Ladies Almanack* (New York: New York University Press, 1992), n.p.; see Explanatory Notes, note to p. 238.

[19] Leonard Woolf, 'The World of Books: The Well of Loneliness', *Nation and Athenaeum*, 4 Aug. 1928, 593; Forster and Woolf, 'The New Censorship', 726.

Their private comments on Hall and her novel were as caustic and as quotable as Douglas's own. Woolf's diary records an evening where 'we got drunk, & talked of sodomy, and sapphism, with emotion. [. . . Forster] saw [Hall] & she screamed like a herring gull, mad with egotism and vanity'.[20] Her own view was that 'The dulness [*sic*] of the book is such that any indecency may lurk there—one simply can't keep one's eyes on the page'.[21] In a letter to Woolf, Vita Sackville-West—the subject of *Orlando*—revealed that she felt 'very violently about *The Well of Loneliness*. Not on account of what you call my proclivities; not because I think it is a good book; but really on principle. (I think of writing to Jix suggesting that he should suppress Shakespeare's Sonnets)'.[22] In other words, Hall's principles were admirable, but her prose was not.

It is easy to see why readers have criticized the novel's style. The opening paragraphs, like the 'lovely women' they describe, quite clearly 'belong to a bygone generation' (p. 9), and sentences in the Morton scenes drip with sentimentality. Though Hall claimed that the only autobiographical elements were 'certain fundamental emotions that are characteristic of the inverted', the first half of the novel makes an obvious return to both literary and personal history.[23] It was in Malvern, not very far from the 'country seat of the Gordons of Bramley' (p. 9), that Hall wrote and published her early pastoral poems, enjoyed a romance with Violet Hunt, and fell in love and then lived with 'Ladye'. While *The Well of Loneliness* introduces the Malvern Hills as 'great green-girdled mothers of splendid sons' (p. 10), Hall's poems emphasize the queer potential of the natural setting: in 'Malvern, July 23rd, 1906', the evening is 'full of bygone things, | That mingled with emotions newly born', and 'The Meeting-Place' binds together 'my love | And Malvern Hills in Spring!'[24]

[20] Woolf, 31 Aug. 1928, in *The Diary of Virginia Woolf*, ed. Anne Olivier Bell and Andrew McNeillie, 5 vols. (London: Penguin, 1980), iii. 192.

[21] Woolf to Lady Ottoline Morrell, early Nov. 1928, in *A Change of Perspective: The Letters of Virginia Woolf 1923–1928*, ed. Nigel Nicolson and Joanne Trautmann, 5 vols. (London: The Hogarth Press, 1977), iii. 556.

[22] Sackville-West to Woolf, 31 Aug. 1928, in *Love Letters: Virginia Woolf and Vita Sackville-West* (London: Vintage Classics, 2021), 156.

[23] Hall to Gorham Munson, 2 June 1934, printed as *Radclyffe Hall's 1934 Letter About The Well of Loneliness* (New York: Lesbian Herstory Educational Foundation, 1994), 11.

[24] Marguerite Radclyffe-Hall, *A Sheaf of Verses* (London: John and Edward Bumpus, 1908), pp. 58–9, ll. 17–18; *Songs of Three Counties and Other Poems* (London: Chapman & Hall, 1913), pp. 13–4, ll. 19–20.

Writing *The Well of Loneliness* in Kensington a decade after she left Malvern, Hall clearly revisits aspects of her own past via Stephen (not least her old hunting habits), and she does so in an emphatically belated style. Stephen is a Victorian child, born in 1886, and Hall describes the events of her childhood in a manner and tone suited to the spirit and the literature of the age.

As the novel moves away from Morton and towards the metropolises of London and Paris, Hall's prose gathers pace and precision. Books One and Two are laden with ornate descriptions, but the long, nostalgia-heavy sentence beginning 'The good, sweet-smelling meadows with their placid cattle, she was going to leave them' (p. 202) in the final chapter of Book Two appears as a farewell to nineteenth-century aesthetics. Hall can never quite let go of archaic language ('anent', p. 355), dated structures ('Came the day', p. 421), or the opener 'And', which gives sentences the weight and solemnity of Bible verses, but the narrative voice—like Stephen—takes on a sharper and more modern character. For Leonard Woolf, 'as the book goes on, life and emotion die out of the language, and Miss Hall drops into journalese or the tell-tale novelist's cliches', but we might interpret the novel's stylistic development more generously.[25] While Hall favours readability over radical innovation, she experiments with both voice and perspective. From the deathly rhythms of war ('Dead streets— streets of death—death in streets and their houses; yet people still able to sleep and still sleeping', p. 272) to the catalogue of sights, sounds, and smells in the Passage Choiseul (pp. 252–53)—where the energetic prose, like an eager shopkeeper, beckons the reader in—Hall adopts new styles and sentence structures to keep up with the novel's changing events. There is a subtle Scottish quality to the narrator's voice when describing Barbara and Jamie's history ('dour', p. 349, 'timorous', p. 343); at other times, characters are held at a distance, and general observations allow for reflection or objective analysis: 'THERE comes a time in all passionate attachments' (p. 327). While the first half of the novel is overloaded with biblical and sexological allusions, and though Hall resurrects the portentous biblical tone in its closing chapters, the prose in the London, Paris, Compiègne, and La Orotava scenes is as varied as the locations themselves.

[25] Woolf, 'The World of Books', 593.

A counterpoint to Woolf's well-known 'dulness' remark is provided, perhaps surprisingly, by a breezy column in *The Tatler* in September 1928.[26] 'Priscilla in Paris' discusses having read *The Well of Loneliness* 'from cover to cover with breathless interest', finding that rarely had Paris been 'so well done'.[27] Hurried reports on the scandal surrounding Hall's 'Sex Book' or 'Sex Novel Dealing with Perversion' make it clear why Hall would insist on the high seriousness of her novel: hers was not a salacious page-turner, and she later took aim at books written 'with flippancy' or 'with an eye to sales, dirty, unworthy, lewd little books that their authors should have strangled at birth'.[28] But accounts like 'Priscilla's', from readers gripped by and keen to revisit Hall's prose—'very soon, no doubt, I shall read it again'—highlight not only the novel's broad appeal but also its multifaceted identity. *The Well of Loneliness* begins as a Victorian country house novel, but it goes on to capture 'the whole atmosphere' of Paris in the 1910s and 1920s, from scenes of decadence and debauchery in sapphic salons and gay bars to Adèle and Jean's traditional wedding in the Notre-Dame-des-Victoires.[29] *The Well of Loneliness* is a travel guide, taking its readers on a tour of Versailles and to the volcanic hills of northern Tenerife. It is a war novel, recording the extraordinary contribution of women who served in ambulance units at the front. It is a novel about the natural world, demonstrating the non-normative potential of plants and trees: Angela is 'like some queer flower' (p. 130), the 'queer, sensitive' Martin Hallam is stirred by 'erect, towering firs, [. . .] their girth that of giants' (p. 94), Mrs Breakspeare warns that love between women may spring up like 'mushroom growths' (p. 281), and Jamie and Barbara are like two saplings whose 'branches had quietly intertwined' (p. 342). It is a novel that examines the strength of human–animal connections: five years before Woolf published *Flush* (1933), her biography of Elizabeth Barrett-Browning's cocker spaniel, Hall (who, with Troubridge, was a celebrated breeder of champion dachshunds) imagines convincing and genuinely moving

[26] See Explanatory Notes, note to p. 357.

[27] 'Priscilla in Paris', *The Tatler*, 12 Sept. 1928, 482.

[28] 'Sex Book to be Withdrawn', *North-Eastern Daily Gazette*, 23 Aug. 1928; 'English Reformers get Way; Sex Novel Dealing with Perversion Barred', *Chicago Tribune* (Paris), 24 Aug. 1928; Hall, *Radclyffe Hall's 1934 Letter*, 10. Reports and reviews are collected in a scrapbook in Hall–Troubridge Papers, 24.3.

[29] 'Priscilla in Paris', 482.

communication and communion with Raftery (p. 125) and David (p. 329). Though *The Well of Loneliness* is 'seriously-minded', to quote Forster and Woolf, it is also funny: Hall may have thought it wise to reconsider Stephen's witty response to Humphrey Brock, but she does not omit moments of irony and comic relief (particularly in exchanges with Mademoiselle Duphot), and Brockett provides both sardonic humour and camp frivolity.[30] In short, *The Well of Loneliness* is far more sophisticated and stylish—and significantly less sombre—than readers have acknowledged.

Sexology and Sexual Inversion

At its heart, of course, *The Well of Loneliness* is a novel about congenital sexual inversion. The term originates in sexology, an interdisciplinary field of knowledge that emerged towards the end of the nineteenth century to explain the 'normal' and 'abnormal manifestation of the sexual instinct'.[31] Due to the slow and uneven dissemination of sexological knowledge in Britain, many of Hall's readers would have been unfamiliar with the new scientific language that she dared to use. According to Douglas, the theme of sexual inversion might have its place in 'scientific textbooks' but was 'utterly inadmissible in the novel'.[32]

It was Troubridge, not Hall, who first encountered sexology in 1913 when she consulted psychiatrist Hugh Crichton-Miller. To treat his client's sleeplessness, nausea, and depression, Crichton-Miller introduced Troubridge to hypnotherapy. The two 'talked psychology', and Troubridge immersed herself in studies of hypnotism by Auguste Forel and Albert Moll, pioneering figures in the field of sexology.[33] In 1918, as new members of the SPR, Hall and Troubridge studied psychoanalytic publications by Sigmund Freud, Sándor Ferenczi, and Carl Gustav Jung.[34] When Hall decided to write a novel provisionally entitled 'Stephen', the couple read Ellis and Jacobus X together, anticipating Stephen and Mary's shared enjoyment of books in

[30] Forster and Woolf, 'The New Censorship', 726.

[31] Havelock Ellis, *Sexual Inversion* (3rd edn., Philadelphia: F. A. Davis Company, 1915), p. v.

[32] Douglas, 'A Book That Must Be Suppressed', 10.

[33] UT Diary, 1913, Lovat Dickson Papers (H-1196 and H-1197), Library and Archives Canada, Ottawa; hereafter cited as UT Diary.

[34] UT Diary, 1918.

The Well of Loneliness.[35] Troubridge's 1928 diary includes notes on the first volume of Hirschfeld's *Geschlechtskunde* (1926), referred to as *A Manual of Sexual Science*.[36] A more personal relationship developed with Ellis. On 23 April 1928, Hall and Troubridge delivered a copy of *The Well of Loneliness* to the elderly sexologist who had promised to read the novel and 'let his opinion be quoted if he approved'.[37] Hall talked to Ellis 'for over an hour'; Troubridge waited outside until she was 'called [. . .] in to tea'.[38] Other sexologists mentioned in diaries, drafts, and notes include Iwan Bloch, Edward Carpenter, Richard von Krafft-Ebing, Karl Heinrich Ulrichs, and Otto Weininger.[39] What the couple encountered in their reading was a mélange of often contradictory terminologies and theories: sexology did not offer a monolithic or uniform framework but instead presented a set of contested terms and debates, which Hall, who identified as a congenital sexual invert herself, negotiated critically and strategically when writing *The Well of Loneliness*.

In the novel, the explanatory power of sexology is established immediately through Ellis's opening commentary, quickly followed by a reference to Ulrichs in the second chapter. Readers are encouraged to follow Philip's lead and turn to sexology to make sense of the 'narrow-hipped, wide-shouldered little tadpole of a baby' (p. 11) named Stephen who has 'nothing in common' with girls and (p. 74) is trying to 'woo' her maid (p. 25). After her father's death, Stephen feels instinctively drawn to his collection of securely locked and hidden sexological publications. The first 'battered old book' she consults is by Krafft-Ebing (p. 203), most likely *Psychopathia Sexualis*, published in 1886, the year of Stephen's birth. Guided by Philip's annotations, Stephen finds in sexology a language to understand herself as a sexual type, part of a community of 'thousands of miserable, unwanted people' (p. 203). That Stephen's initial response is one of despair is unsurprising to readers familiar with Krafft-Ebing's work, which equates the 'abnormality of the sexual function' with 'degeneration' and 'pathology'.[40]

35 UT Diary, 1926. 36 UT Diary, 1928. 37 UT Diary, 1928.

38 UT Diary, 1928. 39 Hall–Troubridge Papers, 12.5, 17.1, 17.3, 50.4.

40 Richard von Krafft-Ebing, *Psychopathia Sexualis: mit besonderer Berücksichtigung der Contraeren Sexualempfindung* (7th edn., Stuttgart: Ferdinand Enke, 1892), 34.

Mercifully, for Stephen, her all-night study of sexology does not end with *Psychopathia Sexualis.* As she pulls 'another of those volumes, and another' (p. 203) from her father's shelf, Stephen familiarizes herself with other sexological approaches. If Stephen initially feels branded with the 'mark' of Cain (p. 203), she is encouraged by Puddle to accept that she is 'as much a part of what people call nature as anyone else' (p. 153). Stephen's evolving understanding of sexology mirrors shifting arguments within the field itself, which Hall and Troubridge had followed. Having read the third revised edition of Ellis's *Sexual Inversion* (first issued in 1915), Hall noted that even Krafft-Ebing 'modifies his early ideas about inverts' in later works.[41] Ellis confirmed that 'It is now widely recognised that we gain little by describing inversion as a degeneration'.[42] According to Hirschfeld and Carpenter, sexual inversion was a 'universal and important natural phenomenon' and 'in a vast number of cases quite instinctive and congenital, mentally and physically'.[43] For these sexologists, as for Hall, sexual inversion was not merely to be tolerated, but to be appreciated. Ellis suggested that 'the congenitally inverted may, I believe, be looked upon as a class of individuals exhibiting nervous characters which to some extent approximate them to persons of artistic genius'.[44] Carpenter insisted that the combination of masculine and feminine traits in 'men and women of an intermediate or mixed temperament' made them uniquely qualified to become 'the world's greatest leaders and artists'.[45] Echoing these ideas, Puddle instructs Stephen to put her 'hyper-sensitive' nervous system (p. 45) and ability to 'write both men and women from a personal knowledge' (p. 204) to good use and claim her 'niche in creation' (p. 153) by becoming a writer. At least some of Hall's readers were already familiar with the image of the naturally gifted invert. Reviewer Cyril Connolly remarked drily: 'Most of us are resigned to the doctrine of homosexuals, that they alone possess all the greatest heroes and all the finer feelings.'[46]

[41] Hall–Troubridge Papers, 12.5.

[42] Ellis, *Sexual Inversion*, 321. The quote is included in Hall's notes (Hall–Troubridge Papers, 12.5).

[43] Magnus Hirschfeld, *Geschlechtskunde*, i (Stuttgart: Julius Püttman, 1926), 599; Edward Carpenter, *The Intermediate Sex: A Study of Some Transitional Types of Men and Women* (London: Swan Sonnenschein & Co., 1908), 55.

[44] Ellis, *Sexual Inversion*, 296.

[45] Carpenter, *Intermediate Sex*, 1, 38.

[46] Cyril Connolly, 'New Novels', *New Statesman*, 25 Aug. 1928, 614–15 (615).

Despite these affirmative uses of sexology, Hall's reliance on sexual scientific taxonomies has confused and frustrated readers. Leonard Woolf remarked that 'Miss Hall rather strangely calls her heroine an "invert"', choosing to refer to Stephen as 'a Sapphic or Lesbian' instead.[47] For Brittain, it was misguided to assume that Stephen was constitutionally different from other women: 'in describing the supposedly sinister predilections of the child Stephen Gordon, much ado is often made about nothing; so many of them appear to be the quite usual preferences of any vigorous young female who happens to possess more vitality and intelligence than her fellows'.[48] A review in the queer feminist journal *Urania,* most likely written by Irene Clyde, criticized Hall for accepting the sexological dictum that lesbian desire was connected to a masculine temperament: 'It was a gratuitous concession to popular foolishness on Radclyffe Hall's part, to make her heroine a little mannish.'[49] Indeed, *The Well of Loneliness* and its author have been credited with—and blamed for—forging an enduring association between lesbian identity and masculinity. Prior to the publication of Hall's novel, 'the uniform woman of the straight masculine silhouette' who donned 'mannish modes' was regularly discussed in English magazines as an icon of fashionable modernity.[50] Hall's own masculine attire inspired a range of interpretations in the 1920s. Newspaper and magazine articles covering the Prix Femina Vie Heureuse award in 1927 commented on Hall's masculine appearance without making a definitive statement about the author's lesbian identity.[51] *Eve: A Ladies Pictorial* praised Hall for being 'in the front rank of those active women who really carry off modern fashion'.[52] For Hall, as for others socially situated in the category of 'woman', masculine attire could serve as a marker of high fashion, emancipation, modernity, and/or lesbian desire. Some of this ambiguity was lost when the muscular, short-haired, cigarette-smoking, suit-wearing Stephen was presented to the world as an exemplary case of sexual

[47] Woolf, 'The World of Books', 593.

[48] Brittain, 'New Fiction: Facing Facts', 765–6.

[49] Anon., '"The Well of Loneliness" or "Cut by the County"', *Urania*, 75–6 (May–Aug. 1929), 1–2 (2).

[50] Lady Forbes-Robertson, 'Dress and the Woman', *Evening Standard*, 21 Apr. 1925, 11; 'Modes on Mannish Lines', *The Sphere*, 30 Oct. 1926, 216.

[51] 'Masculinity', *Glasgow Bulletin and Scots Pictorial*, 13 Apr. 1927.

[52] 'Miss Radclyffe Hall', *Eve: A Ladies Pictorial*, 13 July 1926.

inversion. Combined with Hall's own public persona, *The Well of Loneliness* helped to solidify the image of the 'mannish lesbian' in the popular imagination.

Hall's deliberate engagement with the term 'sexual invert' also raises questions about whether Stephen should be read as a lesbian in the first place. The typology of sexual inversion conflated same-sex desire and gender nonconformity. From 1910, sexologists began to tease apart what would nowadays be described as homosexual and trans identities, introducing new terms like 'transvestitism' (Hirschfeld) and 'sexo-aesthetic inversion' and 'Eonism' (Ellis) to refer to the latter.[53] Ellis suggested in 1915 that the 'inverted woman's masculine element may, in the least degree, consist only in the fact that she makes advances to the woman to whom she is attracted'.[54] Hall, however, remained invested in a conceptualization of sexual inversion that presented gender and sexuality as inseparable. Stephen's masculinity is a vital part of her identity, signalling her attraction to women as well as her orientation towards 'a man's life, the life that should have been hers' (p. 100). She has 'never felt like a woman' (p. 200), finds herself in the 'no-man's-land of sex' (p. 77), and wants others 'to treat her as a man' (p. 99). It is no surprise, then, that Stephen has resonated with readers as a trans masculine or non-binary as well as a lesbian character. Hall's interest in gender inversion is even more pronounced in her short story 'Miss Ogilvy Finds Herself', which was completed in 1926 but published after *The Well of Loneliness* in 1934. Having served in the First World War, the masculine Miss Ogilvy travels in time and finds herself in the body of a Stone Age man. Although Stephen and Miss Ogilvy are different characters, *The Well of Loneliness* and the earlier short story both reveal that trans and lesbian experiences are inextricably entangled in Hall's work.

Even if *The Well of Loneliness* is deeply informed by sexology, it cannot be reduced to a sexological case history. In the novel, references to sexual science sit alongside a wealth of religious, literary, and historical allusions. Certainly, Hall did not require a sexological vocabulary to be able to write queer characters, as Joan Ogden and Elizabeth Rodney in *The Unlit Lamp* (1924) and Sidonia Shore and

[53] Magnus Hirschfeld, *Die Transvestiten* (Berlin: Pulvermacher, 1910); Ellis, *Sexual Inversion*, 2.

[54] Ellis, *Sexual Inversion*, 222–3.

Frances Reide in *A Saturday Life* (1925) demonstrate. Drafts of *The Well of Loneliness* also show that Hall was critical of sexology, understanding its limitations as well as its appeal. In a deleted paragraph from Chapter 44, at the end of a lengthy discussion of sexology, the narrator exclaims: 'Dear Lord, what a truly appalling muddle! So many high-sounding, jaw-breaking names to explain the matter of sexual attraction. Was it strange that these folk with God's mark on their foreheads, often turned in despair from their erudite text-books[?]' (Appendix, p. 438 (5.9)). In the published chapter, Hall plays with and appears to poke fun at sexological language when referring to one of Stephen's acquaintances as a 'congenital poacher' (p. 344). Hall ultimately wrote *The Well of Loneliness* to correct what she saw as a shortcoming in sexology, a field that could only depict sexual inversion through a detached clinical lens. As Adolphe Blanc reminds Stephen, 'what doctor can know the entire truth? [. . .] the whole truth is known only to the normal invert' (p. 379). Hall asserted that 'being myself a congenital invert, I understood the subject from the inside as well as from medical and psychological text-books'.[55] Her hope was that 'by telling readers the truth, "The Well of Loneliness" would carry conviction'.[56]

In many ways, Hall's decision to use sexology to legitimize *The Well of Loneliness* was unsuccessful. The argument that sexual inversion was not only natural, but also inborn and unchanging, was intended to assuage persistent anxieties around seduction and corruption that underpinned definitions of obscenity. As Troubridge noted in her diary after reading Hirschfeld: 'there is a homo-sexual constitution, but there is no such thing as a true homosexual seduction'.[57] Douglas would have none of the 'born this way' narrative, asserting that 'moral derelicts are not cursed from their birth' but rather 'choose to be damned'.[58] Though Hall did not believe that anyone could become a 'true sexual invert' by choice, influence, or seduction, her novel raises knotty questions around the origins of sexual desire. Stephen's unconventional upbringing left some reviewers wondering whether her parents' 'intense longing for a boy may have had some psychological influence upon the character of their child

[55] Hall–Troubridge Papers, 17.3.
[56] Hall–Troubridge Papers, 17.5.
[57] UT Diary, 1928.
[58] Douglas, 'A Book That Must Be Suppressed', 10.

while yet in her mother's womb'.[59] Importantly, congenital sexual inversion is not the only sexological framework deployed in the novel. The fact that Stephen's lovers do not fit the typology of the inborn sexual invert was exploited during the censorship trial: in his judgement, Biron suggested that Stephen 'first seduced a married woman' before turning her attention towards Mary, 'a perfectly innocent girl' whom she 'debauches'.[60]

Hall took a risk in presenting Mary as a 'perfectly normal young woman' (p. 334), 'not much more than nineteen or twenty' (p. 270) when she falls in love with the older Stephen. Mary's 'normality' may signal heterosexuality, but Hall was also well versed in long-standing sexological and psychoanalytical discussions of bisexuality. She jotted down Hirschfeld's statistical estimate that 'there are more than 4 per cent (40 per thousand) who are bisexual' and, in 1934, informed her lover Evguenia Souline, with whom she conducted a nine-year love affair, that bisexuality 'is merely a very common fact in Nature', possibly 'the true normal'.[61] Although the novel's depiction of Mary as 'perfect woman [. . .] rest[ing] without thought, without exultation, without question' (p. 306) appears troublingly limiting, she is a complex and compelling character. Hall goes to great lengths to describe Mary's powerful attraction to Stephen, who is anything but 'maimed and ugly' (p. 203) when seen through her lover's eyes, and it is Mary who initiates physical intimacy with Stephen, 'stirred by some irresistible impulse, quite beyond the realms of her own understanding' (p. 276). While some of the eroticism of earlier drafts is lost in the published novel, *The Well of Loneliness* leaves no doubt that theirs is a sexual—and sexually fulfilling—relationship. In a letter to the Danish translator of the novel, Karin Michaëlis, Hall made the importance of intimacy clear: 'the book must not be shortened or altered by so much as a word. [. . .] Only, remember you will break my heart if you allow your public to think that I did not mean them to understand that actual physical relations existed. Stephen and Mary were lovers.'[62]

[59] Richard King, 'With Silent Friends', *The Tatler*, 15 Aug. 1928, 299–300 (299).

[60] Biron, 'Judgment', 45.

[61] Hall–Troubridge Papers, 17.3; Hall to Souline, 19 Aug. 1934, Hall–Troubridge Papers, 46.5.

[62] Hall to Michaëlis, 4 Mar. 1929, Lovat Dickson Papers (H-1198), Library and Archives Canada, Ottawa.

Other characters in the novel are entirely unburdened by sexological taxonomies. Though familiar with the language of inversion, Valérie Seymour, modelled on Hall's friend and lesbian extraordinaire Natalie Clifford Barney, is more inclined to find herself in the lyrical world of Sappho and ancient Greece than the sexological clinic. Through Valérie, Hall acknowledges that many of her contemporaries disturbed or dismissed the new identity categories provided by sexology. In this regard, *The Well of Loneliness* exists in conversation with other queer modernist texts, including *Orlando* and *Ladies Almanack*, and raises enduring questions about definitions and representations of sex, gender, and sexuality.

Claiming Kinship

In terms of its politics, *The Well of Loneliness*, like its protagonist, seems 'all contradictions' (p. 30). It is the great tragedy of Stephen's life that she combines, as Valérie puts it, 'the nerves of the abnormal' with 'all the respectable county instincts of the man who cultivates children and acres' (p. 397). While Stephen enjoys many of the privileges afforded to the landed English gentry, she is repeatedly marked as an outsider. Within the racialized logic of the novel, the 'warm Celtic blood' (p. 31) she shares with her Irish mother exists in tension with the English temperament she has inherited from her 'scholarly' father (p. 203). The novel insists on associations between Englishness and whiteness: Stephen and Anna are drawn to the 'white smell' (p. 30) of the English meadows, and the 'white Swan called Peter' (p. 185), described as 'the spirit of Morton' in an early draft, is 'proud in his splendid, incredible whiteness' (p. 101).[63] But although Stephen's body is 'so white, so strong and so self-sufficient' (p. 186), her relationship to Englishness is compromised. On two occasions, she is likened to 'some primitive thing conceived in a turbulent age of transition' (pp. 51 and 149). Echoing sexological associations of queerness with a 'primitive ancestral phase', Stephen's intense emotionality places her closer to nature and at a further remove from the civilized and restrained Englishness that she seeks to embody.[64] To consummate their relationship, Stephen and Mary must leave England and travel to La Orotava, where their desires appear as 'primitive and

[63] Hall–Troubridge Papers, 13.3.

[64] Ellis, *Sexual Inversion*, 313.

age-old as Nature herself' (p. 305). Instead of returning to England, they seek exile in Paris, making a home as 'lovers' (p. 319) on the Rue Jacob. Suggesting that queer desire cannot thrive in Stephen's homeland, *The Well of Loneliness* appears to confirm Douglas's claim that the 'battle against homosexuality had been lost in France and Germany' but not (yet) in England.[65]

This was a situation that Hall was eager to change. Her long-term success in doing so may be measured by a 1982 article by Kay Dick, who claimed upon rereading the novel that 'one appreciates why it shocked the English judicial establishment. [. . . Hall] was English, to her backbone, not some foreigner with odd moral values, and she dared to state what everyone [. . .] knew, that women did often fall in love with women, even in the shires'.[66] In the English Stephen Gordon, Hall depicted what she considered to be 'the finest type of the inverted woman'.[67] She hoped that *The Well of Loneliness* would succeed in 'spurring all classes of inverts to prove that they are capable of being as good and useful citizens as the best of the so-called normal men and women'.[68] In a manuscript entitled 'Ghosts', Hall argues that the First World War was 'like a Godsend' for inverted women: 'For the first time in their lives they were given a chance to justify their abhorred existence, nor were they slow to recognize their chance, and to serve their country with skill and courage.'[69] *The Well of Loneliness* imagines the war as a watershed moment giving Stephen and other sexual inverts the opportunity to 'come into the daylight' (p. 266) and prove their worth to the nation. In addition to her war work, for which she is awarded the Croix de Guerre, Stephen demonstrates her value to society in her role as 'a great author' (p. 355). Despite her considerable accomplishments, however, she feels tormented by her inability to offer Mary protection and social respectability through marriage.

Understandably, Stephen's 'inherent respect of the normal' (p. 420) has been a source of frustration for readers hoping to find in Hall's so-called Lesbian Bible a more radical and non-assimilationist queer politics. In *Ladies Almanack*, Barnes lampooned not only Hall's (allegedly) conservative style but also her conservative values, not

[65] Douglas, 'A Book That Must Be Suppressed', 10.

[66] Kay Dick, 'Man's Pyjamas', *The Spectator*, 18 Dec. 1982, 39.

[67] Hall, *Radclyffe Hall's 1934 Letter*, 2.

[68] Hall, *Radclyffe Hall's 1934 Letter*, 3.

[69] Hall–Troubridge Papers, 18.8.

least her idealization of 'Marriage'.[70] Hall was undeterred and remained convinced that most inverts wish 'to legalise their unions' and 'form a part of the social scheme, to conform in all ways to the social code'.[71] But even if Hall's assimilationist politics find ample expression in *The Well of Loneliness*, the novel also presents a damning criticism of 'securely established, self-satisfied people' (p. 357–58) like Violet Antrim and Lady Massey. In contrast to her upper-class neighbours, Stephen's personal and artistic development hinges on her ability to recognize as 'brethren' (p. 341) individuals who are unlike her. Her deep friendship with Jamie and profound bond with Puddle offer touching portrayals of relationships negotiated across differences in status, wealth, and age. In a pivotal scene, Stephen overcomes her instinct to disavow the decidedly unrespectable young invert in Alec's Bar in Paris, addressing him as ('My brother', p. 378) instead.

This is not to deny that Stephen's claims to kinship are often fraught with difficulty and tension. Like other white modernists, Hall was fascinated by Black artists of the Harlem Renaissance. On 20 June 1927, Hall and Troubridge attended a performance of spirituals by American singers Taylor Gordon, J. Rosamund Johnson, and Florence Mills at Wigmore Hall in London. An aftershow party hosted by the soprano and folk-song singer Ursula Greville provided an opportunity for the couple to meet the artists. After attending a second public concert on 27 June, Hall and Troubridge invited Johnson and Gordon to a private performance and dinner at their Kensington home on 14 July.[72] In her diary, Troubridge describes the dinner as 'very successful' and the party a 'huge success till 2.30' with 'nearly 70 people' in attendance.[73] Judging by an account in his 1929 memoir, Gordon also enjoyed the evening: 'we were invited to a dinner party by Lady Trowbridge [*sic*] and Radclyffe Hall, the writers, two very very interesting people—so singular. [. . .] Ursula Greville, who can sing old Irish and Scottish Folklore better than anyone I have ever heard held all spellbound, and our spirituals were well received.'[74] In *The Well of Loneliness*, Johnson and Gordon are fictionalized as the brothers Henry and Lincoln who perform for Stephen and her friends in Jamie's flat in Paris. The white audience imagines that the

70 Barnes, *Ladies Almanack*, 18.
71 Hall, *Radclyffe Hall's 1934 Letter*, 8.
72 UT Diary, 1927.
73 UT Diary, 1927.
74 Taylor Gordon, *Born to Be* (Lincoln: Nebraska Press, 1995), 214–15.

Black spirituals express a shared experience of being 'among the hopeless' (p. 351). The crass, racist description of Henry as a 'crude animal' and 'primitive force [. . .] rendered offensive by civilization' (p. 351) echoes the primitivist language used elsewhere in the novel to describe Stephen. Inspired by Henry and Lincoln, Stephen learns to embrace her own voice as an author to demonstrate her value to society and give expression to the struggles faced by 'her kind' (p. 369). Though apparently eager to reach across racialized divides, Hall engages with Black culture mainly to further Stephen's artistic growth. In many ways, *The Well of Loneliness* falls short of interrogating the racist ideologies and typologies that shape its narrative. This did not stop Black writers and artists of the Harlem Renaissance from engaging, sincerely and subversively, with the novel. Richard Bruce Nugent considered it 'a superbly written and conceived work' that was 'so very different from most novels on inversion, there is nothing sensational. Merely a story of an invert told psychologically and incidently [*sic*] with beauty and strength'.[75] Alain Locke was only unsure 'whether to admire most its beauty or its quiet bravery'.[76] Gladys Bentley's 1937 revue *Brevities in Bronze* included a number entitled 'In My Well of Loneliness', and Geraldyn Dismond reassured readers of the *Inter-State Tattler* that there were 'never no wells of loneliness in Harlem'.[77]

Endings and Beginnings

The much-maligned ending of *The Well of Loneliness* makes it clear that, for Hall, sexual inversion must be understood as a collective rather than an individual identity. Though Stephen sacrifices her relationship with Mary, she does not end the novel alone. Accepting the plea of the sexual inverts she 'dare not disown' (p. 427), Stephen will take up the responsibility to write on behalf of her kin, using her skills as a novelist—and her 'curious double insight' (p. 204), as

[75] Correspondence between Richard Bruce Nugent and Alain Locke, quoted in *Genny Beemyn, A Queer Capital: A History of Gay Life in Washington, D.C.* (New York: Routledge, 2015), 64.

[76] Quoted in Beemyn, *A Queer Capital*, 64.

[77] Ken Jessamy, 'Club Revue is Entertaining and Brilliant', *New York Amsterdam News*, 3 Apr. 1937, 16; Geraldyn Dismond, 'Social Snapshots', *Inter-State Tattler*, 29 Feb. 1929, 5.

Puddle defines it—to demand from God and her readers the 'right to our existence' (p. 428).

Novelist Arnold Bennett could not have been more wrong when he predicted, ten days before Douglas's attack, that Hall's 'cry for unprejudiced social recognition of the victims' would not be 'effectively heard'.[78] Though *The Well of Loneliness* was defeated in Britain, its rallying call reached sympathetic readers across the globe. Before the British trial, Jonathan Cape arranged for moulds of the type to be delivered to the Pegasus Press in Paris, where orders flooded in; on 16 December, two days after the failed appeal, *The Well of Loneliness* was issued in the US by newly formed publishing partnership Covici Friede. By January 1929, Hall had received more than 5,000 letters of support. 'In all these circumstances with letters still pouring in from all over the world,' wrote Troubridge to Ellis on 7 March, 'I do think we can all feel that as you said from the first, persecution has only served a good purpose & helped the book to do its work—at least 60,000 copies are now in circulation & it cannot now be killed or forgotten.'[79] When the novel was successfully defended against a charge of obscenity in the US in April 1929, Friede prepared a run of 225 copies of a special 'Victory Edition' to be signed by its triumphant author. Hall and Troubridge received the happy news of the verdict in Paris, where the novel was selling more than a hundred copies a day. They were delighted to see the text translated into eleven languages including Czech, Dutch, French (by Troubridge herself), and German. Nevertheless, Hall was deeply disappointed that *The Well of Loneliness* could not be sold legally in Britain: 'Until my book is permitted to come home I shall feel that I have a blot on my escutcheon.'[80] Her ambition was finally realized in 1949, when Troubridge found a publisher willing to take the risk: six years after Hall's death, London's Falcon Press issued a new edition without legal challenge or complaint.

The Well of Loneliness, after all, was a book that would not be suppressed. Despite the best efforts of Douglas, Jix, and Biron, Hall's novel would not only survive but would also give life, purpose, and

[78] Arnold Bennett, 'My *Brilliant* but *Bewildering* Niece', *London Evening Standard*, 9 Aug. 1928, 7.

[79] Troubridge to Ellis, 7 Mar. 1929, in the Havelock Ellis Papers, London, British Library, Add. MS 70539.

[80] Hall, *Radclyffe Hall's 1934 Letter*, 9.

a sense of belonging to readers of all nationalities, classes, and ages—including healthy boys and healthy girls. For the heroine of Alison Bechdel's 'family tragicomic' *Fun Home* (2006), published by Jonathan Cape, reading Hall's novel is a formative experience: 'my realisation at nineteen that I was a lesbian came about in a manner consistent with my bookish upbringing', reflects Alison, before an illustration depicts her hand taking a copy of *The Well of Loneliness* from a bookshelf.[81] Alison (or Bechdel) is one of countless young readers who have sought selfhood, self-help, and solidarity in Hall's novel. Among the correspondence that Hall and Troubridge compiled in 1928 is a letter from an English supporter who notes that they are 'yet almost a child, being not quite nineteen years, but for all that I have experienced many of the terrors of the invert. It being already some years since I realised my peculiarity'.[82] More powerfully still, a Jewish reader who encountered the Polish translation of *The Well of Loneliness* at the age of 12 or 13, prior to being held in a concentration camp, recalled that 'one of the ways I survived in the camp was by remembering that book. I wanted to live long enough to kiss a woman'.[83]

Though legions of LGBTQ+ readers have mocked the novel's style and despaired of its ostensibly bleak ending—Terry Castle reflects that 'Like many bookish lesbians I seem to have spent much of my adult life making jokes about it, as if to fend it off once and for all'—its continued role in the formation of lesbian, queer, and trans identities and connections is impossible to overstate.[84] It is significant that the closing paragraphs of *The Well of Loneliness* look to the future. The 'yet unborn' (p. 427) inverts who occupy Stephen's 'barren womb' (p. 427) will go on to gain recognition and acceptance. Stephen's novel, just like the one that we hold in our hands, will represent the voices of 'millions' (p. 427). Its articulation of sexual difference may well be of its time, but new generations of readers, of all sexualities and genders, will find themselves in its story.

[81] Alison Bechdel, *Fun Home: A Family Tragicomic* (London: Jonathan Cape 2006), 74–5.

[82] Hall–Troubridge Papers, 17.3.

[83] Quoted in Joan Nestle, 'Into the Mainstream', *Bridges*, 1/1 (Spring 1990), 98–104 (98).

[84] Terry Castle, 'Afterword: It was Good, Good, *Good*', in *Palatable Poison*, 394–402 (394).

NOTE ON THE TEXT

The Well of Loneliness was published by Jonathan Cape on 27 July 1928. This Oxford World's Classic reproduces the 1928 Pegasus Press edition, which was printed in Paris using moulds of the text supplied by Cape before the novel was banned as obscene in Britain.

Hall's handwritten and typed drafts, housed in the Radclyffe Hall and Una Vincenzo, Lady Troubridge Papers, Harry Ransom Center, University of Texas at Austin, show that the novel was extensively revised and entire chapters refocused or omitted before publication. The multiple drafts, along with Hall's detailed notebooks and records of Stephen Gordon's activities, reveal the finished novel to be much more polished and carefully plotted than has previously been acknowledged. The Appendix to this edition provides selected extracts from the drafts, allowing readers to note significant revisions and omissions, but it by no means offers a comprehensive comparative analysis. The editors hope that the Explanatory Notes and Appendix will serve as a springboard for future scholarship on Hall and her archive.

Some of the terms used in Hall's work and other sources discussed in this edition are outdated or offensive. In most cases, the editors have reproduced them faithfully for historical accuracy.

SELECT BIBLIOGRAPHY

Biography

Baker, Michael, *Our Three Selves: The Life of Radclyffe Hall* (New York: William Morrow and Co., 1985).

Castle, Terry, *Noël Coward and Radclyffe Hall: Kindred Spirits* (New York: Columbia University Press, 1996).

Cline, Sally, *Radclyffe Hall: A Woman Called John* (London: John Murray, 1997).

Dickson, Lovat, *Radclyffe Hall at the Well of Loneliness: A Sapphic Chronicle* (London: Collins, 1975).

Ormrod, Richard, *Una Troubridge: The Friend of Radclyffe Hall* (London: Jonathan Cape, 1984).

Souhami, Diana, *The Trials of Radclyffe Hall* (London: Weidenfeld & Nicolson, 1998).

Troubridge, Una, Lady, *The Life and Death of Radclyffe Hall* (London: Hammond, Hammond and Co., 1961).

General Criticism

Ahmed, Sara, 'Unhappy Queers', in Ahmed, *The Promise of Happiness* (Durham, NC: Duke University Press, 2010), 88–120.

Backus, Margot Gayle, 'Sexual Orientation in the (Post)Imperial Nation: Celticism and Inversion Theory in Radclyffe Hall's *The Well of Loneliness*', *Tulsa Studies in Women's Literature*, 15/2 (Autumn 1996), 253–66.

Baer, Brian James, and Liu, Yingmei, '"Queer" in Translation: The Case of Radclyffe Hall's *The Well of Loneliness*', *Transcultural*, 14/1 (Jan. 2002), 4–20.

Bauer, Heike, 'In the Canine Archives of Sex: Radclyffe Hall, Una Troubridge and Their Dogs', *Gender & History* (June 2022), 1–18.

Bauer, Heike, 'Stephen Gordon Super-Invert: The Sexology of Radclyffe Hall', in Bauer, *English Literary Sexology: Translations of Inversion, 1860–1930* (Basingstoke: Palgrave, 2009).

Breen, Margaret Soenser, 'Obscenity, Modernity, Identity: Legalizing *The Well of Loneliness* and *Nightwood*', *Journal of the History of Sexuality*, 4/4 (Apr. 1994), 603–24.

Brittain, Vera, *Radclyffe Hall: A Case of Obscenity?* (London: Femina, 1968).

Buck, Claire, '"Still Some Obstinate Emotion Remains": Radclyffe Hall and the Meanings of Service', in Suzanne Raitt and Trudi Tate (eds.), *Women's Fiction and the Great War* (Oxford: Clarendon Press, 1997), 174–96.

Cohler, Deborah, 'Boy-Girls and Girl-Boys: Postwar Lesbian Literary Representations', in Cohler, *Citizen, Invert, Queer: Lesbianism and War in Early Twentieth-Century Britain* (Minneapolis: University of Minnesota Press, 2010), 151–96.

Dellamora, Richard, 'Engendering Modernism: The Vernacular Modernism of Radclyffe Hall', in Lynne Hapgood and Nancy L. Paxton (eds.), *Outside Modernism: In Pursuit of the English Novel, 1900–1930* (Basingstoke: Palgrave, 2000), 85–103.

Dellamora, Richard, *Radclyffe Hall: A Life in the Writing* (Philadelphia: University of Pennsylvania Press, 2011).

Doan, Laura, *Fashioning Sapphism: The Origins of a Modern English Lesbian Subculture* (New York: Columbia University Press, 2001).

Doan, Laura, '"Miss Ogilvy Finds Herself": The Queer Navigational Systems of Radclyffe Hall', *English Language Notes*, 45/2 (Sept. 2007), 9–22.

Doan, Laura, '"Woman's Place *Is* the Home": Conservative Sapphic Modernity', in Doan and Jane Garrity (eds.), *Sapphic Modernities: Sexuality, Women and National Culture* (Basingstoke: Palgrave Macmillan, 2006), 91–107.

Doan, Laura, and Prosser, Jay (eds.), *Palatable Poison: Critical Perspectives on The Well of Loneliness* (New York: Columbia University Press, 2001).

Faderman, Lillian, 'The Spread of Medical "Knowledge"', in Faderman, *Surpassing the Love of Men: Romantic Friendship and Love Between Women from the Renaissance to the Present* (London: Junction Books, 1980), 314–31.

Franks, Claudia, *Beyond* The Well of Loneliness*: The Fiction of Radclyffe Hall* (Amersham: Avebury Publishing Company, 1982).

Funke, Jana, 'Introduction', in *'The World' and Other Unpublished Works of Radclyffe Hall*, ed. Jana Funke (Manchester: Manchester University Press, 2016), 1–46.

Glasgow, Joanne, 'What's A Nice Lesbian Like You Doing in the Church of Torquemada? Radclyffe Hall and Other Catholic Converts', in Karla Jay and Joanne Glasgow (eds.), *Lesbian Texts and Contexts: Radical Revisions* (New York: New York University Press, 1990), 217–40.

Glasgow, Joanne, 'Introduction', in Joanne Glasgow (ed.), *Your John: The Love Letters of Radclyffe Hall* (New York: New York University Press, 1997), 1–17.

Green, Laura, 'Hall of Mirrors: Radclyffe Hall's *The Well of Loneliness* and Modernist Fictions of Identity', *Twentieth Century Literature*, 49/3 (Autumn 2003), 277–97.

Halberstam, Jack, '"A Writer of Misfits": John Radclyffe Hall and the Discourse of Inversion', in Halberstam, *Female Masculinity* (Durham, NC: Duke University Press, 1998), 75–110.

Hill, Emily S., 'God's Miserable Army: Love, Suffering, and Queer Faith in Radclyffe Hall's *The Well of Loneliness*', *Literature and Theology*, 30/3 (2016), 359–74.

Hovey, Jaime E., 'Gallantry and Its Discontents: Joan of Arc and Virtuous Transmasculinity in Radclyffe Hall and Vita Sackville-West', *Feminist Modernist Studies*, 1/1–2 (2018), 113–37.

Love, Heather, 'Spoiled Identity: Radclyffe Hall's Unwanted Being', in Love, *Feeling Backward: Loss and the Politics of Queer History* (Cambridge, MA: Harvard University Press, 2007), 100–28.

Macnamara, Steven, 'Inverting the Gaze: Radclyffe Hall and Male Sexual Identities', in Elizabeth English, Jana Funke, and Sarah Parker (eds.), *Interrogating Lesbian Modernism: Histories, Forms, Genres* (Edinburgh: Edinburgh University Press, 2023), 145–62.

MacPike, Loralee, 'A Geography of Radclyffe Hall's Lesbian Country', *Historical Reflections/Réflexions historiques*, 20/2 (Summer 1994), 217–42.

MacPike, Loralee, 'Is Mary Llewellyn an Invert? The Modernist Supertext of *The Well of Loneliness*', in Elizabeth Jane Harrison and Shirley Peterson (eds.), *Unmanning Modernism: Gendered Re-Readings* (Knoxville: University of Tennessee Press, 1997), 73–89.

Madden, Ed, '*The Well of Loneliness*, or The Gospel According to Radclyffe Hall', *Journal of Homosexuality*, 33/3–4 (1997), 163–86.

Marcus, Jane, 'Sapphistory: The Woolf and the Well', in Karla Jay and Joanne Glasgow (eds.), *Lesbian Texts and Contexts: Radical Revisions* (New York: New York University Press, 1990), 164–79.

Marshik, Celia, 'History's "Abrupt Revenges": Censoring War's Perversions in *The Well of Loneliness* and *Sleeveless Errand*', *Journal of Modern Literature*, 26/2 (2003), 145–59.

Medd, Jodie, 'Bloomsbury and the Scandal of *The Well of Loneliness*', in Medd, *Lesbian Scandal and the Culture of Modernism* (New York: Cambridge University Press, 2012), 151–91.

Medd, Jodie, 'Séances and Slander: Radclyffe Hall in 1920', in Laura Doan and Jane Garrity (eds.), *Sapphic Modernities: Sexuality, Women and National Culture* (Basingstoke: Palgrave, 2006), 201–16.

Micir, Melanie, 'Intimacy Issues' and 'Claiming Radclyffe Hall: An Almost Archival Story', in Micir, *The Passion Projects: Modernist Women, Intimate Archives, Unfinished Lives* (Princeton: Princeton University Press, 2019), 21–4 and 24–32.

Mortimer-Sandilands, Catriona, 'Masculinity, Modernism, and the Ambivalence of Nature: Sexual Inversion as Queer Ecology in *The Well of Loneliness*', *Left History*, 13/1 (Spring–Summer 2008), 35–58.

Newton, Esther, 'The Mythic Mannish Lesbian: Radclyffe Hall and the New Woman', *Signs*, 9/4 (1984), 557–75.

Nicholls, Ben, 'Normative', in *Same Old: Queer Theory, Literature and the Politics of Sameness* (Manchester: Manchester University Press, 2020), 114–50.

O'Rourke, Rebecca, *Reflecting on The Well of Loneliness* (New York: Routledge, 1989).

Pająk, Paulina, '"Echo Texts": Woolf, Krzywicka, and *The Well of Loneliness*', *Woolf Studies Annual*, 24 (2018), 11–34.

Parkes, Adam, '"Suppressed Randiness": *Orlando* and *The Well of Loneliness*', in Parkes, *Modernism and the Theater of Censorship* (New York: Oxford University Press, 1996), 144–80.

Prince-Hughes, Tara, '"A Curious Double Insight": *The Well of Loneliness* and Native American Alternative Gender Traditions', *Rocky Mountain Review of Language and Literature*, 53/2 (1999), 31–43.

Prosser, Jay, '"Some Primitive Thing Conceived in a Turbulent Age of Transition": The Invert, *The Well of Loneliness*, and the Narrative Origins of Transsexuality', in Prosser, *Second Skins* (Columbia: Columbia University Press, 1998), 135–69.

Radford, Jean, 'An Inverted Romance: *The Well of Loneliness* and Sexual Ideology', in Radford (ed.), *The Progress of Romance: The Politics of Popular Fiction* (London: Routledge, 1986), 97–111.

Roche, Hannah, 'Strange Soil and Novel Ground: Radclyffe Hall's Romance Plots' and 'Romantic Emblems and "the Real Thing"', in Roche, *The Outside Thing: Modernist Lesbian Romance* (New York: Columbia University Press, 2019), 75–104 and 105–28.

Roche, Hannah, 'Writing Widows of Lesbian Modernism', in Elizabeth English, Jana Funke, and Sarah Parker (eds.), *Interrogating Lesbian Modernism: Histories, Forms, Genres* (Edinburgh: Edinburgh University Press, 2023), 165–82.

Rohy, Valerie, 'Desire and the Scene of Reading', in Rohy, *Lost Causes: Narrative, Etiology, and Queer Theory* (Oxford: Oxford University Press, 2014), 104–37.

Ruehl, Sonja, 'Inverts and Experts: Radclyffe Hall and the Lesbian Identity', in Rosalind Brunt and Caroline Rowan (eds.), *Feminism, Culture, and Politics* (London: Lawrence and Wishart, 1982), 15–36.

Stockton, Kathryn Bond, 'Why the (Lesbian) Child Requires an Interval of Animal: The Family Dog as a Time Machine', in Stockton, *The Queer Child, or Growing Sideways in the Twentieth Century* (Durham, NC: Duke University Press, 2009), 89–116.

Vicinus, Martha, '"A Love of Domination": The Mannish Invert and Sexual Danger', in Vicinus, *Intimate Friends: Women Who Loved Women, 1778–1928* (Chicago: Chicago University Press, 2004), 202–28.

Walker, Lisa, 'Martyred Butches and Impossible Femmes: Radclyffe Hall and the Modern Lesbian', in Walker, *Looking Like What You Are: Sexual Style, Race, and Lesbian Identity* (New York: New York University Press, 2001), 12–57.

Whitlock, Gillian, '"Everything Is Out of Place": Radclyffe Hall and the Lesbian Literary Tradition', *Feminist Studies*, 13/3 (Autumn 1987), 554–82.

Wilson, James F. '"In My Well of Loneliness": Gladys Bentley's Bulldykin' Blues', in Wilson, *Bulldaggers, Pansies, and Chocolate Babies: Performance, Race, and Sexuality in the Harlem Renaissance* (Ann Arbor: University of Michigan Press, 2010), 154–91.

Further Reading in Oxford World's Classics

Mansfield, K., *Selected Stories*, ed. Angela Smith.

Woolf, V., *A Room of One's Own and Three Guineas*, ed. Anna Snaith.

Woolf, V., *Between the Acts*, ed. Frank Kermode.

Woolf, V., *Flush*, ed. Kate Flint.

Woolf, V., *Jacob's Room*, ed. Urmila Seshagiri.

Woolf, V., *Mrs Dalloway*, ed. David Bradshaw.

Woolf, V., *Night and Day*, ed. Suzanne Raitt.

Woolf, V., *Orlando*, ed. Michael H. Whitworth.

Woolf, V., *Selected Essays*, ed. David Bradshaw.

Woolf, V., *The Mark on the Wall and Other Short Fiction*, ed. David Bradshaw.

Woolf, V., *The Voyage Out*, ed. Lorna Sage.

Woolf, V., *To the Lighthouse*, ed. David Bradshaw.

Woolf, V., *The Waves*, ed. David Bradshaw.

Woolf, V., *Kew Gardens and Other Short Fiction*, ed. Bryony Randall and David Bradshaw.

Woolf, V., *The Years*, ed. Hermione Lee and Sue Asbee.

A CHRONOLOGY OF RADCLYFFE HALL

	Life	*Historical and Cultural Background*
1880	(12 Aug.) Marguerite Antonia Radclyffe-Hall, later John Radclyffe Hall (RH), born at Sunny Lawn, Durley Road, Bournemouth; (5 Sept.) older sister Florence Maude dies.	Deaths of G. Eliot and Flaubert; L. Strachey and van Vechten born; Gladstone prime minister; Elementary Education Act; Charles Parnell demands home rule for Ireland. Gissing, *Workers in the Dawn* Tennyson, *Ballads and Other Poems* Trollope, *The Duke's Children* Zola, *Nana*
1882	RH's father, Radclyffe Radclyffe-Hall, abandons RH and her mother, Mary Jane Diehl (later Visetti).	Deaths of Darwin, Trollope, and D. G. Rossetti; Joyce and Woolf born; Married Women's Property Act; Society for Psychical Research (SPR) founded.
1886		H.D. born; Gascoyne-Cecil prime minister; Repeal of the Contagious Diseases Act; Irish Home Rule Bill defeated. Hardy, *The Mayor of Casterbridge* H. James, *The Bostonians* Krafft-Ebing, *Psychopathia Sexualis* Stevenson, *Strange Case of Dr. Jekyll and Mr. Hyde*
1887	(8 Mar.) Margot Elena Gertrude Taylor, later Una Vincenzo, Lady Troubridge (UT), born in London.	S. Beach and R. Brooke born; Victoria's Golden Jubilee. Corelli, *Thelma* Nietzsche, *On the Genealogy of Morality*
1888	(Dec.) divorce of parents.	Death of Arnold; T. S. Eliot born. Hardy, *Wessex Tales* Wilde, *The Happy Prince and Other Tales*
1889	RH stays in Bruges, Belgium, with her mother and grand-mother Sarah Diehl; mother's engagement and marriage to Alberto Visetti (*c.*1889).	Death of Browning; Cocteau born; London dock strike. Bergson, *Time and Free Will* Carpenter, *Civilization: Its Cause and Cure*
1890	RH moves to 14 Addison Road, Kensington, with mother and Visetti.	Christie born; decline of the circulating libraries and death of the three-volume novel; Housing of the Working Classes Act. Frazer, *The Golden Bough* Ibsen, *Hedda Gabler* Wilde, *The Picture of Dorian Gray*

	Life	*Historical and Cultural Background*
1894	*Poems dedicated to Sir Arthur Sullivan* privately printed; ongoing education at Mrs Cole's day school, Earls Court.	Bryher born; Primrose prime minister. Carpenter, *Homogenic Love and Its Place in a Free Society* G. du Maurier, *Trilby* Kipling, *The Jungle Book* Louÿs, *Chansons de Bilitis*
1895		Death of T. H. Huxley; Gascoyne-Cecil prime minister; X-rays discovered; invention of the cinematograph and wireless telegraphy; first Bristol electric tramway; arrest, trials, and conviction of Oscar Wilde. Allen, *The Women Who Did* Freud and Breuer, *Studies on Hysteria* Meredith, *Diana of the Crossways* Wilde, *The Importance of Being Earnest* and *An Ideal Husband*
1897		National Union of Women's Suffrage Societies (NUWS) founded; Queen Victoria's Diamond Jubilee; Wilde released from prison. Ellis and Symonds, *Sexual Inversion* H. James, *What Maisie Knew* Stoker, *Dracula*
1898	(29 Oct.) Death of father.	Deaths of Gladstone and L. Carroll; radium and plutonium discovered; Germany begins building large battle fleet and Britain responds by doing the same. Wells, *The War of the Worlds* Wilde, *The Ballad of Reading Gaol*
1900		Deaths of Nietzsche, Ruskin, and Wilde; Planck announces quantum theory; Boer War in South Africa (1899–1902); Labour Representation Committee set up. Colette, *Claudine à l'école* Conrad, *Lord Jim*
1901	(12 Aug.) RH receives inheritance; purchases lease on Campden Hill Terrace, Kensington, and Highfield House, Malvern Wells.	Death of Queen Victoria; accession of Edward VII; first wireless communication between Europe and US. Kipling, *Kim*

	Life	*Historical and Cultural Background*
1903		Deaths of Gissing, Spencer, and Weininger; Wright brothers make their first aeroplane flight; Emmeline Pankhurst founds the Women's Social and Political Union (WSPU); Motor Car Act raises speed limit to 20 m.p.h. H. James, *The Ambassadors* Moore, *Principia Ethica* Weininger, *Sex and Character* Vivien, *Évocations, Sapho*, and *Du Vert au Violet* Stein writes *Q.E.D.* (published 1950)
1906	*Twixt Earth and Stars* published; (Sept.) RH sees Mabel 'Ladye' Batten in Edinburgh.	Death of Ibsen; Beckett born; Liberal government elected; launch of HMS *Dreadnought*.
1907	(22 Aug.) RH meets Ladye in Homburg, Germany; (10 Oct.) UT marries Ernest Troubridge.	Auden born; Anglo-Russian Entente; first London cinema. Conrad, *The Secret Agent* Forster, *The Longest Journey*
1908	*A Sheaf of Verses: Poems* published; (summer) RH travels to Bruges and begins relationship with Ladye; (24 Dec.) sustains concussion and leg injury during riding accident.	Asquith prime minister; Old Age Pensions Act. Bennett, *The Old Wives' Tale* Carpenter, *The Intermediate Sex: A Study of Some Transitional Types of Men and Women* Forster, *A Room with a View*
1909	RH moves to Shelley Court, Tite Street, Chelsea; first trip to Tenerife with Ladye.	Deaths of Swinburne and Vivien; English Channel flown by Blériot; Housing and Town Planning Act; Labour Exchanges Act; Barney establishes literary salon in Paris. Marinetti, *Futurist Manifesto* Stein, *Three Lives*
1910	*Poems of the Past & Present* published; (18 Oct.) death of grandmother Diehl; (24 Oct.) death of George Batten, Ladye's husband; (5 Nov.) UT gives birth to daughter Andrea Theodosia.	Deaths of Edward VII, Tolstoy, and Nightingale; accession of George V; Fry's Post-Impressionist Exhibition. Forster, *Howards End* Freud, *Leonardo da Vinci: A Memory of His Childhood* Yeats, *The Green Helmet*
1911	(May) RH purchases lease of 59 Cadogan Square to set up joint home with Ladye; (29 June) RH and Ladye attend Ethel Smyth's Suffragette concert in London.	National Insurance Act; Pioneer Players founded; Suffragette riots. Ford, *Lady Whose Bright Eyes* Lawrence, *The White Peacock* K. Mansfield, *In a German Pension*

	Life	*Historical and Cultural Background*
1912	(5 Feb.) RH converts to Catholicism; (4 Mar.) publishes anti-Suffragette letter in *Pall Mall Gazette*; (4 Aug.) moves into the White Cottage, Malvern, with Ladye after sale of Highfield House; begins to use first name 'John' or 'Johnnie'.	Second Post-Impressionist Exhibition; Suffragettes active; strikes by dockers, coal-miners, and transport workers; Irish Home Bill again rejected by Lords; sinking of SS *Titanic;* William Morris produces first affordable Morris Oxford car. A. Lowell, *A Dome of Many-Coloured Glass*
1913	*Songs of Three Counties and Other Poems* published; (Jan.) UT begins hypnotherapy with Hugh Crichton-Miller; (10 Dec.) audience with Pope Pius X in Rome.	British Society for the Study of Sex Psychology founded; Suffragettes active. Forster begins *Maurice* (published in 1971) Lawrence, *Sons and Lovers*
1914	RH and Ladye house wounded soldiers at the White Cottage; RH writes First World War recruiting leaflets and runs enlistment campaigns; at work on short stories; (22 Sept.) Ladye seriously injured in car accident.	Irish Home Rule Bill passed by Parliament; First World War begins (28 July). Bell, *Art* Carpenter, *Intermediate Types Among Primitive Folk: A Study in Social Evolution* Hirschfeld, *Die Homosexualität des Mannes und des Weibes* Joyce, *Dubliners* Lewis, *Blast* A. Lowell, *Sword Blades and Poppy Seed* Sinclair, *The Three Sisters* Stein, *Tender Buttons* Yeats, *Responsibilities*
1915	*The Forgotten Island* published; at work on *The Cunninghams* and *Michael West* (both unpublished) and short fiction; (May) Ladye sends RH's short stories to William Heinemann; (1 Aug.) meets UT; (autumn) RH begins relationship with UT; (Nov.) sale negotiations for Cadogan Square and the White Cottage.	Death of R. Brooke; Einstein's General Theory of Relativity; Second Battle of Ypres; Dardanelles Campaign; sinking of SS *Lusitania*; air attacks on London. Barnes, *The Book of Repulsive Women* Brooke, *1914 and Other Poems* Ford, *The Good Soldier* Lawrence, *The Rainbow* (13 Nov. banned as obscene) Richardson, *Pointed Roofs* (beginning of *Pilgrimage* series) Woolf, *The Voyage Out*

	Life	*Historical and Cultural Background*
1916	(25 May) Death of Ladye; moves into 22 Cadogan Court, Chelsea; RH and UT begin to attend seances with Gladys Leonard.	Death of H. James; Lloyd George prime minister; First Battle of the Somme; Battle of Verdun; Gallipoli Campaign; Easter Rising in Dublin. H.D., *Sea Garden* A. Lowell, *Men, Women, and Ghosts* Hunt, *Their Lives* Joyce, *A Portrait of the Artist as a Young Man* Lodge, *Raymond, or Life and Death*
1917	(22 Mar.) RH contracts German measles; first holiday at Lynton with UT; (Nov.) UT leases villa in Datchet.	Third Battle of Ypres; T. E. Lawrence's campaigns in Arabia; US enters First World War; Revolution in Russia; Balfour Declaration; Hogarth Press founded. Dane, *Regiment of Women* T. S. Eliot, *Prufrock and Other Observations*
1918	RH elected to Council of the SPR; (31 Jan. and 22 Mar.) delivers paper to SPR Council members.	Death of Owen; Second Battle of the Somme; final German offensive collapses; (11 Nov.) Armistice with Germany; Representation of the People Act grants vote to men over 21 and some women over 30; Education Act raises school-leaving age to 14 and extends education for some to 16; influenza pandemic. Lewis, *Tarr* A. Lowell, *Can Grande's Castle* Stopes, *Married Love* Strachey, *Eminent Victorians* West, *The Return of the Soldier*
1919	(2 Jan.) purchase of Chip Chase in Hadley Wood to set up first home with UT; (Feb.) separation of UT and Ernest Troubridge formalized; (June) Troubridge made Knight Commander of the Order of St Michael and St George, UT takes title 'Lady'; RH begins work on *Octopi* (working title for *The Unlit Lamp*).	Treaty of Versailles; Alcock and Brown fly the Atlantic; Russian Revolution; Irish War of Independence (1919–1921); Hirschfeld opens Institute of Sexual Science in Berlin. A. Lowell, *Pictures of the Floating World* Sackville-West, *Heritage* Shaw, *Heartbreak House* Sinclair, *Mary Olivier: A Life* Woolf, *Night and Day*

	Life	*Historical and Cultural Background*
1920	(June) stomach and gynaecological illness; (Nov.) slander case against George Lane Fox-Pitt, council member of the SPR; (17 Dec.) cuts off long hair; sale of Cadogan Court.	League of Nations established; Unemployment Insurance Act; National Socialist Party founded in Germany. Barney, *Pensées d'une Amazone* and *Poems & Poèmes: Autres Alliances* Bryher, *Development* Colette, *Chéri* Freud, *Beyond the Pleasure Principle* Fry, *Vision and Design* Lawrence, *Women in Love* Pound, *Hugh Selwyn Mauberley* Sackville-West, *Challenge*
1921	RH begins to suffer eye strain; (Jan.) sale of Chip Chase; (May) purchases 10 Sterling Street, Knightsbridge; (Nov.) first trip to Florence with UT; RH and UT listed as 'joint head of household' on census.	Irish Free State declared; Stopes opens first birth control clinic in London; attempt to criminalize 'gross indecency between female persons' fails. H.D., *Hymen* Hunt, *Their Hearts* Huxley, *Crome Yellow* A. Lowell, *Legends* and *Fir-Flower Tablets*
1922	(Jan.) meets Natalie Clifford Barney in Paris; elected member of PEN Club.	Death of Proust; Bonar Law prime minister; Mussolini forms Fascist government in Italy; BBC founded. T. S. Eliot, *The Waste Land* Galsworthy, *The Forsyte Saga* Joyce, *Ulysses* (banned as obscene in US) K. Mansfield, *The Garden Party* Lawrence, 'The Fox' A. Lowell, *A Critical Fable* Sinclair, *Life and Death of Harriett Frean* Woolf, *Jacob's Room*
1923	RH engages agent A. M. Heath; (Jan.) begins work on *Chains* (working title of *The Forge*).	Death of K. Mansfield; Baldwin prime minister; (Nov.) BBC radio first broadcast. Bryher, *Two Selves*
1924	(25 Jan.) *The Forge* published; (May) finishes first draft of *A Saturday Life*; (May–June) Romaine Brooks paints UT's portrait; (Sept.) *The Unlit Lamp* published; (Oct.) RH begins *The World* (posthumously published); (4 Dec.) moves into 37 Holland Street, Kensington, with UT.	Deaths of Lenin, Kafka, and Conrad; first (minority) Labour government; MacDonald and later Baldwin prime minister. Coward, *The Vortex* H.D., *Heliodora and Other Poems* Ford, *Some Do Not* Forster, *Passage to India*

	Life	*Historical and Cultural Background*
1925	(Jan.) RH at work on *Food* (working title for *Adam's Breed*); (Apr.) *A Saturday Life* published; (Dec.) suffers from influenza.	Death of A. Lowell. Ford, *No More Parades* H.D., *Collected Poems of H.D.* Huxley, *Those Barren Leaves* A. Lowell, *What's O'Clock* Locke, *The New Negro* Stein, *The Making of Americans* Woolf, *Mrs Dalloway* and *The Common Reader*
1926	(28 Jan.) Death of Ernest Troubridge; (Mar.) *Adam's Breed* published; (July) RH begins work on *The Well of Loneliness*; (3 Aug.) gives broadcast for BBC.	(3–12 May) General Strike; first television demonstration. Ford, *A Man Could Stand Up* A. Lowell, *East Wind* Nugent, 'Smoke, Lilies and Jade' Sackville-West, *The Land* Townsend Warner, *Lolly Willowes*
1927	*Adam's Breed* wins (Apr.) Prix Femina Vie Heureuse and (Dec.) James Tait Black Memorial Prize.	Lindburgh flies solo across the Atlantic; first 'talkie' films. Lehman, *Dusty Answer* A. Lowell, *Ballads for Sale* Townsend Warner, *Mr. Fortune's Maggot* Woolf, *To the Lighthouse*
1928	(27 July) *The Well* published; (Nov.) *The Well* banned as obscene in UK; (13 Nov.) RH forced to sell Holland House and decides to relocate to Rye; (20 Nov.) threatens to resign from PEN club; (14 Dec.) verdict of trial upheld on appeal; (16 Dec.) *The Well* published in US; death of Visetti.	Death of Hardy; Equal Franchise Act grants votes to women over 21; Third Congress of the World League for Sexual Reform in London; Brontë Parsonage Museum opens. Barnes, *Ladies Almanack* and *Ryder* Bell, *Civilization* Egan, *The Sink of Solitude* (verse lampoon of *The Well*) Larsen, *Quicksand* Lawrence, *Lady Chatterley's Lover* Mackenzie, *Extraordinary Women* Waugh, *Decline and Fall* Woolf, *Orlando* Yeats, *The Tower*
1929	(25 Jan.) RH gives lecture on sexual inversion to the National Council of Labour Colleges' Students Association; (29 Feb.) *The Well* found obscene in US trial; (19 Apr.) US court decision reversed; US 'Victory Edition' of	Death of Carpenter; second Labour government, MacDonald prime minister; collapse of New York Stock Exchange; start of world economic depression. Aldington, *Death of a Hero* Larsen, *Passing* Woolf, *A Room of One's Own*

	Life	*Historical and Cultural Background*
	The Well published; (summer) stays in South of France and begins work on *The Carpenter's Son* (working title of *The Master of the House*); (Nov.) purchases the Black Boy in Rye.	
1930	(12 Aug.) RH moves into the Black Boy in Rye with UT; (Sept.) UT finishes French translation of *The Well*; (2 Sept.) pirated stage production of *The Well* premieres in Paris.	Death of Doyle and D. H. Lawrence; mass unemployment; television in US. Auden, *Poems* Barney, *The One Who is Legion* Coward, *Private Lives* T. S. Eliot, *Ash Wednesday* Freud, *Civilization and Its Discontents* Lewis, *Apes of God* Sackville-West, *The Edwardians* Waugh, *Vile Bodies*
1931	(Sept.) RH permanently resigns from PEN club.	Death of Bennett; formation of First National Government, MacDonald prime minister; abandonment of Gold Standard; Japan invades China. Sackville-West, *All Passion Spent* Woolf, *The Waves*
1932	(Feb.) *The Master of the House* published; (May) RH suffers from eye problems.	Roosevelt elected president of US; hunger marches start in Britain. Huxley, *Brave New World*
1933	(18 May) RH takes possession of flat at 17 Talbot House, St Martin's Lane; (Dec.) purchases the Forecastle, Rye, after putting Black Boy up for sale; at work on *Miss Ogilvy Finds Herself*.	Deaths of Galsworthy and G. Moore; Hitler Chancellor of Germany; Nazis raid and destroy Hirschfeld's Institute in Berlin. Stein, *The Autobiography of Alice B. Toklas* Wells, *The Shape of Things to Come* Woolf, *Flush*
1934	(Mar.) *Miss Ogilvy Finds Herself* published; (2 July) RH meets Evguenia Souline in Bagnoles, France; (31 July) informs UT of affair with Souline; (summer) stay in Sirmione, Italy; (10 Aug.) begins work on *Emblem Hurlstone* (unpublished).	Death of Fry. Beckett, *More Pricks than Kicks* Burdekin, *Proud Man* Graves, *I, Claudius* Sackville-West, *The Dark Island* Waugh, *A Handful of Dust*
1935	(Apr.) RH begins work on *The Sixth Beatitude*; decides to sell Talbot House flat.	Death of Hirschfeld; George V's Silver Jubilee; Baldwin prime minister of National Government; Germany rearms; Italian invasion of Abyssinia (Ethiopia). Isherwood, *Mr Norris Changes Trains* T. S. Eliot, *Murder in the Cathedral*

	Life	*Historical and Cultural Background*
1936	(Apr.) *The Sixth Beatitude* published; (Sept.) RH begins stay in Merano and works on *The Merano Shoemaker* (unpublished and destroyed).	Deaths of George V, Housman, and Kipling; accession of Edward VIII; abdication crisis; accession of George VI; Civil War in Spain; Germany reoccupies the Rhineland; (2 Nov.) BBC television. Barnes, *Nightwood*
1937	(summer) RH signs lease on 18 Lungarno Acciaivoli, Florence; (Aug.) suffers from ongoing painful eye spasms; hospitalized with fractured ankle.	Death of Barrie; Chamberlain prime minister; destruction of Guernica. Burdekin, *Swastika Night* Hurston, *Their Eyes Were Watching God* Stein, *Everybody's Autobiography* Woolf, *The Years*
1939	(June) RH threatens suicide after fight with Souline; (summer) gives up smoking after X-ray reveals lung scarring; sale of the Forecastle.	Deaths of Ellis, Ford, Freud, and Yeats; end of Civil War in Spain; (1 Sept.) Germany invades Poland; (3 Sept.) Britain and France declare war on Germany. Freud, *Moses and Monotheism* Isherwood, *Goodbye to Berlin* Joyce, *Finnegans Wake*
1940	RH suffers from influenza, failing eyesight, and eye spasms, severe colitis; stays at the Wayside, Lynton, with UT.	Churchill prime minister; Germany invades north-west Europe; fall of France; evacuation of British troops from Dunkirk; Battle of Britain; beginning of 'the Blitz'. Woolf, *Roger Fry*
1941	(Aug.) RH undergoes eye operation in Bath; (winter) suffers from toothache, double pneumonia, haemorrhoids, and severe influenza.	Death of Joyce; Germany invades USSR; Japanese destroy US Fleet at Pearl Harbor. Woolf, *Between the Acts*
1943	(Apr.) RH leaves Lynton for London and is diagnosed with cancer; (7 Oct.) dies in London after two operations; (14 Oct.) interred at Highgate Cemetery.	Casablanca Conference; Warsaw Ghetto Uprising; Mussolini dismissed and arrested; signing of Moscow Declaration. T. S. Eliot, *Four Quartets* Sartre, *Being and Nothingness*

THE WELL OF LONELINESS

'. . . . . nothing extenuate,
Nor set down aught in malice.'*

with a commentary by

HAVELOCK ELLIS

Dedicated to
*Our Three Selves**

COMMENTARY*

I HAVE read *The Well of Loneliness* with great interest because—apart from its fine qualities as a novel by a writer of accomplished art—it possesses a notable psychological and sociological significance. So far as I know, it is the first English novel which presents, in a completely faithful and uncompromising form, one particular aspect of sexual life as it exists among us to-day. The relation of certain people—who while different from their fellow human beings, are sometimes of the highest character and the finest aptitudes—to the often hostile society in which they move, presents difficult and still unsolved problems. The poignant situations which thus arise are here set forth so vividly, and yet with such complete absence of offence, that we must place Radclyffe Hall's book on a high level of distinction.

HAVELOCK ELLIS

AUTHOR'S NOTE

ALL the characters in this book are purely imaginary, and if the author in any instance has used names that may suggest a reference to living persons, she has done so inadvertently.

A motor ambulance unit of British women drivers* did very fine service upon the Allied front in France during the later months of the war, but although the unit mentioned in this book, of which Stephen Gordon becomes a member, operates in much the same area, it has never had any existence save in the author's imagination.

BOOK ONE

CHAPTER 1

I

Not very far from Upton-on-Severn—between it, in fact, and the Malvern Hills*—stands the country seat of the Gordons of Bramley; well-timbered, well-cottaged, well-fenced and well-watered, having, in this latter respect, a stream that forks in exactly the right position to feed two large lakes in the grounds.

The house itself is of Georgian red brick, with charming circular windows near the roof. It has dignity and pride without ostentation, self-assurance without arrogance, repose without inertia; and a gentle aloofness that, to those who know its spirit, but adds to its value as a home. It is indeed like certain lovely women who, now old, belong to a bygone generation—women who in youth were passionate but seemly; difficult to win but when won, all-fulfilling. They are passing away, but their homesteads remain, and such an homestead is Morton.

To Morton Hall* came the Lady Anna Gordon as a bride of just over twenty. She was lovely as only an Irish woman can be, having that in her bearing that betokened quiet pride, having that in her eyes that betokened great longing, having that in her body that betokened happy promise—the archetype of the very perfect woman, whom creating God has found good. Sir Philip had met her away in County Clare—Anna Molloy, the slim virgin thing,* all chastity, and his weariness had flown to her bosom as a spent bird will fly to its nest—as indeed such a bird had once flown to her, she told him, taking refuge from the perils of a storm.

Sir Philip was a tall man and exceedingly well-favoured, but his charm lay less in feature than in a certain wide expression, a tolerant expression that might almost be called noble, and in something sad yet gallant in his deep-set hazel eyes. His chin, which was firm, was very slightly cleft, his forehead intellectual, his hair tinged with auburn. His wide-nostrilled nose was indicative of temper, but his lips were well-modelled and sensitive and ardent—they revealed him as a dreamer and a lover.

Twenty-nine when they had married, he had sown no few wild oats, yet Anna's true instinct made her trust him completely. Her guardian had disliked him, opposing the engagement, but in the end she had had her own way. And as things turned out her choice had been happy, for seldom had two people loved more than they did; they loved with an ardour undiminished by time; as they ripened, so their love ripened with them.

Sir Philip never knew how much he longed for a son until, some ten years after marriage, his wife conceived a child; then he knew that this thing meant complete fulfilment, the fulfilment for which they had both been waiting. When she told him, he could not find words for expression, and must just turn and weep on her shoulder. It never seemed to cross his mind for a moment that Anna might very well give him a daughter; he saw her only as a mother of sons, nor could her warnings disturb him. He christened the unborn infant Stephen, because he admired the pluck of that Saint.* He was not a religious man by instinct, being perhaps too much of a student, but he read the Bible for its fine literature, and Stephen had gripped his imagination. Thus he often discussed the future of their child: 'I think I shall put Stephen down for Harrow,'* or: 'I'd rather like Stephen to finish off abroad, it widens one's outlook on life.'

And listening to him, Anna also grew convinced; his certainty wore down her vague misgivings, and she saw herself playing with this little Stephen, in the nursery, in the garden, in the sweet-smelling meadows. 'And himself the lovely young man,' she would say, thinking of the soft Irish speech of her peasants; 'And himself with the light of the stars in his eyes, and the courage of a lion in his heart!'

When the child stirred within her she would think it stirred strongly because of the gallant male creature she was hiding; then her spirit grew large with a mighty new courage, because a man-child would be born. She would sit with her needlework dropped on her knees, while her eyes turned away to the long line of hills that stretched beyond the Severn valley. From her favourite seat underneath an old cedar, she would see these Malvern Hills in their beauty, and their swelling slopes seemed to hold a new meaning. They were like pregnant women, full-bosomed, courageous, great green-girdled mothers of splendid sons! Thus through all those summer months, she sat and watched the hills, and Sir Philip would sit with her—they would sit hand in hand. And because she felt grateful she gave much to the poor, and Sir Philip went to church, which was seldom his custom, and the Vicar came to dinner, and just towards the end many matrons called to give good advice to Anna.

But: 'Man proposes—God disposes,'* and so it happened that on Christmas Eve,* Anna Gordon was delivered of a daughter; a narrow-hipped, wide-shouldered little tadpole of a baby, that yelled and yelled for three hours without ceasing, as though outraged to find itself ejected into life.

2

Anna Gordon held her child to her breast, but she grieved while it drank, because of her man who had longed so much for a son. And seeing her grief, Sir Philip hid his chagrin, and he fondled the baby and examined its fingers.

'What a hand!' he would say. 'Why it's actually got nails on all its ten fingers: little, perfect, pink nails!'

Then Anna would dry her eyes and caress it, kissing the tiny hand.

He insisted on calling the infant Stephen, nay more, he would have it baptized by that name. 'We've called her Stephen so long,' he told Anna, 'that I really can't see why we shouldn't go on—'

Anna felt doubtful, but Sir Philip was stubborn, as he could be at times over whims.

The Vicar said that it was rather unusual, so to mollify him they must add female names. The child was baptized in the village church as Stephen Mary Olivia Gertrude—and she throve, seeming strong, and when her hair grew it was seen to be auburn like Sir Philip's. There was also a tiny cleft in her chin, so small just at first that it looked like a shadow; and after a while when her eyes lost the blueness that is proper to puppies and other young things, Anna saw that her eyes were going to be hazel—and thought that their expression was her father's. On the whole she was quite a well-behaved baby, owing, no doubt, to a fine constitution. Beyond that first energetic protest at birth she had done very little howling.

It was happy to have a baby at Morton, and the old house seemed to become more mellow as the child, growing fast now and learning to walk, staggered or stumbled or sprawled on the floors that had long known the ways of children. Sir Philip would come home all muddy from hunting and would rush into the nursery before pulling off his boots, then down he would go on his hands and knees while Stephen clambered on to his back. Sir Philip would pretend to be well corned up,* bucking and jumping and kicking wildly, so that Stephen must cling to his hair or his collar, and thump him with hard little arrogant fists. Anna, attracted by the outlandish hubbub, would find them, and would point to the mud on the carpet.

She would say: 'Now, Philip, now, Stephen, that's enough! It's time for your tea,' as though both of them were children. Then Sir Philip would reach up and disentangle Stephen, after which he would kiss Stephen's mother.

3

The son that they waited for seemed long a-coming; he had not arrived when Stephen was seven. Nor had Anna produced other female offspring. Thus Stephen remained cock of the roost. It is doubtful if any only child is to be envied, for the only child is bound to become introspective; having no one of its own ilk in whom to confide, it is apt to confide in itself. It cannot be said that at seven years old the mind is beset by serious problems, but nevertheless it is already groping, may already be subject to small fits of dejection, may already be struggling to get a grip on life—on the limited life of its surroundings.* At seven there are miniature loves and hatreds, which, however, loom large and are extremely disconcerting. There may even be present a dim sense of frustration, and Stephen was often conscious of this sense, though she could not have put it into words. To cope with it, however, she would give way at times to sudden fits of hot temper,* working herself up over everyday trifles that usually left her cold. It relieved her to stamp and then burst into tears at the first sign of opposition. After such outbreaks she would feel much more cheerful, would find it almost easy to be docile and obedient. In some vague, childish way she had hit back at life, and this fact had restored her self-respect.

Anna would send for her turbulent offspring and would say: 'Stephen darling, Mother's not really cross—tell Mother what makes you give way to these tempers; she'll promise to try to understand if you'll tell her—'

But her eyes would look cold, though her voice might be gentle, and her hand when it fondled would be tentative, unwilling. The hand would be making an effort to fondle, and Stephen would be conscious of that effort. Then looking up at the calm, lovely face, Stephen would be filled with a sudden contrition, with a sudden deep sense of her own shortcomings; she would long to blurt all this out to her mother, yet would stand there tongue-tied, saying nothing at all. For these two were strangely shy with each other—it was almost grotesque, this shyness of theirs, as existing between mother and child. Anna would feel it, and through her Stephen, young as she was, would become conscious of it; so that they held a little aloof when they should have been drawing together.

Stephen, acutely responsive to beauty, would be dimly longing to find expression for a feeling almost amounting to worship, that her mother's face had awakened. But Anna, looking gravely at her daughter, noting the plentiful auburn hair, the brave hazel eyes that were so like the father's, as indeed were the child's whole expression and bearing, would be filled with a sudden antagonism that came very near to anger.

She would lie awake at night and ponder this thing, scourging herself in an access of contrition; accusing herself of hardness of spirit, of being an unnatural mother.* Sometimes she would shed slow, miserable tears, remembering the inarticulate Stephen.

She would think: 'I ought to be proud of the likeness, proud and happy and glad when I see it!' Then back would come flooding that queer antagonism that amounted almost to anger.

It would seem to Anna that she must be going mad, for this likeness to her husband would strike her as an outrage—as though the poor, innocent seven-year-old Stephen were in some way a caricature of Sir Philip; a blemished, unworthy, maimed reproduction*—yet she knew that the child was handsome. But now there were times when the child's soft flesh would be almost distasteful to her; when she hated the way Stephen moved or stood still, hated a certain largeness about her, a certain crude lack of grace in her movements, a certain unconscious defiance. Then the mother's mind would slip back to the days when this creature had clung to her breast, forcing her to love it by its own utter weakness; and at this thought her eyes must fill again, for she came of a race of devoted mothers. The thing had crept on her like a foe in the dark—it had been slow, insidious, deadly; it had waxed strong as Stephen herself had waxed strong, being part, in some way, of Stephen.

Restlessly tossing from side to side, Anna Gordon would pray for enlightenment and guidance; would pray that her husband might never suspect her feelings towards his child. All that she was and had been he knew; in all the world she had no other secret save this one most unnatural and monstrous injustice that was stronger than her will to destroy it. And Sir Philip loved Stephen, he idolized her; it was almost as though he divined by instinct that his daughter was being secretly defrauded, was bearing some unmerited burden. He never spoke to his wife of these things, yet watching them together, she grew daily more certain that his love for the child held an element in it that was closely akin to pity.

CHAPTER 2

I

At about this time Stephen first became conscious of an urgent necessity to love. She adored her father, but that was quite different; he was part of herself, he had always been there, she could not envisage the world without him—it was other with Collins, the housemaid. Collins was what was called 'second of three';* she might one day hope for promotion. Meanwhile she was florid, full-lipped and full-bosomed,* rather ample indeed for a young girl of twenty, but her eyes were unusually blue and arresting, very pretty inquisitive eyes. Stephen had seen Collins sweeping the stairs for two years, and had passed her by quite unnoticed; but one morning, when Stephen was just over seven, Collins looked up and suddenly smiled, then all in a moment Stephen knew that she loved her—a staggering revelation!*

Collins said politely: 'Good morning, Miss Stephen.'

She had always said: 'Good morning, Miss Stephen,' but on this occasion it sounded alluring—so alluring that Stephen wanted to touch her, and extending a rather uncertain hand she started to stroke her sleeve.

Collins picked up the hand and stared at it. 'Oh, my!' she exclaimed, 'what very dirty nails!' Whereupon their owner flushed painfully crimson and dashed upstairs to repair them.

'Put them scissors down this minute, Miss Stephen!' came the nurse's peremptory voice, while her charge was still busily engaged on her toilet.

But Stephen said firmly: 'I'm cleaning my nails 'cause Collins doesn't like them—she says they're dirty!'

'What impudence!' snapped the nurse, thoroughly annoyed. 'I'll thank her to mind her own business!'

Having finally secured the large cutting-out scissors, Mrs. Bingham went forth in search of the offender; she was not one to tolerate any interference with the dignity of her status. She found Collins still on the top flight of stairs, and forthwith she started to upbraid her: 'putting her back in her place,' the nurse called it; and she did it so thoroughly that in less than five minutes the 'second-of-three' had been told of every fault that was likely to preclude promotion.

Stephen stood still in the nursery doorway. She could feel her heart thumping against her side, thumping with anger and pity for Collins, who was answering never a word. There she knelt mute, with her brush suspended, with her mouth slightly open and her eyes rather scared; and when at long last she did manage to speak, her voice sounded humble and frightened. She was timid by nature, and the nurse's sharp tongue was a byword throughout the household.

Collins was saying: 'Interfere with your child? Oh, no, Mrs. Bingham, never! I hope I knows my place better than that—Miss Stephen herself showed me them dirty nails; she said: "Collins, just look, aren't my nails awful dirty!" And I said: "You must ask Nanny about that, Miss Stephen." Is it likely that I'd interfere with your work? I'm not that sort, Mrs. Bingham.'

Oh, Collins, Collins, with those pretty blue eyes and that funny alluring smile! Stephen's own eyes grew wide with amazement, then they clouded with sudden and disillusioned tears, for far worse than Collins' poorness of spirit was the dreadful injustice of those lies—yet this very injustice seemed to draw her to Collins, since despising, she could still love her.

For the rest of that day Stephen brooded darkly over Collins' unworthiness; and yet all through that day she still wanted Collins, and whenever she saw her she caught herself smiling, quite unable, in her turn, to muster the courage to frown her innate disapproval. And Collins smiled too, if the nurse was not looking, and she held up her plump red fingers, pointing to her nails and making a grimace at the nurse's retreating figure. Watching her, Stephen felt unhappy and embarrassed, not so much for herself as for Collins; and this feeling increased, so that thinking about her made Stephen go hot down her spine.

In the evening, when Collins was laying the tea, Stephen managed to get her alone. 'Collins,' she whispered, 'you told an untruth—I never showed you my dirty nails!'

'Course not!' murmured Collins, 'but I had to say something—you didn't mind, Miss Stephen, did you?' And as Stephen looked doubtfully up into her face, Collins suddenly stooped and kissed her.

Stephen stood speechless from a sheer sense of joy, all her doubts swept completely away. At that moment she knew nothing but beauty and Collins, and the two were as one, and the one was Stephen—and yet not Stephen either, but something more vast, that the mind of seven years found no name for.*

The nurse came in grumbling: 'Now then, hurry up, Miss Stephen! Don't stand there as though you were daft! Go and wash your face and hands before tea—how many times must I tell you the same thing?'

'I don't know—' muttered Stephen. And indeed she did not; she knew nothing of such trifles at that moment.

2

From now on Stephen entered a completely new world, that turned on an axis of Collins. A world full of constant exciting adventures; of elation, of joy, of incredible sadness, but withal a fine place to be dashing about in like a moth who is courting a candle. Up and down went the days; they resembled a swing that soared high above the tree-tops, then dropped to the depths, but seldom if ever hung midway. And with them went Stephen, clinging to the swing, waking up in the mornings with a thrill of vague excitement—the sort of excitement that belonged by rights to birthdays, and Christmas, and a visit to the pantomime at Malvern. She would open her eyes and jump out of bed quickly, still too sleepy to remember why she felt so elated; but then would come memory—she would know that this day she was actually going to see Collins. The thought would set her splashing in her sitz-bath,* and tearing the buttons off her clothes in her haste, and cleaning her nails with such ruthlessness and vigour that she made them quite sore in the process.

She began to be very inattentive at her lessons, sucking her pencil, staring out of the window, or what was far worse, not listening at all, except for Collins' footsteps. The nurse slapped her hands, and stood her in the corner, and deprived her of jam, but all to no purpose; for Stephen would smile, hugging closer her secret—it was worth being punished for Collins.

She grew restless and could not be induced to sit still even when her nurse read aloud. At one time she had very much liked being read to, especially from books that were all about heroes; but now such stories so stirred her ambition, that she longed intensely to live them. She, Stephen, now longed to be William Tell, or Nelson, or the whole Charge of Balaclava;* and this led to much foraging in the nursery rag-bag, much hunting up of garments once used for charades, much swagger and noise, much strutting and posing, and much staring into the mirror. There ensued a period of general confusion when the nursery looked as though smitten by an earthquake; when the chairs and the floor would be littered with oddments that Stephen had dug out but discarded. Once dressed, however, she would walk away grandly, waving the nurse peremptorily aside, going, as always, in search of Collins, who might have to be stalked to the basement.

Sometimes Collins would play up, especially to Nelson. 'My, but you do look fine!' she would exclaim. And then to the cook: 'Do come here, Mrs. Wilson! Doesn't Miss Stephen look exactly like a boy? I believe she must be a boy with them shoulders, and them funny gawky legs she's got on her!'

And Stephen would say gravely: 'Yes, of course I'm a boy. I'm young Nelson, and I'm saying: "What is fear?"* you know, Collins—I must be a boy, 'cause I feel exactly like one, I feel like young Nelson in the picture upstairs.'

Collins would laugh and so would Mrs. Wilson, and after Stephen had gone they would get talking, and Collins might say: 'She is a queer kid,* always dressing herself up and play-acting—it's funny.'

But Mrs. Wilson might show disapproval: 'I don't hold with such nonsense, not for a young lady. Miss Stephen's quite different from other young ladies—she's got none of their pretty little ways—it's a pity!'

There were times, however, when Collins seemed sulky, when Stephen could dress up as Nelson in vain. 'Now, don't bother me, Miss, I've got my work to see to!' or: 'You go and show Nurse—yes, I know you're a boy, but I've got my work to get on with. Run away.'

And Stephen must slink upstairs thoroughly deflated, strangely unhappy and exceedingly humble, and must tear off the clothes she so dearly loved donning, to replace them by the garments she hated.* How she hated soft dresses and sashes, and ribbons, and small coral beads, and openwork stockings! Her legs felt so free and comfortable in breeches;* she adored pockets too, and these were forbidden—at least really adequate pockets. She would gloom about the nursery because Collins had snubbed her, because she was conscious of feeling all wrong, because she so longed to be some one quite real, instead of just Stephen pretending to be Nelson. In a quick fit of anger she would go to the cupboard, and getting out her dolls* would begin to torment them. She had always despised the idiotic creatures which, however, arrived with each Christmas and birthday.

'I hate you! I hate you! I hate you!' she would mutter, thumping their innocuous faces.

But one day, when Collins had been crosser than usual, she seemed to be filled with a sudden contrition. 'It's me housemaid's knee,'* she confided to Stephen, 'It's not you, it's me housemaid's knee, dearie.'

'Is that dangerous?' demanded the child, looking frightened.

Then Collins, true to her class, said: 'It may be—it may mean an 'orrible operation, and I don't want no operation.'

'What's that?' inquired Stephen.

'Why, they'd cut me,' moaned Collins; 'they'd 'ave to cut me to let out the water.'

'Oh, Collins! What water?'

'The water in me kneecap—you can see if you press it, Miss Stephen.'

They were standing alone in the spacious night-nursery, where Collins was limply making the bed. It was one of those rare and delicious occasions when Stephen could converse with her goddess undisturbed, for the nurse had gone out to post a letter. Collins rolled down a coarse woollen stocking and displayed the afflicted member; it was blotchy and swollen and far from attractive, but Stephen's eyes filled with quick, anxious tears as she touched the knee with her finger.

'There now!' exclaimed Collins, 'See that dent? That's the water!' And she added: 'It's so painful it fair makes me sick. It all comes from polishing them floors, Miss Stephen; I didn't ought to polish them floors.'

Stephen said gravely: 'I do wish I'd got it—I wish I'd got your housemaid's knee, Collins, 'cause that way I could bear it instead of you. I'd like to be awfully hurt for you, Collins, the way that Jesus was hurt for sinners.* Suppose I pray hard, don't you think I might catch it? Or supposing I rub my knee against yours?'

'Lord bless you!' laughed Collins, 'it's not like the measles; no, Miss Stephen, it's caught from them floors.'

That evening Stephen became rather pensive, and she turned to the Child's Book of Scripture Stories* and she studied the picture of the Lord on His Cross, and she felt that she understood Him. She had often been rather puzzled about Him, since she herself was fearful of pain—when she barked her shins* on the gravel in the garden, it was not always easy to keep back her tears—and yet Jesus had chosen to bear pain for sinners, when He might have called up all those angels! Oh, yes, she had wondered a great deal about Him, but now she no longer wondered.

At bedtime, when her mother came to hear her say her prayers—as custom demanded—Stephen's prayers lacked conviction. But when Anna had kissed her and had turned out the light, then it was that Stephen prayed in good earnest—with such fervour, indeed, that she dripped perspiration in a veritable orgy of prayer.

'Please, Jesus, give me a housemaid's knee instead of Collins—do, *do*, Lord Jesus. Please, Jesus, I would like to bear all Collins' pain the way You did, and I don't want any angels! I would like to wash Collins in my blood,* Lord Jesus—I would like very much to be a Saviour to Collins—I love her, and I want to be hurt like You were; please, dear Lord Jesus, do let me. Please give me a knee that's all full of water, so that I can have Collins' operation. I want to have it instead of her, 'cause she's frightened—I'm not a bit frightened!'

This petition she repeated until she fell asleep, to dream that in some queer way she was Jesus, and that Collins was kneeling and kissing her hand, because she, Stephen, had managed to cure her by cutting off her knee with a bone paper-knife and grafting it on to her own. The dream* was a mixture of rapture and discomfort, and it stayed quite a long time with Stephen.

The next morning she awoke with the feeling of elation that comes only in moments of perfect faith. But a close examination of her knees in the bath, revealed them to be flawless except for old scars and a crisp, brown scab from a recent tumble—this, of course, was very disappointing. She picked off the scab, and that hurt her a little, but not, she felt sure, like a real housemaid's knee. However, she decided to continue in prayer, and not to be too easily downhearted.

For more than three weeks she sweated and prayed, and pestered poor Collins with endless daily questions: 'Is your knee better yet?' 'Don't you think my knee's swollen?' 'Have you faith? 'Cause I have—' 'Does it hurt you less, Collins?'

But Collins would always reply in the same way: 'It's no better, thank you, Miss Stephen.'

At the end of the fourth week Stephen suddenly stopped praying, and she said to Our Lord: 'You don't love Collins, Jesus, but I do, and I'm going to get housemaid's knee. You see if I don't!' Then she felt rather frightened, and added more humbly: 'I mean, I do want to—You don't mind, do You, Lord Jesus?'

The nursery floor was covered with carpet, which was obviously rather unfortunate for Stephen; had it only been parquet like the drawing-room and study, she felt it would better have served her purpose. All the same it was hard if she knelt long enough—it was so hard, indeed, that she had to grit her teeth if she stayed on her knees for more than twenty minutes. This was much worse than barking one's shins in the garden; it was much worse even than picking off a scab! Nelson helped her a little. She would think: 'Now I'm Nelson. I'm in the middle of the Battle of Trafalgar*—I've got shots in my knees!' But then she would remember that Nelson had been spared such torment. However, it was really rather fine to be suffering—it certainly seemed to bring Collins much nearer; it seemed to make Stephen feel that she owned her by right of this diligent pain.

There were endless spots on the old nursery carpet, and these spots Stephen could pretend to be cleaning; always careful to copy Collins' movements, rubbing backwards and forwards while groaning a little. When she got up at last, she must hold her left leg and limp, still groaning a little. Enormous new holes appeared in her stockings, through which she could examine her aching knees, and this led to rebuke: 'Stop your nonsense, Miss Stephen! It's scandalous the way you're tearing your stockings!' But Stephen smiled grimly and went on with the nonsense, spurred by love to an open defiance. On the eighth day,* however, it dawned upon Stephen that Collins should be shown the proof of her devotion. Her knees were particularly scarified that morning, so she limped off in search of the unsuspecting housemaid.

Collins stared: 'Good gracious, whatever's the matter? Whatever have you been doing, Miss Stephen?'

Then Stephen said, not without pardonable pride: 'I've been getting a housemaid's knee, like you, Collins!' And as Collins looked stupid and rather bewildered—'You see, I wanted to share your suffering. I've prayed quite a lot, but Jesus won't listen, so I've got to get housemaid's knee my own way—I can't wait any longer for Jesus!'

'Oh, hush!' murmured Collins, thoroughly shocked. 'You mustn't say such things: it's wicked, Miss Stephen.' But she smiled a little in spite of herself, then she suddenly hugged the child warmly.

All the same, Collins plucked up her courage that evening and spoke to the nurse about Stephen. 'Her knees was all red and swollen, Mrs. Bingham. Did ever you know such a queer fish as she is? Praying about my knee too. She's a caution!* And now if she isn't trying to get one! Well, if that's not real loving then I don't know nothing.' And Collins began to laugh weakly.

After this Mrs. Bingham rose in her might, and the self-imposed torture was forcibly stopped. Collins, on her part, was ordered to lie, if Stephen continued to question. So Collins lied nobly: 'It's better, Miss Stephen, it must be your praying—you see Jesus heard you. I expect He was sorry to see your poor knees—I know as I was when I saw them!'

'Are you telling me the truth?' Stephen asked her, still doubting, still mindful of that first day of Love's young dream.*

'Why, of course I'm telling you the truth, Miss Stephen.'

And with this Stephen had to be content.

3

Collins became more affectionate after the incident of the housemaid's knee; she could not but feel a new interest in the child whom she and the cook had now labelled as 'queer,' and Stephen basked in much surreptitious petting, and her love for Collins grew daily.

It was spring, the season of gentle emotions, and Stephen, for the first time, became aware of spring. In a dumb, childish way she was conscious of its fragrance, and the house irked her sorely, and she longed for the meadows, and the hills that were white with thorn-trees. Her active young body was for ever on the fidget, but her mind was bathed in a kind of soft haze, and this she could never quite put into words, though she tried to tell Collins about it. It was all part of Collins, yet somehow quite different—it had nothing to do with Collins' wide smile, nor her hands which were red, nor even her eyes which were blue, and very arresting. Yet all that was Collins, Stephen's Collins, was also a part of these long, warm days, a part of the twilights that came in and lingered for hours after Stephen had been put to bed; a part too, could Stephen have only known it, of her own quickening childish perceptions. This spring, for the first time, she thrilled to the cuckoo, standing quite still to listen, with her head on one side; and the lure of that far-away call was destined to remain with her all her life.

There were times when she wanted to get away from Collins, yet at others she longed intensely to be near her, longed to force the response that her loving craved for, but quite wisely was very seldom granted.

She would say: 'I do love you awfully, Collins. I love you so much that it makes me want to cry.'

And Collins would answer: 'Don't be silly, Miss Stephen,' which was not satisfactory—not at all satisfactory.

Then Stephen might suddenly push her, in anger: 'You're a beast! How I hate you, Collins!'

And now Stephen had taken to keeping awake every night, in order to build up pictures: pictures of herself companioned by Collins in all sorts of happy situations. Perhaps they would be walking in the garden, hand in hand, or pausing on a hill-side to listen to the cuckoo; or perhaps they would be skimming over miles of blue ocean in a queer little ship with a leg-of-mutton sail, like the one in the fairy story.* Sometimes Stephen pictured them living alone in a low thatched cottage by the side of a mill stream—she had seen such a cottage not very far from Upton—and the water flowed quickly and made talking noises; there were sometimes dead leaves on the water. This last was a very intimate picture, full of detail, even to the red china dogs that stood one at each end of the high mantelpiece, and the grandfather clock that ticked loudly. Collins would sit by the fire with her shoes off. 'Me feet's that swollen and painful,' she would say. Then Stephen would go and cut rich bread and butter—the drawing-room kind, little bread and much butter—and would put on the kettle and brew tea for Collins, who liked it very strong and practically boiling, so that she could sip it from her saucer. In this picture it was Collins who talked about loving, and Stephen who gently but firmly rebuked her: 'There, there, Collins, don't be silly, you are a queer fish!' And yet all the while she would be longing to tell her how wonderful it was, like honeysuckle blossom—something very sweet like that—or like fields smelling strongly of new-mown hay, in the sunshine. And perhaps she *would* tell her, just at the very end—just before this last picture faded.

4

In these days Stephen clung more closely to her father, and this in a way was because of Collins. She could not have told you why it should be so, she only felt that it was. Sir Philip and his daughter would walk on the hill-sides, in and out of the blackthorn and young green bracken; they would walk hand in hand with a deep sense of friendship, with a deep sense of mutual understanding.

Sir Philip knew all about wild flowers and berries, and the ways of young foxes and rabbits and such people. There were many rare birds, too, on the hills near Malvern, and these he would point out to Stephen. He taught her the simpler laws of nature, which, though simple, had always filled him with wonder: the law of the sap as it flowed through the branches, the law of the wind that came stirring the sap, the law of bird life and the building of nests, the law of the cuckoo's varying call, which in June changed to 'Cuckoo-kook!' He taught out of love for both subject and pupil, and while he thus taught he watched Stephen.

Sometimes, when the child's heart would feel full past bearing, she must tell him her problems in small, stumbling phrases. Tell him how much she longed to be different, longed to be some one like Nelson.

She would say: 'Do you think that I *could* be a man, supposing I thought very hard—or prayed, Father?'

Then Sir Philip would smile and tease her a little, and would tell her that one day she would want pretty frocks, and his teasing was always excessively gentle, so that it hurt not at all.

But at times he would study his daughter gravely, with his strong, cleft chin tightly cupped in his hand. He would watch her at play with the dogs in the garden, watch the curious suggestion of strength in her movements, the long line of her limbs—she was tall for her age—and the poise of her head on her over-broad shoulders. Then perhaps he would frown and become lost in thought, or perhaps he might suddenly call her:

'Stephen, come here!'

She would go to him gladly, waiting expectant for what he should say; but as likely as not he would just hold her to him for a moment, and then let go of her abruptly. Getting up he would turn to the house and his study, to spend all the rest of that day with his books.

A queer mixture, Sir Philip, part sportsman, part student. He had one of the finest libraries in England, and just lately he had taken to reading half the night, which had not hitherto been his custom. Alone in that grave-looking, quiet study, he would unlock a drawer in his ample desk, and would get out a slim volume recently acquired, and would read and re-read it in the silence. The author was a German, Karl Heinrich Ulrichs,* and reading, Sir Philip's eyes would grow puzzled; then groping for a pencil he would make little notes all along the immaculate margins. Sometimes he would jump up and pace the room quickly, pausing now and again to stare at a picture—the portrait of Stephen painted with her mother, by Millais,* the previous year. He would notice the gracious beauty of Anna, so perfect a thing, so completely reassuring; and then that indefinable quality in Stephen that made her look wrong in the clothes she was wearing, as though she and they had no right to each other, but above all no right to Anna. After a while he would steal up to bed, being painfully careful to tread very softly, fearful of waking his wife who might question: 'Philip darling, it's so late—what have you been reading?' He would not want to answer, he would not want to tell her; that was why he must tread very softly.

The next morning, he would be very tender to Anna—but even more tender to Stephen.

5

As the spring waxed more lusty and strode into summer, Stephen grew conscious that Collins was changing. The change was almost intangible at first, but the instinct of children is not mocked. Came a day when Collins turned on her quite sharply, nor did she explain it by a reference to her knee.

'Don't be always under my feet now, Miss Stephen. Don't follow me about and don't be always staring. I 'ates being watched—you run up to the nursery, the basement's no place for young ladies.' After which such rebuffs were of frequent occurrence, if Stephen went anywhere near her.

Miserable enigma! Stephen's mind groped about it like a little blind mole that is always in darkness. She was utterly confounded, while her love grew the stronger for so much hard pruning, and she tried to woo Collins by offerings of bull's-eyes* and chocolate drops, which the maid took because she liked them. Nor was Collins so blameworthy as she appeared, for she, in her turn, was the puppet of emotion. The new footman was tall and exceedingly handsome. He had looked upon Collins with eyes of approval. He had said: 'Stop that damned kid hanging around you; if you don't she'll go blabbing about us.'

And now Stephen knew very deep desolation because there was no one in whom to confide. She shrank from telling even her father—he might not understand, he might smile, he might tease her—if he teased her, however gently, she knew that she could not keep back her tears. Even Nelson had suddenly become quite remote. What was the good of trying to be Nelson? What was the good of dressing up any more—what was the good of pretending? She turned from her food, growing pasty and languid; until, thoroughly alarmed, Anna sent for the doctor. He arrived, and prescribed a dose of Gregory powder,* finding nothing much wrong with the patient. Stephen tossed off the foul brew without a murmur—it was almost as though she liked it!

The end came abruptly, as is often the way, and it came when the child was alone in the garden, still miserably puzzling over Collins, who had been avoiding her for days. Stephen had wandered to an old potting-shed, and there, whom should she see but Collins and the footman; they appeared to be talking very earnestly together, so earnestly that they failed to hear her. Then a really catastrophic thing happened, for Henry caught Collins roughly by the wrists, and he dragged her towards him, still handling her roughly, and he kissed her full on the lips. Stephen's head felt suddenly hot and dizzy, she was filled with a blind, uncomprehending rage; she wanted to cry out, but her voice failed completely, so that all she could do was to splutter. But the very next moment she had seized a broken flower-pot and had hurled it hard and straight at the footman. It struck him in the face, cutting open his cheek, down which the blood trickled slowly. He stood as though stunned, gently mopping the cut, while Collins stared dumbly at Stephen. Neither of them spoke, they were feeling too guilty—they were also too much astonished.

Then Stephen turned and fled from them wildly. Away and away, anyhow, anywhere, so long as she need not see them! She sobbed as she ran and covered her eyes, tearing her clothes on the shrubs in passing, tearing her stockings and the skin of her legs as she lunged against intercepting branches. But suddenly the child was caught in strong arms, and her face was pressing against her father, and Sir Philip was carrying her back to the house, and along the wide passage to his study. He held her on his knee, forbearing to question, and at first she crouched there like a little dumb creature that had somehow got itself wounded. But her heart was too young to contain this new trouble—too heavy it felt, too much overburdened, so the trouble came bubbling up from her heart and was told on Sir Philip's shoulder.

He listened very gravely, just stroking her hair. 'Yes—yes—' he said softly; and then, 'go on, Stephen.' And when she had finished he was silent for some moments, while he went on stroking her hair. Then he said: 'I think I understand, Stephen—this thing seems more dreadful than anything else that has ever happened, more utterly dreadful—but you'll find that it will pass and be completely forgotten—you must try to believe me, Stephen. And now I'm going to treat you like a boy, and a boy must always be brave, remember. I'm not going to pretend as though you were a coward; why should I, when I know that you're brave? I'm going to send Collins away to-morrow; do you understand, Stephen? I shall send her away. I shan't be unkind, but she'll go away to-morrow, and meanwhile I don't want you to see her again. You'll miss her at first, that will only be natural, but in time you'll find that you'll forget all about her; this trouble will just seem like nothing at all. I am telling you the truth, dear, I swear it. If you need me, remember that I'm always near you—you can come to my study whenever you like. You can talk to me about it whenever you're unhappy, and you want a companion to talk to.' He paused, then finished rather abruptly: 'Don't worry your mother, just come to me, Stephen.'

And Stephen, still catching her breath, looked straight at him. She nodded, and Sir Philip saw his own mournful eyes gazing back from his daughter's tear-stained face. But her lips set more firmly, and the cleft in her chin grew more marked with a new, childish will to courage.

Bending down, he kissed her in absolute silence—it was like the sealing of a sorrowful pact.

6

Anna, who had been out at the time of the disaster, returned to find her husband waiting for her in the hall.

'Stephen's been naughty, she's up in the nursery; she's had one of her fits of temper,' he remarked.

In spite of the fact that he had obviously been waiting to intercept Anna, he now spoke quite lightly. Collins and the footman must go, he told her. As for Stephen, he had had a long talk with her already—Anna had better just let the thing drop, it had only been childish temper—

Anna hurried upstairs to her daughter. She, herself, had not been a turbulent child, and Stephen's outbursts always made her feel helpless; however, she was fully prepared for the worst. But she found Stephen sitting with her chin on her hand, and calmly staring out of the window; her eyes were still swollen and her face very pale, otherwise she showed no great signs of emotion; indeed she actually smiled up at Anna—it was rather a stiff little smile. Anna talked kindly and Stephen listened, nodding her head from time to time in acquiescence. But Anna felt awkward, and as though for some reason the child was anxious to reassure her; that smile had been meant to be reassuring—it had been such a very unchildish smile. The mother was doing all the talking, she found. Stephen would not discuss her affection for Collins; on this point she was firmly, obdurately silent. She neither excused nor upheld her action in throwing a broken flower-pot at the footman.

'She's trying to keep something back,' thought Anna, feeling more nonplussed every moment.

In the end Stephen took her mother's hand gravely and proceeded to stroke it, as though she were consoling. She said: 'Don't feel worried, 'cause that worries Father—I promise I'll try not to get into tempers, but you promise that you won't go on feeling worried.'

And absurd though it seemed, Anna heard herself saying: 'Very well then—I do promise, Stephen.'

CHAPTER 3

I

STEPHEN never went to her father's study in order to talk of her grief over Collins. A reticence strange in so young a child, together with a new, stubborn pride, held her tongue-tied, so that she fought out her battle alone, and Sir Philip allowed her to do so. Collins disappeared and with her the footman, and in Collins' stead came a new second housemaid, a niece of Mrs. Bingham's, who was even more timid than her predecessor, and who talked not at all. She was ugly, having small, round black eyes like currants—not inquisitive blue eyes like Collins.

With set lips and tight throat Stephen watched this intruder as she scuttled to and fro doing Collins' duties. She would sit and scowl at poor Winefred darkly, devising small torments to add to her labours—such as stepping on dustpans and upsetting their contents, or hiding away brooms and brushes and slop-cloths—until Winefred, distracted, would finally unearth them from the most inappropriate places.

''Owever did them slop-cloths get in 'ere!' she would mutter, discovering them under a nursery cushion. And her face would grow blotched with anxiety and fear as she glanced towards Mrs. Bingham.

But at night, when the child lay lonely and wakeful, these acts that had proved a consolation in the morning, having sprung from a desperate kind of loyalty to Collins—these acts would seem trivial and silly and useless, since Collins could neither know of them nor see them, and the tears that had been held in check through the day would well under Stephen's eyelids. Nor could she, in those lonely watches of the night-time, pluck up courage enough to reproach the Lord Jesus, who, she felt, could have helped her quite well had He chosen to accord her a housemaid's knee.

She would think: 'He loves neither me nor Collins—He wants all the pain for Himself; He won't share it!'

And then she would feel contrite: 'Oh, I'm sorry, Lord Jesus, 'cause I *do* know You love all miserable sinners!' And the thought that perhaps she had been unjust to Jesus would reduce her to still further tears.

Very dreadful indeed were those nights spent in weeping, spent in doubting the Lord and His servant Collins. The hours would drag by in intolerable blackness, that in passing seemed to envelop Stephen's body, making her feel now hot and now cold. The grandfather clock on the stairs ticked so loudly that her head ached to hear its unnatural ticking—when it chimed, which it did at the hours and the half-hours, its voice seemed to shake the whole house with terror, until Stephen would creep down under the bed-clothes to hide from she knew not what. But presently, huddled beneath the blankets, the child would be soothed by a warm sense of safety, and her nerves would relax, while her body grew limp with the drowsy softness of bed. Then suddenly a big and most comforting yawn, and another, and another, until darkness and Collins and tall clocks that menaced, and Stephen herself, were all blended and merged into something quite friendly, a harmonious whole, neither fearful nor doubting—the blessèd illusion we call sleep.

2

In the weeks that followed on Collins' departure, Anna tried to be very gentle with her daughter, having the child more frequently with her, more diligently fondling Stephen. Mother and daughter would walk in the garden, or wander about together through the meadows, and Anna would remember the son of her dreams, who had played with her in those meadows. A great sadness would cloud her eyes for a moment, an infinite regret as she looked down at Stephen; and Stephen, quick to discern that sadness, would press Anna's hand with small, anxious fingers; she would long to inquire what troubled her mother, but would be held speechless through shyness.*

The scents of the meadows would move those two strangely—the queer, pungent smell from the hearts of dog-daisies; the buttercup smell, faintly green like the grass; and then meadow-sweet that grew close by the hedges.* Sometimes Stephen must tug at her mother's sleeve sharply—intolerable to bear that thick fragrance alone!

One day she had said: 'Stand still or you'll hurt it—it's all round us—it's a white smell, it reminds me of you!' And then she had flushed, and had glanced up quickly, rather frightened in case she should find Anna laughing.

But her mother had looked at her curiously, gravely, puzzled by this creature who seemed all contradictions—at one moment so hard, at another so gentle, gentle to tenderness, even. Anna had been stirred, as her child had been stirred, by the breath of the meadow-sweet under the hedges; for in this they were one, the mother and daughter, having each in her veins the warm Celtic blood that takes note of such things—could they only have divined it, such simple things might have formed a link between them.

A great will to loving had suddenly possessed Anna Gordon, there in that sunlit meadow—had possessed them both as they stood together, bridging the gulf between maturity and childhood. They had gazed at each other as though asking for something, as though seeking for something, the one from the other; then the moment had passed—they had walked on in silence, no nearer in spirit than before.

3

Sometimes Anna would drive Stephen into Great Malvern,* to the shops, with lunch at the Abbey Hotel on cold beef and wholesome rice pudding. Stephen loathed these excursions, which meant dressing up, but she bore them because of the honour which she felt to be hers when escorting her mother through the streets, especially Church Street with its long, busy hill, because every one saw you in Church Street. Hats would be lifted with obvious respect, while a humbler finger might fly to a forelock; women would bow, and a few even curtsy to the lady of Morton—women in from the country with speckled sunbonnets that looked like their hens, and kind faces like brown, wrinkled apples. Then Anna must stop to inquire about calves and babies and foals, indeed all such young creatures as prosper on farms, and her voice would be gentle because she loved such young creatures.

Stephen would stand just a little behind her, thinking how gracious and lovely she was; comparing her slim and elegant shoulders with the toil-thickened back of old Mrs. Bennett, with the ugly, bent spine of young Mrs. Thompson who coughed when she spoke and then said: 'I beg pardon!' as though she were conscious that one did not cough in front of a goddess like Anna.

Presently Anna would look round for Stephen: 'Oh, there you are, darling! We must go into Jackson's and change mother's books'; or, 'Nanny wants some more saucers; let's walk on and get them at Langley's.'

Stephen would suddenly spring to attention, especially if they were crossing the street. She would look right and left for imaginary traffic, slipping a hand under Anna's elbow.

'Come with me,' she would order, 'and take care of the puddles, 'cause you might get your feet wet—hold on by me, Mother!'

Anna would feel the small hand at her elbow, and would think that the fingers were curiously strong; strong and efficient they would feel, like Sir Philip's, and this always vaguely displeased her. Nevertheless she would smile at Stephen while she let the child guide her in and out between the puddles.

She would say: 'Thank you, dear; you're as strong as a lion!'* trying to keep that displeasure from her voice.

Very protective* and careful was Stephen when she and her mother were out alone together. Not all her queer shyness could prevent her protecting, nor could Anna's own shyness save her from protection. She was forced to submit to a quiet supervision that was painstaking, gentle but extremely persistent. And yet was this love? Anna often wondered. It was not, she felt sure, the trusting devotion that Stephen had always felt for her father; it was more like a sort of instinctive admiration, coupled with a large, patient kindness.

'If she'd only talk to me as she talks to Philip, I might get to understand her,' Anna would muse, 'It's so odd not to know what she's feeling and thinking, to suspect that something's always being kept in the background.'

Their drives home from Malvern were usually silent, for Stephen would feel that her task was accomplished, her mother no longer needing her protection now that the coachman had the care of them both—he, and the arrogant-looking grey cobs that were yet so mannerly and gentle. As for Anna, she would sigh and lean back in her corner, weary of trying to make conversation. She would wonder if Stephen were tired or just sulky, or if, after all, the child might be stupid. Ought she, perhaps, to feel sorry for the child? She could never quite make up her mind.

Meanwhile, Stephen, enjoying the comfortable brougham,* would begin to indulge in kaleidoscopic musings, those musings that belong to the end of the day, and occasionally visit children. Mrs. Thompson's bent spine, it looked like a bow—not a rainbow but one of the archery kind; if you stretched a tight string from her feet to her head, could you shoot straight with Mrs. Thompson? China dogs—they had nice china dogs at Langley's—that made you think of someone; oh, yes, of course, Collins—Collins and a cottage with red china dogs. But you tried not to think about Collins! There was such a queer light slanting over the hills, a kind of gold glory, and it made you feel sorry—why should a gold glory make you feel sorry when it shone that way on the hills? Rice pudding, almost as bad as tapioca—not quite though, because it was not so slimy—tapioca evaded your efforts to chew it, it felt horrid, like biting down on your own gum. The lanes smelt of wetness, a wonderful smell! Yet when Nanny washed things they only smelt soapy—but then, of course, God washed the world without soap; being God, perhaps He didn't need any—you needed a lot, especially for hands—did God wash His hands without soap? Mother, talking about calves and babies, and looking like the Virgin Mary in church, the one in the stained-glass window with Jesus, which reminded you of Church Street, not a bad place after all; Church Street was really rather exciting—what fun it must be for men to have hats that they could take off, instead of just smiling—a bowler must be much more fun than a Leghorn*—you couldn't take that off to Mother—

The brougham would roll smoothly along the white road, between stout leafy hedges starred with dog-roses; blackbirds and thrushes would be singing loudly, so loudly that Stephen could hear their voices above the quick clip, clip, of the cobs and the muffled sounds of the carriage. Then from under her brows she must glance across at Anna, who she knew loved the songs of blackbirds and thrushes; but Anna's face would be hidden in shadow, while her hands lay placidly folded.

And now the horses, nearing their stables, would redouble their efforts as they swung through the gates, the tall, iron gates of the parklands of Morton, faithful gates that had always meant home. Old trees would fly past, then the paddocks with their cattle—Worcestershire cattle with uncanny white faces; then the two quiet lakes where the swans reared their cygnets; then the lawns, and at last the wide curve in the drive, near the house, that would lead to the massive entrance.

The child was too young to know why the beauty of Morton would bring a lump to her throat when seen thus in the gold haze of late afternoon, with its thoughts of evening upon it. She would want to cry out in a kind of protest that was very near tears: 'Stop it—stop it, you're hurting!' But instead she would blink hard and shut her lips tightly, unhappy yet happy. It was a queer feeling; it was too big for Stephen, who was still rather little when it came to affairs of the spirit. For the spirit of Morton would be part of her then, and would always remain somewhere deep down within her, aloof and untouched by the years that must follow, by the stress and the ugliness of life. In those after-years certain scents would evoke it—the scent of damp rushes growing by water; the kind, slightly milky odour of cattle; the smell of dried rose-leaves and orris-root* and violets, that together with a vague suggestion of beeswax always hung about Anna's rooms. Then that part of Stephen that she still shared with Morton would know what it was to feel terribly lonely, like a soul that wakes up to find itself wandering, unwanted, between the spheres.

4

Anna and Stephen would take off their coats, and go to the study in search of Sir Philip, who would usually be there waiting.

'Hallo, Stephen!' he would say in his pleasant, deep voice, but his eyes would be resting on Anna.

Stephen's eyes invariably followed her father's, so that she too would stand looking at Anna, and sometimes she must catch her breath in surprise at the fullness of that calm beauty. She never got used to her mother's beauty, it always surprised her each time she saw it; it was one of those queerly unbearable things, like the fragrance of meadow-sweet under the hedges.

Anna might say: 'What's the matter, Stephen? For goodness' sake darling, do stop staring!' And Stephen would feel hot with shame and confusion because Anna had caught her staring.

Sir Philip usually came to her rescue: 'Stephen, here's that new picture-book about hunting'; or, 'I know of a really nice print of young Nelson; if you're good I'll order it for you to-morrow.'

But after a little he and Anna must get talking, amusing themselves irrespective of Stephen, inventing absurd little games, like two children, which games did not always include the real child. Stephen would sit there silently watching, but her heart would be a prey to the strangest emotions—emotions that seven-years-old could not cope with, and for which it could find no adequate names. All she would know was that seeing her parents together in this mood, would fill her with longings for something that she wanted yet could not define—a something that would make her as happy as they were. And this something would always be mixed up with Morton, with grave, stately rooms like her father's study, with wide views from windows that let in much sunshine, and the scents of a spacious garden. Her mind would go groping about for a reason, and would find no reason—unless it were Collins—but Collins would refuse to fit into these pictures; even love must admit that she did not belong there any more than the brushes and buckets and slop-cloths belonged in that dignified study.

Presently Stephen must go off to her tea, leaving the two grown-up children together; secretly divining that neither of them would miss her—not even her father.

Arrived in the nursery she would probably be cross, because her heart felt very empty and tearful; or because, having looked at herself in the glass, she had decided that she loathed her abundant long hair. Snatching at a slice of thick bread and butter, she would upset the milk jug, or break a new tea-cup, or smear the front of her dress with her fingers, to the fury of Mrs. Bingham. If she spoke at such times it was usually to threaten: 'I shall cut all my hair off, you see if I don't!' or, 'I *hate* this white dress and I'm going to burn it—it makes me feel idiotic!' But once launched she would dig up the grievances of months, going back to the time of the would-be young Nelson, loudly complaining that being a girl spoilt everything—even Nelson. The rest of the evening would be spent in grumbling, because one does grumble when one is unhappy—at least one does grumble when one is seven—later on it may seem rather useless.

At last the hour of the bath would arrive, and still grumbling, Stephen must submit to Mrs. Bingham, fidgeting under the nurse's rough fingers like a dog in the hands of a trimmer. There she would stand pretending to shiver, a strong little figure, narrow-hipped and wide-shouldered;* her flanks as wiry and thin as a greyhound's and even more ceaselessly restless.

'God doesn't use soap!' she might suddenly remark.

At which Mrs. Bingham must smile, none too kindly: 'Maybe not, Miss Stephen—He don't 'ave to wash *you*; if He did He'd need plenty of soap, I'll be bound!'

The bath over, and Stephen garbed in her nightgown, a long pause would ensue, known as: 'Waiting for Mother,' and if mother, for some reason, did not happen to arrive, the pause could be spun out for quite twenty minutes, or for half an hour even, if luck was with Stephen, and the nursery clock not too precise and old-maidish.

'Now come on, say your prayers'; Mrs. Bingham would order, 'and you'd better ask the dear Lord to forgive you—impious I calls it, and you a young lady! Carrying on because you can't be a boy!'

Stephen would kneel by the side of the bed, but in such moods as these her prayers would sound angry. The nurse would protest: 'Not so loud, Miss Stephen! Pray slower, and don't shout at the Lord, He won't like it!'

But Stephen would continue to shout at the Lord in a kind of impotent defiance.

CHAPTER 4

I

THE sorrows of childhood are mercifully passing, for it is only when maturity has rendered soil mellow that grief will root very deeply. Stephen's grief for Collins, in spite of its violence, or perhaps because of that very violence, wore itself out like a passing tempest and was all but spent by the autumn. By Christmas, the gusts when they came were quite gentle, rousing nothing more disturbing than a faint melancholy—by Christmas it required quite an effort of will to recapture the charm of Collins.

Stephen was nonplussed and rather uneasy; to have loved so greatly and now to forget! It made her feel childish and horribly silly, as though she had cried over cutting her finger. As on all grave occasions, she considered the Lord, remembering His love for miserable sinners:

'Teach me to love Collins Your way,' prayed Stephen, trying hard to squeeze out some tears in the process, 'teach me to love her 'cause she's mean and unkind and won't be a proper sinner that repenteth.' But the tears would not come, nor was prayer what it had been; it lacked something—she no longer sweated when she prayed.

Then an awful thing happened, the maid's image was fading, and try as she would Stephen could not recall certain passing expressions that had erstwhile allured her. Now she could not see Collins' face at all clearly even if she willed very hard in the dark. Thoroughly disgruntled, she bethought her of books, books of fairy tales, hitherto not much in favour, especially of those that treated of spells, incantations and other unlawful proceedings. She even requested the surprised Mrs. Bingham to read from the Bible:

'You know where,' coaxed Stephen, 'it's the place they were reading in church last Sunday, about Saul and a witch with a name like Edna—the place where she makes some person come up, 'cause the king had forgotten what he looked like.'*

But if prayer had failed Stephen, her spells also failed her; indeed they behaved as spells do when said backwards, making her see, not the person she wished to, but a creature entirely different. For Collins now had a most serious rival, one who had lately appeared at the stables. He was not possessed of a real housemaid's knee, but instead, of four deeply thrilling brown legs—he was two up on legs, and one up on a tail, which was rather unfair on Collins! That Christmas, when Stephen was eight years old, Sir Philip had bought her a hefty bay pony; she was learning to ride him, could ride him already, being naturally skilful and fearless. There had been quite a heated discussion with Anna, because Stephen had insisted on riding astride.* In this she had shown herself very refractory, falling off every time she tried the side-saddle—quite obvious, of course, this falling off process, but enough to subjugate Anna.

And now Stephen would spend long hours at the stables, swaggering largely in corduroy breeches, hobnobbing with Williams, the old stud groom, who had a soft place in his heart for the child.

She would say: 'Come up, horse!' in the same tone as Williams; or, pretending to a knowledge she was far from possessing: 'Is that fetlock* a bit puffy? It looks to me puffy; supposing we put on a nice wet bandage.'

Then Williams would rub his rough chin as though thinking: 'Maybe yes—maybe no—' he would temporize, wisely.

She grew to adore the smell of the stables; it was far more enticing than Collins' perfume—the Erasmic* she had used on her afternoons out, and which had once smelt so delicious. And the pony! So strong, so entirely fulfilling, with his round, gentle eyes, and his heart big with courage—he was surely more worthy of worship than Collins, who had treated you badly because of the footman! And yet—and yet—you owed something to Collins, just because you had loved her, though you couldn't any more. It was dreadfully worrying, all this hard thinking, when you wished to enjoy a new pony! Stephen would stand there rubbing her chin in an almost exact imitation of Williams. She could not produce the same scrabbly sound, but in spite of this drawback the movement would soothe her.

Then one morning she had a bright inspiration: 'Come up, horse!' she commanded, slapping the pony, 'Come up, horse, and let me get close to your ear, 'cause I'm going to whisper something dreadfully important.' Laying her cheek against his firm neck she said softly: 'You're not *you* any more, you're Collins!'

So Collins was comfortably transmigrated.* It was Stephen's last effort to remember.

2

Came the day when Stephen rode out with her father to a meet,* a glorious and memorable day. Side by side the two of them jogged through the gates, and the lodgekeeper's wife must smile to see Stephen sitting her smart bay pony astride, and looking so comically like Sir Philip.

'It do be a pity as her isn't a boy, our young lady,' she told her husband.

It was one of those still, slightly frosty mornings when the landing is tricky on the north side of the hedges; when the smoke from farm chimneys rises straight as a ramrod; when the scent of log fires or of burning brushwood, though left far behind, still persists in the nostrils. A crystal clear morning, like a draught of spring water, and such mornings are good when one is young.

The pony tugged hard and fought at his bridle; he was trembling with pleasure, for he was no novice; he knew all about signs and wonders in stables, such as large feeds of corn administered early, and extra long groomings, and pink coats with brass buttons, like the hunt coat Sir Philip was wearing. He frisked down the road, a mass of affectation, demanding some skill on the part of his rider; but the child's hands were strong yet exceedingly gentle—she possessed that rare gift, perfect hands on a horse.

'This is better than being young Nelson,' thought Stephen, ''cause this way I'm happy just being myself.'

Sir Philip looked down at his daughter with contentment; she was good to look upon, he decided. And yet his contentment was not quite complete, so that he looked away again quickly, sighing a little, because, somehow these days, he had taken to sighing over Stephen.

The meet was a large one. People noticed the child; Colonel Antrim, the Master, rode up and spoke kindly: 'You've a fine pony there, but he'll need a bit of holding!' And then to her father: 'Is she safe astride, Philip? Violet's learning to ride, but side-saddle, I prefer it—I never think girl children get the grip astride; they aren't built for it, haven't the necessary muscle; still, no doubt she'll stick on by balance.'

Stephen flushed: 'No doubt she'll stick on by balance!' The words rankled, oh, very deeply they rankled. Violet was learning to ride side-saddle, that small, flabby lump who squealed if you pinched her; that terrified creature of muslins and ribbons and hair that curled over the nurse's finger! Why, Violet could never come to tea without crying, could never play a game without getting herself hurt! She had fat, wobbly legs too, just like a rag doll—and you, Stephen, had been compared to Violet! Ridiculous of course, and yet all of a sudden you felt less impressive in your fine riding breeches. You felt—well, not foolish exactly, but self-conscious—not quite at your ease, a little bit wrong. It was almost as though you were playing at young Nelson again, were only pretending.

But you said: 'I've got muscles, haven't I, Father? Williams says I've got riding muscles already!' Then you dug your heels sharply into the pony, so that he whisked round, bucking and rearing. As for you, you stuck to his back like a limpet. Wasn't that enough to convince them?

'Steady on, Stephen!' came Sir Philip's voice, warning. Then the Master's: 'She's got a fine seat. I'll admit it—Violet's a little bit scared on a horse, but I think she'll get confidence later; I hope so.'

And now hounds were moving away towards cover, tails waving—they looked like an army with banners. 'Hi, Starbright—Fancy! Get in, little bitch! Hi, Frolic, get on with it, Frolic!'

The long lashes shot out with amazing precision, stinging a flank or stroking a shoulder, while the four-legged Amazons* closed up their ranks for the serious business ahead. 'Hi, Starbright!' Whips cracked and horses grew restless; Stephen's mount required undivided attention. She had no time to think of her muscles or her grievance, but only of the creature between her small knees.

'All right, Stephen?'

'Yes, Father.'

'Well, go steady at your fences; it may be a little bit slippery this morning.' But Sir Philip's voice did not sound at all anxious; indeed there was a note of deep pride in his voice.

'He knows that I'm not just a rag doll, like Violet; he knows that I'm different to her!' thought Stephen.

3

The strange, implacable heart-broken music of hounds giving tongue* as they break from cover; the cry of the huntsman as he stands in his stirrups; the thud of hooves pounding ruthlessly forward over long, green, undulating meadows. The meadows flying back as though seen from a train, the meadows streaming away behind you; the acrid smell of horse sweat caught in passing; the smell of damp leather, of earth and bruised herbage—all sudden, all passing—then the smell of wide spaces, the air smell, cool yet as potent as wine.

Sir Philip was looking back over his shoulder: 'All right, Stephen?'

'Oh, yes—' Stephen's voice sounded breathless.

'Steady on! Steady on!'

They were coming to a fence, and Stephen's grip tightened a little. The pony took the fence in his stride, very gaily; for an instant he seemed to stay poised in mid-air as though he had wings, then he touched earth again, and away without even pausing.

'All right, Stephen?'

'Yes, yes!'

Sir Philip's broad back was bent forward over the shoulder of his hunter;* the crisp auburn hair in the nape of his neck showed bright where the winter sunshine touched it; and as the child followed that purposeful back, she felt that she loved it utterly, entirely. At that moment it seemed to embody all kindness, all strength, and all understanding.

4

They killed not so very far from Worcester; it had been a stiff run, the best of the season. Colonel Antrim came jogging along to Stephen, whose prowess had amused and surprised him.

'Well, well,' he said, grinning, 'so here you are, madam, still with a leg on each side of your horse—I'm going to tell Violet she'll have to buck up. By the way, Philip, can Stephen come to tea on Monday, before Roger goes back to school? She can? Oh, splendid! And now where's that brush?* I think our young Stephen here, takes it.'

Strange it is, but unforgettable moments are often connected with very small happenings, happenings that assume fictitious proportions, especially when we are children. If Colonel Antrim had offered Stephen the crown of England on a red velvet cushion, it is doubtful whether her pride would have equalled the pride that she felt when the huntsman came forward and presented her with her first hunting trophy—the rather pathetic, bedraggled little brush, that had weathered so many hard miles. Just for an instant the child's heart misgave her, as she looked at the soft, furry thing in her hand; but the joy of attainment was still hot upon her, and that incomparable feeling of elation that comes from the knowledge of personal courage, so that she forgot the woes of the fox in remembering the prowess of Stephen.

Sir Philip fastened the brush to her saddle. 'You rode well,' he said briefly, then turned to the Master.

But she knew that that day she had not failed him, for his eyes had been bright when they rested on hers; she had seen great love in those melancholy eyes, together with a curiously wistful expression of which her youth lacked understanding. And now many people smiled broadly at Stephen, patting her pony and calling him a flier.

One old farmer remarked: ''E do be a good plucked un, and so be 'is rider—beggin' your pardon.'

At which Stephen must blush and grow slightly mendacious, pretending to give all the credit to the pony, pretending to feel very humble of spirit, which she knew she was far from feeling.

'Come along!' called Sir Philip, 'No more to-day, Stephen, your poor little fellow's had enough for one day.' Which was true, since Collins was all of a tremble, what with excitement and straining short legs to keep up with vainglorious hunters.

Whips touched hats: 'Good-bye, Stephen, come out soon again—See you on Tuesday, Sir Philip, with the Croome.'* And the field settled down to the changing of horses, before drawing yet one more cover.

5

Father and daughter rode home through the twilight, and now there were no dog-roses in the hedges, the hedges stood leafless and grey with frost rime,* a network of delicate branches. The earth smelt as clean as a newly washed garment—it smelt of 'God's washing,' as Stephen called it—while away to the left, from a distant farm-house, came the sound of a yard-dog, barking. Small lights were glowing in cottage windows as yet uncurtained, as yet very friendly; and beyond, where the great hills of Malvern showed blue against the pale sky, many small lights were burning—lights of home newly lit on the altar of the hills to the God of both hills and homesteads. No birds were singing in the trees by the roadside, but a silence prevailed, more lovely than bird song; the thoughtful and holy silence of winter, the silence of trustfully waiting furrows. For the soil is the greatest saint of all ages, knowing neither impatience, nor fear, nor doubting; knowing only faith, from which spring all blessings that are needful to nurture man.

Sir Philip said: 'Are you happy, my Stephen?'

And she answered: 'I'm dreadfully happy, Father. I'm so dreadfully happy that it makes me feel frightened, 'cause I mayn't always last happy—not this way.'

He did not ask why she might not last happy; he just nodded, as though he admitted of a reason; but he laid his hand over hers on the bridle for a moment, a large and comforting hand. Then the peace of the evening took possession of Stephen, that and the peace of a healthy body tired out with fresh air and much vigorous movement, so that she swayed a little in her saddle and came near to falling asleep. The pony, even more tired than his rider, jogged along with neck drooping and reins hanging slackly, too weary to shy at the ogreish shadows that were crouching ready to scare him. His small mind was doubtless concentrated on fodder; on the bucket of water nicely seasoned with gruel; on the groom's soothing hiss as he rubbed down and bandaged; on the warm blanket clothing, so pleasant in winter, and above all on that golden bed of deep straw that was sure to be waiting in his stable.

And now a great moon had swung up very slowly; and the moon seemed to pause, staring hard at Stephen, while the frost rime turned white with the whiteness of diamonds, and the shadows turned black and lay folded like velvet round the feet of the drowsy hedges. But the meadows beyond the hedges turned silver, and so did the road to Morton.

6

It was late when they reached the stables at last, and old Williams was waiting in the yard with a lantern.

'Did you kill?' he inquired, according to custom; then he saw Stephen's trophy and chuckled.

Stephen tried to spring easily out of the saddle as her father had done, but her legs seemed to fail her. To her horror and chagrin her legs hung down stiffly as though made of wood; she could not control them; and to make matters worse, Collins now grew impatient and began to walk off to his loose-box.* Then Sir Philip put two strong arms around Stephen, and he lifted her bodily as though she were a baby, and he carried her, only faintly protesting, right up to the door of the house and beyond it—right up, indeed, to the warm pleasant nursery where a steaming hot bath was waiting. Her head fell back and lay on his shoulder, while her eyelids drooped, heavy with well-earned sleep; she had to blink very hard several times over in order to get the better of that sleep.

'Happy, darling?' he whispered, and his grave face bent nearer. She could feel his cheek, rough at the end of the day, pressed against her forehead, and she loved that kind roughness, so that she put up her hand and stroked it.

'So dreadfully, dreadfully happy, Father,' she murmured, 'so—dreadfully happy—'

CHAPTER 5

I

On the Monday that followed Stephen's first day out hunting she woke with something very like a weight on her chest; in less than two minutes she knew why this was—she was going to tea with the Antrims. Her relations with other children were peculiar, she thought so herself and so did the children; they could not define it and neither could Stephen, but there it was all the same. A high-spirited child, she should have been popular, and yet she was not, a fact which she divined, and this made her feel ill at ease with her playmates, who in their turn felt ill at ease. She would think that the children were whispering about her, whispering and laughing for no apparent reason; but although this had happened on one occasion, it was not always happening as Stephen imagined. She was painfully hyper-sensitive at times, and she suffered accordingly.

Of all the children that Stephen most dreaded, Violet and Roger Antrim took precedence; especially Roger, who was ten years old, and already full to the neck of male arrogance—he had just been promoted to Etons* that winter, which added to his overbearing pride. Roger Antrim had round, brown eyes like his mother, and a short, straight nose that might one day be handsome; he was rather a thick-set, plump little boy, whose buttocks looked too large in a short Eton jacket, especially when he stuck his hands in his pockets and strutted, which he did very often.

Roger was a bully; he bullied his sister, and would dearly have loved to bully Stephen; but Stephen nonplussed him, her arms were so strong, he could never wrench Stephen's arms backwards like Violet's; he could never make her cry or show any emotion when he pinched her, or tugged roughly at her new hair ribbon, and then Stephen would often beat him at games, a fact which he deeply resented. She could bowl at cricket much straighter than he could; she climbed trees with astonishing skill and prowess, and even if she did tear her skirts in the process it was obviously cheek for a girl to climb at all. Violet never climbed trees; she stood at the bottom admiring the courage of Roger. He grew to hate Stephen as a kind of rival, a kind of intruder into his especial province; he was always longing to take her down a peg, but being slow-witted he was foolish in his methods—no good daring Stephen, she responded at once, and usually went one better. As for Stephen, she loathed him, and her loathing was increased by a most humiliating consciousness of envy. Yes, despite his shortcomings she envied young Roger with his thick, clumping boots, his cropped hair and his Etons; envied his school and his masculine companions of whom he would speak grandly as: 'all the other fellows!'; envied his right to climb trees and play cricket and football—his right to be perfectly natural; above all she envied his splendid conviction that being a boy constituted a privilege in life; she could well understand that conviction, but this only increased her envy.

Stephen found Violet intolerably silly, she cried quite as loudly when she bumped her own head as when Roger applied his most strenuous torments. But what irritated Stephen, was the fact that she suspected that Violet almost enjoyed those torments.

'He's so dreadfully strong!' she had confided to Stephen, with something like pride in her voice.

Stephen had longed to shake her for that: 'I can pinch quite as hard as he can!' she had threatened, 'If you think he's stronger than I am, I'll show you!' At which Violet had rushed away screaming.

Violet was already full of feminine poses; she loved dolls, but not quite so much as she pretended. People said: 'Look at Violet, she's like a little mother; it's so touching to see that instinct in a child!' Then Violet would become still more touching. She was always thrusting her dolls upon Stephen, making her undress them and put them to bed. 'Now you're Nanny, Stephen, and I'm Gertrude's mother, or you can be mother this time if you'd rather—Oh, be careful, you'll break her! Now you've pulled off a button! I do think you might play more like I do!' And then Violet knitted, or said that she knitted—Stephen had never seen anything but knots. 'Can't *you* knit?' she would say, looking scornfully at Stephen, 'I can—Mother called me a dear little housewife!' Then Stephen would lose her temper and speak rudely: 'You're a dear little sop, that's what you are!' For hours she must play stupid doll-games with Violet, because Roger would not always play real games in the garden. He hated to be beaten, yet how could she help it? Could she help throwing straighter than Roger?

They had nothing whatever in common, these children, but the Antrims were neighbours, and even Sir Philip, indulgent though he was, insisted that Stephen should have friends of her own age to play with. He had spoken quite sharply on several occasions when the child had pleaded to be allowed to stay at home. Indeed he spoke sharply that very day at luncheon:

'Eat your pudding please, Stephen; come now, finish it quickly! If all this fuss is about the little Antrims, then Father won't have it, it's ridiculous, darling.'

So Stephen had hastily swallowed her pudding, and escaped upstairs to the nursery.

2

The Antrims lived half a mile from Ledbury,* on the other side of the hills. It was quite a long drive to their house from Morton—Stephen was driven over in the dog-cart.* She sat beside Williams in gloomy silence, with the collar of her coat turned up to her ears. She was filled with a sense of bitter injustice; why should they insist on this stupid expedition? Even her father had been cross at luncheon because she preferred to stay at home with him. Why should she be forced to know other children? They didn't want her nor she them. And above all the Antrims! That idiotic Violet—Violet who was learning to ride side-saddle—and Roger strutting about in his Etons, and bragging, always bragging because he was a boy—and their mother who was quite sure to patronize Stephen, because being grown-up made her put on a manner. Stephen could hear her infuriating voice, the voice she reserved for children. 'Ah, here you are, Stephen! Now then, little people, run along and have a good feed in the schoolroom. There's plenty of cake; I knew Stephen was coming; we all know Stephen's capacity for cake!'

Stephen could hear Violet's timorous giggle and Roger's guffaw as they greeted this sally. She could feel his fat fingers pinching her arm; pinching cruelly, slyly, as he strutted beside her. Then his whisper: 'You're a pig! You eat much more than I do, mother said so to-day, and boys need more than girls!' Then Violet: 'I'm not very fond of plum cake, it makes me feel sicky—mother says it's indigestion. I could never eat big bits of plum cake like Stephen. Nanny says I'm a dainty feeder.' Then Stephen herself, saying nothing at all, but glaring sideways at Roger.

The dog-cart was slowly climbing British Camp,* that long, steep hill out of Little Malvern. The cold air grew colder, but marvellously pure it was, up there above the valleys. The peak of the Camp stood out clearly defined by snow that had fallen lightly that morning, and as they breasted the crest of the hill, the sun shone out on the snow. Away to the right lay the valley of the Wye, a long, lovely valley of deep blue shadows; a valley of small homesteads and mothering trees, of soft undulations and wide, restful spaces leading away to a line of dim mountains—leading away to the mountains of Wales, that lay just over the border. And because she loved this kind English valley, Stephen's sulky eyes must turn and rest upon it; not all her apprehension and sense of injustice could take from her eyes the joy of that seeing. She must gaze and gaze, she must let it possess her, the peace, the wonder that lay in such beauty; while the unwilling tears welled up under her lids—she not knowing why they had come there.

And now they were trotting swiftly downhill; the valley had vanished, but the woods of Eastnor* stood naked and lovely, and the forms of their trees were more perfect than forms that are made with hands—unless with the hands of God. Stephen's eyes turned again; she could not stay sulky, for these were the woods where she drove with her father. Twice every spring they drove up to these woods and through them to the stretching parkland beyond. There were deer in the park—they would sometimes get out of the dog-cart so that Stephen could feed the does.

She began to whistle softly through her teeth, an accomplishment in which she took a great pride.* Impossible to go on feeling resentful when the sun was shining between the bare branches, when the air was as clear and as bright as crystal, when the cob was literally flying through the air, taking all Williams' strength to hold him.

'Steady boy—steady on! He be feeling the weather—gets into his blood and makes him that skittish—Now go quiet, you young blight! Just look at him, will you, he's got himself all of a lather!'

'Let me drive,' pleaded Stephen, 'Oh, please, *please* Williams!'

But Williams shook his head as he grinned at her broadly: 'I've got old bones, Miss Stephen, and old bones breaks quick when it's frosty, so I've heard tell.'

3

Mrs. Antrim was waiting for Stephen in the lounge—she was always waiting to waylay her in the lounge, or so it appeared to Stephen. The lounge was a much over-dressed apartment, full of small, useless tables and large, clumsy chairs. You bumped into the chairs and tripped over the tables; at least you did if you were Stephen. There was one deadly pitfall you never could avoid, a huge polar bear skin that lay on the floor. Its stuffed head protruded at a most awkward angle; you invariably stubbed your big toe on that head. Stephen, true to tradition, stubbed her toe rather badly as she blundered towards Mrs. Antrim.

'Dear me,' remarked her hostess, 'you are a great girl; why your feet must be double the size of Violet's! Come here and let me have a look at your feet.' Then she laughed as though something amused her.

Stephen was longing to rub her big toe, but she thought better of it, enduring in silence.

'Children!' called Mrs. Antrim, 'Here's Stephen, I'm sure she's as hungry as a hunter!'

Violet was wearing a pale blue silk frock; even at seven she was vain of her appearance. She had cried until she had got permission to wear that particular pale blue frock, which was usually reserved for parties. Her brown hair was curled into careful ringlets, and tied with a very large bow of blue ribbon. Mrs. Antrim glanced quickly from Stephen to Violet with a look of maternal pride.

Roger was bulging inside his Etons; his round cheeks were puffed, very pink and aggressive. He eyed Stephen coldly from above a white collar that was obviously fresh from the laundry. On their way upstairs he pinched Stephen's leg, and Stephen kicked backwards, swiftly and neatly.

'I suppose you think you can kick!' grunted Roger, who was suffering acutely at that moment from his shin, 'You've not got the strength of a flea; I don't feel it!'

At Violet's request they were left alone for tea; she liked playing the hostess, and her mother spoilt her. A special small teapot had had to be unearthed, in order that Violet could lift it.

'Sugar?' she inquired with tongs poised in mid air, '*And* milk?' she added, imitating her mother. Mrs. Antrim always said: '*And* milk,' in that tone—it made you feel that you must be rather greedy.

'Oh, chuck it!' growled Roger, whose shin was still aching, 'You know I want milk and four lumps of sugar.'

Violet's underlip began to tremble, but she held her ground with unexpected firmness. 'May I give you a little more milk, Stephen dear? Or would you prefer no milk, only lemon?'

'There isn't any lemon and you know it!' bawled Roger. 'Here, give me my tea or I'll spoil your hair ribbon.' He grabbed at his cup and nearly upset it.

'Oh, oh!' shrilled Violet, 'My dress!'

They settled down to the meal at last, but Stephen observed that Roger was watching; every mouthful she ate she could feel him watching, so that she grew self-conscious. She was hungry, not having eaten much luncheon, but now she could not enjoy her cake; Roger himself was stuffing like a grampus,* but his eyes never left her face. Then Roger, the slow-witted in his dealings with Stephen, all but choked in the throes of a great inspiration.

'I say, *you*,' he began, with his mouth very full, 'what about a certain young lady out hunting? What about a fat leg on each side of her horse like a monkey on a stick, and everybody laughing!'

'They were not!' exclaimed Stephen, growing suddenly red.

'Oh, yes, but they were, though!' mocked Roger.

Now had Stephen been wise she would have let the thing drop, for no fun is derived from a one-sided contest, but at eight years old one is not always wise, and moreover her pride had been stung to the quick.

She said: 'I'd like to see you get the brush; why you can't stick on just riding round the paddock! I've seen you fall off jumping nothing but a hurdle; I'd like to see *you* out hunting!'

Roger swallowed some more cake; there was now no great hurry; he had thrown his sprat and had landed his mackerel.* He had very much feared that she might not be drawn—it was not always easy to draw Stephen.

'Well now, listen,' he drawled, 'and I'll tell you something. You thought they admired you squatting on your pony; you thought you were being very grand, I'll bet, with your new riding breeches and your black velvet cap; you thought they'd suppose that you looked like a boy, just because you were trying to be one. As a matter of fact, if you really want to know, they were busting their sides; why, my father said so. He was laughing all the time at your looking so funny on that rotten old pony that's as fat as a porpoise. Why, he only gave you the brush for fun, because you were such a small kid—he said so. He said: "I gave Stephen Gordon the brush because I thought she might cry if I didn't." '

'You're a liar,' breathed Stephen, who had turned very pale.

'Oh, am I? Well, you ask father.'

'Do stop—' whimpered Violet, beginning to cry; 'you're horrid, you're spoiling my party.'

But Roger was launched on his first perfect triumph; he had seen the expression in Stephen's eyes: 'And my mother said,' he continued more loudly, 'that your mother must be funny to allow you to do it; she said it was horrid to let girls ride that way; she said she was awfully surprised at your mother; she said that she'd have thought that your mother had more sense; she said that it wasn't modest; she said—'

Stephen had suddenly sprung to her feet: 'How dare you! How dare you—my mother!' she spluttered. And now she was almost beside herself with rage, conscious only of one overwhelming impulse, and that to belabour Roger.

A plate crashed to the ground and Violet screamed faintly. Roger, in his turn, had pushed back his chair; his round eyes were staring and rather frightened; he had never seen Stephen quite like this before. She was actually rolling up the sleeves of her smock.

'You cad!' she shouted, 'I'll fight you for this!' And she doubled up her fist and shook it at Roger while he edged away from the table.

She stood there an enraged and ridiculous figure in her Liberty smock,* with her hard, boyish forearms. Her long hair had partly escaped from its ribbon, and the bow sagged down limply, crooked and foolish. All that was heavy in her face sprang into view, the strong line of the jaw, the square, massive brow, the eyebrows, too thick and too wide for beauty. And yet there was a kind of large splendour about her—absurd though she was, she was splendid at that moment—grotesque and splendid, like some primitive thing conceived in a turbulent age of transition.

'Are you going to fight me, you coward?' she demanded, as she stepped round the table and faced her tormentor.

But Roger thrust his hands deep into his pockets: 'I don't fight with girls!' he remarked very grandly. Then he sauntered out of the schoolroom.

Stephen's own hands fell and hung at her sides; her head drooped, and she stood staring down at the carpet. The whole of her suddenly drooped and looked helpless, as she stood staring down at the carpet.

'How could you!' began Violet, who was plucking up courage. 'Little girls don't have fights—I don't, I'd be frightened—'

But Stephen cut her short: 'I'm going,' she said thickly; 'I'm going home to my father.'

She went heavily downstairs and out into the lobby, where she put on her hat and coat; then she made her way round the house to the stables, in search of old Williams and the dog-cart.

4

'You're home very early, Stephen,' said Anna, but Sir Philip was staring at his daughter's face.

'What's the matter?' he inquired, and his voice sounded anxious. 'Come here and tell me about it.'

Then Stephen quite suddenly burst into tears, and she wept and she wept as she stood there before them, and she poured out her shame and humiliation, telling all that Roger had said about her mother, telling all that she, Stephen, would have done to defend her, had it not been that Roger would not fight with a girl. She wept and she wept without any restraint, scarcely knowing what she said—at that moment not caring. And Sir Philip listened with his head on his hand, and Anna listened bewildered and dumbfounded. She tried to kiss Stephen, to hold her to her, but Stephen, still sobbing, pushed her away; in this orgy of grief she resented consolation, so that in the end Anna took her to the nursery and delivered her over to the care of Mrs. Bingham, feeling that the child did not want her.

When Anna went quietly back to the study, Sir Philip was still sitting with his head on his hand. She said: 'It's time you realized, Philip, that if you're Stephen's father, I'm her mother. So far you've managed the child your own way, and I don't think it's been successful. You've treated Stephen as though she were a boy—perhaps it's because I've not given you a son—' Her voice trembled a little but she went on gravely: 'It's not good for Stephen; I know it's not good, and at times it frightens me, Philip.'

'No, no!' he said sharply.

But Anna persisted: 'Yes, Philip, at times it makes me afraid—I can't tell you why, but it seems all wrong—it makes me feel—strange with the child.'

He looked at her out of his melancholy eyes: 'Can't you trust me? Won't you try to trust me, Anna?'

But Anna shook her head: 'I don't understand, why shouldn't you trust *me*, Philip?'

And then in his terror for this well-beloved woman, Sir Philip committed the first cowardly action of his life—he who would not have spared himself pain, could not bear to inflict it on Anna. In his infinite pity for Stephen's mother, he sinned very deeply and gravely against Stephen, by withholding from that mother his own conviction that her child was not as other children.

'There's nothing for you to understand,' he said firmly, 'but I like you to trust me in all things.'

After this they sat talking about the child, Sir Philip very quiet and reassuring.

'I've wanted her to have a healthy body,' he explained, 'that's why I've let her run more or less wild; but perhaps we'd better have a governess now, as you say; a French governess, my dear, if you'd prefer one—Later on I've always meant to engage a bluestocking,* some woman who's been to Oxford. I want Stephen to have the finest education that care and money can give her.'

But once again Anna began to protest. 'What's the good of it all for a girl?' she argued. 'Did you love me any less because I couldn't do mathematics? Do you love me less now because I count on my fingers?'

He kissed her. 'That's different, you're you,' he said, smiling, but a look that she knew well had come into his eyes, a cold, resolute expression, which meant that all persuasion was likely to be unavailing.

Presently they went upstairs to the nursery, and Sir Philip shaded the candle with his hand, while they stood together gazing down at Stephen—the child was heavily asleep.

'Look, Philip,' whispered Anna, pitiful and shaken, 'look, Philip—she's got two big tears on her cheek!'

He nodded, slipping his arm around Anna: 'Come away, he muttered, 'we may wake her.'

CHAPTER 6

I

Mrs. Bingham departed unmourned and unmourning, and in her stead reigned Mademoiselle Duphot, a youthful French governess with a long, pleasant face that reminded Stephen of a horse. This equine resemblance was fortunate in one way—Stephen took to Mademoiselle Duphot at once—but it did not make for respectful obedience. On the contrary, Stephen felt very familiar, kindly familiar and quite at her ease; she petted Mademoiselle Duphot. Mademoiselle Duphot was lonely and homesick, and it must be admitted that she liked being petted. Stephen would rush off to get her a cushion, or a footstool or her glass of milk at eleven.

'Comme elle est gentille, cette drôle de petite fille, elle a si bon cœur,'* would think Mademoiselle Duphot, and somehow geography would not seem to matter quite so much, or arithmetic either—in vain did Mademoiselle try to be strict, her pupil could always beguile her.

Mademoiselle Duphot knew nothing about horses, in spite of the fact that she looked so much like one, and Stephen would complacently entertain her with long conversations anent splints and spavins, cow hocks and colic,* all mixed up together in a kind of wild veterinary jumble. Had Williams been listening, he might well have rubbed his chin, but Williams was not there to listen.

As for Mademoiselle Duphot, she was genuinely impressed: 'Mais quel type, quel type!' she was always exclaiming. 'Vous êtes déjà une vraie petite Amazone, Stévenne.'

'N'est-ce pas?'* agreed Stephen, who was picking up French.

The child showed a real ability for French, and this delighted her teacher; at the end of six months she could gabble quite freely, making quick little gestures and shrugging her shoulders. She liked talking French, it rather amused her, nor was she averse to mastering the grammar; what she could not endure were the long, foolish dictées from the edifying Bibliothèque Rose.* Weak in all other respects with Stephen, Mademoiselle Duphot clung to these dictées; the Bibliothèque Rose became her last trench of authority, and she held it.

'"Les Petites Filles Modèles,"' Mademoiselle would announce, while Stephen yawned out her ineffable boredom; 'Maintenant nous allons retrouver Sophie—Where to did we arrive? Ah, oui, I remember: "Cette preuve de confiance toucha Sophie et augmenta encore son regret d'avoir été si méchante.

'"Comment, se dit-elle, ai-je pu me livrer à une telle colère? Comment ai-je été si méchante avec des amies aussi bonnes que celles que j'ai ici, et si hardie envers une personne aussi douce, aussi tendre que Mme. de Fleurville!"'*

From time to time the programme would be varied by extracts of an even more edifying nature, and 'Les Bons Enfants'* would be chosen for dictation, to the scorn and derision of Stephen.

'*La Maman.* Donne-lui ton cœur, mon Henri; c'est ce que tu pourras lui donner de plus agréable.

'—Mon cœur? Dit Henri en déboutonnant son habit et en ouvrant sa chemise. Mais comment faire? il me faudrait un couteau.'* At which Stephen would giggle.

One day she had added a comment of her own in the margin: 'Little beast, he was only shamming!'* and Mademoiselle, coming on this unawares, had been caught in the act of laughing by her pupil. After which there was naturally less discipline than ever in the schoolroom, but considerably more friendship.

However, Anna seemed quite contented, since Stephen was becoming so proficient in French; and observing that his wife looked less anxious these days, Sir Philip said nothing, biding his time. This frank, jaunty slacking on the part of his daughter should be checked later on, he decided. Meanwhile, Stephen grew fond of the mild-faced Frenchwoman, who in her turn adored the unusual child. She would often confide her troubles to Stephen, those family troubles in which governesses abound—her Maman was old and delicate and needy; her sister had a wicked and spendthrift husband, and now her sister must make little bags for the grand shops in Paris that paid very badly, her sister was gradually losing her eyesight through making those little bead bags for the shops that cared nothing, and paid very badly. Mademoiselle sent Maman a part of her earnings, and sometimes, of course, she must help her sister. Her Maman must have her chicken on Sundays: 'Bon Dieu, il faut vivre—il faut manger, au moins—'* And afterwards that chicken came in very nicely for Petite Marmite,* which was made from his carcass and a few leaves of cabbage—Maman loved Petite Marmite, the warmth of it eased her old gums.

Stephen would listen to these long dissertations with patience and with apparent understanding. She would nod her head wisely: 'Mais c'est dur,' she would comment, 'c'est terriblement dur, la vie!'*

But she never confided her own special troubles, and Mademoiselle Duphot sometimes wondered about her: 'Est-elle heureuse, cet étrange petit être?' she would wonder. 'Sera-t-elle heureuse plus tard? Qui sait!'*

2

Idleness and peace had reigned in the schoolroom for more than two years, when ex-Sergeant Smylie sailed over the horizon and proceeded to announce that he taught gymnastics and fencing.* From that moment peace ceased to reign in the schoolroom, or indeed anywhere in the house for that matter. In vain did Mademoiselle Duphot protest that gymnastics and fencing thickened the ankles, in vain did Anna express disapproval, Stephen merely ignored them and consulted her father.

'I want to go in for Sandowing,'* she informed him, as though they were discussing a career.

He laughed: 'Sandowing? Well, and how will you start it?'

Then Stephen explained about ex-Sergeant Smylie.

'I see,' nodded Sir Philip, 'you want to learn fencing.'

'And how to lift weights with my stomach,' she said quickly.

'Why not with your large front teeth?' he teased her. 'Oh, well,' he added, 'there's no harm in fencing or gymnastics either—provided, of course, that you don't try to wreck Morton Hall like a Samson wrecking the house of the Philistines;* I foresee that that might easily happen—'

Stephen grinned: 'But it mightn't if I cut off my hair!* May I cut off my hair? Oh, do let me, Father!'

'Certainly not, I prefer to risk it,' said Sir Philip, speaking quite firmly.

Stephen went pounding back to the schoolroom. 'I'm going to those classes!' she announced in triumph. 'I'm going to be driven over to Malvern next week; I'm going to begin on Tuesday, and I'm going to learn fencing so as I can kill your brother-in-law who's a beast to your sister, I'm going to fight duels for wives in distress, like men do in Paris, and I'm going to learn how to lift pianos on my stomach by expanding something—the diapan muscles*—and I'm going to cut my hair off!' she mendaciously concluded, glancing sideways to observe the effect of this bomb-shell.

'Bon Dieu, soyez clément!'* breathed Mademoiselle Duphot, casting her eyes to heaven.

3

It was not very long before ex-Sergeant Smylie discovered that in Stephen he had a star pupil. 'Some day you ought to make a champion fencer, if you work really hard at it, Miss,' he told her.

Stephen did not learn to lift pianos with her stomach, but as time went on she did become quite an expert gymnast and fencer; and as Mademoiselle Duphot confided to Anna, it was after all very charming to watch her, so supple and young and quick in her movements.

'And she fence like an angel,' said Mademoiselle fondly, 'she fence now almost as well as she ride.'

Anna nodded. She herself had seen Stephen fencing many times, and had thought it a fine performance for so young a child, but the fencing displeased her, so that she found it hard to praise Stephen.

'I hate all that sort of thing for girls,' she said slowly.

'But she fence like a man, with such power and such grace,' babbled Mademoiselle Duphot, the tactless.

And now life was full of new interest for Stephen, an interest that centred entirely in her body. She discovered her body for a thing to be cherished, a thing of real value since its strength could rejoice her;* and young though she was she cared for her body with great diligence, bathing it night and morning in dull, tepid water—cold baths were forbidden,* and hot baths, she had heard, sometimes weakened the muscles. For gymnastics she wore her hair in a pigtail, and somehow that pigtail began to intrude on other occasions. In spite of protests, she always forgot and came down to breakfast with a neat, shining plait, so that Anna gave in in the end and said, sighing:

'Have your pigtail, do, child, if you feel that you must—but I can't say it suits you, Stephen.'

And Mademoiselle Duphot was foolishly loving. Stephen would stop in the middle of lessons to roll back her sleeves and examine her muscles; then Mademoiselle Duphot, instead of protesting, would laugh and admire her absurd little biceps. Stephen's craze for physical culture increased, and now it began to invade the schoolroom. Dumb-bells appeared in the schoolroom bookcases, while half worn-out gym shoes skulked in the corners. Everything went by the board but this passion of the child's for training her body. And what must Sir Philip elect to do next, but to write out to Ireland and purchase a hunter for his daughter to ride—a real, thoroughbred hunter. And what must he say but: 'That's one for young Roger!' So that Stephen found herself comfortably laughing at the thought of young Roger; and that laugh went a long way towards healing the wound that had rankled within her—perhaps this was why Sir Philip had written out to Ireland for that thoroughbred hunter.

The hunter, when he came, was grey-coated and slender, and his eyes were as soft as an Irish morning, and his courage was as bright as an Irish sunrise, and his heart was as young as the wild heart of Ireland, but devoted and loyal and eager for service, and his name was sweet on the tongue as you spoke it—being Raftery, after the poet.* Stephen loved Raftery and Raftery loved Stephen. It was love at first sight, and they talked to each other for hours in his loose box—not in Irish or English, but in a quiet language having very few words but many small sounds and many small movements, which to both of them meant more than words.* And Raftery said: 'I will carry you bravely, I will serve you all the days of my life.' And she answered: 'I will care for you night and day, Raftery—all the days of your life.' Thus Stephen and Raftery pledged their devotion, alone in his fragrant, hay-scented stable. And Raftery was five and Stephen was twelve when they solemnly pledged their devotion.

Never was rider more proud or more happy than Stephen, when first she and Raftery went a-hunting;* and never was youngster more wise or courageous than Raftery proved himself at his fences; and never can Bellerophon* have thrilled to more daring than did Stephen, astride of Raftery that day, with the wind in her face and a fire in her heart that made life a thing of glory. At the very beginning of the run the fox turned in the direction of Morton, actually crossing the big north paddock before turning once more and making for Upton. In the paddock was a mighty, upstanding hedge, a formidable place concealing timber, and what must they do, these two young creatures, but go straight at it and get safely over—those who saw

Raftery fly that hedge could never afterwards doubt his valour. And when they got home there was Anna waiting to pat Raftery, because she could not resist him. Because, being Irish, her hands loved the feel of fine horse-flesh under their delicate fingers—and because she did very much want to be tender to Stephen, and understanding. But as Stephen dismounted, bespattered and dishevelled, and yet with that perversive look of her father, the words that Anna had been planning to speak died away before they could get themselves spoken—she shrank back from the child; but the child was too overjoyed at that moment to perceive it.

4

Happy days, splendid days of childish achievements; but they passed all too soon, giving place to the seasons, and there came the winter when Stephen was fourteen.

On a January afternoon of bright sunshine, Mademoiselle Duphot sat dabbing her eyes; for Mademoiselle Duphot must leave her loved Stévenne, must give place to a rival who could teach Greek and Latin—she would go back to Paris, the poor Mademoiselle Duphot, and take care of her ageing Maman.

Meanwhile, Stephen, very angular and lanky at fourteen, was standing before her father in his study. She stood still, but her glance kept straying to the window, to the sunshine that seemed to be beckoning through the window. She was dressed for riding in breeches and gaiters, and her thoughts were with Raftery.

'Sit down,' said Sir Philip, and his voice was so grave that her thoughts came back with a leap and a bound; 'you and I have got to talk this thing out, Stephen.'

'What thing, Father?' she faltered, sitting down abruptly.

'Your idleness, my child. The time has now come when all play and no work will make a dull Stephen,* unless we pull ourselves together.'

She rested her large, shapely hands on her knees and bent forward, searching his face intently. What she saw there was a quiet determination that spread from his lips to his eyes. She grew suddenly uneasy, like a youngster who objects to the rather unpleasant process of mouthing.*

'I speak French,' she broke out, 'I speak French like a native; I can read and write French as well as Mademoiselle does.'

'And beyond that you know very little,' he informed her; 'it's not enough, Stephen, believe me.'

There ensued a long silence, she tapping her leg with her whip, he speculating about her. Then he said, but quite gently: 'I've considered this thing—I've considered this matter of your education. I want you to have the same education, the same advantages as I'd give to my son—that is as far as possible—' he added, looking away from Stephen.

'But I'm not your son, Father,' she said very slowly, and even as she said it her heart felt heavy—heavy and sad as it had not done for years, not since she was quite a small child.

And at this he looked back at her with love in his eyes, love and something that seemed like compassion; and their looks met and mingled and held for a moment, speechless yet somehow expressing their hearts. Her own eyes clouded and she stared at her boots, ashamed of the tears that she felt might flow over. He saw this and went on, speaking more quickly, as though anxious to cover her confusion.

'You're all the son that I've got,' he told her. 'You're brave and strong-limbed, but I want you to be wise—I want you to be wise for your own sake, Stephen, because at the best life requires great wisdom. I want you to learn to make friends of your books; some day you may need them, because—' He hesitated, 'because you mayn't find life at all easy, we none of us do, and books are good friends. I don't want you to give up your fencing and gymnastics or your riding, but I want you to show moderation. You've developed your body, now develop your mind; let your mind and your muscles help, not hinder each other—it can be done, Stephen, I've done it myself, and in many respects you're like me. I've brought you up very differently from most girls, you must know that—look at Violet Antrim. I've indulged you, I suppose, but I don't think I've spoilt you, because I believe in you absolutely. I believe in myself too, where you're concerned; I believe in my own sound judgment. But you've now got to prove that my judgment's been sound, we've both got to prove it to ourselves and to your mother—she's been very patient with my unusual methods—I'm going to stand trial now, and she'll be my judge. Help me, I'm going to need all your help; if you fail then I fail, we shall go down together. But we're not going to fail, you're going to work hard when your new governess comes, and when you're older you're going to become a fine woman, you must; dear—I love you so much that you can't disappoint me.' His voice faltered a little, then he held out his hand: 'and Stephen, come here—look me straight in the eyes—what is honour, my daughter?'

She looked into his anxious, questioning eyes: 'You are honour,' she said quite simply.

5

When Stephen kissed Mademoiselle Duphot good-bye, she cried, for she felt that something was going that would never come back—irresponsible childhood. It was going, like Mademoiselle Duphot. Kind Mademoiselle Duphot, so foolishly loving, so easily coerced, so glad to be persuaded; so eager to believe that you were doing your best, in the face of the most obvious slacking. Kind Mademoiselle Duphot who smiled when she shouldn't, who laughed when she shouldn't, and now she was weeping—but weeping as only a Latin can weep, shedding rivers of tears and sobbing quite loudly.

'Chérie—mon bébé, petit chou!'* she was sobbing, as she clung to the angular Stephen.

The tears ran down on to Mademoiselle's tippet,* and they wet the poor fur which already looked jaded, and the fur clogged together, turning black with those tears, so that Mademoiselle tried to wipe it. But the more she wiped it the wetter it grew, since her handkerchief only augmented the trouble; nor was Stephen's large handkerchief very dry either, as she found when she started to help.

The old station fly* that had come out from Malvern, drove up, and the footman seized Mademoiselle's luggage. It was such meagre luggage that he waved back assistance from the driver, and lifted the trunk single-handed. Then Mademoiselle Duphot broke out into English—heaven only knew why, perhaps from emotion.

'It's not farewell, it shall not be for ever—' she sobbed. 'You come, but I feel it, to Paris. We meet once more, Stévenne, my poor little baby, when you grow up bigger, we two meet once more—' And Stephen, already taller than she was, longed to grow small again, just to please Mademoiselle. Then, because the French are a practical people even in moments of real emotion, Mademoiselle found her handbag, and groping in its depths she produced a half sheet of paper.

'The address of my sister in Paris,' she said, snuffling; 'the address of my sister who makes little bags—if you should hear of anyone, Stévenne—any lady who would care to buy one little bag—'

'Yes, yes, I'll remember,' muttered Stephen.

At last she was gone; the fly rumbled away down the drive and finally turned the corner. To the end a wet face had been thrust from the window, a wet handkerchief waved despondently at Stephen. The rain must have mingled with Mademoiselle's tears, for the weather had broken and now it was raining. It was surely a desolate day for departure, with the mist closing over the Severn Valley and beginning to creep up the hill-sides. . . .

Stephen made her way to the empty schoolroom, empty of all save a general confusion; the confusion that stalks in some people's trail—it had always stalked Mademoiselle Duphot. On the chairs, which stood crooked, lay odds and ends meaning nothing—crumpled paper, a broken shoehorn, a well-worn brown glove that had lost its fellow and likewise two of its buttons. On the table lay a much abused pink blotting pad,* from which Stephen had torn off the corners, unchidden*—it was crossed and re-crossed with elegant French script until its scarred face had turned purple. And there stood the bottle of purple ink, half-empty, and green round its neck with dribbles; and a pen with a nib as sharp as a pin point, a thin, peevish nib that jabbed at the paper. Chock-a-block* with the bottle of purple ink lay a little piety card of St. Joseph that had evidently slipped out of Mademoiselle's missal—St. Joseph looked very respectable and kind, like the fishmonger in Great Malvern. Stephen picked up the card and stared at St. Joseph; something was written across his corner; looking closer she read the minute handwriting: 'Priez pour ma petite Stévenne.'*

She put the card away in her desk; the ink and the blotter she hid in the cupboard together with the peevish steel nib that jabbed paper, and that richly deserved cremation. Then she straightened the chairs and threw away the litter, after which she went in search of a duster; one by one she dusted the few remaining volumes in the bookcase, including the Bibliothèque Rose. She arranged her dictation note-books in a pile with others that were far less accurately written—books of sums, mostly careless and marked with a cross; books of English history, in one of which Stephen had begun to write the history of the horse! Books of geography with Mademoiselle's comments in strong purple ink: 'Grand manque d'attention.'* And lastly she collected the torn lesson books that had lain on their backs, on their sides, on their bellies—anyhow, anywhere in drawers or in cupboards, but not very often in the bookcase. For the bookcase was harbouring quite other things, a motley and most unstudious collection; dumb-bells, wooden and iron, of varying sizes—some Indian clubs, one split off at the handle—cotton laces, for gym shoes, the belt of a tunic. And then stable keepsakes, including a headband that Raftery had worn on some special occasion; a miniature horseshoe kicked sky-high by Collins; a half-eaten carrot, now withered and mouldy, and two hunting crops that had both lost their lashes and were waiting to visit the saddler.

Stephen considered, rubbing her chin—a habit which by now had become automatic—she finally decided on the ample box-sofa* as a seemly receptacle. Remained only the carrot, and she stood for a long time with it clasped in her hand, disturbed and unhappy—this clearing of decks for stern mental action was certainly very depressing. But at last she threw the thing into the fire, where it shifted distressfully, sizzling and humming. Then she sat down and stared rather grimly at the flames that were burning up Raftery's first carrot.

CHAPTER 7

I

SOON after the departure of Mademoiselle Duphot, there occurred two distinct innovations at Morton. Miss Puddleton arrived to take possession of the schoolroom, and Sir Philip bought himself a motor-car. The motor was a Panhard,* and it caused much excitement in the neighbourhood of Upton-on-Severn. Conservative, suspicious of all innovations, people had abstained from motors in the Midlands, and, incredible as it now seems to look back on, Sir Philip was regarded as a kind of pioneer. The Panhard was a high-shouldered, snub-nosed abortion with a loud, vulgar voice and an uncertain temper. It suffered from frequent fits of dyspepsia,* brought about by an unhealthy spark-plug. Its seats were the very acme of discomfort, its primitive gears unhandy and noisy, but nevertheless it could manage to attain to a speed of about fifteen miles per hour—given always that, by God's good grace and the chauffeur's, it was not in the throes of indigestion.

Anna felt doubtful regarding this new purchase. She was one of those women who, having passed forty, were content to go on placidly driving in their broughams, or, in summer, in their charming little French victorias.* She detested the look of herself in large goggles, detested being forced to tie on her hat, detested the heavy, mannish coat of rough tweed that Sir Philip insisted she must wear when motoring. Such things were not of her; they offended her sense of the seemly, her preference for soft, clinging garments, her instinct for quiet, rather slow, gentle movements, her love of the feminine and comely. For Anna at forty-four was still slender, and her dark hair, as yet, was untouched with grey, and her blue Irish eyes were as clear and candid as when she had come as a bride to Morton. She was beautiful still, and this fact rejoiced her in secret, because of her husband. Yet Anna did not ignore middle age; she met it half-way with dignity and courage; and now her soft dresses were of reticent colours, and her movements a little more careful than they had been, and her mind more severely disciplined and guarded—too much guarded these days, she was gradually growing less tolerant as her interests narrowed. And the motor, an unimportant thing in itself, served nevertheless to crystallize in Anna a certain tendency towards retrogression, a certain instinctive dislike of the unusual, a certain deep-rooted fear of the unknown.

Old Williams was openly disgusted and hostile; he considered the car to be an outrage to his stables—those immaculate stables with their spacious coach-houses, their wide plaits of straw neatly interwoven with yards of red and blue saddler's tape, and their fine stable-yard hitherto kept so spotless. Came the Panhard, and behold, pools of oil on the flagstones, greenish, bad-smelling oil that defied even scouring; and a medley of odd-looking tools in the coach-house, all greasy, all soiling your hands when you touched them; and large tins of what looked like black vaseline; and spare tyres for which nails had been knocked into the woodwork; and a bench with a vice for the motor's insides which were frequently being dissected. From this coach-house the dog-cart had been ruthlessly expelled, and now it must stand chock-a-block with the phaeton,* so that room might be made for the garish intruder together with its young body-servant. The young body-servant was known as a chauffeur—he had come down from London and wore clothes made of leather. He talked Cockney, and openly spat before Williams in the coach-house, then rubbed his foot over the spittle.

'I'll 'ave none of yer expectoration 'ere in me coach-house, I tells ee!' bawled Williams, apoplectic with temper.

'Oh, come orf it, do, Grandpa; we're not in the ark!' was how the new blood answered Williams.

There was war to the knife between Williams and Burton—Burton who expressed large disdain of the horses.

'Yer time's up now, Grandpa,' he was constantly remarking; 'it's all up with the gees—better learn to be a shovver!'*

''Opes I'll die afore ever I demean meself that way, you young blight!' bawled the outraged Williams. Very angry he grew, and his dinner fermented, dilating his stomach and causing discomfort, so that his wife became anxious about him.

'Now don't ee go worryin', Arth-thur,' she coaxed; 'us be old, me and you, and the world be progressin'.'

'It be goin' to the devil, that's what it be doin'!' groaned Williams, rubbing his stomach.

To make matters worse, Sir Philip's behaviour was that of a schoolboy with some horrid new contraption. He was caught by his stud-groom lying flat on his back with his feet sticking out beneath the bonnet of the motor, and when he emerged there was soot on his cheek-bones, on his hair, and even on the tip of his nose. He looked terribly sheepish, and as Williams said later to his wife:

'It were somethin' aw-ful to see 'im all mucked up, and 'im such a neat gentleman, and 'im in a filthy old coat of that Burton's, and that Burton agrinnin' at me and just pointin', silent, because the master couldn't see 'im, and the master a-callin' up familiar-like to Burton: "I say! She's got somethin' all wrong with 'er exhaust pipe!" and Burton a-contradictin' the master: "It's that piston," says 'e, as cool as yer please.'

Nor was Stephen less thrilled by the car than was her father. Stephen made friends with the execrable Burton, and Burton, who was only too anxious to gain allies, soon started to teach her the parts of the engine; he taught her to drive too, Sir Philip being willing, and off they would go, the three of them together, leaving Williams to glare at the disappearing motor.

'And 'er such a fine 'orse-woman and all!' he would grumble, rubbing a disconsolate chin.

It is not too much to say that Williams felt heart-broken, he was like a very unhappy old baby; quite infantile he was in his fits of bad temper, in his mouthings and his grindings of toothless gums. And all about nothing, for Sir Philip and his daughter had the lure of horse-flesh in their very bones—and then there was Raftery, and Raftery loved Stephen, and Stephen loved Raftery.

2

The motoring, of course, was the most tremendous fun, but—and it was a very large but indeed—when Stephen got home to Morton and the schoolroom, a little grey figure would be sitting at the table correcting an exercise book, or preparing some task for the following morning. The little grey figure might look up and smile, and when it did this its face would be charming; but if it refrained from smiling, then its face would be ugly, too hard and too square in formation—except for the brow, which was rounded and shiny like a bare intellectual knee. If the little grey figure got up from the table, you were struck by the fact that it seemed square all over—square shoulders, square hips, a flat, square line of bosom; square tips to the fingers, square toes to the shoes, and all tiny; it suggested a miniature box that was neatly spliced at the corners. Of uncertain age, pale, with iron-grey hair, grey eyes, and invariably dressed in dark grey, Miss Puddleton did not look very inspiring—not at all as one having authority, in fact. But on close observation it had to be admitted that her chin, though minute, was extremely aggressive. Her mouth, too, was firm, except when its firmness was melted by the warmth and humour of her smile—a smile that mocked, pitied and questioned the world, and perhaps Miss Puddleton as well.

From the very first moment of Miss Puddleton's arrival, Stephen had had an uncomfortable conviction that this queer little woman* was going to mean something, was going to become a fixture. And sure enough she had settled down at once, so that in less than two months it seemed to Stephen that Miss Puddleton must always have been at Morton, must always have been sitting at the large walnut table, must always have been saying in that dry, toneless voice with the Oxford accent: 'You've forgotten something, Stephen,' and then, 'the books can't walk to the bookcase, but you can, so suppose that you take them with you.'

It was truly amazing, the change in the schoolroom, not a book out of place, not a shelf in disorder; even the box lounge had had to be opened and its dumb-bells and clubs paired off nicely together—Miss Puddleton always liked things to be paired, perhaps an unrecognized matrimonial instinct. And now Stephen found herself put into harness for the first time in her life, and she loathed the sensation. There were so many rules that a very large time-sheet had had to be fastened to the blackboard in the schoolroom.

'Because,' said Miss Puddleton as she pinned the thing up, 'even my brain won't stand your complete lack of method, it's infectious; this time-sheet is my anti-toxin, so please don't tear it to pieces!'

Mathematics and algebra, Latin and Greek, Roman history, Greek history, geometry, botany, they reduced Stephen's mind to a species of beehive in which every bee buzzed on the least provocation. She would gaze at Miss Puddleton in a kind of amazement; that tiny, square box to hold all this grim knowledge! And seeing that gaze Miss Puddleton would smile her most warm, charming smile, and would say as she did so:

'Yes, I know—but it's only the first effort, Stephen; presently your mind will get neat like the schoolroom, and then you'll be able to find what you want without all this rummaging and bother.'

But her tasks being over, Stephen must often slip away to visit Raftery in the stables: 'Oh, Raftery, I'm hating it so!' she would tell him. 'I feel like you'd feel if I put you in harness—hard wooden shafts and a kicking strap, Raftery—but my darling, I'd never put you into harness!'

And Raftery would hardly know what he should answer, since all human creatures, so far as he knew them, must run between shafts—God-like though they were, they undoubtedly had to run between shafts.*. . .

Nothing but Stephen's great love for her father helped her to endure the first six months of learning—that and her own stubborn, arrogant will that made her hate to be beaten. She would swing clubs and dumb-bells in a kind of fury, consoling herself with the thought of her muscles, and, finding her at it, Miss Puddleton had laughed.

'You must feel that your teacher's some sort of midge, Stephen—a tiresome midge that you want to brush off!'

Then Stephen had laughed too: 'Well, you are little, Puddle—oh, I'm sorry—'

'I don't mind,' Miss Puddleton had told her; 'call me Puddle if you like, it's all one to me.' After which Miss Puddleton disappeared somehow, and Puddle took her place in the household.

An insignificant creature this Puddle, yet at moments unmistakably self-assertive. Always willing to help in domestic affairs, such as balancing Anna's chaotic account books, or making out library lists for Jackson's, she was nevertheless very guardful of her rights, very quick to assert and maintain her position. Puddle knew what she wanted and saw that she got it, both in and out of the schoolroom. Yet every one liked her; she took what she gave and she gave what she took, yes, but sometimes she gave just a little bit more—and that little bit more is the whole art of teaching, the whole art of living, in fact, and Miss Puddleton knew it. Thus gradually, oh, very gradually at first, she wore down her pupil's unconscious resistance. With small, dexterous fingers she caught Stephen's brain, and she stroked it and modelled it after her own fashion. She talked to that brain and showed it new pictures; she gave it new thoughts, new hopes and ambitions; she made it feel certain and proud of achievement. Nor did she belittle Stephen's muscles in the process, never once did Puddle make game of the athlete, never once did she show by so much as the twitch of an eyelid that she had her own thoughts about her pupil. She appeared to take Stephen as a matter of course, nothing surprised or even amused her it seemed, and Stephen grew quite at ease with her.

'I can always be comfortable with you, Puddle,' Stephen would say in a tone of satisfaction, 'you're like a nice chair; though you are so tiny yet one's got room to stretch, I don't know how you do it.'

Then Puddle would smile, and that smile would warm Stephen while it mocked her a little; but it also mocked Puddle—they would share that warm smile with its fun and its kindness, so that neither of them could feel hurt or embarrassed. And their friendship took root, growing strong and verdant, and it flourished like a green bay-tree in the schoolroom.

Came the time when Stephen began to realize that Puddle had genius—the genius of teaching; the genius of compelling her pupil to share in her own enthusiastic love of the Classics.

'Oh, Stephen, if only you could read this in Greek!' she would say, and her voice would sound full of excitement; 'the beauty, the splendid dignity of it—it's like the sea, Stephen, rather terrible but splendid; that's the language, it's far more virile than Latin.' And Stephen would catch that sudden excitement, and determine to work even harder at Greek.

But Puddle did not live by the ancients alone, she taught Stephen to appreciate all literary beauty, observing in her pupil a really fine judgment, a great feeling for balance in sentences and words. A vast tract of new interest was thus opened up, and Stephen began to excel in composition; to her own deep amazement she found herself able to write many things that had long lain dormant in her heart—all the beauty of nature, for instance, she could write it. Impressions of childhood—gold light on the hills; the first cuckoo,* mysterious, strangely alluring; those rides home from hunting together with her father—bare furrows, the meaning of those bare furrows. And later, how many queer hopes and queer longings, queer joys and even more curious frustrations. Joy of strength, splendid physical strength and courage; joy of health and sound sleep and refreshed awakening; joy of Raftery leaping under the saddle, joy of wind racing backward as Raftery leapt forward. And then, what? A sudden impenetrable darkness, a sudden vast void all nothingness and darkness; a sudden sense of acute apprehension: 'I'm lost, where am I? Where am I? I'm nothing—yes I am, I'm Stephen—but that's being nothing—'* then that horrible sense of apprehension.

Writing, it was like a heavenly balm, it was like the flowing out of deep waters, it was like the lifting of a load from the spirit; it brought with it a sense of relief, of assuagement. One could say things in writing without feeling self-conscious, without feeling shy and ashamed and foolish—one could even write of the days of young Nelson, smiling a very little as one did so.

Sometimes Puddle would sit alone in her bedroom reading and re-reading Stephen's strange compositions; frowning, or smiling a little in her turn, at those turbulent, youthful outpourings.

She would think: 'Here's real talent, real red-hot talent—interesting to find it in that great, athletic creature; but what is she likely to make of her talent? She's up agin the world, if she only knew it!' Then Puddle would shake her head and look doubtful, feeling sorry for Stephen and the world in general.

3

This then was how Stephen conquered yet another kingdom, and at seventeen was not only athlete but student. Three years under Puddle's ingenious tuition, and the girl was as proud of her brains as of her muscles—a trifle too proud, she was growing conceited, she was growing self-satisfied, arrogant even, and Sir Philip must tease her: 'Ask Stephen, she'll tell us. Stephen, what's that reference to Adeimantus, something about a mind fixed on true being—doesn't it come in Euripides, somewhere? Oh, no, I'm forgetting, of course it's Plato;* really my Greek is disgracefully rusty!' Then Stephen would know that Sir Philip was laughing at her, but very kindly.

In spite of her newly acquired book learning, Stephen still talked quite often to Raftery. He was now ten years old and had grown much in wisdom himself, so he listened with care and attention.

'You see,' she would tell him, 'it's very important to develop the brain as well as the muscles; I'm now doing both—stand still, will you, Raftery! Never mind that old corn-bin, stop rolling your eye round—it's very important to develop the brain because that gives you an advantage over people, it makes you more able to do as you like in this world, to conquer conditions, Raftery.'

And Raftery, who was not really thinking of the corn-bin, but rolling his eye in an effort to answer, would want to say something too big for his language, which at best must consist of small sounds and small movements; would want to say something about a strong feeling he had that Stephen was missing the truth. But how could he hope to make her understand the age-old wisdom of all the dumb creatures? The wisdom of plains and primeval forests, the wisdom come down from the youth of the world.

CHAPTER 8

I

At seventeen Stephen was taller than Anna, who had used to be considered quite tall for a woman, but Stephen was nearly as tall as her father—not a beauty this, in the eyes of the neighbours.

Colonel Antrim would shake his head and remark: 'I like 'em plump and compact, it's more taking.'

Then his wife, who was certainly plump and compact, so compact in her stays* that she felt rather breathless, would say: 'But then Stephen is very unusual, almost—well, almost a wee bit unnatural—such a pity, poor child, it's a terrible drawback; young men do hate that sort of thing, don't they?'

But in spite of all this Stephen's figure was handsome in a flat,* broad-shouldered and slim flanked fashion; and her movements were purposeful, having fine poise, she moved with the easy assurance of the athlete. Her hands, although large for a woman, were slender and meticulously tended; she was proud of her hands. In face she had changed very little since childhood, still having Sir Philip's wide, tolerant expression. What change there was only tended to strengthen the extraordinary likeness between father and daughter, for now that the bones of her face showed more clearly, as the childish fullness had gradually diminished, the formation of the resolute jaw was Sir Philip's. His too the strong chin with its shade of a cleft; the well modelled, sensitive lips were his also. A fine face, very pleasing, yet with something about it that went ill with the hats on which Anna insisted—large hats trimmed with ribbons or roses or daisies, and supposed to be softening to the features.*

Staring at her own reflection in the glass, Stephen would feel just a little uneasy: '*Am* I queer looking or not?' she would wonder, 'Suppose I wore my hair more like Mother's?' and then she would undo her splendid, thick hair, and would part it in the middle and draw it back loosely.

The result was always far from becoming, so that Stephen would hastily plait it again. She now wore the plait screwed up very tightly in the nape of her neck with a bow of black ribbon. Anna hated this fashion and constantly said so, but Stephen was stubborn: 'I've tried your way, Mother, and I look like a scarecrow; you're beautiful, darling, but your young daughter isn't, which is jolly hard on you.'

'She makes no effort to improve her appearance,' Anna would reproach, very gravely.

These days there was constant warfare between them on the subject of clothes; quite a seemly warfare, for Stephen was learning to control her hot temper, and Anna was seldom anything but gentle. Nevertheless it was open warfare, the inevitable clash of two opposing natures who sought to express themselves in apparel, since clothes, after all, are a form of self-expression. The victory would be now on this side, now on that; sometimes Stephen would appear in a thick woollen jersey, or a suit of rough tweeds surreptitiously ordered from the excellent tailor in Malvern. Sometimes Anna would triumph, having journeyed to London to procure soft and very expensive dresses, which her daughter must wear in order to please her, because she would come home quite tired by such journeys. On the whole, Anna got her own way at this time, for Stephen would suddenly give up the contest, reduced to submission by Anna's disappointment, always more efficacious than mere disapproval.

'Here, give it to me!' she would say rather gruffly, grabbing the delicate dress from her mother.

Then off she would rush and put it on all wrong, so that Anna would sigh in a kind of desperation, and would pat, readjust, unfasten and fasten, striving to make peace between wearer and model, whose inimical feelings were evidently mutual.

Came a day when Stephen was suddenly outspoken: 'It's my face,' she announced, 'something's wrong with my face.'

'Nonsense!' exclaimed Anna, and her cheeks flushed a little, as though the girl's words had been an offence, then she turned away quickly to hide her expression.

But Stephen had seen that fleeting expression, and she stood very still when her mother had left her, her own face growing heavy and sombre with anger, with a sense of some uncomprehended injustice. She wrenched off the dress and hurled it from her, longing intensely to rend it, to hurt it, longing to hurt herself in the process, yet filled all the while with that sense of injustice. But this mood changed abruptly to one of self pity; she wanted to sit down and weep over Stephen; on a sudden impulse she wanted to pray over Stephen as though she were some one apart, yet terribly personal too in her trouble. Going over to the dress she smoothed it out slowly; it seemed to have acquired an enormous importance; it seemed to have acquired the importance of prayer, the poor, crumpled thing lying crushed and dejected. Yet Stephen, these days, was not given to prayer, God had grown so unreal, so hard to believe in since she had studied Comparative Religion; engrossed in her studies she had somehow mislaid Him. But now, here she was, very wishful to pray, while not knowing how to explain her dilemma: 'I'm terribly unhappy, dear, improbable God—' would not be a very propitious beginning. And yet at this moment she was wanting a God and a tangible one, very kind and paternal; a God with a white flowing beard and wide forehead, a benevolent parent Who would lean out of Heaven and turn His face sideways the better to listen from His cloud, upheld by cherubs and angels. What she wanted was a wise old family God, surrounded by endless heavenly relations. In spite of her troubles she began to laugh weakly, and the laughter was good, for it killed self pity; nor can it have offended that Venerable Person whose image persists in the hearts of small children.

She donned the new dress with infinite precaution, pulling out its bows and arranging its ruffles. Her large hands were clumsy but now they were willing, very penitent hands full of deep resignation. They fumbled and paused, then continued to fumble with the endless small fastenings so cunningly hidden. She sighed once or twice, but the sighs were quite patient, so perhaps in this wise, after all, Stephen prayed.

2

Anna worried continually over her daughter; for one thing Stephen was a social disaster, yet at seventeen many a girl was presented,* but the bare idea of this had terrified Stephen, and so it had had to be abandoned. At garden parties she was always a failure, seemingly ill at ease and ungracious. She shook hands much too hard, digging rings into fingers, this from sheer automatic nervous reaction. She spoke not at all, or else gabbled too freely, so that Anna grew vague in her own conversation; all eyes and ears she would be as she listened—it was certainly terribly hard on Anna. But if hard on Anna, it was harder on Stephen who dreaded these festive gatherings intensely;

indeed her dread of them lacked all proportion, becoming a kind of unreasoning obsession. Every vestige of self-confidence seemed to desert her, so that Puddle, supposing she happened to be present would find herself grimly comparing this Stephen with the graceful, light-footed, proficient young athlete, with the clever and somewhat opinionated student who was fast outstripping her own powers as a teacher. Yes, Puddle would sit there grimly comparing, and would feel not a little uneasy as she did so. Then something of her pupil's distress would reach her, so that perforce she would have to share it and as like as not she would want to shake Stephen.

'Good Lord,' she would think, 'why can't she hit back? It's absurd, it's outrageous to be so disgruntled by a handful of petty, half-educated yokels—a girl with her brain too, it's simply outrageous! She'll have to tackle life more forcibly than this, if she's not going to let herself go under!'

But Stephen, completely oblivious of Puddle, would be deep in the throes of her old suspicion, the suspicion that had haunted her ever since childhood—she would fancy that people were laughing at her. So sensitive was she, that a half-heard sentence, a word, a glance, made her inwardly crumble. It might well be that people were not even thinking about her, much less discussing her appearance—no good, she would always imagine that the word, the glance, had some purely personal meaning. She would twitch at her hat with inadequate fingers, or walk clumsily, slouching a little as she did so, until Anna would whisper:

'Hold your back up, you're stooping.'

Or Puddle exclaim crossly: 'What on earth's the matter, Stephen!'

All of which only added to Stephen's tribulation by making her still more self-conscious.

With other young girls she had nothing in common, while they, in their turn, found her irritating. She was shy to primness regarding certain subjects, and would actually blush if they happened to be mentioned. This would strike her companions as queer and absurd—after all, between girls—surely every one knew that at times one ought not to get one's feet wet, that one didn't play games, not at certain times*—there was nothing to make all this fuss about surely! To see Stephen Gordon's expression of horror if one so much as threw out a hint on the subject, was to feel that the thing must in some way be shameful, a kind of disgrace, a humiliation! And then she was odd about other things too; there were so many things that she didn't like mentioned.

In the end, they completely lost patience with her, and they left her alone with her fads and her fancies, disliking the check that her presence imposed, disliking to feel that they dare not allude to even the necessary functions of nature without being made to feel immodest.

But at times Stephen hated her own isolation, and then she would make little awkward advances, while her eyes would grow rather apologetic, like the eyes of a dog who has been out of favour. She would try to appear quite at ease with her companions, as she joined in their light-hearted conversation. Strolling up to a group of young girls at a party, she would grin as though their small jokes amused her, or else listen gravely while they talked about clothes or some popular actor who had visited Malvern. As long as they refrained from too intimate details, she would fondly imagine that her interest passed muster. There she would stand with her strong arms folded, and her face somewhat strained in an effort of attention. While despising these girls, she yet longed to be like them—yes, indeed, at such moments she longed to be like them. It would suddenly strike her that they seemed very happy, very sure of themselves as they gossiped together. There was something so secure in their feminine conclaves, a secure sense of oneness, of mutual understanding; each in turn understood the other's ambitions. They might have their jealousies, their quarrels even, but always she discerned, underneath, that sense of oneness.

Poor Stephen! She could never impose upon them; they always saw through her as though she were a window. They knew well enough that she cared not so much as a jot about clothes and popular actors. Conversation would falter, then die down completely, her presence would dry up their springs of inspiration. She spoilt things while trying to make herself agreeable; they really liked her better when she was grumpy.

Could Stephen have met men on equal terms, she would always have chosen them as her companions; she preferred them because of their blunt, open outlook, and with men she had much in common—sport for instance. But men found her too clever if she ventured to expand, and too dull if she suddenly subsided into shyness. In addition to this there was something about her that antagonized slightly, an unconscious presumption. Shy though she might be, they sensed this presumption; it annoyed them, it made them feel on the defensive. She was handsome but much too large and unyielding both in body and mind, and they liked clinging women. They were oak-trees, preferring the feminine ivy. It might cling rather close, it might finally strangle, it frequently did, and yet they preferred it, and this being so, they resented Stephen, suspecting something of the acorn about her.

3

Stephen's worst ordeals at this time were the dinners given in turn by a hospitable county. They were long, these dinners, overloaded with courses; they were heavy, being weighted with polite conversation; they were stately, by reason of the family silver; above all they were firmly conservative in spirit, as conservative as the marriage service itself, and almost as insistent upon sex distinction.

'Captain Ramsay, will you take Miss Gordon in to dinner?'

A politely crooked arm: 'Delighted, Miss Gordon.'

Then the solemn and very ridiculous procession, animals marching into Noah's Ark two by two, very sure of divine protection—male and female created He them!* Stephen's skirt would be long and her foot might get entangled, and she with but one free hand at her disposal—the procession would stop and she would have stopped it! Intolerable thought, she had stopped the procession!

'I'm so sorry, Captain Ramsay!'

'I say, can I help you?'

'No—it's really—all right, I think I can manage—'

But oh, the utter confusion of spirit, the humiliating feeling that some one must be laughing, the resentment at having to cling to his arm for support, while Captain Ramsay looked patient.

'Not much damage, I think you've just torn the frill, but I often wonder how you women manage. Imagine a man in a dress like that, too awful to think of—imagine me in it!' Then a laugh, not unkindly but a trifle self-conscious, and rather more than a trifle complacent.

Safely steered to her seat at the long dinner-table, Stephen would struggle to smile and talk brightly, while her partner would think: 'Lord, she's heavy in hand; I wish I had the mother; now there's a lovely woman!'

And Stephen would think: 'I'm a bore, why is it?' Then, 'But if I were he I wouldn't be a bore, I could just be myself, I'd feel perfectly natural.'

Her face would grow splotched with resentment and worry; she would feel her neck flush and her hands become awkward. Embarrassed, she would sit staring down at her hands, which would seem to be growing more and more awkward. No escape! No escape! Captain Ramsay was kind-hearted, he would try very hard to be complimentary; his grey eyes would try to express admiration, polite admiration as they rested on Stephen. His voice would sound softer and more confidential, the voice that nice men reserve for good women, protective, respectful, yet a little sex-conscious, a little expectant of a tentative response. But Stephen would feel herself growing more rigid with every kind word and gallant allusion. Openly hostile she would be feeling, as poor Captain Ramsay or some other victim was manfully trying to do his duty.

In such a mood as this she had once drunk champagne, one glass only, the first she had ever tasted. She had gulped it all down in sheer desperation—the result had not been Dutch courage but hiccups. Violent, insistent, incorrigible hiccups had echoed along the whole length of the table. One of those weird conversational lulls had been filled, as it were, to the brim with her hiccups. Then Anna had started to talk very loudly; Mrs. Antrim had smiled and so had their hostess. Their hostess had finally beckoned to the butler: 'Give Miss Gordon a glass of water,' she had whispered. After that Stephen shunned champagne like the plague—better hopeless depression, she decided, than hiccups!

It was strange how little her fine brain seemed able to help her when she was trying to be social; in spite of her confident boasting to Raftery, it did not seem able to help her at all. Perhaps it was the clothes, for she lost all conceit the moment she was dressed as Anna would have her; at this period clothes greatly influenced Stephen, giving her confidence or the reverse. But be that as it might, people thought her peculiar, and with them that was tantamount to disapproval.

And thus, it was being borne in upon Stephen, that for her there was no real abiding city* beyond the strong, friendly old gates of Morton, and she clung more and more to her home and to her father. Perplexed and unhappy, she would seek out her father on all social occasions and would sit down beside him. Like a very small child this large muscular creature would sit down beside him because she felt lonely, and because youth most rightly resents isolation, and because she had not yet learnt her hard lesson—she had not yet learnt that the loneliest place in this world is the no-man's-land of sex.*

CHAPTER 9

I

SIR PHILIP and his daughter had a new common interest; they could now discuss books and the making of books and the feel and the smell and the essence of books—a mighty bond this, and one full of enchantment. They could talk of these things with mutual understanding; they did so for hours in the father's study, and Sir Philip discovered a secret ambition that had lain in the girl like a seed in deep soil;* and he, the good gardener of her body and spirit, hoed the soil and watered this seed of ambition. Stephen would show him her queer compositions, and would wait very breathless and still while he read them; then one evening he looked up and saw her expression, and he smiled:

'So that's it, you want to be a writer. Well, why not? You've got plenty of talent, Stephen; I should be a proud man if you were a writer.' After which their discussions on the making of books held an even more vital enchantment.

But Anna came less and less often to the study, and she would be sitting alone and idle. Puddle, upstairs at work in the schoolroom, might be swatting at her Greek to keep pace with Stephen, but Anna would be sitting with her hands in her lap in the vast drawing-room so beautifully proportioned, so restfully furnished in old polished walnut, so redolent of beeswax and orris root and violets—all alone in its vastness would Anna be sitting, with her white hands folded and idle.

A lovely and most comfortable woman she had been, and still was, in spite of her gentle ageing, but not learned, oh, no, very far from learned—that, indeed, was why Sir Philip had loved her, that was why he had found her so infinitely restful, that was why he still loved her after very many years; her simplicity was stronger to hold him than learning. But now Anna went less and less often to the study.

It was not that they failed to make her feel welcome, but rather that they could not conceal their deep interest in subjects of which she knew little or nothing. What did she know of or care for the Classics? What interest had she in the works of Erasmus?* Her theology needed no erudite discussion, her philosophy consisted of a home swept and garnished, and as for the poets, she liked simple verses; for the rest her poetry lay in her husband. All this she well knew and had no wish to alter, yet lately there had come upon Anna an aching, a tormenting aching that she dared give no name to. It nagged at her heart when she went to that study and saw Sir Philip together with their daughter, and knew that her presence contributed nothing to his happiness when he sat reading to Stephen.

Staring at the girl, she would see the strange resemblance, the invidious likeness of the child to the father, she would notice their movements so grotesquely alike; their hands were alike, they made the same gestures, and her mind would recoil with that nameless resentment, the while she reproached herself, penitent and trembling. Yet penitent and trembling though Anna might be, she would sometimes hear herself speaking to Stephen in a way that would make her feel secretly ashamed. She would hear herself covertly, cleverly gibing,* with such skill that the girl would look up at her bewildered; with such skill that even Sir Philip himself could not well take exception to what she was saying; then, as like as not, she would laugh if off lightly, as though all the time she had only been jesting, and Stephen would laugh too, a big, friendly laugh. But Sir Philip would not laugh, and his eyes would seek Anna's, questioning, amazed, incredulous and angry. That was why she now went so seldom to the study when Sir Philip and his daughter were together.

But sometimes, when she was alone with her husband, Anna would suddenly cling to him in silence. She would hide her face against his hard shoulder clinging closer and closer, as though she were frightened, as though she were afraid for this great love of theirs. He would stand very still, forbearing to move, forbearing to question, for why should he question? He knew already, and she knew that he knew. Yet neither of them spoke it, this most unhappy thing, and their silence spread round them like a poisonous miasma. The spectre that was Stephen would seem to be watching, and Sir Philip would gently release himself from Anna, while she, looking up, would see his tired eyes, not angry any more, only very unhappy. She would think that those eyes were pleading, beseeching; she would think: 'He's pleading with me for Stephen.' Then her own eyes would fill with tears of contrition, and that night she would kneel long in prayer to her Maker:

'Give me peace,' she would entreat, 'and enlighten my spirit, so that I may learn how to love my own child.'*

2

Sir Philip looked older now than his age, and seeing this, Anna could scarcely endure it. Everything in her cried out in rebellion so that she wanted to thrust back the years, to hold them at bay with her own weak body. Had the years been an army of naked swords she would gladly have held them at bay with her body.

He would constantly now remain in his study right into the early hours of the morning. This habit of his had been growing on him lately, and Anna, waking to find herself alone, and feeling uneasy would steal down to listen. Backwards and forwards, backwards and forwards! She would hear his desolate sounding footsteps. Why was he pacing backwards and forwards, and why was she always afraid to ask him? Why was the hand she stretched out to the door always fearful when it came to turning the handle? Oh, but it was strong, this thing that stood between them, strong with the strength of their united bodies. It had drawn its own life from their youth, their passion, from the splendid and purposeful meaning of their passion—that was how it had leapt full of power into life, and now it had thrust in between them. They were ageing, they had little left but their loving—that gentler loving, perhaps the more perfect—and their faith in each other, which was part of that loving, and their peace, which was part of the peace of Morton. Backwards and forwards, backwards and forwards! Those incessant and desolate sounding footsteps. Peace? There was surely no peace in that study, but rather some affliction, menacing, prophetic! Yet prophetic of what? She dared not ask him, she dared not so much as turn the door-handle, a haunting premonition of disaster would make her creep away with her question unasked.

Then something would draw her, not back to her bedroom, but on up the stairs to the room of their daughter. She would open that door very gently—by inches. She would hold her hand so that it shaded the candle, and would stand looking down at the sleeping Stephen as she and her husband had done long ago. But now there would be no little child to look down on, no small helplessness to arouse mother-pity. Stephen would be lying very straight, very large, very long, underneath the neatly drawn covers. Quite often an arm would be outside the bedspread, the sleeve having fallen away as it lay there, and that arm would look firm and strong and possessive, and so would the face by the light of the candle. She slept deeply. Her breathing would be even and placid. Her body would be drinking in its fill of refreshment. It would rise up clean and refreshed in the morning; it would eat, speak, move—it would move about Morton. In the stables, in the gardens, in the neighbouring paddocks, in the study—it would move about Morton. Intolerable dispensation of nature, Anna would stare at that splendid young body, and would feel, as she did so, that she looked on a stranger. She would scourge her heart and her anxious spirit with memories drawn from this stranger's beginnings: 'Little—you were so very little!' she would whisper, 'and you sucked from my breast because you were hungry—little and always so terribly hungry—a good baby though, a contented little baby—'

And Stephen would sometimes stir in her sleep as though she were vaguely conscious of Anna. It would pass and she would lie quiet again, breathing in those deep, placid draughts of refreshment. Then Anna, still ruthlessly scourging her heart and her anxious spirit, would stoop and kiss Stephen, but lightly and very quickly on the forehead, so that the girl should not be awakened. So that the girl should not wake and kiss back, she would kiss her lightly and quickly on the forehead.

3

The eye of youth is very observant. Youth has its moments and keen intuition, even normal youth—but the intuition of those who stand midway between the sexes, is so ruthless, so poignant, so accurate, so deadly, as to be in the nature of an added scourge; and by such an intuition did Stephen discover that all was not well with her parents.

Their outward existence seemed calm and unruffled; so far nothing had disturbed the outward peace of Morton. But their child saw their hearts with the eyes of the spirit; flesh of their flesh,* she had sprung from their hearts, and she knew that those hearts were heavy. They said nothing, but she sensed that some deep, secret trouble was afflicting them both; she could see it in their eyes. In the words that they left unspoken she could hear it—it would be there, filling the small gaps of silence. She thought that she discerned it in her father's slow movements—surely his movements had grown slower of late? And his hair was quite grey; it was quite grey all over. She realized this with a slight shock one morning as he sat in the sunlight—it had used to look auburn in the nape of his neck when the sun fell upon it—and now it was dull grey all over.

But this mattered little. Even their trouble mattered little in comparison with something more vital, with their love—that, she felt, was the only thing that mattered, and that was the thing that now stood most in danger. This love of theirs had been a great glory; all her life she had lived with it side by side, but never until it appeared to be threatened, did she feel that she had really grasped its true meaning—the serene and beautiful spirit of Morton clothed in flesh, yes, that had been its true meaning. Yet that had been only a part of its meaning for her, it had meant something greater than Morton, it had stood for the symbol of perfect fulfilment—she remembered that even as a very small child she had vaguely discerned that perfect fulfilment. This love had been glowing like a great friendly beacon, a thing that was steadfast and very reassuring. All unconscious, she must often have warmed herself at it, must have thawed out her doubts and her vague misgivings. It had always been their love, the one for the other; she knew this, and yet it had been her beacon. But now those flames were no longer steadfast; something had dared to blemish their brightness. She longed to leap up in her youth and strength and cast this thing out of her holy of holies.* The fire must not die and leave her in darkness.

And yet she was utterly helpless, and she knew it. All that she did seemed inadequate and childish: 'When I was a child I spake as a child, I understood as a child, I thought as a child.'* Remembering Saint Paul, she decided grimly that surely she had remained as a child. She could sit and stare at them—these poor, stricken lovers—with eyes that were scared and deeply reproachful: 'You must not let anything spoil your loving, I need it,' her eyes could send them that message. She could love them in her turn, possessively, fiercely: 'You're mine, mine, mine, the one perfect thing about me. You're one and you're mine, I'm frightened, I need you!' Her thoughts could send them that message. She could start to caress them, awkwardly, shyly, stroking their hands with her strong, bony fingers—first his hand, then hers, then perhaps both together, so that they smiled in spite of their trouble. But she dared not stand up before them accusing, and say: 'I'm Stephen, I'm you, for you bred me. You shall not fail me by failing yourselves. I've a right to demand that you shall not fail me!' No, she dared not stand up and speak such words as these—she had never demanded anything from them.

Sometimes she would think them quietly over as two fellow creatures whom chance had made her parents. Her father, her mother—a man, a woman; and then she would be amazed to discover how little she knew of this man and this woman. They had once been babies, and later small children, ignorant of life and utterly dependent. That seemed so curious, ignorant of life—her father utterly weak and dependent. They had come to adolescence even as she had, and perhaps at times they too had felt unhappy. What had their thoughts been, those thoughts that lie hidden, those nebulous misgivings that never get spoken? Had her mother shrunk back resentful, protesting, when the seal of her womanhood had been stamped upon her? Surely not, for her mother was somehow so perfect, that all that befell her must in its turn, be perfect—her mother gathered nature into her arms and embraced it as a friend, as a well loved companion. But she, Stephen, had never felt friendly like that, which must mean, she supposed, that she lacked some fine instinct.

There had been those young years of her mother's in Ireland; she spoke of them sometimes but only vaguely, as though they were now very far away, as though they had never seriously counted. And yet she had been lovely, lovely Anna Molloy, much admired, much loved and constantly courted—And her father, he too had been in the world, in Rome, in Paris, and often in London—he had not lived much at Morton in those days; and how queer it seemed, there had been a time when her father had actually not known her mother. They had been completely unconscious of each other, he for twenty-nine years, she for just over twenty, and yet all the while had been drawing together, in spite of themselves, always nearer together. Then had come that morning away in County Clare, when those two had suddenly seen each other, and had known from that moment the meaning of life, of love, just because they had seen each other. Her father spoke very seldom of such things, but this much he had told her, it had all grown quite clear—What had it felt like when they realized each other? What did it feel like to see things quite clearly, to know the innermost reason for things?

Morton—her mother had come home to Morton, to wonderful, gently enfolding Morton. She had passed for the first time through the heavy white doorway under the shining semicircular fanlight. She had walked into the old square hall with its bear-skins, and its pictures of funny, dressed-up looking Gordons—the hall with the whip-rack where Stephen kept her whips—the hall with the beautiful iridescent window, that looked over the lawns and herbaceous borders.

Then, perhaps hand in hand,* they had passed beyond the hall, her father a man, her mother a woman, with their destiny already upon them—and that destiny of theirs had been Stephen.

Ten years. For ten years they had just had each other, each other and Morton—surely wonderful years. But what had they been thinking about all those years? Had they perhaps thought a little about Stephen? Oh, but what could she hope to know of these things, their thoughts, their feelings, their secret ambitions—she, who had not even been conceived, she, who had not yet come into existence? They had lived in a world that her eyes had not looked on; days and nights had slipped into the weeks, months and years. Time had existed, but she, Stephen, had not. They had lived through that time; it had gone to their making; their present had been the result of its travail, had sprung from its womb as she from her mother's, only she had not been a part of that travail, as she had been a part of her mother's. Hopeless! And yet she must try to know them, these two, every inch of their hearts, of their minds; and knowing them, she must then try to guard them—but him first, oh, him first—she did not ask why, she only knew that because she loved him as she did, he would always have to come first. Love was simple like that; it just followed its impulse and asked no questions—it was beautifully simple. But for his sake she must also love the thing that he loved, her mother, though this love was somehow quite different; it was less hers than his, he had thrust it upon her; it was not an integral part of her being. Nevertheless it too must be served, for the happiness of one was that of the other. They were indivisible, one flesh, one spirit,* and whatever it was that had crept in between them was trying to tear asunder this oneness—that was why she, their child, must rise up and help them if she could, for was she not the fruit of their oneness?

4

There were times when she would think that she must have been mistaken, that no trouble was overshadowing her father; these would be when they two were sitting in his study, for then he would seem contented. Surrounded by his books, caressing their bindings, Sir Philip would look care-free again and light-hearted.

'No friends in the world like books,' he would tell her. 'Look at this fellow in his old leather jacket!'

There were times, too, out hunting when he seemed very young, as Raftery had been that first season. But the ten-year-old Raftery was now wiser than Sir Philip, who would often behave like a foolhardy schoolboy. He would give Stephen leads over hair-raising places, and then, she safely landed, turn round and grin at her. He liked her to ride the pick of his hunters these days, and would slyly show off her prowess. The sport would bring back the old light to his eyes, and his eyes would look happy as they rested on his daughter.

She would think: 'I must have been terribly mistaken,' and would feel a great peace surge over her spirit.

He might say, as they slowly jogged home to Morton: 'Did you notice my youngster here take that stiff timber?* Not bad for a five-year-old, he'll do nicely.' And perhaps he might add: 'Put a three on that five, and then tell your old sire that he's not so bad either! I'm fifty-three, Stephen, I'll be going in the wind* if I don't knock off smoking quite soon, and that's certain!'

Then Stephen would know that her father felt young, very young, and was wanting her to flatter him a little.

But this mood would not last; it had often quite changed by the time that the two of them reached the stables. She would notice with a sudden pain in her heart that he stooped when he walked, not much yet, but a little. And she loved his broad back, she had always loved it—a kind, reassuring protective back. Then the thought would come that perhaps its great kindness had caused it to stoop as though bearing a burden; and the thought would come: 'He *is* bearing a burden, not his own, it's some one else's—but whose?'*

CHAPTER 10

I

CHRISTMAS came and with it the girl's eighteenth birthday, but the shadows that clung round her home did not lessen; nor could Stephen, groping about in those shadows, find a way to win through to the light. Every one tried to be cheerful and happy, as even sad people will do at Christmas, while the gardeners brought in huge bundles of holly with which to festoon the portraits of Gordons—rich, red-berried holly that came from the hills, and that year after year would be sent down to Morton. The courageous-eyed Gordons looked out from their wreaths unsmiling, as though they were thinking of Stephen.

In the hall stood the Christmas-tree of her childhood, for Sir Philip loved the old German custom* which would seem to insist that even the aged be as children and play with God on His birthday. At the top of the tree swung the little wax Christ-child in His spangled night-gown with gold and blue ribbons; and the little wax Christ-child bent downwards and sideways because, although small, He was rather heavy—or, as Stephen had thought when she too had been small, because He was trying to look for His presents.

In the morning they all went to church in the village, and the church smelt of coldness and freshly bruised greenstuff—of the laurel and holly and pungent pine branches, that wreathed the oak pulpit and framed the altar; and the anxious-faced eagle* who must carry the Scriptures on his wings, he too was looking quite festive. Very redolent of England it was, that small church, with its apple-cheeked choir-boys in newly washed garments; with its young Oxford parson who in summer played cricket to the glory of God and the good of the county; with its trim congregation of neighbouring gentry who had recently purchased an excellent organ, so that now they could hear the opening bars of the hymns with a feeling of self-satisfaction, but with something else too that came nearer to Heaven, because of those lovely old songs of Christmas. The choir raised their sexless, untroubled voices: 'While shepherds watched their flocks . . .' sang the choir; and Anna's soft mezzo mingled and blended with her husband's deep boom and Puddle's soprano. Then Stephen sang too for the sheer joy of singing, though her voice at best was inclined to be husky: 'While shepherds watched their flocks by night,'* carolled Stephen—for some reason thinking of Raftery.

After church the habitual Christmas greetings: 'Merry Christmas.' 'Merry Christmas.' 'Same to you, many of them!' Then home to Morton and the large mid-day dinner—turkey, plum pudding with its crisp brandy butter, and the mince-pies that invariably gave Puddle indigestion. Then dessert with all sorts of sweet fruits out of boxes, crystallized fruits that made your hands sticky, together with fruit from the Morton green-houses; and from somewhere that no one could ever remember, the elegant miniature Lady-apples* that you ate skins and all in two bites if you were greedy.

A long afternoon spent in waiting for darkness when Anna could light the Christmas-tree candles; and no ringing of bells to disturb the servants, not until they must all file in for their presents which were piled up high round the base of the tree on which Anna would light the small candles. Dusk—draw the curtains, it was dark enough now, and some one must go and fetch Anna the taper, but she must take care of the little wax Christ-child, Who liked many lights even though they should melt Him.

'Stephen, climb up, will you, and tie back the Christ-child, His toe is almost touching that candle!'

Then Anna applying the long lighted taper from branch to branch, very slowly and gravely, as though she accomplished some ritual, as though she herself were a ministering priestess—Anna very slender and tall in a dress whose soft folds swept her limbs and lay round her ankles.

'Ring three times, will you, Philip? I think they're all lighted—no, wait—all right now, I'd missed that top candle. Stephen, begin to sort out the presents, please, dear, your father's just rung for the servants. Oh, and Puddle, you might push over the table, I may need it—no, not that one, the table by the window—'

A subdued sound of voices, a stifled giggle. The servants filing in through the green baize door, and only the butler and footmen familiar in appearance, the others all strangers, in mufti.* Mrs. Wilson, the cook, in black silk with jet trimming, the scullery maid in electric blue cashmere, one housemaid in mauve, another in green, and the upper of three in dark terracotta, while Anna's own maid wore an old dress of Anna's. Then the men from outside, from the gardens and stables—men bare-headed who were usually seen in their caps—old Williams displaying a widening bald patch, and wearing tight trousers instead of his breeches; old Williams walking stiffly because his new suit felt like cardboard, and because his white collar was too high, and because his hard, made-up black bow would slip crooked. The grooms and the boys, all exceedingly shiny from their neatly oiled heads to their well polished noses—the boys very awkward, short-sleeved and rough-handed, shuffling a little because trying not to. And the gardeners led in by the grave Mr. Hopkins, who wore black of a Sunday and carried a Church Service, and whose knowledge of the ills that all grape-flesh is heir to,* had given his face a patient, pained expression. Men smelling of soil these, in spite of much scrubbing; men whose necks and whose hands were crossed and re-crossed by a network of tiny and earth-clogged furrows—men whose backs would bend early from tending the earth. There they stood in the wake of the grave Mr. Hopkins, with their eyes on the big, lighted Christmas-tree, while they never so much as glanced at the flowers that had sprung from many long hours of their labour. No, instead they must just stand and gape at the tree, as though with its candles and Christ-child and all, it were some strange exotic plant in Kew Gardens.*

Then Anna called her people by name, and to each one she gave the gifts of that Christmas; and they thanked her, thanked Stephen and thanked Sir Philip; and Sir Philip thanked them for their faithful service, as had always been the good custom at Morton for more years than Sir Philip himself could remember. Thus the day had passed by in accordance with tradition, every one from the highest to the lowest remembered; nor had Anna forgotten her gifts for the village—warm shawls, sacks of coal, cough mixture and sweets. Sir Philip had sent a cheque to the vicar, which would keep him for a long time in cricketing flannels; and Stephen had carried a carrot to Raftery and two lumps of sugar to the fat, aged Collins, who because he was all but blind of one eye, had bitten her hand in place of his sugar. And Puddle had written at great length to a sister who lived down in Cornwall and whom she neglected, except on such memory-jogging occasions as Christmas, when somehow we always remember. And the servants had gorged themselves to repletion, and the hunters had rested in their hay-scented stables; while out in the fields, sea-gulls, come far inland, had feasted in their turn on humbler creatures—grubs and slugs, and other unhappy small fry, much relished by birds and hated by farmers.

Night closed down on the house, and out of the darkness came the anxious young voices of village schoolchildren: 'Noël, Noël—'* piped the anxious young voices, lubricated by sweets from the lady of Morton. Sir Philip stirred the logs in the hall to a blaze, while Anna sank into a deep chair and watched them. Her hands that were wearied by much ministration, lay over the arms of the chair in the firelight, and the firelight sought out the rings on her hands, and it played with the whiter flames in her diamonds. Then Sir Philip stood up, and he gazed at his wife, while she stared at the logs, not appearing to notice him; but Stephen, watching in silence from her corner, seemed to see a dark shadow that stole in between them—beyond this her vision was mercifully dim, otherwise she must surely have recognized that shadow.

2

On New Year's Eve Mrs. Antrim gave a dance in order, or so she said, to please Violet, who was still rather young to attend the hunt balls, but who dearly loved gaiety, especially dancing. Violet was plump, pert and adolescent, and had lately insisted on putting her hair up. She liked men, who in consequence always liked her, for like begets like when it comes to the sexes, and Violet was full of what people call 'allure,' or in simpler language, of sexual attraction. Roger was home for Christmas from Sandhurst,* so that he would be there to assist his mother. He was now nearly twenty, a good-looking youth with a tiny moustache which he tentatively fingered. He assumed the grand air of the man of the world who has actually weathered about nineteen summers. He was hoping to join his regiment quite soon, which greatly augmented his self-importance.

Could Mrs. Antrim have ignored Stephen Gordon's existence, she would almost certainly have done so. She disliked the girl; she had always disliked her; what she called Stephen's 'queerness' aroused her suspicion—she was never quite clear as to what she suspected, but felt sure that it must be something outlandish: 'A young woman of her age to ride like a man, I call it preposterous!' declared Mrs. Antrim.*

It can safely be said that Stephen at eighteen had in no way outgrown her dread of the Antrims; there was only one member of that family who liked her, she knew, and that was the small, henpecked Colonel. He liked her because, a fine horseman himself, he admired her skill and her courage out hunting.

'It's a pity she's so tall, of course—' he would grumble, 'but she does know a horse and how to stick on one. Now my children might have been brought up at Margate,* they're just about fitted to ride the beach donkeys!'

But Colonel Antrim would not count at the dance; indeed in his own house he very seldom counted. Stephen would have to endure Mrs. Antrim and Violet—and then Roger was home from Sandhurst. Their antagonism had never quite died, perhaps because it was too fundamental. Now they covered it up with a cloak of good manners, but these two were still enemies at heart, and they knew it. No, Stephen did not want to go to that dance, though she went in order to please her mother. Nervous, awkward and apprehensive, Stephen arrived at the Antrims that night, little thinking that Fate, the most expert of tricksters, was waiting to catch her just round the corner. Yet so it was, for during that evening Stephen met Martin and Martin met Stephen, and their meeting was great with portent for them both, though neither of them could know it.

It all happened quite simply as such things will happen. It was Roger who introduced Martin Hallam;* it was Stephen who explained that she danced very badly; it was Martin who suggested that they sit out their dances. Then—how quickly it occurs if the thing is predestined—they suddenly knew that they liked each other, that some chord had been struck to a pleasant vibration; and this being so they sat out many dances, and they talked for quite a long while that evening.

Martin lived in British Columbia,* it seemed, where he owned several farms and a number of orchards. He had gone out there after the death of his mother, for six months, but had stayed on for love of the country. And now he was having a holiday in England—that was how he had got to know young Roger Antrim, they had met up in London and Roger had asked him to come down for a week, and so here he was—but it felt almost strange to be back again in England. Then he talked of the vastness of that new country that was yet so old; of its snow-capped mountains, of its canyons and gorges, of its deep, princely rivers, of its lakes, above all of its mighty forests. And when Martin spoke of those mighty forests, his voice changed, it became almost reverential; for this young man loved trees with a primitive instinct, with a strange and inexplicable devotion. Because he liked Stephen he could talk of his trees, and because she liked him she could listen while he talked, feeling that she too would love his great forests.

His face was very young, clean-shaven and bony; he had bony, brown hands with spatulate fingers; for the rest, he was tall with a loosely knit figure, and he slouched a little when he walked, from much riding. But his face had a charming quality about it, especially when he talked of his trees; it glowed, it seemed to be inwardly kindled, and it asked for a real and heart-felt understanding of the patience and the beauty and the goodness of trees—it was eager for your understanding. Yet in spite of this touch of romance in his make-up, which he could not keep out of his voice at moments, he spoke simply, as one man will speak to another, very simply, not trying to create an impression. He talked about trees as some men talk of ships, because they love them and the element they stand for. And Stephen, the awkward, the bashful, the tongue-tied, heard herself talking in her turn, quite freely, heard herself asking him endless questions about forestry, farming and the care of vast orchards; thoughtful questions, unromantic but apt—such as one man will ask of another.

Then Martin wished to learn about her, and they talked of her fencing, her studies, her riding, and she told him about Raftery who was named for the poet. And all the while she felt natural and happy because here was a man who was taking her for granted, who appeared to find nothing eccentric about her or her tastes, but who quite simply took her for granted. Had you asked Martin Hallam to explain why it was that he accepted the girl at her own valuation, he would surely have been unable to tell you—it had happened, that was all, and there the thing ended. But whatever the reason, he felt drawn to this friendship that had leapt so suddenly into being.

Before Anna left the dance with her daughter, she invited the young man to drive over and see them; and Stephen felt glad of that invitation, because now she could share her new friend with Morton. She said to Morton that night in her bedroom: 'I know you're going to like Martin Hallam.'

CHAPTER 11

I

MARTIN went to Morton, he went very often, for Sir Philip liked him and encouraged the friendship. Anna liked Martin too, and she made him feel welcome because he was young and had lost his mother. She spoilt him a little, as a woman will spoil who, having no son must adopt some one else's, so to Anna he went with all his small troubles, and she doctored him when he caught a bad chill out hunting. He instinctively turned to her in such things, but never, in spite of their friendship, to Stephen.

Yet now he and Stephen were always together, he was staying on and on at the hotel in Upton; ostensibly staying because of the hunting; in reality staying because of Stephen who was filling a niche in his life long empty, the niche reserved for the perfect companion. A queer, sensitive fellow* this Martin Hallam, with his strange love of trees and primitive forests—not a man to make many intimate friends, and in consequence a man to be lonely. He knew little about books and had been a slack student, but Stephen and he had other things in common; he rode well, and he cared for and understood horses; he fenced well and would quite often now fence with Stephen; nor did he appear to resent it when she beat him; indeed he seemed to accept it as natural, and would merely laugh at his own lack of skill. Out hunting these two would keep close to each other, and would ride home together as far as Upton; or perhaps he would go on to Morton with her, for Anna was always glad to see Martin. Sir Philip gave him the freedom of the stables, and even old Williams forbore to grumble:

''E be trusty, that's what 'e be,' declared Williams, 'and the horses knows it and acts accordin'.'

But sport was not all that drew Stephen to Martin, for his mind, like hers, was responsive to beauty, and she taught him the countryside that she loved, from Upton to Castle Morton* common—the common that lies at the foot of the hills. But far beyond Castle Morton she took him. They would ride down the winding lane to Bromsberrow, then crossing the small stream at Clincher's Mill, jog home through the bare winter woods of Eastnor.* And she taught him the hills whose plentiful bosoms had made Anna think of green-girdled mothers, mothers of sons, as she sat and watched them, great with the child who should have been her son. They climbed the venerable Worcestershire Beacon* that stands guardian of all the seven Malverns, or wandered across the hills of the Wells to the old British Camp above the Wye Valley. The Valley would lie half in light, half in shadow, and beyond would be Wales and the dim Black Mountains. Then Stephen's heart would tighten a little, as it always had done because of that beauty, so that one day she said:

'When I was a child, this used to make me want to cry, Martin.'

And he answered: 'Some part of us always sheds tears when we see lovely things—they make us regretful.' But when she asked him why this should be, he shook his head slowly, unable to tell her.

Sometimes they walked through Hollybush woods, then on up Raggedstone, a hill grim with legend—its shadow would bring misfortune or death to those it fell on, according to legend.* Martin would pause to examine the thorn trees, ancient thorns that had weathered many a hard winter. He would touch them with gentle, pitying fingers:

'Look, Stephen—the courage of these old fellows! They're all twisted and crippled; it hurts me to see them, yet they go on patiently doing their bit—have you ever thought about the enormous courage of trees? I have, and it seems to me amazing. The Lord dumps them down and they've just got to stick it, no matter what happens—that must need some courage!' And one day he said: 'Don't think me quite mad, but if we survive death then the trees will survive it; there must be some sort of a forest heaven for all the faithful—the faithful of trees. I expect they take their birds along with them; why not? "And in death they were not divided." '* Then he laughed, but she saw that his eyes were quite grave, so she asked him:

'Do you believe in God, Martin?'

And he answered: 'Yes, because of His trees. Don't you?'

'I'm not sure—'

'Oh, my poor, blind Stephen!* Look again, go on looking until you do believe.'

They discussed many things quite simply together, for between these two was no vestige of shyness. His youth met hers and walked hand in hand with it, so that she knew how utterly lonely her own youth had been before the coming of Martin.

She said: 'You're the only real friend I've ever had, except Father—our friendship's so wonderful, somehow—we're like brothers, we enjoy all the same sort of things.'

He nodded: 'I know, a wonderful friendship.'

The hills must let Stephen tell him their secrets, the secrets of by-paths most cunningly hidden; the secrets of small, unsuspected green hollows; the secrets of ferns that live only by hiding. She might even reveal the secrets of birds, and show him the playground of shy, spring cuckoos.

'They fly quite low up here, one can see them; last year a couple flew right past me, calling.* If you were not going away so soon, Martin, we'd come later on—I'd love you to see them.'

'And I'd love you to see my huge forests,' he told her, 'why can't you come back to Canada with me? What rot it is, all this damned convention; we're such pals you and I, I'll be desperately lonely—Lord, what a fool of a world we live in!'

And she said quite simply: 'I'd love to come with you.'

Then he started to tell her about his huge forests, so vast that their greenness seemed almost eternal. Great trees he told of, erect, towering firs, many centuries old and their girth that of giants. And then there were all the humbler tree-folk whom he spoke of as friends that were dear and familiar; the hemlocks that grow by the courses of rivers, in love with adventure and clear running water; the slender white spruces that border the lakes; the red pines, that glow like copper in the sunset. Unfortunate trees these beautiful red pines, for their tough, manly wood is coveted by builders.

'But I won't have my roof-tree* hacked from their sides,' declared Martin, 'I'd feel like a positive assassin!'

Happy days spent between the hills and the stables, happy days for these two who had always been lonely until now, and now this wonderful friendship—there had never been anything like it for Stephen. Oh, but it was good to have him beside her, so young, so strong and so understanding. She liked his quiet voice with its careful accent, and his thoughtful blue eyes that moved rather slowly, so that his glance when it came, came slowly—sometimes she would meet his glance half-way, smiling. She who had longed for the companionship of men, for their friendship, their good-will, their toleration, she had it all now and much more in Martin, because of his great understanding.

She said to Puddle one night in the schoolroom: 'I've grown fond of Martin—isn't that queer after only a couple of months of friendship? But he's different somehow—when he's gone I shall miss him.'

And her words had the strangest effect on Puddle who quite suddenly beamed at Stephen and kissed her—Puddle who never betrayed her emotions, quite suddenly beamed at Stephen and kissed her.

2

People gossiped a little because of the freedom allowed Martin and Stephen by her parents; but on the whole they gossiped quite kindly, with a great deal of smiling and nodding of heads. After all the girl was just like other girls—they almost ceased to resent her. Meanwhile Martin continued to stay on in Upton, held fast by the charm and the strangeness of Stephen—her very strangeness it was that allured him, yet all the while he must think of their friendship, not even admitting that strangeness. He deluded himself with these thoughts of friendship, but Sir Philip and Anna were not deluded. They looked at each other almost shyly at first, then Anna grew bold, and she said to her husband:

'Is it possible the child is falling in love with Martin? Of course he's in love with her. Oh, my dear, it would make me so awfully happy—' And her heart went out in affection to Stephen, as it had not done since the girl was a baby.

Her hopes would go flying ahead of events; she would start making plans for her daughter's future. Martin must give up his orchards and forests and buy Tenley Court* that was now in the market; it had several large farms and some excellent pasture, quite enough to keep any man happy and busy. Then Anna would suddenly grow very thoughtful; Tenley Court was also possessed of fine nurseries, big, bright, sunny rooms facing south, with their bath-room, there were bars to the windows—it was all there and ready.

Sir Philip shook his head and warned Anna to go slowly, but he could not quite keep the great joy from his eyes, nor the hope from his heart. Had he been mistaken? Perhaps after all he had been mistaken—the hope thudded ceaselessly now in his heart.

3

Came a day when winter must give place to spring, when the daffodils marched across the whole country from Castle Morton Common to Ross* and beyond, pitching camps by the side of the river. When the hornbeam* made patches of green in the hedges, and the hawthorn broke out into small, budding bundles; when the old cedar tree on the lawn at Morton grew reddish pink tips to its elegant fingers; when the wild cherry trees on the sides of the hills were industriously putting forth both leaves and blossoms; when Martin looked into his heart and saw Stephen—saw her suddenly there as a woman.

Friendship! He marvelled now at his folly, at his blindness, his coldness of body and spirit. He had offered this girl the cold husks of his friendship, insulting her youth, her womanhood, her beauty—for he saw her now with the eyes of a lover. To a man such as he was, sensitive, restrained, love came as a blinding revelation. He knew little about women, and the little he did know was restricted to episodes that he thought best forgotten. On the whole he had led a fairly chaste life—less from scruple than because he was fastidious by nature. But now he was very deeply in love, and those years of restraint took their toll of poor Martin, so that he trembled before his own passion, amazed at its strength, not a little disconcerted. And being by habit a quiet, reserved creature, he must quite lose his head and become the reverse. So impatient was he that he rushed off to Morton very early one morning to look for Stephen, tracking her down in the end at the stables, where he found her talking to Williams and Raftery.

He said: 'Never mind about Raftery, Stephen—let's go into the garden, I've got something to tell you.' And she thought that he must have had bad news from home, because of his voice and his curious pallor.

She went with him and they walked on in silence for awhile, then Martin stood still, and began to talk quickly; he was saying amazing, incredible things: 'Stephen, my dear—I do utterly love you.' He was holding out his arms, while she shrank back bewildered: 'I love you, I'm deeply in love with you, Stephen—look at me, don't you understand me, belovèd? I want you to marry me—you do love me, don't you?' And then, as though she had suddenly struck him, he flinched: 'Good God! What's the matter, Stephen?'

She was staring at him in a kind of dumb horror, staring at his eyes that were clouded by desire, while gradually over her colourless face there was spreading an expression of the deepest repulsion—terror and repulsion he saw on her face, and something else too, a look as of outrage. He could not believe this thing that he saw, this insult to all that he felt to be sacred; for a moment he in his turn, must stare, then he came a step nearer, still unable to believe. But at that she wheeled round and fled from him wildly, fled back to the house that had always protected; without so much as a word she left him, nor did she once pause in her flight to look back. Yet even in this moment of headlong panic, the girl was conscious of something like amazement, amazement at herself, and she gasped as she ran: 'It's Martin—Martin—' And again: 'It's Martin!'

He stood perfectly still until the trees hid her. He felt stunned, incapable of understanding. All that he knew was that he must get away, away from Stephen, away from Morton, away from the thoughts that would follow after. In less than two hours he was motoring to London; in less than two weeks he was standing on the deck of the steamer that would carry him back to his forests that lay somewhere beyond the horizon.

CHAPTER 12

I

No one questioned at Morton; they spoke very little. Even Anna forbore to question her daughter, checked by something that she saw in the girl's pale face.

But alone with her husband she gave way to her misgivings, to her deep disappointment: 'It's heartbreaking, Philip. What's happened? They seemed so devoted to each other. Will you ask the child? Surely one of us ought to—'

Sir Philip said quietly: 'I think Stephen will tell me.' And with that Anna had perforce to be content.

Very silently Stephen now went about Morton, and her eyes looked bewildered and deeply unhappy. At night she would lie awake thinking of Martin, missing him, mourning him as though he were dead. But she could not accept this death without question, without feeling that she was in some way blameworthy. What was she, what manner of curious creature, to have been so repelled by a lover like Martin? Yet she had been repelled, and even her pity for the man could not wipe out that stronger feeling. She had driven him away because something within her was intolerant of that new aspect of Martin.

Oh, but she mourned his good, honest friendship; he had taken that from her, the thing she most needed—but perhaps after all it had never existed except as a cloak for this other emotion. And then, lying there in the thickening darkness, she would shrink from what might be waiting in the future, for all that had just happened might happen again—there were other men in the world beside Martin. Fool, never to have visualized this thing before, never to have faced the possibility of it; now she understood her resentment of men when their voices grew soft and insinuating. Yes, and now she knew to the full the meaning of fear, and Martin it was, who had taught her its meaning—her friend—the man she had utterly trusted had pulled the scales from her eyes and revealed it. Fear, stark fear, and the shame of such fear—that was the legacy left her by Martin. And yet he had made her so happy at first, she had felt so contented, so natural with him; but that was because they had been like two men, companions, sharing each other's interests.* And at this thought her bitterness would all but flow over; it was cruel, it was cowardly of him to have deceived her, when all the time he had only been waiting for the chance to force this other thing on her.

But what was she? Her thoughts slipping back to her childhood, would find many things in her past that perplexed her. She had never been quite like the other small children, she had always been lonely and discontented, she had always been trying to be some one else—that was why she had dressed herself up as young Nelson. Remembering those days she would think of her father, and would wonder if now, as then, he could help her. Supposing she should ask him to explain about Martin? Her father was wise, and had infinite patience—yet somehow she instinctively dreaded to ask him. Alone—it was terrible to feel so much alone—to feel oneself different from other people. At one time she had rather enjoyed this distinction—she had rather enjoyed dressing up as young Nelson. Yet had she enjoyed it? Or had it been done as some sort of inadequate, childish protest? But if so against what had she been protesting when she strutted about the house, masquerading? In those days she had wanted to be a boy—had that been the meaning of the pitiful young Nelson? And what about now? She had wanted Martin to treat her as a man, had expected it of him. . . . The questions to which she could find no answers, would pile themselves up and up in the darkness; oppressing, stifling by sheer weight of numbers, until she would feel them getting her under: 'I don't know—oh, God, I don't know!' she would mutter, tossing as though to fling off those questions.

Then one night towards dawn she could bear it no longer; her dread must give place to her need of consolation. She would ask her father to explain her to herself; she would tell him her deep desolation over Martin. She would say: 'Is there anything strange about me, Father, that I should have felt as I did about Martin?' And then she would try to explain very calmly what it was she had felt, the intensity of it. She would try to make him understand her suspicion that this feeling of hers was a thing fundamental, much more than merely not being in love; much, much more than not wanting to marry Martin. She would tell him why she found herself so utterly bewildered; tell him how she had loved Martin's strong, young body, and his honest brown face, and his slow thoughtful eyes, and his careless walk—all these things she had loved. Then suddenly terror and deep repugnance because of that unforeseen change in Martin, the change that had turned the friend into the lover—in reality it had been no more than that, the friend had turned lover and had wanted from her what she could not give him, or indeed any man, because of that deep repugnance. Yet there should have been nothing repugnant about Martin, nor was she a child to have felt such terror. She had known certain facts about life for some time and they had not repelled her in other people—not until they had been brought home to herself had these facts both terrified and repelled her.

She got up. No good in trying to sleep, those eternal questions kept stifling, tormenting. Dressing quickly, she stole down the wide, shallow stairs to the garden door, then out into the garden. The garden looked unfamiliar in the sunrise, like a well-known face that is suddenly transfigured. There was something aloof and awesome about it, as though it were lost in ecstatic devotion. She tried to tread softly, for she felt apologetic, she and her troubles were there as intruders; their presence disturbed this strange hush of communion, this oneness with something beyond their knowledge, that was yet known and loved by the soul of the garden. A mysterious and wonderful thing this oneness, pregnant with comfort could she know its true meaning—she felt this somewhere deep down in herself, but try as she would her mind could not grasp it; perhaps even the garden was shutting her out of its prayers, because she had sent away Martin. Then a thrush began to sing in the cedar, and his song was full of wild jubilation: 'Stephen, look at me, look at me!' sang the thrush, 'I'm happy, happy, it's all very simple!' There was something heartless about that singing which only served to remind her of Martin. She walked on disconsolate, thinking deeply. He had gone, he would soon be back in his forests—she had made no effort to keep him beside her because he had wanted to be her lover. . . . 'Stephen, look at us, look at us!' sang the birds, 'We're happy, happy, it's all very simple!' Martin walking in dim, green places—she could picture his life away in the forests, a man's life, good with the goodness of danger, a primitive, strong, imperative thing—a man's life, the life that should have been hers—And her eyes filled with heavy, regretful tears, yet she did not quite know for what she was weeping. She only knew that some great sense of loss, some great sense of incompleteness possessed her, and she let the tears trickle down her face, wiping them off one by one with her finger.

And now she was passing the old potting shed where Collins had lain in the arms of the footman. Choking back her tears she paused by the shed, and tried to remember the girl's appearance. Grey eyes—no, blue, and a round-about figure—plump hands, with soft skin always puckered from soap-suds—a housemaid's knee that had pained very badly: 'See that dent? That's the water. . . . It fair makes me sick.' Then a queer little girl dressed up as young Nelson: 'I'd like to be awfully hurt for you, Collins, the way that Jesus was hurt for sinners. . . .' The potting shed smelling of earth and dampness, sagging a little on one side, lop-sided—Collins lying in the arms of the footman, Collins being kissed by him, wantonly, crudely—a broken flower pot in the hand of a child—rage, deep rage—a great anguish of spirit—blood on a face that was pale with amazement, very bright red blood that kept trickling and trickling—flight, wild, inarticulate flight, away and away, anyhow, anywhere—the pain of torn skin, the rip of torn stockings—

She had not remembered these things for years, she had thought that all this had been quite forgotten; there was nothing to remind her of Collins these days but a fat, half-blind and pampered old pony. Strange how these memories came back this morning; she had lain in bed lately trying to recapture the childish emotions aroused in her by Collins and had failed, yet this morning they came back quite clearly. But the garden was full of a new memory now; it was full of the sorrowful memory of Martin. She turned abruptly, and leaving the shed walked towards the lakes that gleamed faintly in the distance.

Down by the lakes there was a sense of great stillness which the songs of the birds could in no way lessen, for this place had that curious stillness of spirit that seems to interpenetrate sound. A swan paddled about in front of his island, on guard, for his mate had a nest full of cygnets; from time to time he glanced crossly at Stephen though he knew her quite well, but now there were cygnets. He was proud in his splendid, incredible whiteness, and paternity made him feel overbearing, so that he refused to feed from Stephen's hand although she found a biscuit in her pocket.

'Coup, c-o-u-p!' she called, but he swung his neck sideways as he swam—it was like a disdainful negation. 'Perhaps he thinks I'm a freak,' she mused grimly, feeling more lonely because of the swan.

The lakes were guarded by massive old beech trees, and the beech trees stood ankle-deep in their foliage; a lovely and luminous carpet of leaves they had spread on the homely brown earth of Morton. Each spring came new little shuttles of greenness that in time added warp and woof to the carpet, so that year by year it grew softer and deeper, and year by year it glowed more resplendent. Stephen had loved this spot from her childhood, and now she instinctively went to it for comfort, but its beauty only added to her melancholy, for beauty can wound like a two-edged sword. She could not respond to its stillness of spirit, since she could not lull her own spirit to stillness.

She thought: 'I shall never be one with great peace any more, I shall always stand outside this stillness—wherever there is absolute stillness and peace in this world, I shall always stand just outside it.' And as though these thoughts were in some way prophetic, she inwardly shivered a little.

Then what must the swan do but start to hiss loudly, just to show her that he was really a father: 'Peter,' she reproached him, 'I won't hurt your babies—can't you trust me? I fed you the whole of last winter!'

But apparently Peter could not trust her at all, for he squawked to his mate who came out through the bushes, and she hissed in her turn, flapping strong angry wings, which meant in mere language: 'Get out of this, Stephen, you clumsy, inadequate, ludicrous creature; you destroyer of nests, you disturber of young, you great wingless blot on a beautiful morning!' Then they both hissed together: 'Get out of this, Stephen!' So Stephen left them to the care of their cygnets.

Remembering Raftery, she walked to the stables, where all was confusion and purposeful bustle. Old Williams was ruthlessly out on the warpath; he was scolding: 'Drat* the boy, what be 'e a-doin'? Come on, do! 'Urry up, get them two horses bridled, and don't go forgettin' their knee-caps this mornin'—and that bucket there don't belong where it's standin', nor that broom! Did Jim take the roan* to the blacksmith's? Gawd almighty, why not? 'Er shoes is like paper! 'Ere, you Jim, don't you go on ignorin' my orders, if you do—Come on, boy, got them two horses ready? Right, well then, up you go! You don't want no saddle, like as not you'd give 'im a gall* if you 'ad one!'

The sleek, good-looking hunters were led out in clothing—for the early spring mornings were still rather nippy—and among them came Raftery, slender and skittish; he was wearing his hood, and his eyes peered out bright as a falcon's from the two neatly braided eyeholes. From a couple more holes in the top of his head-dress, shot his small, pointed ears, which now worked with excitement.

''Old on!' bellowed Williams, 'What the 'ell be you doin'? Quick, shorten 'is bridle, yer not in a circus!' And then seeing Stephen: 'Beg pardon, Miss Stephen, but it be a fair crime not to lead that horse close, and 'im all corned up until 'e's fair dancin'!'

They stood watching Raftery skip through the gates, then old Williams said softly: ''E do be a wonder—more nor fifty odd years 'ave I worked in the stables, and never no beast 'ave I loved like Raftery. But 'e's no common horse, 'e be some sort of Christian, and a better one too than a good few I knows on—'

And Stephen answered: 'Perhaps he's a poet like his namesake; I think if he could write he'd write verses. They say all the Irish are poets at heart, so perhaps they pass on the gift to their horses.'

Then the two of them smiled, each a little embarrassed, but their eyes held great friendship the one for the other, a friendship of years now cemented by Raftery whom they loved—and small wonder, for assuredly never did more gallant or courteous horse step out of stable.

'Oh, well,' sighed Williams, 'I be gettin' that old—and Raftery, 'e do be comin' eleven, but 'e don't feel it yet in 'is limbs the way I does—me rheumatics 'as troubled me awful this winter.'

She stayed on a little while, comforting Williams, then made her way back to the house, very slowly. 'Poor Williams,' she thought, 'he is getting old, but thank the Lord nothing's the matter with Raftery.'

The house lay full in a great slant of sunshine; it looked as though it was sunning its shoulders. Glancing up, she came eye to eye with the house, and she fancied that Morton was thinking about her, for its windows seemed to be beckoning, inviting: 'Come home, come home, come inside quickly, Stephen!' And as though they had spoken, she answered: 'I'm coming,' and she quickened her lagging steps to a run, in response to this most compassionate kindness. Yes, she actually ran through the heavy white doorway under the semicircular fanlight, and on up the staircase that led from the hall in which hung the funny old portraits of Gordons—men long dead and gone but still wonderfully living, since their thoughts had fashioned the comeliness of Morton; since their loves had made children from father to son—from father to son until the advent of Stephen.

2

That evening she went to her father's study, and when he looked up she thought she was expected.

She said: 'I want to talk to you, Father.'

And he answered: 'I know—sit close to me, Stephen.'

He shaded his face with his long, thin hand, so that she could not see his expression, yet it seemed to her that he knew quite well why she had come to him in that study. Then she told him about Martin, told him all that had happened, omitting no detail, sparing him nothing. She openly mourned the friend who had failed her, and herself she mourned for failing the lover—and Sir Philip listened in absolute silence.

After she had spoken for quite a long time, she at length found the courage to ask her question: 'Is there anything strange about me, Father, that I should have felt as I did about Martin?'

It had come. It fell on his heart like a blow. The hand that was shading his pale face trembled, for he felt a great trembling take hold of his spirit. His spirit shrank back and cowered in his body, so that it dared not look out on Stephen.

She was waiting, and now she was asking again: 'Father, is there anything strange about me? I remember when I was a little child—I was never quite like all the other children—'

Her voice sounded apologetic, uncertain, and he knew that the tears were not far from her eyes, knew that if he looked now he would see her lips shaking, and the tears making ugly red stains on her eyelids. His loins ached with pity for this fruit of his loins—an insufferable aching, an intolerable pity.* He was frightened, a coward because of his pity, as he had been once long ago with her mother. Merciful God! How could a man answer? What could he say, and that man a father? He sat there inwardly grovelling before her: 'Oh, Stephen, my child, my little, little Stephen.' For now in his pity she seemed to him little, little and utterly helpless again—he remembered her hands as the hands of a baby, very small, very pink, with minute perfect nails—he had played with her hands, exclaiming about them, astonished because of their neat perfection: 'Oh, Stephen, my little, little Stephen.' He wanted to cry out against God for this thing; he wanted to cry out: 'You have maimed my Stephen! What had I done or my father before me, or my father's father, or his father's father? Unto the third and fourth generations. . . .'* And Stephen was waiting for his answer. Then Sir Philip set the lips of his spirit to the cup, and his spirit must drink the gall* of deception: 'I will not tell her, You cannot ask it—there are some things that even God should not ask.'

And now he turned round and deliberately faced her; smiling right into her eyes he lied glibly: 'My dear, don't be foolish, there's nothing strange about you, some day you may meet a man you can love. And supposing you don't, well, what of it, Stephen? Marriage isn't the only career for a woman. I've been thinking about your writing just lately, and I'm going to let you go up to Oxford; but meanwhile you mustn't get foolish fancies, that won't do at all—it's not like you, Stephen.' She was gazing at him and he turned away quickly: 'Darling, I'm busy, you must leave me,' he faltered.

'Thank you,' she said very quietly and simply, 'I felt that I had to ask you about Martin—'

3

After she had gone he sat on alone, and the lie was still bitter to his spirit as he sat there, and he covered his face for the shame that was in him—but because of the love that was in him he wept.

CHAPTER 13

I

THERE was gossip in plenty over Martin's disappearance, and to this Mrs. Antrim contributed her share, even more than her share, looking wise and mysterious whenever Stephen's name was mentioned. Every one felt very deeply aggrieved. They had been so eager to welcome the girl as one of themselves, and now this strange happening—it made them feel foolish which in turn made them angry.

The spring meets were heavy with tacit disapproval—nice men like young Hallam did not run away for nothing; and then what a scandal if those two were not engaged; they had wandered all over the country together. This tacit disapproval was extended to Sir Philip, and via him to Anna for allowing too much freedom; a mother ought to look after her daughter, but then Stephen had always been allowed too much freedom. This, no doubt, was what came of her riding astride and fencing and all the rest of the nonsense; when she did meet a man she took the bit between her teeth and behaved in a most amazing manner. Of course, had there been a proper engagement—but obviously that had never existed. They marvelled, remembering their own toleration, they had really been extremely broad-minded. An extraordinary girl, she had always been odd, and now for some reason she seemed odder than ever. Not so much as a word was said in her hearing that could possibly offend, and yet Stephen well knew that her neighbours' good-will had been only fleeting, a thing entirely dependent upon Martin. He it was who had raised her status among them—he, the stranger, not even connected with their county. They had all decided that she meant to marry Martin, and that fact had at once made them welcoming and friendly; and suddenly Stephen longed intensely to be welcomed, and she wished from her heart that she could have married Martin.

The strange thing was that she understood her neighbours in a way, and was therefore too just to condemn them; indeed had nature been less daring with her, she might well have become very much what they were—a breeder of children, an upholder of home, a careful and diligent steward of pastures. There was little of the true pioneer about

Stephen, in spite of her erstwhile longing for the forests. She belonged to the soil and the fruitfulness of Morton, to its pastures and paddocks, to its farms and its cattle, to its quiet and gentlemanly ordered traditions, to the dignity and pride of its old red brick house, that was yet without ostentation.* To these things she belonged and would always belong by right of those past generations of Gordons whose thoughts had fashioned the comeliness of Morton, whose bodies had gone to the making of Stephen. Yes, she was of them, those bygone people; they might spurn her—the lusty breeders of sons that they had been—they might even look down from Heaven with raised eyebrows, and say: 'We utterly refuse to acknowledge this curious creature called Stephen.' But for all that they could not drain her of blood, and her blood was theirs also, so that do what they would they could never completely rid themselves of her nor she of them—they were one in their blood.

But Sir Philip, that other descendant of theirs, found little excuse for his critical neighbours. Because he loved much he must equally suffer, consuming himself at times with resentment. And now when he and Stephen were out hunting he would be on his guard, very anxious and watchful lest any small incident should occur to distress her, lest at any time she should find herself lonely. When hounds checked and the field collected together,* he would make little jokes to amuse his daughter, he would rack his brain for these poor little jokes, in order that people should see Stephen laughing.

Sometimes he would whisper: 'Let 'em have it hot, Stephen, that youngster you're on loves a good bit of timber*—don't mind me, I know you won't damage his knees, just you give 'em a lead and let's see if they'll catch you!' And because it was seldom indeed that they caught her, his sore heart would know a fleeting contentment.

Yet people begrudged her even this triumph, pointing out that the girl was magnificently mounted: 'Anyone could get there on that sort of horse,' they would murmur, when Stephen was out of hearing.

But small Colonel Antrim, who was not always kind, would retort if he heard them: 'Damn it, *no*, it's the riding. The girl rides, that's the point; as for some of you others—' And then he would let loose a flood of foul language. 'If some bloody fools that I know rode like Stephen, we'd have bloody well less to pay to the farmers,'* and much more he would say to the same effect, with rich oaths interlarding his every sentence—the foulest-mouthed master in the whole British Isles he was said to be, this small Colonel Antrim.

Oh, but he dearly loved a fine rider, and he cursed and he swore his appreciation. Even in the presence of a sporting bishop one day, he had failed to control his language; indeed, he had sworn in the face of the bishop with enthusiasm, as he pointed to Stephen. An ineffectual and henpecked little fellow—in his home he was hardly allowed to say 'damn.' He was never permitted to smoke a cigar outside of his dark, inhospitable study. He must not breed Norwich canaries, which he loved, because they brought mice, declared Mrs. Antrim; he must not keep a pet dog in the house, and the 'Pink 'Un'* was anathema because of Violet. His taste in art was heavily censored, even on the walls of his own water-closet, where nothing might hang but a family group taken sixteen odd years ago with the children.

On Sundays he sat in an uncomfortable pew while his wife chanted psalms in the voice of a peacock. 'Oh come, let us sing unto the Lord,'* she would chant, as she heartily rejoiced in the strength of her salvation. All this and a great deal more he endured, indeed most of his life was passed in endurance—had it not been for those red-letter days out hunting, he might well have become melancholic from boredom. But those days, when he actually found himself master, went far to restore his anæmic manhood, and on them he would speak the good English language as some deep-seated complex knew it ought to be spoken—ruddily, roundly, explosively spoken, with elation, at times with total abandon—especially if he should chance to remember Mrs. Antrim would he speak it with total abandon.

But his oaths could not save Stephen now from her neighbours, nothing could do that since the going of Martin—for quite unknown to themselves they feared her; it was fear that aroused their antagonism. In her they instinctively sensed an outlaw, and theirs was the task of policing nature.

2

In her vast drawing-room so beautifully proportioned, Anna would sit with her pride sorely wounded, dreading the thinly veiled questions of her neighbours, dreading the ominous silence of her husband. And the old aversion she had felt for her child would return upon her like the unclean spirit who gathered to himself seven others more wicked,* so that her last state was worse than her first, and at times she must turn away her eyes from Stephen.

Thus tormented, she grew less tactful with her husband, and now she was always plying him with questions: 'But why can't you tell me what Stephen said to you, Philip, that evening when she went to your study?'

And he, with a mighty effort to be patient, would answer: 'She said that she couldn't love Martin—there was no crime in that. Leave the child alone, Anna, she's unhappy enough; why not let her alone?' And then he would hastily change the subject.

But Anna could not let Stephen alone, could never keep off the topic of Martin. She would talk at the girl until she grew crimson; and seeing this, Sir Philip would frown darkly, and when he and his wife were alone in their bedroom he would often reproach her with violence.

'Cruel—it's abominably cruel of you, Anna. Why in God's name must you go on nagging Stephen?'

Anna's taut nerves would tighten to breaking, so that she, when she answered, must also speak with violence.

One night he said abruptly: 'Stephen won't marry—I don't want her to marry; it would only mean disaster.'

And at this Anna broke out in angry protest. Why shouldn't Stephen marry? She wished her to marry. Was he mad? And what did he mean by disaster? No woman was ever complete without marriage—what on earth did he mean by disaster? He frowned and refused to answer her question. Stephen, he said, must go up to Oxford. He had set his heart on a good education for the child, who might some day become a fine writer. Marriage wasn't the only career for a woman. Look at Puddle, for instance; she'd been at Oxford—a most admirable, well-balanced, sensible creature. Next year he was going to send Stephen to Oxford. Anna scoffed. Yes, indeed, he might well look at Puddle! She was what came of this higher education—a lonely, unfulfilled, middle-aged spinster. Anna didn't want that kind of life for her daughter.

And then: 'It's a pity you can't be frank, Philip, about what was said that night in your study. I feel that there's something you're keeping back from me—it's so unlike Martin to behave as he has done; there must have been something that you haven't told me, to have made him go off without even a letter—'

He flared up at once because he felt guilty. 'I don't care a damn about Martin!' he said hotly. 'All I care about is Stephen, and she's going to Oxford next year; she's my child as well as yours, Anna!'

Then quite suddenly Anna's self-control left her, and she let him see into her tormented spirit; all that had lain unspoken between them she now put into crude, ugly words for his hearing: 'You care nothing for me any more—you and Stephen are enleagued against me—you have been for years.' Aghast at herself, she must yet go on speaking: 'You and Stephen—oh, I've seen it for years—you and Stephen.' He looked at her, and there was warning in his eyes, but she babbled on wildly: 'I've seen it for years—the cruelty of it; she's taken you from me, my own child—the unspeakable cruelty of it!'

'Cruelty, yes, but not Stephen's, Anna—it's yours; for in all the child's life you've never loved her.'

Ugly, degrading, rather terrible half-truths; and he knew the whole truth, yet he dared not speak it. It is bad for the soul to know itself a coward, it is apt to take refuge in mere wordy violence.

'Yes, you, her mother, you persecute Stephen, you torment her; I sometimes think you hate her!'

'Philip—good God!'

'Yes, I think you hate her; but be careful, Anna, for hatred breeds hatred, and remember I stand for the rights of my child—if you hate her you've got to hate me; she's my child. I won't let her face your hatred alone.'

Ugly, degrading, rather terrible half-truths. Their hearts ached while their lips formed recriminations. Their hearts burst into tears while their eyes remained dry and accusing, staring in hostility and anger. Far into the night they accused each other, they who before had never seriously quarrelled; and something very like the hatred he spoke of leapt out like a flame that seared them at moments.

'Stephen, my own child—she's come between us.'

'It's you who have thrust her between us, Anna.'

Mad, it was madness! They were such faithful lovers, and their love it was that had fashioned their child. They knew it was madness and yet they persisted, while their anger dug out for itself a deep channel, so that future angers might more easily follow. They could not forgive and they could not sleep, for neither could sleep without the other's forgiveness, and the hatred that leapt out at moments between them would be drowned in the tears that their hearts were shedding.

3

Like some vile and prolific thing, this first quarrel bred others, and the peace of Morton was shattered. The house seemed to mourn, and withdraw into itself, so that Stephen went searching for its spirit in vain. 'Morton,' she whispered, 'where are you, Morton? I must find you, I need you so badly.'

For now Stephen knew the cause of their quarrels, and she recognized the form of the shadow that had seemed to creep in between them at Christmas, and knowing, she stretched out her arms to Morton for comfort: 'My Morton, where are you? I need you.'

Grim and exceedingly angry grew Puddle, that little grey box of a woman in her schoolroom; angry with Anna for her treatment of Stephen, but even more deeply angry with Sir Philip, who knew the whole truth, or so she suspected, and who yet kept that truth back from Anna.

Stephen would sit with her head in her hands. 'Oh, Puddle, it's my fault; I've come in between them, and they're all I've got—they're my one perfect thing—I can't bear it—why have I come in between them?'

And Puddle would flush with reminiscent anger as her mind slipped back and back over the years to old sorrows, old miseries, long decently buried but now disinterred by this pitiful Stephen. She would live through those years again, while her spirit would cry out, unregenerate, against their injustice.

Frowning at her pupil, she would speak to her sharply: 'Don't be a fool, Stephen. Where's your brain, where's your backbone? Stop holding your head and get on with your Latin. My God, child, you'll have worse things than this to face later—life's not all beer and skittles,* I do assure you. Now come along, do, and get on with that Latin. Remember you'll soon be going up to Oxford.' But after a while she might pat the girl's shoulder and say rather gruffly: 'I'm not angry, Stephen—I do understand, my dear, I do really—only somehow I've just got to make you have backbone. You're too sensitive, child, and the sensitive suffer—well, I don't want to see you suffer, that's all. Let's go out for a walk—we've done enough Latin for to-day—let's walk over the meadows to Upton.'

Stephen clung to this little grey box of a woman as a drowning man will cling to a spar.* Puddle's very hardness was somehow consoling—it seemed concrete, a thing you could trust, could rely on, and their friendship that had flourished as a green bay-tree grew into something more stalwart and much more enduring. And surely the two of them had need of their friendship, for now there was little happiness at Morton; Sir Philip and Anna were deeply unhappy—degraded they would feel by their ceaseless quarrels.

Sir Philip would think: 'I must tell her the truth—I must tell her what I believe to be the truth about Stephen.' He would go in search of his wife, but having found her would stand there tongue-tied, with his eyes full of pity.

And one day Anna suddenly burst out weeping, for no reason except that she felt his great pity. Not knowing and not caring why he pitied, she wept, so that all he could do was to console her.

They clung together like penitent children. 'Anna, forgive me.'

'Forgive me, Philip—' For in between quarrels they were sometimes like children, naïvely asking each other's forgiveness.

Sir Philip's resolution weakened and waned as he kissed the tears from her poor, reddened eyelids. He thought: 'To-morrow—to-morrow I'll tell her—I can't bear to make her more unhappy to-day.'

So the weeks drifted by and still he had not spoken; summer came and went, giving place to the autumn. Yet one more Christmas visited Morton, and still Sir Philip had not spoken.

CHAPTER 14

I

FEBRUARY came, bringing snowstorms with it, the heaviest known for many a year. The hills lay folded in swathes of whiteness, and so did the valleys at the foot of the hills, and so did the spacious gardens of Morton—it was all one vast panorama of whiteness. The lakes froze, and the beech trees had crystalline branches, while their luminous carpet of leaves grew brittle so that it crackled now underfoot, the only sound in the frozen stillness of that place that was always infinitely still. Peter, the arrogant swan, turned friendly, and he and his family now welcomed Stephen who fed them every morning and evening, and they glad enough to partake of her bounty. On the lawn Anna set out a tray for the birds, with chopped suet, seed, and small mounds of breadcrumbs; and down at the stables old Williams spread straw in wide rings for exercising the horses who could not be taken beyond the yard, so bad were the roads around Morton.

The gardens lay placidly under the snow, in no way perturbed or disconcerted. Only one inmate of theirs felt anxious, and that was the ancient and wide-boughed cedar,* for the weight of the snow made an ache in its branches—its branches were brittle like an old man's bones; that was why the cedar felt anxious. But it could not cry out or shake off its torment; no, it could only endure with patience, hoping that Anna would take note of its trouble, since she sat in its shade summer after summer—since once long ago she had sat in its shade dreaming of the son she would bear her husband. And one morning Anna did notice its plight, and she called Sir Philip, who hurried from his study.

She said: 'Look, Philip! I'm afraid for my cedar—it's all weighted down—I feel worried about it.'

Then Sir Philip sent in to Upton for chain, and for stout pads of felt to support the branches; and he himself must direct the gardeners while they climbed into the tree and pushed off the snow; and he himself must see to the placing of the stout felt pads, lest the branches be galled.* Because he loved Anna who loved the cedar, he must stand underneath it directing the gardeners.

A sudden and horrible sound of rending. 'Sir, look out! Sir Philip, look out, sir, it's giving!'

A crash, and then silence—a horrible silence, far worse than that horrible sound of rending.

'Sir Philip—oh, Gawd, it's over 'is chest! It's crushed in 'is chest—it's the big branch wot's given! Some one go for the doctor—go quick for Doctor Evans. Oh, Gawd, 'is mouth's bleedin'—it's crushed in 'is chest—Won't nobody go for the doctor?'

The grave, rather pompous voice of Mr. Hopkins: 'Steady, Thomas, it's no good losin' your head. Robert, you'd best slip over to the stables and tell Burton to go in the car for the doctor. You, Thomas, give me a hand with this bough—steady on—ease it off a bit to the right, now lift! Steady on, keep more to the right—now then, gently, gently, man—lift!'

Sir Philip lay very still on the snow, and the blood oozed slowly from between his lips. He looked monstrously tall as he lay on that whiteness, very straight, with his long legs stretched out to their fullest, so that Thomas said foolishly: 'Don't 'e be big—I don't know as I ever noticed before—'

And now some one came scuttling over the snow, panting, stumbling, hopping grotesquely—old Williams, hatless and in his shirt sleeves—and as he came on he kept calling out something: 'Master, oh, Master!' And he hopped grotesquely as he came on over the slippery snow. 'Master, Master—oh, Master!'

They found a hurdle, and with dreadful care they placed the master of Morton upon it, and with dreadful slowness they carried the hurdle over the lawn, and in through the door that Sir Philip himself had left standing ajar.

Slowly they carried him into the hall, and even more slowly his tired eyes opened, and he whispered: 'Where's Stephen? I want—the child.'

And old Williams muttered thickly: 'She's comin', Master—she be comin' down the stairs; she's here, Sir Philip.'

Then Sir Philip tried to move, and he spoke quite loudly: 'Stephen! Where are you? I want you, child—'

She went to him, saying never a word, but she thought: 'He's dying—my Father.'

And she took his large hand in hers and stroked it, but still without speaking, because when one loves there is nothing left in the world to say, when the best belovèd lies dying. He looked at her with the pleading eyes of a dog who is dumb, but who yet asks forgiveness. And she knew that his eyes were asking forgiveness for something beyond her poor comprehension; so she nodded, and just went on stroking his hand.

Mr. Hopkins asked quietly: 'Where shall we take him?'

And as quietly Stephen answered: 'To the study.'

Then she herself led the way to the study, walking steadily, just as though nothing had happened, just as though when she got there she would find her father lolling back in his arm-chair, reading. But she thought all the while: 'He's dying—my Father—' Only the thought seemed unreal, preposterous. It seemed like the thinking of somebody else, a thing so unreal as to be preposterous. Yet when they had set him down in the study, her own voice it was that she heard giving orders.

'Tell Miss Puddleton to go at once to my Mother and break the news gently—I'll stay with Sir Philip. One of you please send a housemaid to me with a sponge and some towels and a basin of cold water. Burton's gone for Doctor Evans, you say? That's quite right. Now I'd like you to go up and fetch down a mattress, the one from the blue room will do—get it quickly. Bring some blankets as well and a couple of pillows—and I may need a little brandy.'

They ran to obey, and before very long she had helped to lift him on to the mattress. He groaned a little, then he actually smiled as he felt her strong arms around him. She kept wiping the blood away from his mouth, and her fingers were stained; she looked at her fingers, but without comprehension—they could not be hers—like her thoughts, they must surely be somebody else's. But now his eyes were growing more restless—he was looking for some one, he was looking for her mother.

'Have you told Miss Puddleton, Williams?' she whispered.

The man nodded.

Then she said: 'Mother's coming, darling; you lie still,' and her voice was softly persuasive as though she were speaking to a small suffering child. 'Mother's coming; you lie quite still, darling.'

And she came—incredulous, yet wide-eyed with horror. 'Philip, oh, Philip!' She sank down beside him and laid her white face against his on the pillow. 'My dear, my dear—it's most terribly hurt you—try to tell me where it hurts; try to tell me, belovèd. The branch gave—it was the snow—it fell on you, Philip—but try to tell me where it hurts most, belovèd.'

Stephen motioned to the servants and they went away slowly with bowed heads, for Sir Philip had been a good friend; they loved him, each in his or her way, each according to his or her capacity for loving.

And always that terrible voice went on speaking, terrible because it was quite unlike Anna's—it was toneless, and it asked and re-asked the same question: 'Try to tell me where it hurts most, belovèd.'

But Sir Philip was fighting the battle of pain; of intense, irresistible, unmanning pain. He lay silent, not answering Anna.

Then she coaxed him in words soft with memories of her country. 'And you the loveliest man,' she whispered, 'and you with the light of God in your eyes.' But he lay there unable to answer.

And now she seemed to forget Stephen's presence, for she spoke as one lover will speak with another—foolishly, fondly, inventing small names, as one lover will do for another. And watching them Stephen beheld a great marvel, for he opened his eyes and his eyes met her mother's, and a light seemed to shine over both their poor faces, transfiguring them with something triumphant, with love—thus those two rekindled the beacon for their child in the shadow of the valley of death.*

2

It was late afternoon before the doctor arrived; he had been out all day and the roads were heavy. He had come the moment he received the news, come as fast as a car clogged with snow could bring him. He did what he could, which was very little, for Sir Philip was conscious and wished to remain so; he would not permit them to ease his pain by administering drugs. He could speak very slowly.

'No—not that—something urgent—I want—to say. No drugs—I know I'm—dying—Evans.'

The doctor adjusted the slipping pillows, then turning he whispered carefully to Stephen. 'Look after your mother. He's going, I think—it can't be long now. I'll wait in the next room. If you need me you've only got to call me.'

'Thank you,' she answered, 'if I need you I'll call you.'

Then Sir Philip paid even to the uttermost farthing,* paid with stupendous physical courage for the sin of his anxious and pitiful heart;

and he drove and he goaded his ebbing strength to the making of one great and terrible effort: 'Anna—it's Stephen—listen.' They were holding his hands. 'It's—Stephen—our child—she's, she's—it's Stephen—not like—'

His head fell back rather sharply, and then lay very still upon Anna's bosom.

Stephen released the hand she was holding, for Anna had stooped and was kissing his lips, desperately, passionately kissing his lips, as though to breathe back the life into his body. And none might be there to witness that thing, save God—the God of death and affliction, Who is also the God of love.* Turning away, she stole out of their presence, leaving them alone in the darkening study, leaving them alone with their deathless devotion—hand in hand, the quick and the dead.*

BOOK TWO*

CHAPTER 15

I

Sir Philip's death deprived his child of three things; of companionship of mind born of real understanding, of a stalwart barrier between her and the world, and above all of love—that faithful love that would gladly have suffered all things for her sake, in order to spare her suffering.

Stephen, recovering from the merciful numbness of shock and facing her first deep sorrow, stood utterly confounded, as a child will stand who is lost in a crowd, having somehow let go of the hand that has always guided. Thinking of her father, she realized how greatly she had leant on that man of deep kindness, how sure she had felt of his constant protection, how much she had taken that protection for granted. And so together with her constant grieving, with the ache for his presence that never left her, came the knowledge of what real loneliness felt like. She would marvel, remembering how often in his lifetime she had thought herself lonely, when by stretching out a finger she could touch him, when by speaking she could hear his voice, when by raising her eyes she could see him before her. And now also she knew the desolation of small things, the power to give infinite pain that lies hidden in the little inanimate objects that persist, in a book, in a well-worn garment, in a half-finished letter, in a favourite arm-chair.

She thought: 'They go on—they mean nothing at all, and yet they go on,' and the handling of them was anguish, and yet she must always touch them. 'How queer, this old arm-chair has outlived him, an old chair—' And feeling the creases in its leather, the dent in its back where her father's head had lain, she would hate the inanimate thing for surviving, or perhaps she would love it and find herself weeping.

Morton had become a place of remembering that closed round her and held her in its grip of remembrance. It was pain, yet now more than ever she adored it, every stone, every blade of grass in its meadows. She fancied that it too grieved for her father and was turning to her for comfort.* Because of Morton the days must go on, all their trifling tasks must be duly accomplished. At times she might wonder that this should be so, might be filled with a fleeting sense of resentment, but then she would think of her home as a creature dependent upon her and her mother for its needs, and the sense of resentment would vanish.

Very gravely she listened to the lawyer from London. 'The place goes to your mother for her lifetime,' he told her; 'on her death, of course, it becomes yours, Miss Gordon. But your father made a separate provision; when you're twenty-one, in about two years time, you'll inherit quite a considerable income.'*

She said: 'Will that leave enough money for Morton?'

'More than enough,' he reassured her, smiling.

In the quiet old house there was discipline and order, death had come and gone, yet these things persisted. Like the well-worn garment and favourite chair, discipline and order had survived the great change, filling the emptiness of the rooms with a queer sense of unreality at times, with a new and very bewildering doubt as to which was real, life or death. The servants scoured and swept and dusted. From Malvern, once a week, came a young clock-winder, and he set the clocks with much care and precision so that when he had gone they all chimed together—rather hurriedly they would all chime together, as though flustered by the great importance of time. Puddle added up the books and made lists for the cook. The tall under-footman polished the windows—the iridescent window that looked out on the lawns and the semicircular fanlight he polished. In the gardens work progressed just as usual. Gardeners pruned and hoed and diligently planted. Spring gained in strength to the joy of the cuckoos, trees blossomed, and outside Sir Philip's study glowed beds of the old-fashioned single tulips he had loved above all the others. According to custom the bulbs had been planted, and now, still according to custom, there were tulips. At the stables the hunters were turned out to grass, and the ceilings and walls had a fresh coat of whitewash. Williams went into Upton to buy tape for the plaits which the grooms were now engaged upon making; while beyond, in a paddock adjoining the beech wood, a couple of mares gave birth to strong foals—thus were all things accomplished in their season at Morton.

But Anna, whose word was now absolute law, had become one of those who have done with smiling; a quiet, enduring, grief-stricken woman, in whose eyes was a patient, waiting expression. She was gentle to Stephen, yet terribly aloof; in their hour of great need they must still stand divided these two, by the old, insidious barrier.* Yet Stephen clung closer and closer to Morton; she had definitely given up all idea of Oxford. In vain did Puddle try to protest, in vain did she daily remind her pupil that Sir Philip had set his heart on her going; no good, for Stephen would always reply:

'Morton needs me; Father would want me to stay, because he taught me to love it.'

And Puddle was helpless. What could she do, bound as she was by the tyranny of silence? She dared not explain the girl to herself, dared not say: 'For your own sake you must go to Oxford, you'll need every weapon your brain can give you; being what you are you'll need every weapon,' for then certainly Stephen would start to question, and her teacher's very position of trust would forbid her to answer those questions.

Outrageous, Puddle would feel it to be, that wilfully selfish tyranny of silence evolved by a crafty old ostrich of a world* for its own well-being and comfort. The world hid its head in the sands of convention, so that seeing nothing it might avoid Truth. It said to itself: 'If seeing's believing, then I don't want to see—if silence is golden, it is also, in this case, very expedient.' There were moments when Puddle would feel sorely tempted to shout out loud at the world.

Sometimes she thought of giving up her post, so weary was she of fretting over Stephen. She would think: 'What's the good of my worrying myself sick? I can't help the girl, but I can help myself—seems to me it's a matter of pure self-preservation.' Then all that was loyal and faithful in her would protest: 'Better stick it, she'll probably need you one day and you ought to be here to help her.' So Puddle decided to stick it.

They did very little work, for Stephen had grown idle with grief and no longer cared for her studies. Nor could she find consolation in her writing, for sorrow will often do one of two things—it will either release the springs of inspiration, or else it will dry up those springs completely, and in Stephen's case it had done the latter. She longed for the comforting outlet of words, but now the words would always evade her.

'I can't write any more, it's gone from me, Puddle—he's taken it with him.' And then would come tears, and the tears would go splashing down on to the paper, blotting the poor inadequate lines that meant little or nothing, as their author well knew, to her own added desolation.

There she would sit like a woebegone child,* and Puddle would think how childish she seemed in this her first encounter with grief, and would marvel because of the physical strength of the creature, that went so ill with those tears. And because her own tears were vexing her eyes she must often speak rather sharply to Stephen. Then Stephen would go off and swing her large dumb-bells, seeking the relief of bodily movement, seeking to wear out her muscular body because her mind was worn out by sorrow.

August came and Williams got the hunters in from grass. Stephen would sometimes get up very early and help with the exercising of the horses, but in spite of this the old man's heart misgave him, she seemed strangely averse to discussing the hunting.

He would think: 'Maybe it's 'er father's death, but the instinct be pretty strong in 'er blood, she'll be all right after 'er's 'ad 'er first gallop.' And perhaps he might craftily point to Raftery. 'Look, Miss Stephen, did ever you see such quarters? 'E's a mighty fine doer,* keeps 'imself fit on grass! I do believe as 'e does it on purpose; I believe 'e's afraid 'e'll miss a day's huntin'.'

But the autumn slipped by and the winter was passing. Hounds met at the very gates of Morton, yet Stephen forbore to send those orders to the stables for which Williams was anxiously waiting. Then one morning in March he could bear it no longer, and he suddenly started reproaching Stephen: 'Yer lettin' my 'orses go stale in their boxes. It's a scandal, Miss Stephen, and you such a rider, and our stables the finest bar none in the county, and yer father so almighty proud of yer ridin'!' And then: 'Miss Stephen—yer'll not give it up? Won't yer' hunt Raftery day after to-morrow? The 'ounds is meetin' quite near by Upton—Miss Stephen, say yer won't give it all up!'

There were actually tears in his worried old eyes, and so to console him she answered briefly: 'Very well then, I'll hunt the day after to-morrow.' But for some strange reason that she did not understand, this prospect had quite ceased to give her pleasure.

2

On a morning of high scudding clouds and sunshine, Stephen rode Raftery into Upton, then over the bridge that spans the river Severn, and on to the Meet at a neighbouring village. Behind her came jogging her second horseman on one of Sir Philip's favourite youngsters, a raw-boned, upstanding, impetuous chestnut,* now all eyes and ears for what might be coming; but beside her rode only memory and heart-ache. Yet from time to time she turned her head quickly as though some one must surely be there at her side.

Her mind was a prey to the strangest fancies. She pictured her father very grave and anxious, not gay and light-hearted as had been his wont when they rode to a Meet in the old days. And because this day was so vibrant with living it was difficult for Stephen to tolerate the idea of death, even for a little red fox, and she caught herself thinking: 'If we find, this morning, there'll be two of us who are utterly alone, with every man's hand against us.'*

At the Meet she was a prey to her self-conscious shyness, so that she fancied people were whispering. There was no one now with bowed, patient shoulders to stand between her and those unfriendly people.

Colonel Antrim came up. 'Glad to see you out, Stephen.' But his voice sounded stiff because he was embarrassed—every one felt just a little embarrassed, as people will do in the face of bereavement.

And then there was something so awkward about her, so aloof that it checked every impulse of kindness. They, in their turn, felt shy, remembering Sir Philip, remembering what his death must have meant to his daughter, so that more than one greeting remained unspoken.

And again she thought grimly: 'Two of us will be alone, with every man's hand against us.'

They found their fox in the very first cover* and went away over the wide, bare meadows. As Raftery leapt forward her curious fancies gained strength, and now they began to obsess her. She fancied that she was being pursued, that the hounds were behind her instead of ahead, that the flushed, bright-eyed people were hunting her down, ruthless, implacable, untiring people—they were many and she was one solitary creature with every man's hand against her. To escape them she suddenly took her own line, putting Raftery over some perilous places; but he, nothing loath, stretched his muscles to their utmost, landing safely—yet always she imagined pursuit, and now it was the world that had turned against her. The whole world was hunting her down with hatred, with a fierce, remorseless will to destruction—the world against one insignificant creature who had nowhere to turn for pity or protection. Her heart tightened with fear, she was terribly afraid of those flushed, bright-eyed people who were hard on her track. She, who had never lacked physical courage in her life, was now actually sweating with terror, and Raftery divining her terror sped on, faster and always faster.

Then Stephen saw something just ahead, and it moved. Checking Raftery sharply she stared at the thing. A crawling, bedraggled streak of red fur, with tongue lolling, with agonized lungs filled to bursting, with the desperate eyes of the hopelessly pursued, bright with terror and glancing now this way now that, as though looking for something; and the thought came to Stephen: 'It's looking for God Who made it.'*

At that moment she felt an imperative need to believe that the stricken beast had a Maker, and her own eyes grew bright, but with blinding tears because of her mighty need to believe, a need that was sharper than physical pain, being born of the pain of the spirit. The thing was dragging its brush in the dust, it was limping, and Stephen sprang to the ground. She held out her hands to the unhappy creature, filled with the will to succour and protect it, but the fox mistrusted her merciful hands, and it crept away into a little coppice. And now in a deathly and awful silence the hounds swept past her, their muzzles to ground. After them galloped Colonel Antrim, crouching low in his saddle, avoiding the branches, and after him came a couple of huntsmen with the few bold riders who had stayed that stiff run. Then a savage clamour broke out in the coppice as the hounds gave tongue in their wild jubilation, and Stephen well knew that that sound meant death—very slowly she remounted Raftery.

Riding home, she felt utterly spent and bewildered. Her thoughts were full of her father again—he seemed very near, incredibly near her. For a moment she thought that she heard his voice, but when she bent sideways trying to listen, all was silence, except for the tired rhythm of Raftery's hooves on the road. As her brain grew calmer, it seemed to Stephen that her father had taught her all that she knew. He had taught her courage and truth and honour in his life, and in death he had taught her mercy—the mercy that he had lacked he had taught her through the mighty adventure of death. With a sudden illumination of vision, she perceived that all life is only one life, that all joy and all sorrow are indeed only one, that all death is only one dying. And she knew that because she had seen a man die in great suffering, yet with courage and love that are deathless, she could never again inflict wanton destruction or pain upon any poor, hapless creature. And so it was that by dying to Stephen, Sir Philip would live on in the attribute of mercy that had come that day to his child.

But the body is still very far from the spirit, and it clings to the primitive joys of the earth—to the sun and the wind and the good rolling grass-lands, to the swift elation of reckless movement, so that Stephen, feeling Raftery between her strong knees, was suddenly filled with regret. Yes, in this her moment of spiritual insight she was infinitely sad, and she said to Raftery: 'We'll never hunt any more, we two, Raftery*—we'll never go out hunting together any more.'

And because in his own way he had understood her, she felt his sides swell with a vast, resigned sigh; heard the creaking of damp girth leather as he sighed because he had understood her. For the love of the chase was still hot in Raftery, the love of splendid, unforeseen danger, the love of crisp mornings and frost-bound evenings, and of long, dusky roads that always led home. He was wise with the age-old wisdom of the beasts, it is true, but that wisdom was not guiltless of slaying, and deep in his gentle and faithful mind lurked a memory bequeathed him by some wild forbear. A memory of vast and unpeopled spaces, of fierce open nostrils and teeth bared in battle, of hooves that struck death with every sure blow, of a great untamed mane that streamed out like a banner, of the shrill and incredibly savage war-cry that accompanied that gallant banner. So now he too felt infinitely sad, and he sighed until his strong girths started creaking, after which he stood still and shook himself largely, in an effort to shake off depression.

Stephen bent forward and patted his neck. 'I'm sorry, sorry, Raftery,' she said gravely.

CHAPTER 16

I

WITH the breaking up of the stables at Morton came the breaking up of their faithful servant. Old age took its toll of Williams at last, and it got him under completely. Sore at heart and gone in both wind and limb, he retired with a pension to his comfortable cottage; there to cough and grumble throughout the winter, or to smoke disconsolate pipes through the summer, seated on a chair in his trim little garden with a rug wrapped around his knees.

'It do be a scandal,' he was now for ever saying, 'and 'er such a splendid woman to 'ounds!'

And then he would start remembering past glories, while his mind would begin to grieve for Sir Philip. He would cry just a little because he still loved him, so his wife must bring Williams a strong cup of tea.

'There, there, Arth-thur, you'll soon be meetin' the master; we be old me and you—it can't be long now.'

At which Williams would glare: 'I'm not thinkin' of 'eaven—like as not there won't be no 'orses in 'eaven—I wants the master down 'ere at me stables. Gawd knows they be needin' a master!'

For now besides Anna's carriage horses, there were only four inmates of those once fine stables; Raftery and Sir Philip's young upstanding chestnut, a cob known as James, and the aged Collins who had taken to vice in senile decay, and persisted in eating his bedding.

Anna had accepted this radical change quite calmly, as she now accepted most things. She hardly ever opposed her daughter these days in matters concerning Morton. But the burden of arranging the sale had been Stephen's; one by one she had said good-bye to the hunters, one by one she had watched them led out of the yard, with a lump in her throat that had almost choked her, and when they were gone she had turned back to Raftery for comfort.

'Oh, Raftery, I'm so unregenerate—I minded so terribly seeing them go! Don't let's look at their empty boxes—'

2

Another year passed, and Stephen was twenty-one, a rich, independent woman. At any time now she could go where she chose, could do entirely as she listed. Puddle remained at her post; she was waiting a little grimly for something to happen. But nothing much happened, beyond the fact that Stephen now dressed in tailor-made clothes* to which Anna had perforce to withdraw her opposition. Yet life was gradually reasserting its claims on the girl, which was only natural, for the young may not be delivered over to the dead, nor to grief that refuses consolation. She still mourned her father, she would always mourn him, but at twenty-one with a healthful body, there came a day when she noticed the sunshine, when she smelt the good earth and was thankful for it, when she suddenly knew herself to be alive and was glad, in despite of death.

On one such morning early that June, Stephen drove her car into Upton. She was meaning to cash a cheque at the bank, she was meaning to call at the local saddler's, she was meaning to buy a new pair of gloves—in the end, however, she did none of these things.

It was outside the butcher's that the dog fight started. The butcher owned an old rip of an Airedale,* and the Airedale had taken up his post in the doorway of the shop, as had long been his custom. Down the street, on trim but belligerent tiptoes, came a very small, snow-white West Highland terrier; perhaps he was looking for trouble, and if so he certainly got it in less than two minutes. His yells were so loud that Stephen stopped the car and turned round in her seat to see what was happening. The butcher ran out to swell the confusion by shouting commands that no one obeyed; he was trying to grasp his dog by the tail which was short and not at all handy for grasping. And then, as it seemed from nowhere at all, there suddenly appeared a very desperate young woman; she was carrying her parasol as though it were a lance with which she intended to enter the battle. Her wails of despair rose above the dog's yells:

'Tony! My Tony! Won't anyone stop them? My dog's being killed, won't any of you stop them?' And she actually tried to stop them herself, though the parasol broke at the first encounter.

But Tony, while yelling, was as game as a ferret, and, moreover, the Airedale had him by the back, so Stephen got hastily out of the car—it seemed only a matter of moments for Tony. She grabbed the old rip by the scruff of his neck, while the butcher dashed off for a bucket of water. The desperate young woman seized her dog by a leg; she pulled, Stephen pulled, they both pulled together. Then Stephen gave a punishing twist which distracted the Airedale, he wanted to bite her; having only one mouth he must let go of Tony, who was instantly clasped to his owner's bosom. The butcher arrived on the scene with his bucket while Stephen was still clinging to the Airedale's collar.

'I'm so sorry, Miss Gordon, I do hope you're not hurt?'

'I'm all right. Here, take this grey devil and thrash him; he's no business to eat up a dog half his size.'

Meanwhile, Tony was dripping all over with gore, and his mistress, it seemed, had got herself bitten. She alternately struggled to staunch Tony's wounds and to suck her own hand which was bleeding freely.

'Better give me your dog and come across to the chemist, your hand will want dressing,' remarked Stephen.

Tony was instantly put into her arms, with a rather pale smile that suggested a breakdown.

'It's quite all right now,' said Stephen quickly, very much afraid the young woman meant to cry.

'Will he live, do you think?' inquired a weak voice.

'Yes, of course; but your hand—come along to the chemist.'

'Oh, never mind that, I'm thinking of Tony!'

'He's all right. We'll take him straight off to the vet when your hand's been seen to; there's quite a good one.'

The chemist applied fairly strong carbolic;* the hand had been bitten on two of the fingers, and Stephen was impressed by the pluck of this stranger, who set her small teeth and endured in silence. The hand bandaged, they drove along to the vet, who was fortunately in and could sew up poor Tony. Stephen held his front paws, while his mistress held his head as best she could in her own maimed condition. She kept pressing his face against her shoulder, presumably so that he should not see the needle.

'Don't look, darling—you mustn't look at it, honey!' Stephen heard her whispering to Tony.

At last he too was carbolicked and bandaged, and Stephen had time to examine her companion. It occurred to her that she had better introduce herself, so she said: 'I'm Stephen Gordon.'

'And I'm Angela Crossby,'* came the reply; 'we've taken The Grange, just the other side of Upton.'

Angela Crossby was amazingly blonde, her hair was not so much golden as silver. She wore it cut short like a mediæval page;* it was straight, and came just to the lobes of her ears, which at that time of pompadours and much curling gave her an unusual appearance. Her skin was very white, and Stephen decided that this woman would never have a great deal of colour, nor would her rather wide mouth be red, it would always remain the tint of pale coral. All the colour that she had seemed to lie in her eyes, which were large and fringed with long fair lashes. Her eyes were of rather an unusual blue that almost seemed to be tinted with purple, and their candid expression was that of a child—very innocent it was, a trustful expression. And Stephen as she looked at those eyes felt indignant, remembering the gossip she had heard about the Crossbys.

The Crossbys, as she knew, were deeply resented. He had been an important Birmingham magnate who had lately retired from some hardware concern, on account of his health, or so ran the gossip. His wife, it was rumoured, had been on the stage in New York, so that her antecedents were doubtful—no one really knew anything at all about her, but her curious hair gave grounds for suspicion. An American wife who had been an actress was a very bad asset* for Crossby. Nor was Crossby himself a prepossessing person; when judged by the county's standards, he bounded.* Moreover he showed signs of unpardonable meanness. His subscription to the Hunt had been a paltry five guineas.* He had written to say that his very poor health would preclude his hunting, and had actually added that he hoped the Hunt would keep clear of his covers! And then every one felt a natural resentment that The Grange should have had to be sacrificed for money—quite a small Tudor house, it was yet very perfect. But Captain Ramsay, its erstwhile owner, had died recently, leaving large debts behind him, so his heir, a young cousin who lived in London, had promptly sold to the first wealthy bidder—hence the advent of Mr. Crossby.

Stephen, looking at Angela, remembered these things, but they suddenly seemed devoid of importance, for now those child-like eyes were upon her, and Angela was saying: 'I don't know how to thank you for saving my Tony, it was wonderful of you! If you hadn't been there they'd have let him get killed, and I'm just devoted to Tony.'

Her voice had the soft, thick drawl of the South, an indolent voice, very lazy and restful. It was quite new to Stephen, that soft, Southern drawl, and she found it unexpectedly pleasant. Then it dawned on the girl that this woman was lovely—she was like some queer flower* that had grown up in darkness, like some rare, pale flower without blemish or stain, and Stephen said flushing:

'I was glad to help you—I'll drive you back to The Grange, if you'll let me?'

'Why, of course we'll let you,' came the prompt answer. 'Tony says he'll be most grateful, don't you, Tony?' Tony wagged his tail rather faintly.

Stephen wrapped him up in a motor rug at the back of the car, where he lay as though prostrate. Angela she placed in the seat beside herself, helping her carefully as she did so.

Presently Angela said: 'Thanks to Tony I've met you at last; I've been longing to meet you!' And she stared rather disconcertingly at Stephen, then smiled as though something she saw had amused her.

Stephen wondered why anyone should have longed to meet her. Feeling suddenly shy, she became suspicious: 'Who told you about me?' she asked abruptly.

'Mrs. Antrim, I think—yes, it was Mrs. Antrim. She said you were such a wonderful rider but that now, for some reason, you'd given up hunting. Oh, yes, and she said you fenced like a man. Do you fence like a man?'

'I don't know,' muttered Stephen.

'Well, I'll tell you whether you do when I've seen you; my father was quite a well-known fencer at one time, so I learnt a lot about fencing in the States—perhaps some day, Miss Gordon, you'll let me see you?'

By now Stephen's face was the colour of a beetroot, and she gripped the wheel as though she meant to hurt it. She was longing to turn round and look at her companion, the desire to look at her was almost overwhelming, but even her eyes seemed too stiff to move, so she gazed at the long dusty road in silence.

'Don't punish the poor, wooden thing that way,' murmured Angela, 'it can't help being just wood!' Then she went on talking as though to herself: 'What should I have done if that brute had killed Tony? He's a real companion to me on my walks—I don't know what I'd do if it weren't for Tony, he's such a devoted, cute little fellow, and these days I'm kind of thrown back on my dog—it's a melancholy business walking alone, yet I've always been fond of walking—'

Stephen wanted to say: 'But I like walking too; let me come with you sometimes as well as Tony.' Then suddenly mustering up her courage, she jerked round in the seat and looked at this woman. As their eyes met and held each other for a moment, something vaguely disturbing stirred in Stephen, so that the car made a dangerous swerve. 'I'm sorry,' she said quickly, 'that was rotten bad driving.'

But Angela did not answer.

3

Ralph Crossby was standing at the open doorway as the car swung up and came to a halt. Stephen noticed that he was immaculately dressed in a grey tweed suit that by rights should have been shabby. But everything about him looked aggressively new, his very hair had a quality of newness—it was thin brown hair that shone as though polished.

'I wonder if he puts it out with his boots,' thought Stephen, surveying him with interest.

He was one of those rather indefinite men, who are neither short nor tall, fat nor thin, old nor young, good-looking nor actually ugly. As his wife would have said, had anybody asked her, he was just 'plain man,' which exactly described him, for his only distinctive features were his newness and the peevish expression about his mouth—his mouth was intensely peevish.

When he spoke his high-pitched voice sounded fretful. 'What on earth have you been doing? It's past two o'clock. I've been waiting since one, the lunch must be ruined; I do wish you'd try and be punctual, Angela!' He appeared not to notice Stephen's existence, for he went on nagging as though no one were present. 'Oh, I see, that damn dog of yours has been fighting again, I've a good mind to give him a thrashing; and what in God's name's the matter with your hand—you *don't* mean to say that you've got yourself bitten? Really, Angela, this is a bit too bad!' His whole manner suggested a personal grievance.

'Well,' drawled Angela, extending the bandaged hand for inspection, 'I've not been getting manicured, Ralph.' And her voice was distinctly if gently provoking, so that he winced with quick irritation. Then she seemed quite suddenly to remember Stephen: 'Miss Gordon, let me introduce my husband.'

He bowed, and pulling himself together: 'Thank you for driving my wife home, Miss Gordon, it was most kind, I'm sure.' But he did not seem friendly, he kept glaring at Angela's dog-bitten hand, and his tone, Stephen thought, was distinctly ungracious.

Getting out of the car she started her engine.

'Good-bye,' smiled Angela, holding out her hand, the left one, which Stephen grasped much too firmly. 'Good-bye—perhaps one day you'll come to tea. We're on the telephone, Upton 25; ring up and suggest yourself some day quite soon.'

'Thanks awfully, I will,' said Stephen.

4

'Had a breakdown or something?' inquired Puddle brightly, as at three o'clock Stephen slouched into the schoolroom.

'No—but Mrs. Crossby's dog had a fight. She got bitten, so I drove her back to The Grange.'

Puddle pricked up her ears: 'What's she like? I've heard rumours—'

'Well, she's not at all like them,' snapped Stephen.

There ensued a long silence while Puddle considered, but consideration does not always bring wise counsel, and now Puddle made a really bad break: 'She's pretty impossible, isn't she, Stephen? They say he unearthed her somewhere in New York; Mrs. Antrim says she was a music-hall actress. I suppose you were obliged to give her a lift, but be careful, I believe she's fearfully pushing.'

Stephen flared up like an emotional schoolgirl: 'I'm not going to discuss her if that's your opinion; Mrs. Crossby is quite as much a lady as you are, or any of the others round here, for that matter. I'm sick unto death of your beastly gossip.' And turning abruptly, she strode from the room.

'Oh, Lord!' murmured Puddle, frowning.

5

That evening Stephen rang up The Grange.* 'Is that Upton 25? It's Miss Gordon speaking—no, *no*, Miss Gordon, speaking from Morton. How is Mrs. Crossby and how is the dog? I hope Mrs. Crossby's hand isn't very painful? Yes, of course I'll hold on while you go and inquire.' She felt shy, yet unusually daring.

Presently the butler came back and said gravely that Mrs. Crossby had just seen the doctor and had now gone to bed, as her hand was aching, but that Tony felt better and sent his love. He added: 'Madam says would you come to tea on Sunday? She'd be very glad indeed if you would.'

And Stephen answered: 'Will you thank Mrs. Crossby and tell her that I'll certainly come on Sunday.' Then she gave the message all over again, very slowly, with pauses. 'Will—you thank—Mrs. Crossby—and tell her—I'll certainly come—on Sunday. Do you quite understand? Have I made it quite clear? Say I'm coming to tea on Sunday.'

CHAPTER 17

I

It was only five days till Sunday, yet for Stephen those five days seemed like as many years. Every evening now she rang up The Grange to inquire about Angela's hand and Tony, so that she grew quite familiar with the butler, with his quality of voice, with his habit of coughing, with the way he hung up the receiver.

She did not stop to analyse her feelings, she only knew that she felt exultant—for no reason at all she was feeling exultant, very much alive too and full of purpose, and she walked for miles alone on the hills, unable to stay really quiet for a moment. She found herself becoming acutely observant, and now she discovered all manner of wonders; the network of veins on the leaves, for instance, and the delicate hearts of the wild dog-roses, the uncertain shimmering flight of the larks as they fluttered up singing, close to her feet. But above all she rediscovered the cuckoo—it was June, so the cuckoo had changed his rhythm—she must often stand breathlessly still to listen: 'Cuckoo-kook, cuckoo-kook,' all over the hills; and at evening the songs of blackbirds and thrushes.*

Her wanderings would sometimes lead her to the places that she and Martin had visited together, only now she could think of him with affection, with toleration, with tenderness even. In a curious way she now understood him as never before, and in consequence condoned. It had just been some rather ghastly mistake, his mistake, yet she understood what he must have felt; and thinking of Martin she might grow rather frightened—what if she should ever make such a mistake? But the fear would be driven into the background by her sense of well-being, her fine exultation. The very earth that she trod seemed exalted, and the green, growing things that sprang out of the earth, and the birds, 'Cuckoo-kook,' all over the hills—and at evening the songs of blackbirds and thrushes.

She became much more anxious about her appearance; for five mornings she studied her face in the glass as she dressed—after all she was not so bad looking. Her hair spoilt her a little, it was too thick and long, but she noticed with pleasure that at least it was wavy—then she suddenly admired the colour of her hair. Opening cupboard after cupboard she went through her clothes. They were old, for the most part distinctly shabby. She would go into Malvern that very afternoon and order a new flannel suit at her tailor's. The suit should be grey with a little white pin stripe, and the jacket, she decided, must have a breast pocket. She would wear a black tie—no, better a grey one to match the new suit with the little white pin stripe. She ordered not one new suit but three, and she also ordered a pair of brown shoes; indeed she spent most of the afternoon in ordering things for her personal adornment. She heard herself being ridiculously fussy about details, disputing with her tailor over buttons; disputing with her bootmaker over the shoes, their thickness of sole, their amount of broguing; disputing regarding the match of her ties with the young man who sold her handkerchiefs and neckties—for such trifles had assumed an enormous importance; she had, in fact, grown quite long-winded about them.

That evening she showed her smart neckties to Puddle, whose manner was most unsatisfactory—she grunted.

And now some one seemed to be always near Stephen, some one for whom these things were accomplished—the purchase of the three new suits, the brown shoes, the six carefully chosen, expensive neckties. Her long walks on the hills were a part of this person, as were also the hearts of the wild dog-roses, the delicate network of veins on the leaves and the queer June break in the cuckoo's rhythm. The night with its large summer stars and its silence, was pregnant with a new and mysterious purpose, so that lying at the mercy of that age-old purpose, Stephen would feel little shivers of pleasure creeping out of the night and into her body. She would get up and stand by the open window, thinking always of Angela Crossby.

2

Sunday came and with it church in the morning; then two interminable hours after lunch, during which Stephen changed her necktie three times, and brushed back her thick chestnut hair with water, and examined her shoes for imaginary dust, and finally gave a hard rub to her nails with a nail pad snatched brusquely away from Puddle.

When the moment for departure arrived at last, she said rather tentatively to Anna: 'Aren't you going to call on the Crossbys, Mother?'

Anna shook her head: 'No, I can't do that, Stephen—I go nowhere these days; you know that, my dear.'

But her voice was quite gentle, so Stephen said quickly: 'Well then, may I invite Mrs. Crossby to Morton?'

Anna hesitated a moment, then she nodded: 'I suppose so—that is if you really wish to.'

The drive only took about twenty minutes, for now Stephen was so nervous that she positively flew. She who had been puffed up with elation and self-satisfaction was crumbling completely—in spite of her careful new necktie she was crumbling at the mere thought of Angela Crossby. Arrived at The Grange she felt over life-size; her hands seemed enormous, all out of proportion, and she thought that the butler stared at her hands.

'Miss Gordon?' he inquired.

'Yes,' she mumbled, 'Miss Gordon.' Then he coughed as he did on the telephone, and quite suddenly Stephen felt foolish.

She was shown into a small oak-panelled parlour whose long, open casements looked on to the herb-garden. A fire of apple wood burnt on the hearth, in spite of the fact that the weather was warm, for Angela was always inclined to feel chilly—the result, so she said, of the English climate. The fire gave off rather a sweet, pungent odour—the odour of slightly damp logs and dry ashes. By way of a really propitious beginning, Tony barked until he nearly burst his stitches, so that Angela, who was lying on the lounge, had perforce to get up in order to soothe him. An extremely round bullfinch in an ornate brass cage, was piping a tune with his wings half extended. The tune sounded something like 'Pop goes the weasel.'* At all events it was an impudent tune, and Stephen felt that she hated that bullfinch. It took all of five minutes to calm down Tony, during which Stephen stood apologetic but tongue-tied. She hardly knew whether to laugh or to cry at this very ridiculous anti-climax.

Then Angela decided the matter by laughing: 'I'm so sorry, Miss Gordon, he's feeling peevish. It's quite natural, poor lamb, he had a bad night, he just hates being all sewn up like a bolster.'

Stephen went over and offered him her hand, which Tony now licked, so that trouble was ended; but in getting up Angela had torn her dress, and this seemed to distress her—she kept fingering the tear.

'Can I help?' inquired Stephen, hoping she'd say no—which she did, quite firmly, after one look at Stephen.

At last Angela settled down again on the lounge. 'Come and sit over here,' she suggested, smiling. Then Stephen sat down on the edge of a chair as though she were sitting in the Prickly Cradle.*

She forgot to inquire about Angela's dog-bite, though the bandaged hand was placed on a cushion; and she also forgot to adjust her new necktie, which in her emotion had slipped slightly crooked. A thousand times in the last few days had she carefully rehearsed this scene of their meeting, making up long and elaborate speeches; assuming, in her mind, many dignified poses; and yet there she sat on the edge of a chair as though it were the Prickly Cradle.

And now Angela was speaking in her soft, Southern drawl: 'So you've found your way here at last,' she was saying. And then, after a pause: 'I'm so glad, Miss Gordon, do you know that your coming has given me real pleasure?'

Stephen said: 'Yes—oh, yes—' Then fell silent again, apparently intent on the carpet.

'Have I dropped my cigarette ash or something?' inquired her hostess, whose mouth twitched a little.

'I don't think so,' murmured Stephen, pretending to look, then glancing up sideways at the impudent bullfinch.

The bullfinch was now being sentimental; he piped very low and with great expression. 'O, Tannebaum, O, Tannebaum, wie grün sind Deine Blätter'* he piped, hopping rather heavily from perch to perch, with one beady black orb fixed on Stephen.

Then Angela said: 'It's a curious thing, but I feel as though I've known you for ages. I don't want to behave as though we were strangers—do you think that's very American of me? Ought I to be formal and stand-offish and British? I will if you say so, but I don't feel British.' And her voice, although quite steady and grave, was somehow distinctly suggestive of laughter.

Stephen lifted troubled eyes to her face: 'I want very much to be your friend if you'll have me,' she said; and then she flushed deeply.

Angela held out her undamaged hand which Stephen took, but in great trepidation. Barely had it lain in her own for a moment, when she clumsily gave it back to its owner. Then Angela looked at her hand.

Stephen thought: 'Have I done something rude or awkward?' And her heart thumped thickly against her side. She wanted to retrieve the lost hand and stroke it, but unfortunately it was now stroking Tony.

She sighed, and Angela, hearing that sigh, glanced up, as though in inquiry.

The butler arrived bringing in the tea.

'Sugar?' asked Angela.

'No, thanks,' said Stephen; then she suddenly changed her mind, 'three lumps,* please,' she had always detested tea without sugar.

The tea was too hot; it burnt her mouth badly. She grew scarlet and her eyes began to water. To cover her confusion she swallowed more tea, while Angela looked tactfully out of the window. But when she considered it safe to turn round, her expression, although still faintly amused, had something about it that was tender.

And now she exerted all her subtlety and skill to make this queer guest of hers talk more freely, and Angela's subtlety was no mean thing, neither was her skill if she chose to exert it. Very gradually the girl became more at her ease; it was up-hill work but Angela triumphed, so that in the end Stephen talked about Morton, and a very little about herself also. And somehow, although Stephen appeared to be talking, she found that she was learning many things about her hostess; for instance, she learnt that Angela was lonely and very badly in need of her friendship. Most of Angela's troubles seemed to centre round Ralph, who was not always kind and seldom agreeable. Remembering Ralph she could well believe this, and she said:

'I don't think your husband liked me.'

Angela sighed: 'Very probably not. Ralph never likes the people I do; he objects to my friends on principle I think.'

Then Angela talked more openly of Ralph. Just now he was staying away with his mother, but next week he would be returning to The Grange, and then he was certain to be disagreeable: 'Whenever he's been with his mother he's that way—she puts him against me, I never know why—unless, of course, it's because I'm not English. I'm the stranger within the gates, it may be that.' And when Stephen protested, 'Oh, yes indeed, I'm quite often made to feel like a stranger. Take the people round here, do you think they like me?'

Then Stephen, who had not yet learnt to dissemble,* stared hard at her shoes, in embarrassed silence.

Just outside the door a clock boomed seven. Stephen started; she had been there nearly three hours. 'I must go,' she said, getting abruptly to her feet, 'you look tired, I've been making a visitation.'*

Her hostess made no effort to detain her: 'Well,' she smiled, 'come again, please come very often—that is if you won't find it dull, Miss Gordon; we're terribly quiet here at The Grange.'

3

Stephen drove home slowly, for now that it was over she felt like a machine that had suddenly run down. Her nerves were relaxed, she was thoroughly tired, yet she rather enjoyed this unusual sensation. The hot June evening was heavy with thunder. From somewhere in the distance came the bleating of sheep, and the melancholy sound seemed to blend and mingle with her mood, which was now very gently depressed. A gentle but persistent sense of depression enveloped her whole being like a soft, grey cloak; and she did not wish to shake off this cloak, but rather to fold it more closely around her.

At Morton she stopped the car by the lakes and sat staring through the trees at the glint of water. For a long while she sat there without knowing why, unless it was that she wished to remember. But she found that she could not even be certain of the kind of dress that Angela had worn—it had been of some soft stuff, that much she remembered, so soft that it had easily torn, for the rest her memories of it were vague—though she very much wanted to remember that dress.

A faint rumble of thunder came out of the west, where the clouds were banking up ominously purple. Some uncertain and rather hysterical swallows flew high and then low at the sound of the thunder. Her sense of depression was now much less gentle, it increased every moment, turning to sadness. She was sad in spirit and mind and body—her body felt dejected, she was sad all over. And now some one was whistling down by the stables, old Williams, she suspected, for the whistle was tuneless. The loss of his teeth had disgruntled his whistle; yes, she was sure that that must be Williams. A horse whinnied as one bucket clanked against another—sounds came clearly this evening; they were watering the horses. Anna's young carriage horses would be pawing their straw, impatient because they were feeling thirsty.

Then a gate slammed. That would be the gate of the meadow where the heifers were pastured—it was yellow with king-cups.* One of the men from the home farm was going his rounds, securing all gates before sunset. Something dropped on the bonnet of the car with a ping. Looking up she met the eyes of a squirrel; he was leaning well forward on his tiny front paws, peering crossly; he had dropped his nut on the bonnet. She got out of the car and retrieved his supper, throwing it under his tree while he waited. Like a flash he was down and then back on his tree, devouring the nut, with his legs well straddled.

All around were the homely activities of evening, the watering of horses, the care of cattle—pleasant, peaceable things that preceded the peace and repose of the coming nightfall. And suddenly Stephen longed to share them, an immense need to share them leapt up within her, so that she ached with this urgent longing that was somehow a part of her bodily dejection.

She drove on and left the car at the stables, then walked round to the house, and when she got there she opened the door of the study and went in, feeling terribly lonely without her father. Sitting down in the old arm-chair that had survived him, she let her head rest where his head had rested; and her hands she laid on the arms of the chair where his hands, as she knew, had lain times without number. Closing her eyes, she tried to visualize his face, his kind face that had sometimes looked anxious; but the picture came slowly and faded at once, for the dead must often give place to the living. It was Angela Crossby's face that persisted as Stephen sat in her father's old chair.

4

In the small panelled room that gave on to the herb-garden, Angela yawned as she stared through the window; then she suddenly laughed out loud at her thoughts; then she suddenly frowned and spoke crossly to Tony.

She could not get Stephen out of her mind, and this irritated while it amused her. Stephen was so large to be tongue-tied and frightened—a curious creature, not devoid of attraction. In a way—her own way—she was almost handsome; no, quite handsome; she had fine eyes and beautiful hair. And her body was supple like that of an athlete, narrow-hipped and wide shouldered,* she should fence very well. Angela was anxious to see her fence; she must certainly try to arrange it somehow.

Mrs. Antrim had conveyed a number of things, while actually saying extremely little; but Angela had no need of her hints, not now that she had come to know Stephen Gordon. And because she was idle, discontented and bored, and certainly not over-burdened with virtue, she must let her thoughts dwell unduly on this girl, while her curiosity kept pace with her thoughts.

Tony stretched and whimpered, so Angela kissed him, then she sat down and wrote quite a short little letter: 'Do come over to lunch the day after tomorrow and advise me about the garden,' ran the letter. And it ended—after one or two casual remarks about gardens—with: 'Tony says *please* come, Stephen!'

CHAPTER 18

I

On a beautiful evening three weeks later, Stephen took Angela over Morton. They had had tea with Anna and Puddle, and Anna had been coldly polite to this friend of her daughter's, but Puddle's manner had been rather resentful—she deeply mistrusted Angela Crossby. But now Stephen was free to show Angela Morton, and this she did gravely, as though something sacred were involved in this first introduction to her home, as though Morton itself must feel that the coming of this small, fair-haired woman was in some way momentous. Very gravely, then, they went over the house—even into Sir Philip's old study.

From the house they made their way to the stables, and still grave, Stephen told her friend about Raftery. Angela listened, assuming an interest she was very far from feeling—she was timid of horses, but she liked to hear the girl's rather gruff voice, such an earnest young voice, it intrigued her. She was thoroughly frightened when Raftery sniffed her and then blew through his nostrils as though disapproving, and she started back with a sharp exclamation, so that Stephen slapped him on his glossy grey shoulder: 'Stop it, Raftery, come up!' And Raftery, disgusted, went and blew on his oats to express his hurt feelings.

They left him and wandered away through the gardens, and quite soon poor Raftery was almost forgotten, for the gardens smelt softly of night-scented stock and of other pale flowers that smell sweetest at evening, and Stephen was thinking that Angela Crossby resembled such flowers—very fragrant and pale she was, so Stephen said to her gently:

'You seem to belong to Morton.'

Angela smiled a slow, questioning smile: 'You think so, Stephen?'

And Stephen answered: 'I do, because Morton and I are one,' and she scarcely understood the portent of her words, but Angela, understanding, spoke quickly:

'Oh, I belong nowhere—you forget I'm the stranger.'

'I know that you're you,' said Stephen.

They walked on in silence while the light changed and deepened, growing always more golden and yet more elusive. And the birds, who loved that strange light, sang singly and then all together: 'We're happy, Stephen!'

And turning to Angela, Stephen answered the birds: 'Your being here makes me so happy.'

'If that's true, then why are you so shy of my name?'

'Angela—' mumbled Stephen.

Then Angela said: 'It's just over three weeks since we met—how quickly our friendship's happened. I suppose it was meant, I believe in Kismet.* You were awfully scared that first day at The Grange; why were you so scared?'

Stephen answered slowly: 'I'm frightened now—I'm frightened of you.'

'Yet you're stronger than I am—'

'Yes, that's why I'm so frightened, you make me feel strong—do you want to do that?'

'Well—perhaps—you're so very unusual, Stephen.'

'Am I?'

'Of course, don't you know that you are? Why, you're altogether different from other people.'

Stephen trembled a little: 'Do you mind?' she faltered.

'I know that you're you,' teased Angela, smiling again, but she reached out and took Stephen's hand.

Something in the queer, vital strength of that hand stirred her deeply, so that she tightened her fingers: 'What in the Lord's name are you?' she murmured.

'I don't know. Go on holding like that to my hand—hold it tighter—I like the feel of your fingers.'

'Stephen, don't be absurd!'

'Go on holding my hand, I like the feel of your fingers.'

'Stephen, you're hurting, you're crushing my rings!'

And now they were under the trees by the lakes, their feet falling softly on the luminous carpet. Hand in hand* they entered that place of deep stillness, and only their breathing disturbed the stillness for a moment, then it folded back over their breathing.

'Look,' said Stephen, and she pointed to the swan called Peter,* who had come drifting past on his own white reflection. 'Look,' she said, 'this is Morton, all beauty and peace—it drifts like that swan does, on calm, deep water. And all this beauty and peace is for you, because now you're a part of Morton.'

Angela said: 'I've never known peace, it's not in me—I don't think I'd find it here, Stephen.' And as she spoke she released her hand, moving a little away from the girl.

But Stephen continued to talk on gently; her voice sounded almost like that of a dreamer: 'Lovely, oh, lovely it is, our Morton. On evenings in winter these lakes are quite frozen, and the ice looks like slabs of gold in the sunset, when you and I come and stand here in the winter. And as we walk back we can smell the log fires long before we can see them, and we love that good smell because it means home, and our home is Morton—and we're happy, happy*—we're utterly contented and at peace, we're filled with the peace of this place—'

'Stephen—don't!'

'We're both filled with the old peace of Morton, because we love each other so deeply—and because we're perfect, a perfect thing, you and I—not two separate people but one.* And our love has lit a great, comforting beacon, so that we need never be afraid of the dark any more—we can warm ourselves at our love, we can lie down together, and my arms will be round you—'

She broke off abruptly, and they stared at each other.

'Do you know what you're saying?' Angela whispered.

And Stephen answered: 'I know that I love you, and that nothing else matters in the world.'

Then, perhaps because of that glamorous evening, with its spirit of queer, unearthly adventure, with its urge to strange, unendurable sweetness, Angela moved a step nearer to Stephen, then another, until their hands were touching. And all that she was, and all that she had been and would be again, perhaps even to-morrow, was fused at that moment into one mighty impulse, one imperative need, and that need was Stephen. Stephen's need was now hers, by sheer force of its blind and uncomprehending will to appeasement.

Then Stephen took Angela into her arms, and she kissed her full on the lips, as a lover.*

CHAPTER 19

I

THROUGH the long years of life that followed after, bringing with them their dreams and disillusions, their joys and sorrows, their fulfilments and frustrations, Stephen was never to forget this summer when she fell quite simply and naturally in love, in accordance with the dictates of her nature.

To her there seemed nothing strange or unholy in the love that she felt for Angela Crossby. To her it seemed an inevitable thing, as much a part of herself as her breathing; and yet it appeared transcendent of self, and she looked up and onward towards her love—for the eyes of the young are drawn to the stars, and the spirit of youth is seldom earth-bound.

She loved deeply, far more deeply than many a one who could fearlessly proclaim himself a lover. Since this is a hard and sad truth for the telling; those whom nature has sacrificed to her ends—her mysterious ends that often lie hidden—are sometimes endowed with a vast will to loving, with an endless capacity for suffering also, which must go hand in hand with their love.

But at first Stephen's eyes were drawn to the stars, and she saw only gleam upon gleam of glory. Her physical passion for Angela Crossby had aroused a strange response in her spirit, so that side by side with every hot impulse that led her at times beyond her own understanding, there would come an impulse not of the body; a fine, selfless thing* of great beauty and courage—she would gladly have given her body over to torment, have laid down her life if need be, for the sake of this woman whom she loved. And so blinded was she by those gleams of glory which the stars fling into the eyes of young lovers, that she saw perfection where none existed; saw a patient endurance that was purely fictitious, and conceived of a loyalty far beyond the limits of Angela's nature.

All that Angela gave seemed the gift of love; all that Angela withheld seemed withheld out of honour: 'If only I were free,' she was always saying, 'but I can't deceive Ralph, you know I can't, Stephen—he's ill.' Then Stephen would feel abashed and ashamed before so much pity and honour.

She would humble herself to the very dust, as one who was altogether unworthy: 'I'm a beast,* forgive me; I'm all, all wrong—I'm mad sometimes these days—yes, of course, there's Ralph.'

But the thought of Ralph would be past all bearing, so that she must reach out for Angela's hand. Then, as likely as not, they would draw together and start kissing, and Stephen would be utterly undone by those painful and terribly sterile kisses.*

'God!' she would mutter, 'I want to get away!'

At which Angela might weep: 'Don't leave me, Stephen! I'm so lonely—why can't you understand that I'm only trying to be decent to Ralph?' So Stephen would stay on for an hour, for two hours, and the next day would find her once more at The Grange, because Angela was feeling so lonely.

For Angela could never quite let the girl go. She herself would be rather bewildered at moments—she did not love Stephen, she was quite sure of that, and yet the very strangeness of it all was an attraction. Stephen was becoming a kind of strong drug, a kind of anodyne against boredom. And then Angela knew her own power to subdue; she could play with fire yet remain unscathed by it. She had only to cry long and bitterly enough for Stephen to grow pitiful and consequently gentle.

'Stephen, don't hurt me—I'm awfully frightened when you're like this—you simply terrify me, Stephen! Is it my fault that I married Ralph before I met you? Be good to me, Stephen!' And then would come tears, so that Stephen must hold her as though she were a child, very tenderly, rocking her backwards and forwards.

They took to driving as far as the hills, taking Tony with them; he liked hunting the rabbits—and while he leapt wildly about in the air to land on nothing more vital than herbage, they would sit very close to each other and watch him. Stephen knew many places where lovers might sit like this, unashamed, among those charitable hills. There were times when a numbness descended upon her as they sat there, and if Angela kissed her cheek lightly, she would not respond, would not even look round, but would just go on staring at Tony. Yet at other times she felt queerly uplifted, and turning to the woman who leant against her shoulder, she said suddenly one day:

'Nothing matters up here. You and I are so small, we're smaller than Tony—our love's nothing but a drop in some vast sea of love—it's rather consoling—don't you think so, belovèd?'

But Angela shook her head: 'No, my Stephen; I'm not fond of vast seas, I'm of the earth earthy,'* and then: 'Kiss me, Stephen.' So Stephen must kiss her many times, for the hot blood of youth stirs quickly, and the mystical sea became Angela's lips that so eagerly gave and took kisses.*

But when they got back to The Grange that evening, Ralph was there—he was hanging about in the hall. He said: 'Had a nice afternoon, you two women? Been motoring Angela round the hills, Stephen, or what?'

He had taken to calling her Stephen, but his voice just now sounded sharp with suspicion as his rather weak eyes peered at Angela, so that for her sake Stephen must lie, and lie well—nor would this be for the first time either.

'Yes, thanks,' she lied calmly, 'we went over to Tewkesbury and had another look at the abbey.* We had tea in the town. I'm sorry we're so late, the carburettor* choked, I couldn't get it right at first, my car needs a good overhauling.'

Lies, always lies! She was growing proficient at the glib kind of lying that pacified Ralph, or at all events left him with nothing to say, nonplussed and at a distinct disadvantage. She was suddenly seized with a kind of horror, she felt physically sick at what she was doing. Her head swam and she caught the jamb of the door for support—at that moment she remembered her father.

2

Two days later as they sat alone in the garden at Morton, Stephen turned to Angela abruptly: 'I can't go on like this, it's vile somehow—it's beastly, it's soiling us both—can't you see that?'

Angela was startled. 'What on earth do you mean?'

'You and me—and then Ralph. I tell you it's beastly—I want you to leave him and come away with me.'

'Are you mad?'

'No, I'm sane. It's the only decent thing, it's the only clean thing; we'll go anywhere you like, to Paris, to Egypt,* or back to the States. For your sake I'm ready to give up my home. Do you hear? I'm ready to give up even Morton. But I can't go on lying about you to Ralph, I want him to know how much I adore you—I want the whole world to know how I adore you. Ralph doesn't understand the first rudiments of loving, he's a nagging, mean-minded cur* of a man, but there's one thing that even he has a right to, and that's the truth. I'm done with these lies—I shall tell him the truth and so will you, Angela; and after we've told him we'll go away, and we'll live quite openly together, you and I, which is what we owe to ourselves and our love.'

Angela stared at her, white and aghast: 'You *are* mad,' she said slowly, 'you're raving mad. Tell him what? Have I let you become my lover? You know that I've always been faithful to Ralph; you know perfectly well that there's nothing to tell him beyond a few rather schoolgirlish kisses. Can I help it if you're—what you obviously are? Oh, no, my dear, you're not going to tell Ralph. You're not going to let all hell loose around me just because you want to save your own pride by pretending to Ralph that you've been my lover. If you're willing to give up your home I'm not willing to sacrifice mine, understand that, please. Ralph's not much of a man but he's better than nothing, and I've managed him so far without any trouble. The great thing with him is to blaze a false trail, that distracts his mind, it works like a charm. He'll follow any trail that I want him to follow—you leave him to me, I know my own husband a darned sight better than you do, Stephen, and I won't have you interfering in my home.' She was terribly frightened, too frightened to choose her words, to consider their effect upon Stephen, to consider anyone but Angela Crossby who stood in such dire and imminent peril. So she said yet again, only now she spoke loudly: 'I won't have you interfering in my home!'

Then Stephen turned on her, white with passion: 'You—you—' she stuttered, 'you're unspeakably cruel. You know how you make me suffer and suffer because I love you the way I do; and because you like the way I love you, you drag the love out of me day after day—Can't you understand that I love you so much that I'd give up Morton? Anything I'd give up—I'd give up the whole world. Angela, listen; I'd take care of you always. Angela, I'm rich—I'd take care of you always. Why won't you trust me? Answer me—why? Don't you think me fit to be trusted?'

She spoke wildly, scarcely knowing what she said; she only knew that she needed this woman with a need so intense, that worthy or unworthy, Angela was all that counted at that moment. And now she stood up, very tall, very strong, yet a little grotesque in her pitiful passion, so that looking at her Angela trembled—there was something rather terrible about her. All that was heavy in her face sprang into view, the strong line of the jaw, the square, massive brow, the eyebrows too thick and too wide for beauty; she was like some curious, primitive thing conceived in a turbulent age of transition.*

'Angela, come very far away—anywhere, only come with me soon—to-morrow.'

Then Angela forced herself to think quickly, and she said just five words: 'Could you marry me, Stephen?'*

She did not look at the girl as she said it—that she could not do, perhaps out of something that, for her, was the nearest she would ever come to pity. There ensued a long, almost breathless silence, while Angela waited with her eyes turned away. A leaf dropped, and she heard its minute, soft falling, heard the creak of the branch that had let fall its leaf as a breeze passed over the garden.

Then the silence was broken by a quiet, dull voice, that sounded to her like the voice of a stranger: 'No—' it said very slowly, 'no—I couldn't marry you, Angela.' And when Angela at last gained the courage to look up, she found that she was sitting there alone.

CHAPTER 20

I

For three weeks they kept away from each other, neither writing nor making any effort to meet. Angela's prudence forbade her to write: 'Litera scripta manet'*—a good motto, and one to which it was wise to adhere when dealing with a firebrand like Stephen. Stephen had given her a pretty bad scare, she realized the necessity for caution; still, thinking over that incredible scene, she found the memory rather exciting. Deprived of her anodyne against boredom, she looked upon Ralph with unfriendly eyes; while he, poor, inadequate, irritable devil, with his vague suspicions and his chronic dyspepsia, did little enough to divert his wife—his days, and a fairly large part of his nights as well, were now spent in nagging.

He nagged about Tony who, as ill luck would have it, had decided that the garden was rampant with moles: 'If you can't keep that bloody dog in order, he goes. I won't have him digging craters round my roses!' Then would come a long list of Tony's misdeeds from the time he had left the litter. He nagged about the large population of green-fly, deploring the existence of their sexual organs: 'Nature's a fool! Fancy procreation being extended to that sort of vermin!' And then he would grow somewhat coarse as he dwelt on the frequent conjugal excesses of green-fly. But most of all he nagged about Stephen, because this as he knew, irritated his wife: 'How's your freak* getting on? I haven't seen her just lately; have you quarrelled or what? Damned good thing if you have. She's appalling; never saw such a girl in my life; comes swaggering round here with her legs in breeches. Why can't she ride like an ordinary woman? Good Lord, it's enough to make any man see red; that sort of thing wants putting down at birth,* I'd like to institute state lethal chambers!'

Or perhaps he would take quite another tack and complain that recently he had been neglected: 'Late for every damned meal—running round with that girl—you don't care what happens to me any more. A lot you care about my indigestion! I've got to eat any old thing these days from cow-hide to bricks. Well, you listen to me, that's not what I pay for; get that into your head! I pay for good meals to be served on time; *on time*, do you hear? And I expect my wife to be in her rightful place at my table to see that the omelette's properly prepared. What's the matter with you that you can't go along and make it yourself? When we were first married you always made my omelettes yourself. I won't eat yellow froth with a few strings of parsley in it—it reminds me of the dog when he's sick, it's disgusting! And I won't go on talking about it either, the next time it happens I'll sack the cook. Damn it all, you were glad enough of my help when I found you practically starving in New York—but now you're for ever racing off with that girl. It's all this damned animal's fault that you met her!' He would kick out sideways at the terrified Tony, who had lately been made to stand proxy for Stephen.

But worst of all was it when Ralph started weeping, because, as he said, his wife did not love him any more, and because, as he did not always say, he felt ill with his painful, chronic dyspepsia. One day he must make feeble love* through his tears: 'Angela, come here—put your arms around me—come and sit on my knee the way you used to.' His wet eyes looked dejected yet rather greedy: 'Put your arms around me, as though you cared—' He was always insistent when most ineffectual.

That night he appeared in his best silk pyjamas—the pink ones that made his complexion look sallow. He climbed into bed with the sly expression that Angela hated—it was so pornographic. 'Well, old girl, don't forget that you've got a man about the house; you haven't forgotten it, have you?' After which followed one or two flaccid embraces together with much arrogant masculine bragging; and Angela, sighing as she lay and endured, quite suddenly thought of Stephen.

2

Pacing restlessly up and down her bedroom, Stephen would be thinking of Angela Crossby—haunted, tormented by Angela's words that day in the garden: 'Could you marry me, Stephen?' and then by those other pitiless words: 'Can I help it if you're—what you obviously are?'

She would think with a kind of despair: 'What am I in God's name—some kind of abomination?'* And this thought would fill her with very great anguish, because, loving much, her love seemed to her sacred. She could not endure that the slur of those words should come anywhere near her love. So now night after night she must pace up and down, beating her mind against a blind problem, beating her spirit against a blank wall—the impregnable wall of non-comprehension: 'Why am I as I am—and what am I?'* Her mind would recoil while her spirit grew faint. A great darkness would seem to descend on her spirit—there would be no light wherewith to lighten that darkness.

She would think of Martin, for now surely she loved just as he had loved—it all seemed like madness. She would think of her father, of his comfortable words: 'Don't be foolish, there's nothing strange about you.' Oh, but he must have been pitifully mistaken—he had died still very pitifully mistaken. She would think yet again of her curious childhood, going over each detail in an effort to remember. But after a little her thoughts must plunge forward once more, right into her grievous present. With a shock she would realize how completely this coming of love had blinded her vision; she had stared at the glory of it so long that not until now had she seen its black shadow. Then would come the most poignant suffering of all, the deepest, the final humiliation. Protection—she could never offer protection to the creature she loved: 'Could you marry me, Stephen?' She could neither protect nor defend nor honour by loving; her hands were completely empty. She who would gladly have given her life, must go empty-handed to love, like a beggar. She could only debase what she longed to exalt, defile what she longed to keep pure and untarnished.

The night would gradually change to dawn; and the dawn would shine in at the open windows, bringing with it the intolerable singing of birds: 'Stephen, look at us, look at us, we're happy!' Away in the distance there would be a harsh crying, the wild, harsh crying of swans by the lakes—the swan called Peter protecting, defending his mate against some unwelcome intruder. From the chimneys of Williams' comfortable cottage smoke would rise—very dark—the first smoke of the morning. Home, that meant home and two people together, respected because of their honourable living. Two people who had had the right to love in their youth, and whom old age had not divided. Two poor and yet infinitely enviable people, without stain, without shame in the eyes of their fellows. Proud people who could face the world unafraid, having no need to fear that world's execration.*

Stephen would fling herself down on the bed, completely exhausted by the night's bitter vigil.

3

There was some one who went every step of the way with Stephen during those miserable weeks, and this was the faithful and anxious Puddle, who could have given much wise advice had Stephen only confided in her. But Stephen hid her trouble in her heart for the sake of Angela Crossby.

With an ever-increasing presage of disaster, Puddle now stuck to the girl like a leech, getting little enough in return for her trouble—Stephen deeply resented this close supervision: 'Can't you leave me alone? No, of course I'm not ill!' she would say, with a quick spurt of temper.

But Puddle, divining her illness of spirit together with its cause, seldom left her alone. She was frightened by something in Stephen's eyes; an incredulous, questioning, wounded expression, as though she were trying to understand why it was that she must be so grievously wounded.* Again and again Puddle cursed her own folly for having shown such open resentment of Angela Crossby; the result was that now Stephen never discussed her, never mentioned her name unless Puddle clumsily dragged it in, and then Stephen would change the subject. And now more than ever Puddle loathed and despised the conspiracy of silence that forbade her to speak frankly. The conspiracy of silence that had sent the girl forth unprotected, right into the arms of this woman. A vain, shallow woman in search of excitement, and caring less than nothing for Stephen.

There were times when Puddle felt almost desperate, and one evening she came to a great resolution. She would go to the girl and say: 'I *know*. I know all about it, you can trust me, Stephen.' And then she would counsel and try to give courage: 'You're neither unnatural, nor abominable, nor mad; you're as much a part of what people call nature as anyone else; only you're unexplained as yet—you've not got your niche in creation. But some day that will come, and meanwhile don't shrink from yourself, but just face yourself calmly and bravely. Have courage; do the best you can with your burden. But above all be honourable. Cling to your honour for the sake of those others who share the same burden. For their sakes show the world that people like you and they can be quite as selfless and fine as the rest of mankind. Let your life go to prove this—it would be a really great life-work, Stephen.'*

But the resolution waned because of Anna, who would surely join hands with the conspiracy of silence. She would never condone such fearless plain speaking. If it came to her knowledge she would turn Puddle out bag and baggage, and that would leave Stephen alone. No, she dared not speak plainly because of the girl for whose sake she should now, above all, be outspoken. But supposing the day should arrive when Stephen herself thought fit to confide in her friend, then Puddle would take the bull by the horns: 'Stephen, I *know*. You can trust me, Stephen.' If only that day were not too long in coming—

For none knew better* than this little grey woman, the agony of mind that must be endured when a sensitive, highly organized nature is first brought face to face with its own affliction. None knew better the terrible nerves of the invert,* nerves that are always lying in wait. Super-nerves, whose response is only equalled by the strain that calls that response into being. Puddle was well acquainted with these things—that was why she was deeply concerned about Stephen.

But all she could do, at least for the present, was to be very gentle and very patient: 'Drink this cocoa, Stephen, I made it myself—' And then with a smile, 'I put four lumps of sugar!'

Then Stephen was pretty sure to turn contrite: 'Puddle—I'm a brute—you're so good to me always.'

'Rubbish! I know you like cocoa made sweet, that's why I put in those four lumps of sugar. Let's go for a really long walk, shall we, dear? I've been wanting a really long walk now for weeks.'

Liar—most kind and self-sacrificing liar! Puddle hated long walks, especially with Stephen who strode as though wearing seven-league boots,* and whose only idea of a country walk was to take her own line across ditches and hedges—yes, indeed, a most kind and self-sacrificing liar! For Puddle was not quite so young as she had been; at times her feet would trouble her a little, and at times she would get a sharp twinge in her knee, which she shrewdly suspected to be rheumatism. Nevertheless she must keep close to Stephen because of the fear that tightened her heart—the fear of that questioning, wounded expression which now never left the girl's eyes for a moment. So Puddle got out her most practical shoes—her heaviest shoes which were said to be damp-proof—and limped along bravely by the side of her charge, who as often as not ignored her existence.

There was one thing in all this that Puddle found amazing, and that was Anna's apparent blindness. Anna appeared to notice no change in

Stephen, to feel no anxiety about her. As always, these two were gravely polite to each other, and as always they never intruded. Still, it did seem to Puddle an incredible thing that the girl's own mother should have noticed nothing. And yet so it was, for Anna had gradually been growing more silent and more abstracted. She was letting the tide of life carry her gently towards that haven on which her thoughts rested. And this blindness of hers troubled Puddle sorely, so that anger must often give way to pity.

She would think: 'God help her, the sorrowful woman; she knows nothing—why didn't he tell her? It was cruel!' And then she would think: 'Yes, but God help Stephen if the day ever comes when her mother does know—what will happen on that day to Stephen?'

Kind and loyal Puddle; she felt torn to shreds between those two, both so worthy of pity. And now in addition she must be tormented by memories dug out of their graves by Stephen—Stephen, whose pain had called up a dead sorrow that for long had lain quietly and decently buried. Her youth would come back and stare into her eyes reproachfully, so that her finest virtues would seem little better than dust and ashes. She would sigh, remembering the bitter sweetness, the valiant hopelessness of her youth—and then she would look at Stephen.

But one morning Stephen announced abruptly: 'I'm going out. Don't wait lunch for me, will you.' And her voice permitted of no argument or question.

Puddle nodded in silence. She had no need to question, she knew only too well where Stephen was going.

4

With head bowed by her mortification of spirit, Stephen rode once more to The Grange. And from time to time as she rode she flushed deeply because of the shame of what she was doing. But from time to time her eyes filled with tears because of the pain of her longing.

She left the cob with a man at the stables, then made her way round to the old herb-garden; and there she found Angela sitting alone in the shade with a book which she was not reading.

Stephen said: 'I've come back.' And then without waiting: 'I'll do anything you want, if you'll let me come back.' And even as she spoke those words her eyes fell.

But Angela answered: 'You had to come back—because I've been wanting you, Stephen.'

Then Stephen went and knelt down beside her, and she hid her face against Angela's knee, and the tears that had never so much as once fallen during all the hard weeks of their separation, gushed out of her eyes. She cried like a child, with her face against Angela's knee.

Angela let her cry on for a while, then she lifted the tear-stained face and kissed it: 'Oh, Stephen, Stephen, get used to the world—it's a horrible place full of horrible people, but it's all there is, and we live in it, don't we? So we've just got to do as the world does, my Stephen.' And because it seemed strange and rather pathetic that this creature should weep, Angela was stirred to something very like love for a moment: 'Don't cry any more—don't cry, honey,' she whispered, 'we're together; nothing else really matters.'

And so it began all over again.

5

Stephen stayed on to lunch, for Ralph was in Worcester. He came home a good two hours before teatime to find them together among his roses; they had followed the shade when it left the herb-garden.

'Oh, it's you!' he exclaimed as his eye lit on Stephen; and his voice was so naïvely disappointed, so full of dismay at her reappearance, that just for a second she felt sorry for him.

'Yes, it's me—' she replied, not quite knowing what to say.

He grunted, and went off for his pruning knife, with which he was soon amputating roses. But in spite of his mood he remained a good surgeon, cutting dexterously, always above the leaf-bud, for the man was fond of his roses. And knowing this Stephen must play on that fondness, since now it was her business to cajole him into friendship. A degrading business, but it had to be done for Angela's sake, lest she suffer through loving. Unthinkable that—'Could you marry me, Stephen?'

'Ralph, look here'; she called, 'Mrs. John Laing's got broken! We may be in time if we bind her with bass.'

'Oh, dear, has she?' He came hurrying up as he spoke, 'Do go down to the shed and get me some, will you?'

She got him the bass and together they bound her, the pink-cheeked, full-bosomed Mrs. John Laing.

'There,' he said, as he snipped off the ends of her bandage, 'that ought to set your leg for you, madam!'

Near by grew a handsome Frau Karl Druschki,* and Stephen praised her luminous whiteness, remarking his obvious pleasure at the praise. He was like a father of beautiful children, always eager to hear them admired by a stranger, and she made a note of this in her mind: 'He likes one to praise his roses.'

He wanted to talk about Frau Karl Druschki: 'She's a beauty! There's something so wonderfully cool—as you say, it's the whiteness—' Then before he could stop himself: 'She reminds me of Angela, somehow.' The moment the words were out he was frowning, and Stephen stared hard at Frau Karl Druschki.

But as they passed from border to border, his brow cleared: 'I've spent over three hundred,' he said proudly, 'never saw such a mess as this garden was in when I bought the place—had to dig in fresh soil for the roses just here, these are all new plants; I motored half across England to get them. See that hedge of York and Lancasters there? They didn't cost much because they're out of fashion. But I like them, they're small but rather distinguished I think—there's something so armorial about them.'

She agreed: 'Yes, I'm awfully fond of them too'; and she listened quite gravely while he explained that they dated as far back as the Wars of the Roses.

'Historical, that's what I mean,' he explained. 'I like everything old, you know, except women.'

She thought with an inward smile of his newness.

Presently he said in a tone of surprise: 'I never imagined that you'd care about roses.'

'Yes, why not? We've got quite a number at Morton. Why don't you come over to-morrow and see them?'

'Do your William Allen Richardsons do well?' he inquired.

'I think so.'

'Mine don't. I can't make it out. This year, of course, they've been damaged by green-fly. Just come here and look at these standards, will you? They're being devoured alive by the brutes!' And then as though he were talking to a friend who would understand him: 'Roses seem good to me—you know what I mean, there's virtue about them—the scent and the feel and the way they grow. I always had some on the desk in my office, they seemed to brighten up the whole place, no end.'

He started to ink in the names on the labels with a gold fountain pen which he took from his pocket. 'Yes,' he murmured, as he bent his face over the labels, 'yes, I always had three or four on my desk. But Birmingham's a foul sort of place for roses.'

And hearing him, Stephen found herself thinking that all men had something simple about them; something that took pleasure in the things that were blameless, that longed, as it were, to contact with Nature. Martin had loved huge, primitive trees; and even this mean little man loved his roses.

Angela came strolling across the lawn: 'Come, you two,' she called gaily, 'tea's waiting in the hall!'

Stephen flinched: 'Come, you two—' the words jarred on and she knew that Angela was thoroughly happy, for when Ralph was out of earshot for a moment she whispered:

'You were clever about his roses!'

At tea Ralph relapsed into sulky silence; he seemed to regret his erstwhile good humour. And he ate quite a lot, which made Angela nervous—she dreaded his attacks of indigestion, which were usually accompanied by attacks of bad temper.

Long after they had all finished tea he lingered, until Angela said: 'Oh, Ralph, that lawn mower. Pratt asked me to tell you that it won't work at all; he thinks it had better go back to the makers. Will you write about it now before the post goes?'

'I suppose so—' he muttered; but he left the room slowly.

Then they looked at each other and drew close together, guiltily, starting at every sound: 'Stephen—be careful for God's sake—Ralph—'

So Stephen's hands dropped from Angela's shoulders, and she set her lips hard, for no protest must pass them any more; they had no right to protest.

CHAPTER 21

I

THAT autumn the Crossbys went up to Scotland, and Stephen went to Cornwall with her mother. Anna was not well, she needed a change, and the doctor had told them of Watergate Bay,* that was why they had gone to Cornwall. To Stephen it mattered very little where she went, since she was not allowed to join Angela in Scotland. Angela had put her foot down quite firmly: 'No, my dear, it wouldn't do. I know Ralph would make hell. I can't let you follow us up to Scotland.' So that there, perforce, the matter had ended.

And now Stephen could sit and gloom over her trouble while Anna read placidly, asking no questions. She seldom worried her daughter with questions, seldom even evinced any interest in her letters.

From time to time Puddle would write from Morton, and then Anna would say, recognizing the writing: 'Is everything all right?'

And Stephen would answer: 'Yes, Mother, Puddle says everything's all right.' As indeed it was—at Morton.

But from Scotland news seemed to come very slowly. Stephen's letters would quite often go unanswered; and what answers she received were unsatisfactory, for Angela's caution was a very strict censor. Stephen herself must write with great care, she discovered, in order to pacify that censor.

Twice daily she visited the hotel porter, a kind, red-faced man with a sympathy for lovers.

'Any letters for me?' she would ask, trying hard to appear rather bored at the mere thought of letters.

'No, miss.'

'There's another post in at seven?'

'Yes, miss.'

'Well—thank you.'

She would wander away, leaving the porter to think to himself: 'She don't look like a girl as would have a young man, but you never can tell. Anyhow she seems anxious—I do hope it's all right for the poor young lady.' He grew to take a real interest in Stephen, and would sometimes talk to his wife about her: 'Have you noticed her,

Alice? A queer-looking girl, very tall, wears a collar and tie—you know, mannish. And she seems just to change her suit of an evening—puts on a dark one—never wears evening dress. The mother's still a beautiful woman; but the girl—I dunno, there's something about her—anyhow I'm surprised she's got a young man; though she must have, the way she watches the posts, I sometimes feel sorry for her.'*

But her calls at his office were not always fruitless: 'Any letters for me?'

'Yes, miss, there's just one.'

He would look at her with a paternal expression, glad enough to think that her young man had written; and Stephen, divining his thoughts from his face, would feel embarrassed and angry. Snatching her letter she would hurry to the beach, where the rocks provided a merciful shelter, and where no one seemed likely to look paternal, unless it should be an occasional sea-gull.

But as she read, her heart would feel empty; something sharp like a physical pain would go through her: 'Dear Stephen. I'm sorry I've not written before, but Ralph and I have been fearfully busy. We're having a positive social orgy up here, I'm so glad he took this large shoot. . . .'* That was the sort of thing Angela wrote these days—perhaps because of her caution.

However, one morning an unusually long letter arrived, telling all about Angela's doings: 'By the way, we've met the Antrim boy, Roger. He's been staying with some people that Ralph knows quite well, the Peacocks, they've got a wonderful old castle; I think I must have told you about them.' Here followed an elaborate description of the castle, together with the ancestral tree of the Peacocks. Then: 'Roger has talked quite a lot about you; he says he used to tease you when you were children. He says that you wanted to fight him one day—that made me laugh awfully, it's so like you, Stephen! He's a good-looking person and rather a nice one. He tells me that his regiment's stationed at Worcester, so I've asked him to come over to The Grange when he likes. It must be pretty dreary, I imagine, in Worcester. . . .'

Stephen finished the letter and sat staring at the sea for a moment, after which she got up abruptly. Slipping the letter into her pocket she buttoned her jacket; she was feeling cold. What she needed was a walk, a really long walk. She set out briskly in the direction of Newquay.

2

During those long, anxious weeks in Cornwall, it was borne in on Stephen as never before how wide was the gulf between her and her mother, how completely they two must always stand divided. Yet looking at Anna's quiet ageing face, the girl would be struck afresh by its beauty, a beauty that seemed to have mollified the years, to have risen triumphant over time and grief. And now as in the days of her childhood, that beauty would fill her with a kind of wonder; so calm it was, so assured, so complete—then her mother's deep eyes,* blue like distant mountains, and now with that far-away look in their blueness, as though they were gazing into the distance. Stephen's heart would suddenly tighten a little; a sense of great loss would descend upon her, together with the sense of not fully understanding just what she had lost or why she had lost it—she would stare at Anna as a thirsty traveller in the desert will stare at a mirage of water.

And one evening there came a preposterous impulse—the impulse to confide in this woman within whose most gracious and perfect body her own anxious body had lain and quickened.* She wanted to speak to that motherhood, to implore, nay, compel its understanding. To say: 'Mother, I need you. I've lost my way—give me your hand to hold in the darkness.' But good God, the folly, the madness of it! The base betrayal of such a confession! Angela delivered over, betrayed—the unthinkable folly, the madness of it.

Yet sometimes as Anna and she sat together looking out at the misty Cornish coast-line, hearing the dull, heavy throb of the sea and the calling of sea-gulls the one to the other—as they sat there together it would seem to Stephen that her heart was so full of Angela Crossby, all the bitterness, all the sweetness of her,* that the mother-heart beating close by her own must surely, in its turn, be stirred to beat faster, for had she not once sheltered under that heart? And so extreme was her need becoming, that now she must often find Anna's cool hand and hold it a moment or two in her own, trying to draw from it some consolation.

But the touch of that cool, pure hand would distress her, causing her spirit to ache with longing for the simple and upright and honourable things that had served many simple and honourable people. Then all that to some might appear uninspiring, would seem to her very fulfilling and perfect. A pair of lovers walking by arm in arm—just a quiet, engaged couple, neither comely nor clever nor burdened with riches; just a quiet, engaged couple—would in her envious eyes be invested with a glory and pride passing all understanding. For were Angela and she those fortunate lovers, they could stand before Anna happy and triumphant. Anna, the mother, would smile and speak gently, tolerant because of her own days of loving. Wherever they went older folk would remember, and remembering would smile on their love and speak gently. To know that the whole world was glad of your gladness, must surely bring heaven very near to the world.

One night Anna looked across at her daughter: 'Are you tired, my dear? You seem a bit fagged.'*

The question was unexpected, for Stephen was supposed not to know what it meant to feel fagged, her physical health and strength were proverbial. Was it possible then that her mother had divined at long last her utter weariness of spirit? Quite suddenly Stephen felt shamelessly childish, and she spoke as a child who wants comforting.

'Yes, I'm dreadfully tired.' Her voice shook a little; 'I'm tired out—I'm dreadfully tired,' she repeated. With amazement she heard herself making this weak bid for pity, and yet she could not resist it. Had Anna held out her arms at that moment, she might soon have learnt about Angela Crossby.

But instead she yawned: 'It's this air, it's too woolly. I'll be very glad when we get back to Morton. What's the time? I'm almost asleep already—let's go up to our beds, don't you think so, Stephen?'

It was like a cold douche; and a good thing too for the girl's self-respect. She pulled herself together: 'Yes, come on, it's past ten. I detest this soft air.' And she flushed, remembering that weak bid for pity.

3

Stephen left Cornwall without a regret; everything about it had seemed to her depressing. Its rather grim beauty which at any other time would have deeply appealed to her virile nature, had but added to the gloom of those interminable weeks spent apart from Angela Crossby. For her perturbation had been growing apace, she was constantly oppressed by doubts and vague fears; bewildered, uncertain of her own power to hold; uncertain, too, of Angela's will to be held by this dangerous yet bloodless loving. Her defrauded body had been troubling her sorely, so that she had tramped over beach and headland, cursing the strength of the youth that was in her, trying to trample down her hot youth and only succeeding in augmenting its vigour.

But now that the ordeal had come to an end at last, she began to feel less despondent. In a week's time Angela would get back from Scotland; then at least the hunger of the eyes* could be appeased—a terrible thing that hunger of the eyes for the sight of the well-loved being. And then Angela's birthday was drawing near, which would surely provide an excuse for a present. She had sternly forbidden the giving of presents, even humble keepsakes, on account of Ralph—still, a birthday was different, and in any case Stephen was quite determined to risk it. For the impulse to give that is common to all lovers, was in her attaining enormous proportions, so that she visualized Angela decked in diadems worthy of Cleopatra;* so that she sat and stared at her bank book with eyes that grew angry when they lit on her balance. What was the good of plenty of money if it could not be spent on the person one loved? Well, this time it should be so spent, and spent largely; no limit was going to be set to this present!

An unworthy and tiresome thing money, at best, but it can at least ease the heart of the lover. When he lightens his purse he lightens his heart, though this can hardly be accounted a virtue, for such giving is perhaps the most insidious form of self-indulgence that is known to mankind.

4

Stephen had said quite casually to Anna: 'Suppose we stay three or four days in London on our way back to Morton? You could do some shopping.' Anna had agreed, thinking of her house linen which wanted renewing; but Stephen had been thinking of the jewellers' shops in Bond Street.*

And now here they actually were in London, established at a quiet and expensive hotel; but the problem of Angela's birthday present had, it seemed, only just begun for Stephen. She had not the least idea what she wanted, or what Angela wanted, which was far more important; and she did not know how to get rid of her mother, who appeared to dislike going out unaccompanied. For three days of the four Stephen fretted and fumed; never had Anna seemed so dependent. At Morton they now led quite separate lives, yet here in London they were always together. Scheme as she might she could find no excuse for a solitary visit to Bond Street. However, on the morning of the fourth and last day, Anna succumbed to a devastating headache.

Stephen said: 'I think I'll go and get some air, if you really don't need me—I'm feeling energetic!'

'Yes, do—I don't want you to stay in,' groaned Anna, who was longing for peace and an aspirin tablet.

Once out on the pavement Stephen hailed the first taxi she met; she was quite absurdly elated. 'Drive to the Piccadilly end of Bond Street,' she ordered, as she jumped in and slammed the door. Then she put her head quickly out of the window: 'And when you get to the corner, please stop. I don't want you to drive along Bond Street, I'll walk. I want you to stop at the Piccadilly corner.'

But when she was actually standing on the corner—the left-hand corner—she began to feel doubtful as to which side of Bond Street she ought to tackle first. Should she try the right side or keep to the left? She decided to try the right side. Crossing over, she started to walk along slowly. At every jeweller's shop she stood still and gazed at the wares displayed in the window. Now she was worried by quite a new problem, the problem of stones, there were so many kinds. Emeralds or rubies or perhaps just plain diamonds? Well, certainly neither emeralds nor rubies—Angela's colouring demanded whiteness. Whiteness—she had it! Pearls*—no, one pearl, one flawless pearl and set as a ring. Angela had once described such a ring with envy, but alas, it had been born in Paris.

People stared at the masculine-looking girl who seemed so intent upon feminine adornments. And some one, a man, laughed and nudged his companion: 'Look at that! What is it?'

'My God! What indeed?'

She heard them and suddenly felt less elated as she made her way into the shop.

She said rather loudly: 'I want a pearl ring.'

'A pearl ring? What kind, madam?'

She hesitated, unable now to describe what she did want: 'I don't quite know—but it must be a large one.'

'For yourself?' And she thought that the man smiled a little.

Of course he did nothing of the kind; but she stammered: 'No—oh, no—it's not for myself, it's for a friend. She's asked me to choose her a large pearl ring.' To her own ears the words sounded foolish and flustered.

There was nothing in that shop that fulfilled her requirements, so once more she must face the guns of Bond Street. Now she quickened her steps and found herself striding; modifying her pace she found herself dawdling; and always she was conscious of people who stared, or whom she imagined were staring. She felt sure that the shop assistants looked doubtful when she asked for a large and flawless pearl ring; and catching a glimpse of her reflection in a glass, she decided that naturally they would look doubtful—her appearance suggested neither pearls nor their price. She slipped a surreptitious hand into her pocket, gaining courage from the comforting feel of her cheque book.

When the east side of the thoroughfare had been exhausted, she crossed over quickly and made her way back towards her original corner. By now she was rather depressed and disgruntled. Supposing that she should not find what she wanted in Bond Street? She had no idea where else to look—her knowledge of London was far from extensive. But apparently the gods were feeling propitious, for a little further on she paused in front of a small, and as she thought, quite humble shop. As a matter of fact it was anything but humble, hence the bars half-way up its unostentatious window. Then she stared, for there on a white velvet cushion lay a pearl that looked like a round gleaming marble, a marble attached to a slender circlet of platinum—some sort of celestial marble! It was just such a ring as Angela had seen in Paris, and had since never ceased to envy.

The person behind this counter was imposing. He was old, and wore glasses with tortoiseshell rims: 'Yes, madam, it's a very fine specimen indeed. The setting's French, just a thin band of platinum, there's nothing to detract from the beauty of the pearl.'

He lifted it tenderly off its cushion, and as tenderly Stephen let it rest on her palm. It shone whiter than white against her skin, which by contrast looked sunburnt and weather-beaten.

Then the dignified old gentleman murmured the price, glancing curiously at the girl as he did so, but she seemed to be quite unperturbed, so he said: 'Will you try the effect of the ring on your finger?'

At this, however, his customer flushed: 'It wouldn't go anywhere near my finger!'

'I can have it enlarged to any size you wish.'

'Thanks, but it's not for me—it's for a friend.'

'Have you any idea what size your friend takes, say in gloves? Is her hand large or small, do you think?'

Stephen answered promptly: 'It's a very small hand,' then immediately looked and felt rather self-conscious.

And now the old gentleman was openly staring: 'Excuse me,' he murmured, 'an extraordinary likeness. . . .' Then more boldly: 'Do you happen to be related to Sir Philip Gordon of Morton Hall, who died—it must be about two years ago—from some accident? I believe a tree fell—'

'Oh, yes, I'm his daughter,' said Stephen.

He nodded and smiled: 'Of course, of course, you couldn't be anything but his daughter.'

'You knew my father?' she inquired, in surprise.

'Very well, Miss Gordon, when your father was young. In those days Sir Philip was a customer of mine. I sold him his first pearl studs while he was at Oxford, and at least four scarf pins—a bit of a dandy* Sir Philip was up at Oxford. But what may interest you is the fact that I made your mother's engagement ring for him; a large half-hoop of very fine diamonds—'

'Did *you* make that ring?'

'I did, Miss Gordon. I remember quite well his showing me a miniature of Lady Anna—I remember his words. He said: "She's so pure that only the purest stones are fit to touch her finger." You see, he'd known me ever since he was at Eton, that's why he spoke of your mother to me—I felt deeply honoured. Ah, yes—dear, dear—your father was young then and very much in love. . . .'

She said suddenly: 'Is this pearl as pure as those diamonds?'

And he answered: 'It's without a blemish.'

Then she found her cheque book and he gave her his pen with which to write out the very large cheque.

'Wouldn't you like some reference?'* she inquired, as she glanced at the sum for which he must trust her.

But at this he laughed: 'Your face is your reference, if I may be allowed to say so, Miss Gordon.'

They shook hands because he had known her father, and she left the shop with the ring in her pocket. As she walked down the street she was lost in thought, so that if people stared she no longer noticed. In her ears kept sounding those words from the past, those words of her father's when long, long ago he too had been a young lover: 'She's so pure that only the purest stones are fit to touch her finger.'

CHAPTER 22

I

WHEN they got back to Morton there was Puddle in the hall, with that warm smile of hers, always just a little mocking yet pitiful too, that queer composite smile that made her face so arresting. And the sight of this faithful little grey woman brought home to Stephen the fact that she had missed her. She had missed her, she found, out of all proportion to the size of the creature, which seemed to have diminished. Coming back to it after those weeks of absence, Puddle's smallness seemed to be even smaller, and Stephen could not help laughing as she hugged her. Then she suddenly lifted her right off her feet with as much ease as though she had been a baby.

Morton smelt good with its log fires burning, and Morton looked good with the goodness of home.* Stephen sighed with something very like contentment: 'Lord! I'm so glad to be back again, Puddle. I must have been a cat in my last incarnation; I hate strange places—especially Cornwall.'

Puddle smiled grimly. She thought that she knew why Stephen had hated Cornwall.

After tea Stephen wandered about the house, touching first this, then that, with affectionate fingers. But presently she went off to the stables with sugar for Collins and carrots for Raftery; and there in his spacious, hay-scented loose box, Raftery was waiting for Stephen. He made a queer little sound in his throat, and his soft Irish eyes said: 'You're home, home, home. I've grown tired with waiting, and with wishing you home.'

And she answered: 'Yes, I've come back to you, Raftery.'

Then she threw her strong arm around his neck, and they talked together for quite a long while—not in Irish or English but in a quiet language having very few words but many small sounds and many small movements, that meant much more than words.

'Since you went I've discovered a wonderful thing,' he told her, 'I've discovered that for me you are God. It's like that sometimes with us humbler people, we may only know God through His human image.'

'Raftery,' she murmured, 'oh, Raftery, my dear—I was so young when you came to Morton. Do you remember that first day out hunting when you jumped the huge hedge in our big north paddock? What a jump! It ought to go down to history. You were splendidly cool and collected about it. Thank the Lord you were—I was only a kid, all the same it was very foolish of us, Raftery.'

She gave him a carrot, which he took with contentment from the hand of his God, and proceeded to munch. And she watched him munch it, contented in her turn, hoping that the carrot was succulent and sweet; hoping that his innocent cup of pleasure* might be full to the brim and overflowing. Like God indeed, she tended his needs, mixing the evening meal in his manger, holding the water bucket to his lips while he sucked in the cool, clear, health-giving water. A groom came along with fresh trusses of straw which he opened and tossed among Raftery's bedding; then he took off the smart blue and red day clothing, and buckled him up in a warm night blanket. Beyond in the far loose box by the window, Sir Philip's young chestnut kicked loudly for supper.

'Woa horse! Get up there! Stop kicking them boards!' And the groom hurried off to attend to the chestnut.

Collins, who had spat out his two lumps of sugar, was now busy indulging his morbid passion. His sides were swollen wellnigh to bursting—blown out like an air balloon was old Collins from the evil and dyspeptic effects of the straw, plus his own woeful lack of molars. He stared at Stephen with whitish-blue eyes that saw nothing, and when she touched him he grunted—a discourteous sound which meant: 'Leave me alone!' So after a mild reproof she left him to his sins and his indigestion.

Last but not least, she strolled down to the home of the two-legged creature who had once reigned supreme in those princely but now depleted stables. And the lamplight streamed out through uncurtained windows to meet her, so that she walked on lamplight. A slim streak of gold led right up to the porch of old Williams' comfortable cottage. She found him sitting with the Bible on his knees, peering crossly down at the Scriptures through his glasses. He had taken to reading the Scriptures aloud to himself—a melancholy occupation. He was at this now. As Stephen entered she could hear him mumbling from Revelation: 'And the heads of the horses were as the heads of lions; and out of their mouths issued fire and smoke and brimstone.'*

He looked up, and hastily twitched off his glasses: 'Miss Stephen!'

'Sit still—stop where you are, Williams.'

But Williams had the arrogance of the humble. He was proud of the stern traditions of his service, and his pride forbade him to sit in her presence, in spite of their long and kind years of friendship. Yet when he spoke he must grumble a little, as though she were still the very small child who had swaggered round the stables rubbing her chin, imitating his every expression and gesture.

'You didn't ought to have no 'orses, Miss Stephen, the way you runs off and leaves them'; he grumbled, 'Raftery's been off 'is feed these last days. I've been talkin' to that Jim what you sets such store by! Impudent young blight, 'e answered me back like as though I'd no right to express me opinion. But I says to 'im: "You just wait, lad," I says, "You wait until I gets 'old of Miss Stephen!" '

For Williams could never keep clear of the stables, and could never refrain from nagging when he got there. Deposed he might be, but not yet defeated even by old age, as grooms knew to their cost. The tap of his heavy oak stick in the yard was enough to send Jim and his underling flying to hide curry-combs and brushes out of sight. Williams needed no glasses when it came to disorder.

'Be this place 'ere a stable or be it a pigsty, I wonder?' was now his habitual greeting.

His wife came bustling in from the kitchen: 'Sit down, Miss Stephen,' and she dusted a chair.

Stephen sat down and glanced at the Bible where it lay, still open, on the table.

'Yes,' said Williams dourly, as though she had spoken, 'I'm reduced to readin' about 'eavenly 'orses. A nice endin' that for a man like me, what's been in the service of Sir Philip Gordon, what's 'ad 'is legs across the best 'unters as ever was seen in this county or any! And I don't believe in them lion-headed beasts breathin' fire and brimstone, it's all agin nature. Whoever it was wrote them Revelations, can't never have been inside of a stable. I don't believe in no 'eavenly 'orses neither—there won't be no 'orses in 'eaven; and a good thing too, judgin' by the description.'

'I'm surprised at you, Arth-thur, bein' so disrespectful to The Book!' his wife reproached him gravely.

'Well, it ain't no encyclopaedee to the stable, and that's a sure thing,' grinned Williams.

Stephen looked from one to the other. They were old, very old, fast approaching completion. Quite soon their circle would be complete, and then Williams would be able to tackle Saint John* on the points of those heavenly horses.

Mrs. Williams glanced apologetically at her: 'Excuse 'im, Miss Stephen, 'e's gettin' rather childish.'E won't read no pretty parts of The Book; all 'e'll read is them parts about chariots and such like. All what's to do with 'orses 'e reads; and then 'e's so unbelievin'—it's aw-ful!' But she looked at her mate with the eyes of a mother, very gentle and tolerant eyes.

And Stephen, seeing those two together, could picture them as they must once have been, in the halcyon days of their youthful vigour. For she thought that she glimpsed through the dust of the years, a faint flicker of the girl who had lingered in the lanes when the young man Williams and she had been courting. And looking at Williams as he stood before her twitching and bowed, she thought that she glimpsed a faint flicker of the youth, very stalwart and comely, who had bent his head downwards and sideways as he walked and whispered and kissed in the lanes. And because they were old yet undivided, her heart ached; not for them but rather for Stephen. Her youth seemed as dross when compared to their honourable age; because they were undivided.

She said: 'Make him sit down, I don't want him to stand.' And she got up and pushed her own chair towards him.

But old Mrs. Williams shook her white head slowly: 'No, Miss Stephen, 'e wouldn't sit down in your presence. Beggin' your pardon, it would 'urt Arth-thur's feelin's to be made to sit down; it would make 'im feel as 'is days of service was really over.'

'I don't need to sit down,' declared Williams.

So Stephen wished them both a good night, promising to come again very soon; and Williams hobbled out to the path which was now quite golden from border to border, for the door of the cottage was standing wide open and the glow from the lamp streamed over the path. Once more she found herself walking on lamplight, while Williams, bareheaded, stood and watched her departure. Then her feet were caught up and entangled in shadows again, as she made her way under the trees.

But presently came a familiar fragrance—logs burning on the wide, friendly hearths of Morton. Logs burning—quite soon the lakes would be frozen—'and the ice looks like slabs of gold in the sunset, when you and I come and stand here in the winter . . . and as we walk back we can smell the log fires long before we can see them, and we love that good smell because it means home, and our home is Morton . . . because it means home and our home is Morton. . . .'*

Oh, intolerable fragrance of log fires burning!

CHAPTER 23

I

ANGELA did not return in a week, she had decided to remain another fortnight in Scotland. She was staying now with the Peacocks, it seemed, and would not get back until after her birthday. Stephen looked at the beautiful ring as it gleamed in its little white velvet box, and her disappointment and chagrin were childish.

But Violet Antrim, who had also been staying with the Peacocks, had arrived home full of importance. She walked in on Stephen one afternoon to announce her engagement to young Alec Peacock. She was so much engaged and so haughty about it that Stephen, whose nerves were already on edge, was very soon literally itching to slap her. Violet was now able to look down on Stephen from the height of her newly gained knowledge of men—knowing Alec she felt that she knew the whole species.

'It's a terrible pity you dress as you do, my dear,' she remarked, with the manner of sixty,* 'a young girl's so much more attractive when she's soft—don't you think you could soften your clothes just a little? I mean, you do want to get married, don't you! No woman's complete until she's married. After all, no woman can really stand alone, she always needs a man to protect her.'

Stephen said: 'I'm all right—getting on nicely, thank you!'

'Oh, no, but you can't be!' Violet insisted. 'I was talking to Alec and Roger about you, and Roger was saying it's an awful mistake for women to get false ideas into their heads. He thinks you've got rather a bee in your bonnet; he told Alec that you'd be quite a womanly woman if you'd only stop trying to ape what you're not.' Presently she said, staring rather hard: 'That Mrs. Crossby—do you really like her? Of course I know you're friends and all that—But why are you friends? You've got nothing in common. She's what Roger calls a thorough man's woman. I think myself she's a bit of a climber. Do you want to be used as a scaling ladder for storming the fortifications of the county? The Peacocks have known old Crossby for years, he's a wonderful shot for an ironmonger,* but they don't care for her very much I believe—Alec says she's man-mad, whatever that means, anyhow she seems desperately keen about Roger.'

Stephen said: 'I'd rather we didn't discuss Mrs. Crossby, because, you see, she's my friend.' And her voice was as icy cold as her hands.

'Oh, of course if you're feeling like that about it—' laughed Violet, 'no, but honest, she is keen on Roger.'

When Violet had gone, Stephen sprang to her feet, but her sense of direction seemed to have left her, for she struck her head a pretty sharp blow against the side of a heavy bookcase. She stood swaying with her hands pressed against her temples. Angela and Roger Antrim—those two—but it couldn't be, Violet had been purposely lying. She loved to torment, she was like her brother, a bully, a devil who loved to torment—it couldn't be—Violet had been lying.

She steadied herself, and leaving the room and the house, went and fetched her car from the stables. She drove to the telegraph office at Upton: 'Come back, I must see you at once,' she wired, taking great care to prepay the reply, lest Angela should find an excuse for not answering.

The clerk counted the words with her stump of a pencil, then she looked at Stephen rather strangely.

2

The next morning came Angela's frigid answer: 'Coming home Monday fortnight not one day sooner please no more wires Ralph very much upset.'

Stephen tore the thing into a hundred fragments and then hurled it away. She was suddenly shaking all over with uncontrollable anger.

3

Right up to the moment of Angela's return that hot anger supported Stephen. It was like a flame that leapt through her veins, a flame that consumed and yet stimulated, so that she purposely fanned the fire from a sense of self preservation.

Then came the actual day of arrival. Angela must be in London by now, she would certainly have travelled by the night express. She would catch the 12.47 to Malvern and then motor to Upton—it was nearly twelve. It was afternoon. At 3.17 Angela's train would arrive at Great Malvern—it had arrived now—in about twenty minutes she would drive past the very gates of Morton. Half-past four. Angela must have got home; she was probably having tea in the parlour—in the little oak parlour with its piping bullfinch whose cage always stood near the casement window. A long time ago, a lifetime ago, Stephen had blundered into that parlour, and Tony had barked, and the bullfinch had piped a sentimental old German tune—but that was surely a lifetime ago. Five o'clock. Violet Antrim had obviously lied; she had lied on purpose to torment Stephen—Angela and Roger—it couldn't be; Violet had lied because she liked to torment. A quarter past five. What was Angela doing now? She was near, just a few miles away—perhaps she was ill, as she had not written; yes, that must be it, of course Angela was ill. The persistent, aching hunger of the eyes. Anger, what was it? A folly, a delusion, a weakness that crumbled before that hunger. And Angela was only a few miles away.

She went up to her room and unlocked a drawer from which she took the little white case. Then she slipped the case into her jacket pocket.

4

She found Angela helping her maid to unpack; they appeared to be all but snowed under by masses of soft, inadequate garments. The bedroom smelt strongly of Angela's scent, which was heavy yet slightly pungent.

She glanced up from a tumbled heap of silk stockings: 'Hallo, Stephen!' Her greeting was casually friendly.

Stephen said: 'Well, how are you after all these weeks? Did you have a good journey down from Scotland?'

The maid said: 'Shall I wash your new crêpe de Chine* night-gowns, ma'am? Or ought they to go to the cleaners?'

Then, somehow, they all fell silent.

To break this suggestive and awkward silence, Stephen inquired politely after Ralph.

'He's in London on business for a couple of days; he's all right, thanks,' Angela answered briefly, and she turned once more to sorting her stockings.

Stephen studied her. Angela was not looking well, her mouth had a childish droop at the corners; there were quite new shadows, too, under her eyes, and these shadows accentuated her pallor. And as though that earnest gaze made her nervous, she suddenly bundled the stockings together with a little sound of impatience.

'Come on, let's go down to my room!' And turning to her maid: 'I'd rather you washed the new nightgowns, please.'

They went down the wide oak stairs without speaking, and into the little oak panelled parlour. Stephen closed the door; then they faced each other.

'Well, Angela?'

'Well, Stephen?' And after a pause: 'What on earth made you send that absurd telegram? Ralph got hold of the thing and began to ask questions. You are such an almighty fool sometimes—you knew perfectly well that I couldn't come back. Why will you behave as though you were six, have you no common sense? What's it all about? Your methods are not only infantile—they're dangerous.'

Then taking Angela firmly by the shoulders, Stephen turned her so that she faced the light. She put her question with youthful crudeness: 'Do you find Roger Antrim physically attractive—do you find that he attracts you that way more than I do?' She waited calmly, it seemed, for her answer.

And because of that distinctly ominous calm, Angela was scared, so she blustered a little: 'Of course I don't! I resent such questions; I won't allow them even from you, Stephen. God knows where you get your fantastic ideas! Have you been discussing me with that girl Violet? If you have, I think it's simply outrageous! She's quite the most evil-minded prig in the county. It was not very gentlemanly of you, my dear, to discuss my affairs with our neighbours, was it?'

'I refused to discuss you with Violet Antrim,' Stephen told her, still speaking quite calmly. But she clung to her point: 'Was it all a mistake? Is there no one between us except your husband? Angela, look at me—I will have the truth.'

For answer Angela kissed her.

Stephen's strong but unhappy arms went round her, and suddenly stretching out her hand, she switched off the little lamp on the table, so that the room was lit only by firelight. They could not see each other's faces very clearly any more, because there was only firelight. And Stephen spoke such words as a lover will speak when his heart is burdened to breaking; when his doubts must bow down and be swept away before the unruly flood of his passion. There in that shadowy, firelit room, she spoke such words as lovers have spoken ever since the divine, sweet madness of God flung the thought of love into Creation.

But Angela suddenly pushed her away: 'Don't, don't—I can't bear it—it's too much, Stephen. It hurts me—I can't bear this thing—for you. It's all wrong, I'm not worth it, anyhow it's all wrong. Stephen, it's making me—can't you understand? It's too much—' She could not, she dared not explain. 'If you were a man—' She stopped abruptly, and burst into uncontrollable weeping.

And somehow this weeping was different from any that had gone before, so that Stephen trembled. There was something frightened and desolate about it; it was like the sobbing of a terrified child. The girl forgot her own desolation in her pity and the need that she felt to comfort. More strongly than ever before she felt the need to protect this woman, and to comfort.

She said, grown suddenly passionless and gentle: 'Tell me—try to tell me what's wrong, belovèd. Don't be afraid of making me angry—we love each other, and that's all that matters. Try to tell me what's wrong, and then let me help you; only don't cry like this—I can't endure it.'

But Angela hid her face in her hands: 'No, no, it's nothing; I'm only so tired. It's been a fearful strain these last months. I'm just a weak, human creature, Stephen—sometimes I think we've been worse than mad. I must have been mad to have allowed you to love me like this—one day you'll despise and hate me. It's my fault, but I was so terribly lonely that I let you come into my life, and now—oh, I can't explain, you wouldn't understand; how could you understand, Stephen?'

And so strangely complex is poor human nature, that Angela really believed in her feelings. At that moment of sudden fear and remorse, remembering those guilty weeks in Scotland, she believed that she felt compassion and regret for this creature who loved her, and whose ardent loving had paved the way for another. In her weakness she could not part from the girl, not yet—there was something so strong about her. She seemed to combine the strength of a man with the gentler and more subtle strength of a woman.* And thinking of the crude young animal Roger, with his brusque, rather brutal appeal to the senses, she was filled with a kind of regretful shame, and she hated herself for what she had done, and for what she well knew she would do again, because of that urge to passion.

Feeling humble, she groped for the girl's kind hand; then she tried to speak lightly: 'Would you always forgive this very miserable sinner, Stephen?'

Stephen said, not apprehending her meaning, 'If our love is a sin,* then heaven must be full of such tender and selfless sinning as ours.'

They sat down close together. They were weary unto death,* and Angela whispered: 'Put your arms around me again—but gently, because I'm so tired. You're a kind lover, Stephen—sometimes I think you're almost too kind.'

And Stephen answered: 'It's not kindness that makes me unwilling to force you—I can't conceive of that sort of love.'

Angela Crossby was silent.

But now she was longing for the subtle easement of confession, so dear to the soul of woman. Her self-pity was augmented by her sense of wrong-doing—she was thoroughly unstrung, almost ill with self-pity—so that lacking the courage to confess the present, she let her thoughts dwell on the past. Stephen had always forborne to question, and therefore that past had never been discussed, but now Angela felt a great need to discuss it. She did not analyse her feelings; she only knew that she longed intensely to humble herself, to plead for compassion, to wring from the queer, strong, sensitive being who loved her, some hope of ultimate forgiveness. At that moment, as she lay there in Stephen's arms, the girl assumed an enormous importance. It was strange, but the very fact of betrayal appeared to have strengthened her will to hold her, and Angela stirred, so that Stephen said softly:

'Lie still—I thought you were fast asleep.'

And Angela answered: 'No, I'm not asleep, dearest, I've been thinking. There are some things I ought to tell you. You've never asked me about my past life—why haven't you, Stephen?'

'Because,' said Stephen, 'I knew that some day you'd tell me.'

Then Angela began at the very beginning. She described a Colonial home in Virginia. A grave, grey house, with a columned entrance, and a garden that looked down on deep, running water, and that water had rather a beautiful name—it was called the Potomac River.* Up the side of the house grew magnolia blossoms, and many old trees gave their shade to its garden. In summer the fire-flies lit lamps on those trees, shifting lamps that moved swiftly among the branches. And the hot summer darkness was splashed with lightning, and the hot summer air was heavy with sweetness.

She described her mother who had died when Angela was twelve—a pathetic, inadequate creature; the descendant of women who had owned many slaves to minister to their most trivial requirements: 'She could hardly put on her own stockings and shoes,' smiled Angela, as she pictured that mother.

She described her father, George Benjamin Maxwell—a charming, but quite incorrigible spendthrift. She said: 'He lived in past glories, Stephen. Because he was a Maxwell—a Maxwell of Virginia—he wouldn't admit that the Civil War had deprived us all of the right to spend money. God knows, there was little enough of it left—the War practically ruined the old Southern gentry! My grandma could remember those days quite well; she scraped lint from her sheets for our wounded soldiers. If Grandma had lived, my life might have been different—but she died a couple of months after Mother.'

She described the eventual cataclysm, when the home had been sold up with everything in it, and she and her father had set out for New York—she just seventeen and he broken and ailing—to rebuild his dissipated fortune. And because she was now painting a picture of real life, untinged by imagination, her words lived, and her voice grew intensely bitter.

'Hell—it was hell! We went under so quickly. There were days when I hadn't enough to eat. Oh, Stephen, the filth, the unspeakable squalor—the heat and the cold and the hunger and the squalor. God, how I hate that great hideous city! It's a monster, it crushes you down, it devours—even now I couldn't go back to New York without feeling a kind of unreasoning terror. Stephen, that damnable city broke my nerve. Father got calmly out of it all by dying one day—and that was so like him! He'd had about enough, so he just lay down and died; but I couldn't do that because I was young—and I didn't want to die, either. I hadn't the least idea what I could do, but I knew that I was supposed to be pretty and that good-looking girls had a chance on the stage, so I started out to look for a job. My God! Shall I ever forget it!'

And now she described the long, angular streets, miles and miles of streets; miles and miles of faces all strange and unfriendly—faces like masks. Then the intimate faces of would-be employers, too intimate when they peered into her own—faces that had suddenly thrown off their masks.

'Stephen, are you listening? I put up a fight, I swear it! I swear I put up a fight—I was only nineteen when I got my first job—nineteen's not so awfully old, is it, Stephen?'

Stephen said: 'Go on,' and her voice sounded husky.

'Oh, my dear—it's so dreadfully hard to tell you. The pay was rotten, not enough to live on—I used to think that they did it on purpose, lots of the girls used to think that way too—they never gave us quite enough to live on. You see, I hadn't a vestige of talent, I could only dress up and try to look pretty. I never got a real speaking part, I just danced, not well, but I'd got a good figure.' She paused and tried to look up through the gloom, but Stephen's face was hidden in shadow. 'Well then, darling—Stephen, I want to feel your arms, hold me closer—well then, I—there was a man who wanted me—not as you want me, Stephen, to protect and care for me; God, no, not that way! And I was so poor and so tired and so frightened; why sometimes my shoes would let in the slush because they were old and I hadn't the money to buy myself new ones—try to think of that, darling. And I'd cry when I washed my hands in the winter because they'd be bleeding from broken chilblains. Well, I couldn't stay the course any longer, that's all. . . .'

The little gilt clock on the desk ticked loudly. Tick, tick! Tick, tick! An astonishing voice to come from so small and fragile a body. Somewhere out in the garden a dog barked—Tony, chasing imaginary rabbits through the darkness.

'Stephen!'

'Yes, my dear?'

'Have you understood me?'*

'Yes—oh, yes, I've understood you. Go on.'

'Well then, after awhile he turned round and left me, and I just had to drag along as I had done, and I sort of crocked up*—couldn't sleep at night, couldn't smile and look happy when I went on to dance—that was how Ralph found me—he saw me dance and came round to the back, the way some men do. I remember thinking that Ralph didn't look like that sort of man; he looked—well, just like Ralph, not a bit like that sort of man. Then he started sending me flowers; never presents or anything like that, just flowers with his card. And we had lunch together a good few times, and he talked about that other man who'd left me. He said he'd like to go out with a horse-whip—imagine Ralph trying to horsewhip a man! They knew each other quite well, I discovered; you see, they were both in the hardware business. Ralph was out after some big contract for his firm, that was why he happened to be in New York—and one day he asked me to marry him, Stephen. I suppose he was really in love with me then, anyhow I thought it was wonderful of him—I thought he was very broad-minded and noble. Good God! He's had his pound of flesh* since; it gave him the hold over me that he wanted. We were married before we sailed for Europe. I wasn't in love, but what could I do? I'd nowhere to turn and my health was crocking; lots of our girls ended up in the hospital wards—I didn't want to end up that way. Well, so you see why I've got to be careful how I act; he's terribly and awfully suspicious. He thinks that because I took a lover when I was literally down and out, I'm likely to do the same thing now. He doesn't trust me, it's natural enough, but sometimes he throws it all up in my face, and when he does that, my God, how I hate him! But oh, Stephen, I could never go through it all again—I haven't got an ounce of fight left in me. That's why, although Ralph's no cinch* as a husband, I'd be scared to death if he really turned nasty. He knows that, I think, so he's not afraid to bully—he's bullied me many a time over you—but of course you're a woman so he couldn't divorce me—I expect that's really what makes him so angry. All the same, when you asked me to leave him for you, I hadn't the courage to face that either. I couldn't have faced the public scandal that Ralph would have made; he'd have hounded us down to the ends of the earth, he'd have branded us, Stephen. I know him, he's revengeful, he'd stop at nothing, that weak sort of man is often that way. It's as though what Ralph lacks in virility, he tries to make up for by being revengeful. My dear, I couldn't go under again—I couldn't be one of those apologetic people who must always exist just under the surface, only coming up for a moment like fish—I've been through that particular hell. I want life, and yet I'm always afraid. Every time that Ralph looks at me I feel frightened, because he knows that I hate him most when he tries to make love—' She broke off abruptly.

And now she was crying a little to herself, letting the tears trickle down unheeded. One of them splashed on to Stephen's coat sleeve and lay there, a small, dark blot on the cloth, while the patient arms never faltered.

'Stephen, say something—say you don't hate me!'

A log crashed, sending up a bright spurt of flame, and Stephen stared down into Angela's face. It was marred by weeping; it looked almost ugly, splotched and reddened as it was by her weeping. And because of that pitiful, blemished face, with the pitiful weakness that lay behind it, the unworthiness even, Stephen loved her so deeply at that moment, that she found no adequate words.

'Say something—speak to me, Stephen!'

Then Stephen gently released her arm, and she found the little white box in her pocket: 'Look, Angela, I got you this for your birthday—Ralph can't bully you about it, it's a birthday present.'

'Stephen—my dear!'

'Yes—I want you to wear it always, so that you'll remember how much I love you. I think you forgot that just now when you talked about hating—Angela, give me your hand, the hand that used to bleed in the winter.'

So the pearl that was pure as her mother's diamonds were pure, Stephen slipped on to Angela's finger. Then she sat very still, while Angela gazed at the pearl wide-eyed, because of its beauty. Presently she lifted her wondering face, and now her lips were quite close to Stephen's, but Stephen kissed her instead on the forehead. 'You must rest,' she said, 'you're' simply worn out. Can't you sleep if I keep you safe in my arms?'

For at moments, such is the blindness and folly yet withal the redeeming glory of love.

CHAPTER 24

1

RALPH said very little about the ring. What could he say? A present given to his wife by the daughter of a neighbour—an unusually costly present of course—still, after all, what could he say? He took refuge in sulky silence. But Stephen would see him staring at the pearl, which Angela wore on her right-hand third finger, and his weak little eyes would look redder than usual, perhaps with anger—one could never quite tell from his eyes whether he was tearful or angry.

And because of those eyes with their constant menace, Stephen must play her conciliatory rôle; and this she must do in spite of his rudeness, for now he was openly rude and hostile. And he bullied. It was almost as though he took pleasure in bullying his wife when Stephen was present; her presence seemed to arouse in the man everything that was ill-bred, petty and cruel. He would make thinly-veiled allusions to the past, glancing sideways at Stephen the while he did so; and one day when she flushed to the roots of her hair with rage to see Angela humble and fearful, he laughed loudly: 'I'm just a plain tradesman, you know; if you don't like my ways, then you'd better not come here.' Catching Angela's eye, Stephen tried to laugh too.

A soul-sickening business. She would feel degraded; she would feel herself gradually losing all sense of pride, of common decency even, so that when she returned in the evening to Morton she would not want to look the old house in the eyes. She would not want to face those pictures of Gordons that hung in its hall, and must turn away, lest they by their very silence rebuke this descendant of theirs who was so unworthy. Yet sometimes it seemed to her that she loved more intensely because she had lost so much—there was nothing left now but Angela Crossby.

2

Watching this deadly decay that threatened all that was fine in her erstwhile pupil, Puddle must sometimes groan loudly in spirit; she must even argue with God about it. Yes, she must actually argue with

God like Job;* and remembering his words in affliction, she must speak those words on behalf of Stephen: 'Thine hands have made me and fashioned me together round about; yet Thou dost destroy me.' For now in addition to everything else, she had learnt of the advent of Roger Antrim. Not that Stephen had confided in her, far from it, but gossip has a way of travelling quickly. Roger spent most of his leisure at The Grange. She had heard that he was always going over from Worcester. So now Puddle, who had not been much given to prayer in the past, must argue with God, like Job. And perhaps, since God probably listens to the heart rather than to the lips, He forgave her.

3

Stupid with misery and growing more inept every day, Stephen found herself no match for Roger. He was calm, self-assured, insolent and triumphant, and his love of tormenting had not waned with his manhood. Roger was no fool; he put two and two together and his masculine instinct deeply resented this creature who might challenge his right of possession. Moreover, that masculine instinct was outraged. He would stare at Stephen as though she were a horse whom he strongly suspected of congenital unsoundness,* and then he would let his eyes rest on Angela's face. They would be the eyes of a lover, possessive, demanding, insistent eyes—if Ralph did not happen to be present. And into Angela's eyes there would come an expression that Stephen had seen many times. A mist would slowly cloud over their blueness; they would dim, as though they were hiding something. Then Stephen would be seized with a violent trembling, so that she could not stand any more but must sit with her hands clasped tightly together, lest those trembling hands betray her to Roger. But Roger would have seen already, and would smile his slow, understanding, masterful smile.

Sometimes he and Stephen would look at each other covertly, and their youthful faces would be marred by a very abominable thing; the instinctive repulsion of two human bodies, the one for the other, which neither could help—not now that those bodies were stirred by a woman. Then into this vortex of secret emotion would come Ralph. He would stare from Stephen to Roger and then at his wife, and his eyes would be red—one never knew whether from tears or from anger. They would form a grotesque triangle for a moment, those three who must share a common desire. But after a little the two male creatures who hated each other, would be shamefully united in the bond of their deeper hatred of Stephen; and divining this, she in her turn would hate.

4

It could not go on without some sort of convulsion, and that Christmas was a time of recriminations. Angela's infatuation was growing, and she did not always hide this from Stephen. Letters would arrive in Roger's handwriting, and Stephen, half crazy with jealousy by now, would demand to see them. She would be refused, and a scene would ensue.

'That man's your lover! Have I gone starving only for this—that you should give yourself to Roger Antrim? Show me that letter!'

'How dare you suggest that Roger's my lover! But if he were it's no business of yours.'

'Will you show me that letter?'

'I will not.'

'It's from Roger.'

'You're intolerable. You can think what you please.'

'What *am* I to think?' Then because of her longing, 'Angela, for God's sake don't treat me like this—I can't bear it. When you loved me it was easier to bear—I endured it for your sake, but now—listen, listen. . . .' Stark naked confessions dragged from lips that grew white the while they confessed: 'Angela, listen. . . .'

And now the terrible nerves of the invert, those nerves that are always lying in wait, gripped Stephen. They ran like live wires through her body, causing a constant and ruthless torment, so that the sudden closing of a door or the barking of Tony would fall like a blow on her shrinking flesh. At night in her bed she must cover her ears from the ticking of the clock, which would sound like thunder in the darkness.

Angela had taken to going up to London on some pretext or another—she must see her dentist; she must fit a new dress.

'Well then, let me come with you.'

'Good heavens, why? I'm only going to the dentist!'

'All right, I'll come too.'

'You'll do nothing of the kind.' Then Stephen would know why Angela was going.

All that day she would be haunted by insufferable pictures. Whatever she did, wherever she went, she would see them together,

Angela and Roger. . . . She would think: 'I'm going mad! I can see them as clearly as though they were here before me in the room.' And then she would cover her eyes with her hands, but this would only strengthen the pictures.

Like some earth-bound spirit she would haunt The Grange on the pretext of taking Tony for a walk. And there, as likely as not, would be Ralph wandering about in his bare rose garden. He would glance up and see her perhaps, and then—most profound shame of all—they would both look guilty, for each would know the loneliness of the other, and that loneliness would draw them together for the moment; they would be almost friends in their hearts.

'Angela's gone up to London, Stephen.'

'Yes, I know. She's gone up to fit her new dress.'

Their eyes would drop. Then Ralph might say sharply: 'If you're after the dog, he's in the kitchen,' and turning his back, he might make a pretence of examining his standard rose-trees.

Calling Tony, Stephen would walk into Upton, then along the mist-swept bank of the river. She would stand very still staring down at the water, but the impulse would pass, and whistling the dog, she would turn and go hurrying back to Upton.

Then one afternoon Roger came with his car to take Angela for a drive through the hills. The New Year was slipping into the spring, and the air smelt of sap and much diligent growing. A warm February had succeeded the winter. Many birds would be astir on those hills where lovers might sit unashamed—where Stephen had sat holding Angela clasped in her arms, while she eagerly took and gave kisses. And remembering these things Stephen turned and left them; unable just then to endure any longer. Going home, she made her way to the lakes, and there she quite suddenly started weeping. Her whole body seemed to dissolve itself in weeping; and she flung herself down on the kind earth of Morton, shedding tears as of blood.* There was no one to witness those tears except the white swan called Peter.

5

Terrible, heart-breaking months. She grew gaunt with her unappeased love for Angela Crossby. And now she would sometimes turn in despair to the thought of her useless and unspent money. Thoughts would come that were altogether unworthy, but nevertheless those thoughts would persist. Roger was not rich; she was rich already and some day she would be even richer.

She went up to London and chose new clothes at a West End tailor's;* the man in Malvern who had made for her father was getting old, she would have her suits made in London in future. She ordered herself a rakish red car; a long-bodied, sixty-horse-power Métallurgique.* It was one of the fastest cars of its year, and it certainly cost her a great deal of money. She bought twelve pairs of gloves, some heavy silk stockings, a square sapphire scarf pin and a new umbrella. Nor could she resist the lure of pyjamas made of white *crêpe de Chine* which she spotted in Bond Street. The pyjamas led to a man's dressing-gown of brocade*—an amazingly ornate garment. Then she had her nails manicured but not polished, and from that shop she carried away toilet water and a box of soap that smelt of carnations* and some cuticle cream for the care of her nails. And last but not least, she bought a gold bag with a clasp set in diamonds for Angela.

All told she had spent a considerable sum, and this gave her a fleeting satisfaction. But on her way back in the train to Malvern, she gazed out of the window with renewed desolation. Money could not buy the one thing that she needed in life; it could not buy Angela's love.

6

That night she stared at herself in the glass;* and even as she did so she hated her body with its muscular shoulders, its small compact breasts, and its slender flanks of an athlete. All her life she must drag this body of hers like a monstrous fetter imposed on her spirit. This strangely ardent yet sterile body that must worship yet never be worshipped in return by the creature of its adoration. She longed to maim it, for it made her feel cruel; it was so white, so strong and so self-sufficient; yet withal so poor and unhappy a thing that her eyes filled with tears and her hate turned to pity. She began to grieve over it, touching her breasts with pitiful fingers, stroking her shoulders, letting her hands slip along her straight thighs—Oh, poor and most desolate body!

Then she, for whom Puddle was actually praying at that moment, must now pray also, but blindly; finding few words that seemed worthy of prayer, few words that seemed to encompass her meaning—for she did not know the meaning of herself. But she loved, and loving groped for the God who had fashioned her,* even unto this bitter loving.

CHAPTER 25

I

STEPHEN'S troubles had begun to be aggravated by Violet, who was always driving over to Morton, ostensibly to talk about Alec, in reality to collect information as to what might be happening at The Grange. She would stay for hours, very skilfully pumping while she dropped unwelcome hints anent Roger.

'Father's going to cut down his allowance,' she declared, 'if he doesn't stop hanging about that woman. Oh, I'm sorry! I always forget she's your friend—' Then looking at Stephen with inquisitive eyes: 'But I can't understand that friendship of yours; for one thing, how *can* you put up with Crossby?' And Stephen knew that yet once again, county gossip was rife about her.

Violet was going to be married in September, they would then live in London, for Alec was a barrister. Their house, it seemed, was already bespoken: 'A perfect duck of a house in Belgravia,'* where Violet intended to entertain largely on the strength of a bountiful parent Peacock. She was in the highest possible fettle these days, invested with an enormous importance in her own eyes, as also in those of her neighbours. Oh, yes, the whole world smiled broadly on Violet and her Alec: 'Such a charming young couple,' said the world, and at once proceeded to shower them with presents. Apostle teaspoons arrived in their dozens, so did coffee-pots, cream-jugs and large fish slices; to say nothing of a heavy silver bowl from the Hunt, and a massive salver from the grateful Scottish tenants.*

On the wedding day not a few eyes would be wet at the sight of so youthful a man and maiden 'joined together in an honourable estate, instituted of God in the time of man's innocency.' For such ancient traditions—in spite of the fact that man's innocency could not even survive one bite of an apple shared with a woman—are none the less apt to be deeply moving. There they would kneel, the young newly wed, ardent yet sanctified by a blessing, so that all, or at least nearly all, they would do, must be considered both natural and pleasing to a God in the image of man created. And the fact that this God, in a thoughtless moment, had created in His turn those pitiful thousands who must stand for ever outside His blessing, would in no way disturb the large congregation or their white-surpliced pastor, or the couple who knelt on the gold-braided, red velvet cushions. And afterwards there would be plentiful champagne to warm the cooling blood of the elders, and much shaking of hands and congratulating, and many kind smiles for the bride and her bridegroom. Some might even murmur a fleeting prayer in their hearts, as the two departed: 'God bless them!'

So now Stephen must actually learn at first hand how straight can run the path of true love,* in direct contradiction to the time-honoured proverb. Must realize more clearly than ever, that love is only permissible to those who are cut in every respect to life's pattern; must feel like some ill-conditioned pariah, hiding her sores* under lies and pretences. And after those visits of Violet Antrim's, her spirits would be at a very low ebb, for she had not yet gained that steel-bright courage which can only be forged in the furnace of affliction, and which takes many weary years in the forging.*

2

The splendid new motor* arrived from London, to the great delight and excitement of Burton. The new suits were completed and worn by their owner, and Angela's costly gold bag was received with apparent delight, which seemed rather surprising considering her erstwhile ban upon presents. Yet could Stephen have known it, this was not so surprising after all, for the bag infuriated Ralph, thereby distracting his facile attention for the moment, from something that was far more dangerous.

Filled with an ever-increasing need to believe, Stephen listened to Angela Crossby: 'You know there's nothing between me and Roger—if you don't, then you above all people ought to,' and her blue, child-like eyes would look up at Stephen, who could never resist the appeal of their blueness.

And as though to bear out the truth of her words, Roger now came to The Grange much less often; and when he did come he was quietly friendly, not at all lover-like if Stephen was present, so that gradually her need to believe had begun to allay her worst fears. Yet she knew with the true instinct of the lover, that Angela was secretly unhappy. She might try to appear light-hearted and flippant, but her smiles and her jests could not deceive Stephen.

'You're miserable. What is it?'

And Angela would answer: 'Ralph's been vile to me again—' But she would not add that Ralph was daily becoming more suspicious and more intolerant of Roger Antrim, so that now her deadly fear of her husband was always at war with her passion.

Sometimes it seemed to the girl that Angela used her as a whip wherewith to lash Ralph. She would lead Stephen on to show signs of affection which would never have been permitted in the past. Ralph's little red eyes would look deeply resentful, and getting up he would slouch from the room. They would hear the front door being closed, and would know that he had gone for a walk with Tony. Yet when they were alone and in comparative safety, there would be something crude, almost cruel in their kisses; a restless, dissatisfied, hungry thing—their lips would seem bent on scourging their bodies. Neither would find deliverance nor ease from the ache that was in them, for each would be kissing with a wellnigh intolerable sense of loss, with a passionate knowledge of separation. After a little they would sit with bent heads, not speaking because of what might not be spoken; not daring to look each other in the eyes nor to touch each other, lest they should cry out against this preposterous love-making.

Completely confounded, Stephen racked her brains for anything that might give them both a respite. She suggested that Angela should see her fence with a celebrated London fencing master whom she had bribed to come down to Morton. She tried to arouse an interest in the car, the splendid new car that had cost so much money. She tried to find out if Angela had an ungratified wish that money could fulfil.

'Only tell me what I can do,' she pleaded, but apparently there was nothing.

Angela came several times to Morton and dutifully attended the fencing lessons. But they did not go well, for Stephen would glimpse her staring abstractedly out of the window; then the sly, agile foil* with its blunt-tipped nose, would slip in under Stephen's guard and shame her.

They would sometimes go far afield in the car, and one night they stopped at an inn and had dinner—Angela ringing up her husband with the old and now threadbare excuse of a breakdown. They dined in a quiet little room by themselves; the scents of the garden came in through the window—warm, significant scents, for now it was May and many flowers multiplied in that garden. Never before had they done such a thing as this, they had never dined all alone at a wayside inn miles away from their homes, just they two, and Stephen stretched out her hand and covered Angela's where it rested very white and still on the table. And Stephen's eyes held an urgent question, for now it was May and the blood of youth leaps and strains with the sap in early summer. The air seemed breathless, since neither would speak, afraid of disturbing the thick, sweet silence—but Angela shook her head very slowly. Then they could not eat, for each was filled with the same and yet with a separate longing; so after a while they must get up and go, both conscious of a sense of painful frustration.

They drove back on a road that was paved with moonlight, and presently Angela fell fast asleep like an unhappy child—she had taken her hat off and her head lay limply against Stephen's shoulder. Seeing her thus, so helpless in sleep, Stephen felt strangely moved, and she drove very slowly, fearful of waking the woman who slept like a child with her fair head against her shoulder. The car climbed the steep hill from Ledbury town, and presently there lay the wide Wye valley whose beauty had saddened a queer little girl long before she had learnt the pain of all beauty. And now the valley was bathed in whiteness, while here and there gleamed a roof or a window, but whitely, as though all the good valley folk had extinguished their lamps and retired to their couches. Far away, like dark clouds coming up out of Wales, rose range upon range of the old Black Mountains,* with the tip of Gadrfawr peering over the others, and the ridge of Pen-cerrig-calch sharp against the skyline. A little wind ruffled the bracken on the hillsides, and Angela's hair blew across her closed eyes so that she stirred and sighed in her sleep. Stephen bent down and began to soothe her.

Then from out of that still and unearthly night, there crept upon Stephen an unearthly longing. A longing that was not any more of the body but rather of the weary and homesick spirit that endured the chains of that body. And when she must drive past the gates of Morton, the longing within her seemed beyond all bearing, for she wanted to lift the sleeping woman in her arms and carry her in through those gates; and carry her in through the heavy white door; and carry her up the wide, shallow staircase, and lay her down on her own bed, still sleeping, but safe in the good care of Morton.

Angela suddenly opened her eyes: 'Where am I?' she muttered, stupid with sleep. Then after a moment her eyes filled with tears, and there she sat all huddled up, crying.

Stephen said gently: 'It's all right, don't cry.'

But Angela went on crying.

CHAPTER 26

I

LIKE a river that has gradually risen to flood, until it sweeps everything before it, so now events rose and gathered in strength towards their inevitable conclusion. At the end of May Ralph must go to his mother, who was said to be dying at her house in Brighton. With all his faults he had been a good son, and the redness of his eyes was indeed from real tears as he kissed his wife good-bye at the station, on his way to his dying mother. The next morning he wired that his mother was dead, but that he could not get home for a couple of weeks. As it happened, he gave the actual day and hour of his return, so that Angela knew it.

The relief of his unexpectedly long absence went to Stephen's head; she grew much more exacting, suggesting all sorts of intimate plans. Supposing they went for a few days to London? Supposing they motored to Symond's Yat* and stayed at the little hotel by the river? They might even push on to Abergavenny and from there motor up and explore the Black Mountains—why not? It was glorious weather.

'Angela, please come away with me, darling—just for a few days—we've never done it, and I've longed to so often. You can't refuse, there's nothing on earth to prevent your coming.'

But Angela would not make up her mind, she seemed suddenly anxious about her husband: 'Poor devil, he was awfully fond of his mother. I oughtn't to go, it would look so heartless with the old woman dead and Ralph so unhappy—'

Stephen said bitterly: 'What about me? Do you think I'm never unhappy?'

So the time slipped by in heartaches and quarrels, for Stephen's taut nerves were like spurs to her temper, and she stormed or reproached in her dire disappointment:

'You pretend that you love me and yet you won't come—and I've waited so long—oh, my God, how I've waited! But you're utterly cruel. And I ask for so little, just to have you with me for a few days and nights—just to sleep with you in my arms; just to feel you beside me when I wake up in the morning—I want to open my eyes and see your face, as though we belonged to each other. Angela, I swear I wouldn't torment you—we'd be just as we are now, if that's what you're afraid of. You must know, after all these months, that you can trust me—'

But Angela set her lips and refused: 'No, Stephen, I'm sorry, but I'd rather not come.'

Then Stephen would feel that life was past bearing, and sometimes she must ride rather wildly for miles—now on Raftery, now on Sir Philip's young chestnut. All alone she would ride in the early mornings, getting up from a sleepless night unrefreshed, yet terribly alive because of those nerves that tortured her luckless body. She would get back to Morton still unable to rest, and a little later would order the motor and drive herself across to The Grange, where Angela would usually be dreading her coming.

Her reception would be cold: 'I'm fairly busy, Stephen—I must pay off all these bills before Ralph gets home'; or: 'I've got a foul headache, so don't scold me this morning; I think if you did that I just couldn't bear it!' Stephen would flinch as though struck in the face; she might even turn round and go back to Morton.

Came the last precious day before Ralph's return, and that day they did spend quite peaceably together, for Angela seemed bent upon soothing. She went out of her way to be gentle to Stephen, and Stephen, quick as always to respond, was very gentle in her turn. But after they had dined in the little herb garden—taking advantage of the hot, still weather—Angela developed one of her headaches.

'Oh, my Stephen—oh, darling, my head's too awful. It must be the thunder—it's been coming on all day. What a perfectly damnable thing to happen, on our last evening too—but I know this kind well; I'll just have to give in and go to my bed. I'll take a cachet* and then try to sleep, so don't ring me up when you get back to Morton. Come to-morrow—come early. I'm so miserable, darling, when I think that this is our last peaceful evening—'

'I know. But are you all right to be left?'

'Yes, of course. All I need is to get some sleep. You won't worry, will you? Promise, my Stephen!'

Stephen hesitated. Quite suddenly Angela was looking very ill, and her hands were like ice. 'Swear you'll telephone to me if you can't get to sleep, then I'll come back at once.'

'Yes, but don't do that, will you, unless I ring up—I should hear you, of course, and that would wake me and start my head throbbing.'

Then as though impelled, in spite of herself, by the girl's strange attraction, she lifted her face: 'Kiss me . . . oh, God . . . Stephen!'

'I love you so much—so much—' whispered Stephen.

2

It was past ten o'clock when she got back to Morton: 'Has Angela Crossby rung up?' she inquired of Puddle, who appeared to have been waiting in the hall.

'No, she hasn't!' snapped Puddle, who was getting to the stage when she hated the mere name of Angela Crossby. Then she added: 'You look like nothing on earth; in your place I'd go to bed at once, Stephen.'

'You go to bed, Puddle, if you're tired—where's Mother?'

'In her bath. For heaven's sake do come to bed! I can't bear to see you looking as you do these days.'

'I'm all right.'

'No, you're not, you're all wrong. Go and look at your face.'

'I don't very much want to, it doesn't attract me,' smiled Stephen.

So Puddle went angrily up to her room, leaving Stephen to sit with a book in the hall near the telephone bell, in case Angela should ring. And there, like the faithful creature she was, she must sit on all through the night, patiently waiting. But when the first tinges of dawn greyed the window and the panes of the semicircular fanlight, she left her chair stiffly, to pace up and down, filled with a longing to be near this woman, if only to stand and keep watch in her garden—Snatching up a coat she went out to her car.

3

She left the motor at the gates of The Grange, and walked up the drive, taking care to tread softly. The air had an indefinable smell of dew and of very newly born morning. The tall, ornate Tudor chimneys of the house stood out gauntly against a brightening sky, and as Stephen crept into the small herb garden, one tentative bird had already begun singing—but his voice was still rather husky from sleep. She stood there and shivered in her heavy coat; the long night of vigil had devitalized her. She was sometimes like this now—she would shiver at the least provocation, the least sign of fatigue, for her splendid physical strength was giving, worn out by its own insistence.

She dragged the coat more closely around her, and stared at the house which was reddening with sunrise. Her heart beat anxiously, fearfully even, as though in some painful anticipation of she knew not what—every window was dark except one or two that were fired by the sunrise. How long she stood there she never knew, it might have been moments, it might have been a lifetime; and then suddenly there was something that moved—the little oak door that led into that garden. It moved cautiously, opening inch by inch, until at last it was standing wide open, and Stephen saw a man and a woman who turned to clasp as though neither of them could endure to be parted from the arms of the other; and as they clung there together and kissed, they swayed unsteadily—drunk with loving.

Then, as sometimes happens in moments of great anguish, Stephen could only remember the grotesque. She could only remember a plump-bosomed housemaid in the arms of a coarsely amorous footman, and she laughed and she laughed like a creature demented—laughed and laughed until she must gasp for breath and spit blood from her tongue, which had somehow got bitten in her efforts to stop her hysterical laughing; and some of the blood remained on her chin, jerked there by that agonized laughter.

Pale as death, Roger Antrim stared out into the garden, and his tiny moustache looked quite black—like an ink stain smeared above his tremulous mouth by some careless, schoolboy finger.

And now Angela's voice came to Stephen, but faintly. She was saying something—what was she saying? It sounded absurdly as though it were a prayer—'Christ!' Then sharply—razor-sharp it sounded as it cut through the air: '*You*, Stephen!'

The laughter died abruptly away, as Stephen turned and walked out of the garden and down the short drive that led to the gates of The Grange, where the motor was waiting. Her face was a mask, quite without expression. She moved stiffly, yet with a curious precision; and she swung up the handle and started the powerful engine without any apparent effort.

She drove at great speed but with accurate judgment, for now her mind felt as clear as spring water, and yet there were strange little gaps in her mind—she had not the least idea where she was going. Every road for miles around Upton was familiar, yet she had not the least idea where she was going. Nor did she know how long she drove, nor when she stopped to procure fresh petrol. The sun rose high and hot in the heavens; it beat down on her without warming her coldness, for always she had the sense of a dead thing that lay close against her heart and oppressed it. A corpse—she was carrying a corpse about with her. Was it the corpse of her love for Angela? If so that love was more terrible dead—oh, far more terrible dead than living.

The first stars were shining, but as yet very faintly, when she found herself driving through the gates of Morton. Heard Puddle's voice calling: 'Wait a minute. Stop, Stephen!' Saw Puddle barring her way in the drive, a tiny yet dauntless figure.

She pulled up with a jerk: 'What's the matter? What is it?'

'Where have you been?'

'I—don't know, Puddle.'

But Puddle had clambered in beside her: 'Listen, Stephen,' and now she was talking very fast, 'listen, Stephen—is it—is it Angela Crossby? It is. I can see the thing in your face. My God, what's that woman done to you, Stephen?'

Then Stephen, in spite of the corpse against her heart, or perhaps because of it, defended the woman: 'She's done nothing at all—it was all my fault, but you wouldn't understand—I got very angry and then I laughed and couldn't stop laughing—' Steady—go steady! She was telling too much: 'No—it wasn't that exactly. Oh, you know my vile temper, it always goes off at half-cock for nothing. Well, then I just drove round and round the country until I cooled down. I'm sorry, Puddle, I ought to have rung up, of course you've been anxious.'

Puddle gripped her arm: 'Stephen, listen, it's your mother—she thinks that you started quite early for Worcester, I lied—I've been nearly distracted, child. If you hadn't come soon, I'd have had to tell her that I didn't know where you were. You must never, *never* go off without a word like this again—But I do understand, oh, I do indeed, Stephen.'

But Stephen shook her head: 'No, my dear, you couldn't—and I'd rather not tell you, Puddle.'

'Some day you must tell me,' said Puddle, 'because—well, because I do understand, Stephen.'

4

That night the weight against Stephen's heart, with its icy coldness, melted; and it flowed out in such a torrent of grief that she could not stand up against that torrent, so that drowning though she was she found pen and paper, and she wrote to Angela Crossby.

What a letter! All the pent-up passion of months, all the terrible, rending, destructive frustrations must burst from her heart: 'Love me, only love me the way I love you. Angela, for God's sake, try to love me a little—don't throw me away, because if you do I'm utterly finished. You know how I love you, with my soul and my body; if it's wrong, grotesque, unholy—have pity. I'll be humble. Oh, my darling, I am humble now; I'm just a poor, heart-broken freak of a creature who loves you and needs you much more than its life, because life's worse than death, ten times worse without you. I'm some awful mistake—God's mistake*—I don't know if there are any more like me, I pray not for their sakes, because it's pure hell. But oh, my dear, whatever I am, I just love you and love you. I thought it was dead, but it wasn't. It's alive—so terribly alive to-night in my bedroom. . . .' And so it went on for page after page.

But never a word about Roger Antrim and what she had seen that morning in the garden. Some fine instinct of utterly selfless protection towards this woman had managed to survive all the anguish and all the madness of that day. The letter was a terrible indictment against Stephen, a complete vindication of Angela Crossby.

5

Angela went to her husband's study, and she stood before him utterly shaken, utterly appalled at what she would do, yet utterly and ruthlessly determined to do it from a primitive instinct of self-preservation. In her ears she could still hear that terrible laughter—that uncanny, hysterical, agonized laughter. Stephen was mad, and God only knew what she might do or say in a moment of madness, and then—but she dared not look into the future. Cringing in spirit and trembling in body, she forgot the girl's faithful and loyal devotion, her will to forgive, her desire to protect, so clearly set forth in that pitiful letter.

She said: 'Ralph, I want to ask your advice. I'm in an awful mess—it's Stephen Gordon. You think I've been carrying on with Roger—good Lord, if you only knew what I've endured these last few months! I have seen a great deal of Roger, I admit—quite innocently of course—still, all the same, I've seen him—I thought it would show her that I'm not—that I'm not—' For one moment her voice seemed about to fail her, then she went on quite firmly: 'that I'm not a pervert; that I'm not that sort of degenerate creature.'*

He sprang up: 'What?' he bellowed.

'Yes, I know, it's too awful. I ought to have asked your advice about it, but I really did like the girl just at first, and after that, well—I set out to reform her. Oh, I know I've been crazy, worse than crazy if you like; it was hopeless right from the very beginning. If I'd only known more about that sort of thing I'd have come to you at once, but I'd never met it. She was our neighbour too, which made it more awkward, and not only that—her position in the county—oh, Ralph, you *must* help me, I'm completely bewildered. How on earth does one answer this sort of thing? It's quite mad—I believe the girl's half mad herself.'

And she handed him Stephen's letter.

He read it slowly, and as he did so his weak little eyes grew literally scarlet—puffy and scarlet all over their lids, and when he had finished reading that letter he turned and spat on the ground. Then Ralph's language became a thing to forget; every filthy invective learnt in the slums of his youth and later on in the workshops, he hurled against Stephen and all her kind. He called down the wrath of the Lord upon them. He deplored the non-existence of the stake, and racked his brains for indecent tortures. And finally: 'I'll answer this letter, yes, by God I will! You leave her to me, I know how I'm going to answer this letter!'

Angela asked him, and now her voice shook: 'Ralph, what will you do to her—to Stephen?'

He laughed loudly: 'I'll hound her out of the county before I've done—and with luck out of England; the same as I'd hound you out if I thought that there'd ever been anything between you two women. It's damned lucky for you that she wrote this letter, damned lucky, otherwise I might have my suspicions. You've got off this time, but don't try your reforming again—you're not cut out to be a reformer. If there's any of that Lamb of God stuff* wanted I'll see to it myself and don't you forget it!' He slipped the letter into his pocket, 'I'll see to it myself next time—with an axe!'

Angela turned and went out of the study with bowed head. She was saved through this great betrayal, yet most strangely bitter she found her salvation, and most shameful the price she had paid for her safety. So, greatly daring, she went to her desk and with trembling fingers took a sheet of paper. Then she wrote in her large, rather childish handwriting: 'Stephen—when you know what I've done, forgive me.'

CHAPTER 27

I

TWO days later Anna Gordon sent for her daughter. Stephen found her sitting quite still in that vast drawing-room of hers, which as always smelt faintly of orris-root, beeswax and violets. Her thin, white hands were folded in her lap, closely folded over a couple of letters; and it seemed to Stephen that all of a sudden she saw in her mother a very old woman—a very old woman with terrible eyes, pitiless, hard and deeply accusing, so that she could but shrink from their gaze, since they were the eyes of her mother.

Anna said: 'Lock the door, then come and stand here.'

In absolute silence Stephen obeyed her. Thus it was that those two confronted each other, flesh of flesh,* blood of blood, they confronted each other across the wide gulf set between them.

Then Anna handed her daughter a letter: 'Read this,' she said briefly.

And Stephen read:

DEAR LADY ANNA,

With deep repugnance I take up my pen, for certain things won't bear thinking about, much less being written. But I feel that I owe you some explanation of my reasons for having come to the decision that I cannot permit your daughter to enter my house again, or my wife to visit Morton. I enclose a copy of your daughter's letter to my wife, which I feel is sufficiently clear to make it unnecessary for me to write further, except to add that my wife is returning the two costly presents given her by Miss Gordon.

I remain, Yours very truly,
RALPH CROSSBY*

Stephen stood as though turned to stone for a moment, not so much as a muscle twitched; then she handed the letter back to her mother without speaking, and in silence Anna received it. 'Stephen—when you know what I've done, forgive me.' The childish scrawl seemed suddenly on fire, it seemed to scorch Stephen's fingers as she touched it in her pocket—so this was what Angela had done. In a blinding flash the girl saw it all; the miserable weakness, the fear of betrayal, the terror of Ralph and of what he would do should he learn of that guilty night with Roger. Oh, but Angela might have spared her this, this last wound to her loyal and faithful devotion; this last insult to all that was best and most sacred in her love—Angela had feared betrayal at the hands of the creature who loved her!

But now her mother was speaking again: 'And this—read this and tell me if you wrote it, or if that man's lying.' And Stephen must read her own misery jibing at her from those pages in Ralph Crossby's stiff and clerical handwriting.

She looked up: 'Yes, Mother, I wrote it.'

Then Anna began to speak very slowly as though nothing of what she would say must be lost; and that slow, quiet voice was more dreadful than anger: 'All your life I've felt very strangely towards you'; she was saying, 'I've felt a kind of physical repulsion, a desire not to touch or be touched by you—a terrible thing for a mother to feel—it has often made me deeply unhappy. I've often felt that I was being unjust, unnatural—but now I know that my instinct was right; it is you who are unnatural, not I. . . .'

'Mother—stop!'

'It is you who are unnatural, not I. And this thing that you are is a sin against creation. Above all is this thing a sin against the father who bred you, the father whom you dare to resemble. You dare to look like your father, and your face is a living insult to his memory, Stephen. I shall never be able to look at you now without thinking of the deadly insult of your face and your body to the memory of the father who bred you. I can only thank God that your father died before he was asked to endure this great shame. As for you, I would rather see you dead at my feet than standing before me with this thing upon you—this unspeakable outrage that you call love in that letter which you don't deny having written. In that letter you say things that may only be said between man and woman, and coming from you they are vile and filthy words of corruption—against nature, against God who created nature. My gorge rises;* you have made me feel physically sick—'

'Mother—you don't know what you're saying—you're my mother—'

'Yes, I am your mother, but for all that, you seem to me like a scourge. I ask myself what I have ever done to be dragged down into the depths by my daughter. And your father—what had he ever done? And you have presumed to use the word love in connection with this—with these lusts of your body; these unnatural cravings of your unbalanced mind and undisciplined body—you have used that word. I have loved—do you hear? I have loved your father, and your father loved me. That was *love*.'

Then, suddenly, Stephen knew that unless she could, indeed, drop dead at the feet of this woman in whose womb she had quickened, there was one thing that she dared not let pass unchallenged, and that was this terrible slur upon her love. And all that was in her rose up to refute it; to protect her love from such unbearable soiling. It was part of herself, and unless she could save it, she could not save herself any more. She must stand or fall by the courage of that love to proclaim its right to toleration.

She held up her hand, commanding silence; commanding that slow, quiet voice to cease speaking, and she said: 'As my father loved you, I loved. As a man loves a woman, that was how I loved—protectively, like my father. I wanted to give all I had in me to give. It made me feel terribly strong . . . and gentle. It was good, good, *good**—I'd have laid down my life a thousand times over for Angela Crossby. If I could have, I'd have married her and brought her home—I wanted to bring her home here to Morton. If I loved her the way a man loves a woman, it's because I can't feel that I am a woman. All my life I've never felt like a woman, and you know it—you say you've always disliked me, that you've always felt a strange physical repulsion. . . . I don't know what I am; no one's ever told me that I'm different and yet I know that I'm different—that's why, I suppose, you've felt as you have done. And for that I forgive you, though whatever it is, it was you and my father who made this body—but what I will never forgive is your daring to try and make me ashamed of my love. I'm not ashamed of it, there's no shame in me.' And now she was stammering a little wildly, 'Good and—and fine it was,' she stammered, 'the best part of myself—I gave all and I asked nothing in return—I just went on hopelessly loving—' she broke off, she was shaking from head to foot, and Anna's cold voice fell like icy water on that angry and sorely tormented spirit.

'You have spoken, Stephen. I don't think there's much more that needs to be said between us except this, we two cannot live together at Morton—not now, because I might grow to hate you. Yes, although you're my child, I might grow to hate you. The same roof mustn't shelter us both any more; one of us must go—which of us shall it be?' And she looked at Stephen and waited.

Morton! They could not both live at Morton. Something seemed to catch hold of the girl's heart and twist it. She stared at her mother, aghast for a moment, while Anna stared back—she was waiting for her answer.

But quite suddenly Stephen found her manhood and she said: 'I understand. I'll leave Morton.'

Then Anna made her daughter sit down beside her, while she talked of how this thing might be accomplished in a way that would cause the least possible scandal: 'For the sake of your father's honourable name, I must ask you to help me, Stephen.' It was better, she said, that Stephen should take Puddle with her, if Puddle would consent to go. They might live in London or somewhere abroad, on the pretext that Stephen wished to study. From time to time Stephen would come back to Morton and visit her mother, and during those visits, they two would take care to be seen together for appearance sake, for the sake of her father. She could take from Morton whatever she needed, the horses, and anything else she wished. Certain of the rent-rolls* would be paid over to her, should her own income prove insufficient. All things must be done in a way that was seemly—no undue haste, no suspicion of a breach between mother and daughter: 'For the sake of your father I ask this of you, not for your sake or mine, but for his. Do you consent to this, Stephen?'

And Stephen answered: 'Yes, I consent.'

Then Anna said: 'I'd like you to leave me now—I feel tired and I want to be alone for a little—but presently I shall send for Puddle to discuss her living with you in the future.'

So Stephen got up, and she went away, leaving Anna Gordon alone.

2

As though drawn there by some strong natal instinct, Stephen went straight to her father's study; and she sat in the old arm-chair that had survived him; then she buried her face in her hands.

All the loneliness that had gone before was as nothing to this new loneliness of spirit. An immense desolation swept down upon her, an immense need to cry out and claim understanding for herself, an immense need to find an answer to the riddle of her unwanted being. All around her were grey and crumbling ruins, and under those ruins her love lay bleeding; shamefully wounded by Angela Crossby, shamefully soiled and defiled by her mother—a piteous, suffering, defenceless thing, it lay bleeding under the ruins.

She felt blind when she tried to look into the future, stupefied when she tried to look back on the past. She must go—she was going away from Morton: 'From Morton—I'm going away from Morton,' the words thudded drearily in her brain: 'I'm going away from Morton.'

The grave, comely house would not know her any more, nor the garden where she had heard the cuckoo with the dawning understanding of a child, nor the lakes where she had kissed Angela Crossby for the first time—full on the lips as a lover. The good, sweet-smelling meadows with their placid cattle, she was going to leave them; and the hills that protected poor, unhappy lovers—the merciful hills; and the lanes with their sleepy dog-roses at evening; and the little, old township of Upton-on-Severn with its battle-scarred church and its yellowish river; that was where she had first seen Angela Crossby. . . .

The spring would come sweeping across Castle Morton, bringing strong, clean winds to the open common. The spring would come sweeping across the whole valley, from the Cotswold Hills right up to the Malverns; bringing daffodils by their hundreds and thousands, bringing bluebells to the beech wood down by the lakes, bringing cygnets for Peter the swan to protect; bringing sunshine to warm the old bricks of the house—but she would not be there any more in the spring. In summer the roses would not be her roses, nor the luminous carpet of leaves in the autumn, nor the beautiful winter forms of the beech trees: 'And on evenings in winter these lakes are quite frozen, and the ice looks like slabs of gold in the sunset, when you and I come and stand here in the winter. . . .' No, no, not that memory, it was too much—'when you and I come and stand here in the winter. . . .'

Getting up, she wandered about the room, touching its kind and familiar objects; stroking the desk, examining a pen, grown rusty from long disuse as it lay there; then she opened a little drawer in the desk and took out the key of her father's locked book-case.* Her mother had told her to take what she pleased—she would take one or two of her father's books. She had never examined this special book-case, and she could not have told why she suddenly did so. As she slipped the key into the lock and turned it, the action seemed curiously automatic.*

She began to take out the volumes slowly and with listless fingers, scarcely glancing at their titles. It gave her something to do, that was all—she thought that she was trying to distract her attention. Then she noticed that on a shelf near the bottom was a row of books standing behind the others; the next moment she had one of these in her hand, and was looking at the name of the author: Krafft Ebing*—she had never heard of that author before. All the same she opened the battered old book, then she looked more closely, for there on its margins were notes in her father's small, scholarly hand and she saw that her own name appeared in those notes—She began to read, sitting down rather abruptly. For a long time she read; then went back to the bookcase and got out another of those volumes, and another. . . . The sun was now setting behind the hills; the garden was growing dusky with shadows. In the study there was little light left to read by, so that she must take her book to the window and must bend her face closer over the page; but still she read on and on in the dusk.

Then suddenly she had got to her feet and was talking aloud—she was talking to her father: 'You knew! All the time you knew this thing, but because of your pity you wouldn't tell me. Oh, Father—and there are so many of us—thousands of miserable, unwanted people, who have no right to love, no right to compassion because they're maimed, hideously maimed and ugly—God's cruel; He let us get flawed in the making.'

And then, before she knew what she was doing, she had found her father's old, well-worn Bible. There she stood demanding a sign from heaven—nothing less than a sign from heaven she demanded. The Bible fell open near the beginning. She read: 'And the Lord set a mark upon Cain. . . .'*

Then Stephen hurled the Bible away, and she sank down completely hopeless and beaten, rocking her body backwards and forwards with a kind of abrupt yet methodical rhythm: 'And the Lord set a mark upon Cain, upon Cain. . . .' she was rocking now in rhythm to those words, 'And the Lord set a mark upon Cain—upon Cain—upon Cain. And the Lord set a mark upon Cain. . . .'

That was how Puddle came in and found her, and Puddle said: 'Where you go, I go, Stephen.* All that you're suffering at this moment I've suffered. It was when I was very young like you—but I still remember.'

Stephen looked up with bewildered eyes: 'Would you go with Cain whom God marked?' she said slowly, for she had not understood

Puddle's meaning, so she asked her once more: 'Would you go with Cain?'

Puddle put an arm round Stephen's bowed shoulders, and she said: 'You've got work to do*—come and do it! Why, just because you are what you are, you may actually find that you've got an advantage. You may write with a curious double insight—write both men and women from a personal knowledge. Nothing's completely misplaced or wasted, I'm sure of that—and we're all part of nature. Some day the world will recognize this, but meanwhile there's plenty of work that's waiting. For the sake of all the others who are like you, but less strong and less gifted perhaps, many of them, it's up to you to have the courage to make good, and I'm here to help you to do it, Stephen.'*

BOOK THREE*

CHAPTER 28

I

A PALE glint of sunshine devoid of all warmth lay over the wide expanse of the river, touching the funnel of a passing tug that tore at the water like a clumsy harrow;* but a field of water is not for the sowing and the river closed back in the wake of the tug, deftly obliterating all traces of its noisy and foolish passing. The trees along the Chelsea Embankment* bent and creaked in a sharp March wind. The wind was urging the sap in their branches to flow with a more determined purpose, but the skin of their bodies was blackened and soot clogged so that when touched it left soot on the fingers, and knowing this they were always disheartened and therefore a little slow to respond to the urge of the wind—they were city trees which are always somewhat disheartened. Away to the right against a toneless sky stood the tall factory chimneys beloved of young artists—especially those whose skill is not great, for few can go wrong over factory chimneys—while across the stream Battersea Park still looked misty as though barely convalescent from fog.

In her large, long, rather low-ceilinged study whose casement windows looked over the river, sat Stephen with her feet stretched out to the fire and her hands thrust into her jacket pockets. Her eyelids drooped, she was all but asleep, although it was early afternoon. She had worked through the night, a deplorable habit and one of which Puddle quite rightly disapproved, but when the spirit of work was on her it was useless to argue with Stephen.

Puddle looked up from her embroidery frame and pushed her spectacles on to her forehead the better to see the drowsy Stephen, for Puddle's eyes had grown very long-sighted so that the room looked blurred through her glasses.

She thought: 'Yes, she's changed a good deal in these two years—' then she sighed half in sadness and half in contentment, 'All the same she is making good,' thought Puddle, remembering with a quick thrill of pride that the long-limbed creature who lounged by the fire had suddenly sprung into something like fame thanks to a fine first novel.

Stephen yawned, and readjusting her spectacles Puddle resumed her wool-work.

It was true that the two long years of exile had left their traces on Stephen's face; it had grown much thinner and more determined, some might have said that the face had hardened, for the mouth was less ardent and much less gentle, and the lips now drooped at the corners. The strong rather massive line of the jaw looked aggressive these days by reason of its thinness. Faint furrows had come between the thick brows and faint shadows showed at times under the eyes; the eyes themselves were the eyes of a writer, always a little tired in expression. Her complexion was paler than it had been in the past, it had lost the look of wind and sunshine—the open-air look—and the fingers of the hand that slowly emerged from her jacket pocket were heavily stained with nicotine—she was now a voracious smoker.* Her hair was quite short. In a mood of defiance she had suddenly walked off to the barber's one morning and had made him crop it close like a man's. And mightily did this fashion become her, for now the fine shape of her head was unmarred by the stiff clumpy plait in the nape of her neck.* Released from the torment imposed upon it, the thick auburn hair could breathe and wave freely, and Stephen had grown fond and proud of her hair—a hundred strokes must it have with the brush every night until it looked burnished. Sir Philip also had been proud of his hair in the days of his youthful manhood.

Stephen's life in London had been one long endeavour, for work to her had become a narcotic. Puddle it was who had found the flat with the casement windows that looked on the river, and Puddle it was who now kept the accounts, paid the rent, settled bills and managed the servants; all these details Stephen calmly ignored and the faithful Puddle allowed her to do so. Like an ageing and anxious Vestal Virgin* she tended the holy fire of inspiration, feeding the flame with suitable food—good grilled meat, light puddings and much fresh fruit, varied by little painstaking surprises from Jackson's or Fortnum and Mason.* For Stephen's appetite was not what it had been in the vigorous days of Morton; now there were times when she could not eat, or if she must eat she did so protesting, fidgeting to go back to her desk. At such times Puddle would steal into the study with a tin of Brand's Essence*—she had even been known to feed the recalcitrant author piecemeal, until Stephen must laugh and gobble up the jelly for the sake of getting on with her writing.

Only one duty apart from her work had Stephen never for a moment neglected, and that was the care and the welfare of Raftery. The cob had been sold, and her father's chestnut she had given away to Colonel Antrim, who had sworn not to let the horse out of his hands for the sake of his lifelong friend, Sir Philip—but Raftery she had brought up to London. She herself had found and rented his stable with comfortable rooms above for Jim, the groom she had taken from Morton. Every morning she rode very early in the Park,* which seemed a futile and dreary business, but now only thus could the horse and his owner contrive to be together for a little. Sometimes she fancied that Raftery sighed as she cantered him round and round the Row, and then she would stoop down and speak to him softly:

'My Raftery, I know, it's not Castle Morton or the hills or the big, green Severn Valley—but I love you.'

And because he had understood her he would throw up his head and begin to prance sideways, pretending that he still felt very youthful, pretending that he was wild with delight at the prospect of cantering round the Row. But after a while these two sorry exiles would droop and move forward without much spirit. Each in a separate way would divine the ache in the other, the ache that was Morton, so that Stephen would cease to urge the beast forward, and Raftery would cease to pretend to Stephen. But when twice a year at her mother's request, Stephen must go back to visit her home, then Raftery went too, and his joy was immense when he felt the good springy turf beneath him, when he sighted the red brick stables of Morton, when he rolled in the straw of his large, airy loose-box. The years would seem to slip from his shoulders, he grew sleeker, he would look like a five-year-old—yet to Stephen these visits of theirs were anguish because of her love for Morton. She would feel like a stranger within the gates, an unwanted stranger there only on sufferance. It would seem to her that the old house withdrew itself from her love very gravely and sadly, that its windows no longer beckoned, invited: 'Come home, come home, come inside quickly, Stephen!' And she would not dare to proffer her love, which would burden her heart to breaking.

She must now pay many calls with her mother, must attend all the formal social functions—this for the sake of appearances, lest the neighbours should guess the breach between them. She must keep up the fiction that she found in a city the stimulus necessary to her work, she who was filled with a hungry longing for the green of the hills, for the air of wide spaces, for the mornings and the noontides and the evenings of Morton. All these things she must do for the sake of her father, aye, and for the sake of Morton.

On her first visit home Anna had said very quietly one day: 'There's something, Stephen, that I think I ought to tell you perhaps, though it's painful to me to reopen the subject. There has been no scandal—that man held his tongue—you'll be glad to know this because of your father. And Stephen—the Crossbys have sold The Grange and gone to America, I believe—' she had stopped abruptly, not looking at Stephen, who had nodded, unable to answer.

So now there were quite different folk at The Grange, folk very much more to the taste of the county—Admiral Carson and his apple-cheeked wife who, childless herself, adored Mothers' Meetings.* Stephen must sometimes go to The Grange with Anna, who liked the Carsons. Very grave and aloof had Stephen become; too reserved, too self-assured, thought her neighbours. They supposed that success had gone to her head, for no one was now allowed to divine the terrible shyness that made social intercourse such a miserable torment. Life had already taught Stephen one thing, and that was that never must human beings be allowed to suspect that a creature fears them. The fear of the one is a spur to the many, for the primitive hunting instinct dies hard—it is better to face a hostile world than to turn one's back for a moment.

But at least she was spared meeting Roger Antrim, and for this she was most profoundly thankful. Roger had gone with his regiment to Malta,* so that they two did not see each other. Violet was married and living in London in the 'perfect duck of a house in Belgravia.' From time to time she would blow in on Stephen, but not often, because she was very much married with one baby already and another on the way. She was somewhat subdued and much less maternal than she had been when first she met Alec.

If Anna was proud of her daughter's achievement she said nothing beyond the very few words that must of necessity be spoken: 'I'm so glad your book has succeeded, Stephen.'*

'Thank you, mother—'

Then as always these two fell silent. Those long and eloquent silences of theirs were now of almost daily occurrence when they found themselves together. Nor could they look each other in the eyes any more, their eyes were for ever shifting, and sometimes Anna's pale cheeks would flush very slightly when she was alone with Stephen—perhaps at her thoughts.

And Stephen would think: 'It's because she can't help remembering.'

For the most part, however, they shunned all contact by common consent, except when in public. And this studied avoidance tore at their nerves; they were now well-nigh obsessed by each other, for ever secretly laying their plans in order to avoid a meeting. Thus it was that these obligatory visits to Morton were a pretty bad strain on Stephen. She would get back to London unable to sleep, unable to eat, unable to write, and with such a despairing and sickening heartache for the grave old house the moment she had left it, that Puddle would have to be very severe in order to pull her together.

'I'm ashamed of you, Stephen; what's happened to your courage? You don't deserve your phenomenal success; if you go on like this, God help the new book. I suppose you're going to be a one-book author!'

Scowling darkly, Stephen would go to her desk—she had no wish to be a one-book author.

2

Yet as everything comes as grist to the mill of those who are destined from birth to be writers—poverty or riches, good or evil, gladness or sorrow, all grist to the mill—so the pain of Morton burning down to the spirit in Stephen had kindled a bright, hot flame, and all that she had written she had written by its light, seeing exceedingly clearly. As though in a kind of self-preservation, her mind had turned to quite simple people, humble people sprung from the soil, from the same kind soil that had nurtured Morton. None of her own strange emotions had touched them, and yet they were part of her own emotions; a part of her longing for simplicity and peace, a part of her curious craving for the normal. And although at this time Stephen did not know it, their happiness had sprung from her moments of joy; their sorrows from the sorrow she had known and still knew; their frustrations from her own bitter emptiness; their fulfilments from her longing to be fulfilled. These people had drawn life and strength from their creator. Like infants they had sucked at her breasts of inspiration, and drawn from them blood, waxing wonderfully strong; demanding, compelling thereby recognition. For surely thus only are fine books written, they must somehow partake of the miracle of blood—the strange and terrible miracle of blood, the giver of life, the purifier, the great final expiation.*

3

But one thing there was that Puddle still feared, and this was the girl's desire for isolation. To her it appeared like a weakness in Stephen; she divined the bruised humility of spirit that now underlay this desire for isolation, and she did her best to frustrate it. It was Puddle who had forced the embarrassed Stephen to let in the Press photographers, and Puddle it was who had given the details for the captions that were to appear with the pictures: 'If you choose to behave like a hermit crab I shall use my own judgment about what I say!'

'I don't care a tinker's darn* what you say! Now leave me in peace, do, Puddle.'

It was Puddle who answered the telephone calls: 'I'm afraid Miss Gordon will be busy working—what name did you say? Oh, *The Literary Monthly*!* I see—well suppose you come on Wednesday.' And on Wednesday morning there was old Puddle waiting to waylay the anxious young man who had been commanded to dig up some copy about the new novelist, Stephen Gordon. Then Puddle had smiled at the anxious young man and had shepherded him into her own little sanctum, and had given him a comfortable chair, and had stirred the fire the better to warm him. And the young man had noticed her charming smile and had thought how kind was this ageing woman, and how damned hard it was to go tramping the streets in quest of erratic, unsociable authors.

Puddle had said, still smiling kindly: 'I'd hate you to go back without your copy, but Miss Gordon's been working overtime lately, I dare not disturb her, you don't mind, do you? Now if you could possibly make shift* with me—I really do know a great deal about her; as a matter of fact I'm her ex-governess, so I really do know quite a lot about her.'

Out had come notebook and copying pencil; it was easy to talk to this sympathetic woman: 'Well, if you could give me some interesting details—say, her taste in books and her recreations, I'd be awfully grateful. She hunts, I believe?'

'Oh, not now!'

'I see—well then, she *did* hunt. And wasn't her father Sir Philip Gordon who had a place down in Worcestershire and was killed by a falling tree or something? What kind of pupil did you find Miss Gordon? I'll send her my notes when I've worked them up, but I really would like to see her, you know.' Then being a fairly sagacious young man: 'I've just read *The Furrow*,* it's a wonderful book!'

Puddle talked glibly while the young man scribbled, and when at last he was just about going she let him out on to the balcony from which he could look into Stephen's study.

'There she is at her desk! What more could you ask?' she said triumphantly, pointing to Stephen, whose hair was literally standing on end, as is sometimes the way with youthful authors. She even managed, occasionally, to make Stephen see the journalists herself.

4

Stephen got up, stretched, and went to the window. The sun had retreated behind the clouds; a kind of brown twilight hung over the Embankment, for the wind had now dropped and a fog was threatening. The discouragement common to all fine writers was upon her, she was hating what she had written. Last night's work seemed inadequate and unworthy; she decided to put a blue pencil through it and to rewrite the chapter from start to finish. She began to give way to a species of panic; her new book would be a ludicrous failure, she felt it, she would never again write a novel possessing the quality of *The Furrow*. *The Furrow* had been the result of shock to which she had, strangely enough, reacted by a kind of unnatural mental vigour. But now she could not react any more, her brain felt like over-stretched elastic, it would not spring back, it was limp, unresponsive. And then there was something else that distracted, something she was longing to put into words yet that shamed her so that it held her tongue-tied. She lit a cigarette and when it was finished found another and kindled it at the stump.

'Stop embroidering that curtain, for God's sake, Puddle. I simply can't stand the sound of your needle; it makes a booming noise like a drum every time you prod that tightly stretched linen.'

Puddle looked up: 'You're smoking too much.'

'I dare say I am. I can't write any more.'

'Since when?'

'Ever since I began this new book.'

'Don't be such a fool!'

'But it's God's truth, I tell you—I feel flat, it's a kind of spiritual dryness. This new book is going to be a failure, sometimes I think I'd better destroy it.' She began to pace up and down the room, dull-eyed yet tense as a tightly drawn bowstring.

'This comes of working all night,' Puddle murmured.

'I must work when the spirit moves me,'* snapped Stephen.

Puddle put aside her wool-work embroidery. She was not much moved by this sudden depression, she had grown quite accustomed to these literary moods, yet she looked a little more closely at Stephen and something that she saw in her face disturbed her.

'You look tired to death; why not lie down and rest?'

'Rot! I want to work.'

'You're not fit to work. You look all on edge, somehow. What's the matter with you?' And then very gently: 'Stephen, come here and sit down by me, please, I must know what's the matter.'

Stephen obeyed as though once again they two were back in the old Morton schoolroom, then she suddenly buried her face in her hands: 'I don't want to tell you—why must I, Puddle?'

'Because,' said Puddle, 'I've a right to know; your career's very dear to me, Stephen.'

Then suddenly Stephen could not resist the blessed relief of confiding in Puddle once more, of taking this great new trouble to the faithful and wise little grey-haired woman whose hand had been stretched out to save in the past. Perhaps yet again that hand might find the strength that was needful to save her.

Not looking at Puddle, she began to talk quickly: 'There's something I've been wanting to tell you, Puddle—it's about my work, there's something wrong with it. I mean that my work could be much more vital; I feel it, I know it, I'm holding it back in some way, there's something I'm always missing. Even in *The Furrow* I feel I missed something—I know it was fine, but it wasn't complete because I'm not complete and I never shall be—can't you understand? I'm not complete. . . .' She paused, unable to find the words she wanted, then blundered on again blindly: 'There's a great chunk of life that I've never known, and I want to know it, I ought to know it if I'm to become a really fine writer. There's the greatest thing perhaps in the world, and I've missed it—that's what's so awful, Puddle, to know that it exists everywhere, all round me, to be constantly near it yet always held back—to feel that the poorest people in the streets, the most ignorant people, know more than I do. And I dare to take up my pen and write, knowing less than these poor men and women in the street! Why haven't I got a right to it, Puddle? Can't you understand that I'm strong and young, so that sometimes this thing that I'm missing torments me, so that I can't concentrate on my work any more? Puddle, help me—you were young yourself once.'

'Yes, Stephen—a long time ago I was young. . . .'

'But can't you remember back for my sake?' And now her voice sounded almost angry in her distress: 'It's unfair, it's unjust. Why should I live in this great isolation of spirit and body—why should I, why? Why have I been afflicted with a body that must never be indulged, that must always be repressed until it grows stronger much than my spirit because of this unnatural repression?* What have I done to be so cursed? And now it's attacking my holy of holies, my work—I shall never be a great writer because of my maimed and insufferable body—' She fell silent, suddenly shy and ashamed, too much ashamed to go on speaking.

And there sat Puddle as pale as death and as speechless, having no comfort to offer—no comfort, that is, that she dared to offer—while all her fine theories about making good for the sake of those others; being noble, courageous, patient, honourable, physically pure, enduring because it was right to endure, the terrible birthright of the invert—all Puddle's fine theories lay strewn around her like the ruins of some false and flimsy temple, and she saw at that moment but one thing clearly—true genius in chains, in the chains of the flesh, a fine spirit subject to physical bondage. And as once before she had argued with God on behalf of this sorely afflicted creature, so now she inwardly cried yet again to the Maker whose will had created Stephen: 'Thine hands have made me and fashioned me together round about; yet Thou dost destroy me.'* Then into her heart crept a bitterness very hard to endure: 'Yet Thou dost destroy me—'

Stephen looked up and saw her face: 'Never mind,' she said sharply, 'it's all right, Puddle—forget it!'

But Puddle's eyes filled with tears, and seeing this, Stephen went to her desk. Sitting down she groped for her manuscript: 'I'm going to turn you out now, I must work. Don't wait for me if I'm late for dinner.'

Very humbly Puddle crept out of the study.

CHAPTER 29

I

SOON after the New Year, nine months later, Stephen's second novel was published. It failed to create the sensation that the first had created, there was something disappointing about it. One critic described this as: 'A lack of grip,' and his criticism, on the whole, was a fair one. However, the Press was disposed to be kind, remembering the merits of *The Furrow*.

But the heart of the Author knoweth its own sorrows* and is seldom responsive to false consolation, so that when Puddle said: 'Never mind, Stephen, you can't expect every book to be *The Furrow*—and this one is full of literary merit,' Stephen replied as she turned away: 'I was writing a novel, my dear, not an essay.'

After this they did not discuss it any more, for what was the use of fruitless discussion? Stephen knew well and Puddle knew also that this book fell far short of its author's powers. Then suddenly, that spring, Raftery went very lame, and everything else was forgotten.

Raftery was aged, he was now eighteen, so that lameness in him was not easy of healing. His life in a city had tried him sorely, he had missed the light, airy stables of Morton, and the cruel-hard bed that lay under the tan of the Row* had jarred his legs badly.

The vet shook his head and looked very grave: 'He's an aged horse, you know, and of course in his youth you hunted him pretty freely—it all counts. Every one comes to the end of their tether, Miss Gordon. Yes, at times I'm afraid it is painful.' Then seeing Stephen's face: 'I'm awfully sorry not to give a more cheerful diagnosis.'

Other experts arrived. Every good vet in London was consulted, including Professor Hobday.* No cure, no cure, it was always the same, and at times, they told Stephen, the old horse suffered; but this she well knew—she had seen the sweat break out darkly on Raftery's shoulders.

So one morning she went into Raftery's loose-box, and she sent the groom Jim out of the stable, and she laid her cheek against the beast's neck, while he turned his head and began to nuzzle. Then they looked at each other very quietly and gravely, and in Raftery's eyes was a strange, new expression—a kind of half-anxious, protesting wonder at this thing men call pain: 'What is it, Stephen?'

She answered, forcing back her hot tears: 'Perhaps, for you, the beginning, Raftery. . . .'

After awhile she went to his manger and let the fodder slip through her fingers; but he would not eat, not even to please her, so she called the groom back and ordered some gruel. Very gently she readjusted the clothing that had slipped to one side, first the under-blanket then the smart blue rug that was braided in red—red and blue, the old stable colours of Morton.

The groom Jim, now a thick-set stalwart young man, stared at her with sorrowful understanding, but he did not speak; he was almost as dumb as the beasts whom his life had been passed in tending—even dumber, perhaps, for his language consisted of words, having no small sounds and small movements such as Raftery used when he spoke with Stephen, and which meant so much more than words.

She said: 'I'm going now to the station to order a horse-box for to-morrow, I'll let you know the time we start, later. And wrap him up well; put on plenty of clothing for the journey, please, he mustn't feel cold.'

The man nodded. She had not told him their destination, but he knew it already; it was Morton. Then the great clumsy fellow must pretend to be busy with a truss of fresh straw for the horse's bedding, because his face had turned a deep crimson, because his coarse lips were actually trembling—and this was not really so very strange, for those who served Raftery loved him.

2

Raftery stepped quietly into his horse-box and Jim with great deftness secured the halter, then he touched his cap and hurried away to his third-class compartment, for Stephen herself would travel with Raftery on this last journey back to the fields of Morton. Sitting down on the seat reserved for a groom she opened the little wooden window into the box, whereupon Raftery's muzzle came up and his face looked out of the window. She fondled the soft, grey plush of his muzzle. Presently she took a carrot from her pocket, but the carrot was rather hard now for his teeth, so she bit off small pieces and these she gave him in the palm of her hand; then she watched him eat them uncomfortably, slowly, because he was old, and this seemed so strange, for old age and Raftery went very ill together.

Her mind slipped back and back over the years until it recaptured the coming of Raftery—grey-coated and slender, and his eyes as soft as an Irish morning, and his courage as bright as an Irish sunrise, and his heart as young as the wild, eternally young heart of Ireland. She remembered what they had said to each other. Raftery had said: 'I will carry you bravely, I will serve you all the days of my life.' She had answered: 'I will care for you night and day, Raftery—all the days of your life.' She remembered their first run with hounds together—she a youngster of twelve, he a youngster of five. Great deeds they had done on that day together, at least they had seemed like great deeds to them—she had had a kind of fire in her heart as she galloped astride of Raftery. She remembered her father, his protective back, so broad, so kind, so patiently protective; and towards the end it had stooped a little as though out of kindness it carried a burden. Now she knew whose burden that back had been bearing so that it stooped a little. He had been very proud of the fine Irish horse, very proud of his small and courageous rider: 'Steady, Stephen!' but his eyes had been bright like Raftery's. 'Steady on, Stephen, we're coming to a stiff one!' but once they were over he had turned round and smiled, as he had done in the days when the impudent Collins had stretched his inadequate legs to their utmost to keep up with the pace of the hunters.

Long ago, it all seemed a long time ago. A long road it seemed, leading where? She wondered. Her father had gone away into its shadows, and now after him, limping a little, went Raftery; Raftery with hollows above his eyes and down his grey neck that had once been so firm; Raftery whose splendid white teeth were now yellowed and too feeble to bite up his carrot.

The train jogged and swayed so that once the horse stumbled. Springing up, she stretched out her hand to soothe him. He seemed glad of her hand: 'Don't be frightened, Raftery. Did that hurt you?' Raftery acquainted with pain on the road that led into the shadows.

Presently the hills showed over on the left, but a long way off, and when they came nearer they were suddenly very near on the right, so near that she saw the white houses on them. They looked dark; a kind of still, thoughtful darkness brooded over the hills and their low white houses. It was always so in the late afternoons, for the sun moved across to the wide Wye Valley—it would set on the western side of the hills, over the wide Wye Valley. The smoke from the chimney-stacks bent downwards after rising a little and formed a blue haze, for the air was heavy with spring and dampness. Leaning from the window she could smell the spring, the time of mating, the time of fruition. When the train stopped a minute outside the station she fancied that she heard the singing of birds; very softly it came but the sound was persistent—yes, surely, that was the singing of birds. . . .

3

They took Raftery in an ambulance from Great Malvern in order to spare him the jar of the roads. That night he slept in his own spacious loose-box, and the faithful Jim would not leave him that night; he sat up and watched while Raftery slept in so deep a bed of yellow-gold straw that it all but reached to his knees when standing. A last inarticulate tribute this to the most gallant horse, the most courteous horse that ever stepped out of stable.

But when the sun came up over Bredon, flooding the breadth of the Severn Valley, touching the slopes of the Malvern Hills that stand opposite Bredon across the valley, gilding the old red bricks of Morton and the weather-vane on its quiet stables, Stephen went into her father's study and she loaded his heavy revolver.

Then they led Raftery out and into the morning; they led him with care to the big north paddock and stood him beside the mighty hedge that had set the seal on his youthful valour. Very still he stood with the sun on his flanks, the groom, Jim, holding the bridle.

Stephen said: 'I'm going to send you away, a long way away, and I've never left you except for a little while since you came when I was a child and you were quite young—but I'm going to send you a long way away because of your pain. Raftery, this is death; and beyond, they say, there's no more suffering.' She paused, then spoke in a voice so low that the groom could not hear her: 'Forgive me, Raftery.'

And Raftery stood there looking at Stephen, and his eyes were as soft as an Irish morning, yet as brave as the eyes that looked into his. Then it seemed to Stephen that he had spoken, that Raftery had said: 'Since to me you are God, what have I to forgive you, Stephen?'

She took a step forward and pressed the revolver high up against Raftery's smooth, grey forehead. She fired, and he dropped to the ground like a stone, lying perfectly still by the mighty hedge that had set the seal on his youthful valour.

But now there broke out a great crying and wailing: 'Oh, me! Oh, me! They've been murderin' Raftery! Shame, shame, I says, on the 'and what done it, and 'im no common horse but a Christian. . . .' Then loud sobbing as though some very young child had fallen down and hurt itself badly. And there in a small, creaky, wicker bath-chair sat Williams, being bumped along over the paddock by a youthful niece, who had come to Morton to take care of the old and now feeble couple; for Williams had had his first stroke that Christmas, in addition to which he was almost childish.* God only knew who had told him this thing; the secret had been very carefully guarded by Stephen, who, knowing his love for the horse, had taken every precaution to spare him. Yet now here he was with his face all twisted by the stroke and the sobs that kept on rising. He was trying to lift his half-paralysed hand which kept dropping back on to the arm of the bath-chair; he was trying to get out of the bath-chair and run to where Raftery lay stretched out in the sunshine; he was trying to speak again, but his voice had grown thick so that no one could understand him. Stephen thought that his mind had begun to wander, for now he was surely not screaming 'Raftery' any more, but something that sounded like: 'Master!' and again, 'Oh, Master, Master!'

She said: 'Take him home,' for he did not know her; 'take him home. You'd no business to bring him here at all—it's against my orders. Who told him about it?'

And the young girl answered: 'It seemed 'e just knowed—it was like as though Raftery told 'im. . . .'

Williams looked up with his blurred, anxious eyes. 'Who be you?' he inquired. Then he suddenly smiled through his tears. 'It be good to be seein' you, Master—seems like a long while. . . .' His voice was now clear but exceedingly small, a small, faraway thing. If a doll had spoken, its voice might have sounded very much as the old man's did at that moment.

Stephen bent over him. 'Williams, I'm Stephen—don't you know me? It's Miss Stephen. You must go straight home and get back to bed—it's still rather cold on these early spring mornings—to please me, Williams, you must go straight home. Why, your hands are frozen!'

But Williams shook his head and began to remember. 'Raftery,' he mumbled, 'something's 'appened to Raftery.' And his sobs and his tears broke out with fresh vigour, so that his niece, frightened, tried to stop him.

'Now, uncle, be qui-et I do be-seech 'e! It's so bad for 'e carryin' on in this wise. What will auntie say when she sees 'e all mucked up with weepin', and yer poor nose all red and dir-ty? I'll be takin' 'e 'ome as Miss Stephen 'ere says. Now, uncle dear, do be qui-et!'

She lugged the bath-chair round with a jolt and trundled it, lurching, towards the cottage. All the way back down the big north paddock Williams wept and wailed and tried to get out, but his niece put one hefty young hand on his shoulder; with the other she guided the lurching bath-chair.

Stephen watched them go, then she turned to the groom. 'Bury him here,' she said briefly.*

4

Before she left Morton that same afternoon, she went once more into the large, bare stables. The stables were now completely empty, for Anna had moved her carriage horses to new quarters nearer the coachman's cottage.

Over one loose-box was a warped oak board bearing Collins' stud-book* title, 'Marcus,' in red and blue letters; but the paint was dulled to a ghostly grey by encroaching mildew, while a spider had spun a large, purposeful web across one side of Collins' manger. A cracked, sticky wine bottle lay on the floor; no doubt used at some time for drenching Collins, who had died in a fit of violent colic a few months after Stephen herself had left Morton. On the window-sill of the farthest loose-box stood a curry comb* and a couple of brushes; the comb was being eaten by rust, the brushes had lost several clumps of bristles. A jam-pot of hoof-polish, now hard as stone, clung tenaciously to a short stick of firewood which time had petrified into the polish. But Raftery's loose-box smelt fresh and pleasant with the curious dry, clean smell of new straw. A deep depression towards the middle showed where his body had lain in sleep, and seeing this Stephen stooped down and touched it for a moment. Then she whispered: 'Sleep peacefully, Raftery.'

She could not weep, for a great desolation too deep for tears lay over her spirit—the great desolation of things that pass, of things that pass away in our lifetime. And then of what good, after all, are our tears, since they cannot hold back this passing away—no, not for so much as a moment? She looked round her now at the empty stables, the unwanted, uncared for stables of Morton. So proud they had been that were now so humbled, even unto cobwebs and dust were they humbled; and they had the feeling of all disused places that have once teemed with life, they felt pitifully lonely. She closed her eyes so as not to see them. Then the thought came to Stephen that this was the end, the end of her courage and patient endurance—that this was somehow the end of Morton. She must not see the place any more; she must, she would, go a long way away. Raftery had gone a long way away—she had sent him beyond all hope of recall—but she could not follow him over that merciful frontier, for her God was more stern than Raftery's; and yet she must fly from her love for Morton. Turning, she hurriedly left the stables.

5

Anna was standing at the foot of the stairs. 'Are you leaving now, Stephen?'

'Yes—I'm going, Mother.'

'A short visit!'

'Yes, I must get back to work.'

'I see. . . .' Then after a long, awkward pause: 'Where would you like him buried?'

'In the large north paddock where he died—I've told Jim.'

'Very well, I'll see that they carry out your orders.' She hesitated, as though suddenly shy of Stephen again, as she had been in the past; but after a moment she went on quickly: 'I thought—I wondered, would you like a small stone with his name and some sort of inscription on it, just to mark the place?'

'If you'd care to put one—I shan't need any stone to remember.'

The carriage was waiting to drive her to Malvern. 'Good-bye, Mother.'

'Good-bye—I shall put up that stone.'

'Thanks, it's a very kind thought of yours.'

Anna said: 'I'm so sorry about this, Stephen.'

But Stephen had hurried into the brougham—the door closed, and she did not hear her mother.

CHAPTER 30

I

At an old-fashioned, Kensington luncheon party, not very long after Raftery's death, Stephen met and renewed her acquaintance with Jonathan Brockett, the playwright.* Her mother had wished her to go to this luncheon, for the Carringtons were old family friends, and Anna insisted that from time to time her daughter should accept their invitations. At their house it was that Stephen had first seen this young man, rather over a year ago. Brockett was a connection of the Carringtons; had he not been Stephen might never have met him, for such gatherings bored him exceedingly, and therefore it was not his habit to attend them. But on that occasion he had not been bored, for his sharp, grey eyes had lit upon Stephen; and as soon as he well could, the meal being over, he had made his way to her side and had remained there. She had found him exceedingly easy to talk to, as indeed he had wished her to find him.

This first meeting had led to one or two rides in the Row together, since they both rode early. Brockett had joined her quite casually one morning; after which he had called, and had talked to Puddle as if he had come on purpose to see her and her only—he had charming and thoughtful manners towards all elderly people. Puddle had accepted him while disliking his clothes, which were always just a trifle too careful; moreover she had disapproved of his cuff-links—platinum links set with tiny emeralds. All the same, she had made him feel very welcome, for to her it had been any port in a storm* just then—she would gladly have welcomed the devil himself, had she thought that he might rouse Stephen.

But Stephen was never able to decide whether Jonathan Brockett attracted or repelled her. Brilliant he could be at certain times, yet curiously foolish and puerile at others; and his hands were as white and soft as a woman's—she would feel a queer little sense of outrage creeping over her when she looked at his hands.* For those hands of his went so ill with him somehow; he was tall, broad-shouldered, and of an extreme thinness. His clean-shaven face was slightly sardonic and almost disconcertingly clever; an inquisitive face too—one felt that it pried into everyone's secrets without shame or mercy. It may have been genuine liking on his part or mere curiosity that had made him persist in thrusting his friendship on Stephen. But whatever it had been it had taken the form of ringing her up almost daily at one time; of worrying her to lunch or dine with him, of inviting himself to her flat in Chelsea, or what was still worse, of dropping in on her whenever the spirit moved him. His work never seemed to worry him at all, and Stephen often wondered when his fine plays got written, for Brockett very seldom if ever discussed them and apparently very seldom wrote them; yet they always appeared at the critical moment when their author had run short of money.

Once, for the sake of peace, she had dined with him in a species of glorified cellar. He had just then discovered the queer little place down in Seven Dials,* and was very proud of it; indeed, he was making it rather the fashion among certain literary people. He had taken a great deal of trouble that evening to make Stephen feel that she belonged to these people by right of her talent, and had introduced her as 'Stephen Gordon, the author of *The Furrow*.' But all the while he had secretly watched her with his sharp and inquisitive grey eyes. She had felt very much at ease with Brockett as they sat at their little dimly lit table, perhaps because her instinct divined that this man would never require of her more than she could give—that the most he would ask for at any time would be friendship.

Then one day he had casually disappeared, and she heard that he had gone to Paris for some months, as was often his custom when the climate of London had begun to get on his nerves. He had drifted away like thistledown,* without so much as a word of warning. He had not said good-bye nor had he written, so that Stephen felt that she had never known him, so completely did he go out of her life during his sojourn in Paris. Later on she was to learn, when she knew him better, that these disconcerting lapses of interest, amounting as they did to a breach of good manners, were highly characteristic of the man, and must of necessity be accepted by all who accepted Jonathan Brockett.

And now here he was back again in England, sitting next to Stephen at the Carringtons' luncheon. And as though they had met but a few hours ago, he took her up calmly just where he had left her. 'May I come in to-morrow?'

'Well—I'm awfully busy.'

'But I want to come, please; I can talk to Puddle.'

'I'm afraid she'll be out.'

'Then I'll just sit and wait until she comes in; I'll be quiet as a mouse.'

'Oh, no, Brockett, please don't; I should know you were there and that would disturb me.'

'I see. A new book?'

'Well, no—I'm trying to write some short stories; I've got a commission from *The Good Housewife*.'*

'Sounds thrifty. I hope you're getting well paid.' Then after a rather long pause: 'How's Raftery?'

For a second she did not answer, and Brockett, with quick intuition, regretted his question. 'Not . . . not. . . .' he stammered.

'Yes,' she said slowly, 'Raftery's dead—he went lame. I shot him.'

He was silent. Then he suddenly took her hand and, still without speaking, pressed it. Glancing up, she was surprised by the look in his eyes, so sorrowful it was, and so understanding. He had liked the old horse, for he liked all dumb creatures. But Raftery's death could mean nothing to him; yet his sharp, grey eyes had now softened with pity because she had had to shoot Raftery.

She thought: 'What a curious fellow he is. At this moment I suppose he actually feels something almost like grief—it's my grief he's getting—and tomorrow, of course, he'll forget all about it.'

Which was true enough. Brockett could compress quite a lot of emotion into an incredibly short space of time; could squeeze a kind of emotional beef-tea* from all those with whom life brought him in contact—a strong brew, and one that served to sustain and revivify his inspiration.

2

For ten days Stephen heard nothing more of Brockett; then he rang up to announce that he was coming to dinner at her flat that very same evening.

'You'll get awfully little to eat,' warned Stephen, who was tired to death and who did not want him.

'Oh, all right, I'll bring some dinner along,' he said blithely, and with that he hung up the receiver.

At a quarter-past eight he arrived, late for dinner and loaded like a pack-mule with brown paper parcels. He looked cross; he had spoilt his new reindeer gloves* with mayonnaise that had oozed through a box containing the lobster salad.

He thrust the box into Stephen's hands. 'Here, you take it—it's dripping. Can I have a wash rag?' But after a moment he forgot the new gloves. 'I've raided Fortnum and Mason—such fun—I do *love* eating things out of cardboard boxes. Hallo, Puddle darling! I sent you a plant. Did you get it? A nice little plant with brown bobbles. It smells good, and it's got a ridiculous name like an old Italian dowager or something. Wait a minute—what's it called? Oh, yes, a baronia*—it's so humble to have such a pompous name! Stephen, do be careful—don't rock the lobster about like that. I told you the thing was dripping!'

He dumped his parcels on to the hall table.

'I'll take them along to the kitchen,' smiled Puddle.

'No, I will,' said Brockett, collecting them again, 'I'll do the whole thing; you leave it to me. I adore other people's kitchens.'

He was in his most foolish and tiresome mood—the mood when his white hands made odd little gestures, when his laugh was too high and his movements too small for the size of his broad-shouldered, rather gaunt body. Stephen had grown to dread him in this mood; there was something almost aggressive about it; it would seem to her that he thrust it upon her, showing off like a child at a Christmas party.

She said sharply: 'If you'll wait, I'll ring for the maid.' But Brockett had already invaded the kitchen.

She followed, to find the cook looking offended.

'I want lots and lots of dishes,' he announced. Then unfortunately he happened to notice the parlourmaid's washing, just back from the laundry.

'Brockett, what on earth are you doing?'

He had put on the girl's ornate frilled cap, and was busily tying on her small apron. He paused for a moment. 'How do I look? What a perfect duck of an apron!'

The parlourmaid giggled and Stephen laughed. That was the worst of Jonathan Brockett, he could make you laugh in spite of yourself—when you most disapproved you found yourself laughing.

The food he had brought was the oddest assortment: lobster, caramels, pâté de foie gras, olives, a tin of rich-mixed biscuits and a Camembert cheese that was smelling loudly. There was also a bottle of Rose's lime-juice* and another of ready-made cocktails. He began to unpack the things one by one, clamouring for plates and entrée dishes. In the process he made a great mess on the table by upsetting most of the lobster salad.

He swore roundly. 'Damn the thing, it's too utterly bloody! It's ruined my gloves, and now look at the table!' In grim silence the cook repaired the damage.

This mishap appeared to have damped his ardour, for he sighed and removed his cap and apron. 'Can anyone open this bottle of olives? And the cocktails? Here, Stephen, you can tackle the cheese; it seems rather shy, it won't leave its kennel.' In the end it was Stephen and the cook who must do all the work, while Brockett sat down on the floor and gave them ridiculous orders.

3

Brockett it was who ate most of the dinner, for Stephen was too overtired to feel hungry; while Puddle, whose digestion was not what it had been, was forced to content herself with a cutlet. But Brockett ate largely, and as he did so he praised himself and his food between mouthfuls.

'Clever of me to have discovered this pâté—I'm so sorry for the geese though, aren't you, Stephen? The awful thing is that it's simply delicious—I wish I knew the esoteric meaning of these mixed emotions!' And he dug with a spoon at the side that appeared to contain the most truffles.

From time to time he paused to inhale the gross little cigarettes he affected. Their tobacco was black, their paper was yellow, and they came from an unpropitious island where, as Brockett declared, the inhabitants died in shoals every year of some tropical fever.* He drank a good deal of the Rose's lime-juice, for this strong, rough tobacco always made him thirsty. Whisky went to his head and wine to his liver, so that on the whole he was forced to be temperate; but when he got home he would brew himself coffee as viciously black as his tobacco.

Presently he said with a sigh of repletion: 'Well, you two, I've finished—let's go into the study.'

As they left the table he seized the mixed biscuits and the caramel creams, for he dearly loved sweet things. He would often go out and buy himself sweets in Bond Street, for solitary consumption.

In the study he sank down on to the divan. 'Puddle dear, do you mind if I put my feet up? It's my new boot-maker, he's given me a corn on my right little toe. It's too heart-breaking. It was such a beautiful toe,' he murmured; 'quite perfect—the one toe without a blemish!'

After this he seemed disinclined to talk. He had made himself a nest with the cushions, and was smoking, and nibbling rich-mixed biscuits, routing about in the tin for his favourites. But his eyes kept straying across to Stephen with a puzzled and rather anxious expression.

At last she said: 'What's the matter, Brockett? Is my necktie crooked?'

'No—it's not your necktie; it's something else.' He sat up abruptly. 'As I came here to say it, I'll get the thing over!'

'Fire away, Brockett.'

'Do you think you'll hate me if I'm frank?'

'Of course not. Why should I hate you?'

'Very well then, listen.' And now his voice was so grave that Puddle put down her embroidery. 'You listen to me, you, Stephen Gordon. Your last book was quite inexcusably bad. It was no more like what we all expected, had a right to expect of you after *The Furrow*, than that plant I sent Puddle is like an oak tree—I won't even compare it to that little plant, for the plant's alive; your book isn't. Oh, I don't mean to say that it's not well written; it's well written because you're just a born writer—you feel words, you've a perfect ear for balance, and a very good all-round knowledge of English. But that's not enough, not nearly enough; all that's a mere suitable dress for a body. And this time you've hung the dress on a dummy—a dummy can't stir our emotions, Stephen. I was talking to Ogilvy* only last night. He gave you a good review, he told me, because he's got such a respect for your talent that he didn't want to put on the damper. He's like that—too merciful I always think—they've all been too merciful to you, my dear. They ought to have literally skinned you alive—that might have helped to show you your danger. My God! and you wrote a thing like *The Furrow*! What's happened? What's undermining your work? Because whatever it is, it's deadly! it must be some kind of horrid dry rot. Ah, no, it's too bad and it mustn't go on—we've got to do something, quickly.'

He paused, and she stared at him in amazement. Until now she had never seen this side of Brockett, the side of the man that belonged to his art, to all art—the one thing in life he respected.

She said: 'Do you really mean what you're saying?'

'I mean every word,' he told her.

Then she asked him quite humbly: 'What must I do to save my work?' for she realized that he had been speaking the stark, bitter truth; that indeed she had needed no one to tell her that her last book had been altogether unworthy—a poor, lifeless thing, having no health in it.

He considered. 'It's a difficult question, Stephen. Your own temperament is so much against you. You're so strong in some ways and yet so timid—such a mixture—and you're terribly frightened of life. Now why? You must try to stop being frightened, to stop hiding your head. You need life, you need people. People are the food that we writers live on; get out and devour them, squeeze them dry, Stephen!'

'My father once told me something like that—not quite in those words—but something very like it.'

'Then your father must have been a sensible man,' smiled Brockett. 'Now I had a perfect beast of a father. Well, Stephen, I'll give you my advice for what it's worth—you want a real change. Why not go abroad somewhere? Get right away for a bit from your England. You'll probably write it a damned sight better when you're far enough off to see the perspective. Start with Paris—it's an excellent jumping-off place. Then you might go across to Italy or Spain—go anywhere, only do get a move on! No wonder you're atrophied here in London. I can put you wise about people in Paris. You ought to know Valérie Seymour, for instance. She's very good fun and a perfect darling; I'm sure you'd like her, every one does. Her parties are a kind of human bran-pie*—you just plunge in your fist and see what happens. You may draw a prize or you may draw blank, but it's always worth while to go to her parties. Oh, but good Lord, there are so many things that stimulate one in Paris.'

He talked on about Paris for a little while longer, then he got up to go. 'Well, good-bye, my dears, I'm off. I've given myself indigestion. And do look at Puddle, she's blind with fury; I believe she's going to refuse to shake hands! Don't be angry, Puddle—I'm very well-meaning.'

'Yes, of course,' answered Puddle, but her voice sounded cold.

4

After he had gone they stared at each other, then Stephen said: 'What a queer revelation. Who would have thought that Brockett could get so worked up? His moods are kaleidoscopic.' She was purposely forcing herself to speak lightly.

But Puddle was angry, bitterly angry. Her pride was wounded to the quick for Stephen. 'The man's a perfect fool!' she said gruffly. 'And I didn't agree with one word he said. I expect he's jealous of your work, they all are. They're a mean-minded lot, these writing people.'

And looking at her Stephen thought sadly, 'She's tired—I'm wearing her out in my service. A few years ago she'd never have tried to deceive me like this—she's losing courage.' Aloud she said: 'Don't be cross with Brockett, he meant to be friendly, I'm quite sure of that. My work will buck up—I've been feeling slack lately, and it's told on my writing—I suppose it was bound to.' Then the merciful lie, 'But I'm not a bit frightened!'

5

Stephen rested her head on her hand as she sat at her desk—it was well past midnight. She was heartsick as only a writer can be whose day has been spent in useless labour. All that she had written that day she would destroy, and now it was well past midnight. She turned, looking wearily round the study, and it came upon her with a slight sense of shock that she was seeing this room for the very first time, and that everything in it was abnormally ugly. The flat had been furnished when her mind had been too much afflicted to care in the least what she bought, and now all her possessions seemed clumsy or puerile, from the small, foolish chairs to the large, roll-top desk; there was nothing personal about any of them. How had she endured this room for so long? Had she really written a fine book in it? Had she sat in it evening after evening and come back to it morning after morning? Then she must have been blind indeed—what a place for any author to work in! She had taken nothing with her from Morton but the hidden books found in her father's study; these she had taken, as though in a way they were hers by some intolerable birthright; for the rest she had shrunk from depriving the house of its ancient and honoured possessions.

Morton—so quietly perfect a thing, yet the thing of all others that she must fly from, that she must forget; but she could not forget it in these surroundings; they reminded by contrast. Curious what

Brockett had said that evening about putting the sea between herself and England. . . . In view of her own half-formed plan to do so, his words had come as a kind of echo of her thoughts; it was almost as though he had peeped through a secret keyhole into her mind, had been spying upon her trouble. By what right did this curious man spy upon her—this man with the soft white hands of a woman, with the movements befitting those soft white hands, yet so ill-befitting the rest of his body? By no right; and how much had the creature found out when his eye had been pressed to that secret keyhole? Clever—Brockett was fiendishly clever—all his whims and his foibles could not disguise it. His face gave him away, a hard, clever face with sharp eyes that were glued to other people's keyholes. That was why Brockett wrote such fine plays, such cruel plays; he fed his genius on live flesh and blood. Carnivorous genius. Moloch,* fed upon live flesh and blood! But she, Stephen, had tried to feed her inspiration upon herbage, the kind, green herbage of Morton. For a little while such food had sufficed, but now her talent had sickened, was dying perhaps—or had she too fed it on blood, her heart's blood when she had written *The Furrow*? If so, her heart would not bleed any more—perhaps it could not—perhaps it was dry. A dry, withered thing; for she did not feel love these days when she thought of Angela Crossby—that must mean that her heart had died within her. A gruesome companion to have, a dead heart.

Angela Crossby—and yet there were times when she longed intensely to see this woman, to hear her speak, to stretch out her arms and clasp them around the woman's body—not gently, not patiently as in the past, but roughly, brutally even. Beastly—it was beastly! She felt degraded. She had no love to offer Angela Crossby, not now, only something that lay like a stain on the beauty of what had once been love. Even this memory was marred and defiled, by herself even more than by Angela Crossby.

Came the thought of that unforgettable scene with her mother. 'I would rather see you dead at my feet.' Oh, yes—very easy to talk about death, but not so easy to manage the dying. 'We two cannot live together at Morton. . . . One of us must go, which of us shall it be?' The subtlety, the craftiness of that question which in common decency could have but one answer! Oh, well, she had gone and would go even farther. Raftery was dead, there was nothing to hold her, she was free—what a terrible thing could be freedom. Trees were free when they were uprooted by the wind; ships were free when they were torn from their moorings; men were free when they were cast out of their homes—free to starve, free to perish of cold and hunger.

At Morton there lived an ageing woman with sorrowful eyes now a little dim from gazing for so long into the distance.* Only once, since her gaze had been fixed on the dead, had this woman turned it full on her daughter; and then her eyes had been changed into something accusing, ruthless, abominably cruel. Through looking upon what had seemed abominable to them, they themselves had become an abomination. Horrible! And yet how dared they accuse? What right had a mother to abominate the child that had sprung from her own secret moments of passion? She the honoured, the fulfilled, the fruitful, the loving and loved, had despised the fruit of her love. Its fruit? No, rather its victim.

She thought of her mother's protected life that had never had to face this terrible freedom. Like a vine* that clings to a warm southern wall it had clung to her father—it still clung to Morton. In the spring had come gentle and nurturing rains, in the summer the strong and health-giving sunshine, in the winter a deep, soft covering of snow—cold yet protecting the delicate tendrils. All, all she had had. She had never gone empty of love in the days of her youthful ardour; had never known longing, shame, degradation, but rather great joy and great pride in her loving. Her love had been pure in the eyes of the world, for she had been able to indulge it with honour. Still with honour, she had borne a child to her mate—but a child who, unlike her, must go unfulfilled all her days, or else live in abject dishonour. Oh, but a hard and pitiless woman this mother must be for all her soft beauty; shamelessly finding shame in her offspring. 'I would rather see you dead at my feet. . . .' 'Too late, too late, your love gave me life. Here am I the creature you made through your loving; by your passion you created the thing that I am. Who are you to deny me the right to love? But for you I need never have known existence.'

And now there crept into Stephen's brain the worst torment of all, a doubt of her father. He had known and knowing he had not told her; he had pitied and pitying had not protected; he had feared and fearing had saved only himself. Had she had a coward for a father? She sprang up and began to pace the room. Not this—she could not face this new torment. She had stained her love, the love of the lover—she dared not stain this one thing that remained, the love of the child for the father. If this light went out the engulfing darkness would consume her, destroying her entirely. Man could not live by darkness alone, one point of light he must have for salvation—one point of light. The most perfect Being of all had cried out for light in His darkness*—even He, the most perfect Being of all. And then as though in answer to prayer, to some prayer that her trembling lips had not uttered, came the memory of a patient, protective back, bowed as though bearing another's burden. Came the memory of horrible, soul-sickening pain: 'No—not that—something urgent—I want—to say. No drugs—I know I'm—dying—Evans.' And again an heroic and tortured effort: 'Anna—it's Stephen—listen.' Stephen suddenly held out her arms to this man who, though dead, was still her father.

But even in this blessed moment of easement, her heart hardened again at the thought of her mother. A fresh wave of bitterness flooded her soul so that the light seemed all but extinguished; very faintly it gleamed like the little lantern on a buoy that is tossed by tempest. Sitting down at her desk she found pen and paper.

She wrote: 'Mother, I am going abroad quite soon, but I shall not see you to say good-bye, because I don't want to come back to Morton. These visits of mine have always been painful, and now my work is beginning to suffer—that I can not allow; I live only for my work and so I intend to guard it in future. There can now be no question of gossip or scandal, for every one knows that I am a writer and as such may have occasion to travel. But in any case I care very little these days for the gossip of neighbours. For nearly three years I have borne your yoke*—I have tried to be patient and understanding. I have tried to think that your yoke was a just one, a just punishment, perhaps, for my being what I am, the creature whom you and my father created; but now I am going to bear it no longer. If my father had lived he would have shown pity, whereas you showed me none, and yet you were my mother. In my hour of great need you utterly failed me; you turned me away like some unclean thing that was unfit to live any longer at Morton. You insulted what to me seemed both natural and sacred. I went, but now I shall not come back any more to you or to Morton. Puddle will be with me because she loves me; if I'm saved at all it is she who has saved me, and so for as long as she wishes to throw in her lot with mine I shall let her. Only one thing more; she will send you our address from time to time, but don't write to me, Mother,

I am going away in order to forget, and your letters would only remind me of Morton.'

She read over what she had written, three times, finding nothing at all that she wished to add, no word of tenderness, or of regret. She felt numb and then unbelievably lonely, but she wrote the address in her firm handwriting: 'The Lady Anna Gordon,' she wrote, 'Morton Hall. Near Upton-on-Severn.' And when she wept, as she presently must do, covering her face with her large, brown hands,* her spirit felt unrefreshed by this weeping, for the hot, angry tears seemed to scorch her spirit. Thus was Anna Gordon baptized through her child as by fire, unto the loss of their mutual salvation.*

CHAPTER 31

I

It was Jonathan Brockett who had recommended the little hotel in the Rue St. Roch,* and when Stephen and Puddle arrived one evening that June, feeling rather tired and dejected, they found their sitting-room bright with roses—roses for Puddle—and on the table two boxes of Turkish cigarettes* for Stephen. Brockett, they learnt, had ordered these things by writing specially from London.

Barely had they been in Paris a week, when Jonathan Brockett turned up in person: 'Hallo, my dears, I've come over to see you. Everything all right? Are you being looked after?' He sat down in the only comfortable chair and proceeded to make himself charming to Puddle. It seemed that his flat in Paris being let, he had tried to get rooms at their hotel but had failed, so had gone instead to the Meurice.* 'But I'm not going to take you to lunch there,' he told them, 'the weather's too fine, we'll go to Versailles.* Stephen, ring up and order your car, there's a darling! By the way, how is Burton getting on? Does he remember to keep to the right and to pass on the left?'* His voice sounded anxious. Stephen reassured him good-humouredly, she knew that he was apt to be nervous in motors.

They lunched at the Hotel des Reservoirs,* Brockett taking great pains to order special dishes. The waiters were zealous, they evidently knew him: 'Oui, monsieur, tout de suite—à l'instant, monsieur!'* Other clients were kept waiting while Brockett was served, and Stephen could see that this pleased him. All through the meal he talked about Paris with ardour, as a lover might talk of a mistress.

'Stephen, I'm not going back for ages. I'm going to make you simply adore her. You'll see, I'll make you adore her so much that you'll find yourself writing like a heaven-born genius. There's nothing so stimulating as love—you've got to have an affair with Paris!' Then looking at Stephen rather intently, 'I suppose you're capable of falling in love?'

She shrugged her shoulders, ignoring his question, but she thought: 'He's putting his eye to the key-hole. His curiosity's positively childish at times,' for she saw that his face had fallen.

'Oh, well, if you don't want to tell me—' he grumbled.

'Don't be silly! There's nothing to tell,' smiled Stephen. But she made a mental note to be careful. Brockett's curiosity was always most dangerous when apparently merely childish.

With quick tact he dropped the personal note. No good trying to force her to confide, he decided, she was too damn clever to give herself away, especially before the watchful old Puddle. He sent for the bill and when it arrived, went over it item by item, frowning.

'Maître d'hotel!'

'Oui, monsieur?'

'You've made a mistake; only one liqueur brandy—and here's another mistake, I ordered two portions of potatoes, *not three*; I do wish to God you'd be careful!' When Brockett felt cross he always felt mean. 'Correct this at once, it's disgusting!' he said rudely. Stephen sighed, and hearing her Brockett looked up unabashed: 'Well, why pay for what we've not ordered?' Then he suddenly found his temper again and left a very large tip for the waiter.

2

There is nothing more difficult to attain to than the art of being a perfect guide. Such an art, indeed, requires a real artist, one who has a keen perception for contrasts, and an eye for the large effects rather than for details, above all one possessed of imagination; and Brockett, when he chose, could be such a guide.

Having waved the professional guides to one side, he himself took them through a part of the palace, and his mind repeopled the place for Stephen so that she seemed to see the glory of the dancers led by the youthful Roi Soleil;* seemed to hear the rhythm of the throbbing violins, and the throb of the rhythmic dancing feet as they beat down the length of the Galerie des Glaces;* seemed to see those other mysterious dancers who followed step by step, in the long line of mirrors. But most skilfully of all did he recreate for her the image of the luckless queen* who came after; as though for some reason this unhappy woman must appeal in a personal way to Stephen. And true it was that the small, humble rooms which the queen had chosen out of all that vast palace, moved Stephen profoundly—so desolate they seemed, so full of unhappy thoughts and emotions that were even now only half forgotten.

Brockett pointed to the simple garniture on the mantelpiece of the little salon, then he looked at Stephen: 'Madame de Lamballe* gave those to the queen,' he murmured softly.

She nodded, only vaguely apprehending his meaning.

Presently they followed him out into the gardens and stood looking across the Tapis Vert* that stretches its quarter mile of greenness towards a straight, lovely line of water.

Brockett said, very low, so that Puddle should not hear him: 'Those two would often come here at sunset. Sometimes they were rowed along the canal in the sunset—can't you imagine it, Stephen? They must often have felt pretty miserable, poor souls; sick to death of the subterfuge and pretences. Don't you ever get tired of that sort of thing? My God, I do!' But she did not answer, for now there was no mistaking his meaning.

Last of all he took them to the Temple d'Amour, where it rests amid the great silence of the years that have long lain upon the dead hearts of its lovers; and from there to the Hameau,* built by the queen for a whim—the tactless and foolish whim of a tactless and foolish but loving woman—by the queen who must play at being a peasant, at a time when her downtrodden peasants were starving. The cottages were badly in need of repair; a melancholy spot it looked, this Hameau, in spite of the birds that sang in its trees and the golden glint of the afternoon sunshine.

On the drive back to Paris they were all very silent. Puddle was feeling too tired to talk, and Stephen was oppressed by a sense of sadness—the vast and rather beautiful sadness that may come to us when we have looked upon beauty, the sadness that aches in the heart of Versailles. Brockett was content to sit opposite Stephen on the hard little let-down seat of her motor. He might have been comfortable next to the driver, but instead he preferred to sit opposite Stephen, and he too was silent, surreptitiously watching the expression of her face in the gathering twilight.

When he left them he said with his cold little smile: 'To-morrow, before you've forgotten Versailles, I want you to come to the Conciergerie.* It's very enlightening—cause and effect.'

At that moment Stephen disliked him intensely. All the same he had stirred her imagination.

3

In the weeks that followed, Brockett showed Stephen just as much of Paris as he wished her to see, and this principally consisted of the tourist's Paris. Into less simple pastures he would guide her later on, always provided that his interest lasted. For the present, however, he considered it wiser to tread delicately, like Agag.* The thought of this girl had begun to obsess him to a very unusual extent. He who had prided himself on his skill in ferreting out other people's secrets, was completely baffled by this youthful abnormal. That she was abnormal he had no doubt whatever, but what he was keenly anxious to find out was just how her own abnormality struck her—he felt pretty sure that she worried about it. And he genuinely liked her. Unscrupulous he might be in his vivisection of men and women; cynical too when it came to his pleasures, himself an invert, secretly hating the world which he knew hated him in secret; and yet in his way he felt sorry for Stephen, and this amazed him, for Jonathan Brockett had long ago, as he thought, done with pity. But his pity was a very poor thing at best, it would never defend and never protect her; it would always go down before any new whim, and his whim at the moment was to keep her in Paris.

All unwittingly Stephen played into his hands, while having no illusions about him. He represented a welcome distraction that helped her to keep her thoughts off England. And because under Brockett's skilful guidance she developed a fondness for the beautiful city, she felt very tolerant of him at moments, almost grateful she felt, grateful too towards Paris. And Puddle also felt grateful.

The strain of the sudden complete rupture with Morton had told on the faithful little grey woman. She would scarcely have known how to counsel Stephen had the girl come to her and asked for her counsel. Sometimes she would lie awake now at nights thinking of that ageing and unhappy mother in the great silent house, and then would come pity, the old pity that had come in the past for Anna—she would pity until she remembered Stephen. Then Puddle would try to think very calmly, to keep the brave heart that had never failed her, to keep her strong faith in Stephen's future—only now there were days when she felt almost old, when she realized that indeed she was ageing. When Anna would write her a calm, friendly letter, but with never so much as a mention of Stephen, she would feel afraid, yes, afraid of this woman, and at moments almost afraid of Stephen. For none might know from those guarded letters what emotions lay in the heart of their writer; and none might know from Stephen's set face when she recognized the writing, what lay in her heart. She would turn away, asking no questions about Morton.

Oh, yes, Puddle felt old and actually frightened, both of which sensations she deeply resented; so being what she was, an indomitable fighter, she thrust out her chin and ordered a tonic. She struggled along through the labyrinths of Paris beside the untiring Stephen and Brockett; through the galleries of the Luxembourg and the Louvre; up the Eiffel Tower—in a lift, thank heaven; down the Rue de la Paix, up the hill to Montmartre*—sometimes in the car but quite often on foot, for Brockett wished Stephen to learn her Paris—and as likely as not, ending up with rich food that disagreed badly with the tired Puddle. In the restaurants people would stare at Stephen, and although the girl would pretend not to notice, Puddle would know that in spite of her calm, Stephen was inwardly feeling resentful, was inwardly feeling embarrassed and awkward. And then because she was tired, Puddle too would feel awkward when she noticed those people staring.

Sometimes Puddle must really give up and rest, in spite of the aggressive chin and the tonic. Then all alone in the Paris hotel, she would suddenly grow very homesick for England—absurd of course and yet there it was, she would feel the sharp tug of England. At such moments she would long for ridiculous things; a penny bun in the train at Dover; the good red faces of English porters—the old ones with little stubby side-whiskers; Harrods Stores; a properly upholstered arm-chair; bacon and eggs; the sea front at Brighton. All alone and via these ridiculous things, Puddle would feel the sharp tug of England.

And one evening her weary mind must switch back to the earliest days of her friendship with Stephen. What a lifetime ago it seemed since the days when a lanky colt of a girl of fourteen had been licked into shape in the schoolroom at Morton. She could hear her own words: 'You've forgotten something, Stephen; the books can't walk to the bookcase, but you can, so suppose that you take them with you,' and then: 'Even my brain won't stand your complete lack of method.' Stephen fourteen—that was twelve years ago. In those years she, Puddle, had grown very tired, tired with trying to see some way out, some way of escape, of fulfilment for Stephen. And always they seemed to be toiling, they two, down an endless road that had no turning; she an ageing woman herself unfulfilled; Stephen still young and as yet still courageous—but the day would come when her youth would fail, and her courage, because of that endless toiling.

She thought of Brockett, Jonathan Brockett, surely an unworthy companion for Stephen; a thoroughly vicious and cynical man, a dangerous one too because he was brilliant. Yet she, Puddle, was actually grateful to this man; so dire were their straits that she was grateful to Brockett. Then came the remembrance of that other man, of Martin Hallam—she had had such high hopes. He had been very simple and honest and good—Puddle felt that there was much to be said for goodness. But for such as Stephen men like Martin Hallam could seldom exist; as friends they would fail her, while she in her turn would fail them as lover. Then what remained? Jonathan Brockett? Like to like. No, no, an intolerable thought! Such a thought as that was an outrage on Stephen. Stephen was honourable and courageous; she was steadfast in friendship and selfless in loving; intolerable to think that her only companions must be men and women like Jonathan Brockett—and yet—after all what else? What remained? Loneliness, or worse still, far worse because it so deeply degraded the spirit, a life of perpetual subterfuge, of guarded opinions and guarded actions, of lies of omission if not of speech, of becoming an accomplice in the world's injustice by maintaining at all times a judicious silence, making and keeping the friends one respected, on false pretences, because if they knew they would turn aside, even the friends one respected.

Puddle abruptly controlled her thoughts; this was no way to be helpful to Stephen. Sufficient unto the day was the evil thereof.* Getting up she went into her bedroom where she bathed her face and tidied her hair.

'I look scarcely human,' she thought ruefully, as she stared at her own reflection in the glass; and indeed at that moment she looked more than her age.

4

It was not until nearly the middle of July that Brockett took Stephen to Valérie Seymour's.* Valérie had been away for some time, and was even now only passing through Paris en route for her villa at St. Tropez.*

As they drove to her apartment on the Quai Voltaire,* Brockett began to extol their hostess, praising her wit, her literary talent. She wrote delicate satires and charming sketches of Greek mœurs*—the latter were very outspoken, but then Valérie's life was very outspoken—she was, said Brockett, a kind of pioneer who would probably go down to history. Most of her sketches were written in French, for among other things Valérie was bi-lingual; she was also quite rich, an American uncle had had the foresight to leave her his fortune; she was also quite young, being just over thirty, and according to Brockett, good-looking. She lived her life in great calmness of spirit, for nothing worried and few things distressed her. She was firmly convinced that in this ugly age one should strive to the top of one's bent after beauty. But Stephen might find her a bit of a free lance, she was libre penseuse* when it came to the heart; her love affairs would fill quite three volumes, even after they had been expurgated. Great men had loved her, great writers had written about her, one had died, it was said, because she refused him, but Valérie was not attracted to men—yet as Stephen would see if she went to her parties, she had many devoted friends among men. In this respect she was almost unique, being what she was, for men did not resent her. But then of course all intelligent people realized that she was a creature apart, as would Stephen the moment she met her.

Brockett babbled away, and as he did so his voice took on the effeminate timbre that Stephen always hated and dreaded: 'Oh, my dear!' he exclaimed with a high little laugh, 'I'm so excited about this meeting of yours, I've a feeling it may be momentous. What fun!' And his soft white hands grew restless, making their foolish gestures.

She looked at him coldly, wondering the while how she could tolerate this young man—why indeed, she chose to endure him.

5

The first thing* that struck Stephen about Valérie's flat was its large and rather splendid disorder. There was something blissfully unkempt about it, as though its mistress were too much engrossed in other affairs to control its behaviour. Nothing was quite where it ought to have been, and much was where it ought not to have been, while over the whole lay a faint layer of dust—even over the spacious salon. The odour of somebody's Oriental scent was mingling with the odour of tuberoses in a sixteenth-century chalice. On a divan, whose truly regal proportions occupied the best part of a shadowy alcove, lay a box of Fuller's peppermint creams and a lute, but the strings of the lute were broken.*

Valérie came forward with a smile of welcome. She was not beautiful nor was she imposing, but her limbs were very perfectly proportioned, which gave her a fictitious look of tallness. She moved well, with the quiet and unconscious grace that sprang from those perfect proportions. Her face was humorous, placid and worldly; her eyes very kind, very blue, very lustrous. She was dressed all in white, and a large white fox skin was clasped round her slender and shapely shoulders. For the rest she had masses of thick fair hair, which was busily ridding itself of its hairpins; one could see at a glance that it hated restraint, like the flat it was in rather splendid disorder.

She said: 'I'm so delighted to meet you at last, Miss Gordon, do come and sit down. And please smoke if you want to,' she added quickly, glancing at Stephen's tell-tale fingers.

Brockett said: 'Positively, this is too splendid! I feel that you're going to be wonderful friends.'

Stephen thought: 'So this is Valérie Seymour.'

No sooner were they seated than Brockett began to ply their hostess with personal questions. The mood that had incubated in the motor was now becoming extremely aggressive, so that he fidgeted about on his chair, making his little inadequate gestures. 'Darling, you're looking perfectly lovely! But do tell me, what have you done with Polinska? Have you drowned her in the blue grotto at Capri?* I hope so, my dear, she *was* such a bore and so dirty! Do tell me about Polinska. How did she behave when you got her to Capri? Did she bite anybody before you drowned her? I always felt frightened; I loathe being bitten!'

Valérie frowned: 'I believe she's quite well.'

'Then you have drowned her, darling!' shrilled Brockett.

And now he was launched on a torrent of gossip about people of whom Stephen had never even heard: 'Pat's been deserted—have you heard that, darling? Do you think she'll take the veil* or cocaine or something? One never quite knows what may happen next with such an emotional temperament, does one? Arabella's skipped off to the Lido* with Jane Grigg. The Griggs' just come into pots and pots of money, so I hope they'll be deliriously happy and silly while it lasts—I mean the money. . . . Oh, and have you heard about Rachel Morris? They say. . . .' He flowed on and on like a brook in spring flood, while Valérie yawned and looked bored, making monosyllabic answers.

And Stephen as she sat there and smoked in silence, thought grimly: 'This is all being said because of me. Brockett wants to let me see that he knows what I am, and he wants to let Valérie Seymour know too—I suppose this is making me welcome.' She hardly knew whether to feel outraged or relieved that here, at least, was no need for pretences.

But after a while she began to fancy that Valérie's eyes had become appraising. They were weighing her up and secretly approving the result, she fancied. A slow anger possessed her. Valérie Seymour was secretly approving, not because her guest was a decent human being with a will to work, with a well-trained brain, with what might some day become a fine talent, but rather because she was seeing before her all the outward stigmata of the abnormal*—verily the wounds of One nailed to a cross—that was why Valérie sat there approving.

And then, as though these bitter thoughts had reached her, Valérie suddenly smiled at Stephen. Turning her back on the chattering Brockett, she started to talk to her guest quite gravely about her work, about books in general, about life in general; and as she did so Stephen began to understand better the charm that many had found in this woman; a charm that lay less in physical attraction than in a great courtesy and understanding, a great will to please, a great impulse towards beauty in all its forms—yes, therein lay her charm. And as they talked on it dawned upon Stephen that here was no mere libertine* in love's garden, but rather a creature born out of her epoch, a pagan* chained to an age that was Christian, one who would surely say with Pierre Louÿs: 'Le monde moderne succombe sous un envahissement de laideur.'* And she thought that she discerned in those luminous eyes, the pale yet ardent light of the fanatic.

Presently Valérie Seymour asked her how long she would be remaining in Paris.

And Stephen answered: 'I'm going to live here,' feeling surprised at the words as she said them, for not until now had she made this decision.

Valérie seemed pleased: 'If you want a house, I know of one in the Rue Jacob;* it's a tumbledown place, but it's got a fine garden. Why not go and see it? You might go to-morrow. Of course you'll have to live on this side, the Rive Gauche is the only possible Paris.'

'I should like to see the old house,' said Stephen.

So Valérie went to the telephone there and then and proceeded to call up the landlord. The appointment was made for eleven the next morning. 'It's rather a sad old house,' she warned, 'no one has troubled to make it a home for some time, but you'll alter all that if you take it, because I suppose you'll make it your home.'

Stephen flushed: 'My home's in England,' she said quickly, for her thoughts had instantly flown back to Morton.

But Valérie answered: 'One may have two homes—many homes. Be courteous to our lovely Paris and give it the privilege of being your second home—it will feel very honoured, Miss Gordon.' She sometimes made little ceremonious speeches like this, and coming from her, they sounded strangely old-fashioned.

Brockett, rather subdued and distinctly pensive as sometimes happened if Valérie had snubbed him, complained of a pain above his right eye: 'I must take some phenacetin,'* he said sadly, 'I'm always getting this curious pain above my right eye—do you think it's the sinus?' He was very intolerant of all pain.

His hostess sent for the phenacetin, and Brockett gulped down a couple of tablets: 'Valérie doesn't love me any more,' he sighed, with a woebegone look at Stephen. 'I do call it hard, but it's always what happens when I introduce my best friends to each other—they foregather at once and leave me in the cold; but then, thank heaven, I'm very forgiving.'

They laughed and Valérie made him get on to the divan where he promptly lay down on the lute.

'Oh God!' he moaned, 'now I've injured my spine—I'm so badly upholstered.' Then he started to strum on the one sound string of the lute.

Valérie went over to her untidy desk and began to write out a list of addresses: 'These may be useful to you, Miss Gordon.'

'Stephen!' exclaimed Brockett, 'Call the poor woman Stephen!'

'May I?'

Stephen acquiesced: 'Yes, please do.'

'Very well then, I'm Valérie. Is that a bargain?'

'The bargain is sealed,' announced Brockett. With extraordinary skill he was managing to strum 'O Sole Mio'* on the single string, when he suddenly stopped: 'I knew there was something—your fencing, Stephen, you've forgotten your fencing. We meant to ask Valérie for Buisson's* address; they say he's the finest master in Europe.'

Valérie looked up: 'Does Stephen fence, then?'

'Does she fence! She's a marvellous, champion fencer.'

'He's never seen me fence,' explained Stephen, 'and I'm never likely to be a champion.'

'Don't you believe her, she's trying to be modest. I've heard that she fences quite as finely as she writes,' he insisted. And somehow Stephen felt touched, Brockett was trying to show off her talents.

Presently she offered him a lift in the car, but he shook his head: 'No, thank you, dear one, I'm staying.' So she wished them good-bye; but as she left them she heard Brockett murmuring to Valérie Seymour, and she felt pretty sure that she caught her own name.

6

'Well, what did you think of Miss Seymour?' inquired Puddle, when Stephen got back about twenty minutes later.

Stephen hesitated: 'I'm not perfectly certain. She was very friendly, but I couldn't help feeling that she liked me because she thought me*—oh, well, because she thought me what I am, Puddle. But I may have been wrong—she was awfully friendly. Brockett was at his very worst though, poor devil! His environment seemed to go to his head.' She sank down wearily on to a chair: 'Oh, Puddle, Puddle, it's a hell of a business.'

Puddle nodded.

Then Stephen said rather abruptly: 'All the same, we're going to live here in Paris. We're going to look at a house to-morrow, an old house with a garden in the Rue Jacob.'

For a moment Puddle hesitated, then she said: 'There's only one thing against it. Do you think you'll ever be happy in a city? You're so fond of the life that belongs to the country.'

Stephen shook her head: 'That's all past now, my dear; there's no country for me away from Morton. But in Paris I might make some sort of a home, I could work here—and then of course there are people. . . .'

Something started to hammer in Puddle's brain: 'Like to like! Like to like! Like to like!' it hammered.

CHAPTER 32

I

STEPHEN bought the house in the Rue Jacob, because as she walked through the dim, grey archway that led from the street to the cobbled courtyard, and saw the deserted house standing before her, she knew at once that there she would live. This will happen sometimes, we instinctively feel in sympathy with certain dwellings.

The courtyard was sunny and surrounded by walls. On the right of this courtyard some iron gates led into the spacious, untidy garden, and woefully neglected though this garden had been, the trees that it still possessed were fine ones. A marble fountain long since choked with weeds, stood in the centre of what had been a lawn. In the farthest corner of the garden some hand had erected a semicircular temple, but that had been a long time ago, and now the temple was all but ruined.

The house itself would need endless repairs, but its rooms were of careful and restful proportions. A fine room with a window that opened on the garden, would be Stephen's study; she could write there in quiet; on the other side of the stone-paved hall was a smaller but comfortable salle à manger;* while past the stone staircase a little round room in a turret would be Puddle's particular sanctum. Above there were bedrooms enough and to spare; there was also the space for a couple of bath-rooms. The day after Stephen had seen this house, she had written agreeing to purchase.

Valérie rang up before leaving Paris to inquire how Stephen had liked the old house, and when she heard that she had actually bought it, she expressed herself as being delighted.

'We'll be quite close neighbours now,' she remarked, 'but I'm not going to bother you until you evince, not even when I get back in the autumn. I know you'll be literally snowed under with workmen for months, you poor dear, I feel sorry for you. But when you can, do let me come and see you—meanwhile if I can help you at all. . . .' And she gave her address at St. Tropez.

And now for the first time since leaving Morton, Stephen turned her mind to the making of a home. Through Brockett she found a young architect who seemed anxious to carry out all her instructions. He was one of those very rare architects who refrain from thrusting their views on their clients. So into the ancient, deserted house in the Rue Jacob streamed an army of workmen, and they hammered and scraped and raised clouds of dust from early morning, all day until evening—smoking harsh Caporals* as they joked or quarrelled or idled or spat or hummed snatches of song. And amazingly soon, wherever one trod one seemed to be treading on wet cement or on dry, gritty heaps of brick-dust and rubble, so that Puddle would complain that she spoilt all her shoes, while Stephen would emerge with her neat blue serge shoulders quite grey, and with even her hair thickly powdered.*

Sometimes the architect would come to the hotel in the evening and then would ensue long discussions. Bending over the little mahogany table, he and Stephen would study the plans intently, for she wished to preserve the spirit of the place intact, despite alterations. She decided to have an Empire study with grey walls and curtains of Empire green, for she loved the great roomy writing tables that had come into being with the first Napoleon.* The walls of the salle à manger should be white and the curtains brown, while Puddle's round sanctum in its turret should have walls and paintwork of yellow, to give the illusion of sunshine.* And so absorbed did Stephen become in these things, that she scarcely had time to notice Jonathan Brockett's abrupt departure for a mountain-top in the Austrian Tyrol.* Having suddenly come to the end of his finances, he must hasten to write a couple of plays that could be produced in London that winter. He sent her three or four picture-postcards of glaciers, after which she heard nothing more from him.

At the end of August, when the work was well under way, she and Puddle fared forth in the motor to visit divers villages and towns, in quest of old furniture, and Stephen was surprised to find how much she enjoyed it. She would catch herself whistling as she drove her car,* and when they got back to some humble auberge in the evening, she would want to eat a large supper. Every morning she diligently swung her dumb-bells; she was getting into condition for fencing. She had not fenced at all since leaving Morton, having been too much engrossed in her work while in London; but now she was going to fence before Buisson, so she diligently swung her dumb-bells. During these two months of holiday-making she grew fond of the wide-eyed, fruitful French country, even as she had grown fond of Paris. She would never love it as she loved the hills and the stretching valleys surrounding Morton, for that love was somehow a part of her being, but she gave to this France, that would give her a home, a quiet and very sincere affection. Her heart grew more grateful with every mile, for hers was above all a grateful nature.

They returned to Paris at the end of October. And now came the selecting of carpets and curtains; of fascinating blankets from the Magasin de Blanc*—blankets craftily dyed to match any bedroom; of fine linen, and other expensive things, including the copper batterie de cuisine,* which latter, however, was left to Puddle. At last the army of workmen departed, its place being taken by a Breton ménage*—brown-faced folk, strong-limbed and capable looking—a mother, father and daughter. Pierre, the butler, had been a fisherman once, but the sea with its hardships had prematurely aged him. He had now been in service for several years, having contracted rheumatic fever which had weakened his heart and made him unfit for the strenuous life of a fisher. Pauline, his wife, was considerably younger, and she it was who would reign in the kitchen, while their daughter Adèle, a girl of eighteen, would help both her parents and look after the housework.

Adèle was as happy as a blackbird in springtime; she would often seem just on the verge of chirping. But Pauline had stood and watched the great storms gather over the sea while her men were out fishing; her father had lost his life through the sea, as had also a brother, so Pauline smiled seldom. Dour she was, with a predilection for dwelling in detail on people's misfortunes. As for Pierre, he was stolid, kind and pious, with the eyes of a man who has looked on vast spaces. His grey stubbly hair was cut short to his head en brosse,* and he had an ungainly figure. When he walked he straddled a little as though he could never believe in a house without motion. He liked Stephen at once, which was very propitious, for one cannot buy the good-will of a Breton.

Thus gradually chaos gave place to order, and on the morning of her twenty-seventh birthday, on Christmas Eve, Stephen moved into her home in the Rue Jacob on the old Rive Gauche, there to start her new life in Paris.

2

All alone in the brown and white salle à manger, Stephen and Puddle ate their Christmas dinner. And Puddle had bought a small Christmas tree and had trimmed it, then hung it with coloured candles. A little wax Christ-child bent downwards and sideways from His branch, as though He were looking for His presents*—only now there were not any presents. Rather clumsily Stephen lit the candles as soon as the daylight had almost faded. Then she and Puddle stood and stared at the tree, but in silence, because they must both remember. But Pierre, who like all who have known the sea was a child at heart, broke into loud exclamations. 'Oh, comme c'est beau, l'arbre de Noël!'* he exclaimed, and he fetched the dour Pauline along from the kitchen, and she too exclaimed; then they both fetched Adèle and they all three exclaimed: 'Comme c'est beau, l'arbre de Noël!' So that after all the little wax Christ-child did not very much miss His presents.

That evening Pauline's two brothers arrived—they were Poilus* stationed just outside Paris—and they brought along with them another young man, one Jean, who was ardently courting Adèle. Very soon came the sound of singing and laughter from the kitchen, and when Stephen went up to her bedroom to look for a book, there was Adèle quite flushed and with very bright eyes because of this Jean—in great haste she turned down the bed and then flew on the wings of love back to the kitchen.

But Stephen went slowly downstairs to her study where Puddle was sitting in front of the fire, and she thought that Puddle sat there as though tired; her hands were quite idle, and after a moment Stephen noticed that she was dozing. Very quietly Stephen opened her book, unwilling to rouse the little grey woman who looked so small in the huge leather chair, and whose head kept guiltily nodding. But the book seemed scarcely worth troubling to read, so that presently Stephen laid it aside and sat staring into the flickering logs that hummed and burnt blue because it was frosty. On the Malvern Hills there would probably be snow; deep snow might be capping the Worcestershire Beacon. The air up at British Camp would be sweet with the smell of winter and open spaces—little lights would be glinting far down in the valley. At Morton the lakes would be still and frozen, so Peter the swan would be feeling friendly—in winter he had always fed from her hand—he must be old now, the swan called Peter. Coup! C-o-u-p! and Peter waddling towards her. He, who was all gliding grace on the water, would come awkwardly waddling towards her hand for the chunk of dry bread that she held in her fingers. Jean with his Adèle along in the kitchen—a nice-looking boy he was, Stephen had seen him—they were young, and both were exceedingly happy, for their parents approved, so some day they would marry. Then children would come, too many, no doubt, for Jean's slender purse, and yet in this life one must pay for one's pleasures—they would pay with their children, and this appeared perfectly fair to Stephen. She thought that it seemed a long time ago since she herself had been a small child, romping about on the floor with her father, bothering Williams down at the stables, dressing up as young Nelson and posing for Collins who had sometimes been cross to young Nelson. She was nearly thirty, and what had she done? Written one good novel and one very bad one, with few mediocre short stories thrown in. Oh, well, she was going to start writing again quite soon—she had an idea for a novel. But she sighed, and Puddle woke up with a start.

'Is that you, my dear? Have I been asleep?'

'Only for a very few minutes, Puddle.'

Puddle glanced at the new gold watch on her wrist; it had been a Christmas present from Stephen. 'It's past ten o'clock—I think I'll turn in.'

'Do. Why not? I hope Adèle's filled your hot water bottle; she's rather light-headed over her Jean.'

'Never mind, I can fill it myself,' smiled Puddle.

She went, and Stephen sat on by the fire with her eyes half closed and her lips set firmly. She must put away all these thoughts of the past and compel herself to think of the future. This brooding over things that were past was all wrong; it was futile, weak-kneed and morbid. She had her work, work that cried out to be done, but no more unworthy books must be written. She must show that being the thing she was, she could climb to success over all opposition, could climb to success in spite of a world that was trying its best to get her under. Her mouth grew hard; her sensitive lips that belonged by rights to the dreamer, the lover, took on a resentful and bitter line which changed her whole face and made it less comely. At that moment the striking likeness of her father appeared to have faded out of her face.

Yes, it was trying to get her under, this world with its mighty self-satisfaction, with its smug rules of conduct, all made to be broken by those who strutted and preened themselves on being what they considered normal. They trod on the necks* of those thousands of others who, for God knew what reason, were not made as they were; they prided themselves on their indignation, on what they proclaimed as their righteous judgments. They sinned grossly; even vilely at times, like lustful beasts—but yet they were normal! And the vilest of them could point a finger of scorn at her, and be loudly applauded.

'God damn them to hell!' she muttered.

Along in the kitchen there was singing again. The young men's voices rose tuneful and happy, and with them blended Adèle's young voice, very sexless as yet, like the voice of a choirboy. Stephen got up and opened the door, then she stood quite still and listened intently. The singing soothed her overstrained nerves as it flowed from the hearts of these simple people. For she did not begrudge them their happiness; she did not resent young Jean with his Adèle, or Pierre who had done a man's work in his time, or Pauline who was often aggressively female. Bitter she had grown in these years since Morton, but not bitter enough to resent the simple. And then as she listened they suddenly stopped for a little before they resumed their singing, and when they resumed it the tune was sad with the sadness that dwells in the souls of most men, above all in the patient soul of the peasant.

'Mais comment ferez vous, l'Abbé,
Ma Doué?'

She could hear the soft Breton words quite clearly.

'Mais comment ferez vous, l'Abbé,
Pour nous dire la Messe?'
'Quand la nuit sera bien tombée
Je tiendrai ma promesse.'

'Mais comment ferez vous, l'Abbé,
Ma Doué,
Mais comment ferez vous, l'Abbé,
Sans nappe de fine toile?'
'Notre Doux Seigneur poserai
Sur un morceau de voile.'

'Mais comment ferez vous, l'Abbé,
Ma Doué,
Mais comment ferez vous, l'Abbé,
Sans chandelle et sans cierge?'
'Les astres seront allumés
Par Madame la Vierge.'

'Mais comment ferez vous, l'Abbé,
Ma Doué,
Mais comment ferez vous, l'Abbé,
Sans orgue résonnante?'
'Jésus touchera le clavier
Des vagues mugissantes.'

'Mais comment ferez vous, l'Abbé,
Ma Doué,
Mais comment ferez vous, l'Abbé,
Si l'Ennemi nous trouble?'
'Une seule fois je vous bénirai,
Les Bleus bénirai double!'*

Closing the study door behind her, Stephen thoughtfully climbed the stairs to her bedroom.

CHAPTER 33

I

WITH the New Year came flowers from Valérie Seymour, and a little letter of New Year's greeting. Then she paid a rather ceremonious call and was entertained by Puddle and Stephen. Before leaving she invited them both to luncheon, but Stephen refused on the plea of her work.

'I'm hard at it again.'

At this Valérie smiled. 'Very well then, à bientôt.* You know where to find me, ring up when you're free, which I hope will be soon.' After which she took her departure.

But Stephen was not to see her again for a very considerable time, as it happened. Valérie was also a busy woman—there are other affairs beside the writing of novels.

Brockett was in London on account of his plays. He wrote seldom, though when he did so he was cordial, affectionate even; but now he was busy with success, and with gathering in the shekels.* He had not lost interest in Stephen again, only just at the moment she did not fit in with his brilliant and affluent scheme of existence.

So once more she and Puddle settled down together to a life that was strangely devoid of people, a life of almost complete isolation, and Puddle could not make up her mind whether she felt relieved or regretful. For herself she cared nothing, her anxious thoughts were as always centred in Stephen. However, Stephen appeared quite contented—she was launched on her book and was pleased with her writing. Paris inspired her to do good work, and as recreation she now had her fencing—twice every week she now fenced with Buisson, that severe but incomparable master.

Buisson had been very rude at first: 'Hideous, affreux, horriblement English!'* he had shouted, quite outraged by Stephen's style. All the same he took a great interest in her. 'You write books; what a pity! I could make you a fine fencer. You have the man's muscles, and the long, graceful lunge when you do not remember that you are a Briton and become—what you say? ah, mais oui, self-conscious. I wish that I had find you out sooner—however, your muscles are young still, pliant.' And one day he said: 'Let me feel the muscles,' then proceeded to pass his hand down her thighs and across her strong loins: 'Tiens, tiens!'* he murmured.

After this he would sometimes look at her gravely with a puzzled expression; but she did not resent him, nor his rudeness, nor his technical interest in her muscles. Indeed, she liked the cross little man with his bristling black beard and his peppery temper, and when he remarked à propos of nothing: 'We are all great imbeciles about nature. We make our own rules and call them la nature; we say she do this, she do that—imbeciles! She do what she please and then make the long nose,'* Stephen felt neither shy nor resentful.

These lessons were a great relaxation from work, and thanks to them her health grew much better. Her body, accustomed to severe exercise, had resented the sedentary life in London. Now, however, she began to take care of her health, walking for a couple of hours in the Bois* every day, or exploring the tall, narrow streets that lay near her home in the Quarter. The sky would look bright at the end of such streets by contrast, as though it were seen through a tunnel. Sometimes she would stand gazing into the shops of the wider and more prosperous Rue des Saints Pères;* the old furniture shops; the crucifix shop with its dozens of crucified Christs in the window—so many crucified ivory Christs! She would think that one must surely exist for every sin committed in Paris. Or perhaps she would make her way over the river, crossing it by the Pont des Arts. And one morning, arrived at the Rue des Petits Champs, what must she suddenly do but discover the Passage Choiseul,* by just stepping inside for shelter, because it had started raining.

Oh, the lure of the Passage Choiseul, the queer, rather gawky attraction of it. Surely the most hideous place in all Paris, with its roof of stark wooden ribs and glass panes—the roof that looks like the vertebral column of some prehistoric monster. The chocolate smell of the patisserie—the big one where people go who have money. The humbler, student smell of Lavrut, where one's grey rubber bands are sold by the gramme and are known as: 'Bracelets de caoutchouc.' Where one buys première qualité blotting paper of a deep ruddy tint and the stiffness of cardboard, and thin but inspiring manuscript books bound in black, with mottled, shiny blue borders. Where pencils and pens are found in their legions, of all makes, all shapes, all colours, all prices; while outside on the trustful trays in the Passage, lives Gomme Onyx, masquerading as marble, and as likely to rub a hole in your paper. For those who prefer the reading of books to the writing of them, there is always Lemerre with his splendid display of yellow bindings. And for those undisturbed by imagination, the taxidermist's shop is quite near the corner—they can stare at a sad and moth-eaten flamingo, two squirrels, three parrots and a dusty canary. Some are tempted by the cheap corduroy at the draper's, where it stands in great rolls as though it were carpet. Some pass on to the little stamp merchant, while a few dauntless souls even enter the chemist's—that shamelessly anatomical chemist's, whose wares do not figure in school manuals on the practical uses of rubber.

And up and down this Passage Choiseul, pass innumerable idle or busy people, bringing in mud and rain in the winter, bringing in dust and heat in the summer, bringing in God knows how many thoughts, some part of which cannot escape with their owners. The very air of the Passage seems heavy with all these imprisoned thoughts.

Stephen's thoughts got themselves entrapped with the others, but hers, at the moment, were those of a schoolgirl, for her eye had suddenly lit on Lavrut, drawn thereto by the trays of ornate india-rubber. And once inside, she could not resist the 'Bracelets de caoutchouc,' or the blotting paper as red as a rose, or the manuscript books with the mottled blue borders. Growing reckless, she gave an enormous order for the simple reason that these things looked different. In the end she actually carried away one of those inspiring manuscript books, and then got herself driven home by a taxi, in order the sooner to fill it.

2

That spring, in the foyer of the Comédie Française,* Stephen stumbled across a link with the past in the person of a middle-aged woman. The woman was stout and wore pince-nez;* her sparse brown hair was already greying; her face, which was long, had a double chin, and that face seemed vaguely familiar to Stephen. Then suddenly Stephen's two hands were seized and held fast in those of the middle-aged woman, while a voice grown loud with delight and emotion was saying:

'Mais oui, c'est ma petite Stévenne!'

Back came a picture of the schoolroom at Morton, with a battered red book on its ink-stained table—the Bibliothèque Rose—'Les

Petites Filles Modèles,' 'Les Bons Enfants,' and Mademoiselle Duphot.

Stephen said: 'To think—after all these years!'

'Ah, quelle joie! Quelle joie!'* babbled Mademoiselle Duphot.

And now Stephen was being embraced on both cheeks, then held at arm's length for a better inspection. 'But how tall, how strong you are, ma petite Stévenne. You remember what I say, that we meet in Paris? I say when I go, "But you come to Paris when you grow up bigger, my poor little baby!" I keep looking and looking, but I knowed you at once. I say, "Oui certainement, that is ma petite Stévenne, no one 'ave such another face what I love, it could only belong to Stévenne," I say. And now voilà! I am correct and I find you.'

Stephen released herself firmly but gently, replying in French to calm Mademoiselle, whose linguistic struggles increased every moment.

'I'm living in Paris altogether,' she told her; 'you must come and see me—come to dinner to-morrow; 35 Rue Jacob.' Then she introduced Puddle, who had been an amused spectator.

The two ex-guardians of Stephen's young mind shook hands with each other very politely, and they made such a strangely contrasted couple that Stephen must smile to see them together. The one was so small, so quiet and so English; the other so portly, so tearful, so French in her generous, if somewhat embarrassing emotion.

As Mademoiselle regained her composure, Stephen was able to observe her more closely, and she saw that her face was excessively childish—a fact which she, when a child, had not noticed. It was more the face of a foal than a horse—an innocent, new-born foal.

Mademoiselle said rather wistfully: 'I will dine with much pleasure to-morrow evening, but when will you come and see me in my home? It is in the Avenue de la Grande Armée,* a small apartment, very small but so pretty—it is pleasant to have one's treasures around one. The bon Dieu has been very good to me, Stévenne, for my Aunt Clothilde left me a little money when she died; it has proved a great consolation.'

'I'll come very soon,' promised Stephen.

Then Mademoiselle spoke at great length of her aunt, and of Maman who had also passed on into glory; Maman, who had had her chicken on Sunday right up to the very last moment, Dieu merci!

Even when her teeth had grown loose in the gums, Maman had asked for her chicken on Sunday. But alas, the poor sister who once made little bags out of beads for the shops in the Rue de la Paix, and who had such a cruel and improvident husband—the poor sister had now become totally blind, and therefore dependent on Mademoiselle Duphot. So after all Mademoiselle Duphot still worked, giving lessons in French to the resident English; and sometimes she taught the American children who were visiting Paris with their parents. But then it was really far better to work; one might grow too fat if one remained idle.

She beamed at Stephen with her gentle brown eyes. 'They are not as you were, ma chère petite Stévenne, not clever and full of intelligence, no; and at times I almost despair of their accent. However, I am not at all to be pitied, thanks to Aunt Clothilde and the good little saints who surely inspired her to leave me that money.'

When Stephen and Puddle returned to their stalls, Mademoiselle climbed to a humbler seat somewhere under the roof, and as she departed she waved her plump hand at Stephen.

Stephen said: 'She's so changed that I didn't know her just at first, or else perhaps I'd forgotten. I felt terribly guilty, because after you came I don't think I ever answered her letters. It's thirteen years since she left. . . .'

Puddle nodded. 'Yes, it's thirteen years since I took her place and forced you to tidy that abominable schoolroom!' And she laughed. 'All the same, I like her,' said Puddle.

3

Mademoiselle Duphot admired the house in the Rue Jacob, and she ate very largely of the rich and excellent dinner. Quite regardless of her increasing proportions, she seemed drawn to all those things that were fattening.

'I cannot resist,' she remarked with a smile, as she reached for her fifth marron glacé.*

They talked of Paris, of its beauty, its charm. Then Mademoiselle spoke yet again of her Maman and of Aunt Clothilde who had left them the money, and of Julie, her blind sister.

But after the meal she quite suddenly blushed. 'Oh, Stévenne, I have never inquired for your parents! What must you think of such great impoliteness? I lose my head the moment I see you and grow selfish—I want you to know about me and my Maman; I babble about my affairs. What must you think of such great impoliteness? How is that kind and handsome Sir Philip? And your mother, my dear, how is Lady Anna?'

And now it was Stephen's turn to grow red. 'My father died. . . .' She hesitated, then finished abruptly, 'I don't live with my mother any more, I don't live at Morton.'

Mademoiselle gasped. 'You no longer live . . .' she began, then something in Stephen's face warned her kind but bewildered guest not to question. 'I am deeply grieved to hear of your father's death, my dear,' she said very gently.

Stephen answered: 'Yes—I shall always miss him.'

There ensued a long, rather painful silence, during which Mademoiselle Duphot felt awkward. What had happened between the mother and daughter? It was all very strange, very disconcerting. And Stephen, why was she exiled from Morton? But Mademoiselle could not cope with these problems, she knew only that she wanted Stephen to be happy, and her kind brown eyes grew anxious, for she did not feel certain that Stephen was happy. Yet she dared not ask for an explanation, so instead she clumsily changed the subject.

'When will you both come to tea with me, Stévenne?'

'We'll come to-morrow if you like,' Stephen told her.

Mademoiselle Duphot left rather early; and all the way home to her apartment her mind felt exercised about Stephen.

She thought: 'She was always a strange little child, but so dear. I remember her when she was little, riding her pony astride like a boy; and how proud he would seem, that handsome Sir Philip—they would look more like father and son, those two. And now—is she not still a little bit strange?'

But these thoughts led her nowhere, for Mademoiselle Duphot was quite unacquainted with the bypaths of nature. Her innocent mind was untutored and trustful; she believed in the legend of Adam and Eve, and no careless mistakes had been made in their garden!

4

The apartment in the Avenue de la Grande Armée was as tidy as Valérie's had been untidy. From the miniature kitchen to the miniature salon, everything shone as though recently polished, for here in spite of restricted finances, no dust was allowed to harbour.

Mademoiselle Duphot beamed on her guests as she herself opened the door to admit them. 'For me this is very real joy,' she declared. Then she introduced them to her sister Julie, whose eyes were hidden behind dark glasses.

The salon was literally stuffed with what Mademoiselle had described as her 'treasures.' On its tables were innumerable useless objects which appeared, for the most part, to be mementoes. Coloured prints of Bouguereaus* hung on the walls, while the chairs were upholstered in a species of velvet so hard as to be rather slippery to sit on, yet that when it was touched felt rough to the fingers. The woodwork of these inhospitable chairs had been coated with varnish until it looked sticky. Over the little inadequate fireplace smiled a portrait of Maman when she was quite young. Maman, dressed in tartan for some strange reason, but in tartan that had never hob-nobbed with the Highlands—a present this portrait had been from a cousin who had wished to become an artist.

Julie extended a white, groping hand. She was like her sister only very much thinner, and her face had the closed rather blank expression that is sometimes associated with blindness.

'Which is Stévenne?' she inquired in an anxious voice; 'I have heard so much about Stévenne!'

Stephen said: 'Here I am,' and she grasped the hand, pitiful of this woman's affliction.

But Julie smiled broadly. 'Yes, I know it is you from the feel,'—she had started to stroke Stephen's coat-sleeve—'my eyes have gone into my fingers these days. It is strange, but I seem to see through my fingers.' Then she turned and found Puddle whom she also stroked. 'And now I know both of you,' declared Julie.

The tea when it came was that straw-coloured liquid which may even now be met with in Paris.

'English tea bought especially for you, my Stévenne,' remarked Mademoiselle proudly. 'We drink only coffee, but I said to my sister, Stévenne likes the good tea, and so, no doubt, does Mademoiselle Puddle. At four o'clock they will not want coffee—you observe how well I remember your England!'

However, the cakes proved worthy of France, and Mademoiselle ate them as though she enjoyed them. Julie ate very little and did not talk much. She just sat there and listened, quietly smiling; and while she listened she crocheted lace as though, as she said, she could see through her fingers. Then Mademoiselle Duphot explained how it was that those delicate hands had become so skilful, replacing the eyes which their ceaseless labour had robbed of the blessèd privilege of sight—explained so simply yet with such conviction, that Stephen must marvel to hear her.

'It is all our little Thérèse,' she told Stephen. 'You have heard of her? No? Ah, but what a pity! Our Thérèse was a nun at the Carmel at Lisieux, and she said: "I will let fall a shower of roses when I die." She died not so long ago, but already her Cause has been presented at Rome by the Very Reverend Father Rodrigo! That is very wonderful, is it not, Stévenne? But she does not wait to become a saint; ah, but no, she is young and therefore impatient. She cannot wait, she has started already to do miracles for all those who ask her. I asked that Julie should not be unhappy through the loss of her eyes—for when she is idle she is always unhappy—so our little Thérèse has put a pair of new eyes in her fingers.'*

Julie nodded. 'It is true,' she said very gravely; 'before that I was stupid because of my blindness. Everything felt very strange, and I stumbled about like an old blind horse. I was terribly stupid, far more so than many. Then one night Véronique asked Thérèse to help me, and the next day I could find my way round our room. From then on my fingers saw what they touched, and now I can even make lace quite well because of this sight in my fingers.' Then turning to the smiling Mademoiselle Duphot: 'But why do you not show her picture to Stévenne?'

So Mademoiselle Duphot went and fetched the small picture of Thérèse, which Stephen duly examined, and the face that she saw was ridiculously youthful—round with youth it still was, and yet very determined. Sœur Thérèse looked as though if she really intended to become a saint, the devil himself would be hard put to it to stop her. Then Puddle must also examine the picture, while Stephen was shown some relics, a piece of the habit and other things such as collect in the wake of sainthood.

When they left, Julie asked them to come again; she said: 'Come often, it will give us such pleasure.' Then she thrust on her guests twelve yards of coarse lace which neither of them liked to offer to pay for.

Mademoiselle murmured: 'Our home is so humble for Stévenne; we have very little to offer.' She was thinking of the house in the Rue Jacob, a grand house, and then too she remembered Morton.

But Julie, with the strange insight of the blind, or perhaps because of those eyes in her fingers, answered quickly: 'She will not care, Véronique, I cannot feel that sort of pride in your Stévenne.'

5

After their first visit they went very often to Mademoiselle's modest little apartment. Mademoiselle Duphot and her quiet blind sister were indeed their only friends now in Paris, for Brockett was in America on business, and Stephen had not rung up Valérie Seymour.

Sometimes when Stephen was busy with her work, Puddle would make her way there all alone. Then she and Mademoiselle would get talking about Stephen's childhood, about her future, but guardedly, for Puddle must be careful to give nothing away to the kind, simple woman. As for Mademoiselle, she too must be careful to accept all and ask no questions. Yet in spite of the inevitable gaps and restraints, a real sympathy sprang up between them, for each sensed in the other a valuable ally who would fight a good fight on behalf of Stephen. And now Stephen would quite often send her car to take the blind Julie for a drive beyond Paris. Julie would sniff the air and tell Burton that through smelling their greenness she could see the trees; he would listen to her broken and halting English with a smile—they were a queer lot these French. Or perhaps he would drive the other Mademoiselle up to Montmartre for early Mass on a Sunday. She belonged to something to do with a heart; it all seemed rather uncanny to Burton. He thought of the Vicar who had played such fine cricket, and suddenly felt very homesick for Morton. Fruit would find its way to the little apartment, together with cakes and large marrons glacés. Then Mademoiselle Duphot would become frankly greedy, eating sweets in bed while she studied her booklets on the holy and very austere Thérèse, who had certainly not eaten marrons glacés.

Thus the spring, that gentle yet fateful spring of 1914, slipped into the summer. With the budding of flowers and the singing of birds it slipped quietly on towards great disaster; while Stephen, whose book was now nearing completion, worked harder than ever in Paris.

CHAPTER 34

I

WAR.* The incredible yet long predicted had come to pass. People woke in the mornings with a sense of disaster, but these were the old who, having known war, remembered. The young men of France, of Germany, of Russia, of the whole world, looked round them amazed and bewildered; yet with something that stung as it leapt in their veins, filling them with a strange excitement—the bitter and ruthless potion of war that spurred and lashed at their manhood.

They hurried through the streets of Paris, these young men; they collected in bars and cafés; they stood gaping at the ominous government placards summoning their youth and strength to the colours.

They talked fast, very fast, they gesticulated: 'C'est la guerre! C'est la guerre!'* they kept repeating.

Then they answered each other: 'Oui, c'est la guerre.'

And true to her traditions the beautiful city sought to hide stark ugliness under beauty, and she decked herself as though for a wedding; her flags streamed out on the breeze in their thousands. With the paraphernalia and pageantry of glory she sought to disguise the true meaning of war.

But where children had been playing a few days before, troops were now encamped along the Champs Elysées.* Their horses nibbled the bark from the trees and pawed at the earth, making little hollows; they neighed to each other in the watches of the night, as though in some fearful anticipation. In by-streets the unreasoning spirit of war broke loose in angry and futile actions; shops were raided because of their German names* and their wares hurled out to lie in the gutters. Around every street corner some imaginary spy must be lurking, until people tilted at shadows.

'C'est la guerre,' murmured women, thinking of their sons.

Then they answered each other: 'Oui, c'est la guerre.'

Pierre said to Stephen: 'They will not take me because of my heart!' And his voice shook with anger, and the anger brought tears which actually splashed the jaunty stripes of his livery waistcoat.

Pauline said: 'I gave my father to the sea and my eldest brother. I have still two young brothers, they alone are left and I give them to France. Bon Dieu! It is terrible being a woman, one gives all!' But Stephen knew from her voice that Pauline felt proud of being a woman.

Adèle said: 'Jean is certain to get promotion, he says so, he will not long remain a Poilu. When he comes back he may be a captain—that will be fine, I shall marry a captain! War, he says, is better than piano-tuning, though I tell him he has a fine ear for music. But Mademoiselle should just see him now in his uniform! We all think he looks splendid.'

Puddle said: 'Of course England was bound to come in, and thank God we didn't take too long about it!'

Stephen said: 'All the young men from Morton will go—every decent man in the country will go.' Then she put away her unfinished novel and sat staring dumbly at Puddle.

2

England, the land of bountiful pastures, of peace, of mothering hills, of home. England was fighting for her right to existence. Face to face with dreadful reality at last, England was pouring her men into battle, her army was even now marching across France. Tramp, tramp; tramp, tramp; the tread of England whose men would defend her right to existence.

Anna wrote from Morton. She wrote to Puddle, but now Stephen took those letters and read them. The agent had enlisted and so had the bailiff. Old Mr. Percival, agent in Sir Philip's lifetime, had come back to help with Morton. Jim the groom, who had stayed on under the coachman after Raftery's death, was now talking of going; he wanted to get into the cavalry, of course, and Anna was using her influence for him. Six of the gardeners had joined up already, but Hopkins was past the prescribed age limit; he must do his small bit by looking after his grape vines—the grapes would be sent to the wounded in London. There were now no men-servants left in the house, and the home farm was short of a couple of hands. Anna wrote that she was proud of her people, and intended to pay those who had enlisted half wages. They would fight for England, but she could not help feeling that in a way they would be fighting for Morton. She had offered Morton to the Red Cross* at once, and they had promised to send her convalescent cases. It was rather isolated for a hospital, it seemed, but would be just the place for convalescents. The Vicar was going as an army chaplain; Violet's husband, Alec, had joined the Flying Corps;* Roger Antrim was somewhere in France already; Colonel Antrim had a job at the barracks in Worcester.

Came an angry scrawl from Jonathan Brockett, who had rushed back to England post-haste from the States: 'Did you ever know anything quite so *stupid* as this war? It's upset my apple-cart completely—can't write jingo plays about St. George and the dragon, and I'm sick to death of "Business as usual!"* Ain't going to be no business, my dear, except killing, and blood always makes me feel faint.' Then the postscript: 'I've just been and gone and done it! Please send me tuck-boxes when I'm sitting in a trench; I like caramel creams and of course mixed biscuits.' Yes, even Jonathan Brockett would go—it was fine in a way that he should have enlisted.

Morton was pouring out its young men, who in their turn might pour out their life-blood for Morton. The agent, the bailiff, in training already. Jim the groom, inarticulate, rather stupid, but wanting to join the cavalry—Jim who had been at Morton since boyhood. The gardeners, kindly men smelling of soil, men of peace with a peaceful occupation; six of these gardeners had gone already, together with a couple of lads from the home farm. There were no men-servants left in the house. It seemed that the old traditions still held, the traditions of England, the traditions of Morton.

The Vicar would soon play a sterner game than cricket, while Alec must put away his law-books and take unto himself a pair of wings—funny to associate wings with Alec. Colonel Antrim had hastily got into khaki and was cursing and swearing, no doubt, at the barracks. And Roger—Roger was somewhere in France already, justifying his manhood. Roger Antrim, who had been so intolerably proud of that manhood—well, now he would get a chance to prove it!

But Jonathan Brockett, with the soft white hands, and the foolish gestures, and the high little laugh—even he could justify his existence, for they had not refused him when he went to enlist. Stephen had never thought to feel envious of a man like Jonathan Brockett.

She sat smoking, with his letter spread out before her on the desk, his absurd yet courageous letter, and somehow it humbled her pride to the dust, for she could not so justify her existence. Every instinct handed down by the men of her race, every decent instinct of courage, now rose to mock her so that all that was male in her make-up seemed to grow more aggressive, aggressive perhaps as never before, because of this new frustration. She felt appalled at the realization of her own grotesqueness; she was nothing but a freak abandoned on a kind of no-man's-land at this moment of splendid national endeavour. England was calling her men into battle, her women to the bedsides of the wounded and dying, and between these two chivalrous, surging forces she, Stephen, might well be crushed out of existence—of less use to her country, she was, than Brockett. She stared at her bony masculine hands,* they had never been skilful when it came to illness; strong they might be, but rather inept; not hands wherewith to succour the wounded. No, assuredly her job, if job she could find, would not lie at the bedsides of the wounded. And yet, good God, one must do something!

Going to the door she called in the servants: 'I'm leaving for England in a few days,' she told them, 'and while I'm away you'll take care of this house. I have absolute confidence in you.'

Pierre said: 'All things shall be done as you would wish, Mademoiselle.' And she knew that it would be so.

That evening she told Puddle of her decision, and Puddle's face brightened: 'I'm so glad, my dear, when war comes one ought to stand by one's country.'

'I'm afraid they won't want my sort . . .' Stephen muttered.

Puddle put a firm little hand over hers: 'I wouldn't be too sure of that, this war may give your sort of woman her chance. I think you may find that they'll need you, Stephen.'

3

There were no farewells to be said in Paris except those to Buisson and Mademoiselle Duphot.

Mademoiselle Duphot shed a few tears: 'I find you only to lose you, Stévenne. Ah, but how many friends will be parted, perhaps for ever, by this terrible war—and yet what else could we do? We are blameless!'

In Berlin people were also saying: 'What else could we do? We are blameless!'

Julie's hand lingered on Stephen's arm: 'You feel so strong,' she said, sighing a little, 'it is good to be strong and courageous these days, and to have one's eyes—alas, I am quite useless.'

'No one is useless who can pray, my sister,' reproved Mademoiselle almost sternly.

And indeed there were many who thought as she did, the churches were crowded all over France. A great wave of piety swept through Paris, filling the dark confessional boxes, so that the priests had now some ado to cope with such shoals of penitent people—the more so as every priest fit to fight had been summoned to join the army. Up at Montmartre the church of the Sacré Cœur echoed and re-echoed with the prayers of the faithful, while those prayers that were whispered with tears in secret, hung like invisible clouds round its altars.

'Save us, most Sacred Heart of Jesus. Have pity upon us, have pity upon France. Save us, oh, Heart of Jesus!'

So all day long must the priests sit and hear the time-honoured sins of body and spirit; a monotonous hearing because of its sameness, since nothing is really new under the sun, least of all our manner of sinning. Men who had not been to Mass for years, now began to remember their first Communion; thus it was that many a hardy blasphemer, grown suddenly tongue-tied and rather sheepish, clumped up to the altar in his new army boots, having made an embarrassed confession.

Young clericals changed into uniform and marched side by side with the roughest Poilus, to share in their hardships, their hopes, their terrors, their deeds of supremest valour. Old men bowed their heads and gave of the strength which no longer animated their bodies, gave of that strength through the bodies of their sons who would charge into battle shouting and singing. Women of all ages knelt down and prayed, since prayer has long been the refuge of women. 'No one is useless who can pray, my sister.' The women of France had spoken through the lips of the humble Mademoiselle Duphot.

Stephen and Puddle said good-bye to the sisters, then went on to Buisson's Academy of Fencing, where they found him engaged upon greasing his foils.*

He looked up, 'Ah, it's you. I must go on greasing. God knows when I shall use these again, to-morrow I join my regiment.' But he wiped his hands on a stained overall and sat down, after clearing a chair for Puddle. 'An ungentlemanly war it will be,' he grumbled. 'Will I lead my men with a sword? Ah, but no! I will lead my men with a dirty revolver in my hand. Parbleu!* Such is modern warfare! A machine could do the whole cursèd thing better—we shall all be nothing but machines in this war. However, I pray that we may kill many Germans.'

Stephen lit a cigarette while the master glared, he was evidently in a very vile temper: 'Go on, go on, smoke your heart to the devil, then come here and ask me to teach you fencing! You smoke in lighting one from the other, you remind me of your horrible Birmingham chimneys*—but of course a woman exaggerates always,' he concluded, with an evident wish to annoy her.

Then he made a few really enlightening remarks about Germans in general, their appearance, their morals, above all their personal habits—which remarks were more seemly in French than they would be in English. For, like Valérie Seymour, this man was filled with a loathing for the ugliness of his epoch, an ugliness to which he felt the Germans were just now doing their best to contribute. Buisson's heart was not buried in Mitylene,* but rather in the glories of a by-gone Paris, where a gentleman lived by the skill of his rapier and the graceful courage that lay behind it.

'In the old days we killed very beautifully,' sighed Buisson, 'now we merely slaughter or else do not kill at all, no matter how gross the insult.'

However, when they got up to go, he relented: 'War is surely a very necessary evil, it thins down the imbecile populations who have murdered their most efficacious microbes.* People will not die, very well, here comes war to mow them down in their tens of thousands. At least for those of us who survive, there will be more breathing space, thanks to the Germans—perhaps they too are a necessary evil.'

Arrived at the door, Stephen turned to look back. Buisson was once more greasing his foils, and his fingers moved slowly yet with great precision—he might almost have been a beauty doctor engaged upon massaging ladies' faces.

Preparations for departure did not take very long, and in less than a week's time Stephen and Puddle had shaken hands with their Breton servants, and were driving at top speed en route for Havre,* from whence they would cross to England.

4

Puddle's prophecy proved to have been correct, work was very soon forthcoming for Stephen. She joined The London Ambulance Column,* which was well under way by that autumn; and presently

Puddle herself got a job in one of the Government departments. She and Stephen had taken a small service flat in Victoria, and here they would meet when released from their hours of duty. But Stephen was obsessed by her one idea, which was, willy-nilly, to get out to the front, and many and varied were the plans and discussions that were listened to by the sympathetic Puddle. An ambulance had managed to slip over to Belgium for a while and had done some very fine service.* Stephen had hit on a similar idea, but in her case the influence required had been lacking. In vain did she offer to form a Unit at her own expense; the reply was polite but always the same, a monotonous reply: England did not send women to the front-line trenches. She disliked the idea of joining the throng who tormented the patient passport officials with demands to be sent out to France at once, on no matter how insufficient a pretext. What was the use of her going to France unless she could find there the work that she wanted? She preferred to stick to her job in England.

And now quite often while she waited at the stations for the wounded, she would see unmistakable figures—unmistakable to her they would be at first sight, she would single them out of the crowd as by instinct. For as though gaining courage from the terror that is war, many a one who was even as Stephen, had crept out of her hole and come into the daylight, come into the daylight and faced her country: 'Well, here I am, will you take me or leave me?' And England had taken her,* asking no questions—she was strong and efficient, she could fill a man's place, she could organize too, given scope for her talent. England had said: 'Thank you very much. You're just what we happen to want . . . at the moment.'

So, side by side with more fortunate women, worked Miss Smith who had been breeding dogs in the country;* or Miss Oliphant* who had been breeding nothing since birth but a litter of hefty complexes; or Miss Tring who had lived with a very dear friend in the humbler purlieus of Chelsea. One great weakness they all had, it must be admitted, and this was for uniforms—yet why not? The good workman is worthy of his Sam Browne belt.* And then too, their nerves were not at all weak, their pulses beat placidly through the worst air raids, for bombs do not trouble the nerves of the invert, but rather that terrible silent bombardment from the batteries of God's good people.*

Yet now even really nice women with hairpins often found their less orthodox sisters quite useful. It would be: 'Miss Smith, do just start up my motor—the engine's so cold I can't get the thing going'; or: 'Miss Oliphant, do glance through these accounts, I've got such a rotten bad head for figures'; or: 'Miss Tring, may I borrow your British Warm?* The office is simply arctic this morning!'

Not that those purely feminine women were less worthy of praise, perhaps they were more so, giving as they did of their best without stint—for they had no stigma to live down in the war, no need to defend their right to respect. They rallied to the call of their country superbly, and may it not be forgotten by England. But the others—since they too gave of their best, may they also not be forgotten. They might look a bit odd, indeed some of them did, and yet in the streets they were seldom stared at, though they strode a little, perhaps from shyness, or perhaps from a slightly self-conscious desire to show off, which is often the same thing as shyness. They were part of the universal convulsion and were being accepted as such, on their merits. And although their Sam Browne belts remained swordless, their hats and their caps without regimental badges, a battalion was formed in those terrible years that would never again be completely disbanded. War and death had given them a right to life, and life tasted sweet, very sweet to their palates. Later on would come bitterness, disillusion,* but never again would such women submit to being driven back to their holes and corners. They had found themselves—thus the whirligig of war brings in its abrupt revenges.

5

Time passed; the first year of hostilities became the second while Stephen still hoped, though no nearer to her ambition. Try as she might she could not get sent to the front; no work at the actual front seemed to be forthcoming for women.

Brockett wrote wonderfully cheerful letters. In every letter was a neat little list telling Stephen what he wished her to send him; but the sweets he loved were getting quite scarce, they were no longer always so easy to come by. And now he was asking for Houbigant soap to be included in his tuck-box.

'Don't let it get near the coffee fondants or it may make them taste like it smells,' he cautioned, 'and do try to send me two bottles of hair-wash, "Eau Athénienne," I used to buy it at Truefitt's.'* He was on a perfectly damnable front, they had sent him to Mesopotamia.*

Violet Peacock, who was now a V.A.D.* with a very imposing Red Cross on her apron, occasionally managed to catch Stephen at home, and then would come reams of tiresome gossip. Sometimes she would bring her over-fed children along, she was stuffing them up like capons.* By fair means or foul Violet always managed to obtain illicit cream for her nursery—she was one of those mothers who reacted to the war by wishing to kill off the useless agèd.

'What's the good of them? Eating up the food of the nation!' she would say, 'I'm going all out on the young, they'll be needed to breed from.' She was very extreme, her perspective had been upset by the air raids.

Raids frightened her as did the thought of starvation, and when frightened she was apt to grow rather sadistic, so that now she would want to rush off and inspect every ruin left by the German marauders. She had also been the first to applaud the dreadful descent of a burning Zeppelin.*

She bored Stephen intensely with her ceaseless prattle about Alec, who was one of London's defenders, about Roger, who had got the Military Cross* and was just on the eve of becoming a major, about the wounded whose faces she sponged every morning, and who seemed so pathetically grateful.

From Morton came occasional letters for Puddle; they were more in the nature of reports now, these letters. Anna had such and such a number of cases; the gardeners had been replaced by young women; Mr. Percival was proving very devoted, he and Anna were holding the estate well together; Williams had been seriously ill with pneumonia. Then a long list of humble names from the farms, from among Anna's staff or from cottage homesteads, together with those from such houses as Morton—for the rich and the poor were in death united. Stephen would read that long list of names, so many of which she had known since her childhood, and would realize that the stark arm of war had struck deep at the quiet heart of the Midlands.

BOOK FOUR*

CHAPTER 35

I

A STUMP of candle in the neck of a bottle flickered once or twice and threatened to go out. Getting up, Stephen found a fresh candle and lit it, then she returned to her packing-case upon which had been placed the remnants of a chair minus its legs and arms.

The room had once been the much prized salon of a large and prosperous villa in Compiègne,* but now the glass was gone from its windows; there remained only battered and splintered shutters which creaked eerily in the bitter wind of a March night in 1918. The walls of the salon had fared little better than its windows, their brocade was detached and hanging, while a recent rainstorm had lashed through the roof making ugly splotches on the delicate fabric—a dark stain on the ceiling was perpetually dripping. The remnants of what had once been a home, little broken tables, an old photograph in a tarnished frame, a child's wooden horse, added to the infinite desolation of this villa that now housed the Breakspeare Unit*—a Unit composed of Englishwomen, that had been serving in France just over six months, attached to the French Army Ambulance Corps.

The place seemed full of grotesquely large shadows cast by figures that sat or sprawled on the floor. Miss Peel in her Jaeger* sleeping-bag snored loudly, then choked because of her cold. Miss Delmé-Howard was gravely engaged upon making the best of a difficult toilet—she was brushing out her magnificent hair which gleamed in the light of the candle. Miss Bless was sewing a button on her tunic; Miss Thurloe was peering at a half-finished letter; but most of the women who were herded together in this, the safest place in the villa and none too safe at that be it said, were apparently sleeping quite soundly. An uncanny stillness had descended on the town; after many hours of intensive bombardment, the Germans were having a breathing space before training their batteries once more upon Compiègne.

Stephen stared down at the girl who lay curled up at her feet in an army blanket. The girl slept the sleep of complete exhaustion, breathing heavily with her head on her arm; her pale and rather triangular face was that of some one who was still very young, not much more than nineteen or twenty. The pallor of her skin was accentuated by the short black lashes which curled back abruptly, by the black arched eyebrows and dark brown hair—sleek hair which grew to a peak on the forehead, and had recently been bobbed for the sake of convenience. For the rest her nose was slightly tip-tilted, and her mouth resolute considering her youth; the lips were well-modelled and fine in texture, having deeply indented corners. For more than a minute Stephen considered the immature figure of Mary Llewellyn. This latest recruit to the Breakspeare Unit had joined it only five weeks ago, replacing a member who was suffering from shell-shock.* Mrs. Breakspeare had shaken her head over Mary, but in these harassed days of the German offensive she could not afford to remain short-handed, so in spite of many misgivings she had kept her.

Still shaking her head she had said to Stephen: 'Needs must when the Boches* get busy, Miss Gordon! Have an eye to her, will you? She may stick it all right, but between you and me I very much doubt it. You might try her out as your second driver.' And so far Mary Llewellyn had stuck it.

Stephen looked away again, closing her eyes, and after a while she forgot about Mary. The events that had preceded her own coming to France began to pass through her brain in procession. Her chief in The London Ambulance Column, through whom she had first met Mrs. Claude Breakspeare—a good sort, the chief, she had been a staunch friend. The great news that she, Stephen, had been accepted and would go to the front as an ambulance driver. Then Puddle's grave face: 'I must write to your mother, this means that you will be in real danger.' Her mother's brief letter: 'Before you leave I should very much like you to come and see me,' the rest of the letter mere polite empty phrases. The impulse to resist, the longing to go, culminating in that hurried visit to Morton. Morton so changed and yet so changeless. Changed because of those blue-clad figures,* the lame, the halt and the partially blinded who had sought its peace and its kindly protection. Changeless because that protection and peace belonged to the very spirit of Morton. Mrs. Williams a widow; her niece melancholic ever since the groom Jim had been wounded and missing—they had married while he had been home on leave, and quite soon the poor soul was expecting a baby. Williams now dead of his third and last stroke, after having survived pneumonia. The swan called Peter no longer gliding across the lake on his white reflection, and in his stead an unmannerly offspring who struck out with his wings and tried to bite Stephen. The family vault where her father lay buried—the vault was in urgent need of repair—'No men left, Miss Stephen, we're that short of stonemasons; her ladyship's bin complainin' already, but it don't be no use complainin' these times.' Raftery's grave—a slab of rough granite: 'In memory of a gentle and courageous friend, whose name was Raftery, after the poet.' Moss on the granite half effacing the words; the thick hedge growing wild for the want of clipping. And her mother—a woman with snow-white hair and a face that was worn almost down to the spirit; a woman of quiet but uncertain movements, with a new trick of twisting the rings on her fingers. 'It was good of you to come.' 'You sent for me, Mother.' Long silences filled with the realization that all they dared hope for was peace between them—too late to go back—they could not retrace their steps even though there was now peace between them. Then those last poignant moments in the study together—memory, the old room was haunted by it—a man dying with love in his eyes that was deathless—a woman holding him in her arms, speaking words such as lovers will speak to each other. Memory—they're the one perfect thing about me. 'Stephen, promise to write when you're out in France, I shall want to hear from you.' 'I promise, Mother.' The return to London; Puddle's anxious voice: 'Well, how was she?' 'Very frail, you must go to Morton.' Puddle's sudden and almost fierce rebellion: 'I would rather not go, I've made my choice, Stephen.' 'But I ask this for my sake, I'm worried about her—even if I weren't going away, I couldn't go back now and live at Morton—our living together would make us remember.' 'I remember too, Stephen, and what I remember is hard to forgive. It's hard to forgive an injury done to some one one loves. . . .' Puddle's face, very white, very stern—strange to hear such words as these on the kind lips of Puddle. 'I know, I know, but she's terribly alone, and I can't forget that my father loved her.' A long silence, and then: 'I've never yet failed you—and you're right—I must go to Morton.'

Stephen's thoughts stopped abruptly. Some one had come in and was stumping down the room in squeaky trench boots. It was Blakeney holding the time-sheet in her hand—funny old monosyllabic Blakeney, with her curly white hair cropped as close as an Uhlan's,* and her face that suggested a sensitive monkey.

'Service, Gordon; wake the kid! Howard—Thurloe—ready?'

They got up and hustled into their trench coats, found their gas masks and finally put on their helmets.

Then Stephen shook Mary Llewellyn very gently: 'It's time.'

Mary opened her clear, grey eyes: 'Who? What?' she stammered.

'It's time. Get up, Mary.'

The girl staggered to her feet, still stupid with fatigue. Through the cracks in the shutters the dawn showed faintly.

2

The grey of a bitter, starved-looking morning. The town like a mortally wounded creature, torn by shells, gashed open by bombs. Dead streets—streets of death—death in streets and their houses; yet people still able to sleep and still sleeping.

'Stephen.'

'Yes, Mary?'

'How far is the Poste?'*

'I think about thirty kilometres; why?'

'Oh, nothing—I only wondered.'

The long stretch of an open country road. On either side of the road wire netting hung with pieces of crudely painted rag—a camouflage this to represent leaves. A road bordered by rag leaves on tall wire hedges. Every few yards or so a deep shell-hole.

'Are they following, Mary? Is Howard all right?'

The girl glanced back: 'Yes, it's all right, she's coming.'

They drove on in silence for a couple of miles. The morning was terribly cold; Mary shivered. 'What's that?' It was rather a foolish question for she knew what it was, knew only too well!

'They're at it again,' Stephen muttered.

A shell burst in a paddock, uprooting some trees. 'All right, Mary?'

'Yes—look out! We're coming to a crater!' They skimmed it by less than an inch and dashed on, Mary suddenly moving nearer to Stephen.

'Don't joggle my arm, for the Lord's sake, child!'

'Did I? I'm sorry.'

'Yes—don't do it again,' and once more they drove forward in silence.

Farther down the road they were blocked by a farm cart: 'Militaires! Militaires! Militaires!'* Stephen shouted.

Rather languidly the farmer got down and went to the heads of his thin, stumbling horses. 'Il faut vivre,'* he explained, as he pointed to the cart, which appeared to be full of potatoes.

In a field on the right worked three very old women; they were hoeing with a diligent and fatalistic patience. At any moment a stray shell might burst and then, presto! little left of the very old women. But what will you? There is war—there has been war so long—one must eat, even under the noses of the Germans; the bon Dieu knows this, He alone can protect—so meanwhile one just goes on diligently hoeing. A blackbird was singing to himself in a tree, the tree was horribly maimed and blasted; all the same he had known it the previous spring and so now, in spite of its wounds, he had found it. Came a sudden lull when they heard him distinctly.

And Mary saw him: 'Look,' she said, 'there's a blackbird!' Just for a moment she forgot about war.

Yet Stephen could now very seldom forget, and this was because of the girl at her side. A queer, tight feeling would come round her heart, she would know the fear that can go hand in hand with personal courage, the fear for another.

But now she looked down for a moment and smiled: 'Bless that blackbird for letting you see him, Mary.' She knew that Mary loved little, wild birds, that indeed she loved all the humbler creatures.

They turned into a lane and were comparatively safe, but the roar of the guns had grown much more insistent. They must be nearing the Poste de Secours, so they spoke very little because of those guns, and after a while because of the wounded.

3

The Poste de Secours was a ruined auberge at the cross-roads, about fifty yards behind the trenches. From what had once been its spacious cellar, they were hurriedly carrying up the wounded, maimed and mangled creatures who, a few hours ago, had been young and vigorous men. None too gently the stretchers were lowered to the ground beside the two waiting ambulances—none too gently because there were so many of them, and because there must come a time in all wars when custom stales even compassion.

The wounded were patient and fatalistic, like the very old women back in the field. The only difference between them being that the men had themselves become as a field laid bare to a ruthless and bloody hoeing. Some of them had not even a blanket to protect them from the biting cold of the wind. A Poilu with a mighty wound in the belly, must lie with the blood congealing on the bandage. Next to him lay a man with his face half blown away, who, God alone knew why, remained conscious. The abdominal case was the first to be handled, Stephen herself helped to lift his stretcher. He was probably dying, but he did not complain except inasmuch as he wanted his mother. The voice that emerged from his coarse, bearded throat was the voice of a child demanding its mother. The man with the terrible face tried to speak, but when he did so the sound was not human. His bandage had slipped a little to one side, so that Stephen must step between him and Mary, and hastily readjust the bandage.

'Get back to the ambulance! I shall want you to drive.'

In silence Mary obeyed her.

And now began the first of those endless journeys from the Poste de Secours to the Field Hospital. For twenty-four hours they would ply back and forth with their light Ford ambulances.* Driving quickly because the lives of the wounded might depend on their speed, yet with every nerve taut to avoid, as far as might be, the jarring of the hazardous roads full of ruts and shell-holes.

The man with the shattered face started again, they could hear him above the throb of the motor. For a moment they stopped while Stephen listened, but his lips were not there . . . an intolerable sound.

'Faster, drive faster, Mary!'

Pale, but with firmly set, resolute mouth, Mary Llewellyn drove faster.

When at last they reached the Field Hospital, the bearded Poilu with the wound in his belly was lying very placidly on his stretcher; his hairy chin pointing slightly upward. He had ceased to speak as a little child—perhaps, after all, he had found his mother.

The day went on and the sun shone out brightly, dazzling the tired eyes of the drivers. Dusk fell, and the roads grew treacherous and vague. Night came—they dared not risk having lights, so that they must just stare and stare into the darkness. In the distance the sky turned ominously red, some stray shells might well have set fire to a village, that tall column of flame was probably the church; and the Boches were punishing Compiègne again, to judge from the heavy sounds of bombardment. Yet by now there was nothing real in the world but that thick and almost impenetrable darkness, and the ache of the eyes that must stare and stare, and the dreadful, patient pain of the wounded—there had never been anything else in the world but black night shot through with the pain of the wounded.

4

On the following morning the two ambulances crept back to their base at the villa in Compiègne. It had been a tough job, long hours of strain, and to make matters worse the reliefs had been late, one of them having had a breakdown. Moving stiffly, and with red rimmed and watering eyes, the four women swallowed large cups of coffee; then just as they were they lay down on the floor, wrapped in their trench coats and army blankets. In less than a quarter of an hour they slept, though the villa shook and rocked with the bombardment.

CHAPTER 36

I

THERE is something that mankind can never destroy in spite of an unreasoning will to destruction, and this is its own idealism, that integral part of its very being. The ageing and the cynical may make wars, but the young and the idealistic must fight them, and thus there are bound to come quick reactions, blind impulses not always comprehended. Men will curse as they kill, yet accomplish deeds of self-sacrifice, giving their lives for others; poets will write with their pens dipped in blood, yet will write not of death but of life eternal; strong and courteous friendships will be born, to endure in the face of enmity and destruction. And so persistent is this urge to the ideal, above all in the presence of great disaster, that mankind, the wilful destroyer of beauty, must immediately strive to create new beauties, lest it perish from a sense of its own desolation; and this urge touched the Celtic soul of Mary.

For the Celtic soul is the stronghold of dreams, of longings come down the dim paths of the ages; and within it there dwells a vague discontent, so that it must for ever go questing. And now as though drawn by some hidden attraction, as though stirred by some irresistible impulse, quite beyond the realms of her own understanding, Mary turned in all faith and all innocence to Stephen. Who can pretend to interpret fate, either his own fate or that of another? Why should this girl have crossed Stephen's path, or indeed Stephen hers, if it came to that matter? Was not the world large enough for them both? Perhaps not—or perhaps the event of their meeting had already been written upon tablets of stone by some wise if relentless recording finger.

An orphan from the days of her earliest childhood, Mary had lived with a married cousin in the wilds of Wales; an unwanted member of a none too prosperous household. She had little education beyond that obtained from a small private school in a neighbouring village. She knew nothing of life or of men and women; and even less did she know of herself, of her ardent, courageous, impulsive nature. Thanks to the fact that her cousin was a doctor, forced to motor over a widely spread practice, she had learnt to drive and look after his car by filling the post of an unpaid chauffeur—she was, in her small way, a good mechanic. But the war had made her much less contented with her narrow life, and although at its outbreak Mary had been not quite eighteen, she had felt a great longing to be independent, in which she had met with no opposition. However, a Welsh village is no field for endeavour, and thus nothing had happened until by a fluke she had suddenly heard of the Breakspeare Unit via the local parson, an old friend of its founder—he himself had written to recommend Mary. And so, straight from the quiet seclusion of Wales, this girl had managed the complicated journey that had finally got her over to France, then across a war-ravaged, dislocated country. Mary was neither so frail nor so timid as Mrs. Breakspeare had thought her.

Stephen had felt rather bored just at first at the prospect of teaching the new member her duties, but after a while it came to pass that she missed the girl when she was not with her. And after a while she would find herself observing the way Mary's hair grew, low on the forehead, the wide setting of her slightly oblique grey eyes, the abrupt sweep back of their heavy lashes; and these things would move Stephen, so that she must touch the girl's hair for a moment with her fingers. Fate was throwing them continually together, in moments of rest as in moments of danger; they could not have escaped this even had they wished to, and indeed they did not wish to escape it. They were pawns in the ruthless and complicated game of existence, moved hither and thither on the board by an unseen hand, yet moved side by side, so that they grew to expect each other.

'Mary, are you there?'

A superfluous question—the reply would be always the same.

'I'm here, Stephen.'

Sometimes Mary would talk of her plans for the future while Stephen listened, smiling as she did so.

'I'll go into an office, I want to be free.'

'You're so little, you'd get mislaid in an office.'

'I'm five foot five!'

'Are you really, Mary? You feel little, somehow.'

'That's because you're so tall. I do wish I could grow a bit!'

'No, don't wish that, you're all right as you are—it's you, Mary.'

Mary would want to be told about Morton, she was never tired of hearing about Morton. She would make Stephen get out the photographs of her father, of her mother whom Mary thought lovely, of Puddle, and above all of Raftery. Then Stephen must tell her of the life in London, and afterwards of the new house in Paris; must talk of her own career and ambitions, though Mary had not read either of her novels—there had never been a library subscription.

But at moments Stephen's face would grow clouded because of the things that she could not tell her; because of the little untruths and evasions that must fill up the gaps in her strange life-history. Looking down into Mary's clear grey eyes, she would suddenly flush through her tan, and feel guilty; and that feeling would reach the girl and disturb her, so that she must hold Stephen's hand for a moment.

One day she said suddenly: 'Are you unhappy?'

'Why on earth should I be unhappy?' smiled Stephen.

All the same there were nights now when Stephen lay awake even after her arduous hours of service, hearing the guns that were coming nearer, yet not thinking of them, but always of Mary. A great gentleness would gradually engulf her like a soft sea mist, veiling reef and headland. She would seem to be drifting quietly, serenely towards some blessèd and peaceful harbour. Stretching out a hand she would stroke the girl's shoulder where she lay, but carefully in case she should wake her. Then the mist would lift: 'Good God! What am I doing?' She would sit up abruptly, disturbing the sleeper.

'Is that you, Stephen?'

'Yes, my dear, go to sleep.'

Then a cross, aggrieved voice: 'Do shut up, you two. It's rotten of you, I was just getting off! Why must you always persist in talking!'

Stephen would lie down again and would think: 'I'm a fool, I go out of my way to find trouble. Of course I've grown fond of the child, she's so plucky, almost anyone would grow fond of Mary. Why shouldn't I have affection and friendship? Why shouldn't I have a real human interest? I can help her to find her feet after the war if we both come through—I might buy her a business.' That gentle mist, hiding both reef and headland; it would gather again blurring all perception, robbing the past of its crude, ugly outlines. 'After all, what harm can it do the child to be fond of me?' It was so good a thing to have won the affection of this young creature.

2

The Germans got perilously near to Compiègne, and the Breakspeare Unit was ordered to retire. Its base was now at a ruined château on the outskirts of an insignificant village, yet not so very insignificant either—it was stuffed to the neck with ammunition. Nearly all the hours that were spent off duty must be passed in the gloomy, damp-smelling dug-outs which consisted of cellars, partly destroyed but protected by sandbags on heavy timbers. Like foxes creeping out of their holes, the members of the Unit would creep into the daylight, their uniforms covered with mould and rubble, their eyes blinking, their hands cold and numb from the dampness—so cold and so numb that the starting up of motors would often present a real problem.

At this time there occurred one or two small mishaps; Bless broke her wrist while cranking her engine; Blakeney and three others at a Poste de Secours, were met by a truly terrific bombardment and took cover in what had once been a brickfield, crawling into the disused furnace. There they squatted for something over eight hours, while the German gunners played hit as hit can with the tall and conspicuous chimney. When at last they emerged, half stifled by brick-dust, Blakeney had got something into her eye, which she rubbed; the result was acute inflammation.

Howard had begun to be irritating, with her passion for tending her beautiful hair. She would sit in the corner of her dug-out as calmly as though she were sitting at a Bond Street hairdresser's; and having completed the ritual brushing, she would gaze at herself in a pocket mirror. With a bandage over her unfortunate eye, Blakeney looked more like a monkey than ever,* a sick monkey, and her strictly curtailed conversation was not calculated to enliven the Unit. She seemed almost entirely bereft of speech these days, as though reverting to species. Her one comment on life was: 'Oh, I dunno . . .' always said with a jaunty, rising inflexion. It meant everything or nothing as you chose to take it, and had long been her panacea for the ills of what she considered a stupid Creation. 'Oh, I dunno. . . .' And indeed she did not; poor, old, sensitive, monosyllabic Blakeney. The Poilu who served out the Unit's rations—cold meat, sardines, bread and sour red Pinard*—was discovered by Stephen in the very act of attempting to unload an aerial bomb. He explained with a smile that the Germans were sly in their methods of loading: 'I cannot discover just how it is done.' Then he showed his left hand—it was minus one of the fingers: 'That,' he told her, still smiling, 'was caused by a shell, a quite little shell, which I was also unloading.' And when she remonstrated none too gently, he sulked: 'But I wish to give this one to Maman!'

Every one had begun to feel the nerve strain, except perhaps Blakeney, who had done with all feeling. Shorthanded by two, the remaining members of the Unit must now work like veritable niggers—on one occasion Stephen and Mary worked for seventy hours with scarcely a respite. Strained nerves are invariably followed by strained tempers, and sudden, hot quarrels would break out over nothing. Bless and Howard loathed each other for two days, then palled up again, because of a grievance that had recently been evolved against Stephen. For every one knew that Stephen and Blakeney were by far the best drivers in the Breakspeare Unit, and as such should be shared by all the members in turn; but poor Blakeney was nursing a very sore eye, while Stephen still continued to drive only with Mary. They were splendidly courageous and great-hearted women, every one of them, glad enough as a rule to help one another to shoulder burdens, to be tolerant and kind when it came to friendships. They petted and admired their youngest recruit, and most of them liked and respected Stephen, all the same they had now grown childishly jealous, and this jealousy reached the sharp ears of Mrs. Breakspeare.

Mrs. Breakspeare sent for Stephen one morning; she was sitting at a Louis Quinze* writing-table which had somehow survived the wreck of the château and was now in her gloomy, official dug-out. Her right hand reposed on an ordnance map, she looked like a very maternal general. The widow of an officer killed in the war, and the mother of two large sons and three daughters, she had led the narrow, conventional life that is common to women in military stations. Yet all the while she must have been filling her sub-conscious reservoir with knowledge, for she suddenly blossomed forth as a leader with a fine understanding of human nature. So now she looked over her ample bosom not unkindly, but rather thoughtfully at Stephen.

'Sit down, Miss Gordon. It's about Llewellyn, whom I asked you to take on as second driver. I think the time has now arrived when she ought to stand more on her own in the Unit. She must take her chance like every one else, and not cling quite so close—don't misunderstand me, I'm most grateful for all you've done for the girl—but of course you are one of our finest drivers, and fine driving counts for a great deal these days, it may mean life or death, as you yourself know. And—well—it seems scarcely fair to the others that Mary should always go out with you. No, it certainly is not quite fair to the others.'

Stephen said: 'Do you mean that she's to go out with every one in turn—with Thurloe for instance?' And do what she would to appear indifferent, she could not quite keep her voice from trembling.

Mrs. Breakspeare nodded: 'That's what I do mean.' Then she said rather slowly: 'These are strenuous times, and such times are apt to breed many emotions which are purely fictitious, purely mushroom growths that spring up in a night and have no roots at all, except in our imaginations. But I'm sure you'll agree with me, Miss Gordon, in thinking it our duty to discourage anything in the nature of an emotional friendship, such as I fancy Mary Llewellyn is on the verge of feeling for you. It's quite natural of course, a kind of reaction, but not wise—no, I cannot think it wise. It savours a little too much of the schoolroom* and might lead to ridicule in the Unit. Your position is far too important for that; I look upon you as my second in command.'

Stephen said quietly: 'I quite understand. I'll go at once and speak to Blakeney about altering Mary Llewellyn's time-sheet.'

'Yes, do, if you will,' agreed Mrs. Breakspeare; then she stooped and studied her ordnance map, without looking again at Stephen.

3

If Stephen had been fearful for Mary's safety before, she was now ten times more so. The front was in a condition of flux and the Postes de Secours were continually shifting. An Allied ambulance driver had been fired on by the Germans, after having arrived at the spot where his Poste had been only the previous evening. There was very close fighting on every sector; it seemed truly amazing that no grave casualties had so far occurred in the Unit. For now the Allies had begun to creep forward, yard by yard, mile by mile, very slowly but surely; refreshed by a splendid transfusion of blood from the youthful veins of a great child-nation.*

Of all the anxieties on Mary's account that now beset Stephen, Thurloe was the gravest; for Thurloe was one of those irritating drivers who stake all on their own inadequate judgment. She was brave to a fault, but inclined to show off when it came to a matter of actual danger. For long hours Stephen would not know what had happened, and must often leave the base before Mary had returned, still in doubt regarding her safety.

Grimly, yet with unfailing courage and devotion, Stephen now went about her duties. Every day the risks that they all took grew graver, for the enemy, nearing the verge of defeat, was less than ever a respecter of persons. Stephen's only moments of comparative peace would be when she herself drove Mary. And as though the girl missed some vitalizing force, some strength that had hitherto been hers to draw on, she flagged, and Stephen would watch her flagging during their brief spells together off duty, and would know that nothing but her Celtic pluck kept Mary Llewellyn from a breakdown. And now, because they were so often parted, even chance meetings became of importance. They might meet while preparing their cars in the morning, and if this should happen they would draw close together for a moment, as though finding comfort in nearness.

Letters from home would arrive for Stephen, and these she would want to read to Mary. In addition to writing, Puddle sent food, even luxuries sometimes, of a pre-war nature. To obtain them she must have used bribery and corruption, for food of all kinds had grown scarce in England. Puddle, it seemed, had a mammoth war map into which she stuck pins with gay little pennants. Every time the lines moved by so much as a yard, out would come Puddle's pins to go in at fresh places; for since Stephen had left her to go to the front, the war had become very personal to Puddle.

Anna also wrote, and from her Stephen learnt of the death of Roger Antrim. He had been shot down while winning his V.C.* through saving the life of a wounded captain. All alone he had gone over to no-man's-land and had rescued his friend where he lay unconscious, receiving a bullet through the head at the moment of flinging the wounded man into safety. Roger—so lacking in understanding, so crude, so cruel and remorseless a bully—Roger had been changed in the twinkling of an eye into something superb because utterly selfless. Thus it was that the undying urge of mankind towards the ideal had come upon Roger. And Stephen as she sat there and read of his passing, suddenly knew that she wished him well, that his courage had wiped one great bitterness out of her heart and her life for ever. And so by dying as he had died, Roger, all unknowing, had fulfilled the law that must be extended to enemy and friend alike—the immutable law of service.

4

Events gathered momentum. By the June of that year 700,000 United States soldiers, strong and comely men plucked from their native prairies, from their fields of tall corn, from their farms and their cities, were giving their lives in defence of freedom on the blood-soaked battlefields of France. They had little to gain and much to lose; it was not their war, yet they helped to fight it because they were young and their nation was young, and the ideals of youth are eternally hopeful.

In July came the Allied counter-offensive,* and now in her moment of approaching triumph France knew to the full her great desolation, as it lay revealed by the retreating armies. For not only had there been a holocaust of homesteads, but the country was strewn with murdered trees, cut down in their hour of most perfect leafing; orchards struck to the ground, an orgy of destruction,* as the mighty forces rolled back like a tide, to recoil on themselves—incredulous, amazed, maddened by the outrage of coming disaster. For mad they must surely have been, since no man is a more faithful lover of trees than the German.

Stephen as she drove through that devastated country would find herself thinking of Martin Hallam—Martin who had touched the old thorns on the hills with such respectful and pitiful fingers: 'Have you ever thought about the enormous courage of trees? I have and it seems to me amazing. The Lord dumps them down and they've just got to stick it, no matter what happens—that must need some courage.' Martin had believed in a heaven for trees, a forest heaven for all the faithful; and looking at those pitiful, leafy corpses, Stephen would want to believe in that heaven. Until lately she had not thought of Martin for years, he belonged to a past that was better forgotten, but now she would sometimes wonder about him. Perhaps he was dead, smitten down where he stood, for many had perished where they stood, like the orchards. It was strange to think that he might have been here in France, have been fighting and have died quite near her. But perhaps he had not been killed after all—she had never told Mary about Martin Hallam.

All roads of thought seemed to lead back to Mary; and these days, in addition to fears for her safety, came a growing distress at what she must see—far more terrible sights than the patient wounded. For everywhere now lay the wreckage of war, sea-wrack spewed up by a poisonous ocean—putrefying, festering in the sun; breeding corruption to man's seed of folly. Twice lately, while they had been driving together, they had come upon sights that Stephen would have spared her. There had been that shattered German gun-carriage with its stiff, dead horses and its three dead gunners—horrible death, the men's faces had been black like the faces of negroes, black and swollen from gas, or was it from putrefaction? There had been the deserted and wounded charger with its fore-leg hanging as though by a rag. Near by had been lying a dead young Uhlan, and Stephen had shot the beast with his revolver,* but Mary had suddenly started sobbing: 'Oh, God! Oh, God! It was dumb—it couldn't speak. It's so awful somehow to see a thing suffer when it can't ask you why!' She had sobbed a long time, and Stephen had not known how to console her.

And now the Unit was creeping forward in the wake of the steadily advancing Allies. Billets would be changed as the base was moved on slowly from devastated village to village. There seldom seemed to be a house left with a roof, or with anything much beyond its four walls, and quite often they must lie staring up at the stars, which would stare back again, aloof and untroubled. At about this time they grew very short of water, for most of the wells were said to have been poisoned; and this shortage of water was a very real torment, since it strictly curtailed the luxury of washing. Then what must Bless do but get herself hit while locating the position of a Poste de Secours which had most inconsiderately vanished. Like the Allied ambulance driver, she was shot at, but in her case she happened to stop a bullet—it was only a flesh wound high up in the arm, yet enough to render her useless for the moment. She had had to be sent back to hospital, so once again the Unit was short-handed.

It turned hot, and in place of the dampness and the cold, came days and nights that seemed almost breathless; days when the wounded must lie out in the sun, tormented by flies as they waited their turn to be lifted into the ambulances. And as though misfortunes attracted each other, as though indeed they were hunting in couples, Stephen's face was struck by a splinter of shell, and her right cheek cut open rather badly. It was neatly stitched up by the little French doctor at the Poste de Secours, and when he had finished with his needle and dressings, he bowed very gravely: 'Mademoiselle will carry an honourable scar* as a mark of her courage,' and he bowed yet again, so that in the end Stephen must also bow gravely. Fortunately, however, she could still do her job, which was all to the good for the short-handed Unit.

5

On an autumn afternoon of blue sky and sunshine, Stephen had the Croix de Guerre* pinned on her breast by a white-haired and white-moustached general. First came the motherly Mrs. Claude

Breakspeare, whose tunic looked much too tight for her bosom, then Stephen and one or two other members of that valiant and untiring Unit. The general kissed each one in turn on both cheeks, while overhead hovered a fleet of Aces;* troops presented arms, veteran troops tried in battle, and having the set look of war in their eyes—for the French have a very nice taste in such matters. And presently Stephen's bronze Croix de Guerre would carry three miniature stars on its ribbon, and each star would stand for a mention in despatches.*

That evening she and Mary walked over the fields to a little town not very far from their billets. They paused for a moment to watch the sunset, and Mary stroked the new Croix de Guerre; then she looked straight up into Stephen's eyes, her mouth shook, and Stephen saw that she was crying. After this they must walk hand in hand for a while. Why not? There was no one just then to see them.

Mary said: 'All my life I've been waiting for something.'

'What was it, my dear?' Stephen asked her gently.

And Mary answered: 'I've been waiting for you, and it's seemed such a dreadful long time, Stephen.'

The barely healed wound across Stephen's cheek flushed darkly, for what could she find to answer?

'For me?' she stammered.

Mary nodded gravely: 'Yes, for you. I've always been waiting for you; and after the war you'll send me away.' Then she suddenly caught hold of Stephen's sleeve: 'Let me come with you—don't send me away, I want to be near you. . . . I can't explain . . . but I only want to be near you, Stephen. Stephen—say you won't send me away. . . .'

Stephen's hand closed over the Croix de Guerre, but the metal of valour felt cold to her fingers; dead and cold it felt at that moment, as the courage that had set it upon her breast. She stared straight ahead of her into the sunset, trembling because of what she would answer.

Then she said very slowly: 'After the war—no, I won't send you away from me, Mary.'*

CHAPTER 37

I

THE most stupendous and heartbreaking folly of our times drew towards its abrupt conclusion. By November the Unit was stationed at St. Quentin* in a little hotel, which although very humble, seemed like paradise after the dug-outs.

A morning came when a handful of the members were together in the coffee-room, huddled round a fire that was principally composed of damp brushwood. At one moment the guns could be heard distinctly, the next, something almost unnatural had happened—there was silence, as though death had turned on himself, smiting his own power of destruction. No one spoke, they just sat and stared at each other with faces entirely devoid of emotion; their faces looked blank, like so many masks from which had been sponged every trace of expression—and they waited—listening to that silence.

The door opened and in walked an untidy Poilu; his manner was casual, his voice apathetic: 'Eh bien, mesdames, c'est l'Armistice.'* But his shining brown eyes were not at all apathetic. 'Oui, c'est l'Armistice,' he repeated coolly; then he shrugged, as a man might do who would say: 'What is all this to me?' After which he grinned broadly in spite of himself, he was still very young, and turning on his heel he departed.

Stephen said: 'So it's over,' and she looked at Mary, who had jumped up, and was looking in her turn at Stephen.

Mary said: 'This means . . .' but she stopped abruptly.

Bless said: 'Got a match, anyone? Oh, thanks!' And she groped for her white-metal cigarette case.

Howard said: 'Well, the first thing *I'm* going to do is to get my hair properly shampooed in Paris.'

Thurloe laughed shrilly, then she started to whistle, kicking the recalcitrant fire as she did so.

But funny, old, monosyllabic Blakeney with her curly white hair cropped as close as an Uhlan's—Blakeney who had long ago done with emotions—quite suddenly laid her arms on the table and her head on her arms, and she wept, and she wept.

2

Stephen stayed with the Unit right up to the eve of its departure for Germany, then she left it, taking Mary Llewellyn with her. Their work was over; remained only the honour of joining the army's triumphal progress, but Mary Llewellyn was completely worn out, and Stephen had no thought except for Mary.

They said farewell to Mrs. Claude Breakspeare, to Howard and Blakeney and the rest of their comrades. And Stephen knew, as indeed did they also, that a mighty event had slipped into the past, had gone from them into the realms of history—something terrible yet splendid, a oneness with life in its titanic struggle against death. Not a woman of them all but felt vaguely regretful in spite of the infinite blessing of peace, for none could know what the future might hold of trivial days filled with trivial actions. Great wars will be followed by great discontents—the pruning knife has been laid to the tree, and the urge to grow throbs through its mutilated branches.

3

The house in the Rue Jacob was *en fête** in honour of Stephen's arrival. Pierre had rigged up an imposing flagstaff, from which waved a brand-new tricolour commandeered by Pauline from the neighbouring baker; flowers had been placed in the study vases, while Adèle had contrived to produce the word 'welcome' in immortelles,* as the *pièce de resistance*, and had hung it above the doorway.

Stephen shook hands with them all in turn, and she introduced Mary, who also shook hands. Then Adèle must start to gabble about Jean, who was quite safe although not a captain; and Pauline must interrupt her to tell of the neighbouring baker who had lost his four sons, and of one of her brothers who had lost his right leg—her face very dour and her voice very cheerful, as was always the way when she told of misfortunes. And presently she must also deplore the long straight scar upon Stephen's cheek: 'Oh, la pauvre! Pour une dame c'est un vrai désastre!'* But Pierre must point to the green and red ribbon in Stephen's lapel: 'C'est la Croix de Guerre!' so that in the end they all gathered round to admire that half-inch of honour and glory.

Oh, yes, this home-coming was as friendly and happy as good will and warm Breton hearts could make it. Yet Stephen was oppressed by a sense of restraint when she took Mary up to the charming bedroom overlooking the garden, and she spoke abruptly.

'This will be your room.'

'It's beautiful, Stephen.'

After that they were silent, perhaps because there was so much that might not be spoken between them.

The dinner was served by a beaming Pierre, an excellent dinner, more than worthy of Pauline; but neither of them managed to eat very much—they were far too acutely conscious of each other. When the meal was over they went into the study where, in spite of the abnormal shortage of fuel, Adèle had managed to build a huge fire which blazed recklessly half up the chimney. The room smelt slightly of hothouse flowers, of leather, of old wood and vanished years, and after a while of cigarette smoke.

Then Stephen forced herself to speak lightly: 'Come and sit over here by the fire,' she said, smiling.

So Mary obeyed, sitting down beside her, and she laid a hand upon Stephen's knee; but Stephen appeared not to notice that hand, for she just let it lie there and went on talking.

'I've been thinking, Mary, hatching all sorts of schemes. I'd like to get you right away for a bit, the weather seems pretty awful in Paris. Puddle once told me about Teneriffe, she went there ages ago with a pupil. She stayed at a place called Orotava;* it's lovely, I believe—do you think you'd enjoy it? I might manage to hear of a villa with a garden, and then you could just slack about in the sunshine.'

Mary said, very conscious of the unnoticed hand: 'Do you really want to go away, Stephen? Wouldn't it interfere with your writing?' Her voice, Stephen thought, sounded strained and unhappy.

'Of course I want to go,' Stephen reassured her, 'I'll work all the better for a holiday. Anyhow, I must see you looking more fit,' and she suddenly laid her hand over Mary's.

The strange sympathy which sometimes exists between two human bodies, so that a touch will stir many secret and perilous emotions, closed down on them both at that moment of contact, and they sat unnaturally still by the fire, feeling that in their stillness lay safety. But presently Stephen went on talking, and now she talked of purely practical matters. Mary must go for a fortnight to her cousins, she had better go almost at once, and remain there while Stephen herself went to Morton. Eventually they would meet in London and from there motor straight away to Southampton, for Stephen would have taken their passages and if possible found a furnished villa, before she went down to Morton. She talked on and on, and as she did so her fingers tightened and relaxed abruptly on the hand that she had continued to hold, so that Mary imprisoned those nervous fingers in her own, and Stephen made no resistance.

Then Mary, like many another before her, grew as happy as she had been downhearted; for the merest trifles are often enough to change the trend of mercurial emotions such as beset the heart in its youth; and she looked at Stephen with gratitude in her eyes, and with something far more fundamental of which she herself was unconscious. And now she began to talk in her turn. She could type fairly well, was a very good speller; she would type Stephen's books, take care of her papers, answer her letters, look after the house, even beard* the lugubrious Pauline in her kitchen. Next autumn she would write to Holland for bulbs—they must have lots of bulbs in their city garden, and in summer they ought to manage some roses—Paris was less cruel to flowers than London. Oh, and might she have pigeons with wide, white tails? They would go so well with the old marble fountain.

Stephen listened, nodding from time to time. Yes, of course she could have her white fan-tailed pigeons, and her bulbs, and her roses, could have anything she pleased, if only she would get quite well and be happy.

At this Mary laughed: 'Oh, Stephen, my dear—don't you know that I'm really terribly happy?'

Pierre came in with the evening letters; there was one from Anna and another from Puddle. There was also a lengthy epistle from Brockett who was praying, it seemed, for demobilization.* Once released, he must go for a few weeks to England, but after that he was coming to Paris.

He wrote: 'I'm longing to see you again and Valérie Seymour. By the way, how goes it? Valérie writes that you never rang her up. It's a pity you're so unsociable, Stephen; unwholesome, I call it, you'll be bagging a shell like a hermit crab, or growing hairs on your chin, or a wart on your nose, or worse still a complex. You might even take to a few nasty habits towards middle life—better read Ferenczi!* Why were you so beastly to Valérie, I wonder? She is such a darling and she likes you so much, only the other day she wrote: "When you see Stephen Gordon give her my love, and tell her that nearly all streets in Paris lead sooner or later to Valérie Seymour." You might write her a line, and you might write to me—already I'm finding your silence suspicious. Are you in love? I'm just crazy to know, so why deny me that innocent pleasure? After all, we're told to rejoice with those who rejoice—may I send my congratulations? Vague but exciting rumours have reached me. And by the way, Valérie's very forgiving, so don't feel shy about telephoning to her. She's one of those highly developed souls who bob up serenely after a snubbing, as do I, your devoted Brockett.'

Stephen glanced at Mary as she folded the letter: 'Isn't it time you went off to bed?'

'Don't send me away.'

'I must, you're so tired. Come on, there's a good child, you look tired and sleepy.'

'I'm not a bit sleepy!'

'All the same it's high time. . . .'

'Are you coming?'

'Not yet, I must answer some letters.'

Mary got up, and just for a moment their eyes met, then Stephen looked away quickly: 'Good night, Mary.'

'Stephen . . . won't you kiss me good night? It's our first night together here in your home. Stephen, do you know that you've never kissed me?'

The clock chimed ten; a rose on the desk fell apart, its overblown petals disturbed by that almost imperceptible vibration. Stephen's heart beat thickly.

'Do you want me to kiss you?'

'More than anything else in the world,' said Mary.

Then Stephen suddenly came to her senses, and she managed to smile: 'Very well, my dear.' She kissed the girl quietly on her cheek, 'And now you really must go to bed, Mary.'

After Mary had gone she tried to write letters; a few lines to Anna, announcing her visit; a few lines to Puddle and to Mademoiselle Duphot—the latter she felt that she had shamefully neglected. But in none of these letters did she mention Mary. Brockett's effusion she left unanswered. Then she took her unfinished novel from its drawer, but it seemed very dreary and unimportant, so she laid it aside again with a sigh, and locking the drawer put the key in her pocket.

And now she could no longer keep it at bay, the great joy, the great pain in her heart that was Mary. She had only to call and Mary would come, bringing all her faith, her youth and her ardour. Yes, she had only to call, and yet—would she ever be cruel enough to call Mary? Her mind recoiled at that word; why cruel? She and Mary loved and needed each other. She could give the girl luxury, make her secure so that she need never fight for her living; she should have every comfort that money could buy. Mary was not strong enough to fight for her living. And then she, Stephen, was no longer a child to be frightened and humbled by this situation. There was many another exactly like her in this very city, in every city; and they did not all live out crucified lives, denying their bodies, stultifying their brains, becoming the victims of their own frustrations. On the contrary, they lived natural lives—lives that to them were perfectly natural. They had their passions like every one else, and why not? They were surely entitled to their passions? They attracted too, that was the irony of it, she herself had attracted Mary Llewellyn—the girl was quite simply and openly in love. 'All my life I've been waiting for something. . . .' Mary had said that, she had said: 'All my life I've been waiting for something. . . . I've been waiting for you.'

Men—they were selfish, arrogant, possessive. What could they do for Mary Llewellyn? What could a man give that she could not? A child? But she would give Mary such a love as would be complete in itself without children. Mary would have no room in her heart, in her life, for a child, if she came to Stephen. All things they would be the one to the other, should they stand in that limitless relationship; father, mother, friend, and lover, all things—the amazing completeness of it; and Mary, the child, the friend, the belovèd.* With the terrible bonds of her dual nature, she could bind Mary fast, and the pain would be sweetness, so that the girl would cry out for that sweetness, hugging her chains always closer to her. The world would condemn but they would rejoice; glorious outcasts, unashamed, triumphant!

She began to pace restlessly up and down the room, as had ever been her wont in moments of emotion. Her face grew ominous, heavy and brooding; the fine line of her mouth was a little marred; her eyes were less clear, less the servants of her spirit than the slaves of her anxious and passionate body; the red scar on her cheek stood out like a wound. Then quite suddenly she had opened the door, and was staring at the dimly lighted staircase. She took a step forward and then stopped; appalled, dumbfounded at herself, at this thing she was doing. And as she stood there as though turned to stone, she remembered another and more spacious study, she remembered a lanky colt of a girl whose glance had kept straying towards the windows; she remembered a man who had held out his hand: 'Stephen, come here. . . . What is honour, my daughter?'*

Honour, good God! Was this her honour? Mary, whose nerves had been strained to breaking! A dastardly thing it would be to drag her through the maze of passion, with no word of warning. Was she to know nothing of what lay before her, of the price she would have to pay for such love? She was young and completely ignorant of life; she knew only that she loved, and the young were ardent. She would give all that Stephen might ask of her and more, for the young were not only ardent but generous. And through giving all she would be left defenceless, neither forewarned nor forearmed against a world that would turn like a merciless beast and rend her. It was horrible. No, Mary must not give until she had counted the cost of that gift, until she was restored in body and mind, and was able to form a considered judgment.

Then Stephen must tell her the cruel truth, she must say: 'I am one of those whom God marked on the forehead. Like Cain, I am marked and blemished. If you come to me, Mary, the world will abhor you, will persecute you, will call you unclean. Our love may be faithful even unto death and beyond—yet the world will call it unclean. We may harm no living creature by our love; we may grow more perfect in understanding and in charity because of our loving; but all this will not save you from the scourge of a world that will turn away its eyes from your noblest actions, finding only corruption and vileness in you. You will see men and women defiling each other, laying the burden of their sins upon their children. You will see unfaithfulness, lies and deceit among those whom the world views with approbation. You will find that many have grown hard of heart, have grown greedy, selfish, cruel and lustful; and then you will turn to me and will say: "You and I are more worthy of respect than these people. Why does the world persecute us, Stephen?" And I shall answer: "Because in this world there is only toleration for the so-called normal." And when you come to me for protection, I shall say: "I cannot protect you, Mary, the world has deprived me of my right to protect; I am utterly helpless, I can only love you." '

And now Stephen was trembling. In spite of her strength and her splendid physique, she must stand there and tremble. She felt deathly cold, her teeth chattered with cold, and when she moved her steps were unsteady. She must climb the wide stairs with infinite care, in case she should inadvertently stumble; must lift her feet slowly, and with infinite care, because if she stumbled she might wake Mary.

4

Ten days later Stephen was saying to her mother: 'I've been needing a change for a very long time. It's rather lucky that a girl I met in the Unit is free and able to go with me. We've taken a villa at Orotava, it's supposed to be furnished and they're leaving the servants, but heaven only knows what the house will be like; it belongs to a Spaniard; however, there'll be sunshine.'

'I believe Orotava's delightful,' said Anna.

But Puddle, who was looking at Stephen, said nothing.

That night Stephen knocked at Puddle's door: 'May I come in?'

'Yes, come in do, my dear. Come and sit by the fire—shall I make you some cocoa?'

'No, thanks.'

A long pause while Puddle slipped into her dressing-gown of soft, grey Viyella.* Then she also drew a chair up to the fire, and after a little: 'It's good to see you—your old teacher's been missing you rather badly.'

'Not more than I've been missing her, Puddle.' Was that quite true? Stephen suddenly flushed, and both of them grew very silent.

Puddle knew quite well that Stephen was unhappy. They had not lived side by side all these years, for Puddle to fail now in intuition; she felt certain that something grave had happened, and her instinct warned her of what this might be, so that she secretly trembled a little. For no young and inexperienced girl sat beside her, but a woman of nearly thirty-two, who was far beyond the reach of her guidance. This woman would settle her problems for herself and in her own way—had indeed always done so. Puddle must try to be tactful in her questions.

She said gently: 'Tell me about your new friend. You met her in the Unit?'

'Yes—we met in the Unit, as I told you this evening—her name's Mary Llewellyn.'

'How old is she, Stephen?'

'Not quite twenty-two.'*

Puddle said: 'Very young—not yet twenty-two . . .' then she glanced at Stephen, and fell silent.

But now Stephen went on talking more quickly: 'I'm glad you asked me about her, Puddle, because I intend to give her a home. She's got no one except some distant cousins, and as far as I can see they don't want her. I shall let her have a try at typing my work, as she's asked to, it will make her feel independent; otherwise, of course, she'll be perfectly free—if it's not a success she can always leave me—but I rather hope it will be a success. She's companionable, we like the same things, anyhow she'll give me an interest in life. . . .'

Puddle thought: 'She's not going to tell me.'

Stephen took out her cigarette case from which she produced a clear little snapshot: 'It's not very good, it was done at the front.'

But Puddle was gazing at Mary Llewellyn. Then she looked up abruptly and saw Stephen's eyes—without a word she handed back the snapshot.

Stephen said: 'Now I want to talk about you. Will you go to Paris at once, or stay here until we come home from Orotava? It's just as you like, the house is quite ready, you've only got to send Pauline a post-card; they're expecting you there at any moment.' And she waited for Puddle's answer.

Then Puddle, that small but indomitable fighter, stood forth all alone to do battle with herself, to strike down a sudden hot jealousy, a sudden and almost fierce resentment. And she saw that self as a tired old woman, a woman grown dull and tired with long service; a woman who had outlived her reason for living, whose companionship was now useless to Stephen. A woman who suffered from rheumatism in the winter and from lassitude in the summer; a woman who when young had never known youth, except as a scourge to a sensitive conscience. And now she was old and what had life left her? Not even the privilege of guarding her friend—for Puddle knew well that her presence in Paris would only embarrass while unable to hinder. Nothing could stay fate if the hour had struck; and yet, from the very bottom of her soul, she was fearing that hour for Stephen. And—who shall presume to accuse or condemn?—she actually found it in her to pray that Stephen might be granted some measure of fulfilment, some palliative for the wound of existence: 'Not like me—don't let her grow old as I've done.' Then she suddenly remembered that Stephen was waiting.

She said quietly: 'Listen, my dear, I've been thinking; I don't feel that I ought to leave your mother, her heart's not very strong—nothing serious, of course—still, she oughtn't to live all alone at Morton; and quite apart from the question of health, living alone's a melancholy business. There's another thing too, I've grown tired and lazy, and I don't want to pull up my roots if I can help it. When one's getting on in years, one gets set in one's ways, and my ways fit in very well with Morton. I didn't want to come here, Stephen, as I told you, but I was all wrong, for your mother needs me—she needs me more now than during the war, because during the war she had occupation. Oh, but good heavens! I'm a silly old woman—did you know that I used to get homesick for England? I used to get homesick for penny buns. Imagine it, and I was living in Paris! Only—' And now her voice broke a little: 'Only, if ever you should feel that you need me, if ever you should feel that you want my advice or my help, you'd send for me, wouldn't you, my dear? Because, old as I am, I'd be able to run if I thought that you really needed me, Stephen.'

Stephen held out her hand and Puddle grasped it. 'There are some things I can't express,' Stephen said slowly; 'I can't express my gratitude to you for all you've done—I can't find any words. But—I want you to know that I'm trying to play straight.'*

'You'd always play straight in the end,' said Puddle.

And so, after nearly eighteen years of life together, these two staunch friends and companions had now virtually parted.

CHAPTER 38

I

THE Villa del Ciprés at Orotava was built on a headland above the Puerto.* It had taken its name from its fine cypress trees, of which there were many in the spacious garden. At the Puerto there was laughter, shouting and singing as the oxen wagons with their crates of bananas came grating and stumbling down to the wharf. At the Puerto one might almost have said there was commerce, for beyond the pier waited the dirty fruit steamers; but the Villa del Ciprés stood proudly aloof like a Spanish grandee who had seen better days—one felt that it literally hated commerce.

The villa was older than the streets of the Puerto, though much grass grew between their venerable cobbles. It was older than the oldest villas on the hill, the hill that was known as old Orotava, though their green latticed shutters were bleached by the suns of innumerable semi-tropical summers. It was so old indeed, that no peasant could have told you precisely when it had come into being; the records were lost, if they had ever existed—for its history one had to apply to its owner. But then its owner was always in Spain, and his agent who kept the place in repair, was too lazy to bother himself over trifles. What could it matter when the first stone was laid, or who laid it? The villa was always well let—he would yawn, roll a cigarette in his fingers, lick the paper with the thick, red tip of his tongue, and finally go to sleep in the sunshine to dream only of satisfactory commissions.

The Villa del Ciprés was a low stone house that had once been tinted a lemon yellow. Its shutters were greener than those on the hill, for every ten years or so they were painted. All its principal windows looked over the sea that lay at the foot of the little headland. There were large, dim rooms with rough mosaic floors and walls that were covered by ancient frescoes. Some of these frescoes were primitive but holy, others were primitive but distinctly less holy; however, they were all so badly defaced, that the tenants were spared what might otherwise have been rather a shock at the contrast. The furniture, although very good of its kind, was sombre, and moreover it was terribly scanty, for its owner was far too busy in Seville to attend to his villa in Orotava. But one glory the old house did certainly possess; its garden, a veritable Eden* of a garden, obsessed by a kind of primitive urge towards all manner of procreation. It was hot with sunshine and the flowing of sap, so that even its shade held a warmth in its greenness, while the virile growth of its flowers and its trees gave off a strangely disturbing fragrance. These trees had long been a haven for birds, from the crested hoopoes to the wild canaries who kept up a chorus of song in the branches.

2

Stephen and Mary arrived at the Villa del Ciprés, not very long after Christmas. They had spent their Christmas Day aboard ship, and on landing had stayed for a week at Santa Cruz* before taking the long, rough drive to Orotava. And as though the fates were being propitious, or unpropitious perhaps—who shall say?—the garden was looking its loveliest, almost melodramatic it looked in the sunset. Mary gazed round her wide-eyed with pleasure; but after a while her eyes must turn, as they always did now, to rest upon Stephen; while Stephen's uncertain and melancholy eyes must look back with great love in their depths for Mary.

Together they made the tour of the villa, and when this was over Stephen laughed a little: 'Not much of anything, is there, Mary?'

'No, but quite enough. Who wants tables and chairs?'

'Well, if you're contented, I am,' Stephen told her. And indeed, so far as the Villa del Ciprés went, they were both very well contented.

They discovered that the indoor staff would consist of two peasants; a plump, smiling woman called Concha, who adhered to the ancient tradition of the island and tied her head up in a white linen kerchief, and a girl whose black hair was elaborately dressed, and whose cheeks were very obviously powdered—Concha's niece she was, by name Esmeralda. Esmeralda looked cross, but this may have been because she squinted so badly.

In the garden worked a handsome person called Ramon, together with Pedro, a youth of sixteen. Pedro was light-hearted, precocious and spotty. He hated his simple work in the garden; what he liked was driving his father's mules for the tourists, according to Ramon. Ramon spoke English passably well; he had picked it up from the numerous tenants and was proud of this fact, so while bringing in the luggage he paused now and then to impart information. It was better to hire mules and donkeys from the father of Pedro—he had very fine mules and donkeys. It was better to take Pedro and none other as your guide, for thus would be saved any little ill-feeling. It was better to let Concha do all the shopping—she was honest and wise as the Blessèd Virgin. It was better never to scold Esmeralda, who was sensitive on account of her squint and therefore inclined to be easily wounded. If you wounded the heart of Esmeralda, she walked out of the house and Concha walked with her. The island women were often like this; you upset them and per Dios,* your dinner could burn! They would not even wait to attend to your dinner.

'You come home,' smiled Ramon, 'and you say, "What burns? Is my villa on fire?" Then you call and you call. No answer . . . all gone!' And he spread out his hands with a wide and distressingly empty gesture.

Ramon said that it was better to buy flowers from him: 'I cut fresh from the garden when you want,' he coaxed gently. He spoke even his broken English with the soft, rather sing-song drawl of the local peasants.

'But aren't they our flowers?' inquired Mary, surprised.

Ramon shook his head: 'Yours to see, yours to touch, but not yours to take, only mine to take—I sell them as part of my little payment. But to you I sell very cheap, Señorita, because you resemble the santa noche* that makes our gardens smell sweet at night. I will show you our beautiful santa noche.' He was thin as a lath and as brown as a chestnut, and his shirt was quite incredibly dirty; but when he walked he moved like a king on his rough bare feet with their broken toe-nails. 'This evening I make you a present of my flowers; I bring you a very big bunch of tabachero,'* he remarked.

'Oh, you mustn't do that,' protested Mary, getting out her purse.

But Ramon looked offended: 'I have said it. I give you the tabachero.'

3

Their dinner consisted of a local fish fried in oil—the fish had a very strange figure, and the oil, Stephen thought, tasted slightly rancid; there was also a small though muscular chicken. But Concha had provided large baskets of fruit; loquats still warm from the tree that bred them, the full flavoured little indigenous bananas, oranges sweet as though dripping honey, custard apples and guavas had Concha provided, together with a bottle of the soft yellow wine* so dearly beloved of the island Spaniards.

Outside in the garden there was luminous darkness. The night had a quality of glory about it, the blue glory peculiar to Africa and seen seldom or never in our more placid climate. A warm breeze stirred the eucalyptus trees, and their crude, harsh smell was persistently mingled with the thick scents of heliotrope and datura,* with the sweet but melancholy scent of jasmine, with the faint, unmistakable odour of cypress.

Stephen lit a cigarette: 'Shall we go out, Mary?'

They stood for a minute looking up at the stars, so much larger and brighter than stars seen in England. From a pond on the farther side of the villa, came the queer, hoarse chirping of innumerable frogs singing their prehistoric love songs. A star fell, shooting swiftly earthward through the darkness.

Then the sweetness that was Mary seemed to stir and mingle with the very urgent sweetness of that garden; with the dim, blue glory of the African night, and with all the stars in their endless courses, so that Stephen could have wept aloud as she stood there, because of the words that must not be spoken. For now that this girl was returning to health, her youth was becoming even more apparent, and something in the quality of Mary's youth, something terrible and ruthless as an unsheathed sword, would leap out at such moments and stand between them.

Mary slipped a small, cool hand into Stephen's, and they walked on towards the edge of the headland. For a long time they gazed out over the sea, while their thoughts were always of one another. But Mary's thoughts were not very coherent, and because she was filled with a vague discontent, she sighed and moved even nearer to Stephen, who suddenly put an arm round her shoulder.

Stephen said: 'Are you tired, you little child?' And her husky voice was infinitely gentle, so that Mary's eyes filled with sudden tears.

She answered: 'I've waited a long, long time, all my life—and now that I've found you at last, I can't get near you. Why is it? Tell me.'

'Aren't you near? It seems to me you're quite near!' And Stephen must smile in spite of herself.

'Yes, but you feel such a long way away.'

'That's because you're not only tired out but foolish!'

Yet they lingered; for when they returned to the villa they would part, and they dreaded these moments of parting. Sometimes they would suddenly remember the night before it had fallen, and when this happened each would be conscious of a very great sadness which their hearts would divine, the one from the other.

But presently Stephen took Mary's arm: 'I believe that big star's moved over more than six inches! It's late—we must have been out here for ages.' And she led the girl slowly back to the villa.

4

The days slipped by, days of splendid sunshine that gave bodily health and strength to Mary. Her pale skin was tanned to a healthful brown, and her eyes no longer looked heavy with fatigue—only now their expression was seldom happy.

She and Stephen would ride far afield on their mules; they would often ride right up into the mountains, climbing the hill to old Orotava where the women sat at their green postigos* through the long, quiet hours of their indolent day and right on into the evening. The walls of the town would be covered with flowers, jasmine, plumbago and bougainvillea. But they would not linger in old Orotava; pressing on they would climb always up and up to the region of heath and trailing arbutus,* and beyond that again to the higher slopes that had once been the home of a mighty forest. Now, only a few Spanish chestnut trees remained to mark the decline of that forest.

Sometimes they took their luncheon along, and when they did this young Pedro went with them, for he it was who must drive the mule that carried Concha's ample lunch-basket. Pedro adored these impromptu excursions, they made an excuse for neglecting the garden. He would saunter along chewing blades of grass, or the stem of some flower he had torn from a wall; or perhaps he would sing softly under his breath, for he knew many songs of his native island. But if the mule Celestino should stumble, or presume, in his turn, to tear flowers from a wall, then Pedro would suddenly cease his soft singing and shout guttural remarks to old Celestino: 'Vaya, burro! Celestino, arre! Arre—boo!'* he would shout with a slap, so that Celestino must swallow his flowers in one angry gulp, before having a sly kick at Pedro.

The lunch would be eaten in the cool upland air, while the beasts stood near at hand, placidly grazing. Against a sky of incredible blueness the Peak would gleam as though powdered with crystal—Teide,* mighty mountain of snow with the heart of fire and the brow of crystal. Down the winding tracks would come goats with their herds, the tinkle of goat-bells breaking the stillness. And as all such things have seemed wonderful to lovers throughout the ages, even so now they seemed very wonderful to Mary and Stephen.

There were days when, leaving the uplands for the vale, they would ride past the big banana plantations and the glowing acres of ripe tomatoes. Geraniums and agaves would be growing side by side in the black volcanic dust of the roadway. From the stretching Valley of Orotava they would see the rugged line of the mountains. The mountains would look blue, like the African nights, all save Teide, clothed in her crystalline whiteness.

And now while they sat together in the garden at evening, there would sometimes come beggars, singing; ragged fellows who played deftly on their guitars and sang songs whose old melodies hailed from Spain, but whose words sprang straight from the heart of the island:

> 'A-a-a-y! Before I saw thee I was at peace,
> But now I am tormented because I have seen thee.
> Take away mine eyes, oh, enemy! Oh, belovèd!
> Take away mine eyes, for they have turned me to fire.
> My blood is as the fire in the heart of Teide.
> A-a-a-y! Before I saw thee I was at peace.'*

The strange minor music, with its restless rhythms, possessed a very potent enchantment, so that the heart beat faster to hear it, and the mind grew mazed with forbidden thoughts, and the soul grew heavy with the infinite sadness of fulfilled desire; but the body knew only the urge towards a complete fulfilment. . . . 'A-a-a-y! Before I saw thee I was at peace.'

They would not understand the soft Spanish words, and yet as they sat there they could but divine their meaning, for love is no slave of mere language. Mary would want Stephen to take her in her arms, so must rest her cheek against Stephen's shoulder, as though they two had a right to such music, had a right to their share in the love songs of the world. But Stephen would always move away quickly.

'Let's go in,' she would mutter; and her voice would sound rough, for that bright sword of youth would have leapt out between them.

5

There came days when they purposely avoided each other, trying to find peace in separation. Stephen would go for long rides alone, leaving Mary to idle about the villa; and when she got back Mary would not speak, but would wander away by herself to the garden. For Stephen had grown almost harsh at times, possessed as she now was by something like terror, since it seemed to her that what she must say to this creature she loved would come as a death-blow, that all youth and all joy would be slain in Mary.

Tormented in body and mind and spirit, she would push the girl away from her roughly: 'Leave me alone, I can't bear any more!'

'Stephen—I don't understand. Do you hate me?'

'Hate you? Of course you don't understand—only, I tell you I simply can't bear it.'

They would stare at each other pale-faced and shaken.

The long nights became even harder to endure, for now they would feel so terribly divided. Their days would be heavy with misunderstandings, their nights filled with doubts, apprehensions and longings. They would often have parted as enemies, and therein would lie the great loneliness of it.

As time went on they grew deeply despondent, their despondency robbing the sun of its brightness, robbing the little goat-bells of their music, robbing the dark of its luminous glory. The songs of the beggars who sang in the garden at the hour when the santa noche smelt sweetest, those songs would seem full of a cruel jibing: 'A-a-a-y! Before I saw thee I was at peace, but now I am tormented because I have seen thee.'

Thus were all things becoming less good in their sight, less perfect because of their own frustration.

6

But Mary Llewellyn was no coward and no weakling, and one night, at long last, pride came to her rescue. She said: 'I want to speak to you, Stephen.'

'Not now, it's so late—to-morrow morning.'

'No, now.' And she followed Stephen into her bedroom.

For a moment they avoided each other's eyes, then Mary began to talk rather fast: 'I can't stay. It's all been a heart-breaking mistake.

I thought you wanted me because you cared. I thought—oh, I don't know what I thought—but I won't accept your charity, Stephen, not now that you've grown to hate me like this—I'm going back home to England. I forced myself on you, I asked you to take me. I must have been mad; you just took me out of pity; you thought that I was ill and you felt sorry for me. Well, now I'm not ill and not mad any more, and I'm going. Every time I come near you you shrink or push me away as though I repelled you. But I want us to part quickly because. . . .' Her voice broke: 'because it torments me to be always with you and to feel that you've literally grown to hate me. I can't stand it; I'd rather not see you, Stephen.'

Stephen stared at her, white and aghast. Then all in a moment the restraint of years was shattered as though by some mighty convulsion. She remembered nothing, was conscious of nothing except that the creature she loved was going.

'You child,' she gasped, 'you don't understand, you can't understand—God help me, I love you!' And now she had the girl in her arms and was kissing her eyes and her mouth: 'Mary . . . Mary. . . .'

They stood there lost to all sense of time, to all sense of reason, to all things save each other, in the grip of what can be one of the most relentless of all the human emotions.

Then Stephen's arms suddenly fell to her sides: 'Stop, stop for God's sake—you've got to listen.'

Oh, but now she must pay to the uttermost farthing* for the madness that had left those words unspoken—even as her father had paid before her. With Mary's kisses still hot on her lips, she must pay and pay unto the uttermost farthing. And because of an anguish that seemed past endurance, she spoke roughly; the words when they came were cruel. She spared neither the girl who must listen to them, nor herself who must force her to stand there and listen.

'Have you understood? Do you realize now what it's going to mean if you give yourself to me?' Then she stopped abruptly . . . Mary was crying.

Stephen said, and her voice had grown quite toneless: 'It's too much to ask—you're right, it's too much. I had to tell you—forgive me, Mary.'

But Mary turned on her with very bright eyes: 'You can say that—you, who talk about loving! What do I care for all you've told me? What do I care for the world's opinion? What do I care for anything but you, and you just as you are—as you are, I love you! Do you think I'm crying because of what you've told me? I'm crying because of your dear, scarred face . . . the misery on it. . . . Can't you understand that all that I am belongs to you, Stephen?'

Stephen bent down and kissed Mary's hands very humbly, for now she could find no words any more . . . and that night they were not divided.*

CHAPTER 39

I

A STRANGE, though to them a very natural thing it seemed, this new and ardent fulfilment; having something fine and urgent about it that lay almost beyond the range of their wills. Something primitive and age-old as Nature herself, did their love appear to Mary and Stephen.* For now they were in the grip of Creation, of Creation's terrific urge to create; the urge that will sometimes sweep forward blindly alike into fruitful and sterile channels.* That wellnigh intolerable life force would grip them, making them a part of its own existence; so that they who might never create a new life, were yet one at such moments with the fountain of living. . . . Oh, great and incomprehensible unreason!

But beyond the bounds of this turbulent river would lie gentle and most placid harbours of refuge; harbours in which the body could repose with contentment, while the lips spoke slow, indolent words, and the eyes beheld a dim, golden haze that blinded the while it revealed all beauty. Then Stephen would stretch out her hand and touch Mary where she lay, happy only to feel her nearness. The hours would slip by towards dawn or sunset; flowers would open and close in the bountiful garden; and perhaps, if it should chance to be evening, beggars would come to that garden, singing; ragged fellows who played deftly on their guitars and sang songs whose old melodies hailed from Spain, but whose words sprang straight from the heart of the island:*

'Oh, thou whom I love, thou art small and guileless;
Thy lips are as cool as the sea at moonrise.
But after the moon there cometh the sun;
After the evening there cometh the morning.
The sea is warmed by the kiss of the sun,
Even so shall my kisses bring warmth to thy lips.
Oh, thou whom I love, thou art small and guileless.'

And now Mary need no longer sigh with unrest, need no longer lay her cheek against Stephen's shoulder; for her rightful place was in

Stephen's arms and there she would be, overwhelmed by the peace that comes at such times to all happy lovers. They would sit together in a little arbour that looked out over miles upon miles of ocean. The water would flush with the after-glow, then change to a soft, indefinite purple; then, fired anew by the African night, would gleam with that curious, deep blue glory for a space before the swift rising of the moon. 'Thy lips are as cool as the sea at moonrise; but after the moon there cometh the sun.'

And Stephen as she held the girl in her arms, would feel that indeed she was all things to Mary; father, mother, friend and lover, all things; and Mary all things to her—the child, the friend, the belovèd, all things. But Mary, because she was perfect woman,* would rest without thought, without exultation, without question; finding no need to question since for her there was now only one thing—Stephen.

2

Time, that most ruthless enemy of lovers, strode callously forward into the spring. It was March, so that down at the noisy Puerto the bougainvilleas were in their full glory, while up in the old town of Orotava bloomed great laden bushes of white camellias. In the garden of the villa the orange trees flowered, and the little arbour that looked over the sea was covered by an ancient wistaria vine whose mighty trunk was as thick as three saplings. But in spite of a haunting shadow of regret at the thought of leaving Orotava, Stephen was deeply and thankfully happy. A happiness such as she had never conceived could be hers, now possessed her body and soul—and Mary also was happy.

Stephen would ask her: 'Do I content you? Tell me, is there anything you want in the world?'

Mary's answer was always the same; she would say very gravely: 'Only you, Stephen.'

Ramon had begun to speculate about them, these two Englishwomen who were so devoted. He would shrug his shoulders—Dios! What did it matter? They were courteous to him and exceedingly generous. If the elder one had an ugly red scar down her cheek, the younger one seemed not to mind it. The younger one was beautiful though, as beautiful as the santa noche . . . some day she would get a real man to love her.

As for Concha and the cross-eyed Esmeralda, their tongues were muted by their ill-gotten gains. They grew rich, thanks to Stephen's complete indifference to the price of such trifles as sugar and candles.

Esmeralda's afflicted eyes were quite sharp, yet she said to Concha: 'I see less than nothing.'

And Concha answered: 'I also see nothing; it is better to suppose that there is nothing to see. They are wealthy and the big one is very careless—she trusts me completely and I do my utmost. She is so taken up with the amighita* that I really believe I could easily rob her! Quien sabe?* They are certainly queer those two—however, I am blind, it is better so; and in any case they are only the English!'

But Pedro was very sorely afflicted, for Pedro had fallen in love with Mary, and now he must stay at home in the garden when she and Stephen rode up to the mountains. Now they wished to be all alone, it seemed, and what food they took would be stuffed into a pocket. It was spring and Pedro was deeply enamoured, so that he sighed as he tended the roses, sighed and stubbed the hard earth with his toes, and made insolent faces at the good-tempered Ramon, and killed flies with a kind of grim desperation, and sang songs of longing under his breath: 'A-a-a-y! Thou art to me as the mountain. Would I could melt thy virginal snows. . . .'

'Would I could kick thy behind!' grinned Ramon.

One evening Mary asked Pedro to sing, speaking to him in her halting Spanish. So Pedro went off and got his guitar; but when he must stand there and sing before Mary he could only stammer a childish old song having in it nothing of passion and longing:

> 'I was born on a reef that is washed by the sea;
> It is a part of Spain that is called Teneriffe.
> I was born on a reef. . . .'

sang the unhappy Pedro.

Stephen felt sorry for the lanky boy with the lovesick eyes, and so to console him she offered him money, ten pesetas*—for she knew that these people set much store by money. But Pedro seemed to have grown very tall as he gently but firmly refused consolation. Then he suddenly burst into tears and fled, leaving his little guitar behind him.

3

The days were too short, as were now the nights—those spring nights of soft heat and incredible moonlight. And because they both felt that something was passing, they would turn their minds to thoughts of the future. The future was drawing very near to the present; in less than three weeks they must start for Paris.

Mary would suddenly cling to Stephen: 'Say that you'll never leave me, belovèd!'

'How could I leave you and go on living?'

Thus their talk of the future would often drift into talk of love, that is always timeless. On their lips, as in their hearts, would be words such as countless other lovers had spoken, for love is the sweetest monotony that was ever conceived of by the Creator.

'Promise you'll never stop loving me, Stephen.'

'Never. You know that I couldn't, Mary.'

Even to themselves their vows would sound foolish, because so inadequate to compass their meaning. Language is surely too small a vessel to contain those emotions of mind and body that have somehow awakened a response in the spirit.

And now when they climbed the long hill to the town of old Orotava on their way to the mountains, they would pause to examine certain flowers minutely, or to stare down the narrow, shadowy by-streets. And when they had reached the cool upland places, and their mules were loosed and placidly grazing, they would sit hand in hand looking out at the Peak, trying to impress such pictures on their minds, because all things pass and they wished to remember. The goat-bells would break the lovely stillness, together with the greater stillness of their dreaming. But the sound of the bells would be lovely also, a part of their dreaming, a part of the stillness; for all things would seem to be welded together, to be one, even as they two were now one.

They no longer felt desolate, hungry outcasts; unloved and unwanted, despised of the world. They were lovers who walked in the vineyard of life, plucking the warm, sweet fruits of that vineyard. Love had lifted them up as on wings of fire, had made them courageous, invincible, enduring. Nothing could be lacking to those who loved—the very earth gave of her fullest bounty. The earth seemed to come alive in response to the touch of their healthful and eager bodies—nothing could be lacking to those who loved.

And thus in a cloud of illusion and glory, sped the last enchanted days at Orotava.

BOOK FIVE

CHAPTER 40

I

Early in April Stephen and Mary returned to the house in Paris. This second home-coming seemed wonderfully sweet by reason of its peaceful and happy completeness, so that they turned to smile at each other as they passed through the door, and Stephen said very softly:

'Welcome home, Mary.'

And now for the first time the old house was home. Mary went quickly from room to room humming a little tune as she did so, feeling that she saw with a new understanding the inanimate objects which filled those rooms—were they not Stephen's? Every now and again she must pause to touch them because they were Stephen's. Then she turned and went into Stephen's bedroom; not timidly, dreading to be unwelcome, but quite without fear or restraint or shyness, and this gave her a warm little glow of pleasure.*

Stephen was busily grooming her hair with a couple of brushes that had been dipped in water. The water had darkened her hair in patches, but had deepened the wide wave above her forehead. Seeing Mary in the glass she did not turn round, but just smiled for a moment at their two reflections. Mary sat down in an arm-chair and watched her, noticing the strong, thin line of her thighs; noticing too the curve of her breasts—slight and compact, of a certain beauty. She had taken off her jacket and looked very tall in her soft silk shirt and her skirt of dark serge.

'Tired?' she inquired, glancing down at the girl.

'No, not a bit tired,' smiled Mary.

Stephen walked over to the stationary basin and proceeded to wash her hands under the tap, spotting her white silk cuffs in the process. Going to the cupboard she got out a clean shirt, slipped in a pair of simple gold cuff-links, and changed; after which she put on a new neck-tie.

Mary said: 'Who's been looking after your clothes—sewing on buttons and that sort of thing?'

'I don't know exactly—Puddle or Adèle. Why?'

'Because I'm going to do it in future. You'll find that I've got one very real talent, and that's darning. When I darn the place looks like a basket, criss-cross. And I know how to pick up a ladder as well as the Invisible Mending people!* It's very important that the darns should be smooth, otherwise when you fence they might give you a blister.'

Stephen's lips twitched a little, but she said quite gravely: 'Thanks awfully, darling, we'll go over my stockings.'

From the dressing-room next door came a series of thuds; Pierre was depositing Stephen's luggage. Getting up, Mary opened the wardrobe, revealing a long, neat line of suits hanging from heavy mahogany shoulders—she examined each suit in turn with great interest. Presently she made her way to the cupboard in the wall; it was fitted with sliding shelves, and these she pulled out one by one with precaution. On the shelves there were orderly piles of shirts, crêpe de Chine pyjamas—quite a goodly assortment, and the heavy silk masculine underwear that for several years now had been worn by Stephen. Finally she discovered the stockings where they lay by themselves in the one long drawer, and these she proceeded to unfurl deftly, with a quick and slightly important movement. Thrusting a fist into toes and heels she looked for the holes that were non-existent.

'You must have paid a lot for these stockings, they're hand knitted silk'; murmured Mary gravely.

'I forget what I paid—Puddle got them from England.'

'Who did she order them from; do you know?'

'I can't remember; some woman or other.'

But Mary persisted: 'I shall want her address.'

Stephen smiled: 'Why? Are you going to order my stockings?'

'Darling! Do you think I'll let you go barefoot? Of course I'm going to order your stockings.'

Stephen rested her elbow on the mantelpiece and stood gazing at Mary with her chin on her hand. As she did so she was struck once again by the look of youth that was characteristic of Mary. She looked much less than her twenty-two years in her simple dress with its leather belt—she looked indeed little more than a schoolgirl. And yet there was something quite new in her face, a soft, wise expression that Stephen had put there, so that she suddenly felt pitiful to see her so young yet so full of this wisdom; for sometimes the coming of passion to youth, in spite of its glory, will be strangely pathetic.

Mary rolled up the stockings with a sigh of regret; alas, they would not require darning. She was at the stage of being in love when she longed to do womanly tasks for Stephen. But all Stephen's clothes were discouragingly neat; Mary thought that she must be very well served, which was true—she was served, as are certain men, with a great deal of nicety and care by the servants.

And now Stephen was filling her cigarette case from the big box that lived on her dressing-table; and now she was strapping on her gold wrist watch; and now she was brushing some dust from her coat; and now she was frowning at herself in the glass for a second as she twitched her immaculate neck-tie. Mary had seen her do all this before, many times, but to-day somehow it was different; for to-day they were in their own home together, so that these little intimate things seemed more dear than they had done at Orotava. The bedroom could only have belonged to Stephen; a large, airy room, very simply furnished—white walls, old oak, and a wide, bricked hearth on which some large, friendly logs were burning. The bed could only have been Stephen's bed; it was heavy and rather austere in pattern. It looked solemn, as Mary had seen Stephen look, and was covered by a bedspread of old blue brocade, otherwise it remained quite guiltless of trimmings. The chairs could only have been Stephen's chairs; a little reserved, not conducive to lounging. The dressing table could only have been hers, with its tall silver mirror and ivory brushes. And all these things had drawn into themselves a species of life derived from their owner, until they seemed to be thinking of Stephen with a dumbness that made their thoughts more insistent, and their thoughts gathered strength and mingled with Mary's so that she heard herself cry out: 'Stephen!' in a voice that was not very far from tears, because of the joy she felt in that name.

And Stephen answered her: 'Mary—'

Then they stood very still, grown abruptly silent. And each of them felt a little afraid, for the realization of great mutual love can at times be so overwhelming a thing, that even the bravest of hearts may grow fearful. And although they could not have put it into words, could not have explained it to themselves or to each other, they seemed at that moment to be looking beyond the turbulent flood of earthly passion; to be looking straight into the eyes of a love that was changed—a love made perfect, discarnate.

But the moment passed and they drew together. . . .*

2

The spring they had left behind in Orotava overtook them quite soon, and one day there it was blowing softly along the old streets of the Quarter—the Rue de Seine, the Rue des Saints Pères, the Rue Bonaparte and their own Rue Jacob. And who can resist the first spring days in Paris? Brighter than ever looked the patches of sky when glimpsed between rows of tall, flat-bosomed houses. From the Pont des Arts could be seen a river that was one wide, ingratiating smile of sunshine; while beyond in the Rue des Petits Champs, spring ran up and down the Passage Choiseul, striking gleams of gold from its dirty glass roof—the roof that looks like the vertebral column of some prehistoric monster.

All over the Bois there was bursting of buds—a positive orgy of growth and greenness. The miniature waterfall lifted its voice in an effort to roar as loud as Niagara. Birds sang. Dogs yapped or barked or bayed according to their size and the tastes of their owners. Children appeared in the Champs Elysées with bright coloured balloons which tried to escape and which, given the ghost of a chance, always did so. In the Tuileries Gardens boys with brown legs and innocent socks were hiring toy boats from the man who provided Bateaux de Location.* The fountains tossed clouds of spray into the air, and just for fun made an occasional rainbow; then the Arc de Triomphe would be seen through an arc that was, thanks to the sun, even more triumphal. As for the very old lady in her kiosk—the one who sells bocks, groseille, limonade,* and such simple food-stuffs as brioches and croissants—as for her, she appeared in a new frilled bonnet and a fine worsted shawl on one memorable Sunday. Smiling she was too, from ear to ear, in spite of the fact that her mouth was toothless, for this fact she only remembered in winter when the east wind started her empty gums aching.

Under the quiet, grey wings of the Madeleine* the flower-stalls were bright with the glory of God—anemones, jonquils, daffodils, tulips; mimosa that left gold dust on the fingers, and the faintly perfumed ascetic white lilac that had come in the train from the Riviera. There were also hyacinths, pink, red and blue, and many small trees of sturdy azalea.

Oh, but the spring was shouting through Paris! It was in the hearts and the eyes of the people. The very dray-horses* jangled their bells more loudly because of the spring in their drivers. The debauched old taxis tooted their horns and spun round the corners as though on a race track. Even such glacial things as the diamonds in the Rue de la Paix, were kindled to fire as the sun pierced their facets right through to their entrails; while the sapphires glowed as those African nights had glowed in the garden at Orotava.

Was it likely that Stephen could finish her book—she who had Paris in springtime with Mary? Was it likely that Mary could urge her to do so—she who had Paris in springtime with Stephen? There was so much to see, so much to show Mary, so many new things to discover together. And now Stephen felt grateful to Jonathan Brockett who had gone to such pains to teach her her Paris.

Idle she was, let it not be denied, idle and happy and utterly carefree. A lover, who, like many another before her, was under the spell of the loved one's existence. She would wake in the mornings to find Mary beside her, and all through the day she would keep beside Mary, and at night they would lie in each other's arms—God alone knows who shall dare judge of such matters; in any case Stephen was too much bewitched to be troubled just then by hair-splitting problems.

Life had become a new revelation. The most mundane things were invested with glory; shopping for instance, shopping with Mary who needed quite a number of dresses. And then there was food that was eaten together—the careful perusal of wine-card and menu. They would lunch or have dinner at Lapérouse;* surely still the most epicurean restaurant in the whole of an epicurean city. So humble it looks with its modest entrance on the Quai des Grands Augustins; so humble that a stranger might well pass it by unnoticed, but not so Stephen, who had been there with Brockett.

Mary loved Prunier's in the Rue Duphot, because of its galaxy of sea-monsters. A whole counter there was of incredible creatures—Oursins, black armoured and covered with prickles; Bigorneaux; serpent-like Anguilles Fumées; and many other exciting things that Stephen mistrusted for English stomachs.* They would sit at their own particular table, one of the tables upstairs by the window, for the manager came very quickly to know them and would smile and bow grandly: 'Bon jour, mesdames.' When they left, the attendant who kept the flower-basket would give Mary a neat little bouquet of roses: 'Au revoir, mesdames. Merci bien—à bientôt!' For every one had pretty manners at Prunier's.

A few people might stare at the tall, scarred woman in her well-tailored clothes and black slouch hat. They would stare first at her and then at her companion: 'Mais regardez moi ça! Elle est belle, la petite; comme c'est rigolo!'* There would be a few smiles, but on the whole they would attract little notice—ils en ont vu bien d'autres*—it was post-war Paris.

Sometimes, having dined, they would saunter towards home through streets that were crowded with others who sauntered—men and women, a couple of women together—always twos—the fine nights seemed prolific of couples. In the air there would be the inconsequent feeling that belongs to the night life of most great cities, above all to the careless night life of Paris, where problems are apt to vanish with sunset. The lure of the brightly lighted boulevards, the lure of the dim and mysterious by-streets would grip them so that they would not turn homeward for quite a long while, but would just go on walking. The moon, less clear than at Orotava, less innocent doubtless, yet scarcely less lovely, would come sailing over the Place de la Concorde, staring down at the dozens of other white moons that had managed to get themselves caught by the standards. In the cafés would be crowds of indolent people, for the French who work hard know well how to idle; and these cafés would smell of hot coffee and sawdust, of rough, strong tobacco, of men and women. Beneath the arcades there would be the shop windows, illuminated and bright with temptation. But Mary would usually stare into Sulka's,* picking out scarves or neck-ties for Stephen.

'That one! We'll come and buy it to-morrow. Oh, Stephen, do wait—look at that dressing-gown!'

And Stephen might laugh and pretend to be bored, though she secretly nurtured a weakness for Sulka's.

Down the Rue de Rivoli they would walk arm in arm, until turning at last, they would pass the old church of St. Germain—the church from whose Gothic tower had been rung the first call to a most bloody slaying.* But now that tower would be grim with silence, dreaming the composite dreams of Paris—dreams that were heavy with blood and beauty, with innocence and lust, with joy and despair, with life and death, with heaven and hell; all the curious composite dreams of Paris.

Then crossing the river they would reach the Quarter and their house, where Stephen would slip her latchkey into the door and would know the warm feeling that can come of a union between door and latchkey. With a sigh of contentment they would find themselves at home once again in the quiet old Rue Jacob.

3

They went to see the kind Mademoiselle Duphot, and this visit seemed momentous to Mary. She gazed with something almost like awe at the woman who had had the teaching of Stephen.

'Oh, but yes,' smiled Mademoiselle Duphot, 'I teached her. She was terribly naughty over her dictée; she would write remarks about the poor Henri*—très impertinente she would be about Henri! Stévenne was a queer little child and naughty—but so dear, so dear—I could never scold her. With me she done everything her own way.'

'Please tell me about that time,' coaxed Mary.

So Mademoiselle Duphot sat down beside Mary and patted her hand: 'Like me, you love her. Well now let me recall—She would sometimes get angry, very angry, and then she would go to the stables and talk to her horse. But when she fence it was marvellous—she fence like a man, and she only a baby but extrèmement strong. And then. . . .' The memories went on and on, such a store she possessed, the kind Mademoiselle Duphot.

As she talked her heart went out to the girl, for she felt a great tenderness towards young things: 'I am glad that you come to live with our Stévenne now that Mademoiselle Puddle is at Morton. Stévenne would be desolate in the big house. It is charming for both of you this new arrangement. While she work you look after the ménage; is it not so? You take care of Stévenne, she take care of you. Oui, oui, I am glad you have come to Paris.'

Julie stroked Mary's smooth young cheek, then her arm, for she wished to observe through her fingers. She smiled: 'Very young, also very kind. I like so much the feel of your kindness—it gives me a warm and so happy sensation, because with all kindness there must be much good.'

Was she quite blind after all, the poor Julie?

And hearing her Stephen flushed with pleasure, and her eyes that could see turned and rested on Mary with a gentle and very profound expression in their depths—at that moment they were calmly thoughtful, as though brooding upon the mystery of life—one might almost have said the eyes of a mother.

A happy and pleasant visit it had been; they talked about it all through the evening.*

CHAPTER 41

I

BURTON, who had enlisted in the Worcesters* soon after Stephen had found work in London, Burton was now back again in Paris, loudly demanding a brand-new motor.

'The car looks awful! Snub-nosed she looks—peculiar—all tucked up in the bonnet'; he declared.

So Stephen bought a touring Renault and a smart little landaulette for Mary.* The choosing of the cars was the greatest fun; Mary climbed in and out of hers at least six times while it stood in the showroom.

'Is it comfortable?' Stephen must keep on asking, 'Do you want them to pad it out more at the back? Are you perfectly sure you like the grey whip-cord? Because if you don't it can be re-upholstered.'

Mary laughed: 'I'm climbing in and out from sheer swank,* just to show that it's mine. Will they send it soon?'

'Almost at once, I hope,' smiled Stephen.

Very splendid it seemed to her now to have money, because of what money could do for Mary; in the shops they must sometimes behave like two children, having endless things dragged out for inspection. They drove to Versailles in the new touring car and wandered for hours through the lovely gardens. The Hameau no longer seemed sad to Stephen, for Mary and she brought love back to the Hameau. Then they drove to the Forest of Fontainebleau, and wherever they went there was singing of birds—challenging, jubilant, provocative singing: 'Look at us, look at us! We're happy, Stephen!'* And Stephen's heart shouted back: 'So are we. Look at us, look at us, look at us! We're happy!'

When they were not driving into the country, or amusing themselves by ransacking Paris, Stephen would fence, to keep herself fit—would fence as never before with Buisson, so that Buisson would sometimes say with a grin:

'Mais voyons, voyons!* I have done you no wrong, yet it almost appears that you wish to kill me!'

The foils laid aside, he might turn to Mary, still grinning: 'She fence very well, eh, your friend? She lunge like a man, so strong and so graceful.' Which considering all things was generous of Buisson.

But suddenly Buisson would grow very angry: 'More than seventy francs have I paid to my cook and for nothing! Bon Dieu! Is this winning the war? We starve, we go short of our butter and chickens, and before it is better it is surely much worse. We are all imbeciles, we kind-hearted French; we starve ourselves to fatten the Germans. Are they grateful? Sacré Nom! Mais oui, they are grateful—they love us so much that they spit in our faces!'* And quite often this mood would be vented on Stephen.

To Mary, however, he was usually polite: 'You like our Paris? I am glad—that is good. You make the home with Mademoiselle Gordon; I hope you prevent her injurious smoking.'

And in spite of his outbursts Mary adored him, because of his interest in Stephen's fencing.

2

One evening towards the end of June, Jonathan Brockett walked in serenely: 'Hallo, Stephen! Here I am, I've turned up again—not that I love you, I positively hate you. I've been keeping away for weeks and weeks. Why did you never answer my letters? Not so much as a line on a picture postcard! There's something in this more than meets the eye. And where's Puddle? She used to be kind to me once—I shall lay my head down on her bosom and weep. . . .' He stopped abruptly, seeing Mary Llewellyn, who got up from her deep arm-chair in the corner.

Stephen said: 'Mary, this is Jonathan Brockett—an old friend of mine; we're fellow-writers. Brockett, this is Mary Llewellyn.'

Brockett shot a swift glance in Stephen's direction, then he bowed and gravely shook hands with Mary.

And now Stephen was to see yet another side of this strange and unexpected creature. With infinite courtesy and tact he went out of his way to make himself charming. Never by so much as a word or a look did he once allow it to be inferred that his quick mind had seized on the situation. Brockett's manner suggested an innocence that he was very far from possessing.

Stephen began to study him with interest; they two had not met since before the war. He had thickened, his figure was more robust, there was muscle and flesh on his wide, straight shoulders. And she thought that his face had certainly aged; little bags were showing under his eyes, and rather deep lines at the sides of his mouth—the war had left its mark upon Brockett. Only his hands remained unchanged; those white and soft-skinned hands of a woman.

He was saying: 'So you two were in the same Unit. That was a great stroke of luck for Stephen; I mean she'd be feeling horribly lonely now that old Puddle's gone back to England. Stephen's distinguished herself I see—Croix de Guerre and a very becoming scar. Don't protest, my dear Stephen, you know it's becoming. All that happened to me was a badly sprained ankle'; he laughed, 'fancy going out to Mesopotamia to slip on a bit of orange peel! I might have done better than that here in Paris. By the way, I'm in my own flat again now; I hope you'll bring Miss Llewellyn to luncheon.'

He did not stay embarrassingly late, nor did he leave suggestively early; he got up to go at just the right moment. But when Mary went out of the room to call Pierre, he quite suddenly put his arm through Stephen's.

'Good luck, my dear, you deserve it;' he murmured, and his sharp grey eyes had grown almost gentle: 'I hope you'll be very, very happy.'

Stephen quietly disengaged her arm with a look of surprise: 'Happy? Thank you, Brockett,' she smiled, as she lighted a cigarette.

3

They could not tear themselves away from their home, and that summer they remained in Paris. There were always so many things to do, Mary's bedroom entirely to refurnish for instance—she had Puddle's old room overlooking the garden. When the city seemed to be growing too airless, they motored off happily into the country, spending a couple of nights at an auberge, for France abounds in green, pleasant places. Once or twice they lunched with Jonathan Brockett at his flat in the Avenue Victor Hugo,* a beautiful flat since his taste was perfect, and he dined with them before leaving for Deauville*—his manner continued to be studiously guarded. The Duphots had gone for their holiday and Buisson was away in Spain for a month—but what did they want that summer with people? On those evenings when they did not go out, Stephen would now read aloud to Mary, leading the girl's adaptable mind into new and hitherto unexplored channels; teaching her the joy that can lie in books, even as Sir Philip had once taught his daughter.* Mary had read so little in her life that the choice of books seemed practically endless, but Stephen must make a start by reading that immortal classic of their own Paris, *Peter Ibbetson*,* and Mary said:

'Stephen—if we were ever parted, do you think that you and I could dream true?'

And Stephen answered: 'I often wonder whether we're not dreaming true all the time—whether the only truth isn't in dreaming.' Then they talked for a while of such nebulous things as dreams, which will seem very concrete to lovers.

Sometimes Stephen would read aloud in French, for she wanted the girl to grow better acquainted with the lure of that fascinating language. And thus gradually, with infinite care, did she seek to fill the more obvious gaps in Mary's none too complete education. And Mary, listening to Stephen's voice, rather deep and always a little husky, would think that words were more tuneful than music and more inspiring, when spoken by Stephen.

At this time many gentle and friendly things began to bear witness to Mary's presence. There were flowers in the quiet old garden for instance, and some large red carp in the fountain's basin, and two married couples of white fantail pigeons* who lived in a house on a tall wooden leg and kept up a convivial cooing. These pigeons lacked all respect for Stephen; by August they were flying in at her window and landing with soft, heavy thuds on her desk where they strutted until she fed them with maize. And because they were Mary's and Mary loved them, Stephen would laugh, as unruffled as they were, and would patiently coax them back into the garden with bribes for their plump little circular crops. In the turret room that had been Puddle's sanctum, there were now three cagefuls of Mary's rescues—tiny bright-coloured birds with dejected plumage, and eyes that had filmed from a lack of sunshine. Mary was always bringing them home from the terrible bird shops along the river, for her love of such helpless and suffering things was so great that she in her turn must suffer. An ill-treated creature would haunt her for days, so that Stephen would often exclaim half in earnest:

'Go and buy up all the animal shops in Paris . . . anything, darling, only don't look unhappy!'

The tiny bright-coloured birds would revive to some extent, thanks to Mary's skilled treatment; but since she always bought the most ailing, not a few of them left this disheartening world for what we must hope was a warm, wild heaven—there were several small graves already in the garden.

Then one morning, when Mary went out alone because Stephen had letters to write to Morton, she chanced on yet one more desolate creature who followed her home to the Rue Jacob, and right into Stephen's immaculate study. It was large, ungainly and appallingly thin; it was coated with mud which had dried on its nose, its back, its legs and all over its stomach. Its paws were heavy, its ears were long, and its tail, like the tail of a rat, looked hairless, but curved up to a point in a miniature sickle. Its face was as smooth as though made out of plush, and its luminous eyes were the colour of amber.

Mary said: 'Oh, Stephen—he wanted to come. He's got a sore paw; look at him, he's limping!'

Then this tramp of a dog hobbled over to the table and stood there gazing dumbly at Stephen, who must stroke his anxious, dishevelled head: 'I suppose this means that we're going to keep him.'

'Darling, I'm dreadfully afraid it does—he says he's sorry to be such a mongrel.'

'He needn't apologize,' Stephen smiled, 'he's all right, he's an Irish water-spaniel,* though what he's doing out here the Lord knows; I've never seen one before in Paris.'

They fed him, and later that afternoon they gave him a bath in Stephen's bath-room. The result of that bath, which was disconcerting as far as the room went, they left to Adèle. The room was a bog, but Mary's rescue had emerged a mass of chocolate ringlets, all save his charming plush-covered face, and his curious tail, which was curved like a sickle. Then they bound the sore pad and took him downstairs; after which Mary wanted to know all about him, so Stephen unearthed an illustrated dog book from a cupboard under the study book-case.

'Oh, look!' exclaimed Mary, reading over her shoulder, 'He's not Irish at all, he's really a Welshman: "We find in the Welsh laws of Howell Dda the first reference to this intelligent spaniel. The Iberians brought the breed to Ireland. . . . "* Of course, that's why he followed me home; he knew I was Welsh the moment he saw me!'

Stephen laughed: 'Yes, his hair grows up from a peak like yours—it must be a national failing. Well, what shall we call him? His name's important; it ought to be quite short.'

'David,'* said Mary.

The dog looked gravely from one to the other for a moment, then he lay down at Mary's feet, dropping his chin on his bandaged paw, and closing his eyes with a grunt of contentment. And so it had suddenly come to pass that they who had lately been two, were now three. There were Stephen and Mary—there was also David.

CHAPTER 42

I

THAT October there arose the first dark cloud. It drifted over to Paris from England, for Anna wrote asking Stephen to Morton but with never a mention of Mary Llewellyn. Not that she ever did mention their friendship in her letters, indeed she completely ignored it; yet this invitation which excluded the girl seemed to Stephen an intentional slight upon Mary. A hot flush of anger spread up to her brow as she read and re-read her mother's brief letter:

'I want to discuss some important points regarding the management of the estate. As the place will eventually come to you, I think we should try to keep more in touch. . . .' Then a list of the points Anna wished to discuss; they seemed very trifling indeed to Stephen.

She put the letter away in a drawer and sat staring darkly out of the window. In the garden Mary was talking to David, persuading him not to retrieve the pigeons.

'If my mother had invited her ten times over I'd never have taken her to Morton,' Stephen muttered.

Oh, but she knew, and only too well, what it would mean should they be there together; the lies, the despicable subterfuges, as though they were little less than criminals. It would be: 'Mary, don't hang about my bedroom—be careful . . . of course while we're here at Morton . . . it's my mother, she can't understand these things; to her they would seem an outrage, an insult. . . .' And then the guard set upon eyes and lips; the feeling of guilt at so much as a hand-touch; the pretence of a careless, quite usual friendship—'Mary, don't look at me as though you cared! you did this evening—remember my mother.'*

Intolerable quagmire of lies and deceit! The degrading of all that to them was sacred—a very gross degrading of love, and through love a gross degrading of Mary. Mary . . . so loyal and as yet so gallant, but so pitifully untried in the war of existence. Warned only by words, the words of a lover, and what were mere words when it came to actions? And the ageing woman with the far-away eyes, eyes that could yet be so cruel, so accusing—they might turn and rest with repugnance on Mary, even as once they had rested on Stephen: 'I would rather see you dead at my feet. . . .'* A fearful saying, and yet she had meant it, that ageing woman with the far-away eyes—she had uttered it knowing herself to be a mother. But that at least should be hidden from Mary.

She began to consider the ageing woman who had scourged her but whom she had so deeply wounded, and as she did so the depth of that wound made her shrink in spite of her bitter anger, so that gradually the anger gave way to a slow and almost reluctant pity. Poor, ignorant, blind, unreasoning woman; herself a victim, having given her body for Nature's most inexplicable whim. Yes, there had been two victims already—must there now be a third—and that one Mary? She trembled. At that moment she could not face it, she was weak, she was utterly undone by loving. Greedy she had grown for happiness, for the joys and the peace that their union had brought her. She would try to minimize the whole thing; she would say: 'It will only be for ten days; I must just run over about this business,' then Mary would probably think it quite natural that she had not been invited to Morton and would ask no questions—she never asked questions. But would Mary think such a slight was quite natural? Fear possessed her; she sat there terribly afraid of this cloud that had suddenly risen to menace—afraid yet determined not to submit, not to let it gain power through her own acquiescence.

There was only one weapon to keep it at bay. Getting up she opened the window: 'Mary!'

All unconscious the girl hurried in with David: 'Did you call?'

'Yes—come close. Closer . . . closer, sweetheart. . . .'

2

Shaken and very greatly humbled, Mary had let Stephen go from her to Morton. She had not been deceived by Stephen's glib words, and had now no illusions regarding Anna Gordon. Lady Anna, suspecting the truth about them, had not wished to meet her. It was all quite clear, cruelly clear if it came to that matter—but these thoughts she had mercifully hidden from Stephen.

She had seen Stephen off at the station with a smile: 'I'll write every day. Do put on your coat, darling; you don't want to arrive at Morton with a chill. And mind you wire when you get to Dover.'

Yet now as she sat in the empty study,* she must bury her face and cry a little because she was here and Stephen in England . . . and then of course, this was their first real parting.

David sat watching with luminous eyes in which were reflected her secret troubles; then he got up and planted a paw on the book, for he thought it high time to have done with this reading. He lacked the language that Raftery had known—the language of many small sounds and small movements—a clumsy and inarticulate fellow he was, but unrestrainedly loving. He nearly broke his own heart between love and the deep gratitude which he felt for Mary. At the moment he wanted to lay back his ears and howl with despair to see her unhappy. He wanted to make an enormous noise, the kind of noise wild folk make in the jungle—lions and tigers and other wild folk that David had heard about from his mother—his mother had been in Africa once a long time ago, with an old French colonel.* But instead he abruptly licked Mary's cheek—it tasted peculiar, he thought, like sea water.

'Do you want a walk, David?' she asked him gently.

And as well as he could, David nodded his head by wagging his tail which was shaped like a sickle. Then he capered, thumping the ground with his paws; after which he barked twice in an effort to amuse her, for such things had seemed funny to her in the past, although now she appeared not to notice his capers. However, she had put on her hat and coat; so, still barking, he followed her through the courtyard.

They wandered along the Quai Voltaire, Mary pausing to look at the misty river.

'Shall I dive in and bring you a rat?' inquired David by lunging wildly backwards and forwards.

She shook her head. 'Do stop, David; be good!' Then she sighed again and stared at the river; so David stared too, but he stared at Mary.

Quite suddenly Paris had lost its charm for her. After all, what was it? Just a big, foreign city—a city that belonged to a stranger people who cared nothing for Stephen and nothing for Mary. They were exiles. She turned the word over in her mind—exiles; it sounded unwanted, lonely. But why had Stephen become an exile? Why had she exiled herself from Morton? Strange that she, Mary, had never asked her—had never wanted to until this moment.

She walked on, not caring very much where she went. It grew dusk, and the dusk brought with it great longing—the longing to see, to hear, to touch—almost a physical pain it was, this longing to feel the nearness of Stephen. But Stephen had left her to go to Morton . . . Morton, that was surely Stephen's real home, and in that real home there was no place for Mary.

She was not resentful. She did not condemn either the world, or herself, or Stephen. Hers was no mind to wrestle with problems, to demand either justice or explanation; she only knew that her heart felt bruised so that all manner of little things hurt her. It hurt her to think of Stephen surrounded by objects that she had never seen—tables, chairs, pictures, all old friends of Stephen's, all dear and familiar, yet strangers to Mary. It hurt her to think of the unknown bedroom in which Stephen had slept since the days of her childhood; of the unknown schoolroom where Stephen had worked; of the stables, the lakes and the gardens of Morton. It hurt her to think of the two unknown women who must now be awaiting Stephen's arrival—Puddle, whom Stephen loved and respected; Lady Anna, of whom she spoke very seldom, and who, Mary felt, could never have loved her. And it came upon Mary with a little shock that a long span of Stephen's life was hidden; years and years of that life had come and gone before they two had finally found each other. How could she hope to link up with a past that belonged to a home which she might not enter? Then, being a woman, she suddenly ached for the quiet, pleasant things that a home will stand for—security, peace, respect and honour, the kindness of parents, the good-will of neighbours; happiness that can be shared with friends, love that is proud to proclaim its existence. All that Stephen most craved for the creature she loved, that creature must now quite suddenly ache for.

And as though some mysterious cord stretched between them, Stephen's heart was troubled at that very moment; intolerably troubled because of Morton, the real home which might not be shared with Mary. Ashamed because of shame laid on another, compassionate and suffering because of her compassion, she was thinking of the girl left alone in Paris—the girl who should have come with her to England, who should have been welcomed and honoured at Morton. Then she suddenly remembered some words from the past, very terrible words: 'Could you marry me, Stephen?'*

Mary turned and walked back to the Rue Jacob. Disheartened and anxious, David lagged beside her. He had done all he could to distract her mind from whatever it was that lay heavy upon it. He had made a pretence of chasing a pigeon, he had barked himself hoarse at a terrified beggar, he had brought her a stick and implored her to throw it, he had caught at her skirt and tugged it politely; in the end he had nearly got run over by a taxi in his desperate efforts to gain her attention. This last attempt had certainly roused her: she had put on his lead—poor, misunderstood David.

3

Mary went into Stephen's study and sat down at the spacious writing-table, for now all of a sudden she had only one ache, and that was the ache of her love for Stephen. And because of her love she wished to comfort, since in every fond woman there is much of the mother. That letter was full of many things which a less privileged pen had best left unwritten—loyalty, faith, consolation, devotion; all this and much more she wrote to Stephen. As she sat there, her heart seemed to swell within her as though in response to some mighty challenge.*

Thus it was that Mary met and defeated the world's first tentative onslaught upon them.

CHAPTER 43

I

THERE comes a time in all passionate attachments when life, real life, must be faced once again with its varied and endless obligations, when the lover knows in his innermost heart that the halcyon days are over. He may well regret this prosaic intrusion, yet to him it will usually seem quite natural, so that while loving not one whit the less, he will bend his neck to the yoke of existence. But the woman, for whom love is an end in itself, finds it harder to submit thus calmly. To every devoted and ardent woman there comes this moment of poignant regretting; and struggle she must to hold it at bay. 'Not yet, not yet—just a little longer'; until Nature, abhorring her idleness, forces on her the labour of procreation.

But in such relationships as Mary's and Stephen's, Nature must pay for experimenting; she may even have to pay very dearly—it largely depends on the sexual mixture.* A drop too little of the male in the lover, and mighty indeed will be the wastage. And yet there are cases—and Stephen's was one—in which the male will emerge triumphant; in which passion combined with a real devotion will become a spur rather than a deterrent; in which love and endeavour will fight side by side in a desperate struggle to find some solution.

Thus it was that when Stephen returned from Morton, Mary divined, as it were by instinct, that the time of dreaming was over and past; and she clung very close, kissing many times—

'Do you love me as much as before you went? Do you love me?' The woman's eternal question.

And Stephen, who, if possible, loved her more, answered almost brusquely: 'Of course I love you.' For her thoughts were still heavy with the bitterness that had come of that visit of hers to Morton, and which at all costs must be hidden from Mary.

There had been no marked change in her mother's manner. Anna had been very quiet and courteous. Together they had interviewed bailiff and agent,* scheming as always for the welfare of Morton; but one topic there had been which Anna had ignored, had refused to discuss, and that topic was Mary. With a suddenness born of exasperation,

Stephen had spoken of her one evening. 'I want Mary Llewellyn to know my real home; some day I must bring her to Morton with me.' She had stopped, seeing Anna's warning face—expressionless, closed; while as for her answer, it had been more eloquent far than words—a disconcerting, unequivocal silence. And Stephen, had she ever entertained any doubt, must have known at that moment past all hope of doubting, that her mother's omission to invite the girl had indeed been meant as a slight upon Mary. Getting up, she had gone to her father's study.

Puddle, who had held her peace at the time, had spoken just before Stephen's departure. 'My dear, I know it's all terribly hard about Morton—about . . .' She had hesitated.

And Stephen had thought with renewed bitterness: 'Even she jibs,* it seems, at mentioning Mary.' She had answered: 'If you're speaking of Mary Llewellyn, I shall certainly never bring her to Morton, that is as long as my mother lives—I don't allow her to be insulted.'

Then Puddle had looked at Stephen gravely. 'You're not working, and yet work's your only weapon. Make the world respect you, as you can do through your work; it's the surest harbour of refuge for your friend, the only harbour—remember that—and it's up to you to provide it, Stephen.'

Stephen had been too sore at heart to reply; but throughout the long journey from Morton to Paris, Puddle's words had kept hammering in her brain: 'You're not working, and yet work's your only weapon.'

So while Mary lay sleeping in Stephen's arms on that first blessèd night of their reunion, her lover lay wide-eyed with sleeplessness, planning the work she must do on the morrow, cursing her own indolence and folly, her illusion of safety where none existed.

2*

They soon settled down to their more prosaic days very much as quite ordinary people will do. Each of them now had her separate tasks—Stephen her writing, and Mary the household, the paying of bills, the filing of receipts, the answering of unimportant letters. But for her there were long hours of idleness, since Pauline and Pierre were almost too perfect—they would smile and manage the house their own way, which it must be admitted was better than Mary's. As for the letters, there were not very many; and as for the bills, there was plenty of money—being spared the struggle to make two ends meet, she was also deprived of the innocent pleasure of scheming to provide little happy surprises, little extra comforts for the person she loved, which in youth can add a real zest to existence. Then Stephen had found her typing too slow, so was sending the work to a woman in Passy;* obsessed by a longing to finish her book, she would tolerate neither let nor hindrance. And because of their curious isolation, there were times when Mary would feel very lonely. For whom did she know? She had no friends in Paris except the kind Mademoiselle Duphot and Julie. Once a week, it is true, she could go and see Buisson, for Stephen continued to keep up her fencing; and occasionally Brockett would come strolling in, but his interest was centred entirely in Stephen; if she should be working, as was often the case, he would not waste very much time over Mary.

Stephen often called her into the study, comforted by the girl's loving presence. 'Come and sit with me, sweetheart, I like you in here.' But quite soon she would seem to forget all about her. 'What . . . what?' she would mutter, frowning a little. 'Don't speak to me just for a minute, Mary. Go and have your luncheon, there's a good child; I'll come when I've finished this bit—you go on!' But Mary's meal might be eaten alone; for meals had become an annoyance to Stephen.

Of course there was David, the grateful, the devoted. Mary could always talk to David, but since he could never answer her back the conversation was very one-sided. Then too, he was making it obvious that he, in his turn, was missing Stephen; he would hang around looking discontented when she failed to go out after frequent suggestions. For although his heart was faithful to Mary, the gentle dispenser of all salvation, yet the instinct that has dwelt in the soul of the male, perhaps ever since Adam left the Garden of Eden, the instinct that displays itself in club windows and in other such places of male segregation, would make him long for the companionable walks that had sometimes been taken apart from Mary.* Above all would it make him long intensely for Stephen's strong hands and purposeful ways; for that queer, intangible something about her that appealed to the canine manhood in him. She always allowed him to look after himself, without fussing; in a word, she seemed restful to David.

Mary, slipping noiselessly out of the study, might whisper: 'We'll go to the Tuileries Gardens.'

But when they arrived there, what was there to do? For of course a dog must not dive after goldfish—David understood this; there were goldfish at home—he must not start splashing about in ponds that had tiresome stone rims and ridiculous fountains. He and Mary would wander along gravel paths, among people who stared at and made fun of David: 'Quel drôle de chien, mais regardez sa queue!'* They were like that, these French; they had laughed at his mother. She had told him never so much as to say: 'Wouf!' For what did they matter? Still, it was disconcerting. And although he had lived in France all his life—having indeed known no other country—as he walked in the stately Tuileries Gardens, the Celt in his blood* would conjure up visions: great beetling mountains with winding courses down which the torrents went roaring in winter; the earth smell, the dew smell, the smell of wild things which a dog might hunt and yet remain lawful—for of all this and more had his old mother told him. These visions it was that had led him astray, that had treacherously led him half starving to Paris; and that, sometimes, even in these placid days, would come back as he walked in the Tuileries Gardens. But now his heart must thrust them aside—a captive he was now, through love of Mary.

But to Mary there would come one vision alone, that of a garden at Orotava; a garden lighted by luminous darkness, and filled with the restless rhythm of singing.

3

The autumn passed, giving place to the winter, with its short, dreary days of mist and rain. There was now little beauty left in Paris. A grey sky hung above the old streets of the Quarter, a sky which no longer looked bright by contrast, as though seen at the end of a tunnel. Stephen was working like some one possessed, entirely re-writing her pre-war novel. Good it had been, but not good enough, for she now saw life from a much wider angle; and moreover, she was writing this book for Mary. Remembering Mary, remembering Morton, her pen covered sheet after sheet of paper; she wrote with the speed of true inspiration, and at times her work brushed the hem of greatness.* She did not entirely neglect the girl for whose sake she was making this mighty effort—that she could not have done even had she wished to, since love was the actual source of her effort. But quite soon there were days when she would not go out, or if she did go, when she seemed abstracted, so that Mary must ask her the same question twice—then as likely as not get a nebulous answer. And soon there were days when all that she did apart from her writing was done with an effort, with an obvious effort to be considerate.

'Would you like to go to a play one night, Mary?'

If Mary said yes, and procured the tickets, they were usually late, because of Stephen who had worked right up to the very last minute.

Sometimes there were poignant if small disappointments when Stephen had failed to keep a promise. 'Listen, Mary darling—will you ever forgive me if I don't come with you about those furs? I've a bit of work here I simply must finish. You do understand?'

'Yes, of course I do.' But Mary, left to choose her new furs alone, had quite suddenly felt that she did not want them.

And this sort of thing happened fairly often.

If only Stephen had confided in her,* had said: 'I'm trying to build you a refuge; remember what I told you in Orotava!' But no, she shrank from reminding the girl of the gloom that surrounded their small patch of sunshine. If only she had shown a little more patience with Mary's careful if rather slow typing, and so given her a real occupation—but no, she must send the work off to Passy, because the sooner this book was finished the better it would be for Mary's future. And thus, blinded by love and her desire to protect the woman she loved, she erred towards Mary.

When she had finished her writing for the day, she frequently read it aloud in the evening. And although Mary knew that the writing was fine, yet her thoughts would stray from the book to Stephen. The deep, husky voice would read on and on, having in it something urgent, appealing, so that Mary must suddenly kiss Stephen's hand, or the scar on her cheek, because of that voice far more than because of what it was reading.

And now there were times when, serving two masters,* her passion for this girl and her will to protect her, Stephen would be torn by conflicting desires, by opposing mental and physical emotions. She would want to save herself for her work; she would want to give herself wholly to Mary.

Yet quite often she would work far into the night.* 'I'm going to be late—you go to bed, sweetheart.'

And when she herself had at last toiled upstairs, she would steal like a thief past Mary's bedroom, although Mary would nearly always hear her.

'Is that you, Stephen?'

'Yes. Why aren't you asleep? Do you realize that it's three in the morning?'

'Is it? You're not angry, are you, darling? I kept thinking of you alone in the study. Come here and say you're not angry with me, even if it is three o'clock in the morning!'

Then Stephen would slip off her old tweed coat and would fling herself down on the bed beside Mary, too exhausted to do more than take the girl in her arms, and let her lie there with her head on her shoulder.

But Mary would be thinking of all those things which she found so deeply appealing in Stephen—the scar on her cheek, the expression in her eyes, the strength and the queer, shy gentleness of her—the strength which at moments could not be gentle. And as they lay there Stephen might sleep, worn out by the strain of those long hours of writing. But Mary would not sleep, or if she slept it would be when the dawn was paling the windows.*

4

One morning Stephen looked at Mary intently. 'Come here. You're not well! What's the matter? Tell me.' For she thought that the girl was unusually pale, thought too that her lips drooped a little at the corners; and a sudden fear contracted her heart. 'Tell me at once what's the matter with you!' Her voice was rough with anxiety, and she laid an imperative hand over Mary's.

Mary protested. 'Don't be absurd; there's nothing the matter, I'm perfectly well—you're imagining things.' For what could be the matter? Was she not here in Paris with Stephen? But her eyes filled with tears, and she turned away quickly to hide them, ashamed of her own unreason.

Stephen stuck to her point. 'You don't look a bit well. We shouldn't have stayed in Paris last summer.' Then because her own nerves were on edge that day, she frowned. 'It's this business of your not eating whenever I can't get in to a meal. I know you don't eat—Pierre's told me about it. You mustn't behave like a baby, Mary! I shan't be able to write a line if I feel you're ill because you're not eating.' Her fear was making her lose her temper. 'I shall send for a doctor,' she finished brusquely.

Mary refused point-blank to see a doctor. What was she to tell him? She hadn't any symptoms. Pierre exaggerated. She ate quite enough—she had never been a very large eater. Stephen had better get on with her work and stop upsetting herself over nothing.

But try as she might, Stephen could not get on—all the rest of the day her work went badly.

After this she would often leave her desk and go wandering off in search of Mary. 'Darling, where are you?'

'Upstairs in my bedroom!'

'Well, come down; I want you here in the study.' And when Mary had settled herself by the fire: 'Now tell me exactly how you feel—all right?'

And Mary would answer, smiling: 'Yes, I'm quite all right; I swear I am, Stephen!'

It was not an ideal atmosphere for work, but the book was by now so well advanced that nothing short of a disaster could have stopped it—it was one of those books that intend to get born,* and that go on maturing in spite of their authors. Nor was there anything really alarming about the condition of Mary's health. She did not look very well, that was all; and at times she seemed a little downhearted, so that Stephen must snatch a few hours from her work in order that they might go out together. Perhaps they would lunch at a restaurant; or drive into the country, to the rapture of David; or just wander about the streets arm in arm as they had done when first they had returned to Paris. And Mary, because she would be feeling happy, would revive for these few hours as though by magic. Yet when she must once more find herself lonely, with nowhere to go and no one to talk to, because Stephen was back again at her desk, why then she would wilt, which was not unnatural considering her youth and her situation.

5

On Christmas Eve Brockett arrived, bringing flowers. Mary had gone for a walk with David, so Stephen must leave her desk with a sigh. 'Come in, Brockett. I say! What wonderful lilac!'*

He sat down, lighting a cigarette. 'Yes, isn't it fine? I brought it for Mary. How is she?'

Stephen hesitated a moment. 'Not awfully well . . . I've been worried about her.'

Brockett frowned, and stared thoughtfully into the fire. There was something that he wanted to say to Stephen, a warning that he was longing to give, but he did not feel certain how she would take it—no wonder that wretched girl was not fit, forced to lead such a deadly dull existence! If Stephen would let him he wanted to advise, to admonish, to be brutally frank if need be. He had once been brutally frank about her work, but that had been a less delicate matter.

He began to fidget with his soft white hands, drumming on the arms of the chair with his fingers. 'Stephen, I've been meaning to speak about Mary. She struck me as looking thoroughly depressed the last time I saw her—when was it? Monday. Yes, she struck me as looking thoroughly depressed.'

'Oh, but surely you were wrong . . .' interrupted Stephen.

'No, I'm perfectly sure I was right,' he insisted. Then he said: 'I'm going to take a big risk—I'm going to take the risk of losing your friendship.'

His voice was so genuinely regretful, that Stephen must ask him: 'Well—what is it, Brockett?'

'You, my dear. You're not playing fair with that girl; the life she's leading would depress a mother abbess. It's enough to give anybody the hump, and it's going to give Mary neurasthenia!'*

'What on earth do you mean?'

'Don't get ratty and I'll tell you. Look here, I'm not going to pretend any more. Of course we all know that you two are lovers. You're gradually becoming a kind of legend—all's well lost for love, and that sort of thing. . . . But Mary's too young to become a legend; and so are you, my dear, for that matter. But you've got your work, whereas Mary's got nothing—not a soul does that miserable kid know in Paris. Don't *please* interrupt, I've not nearly finished; I positively must and will have my say out! You and she have decided to make a *ménage*—as far as I can see it's as bad as marriage! But if you were a man* it would be rather different; you'd have dozens of friends as a matter of course. Mary might even be going to have an infant. Oh, for God's sake, Stephen, do stop looking shocked. Mary's a perfectly normal young woman; she can't live by love alone, that's all rot—especially as I shrewdly suspect that when you're working the diet's pretty meagre. For heaven's sake let her go about a bit! Why on earth don't you take her to Valérie Seymour's? At Valérie's place she'd meet lots of people; and I ask you, what harm could it possibly do? You shun your own ilk as though they were the devil! Mary needs friends awfully badly, and she needs a certain amount of amusement. But be a bit careful of the so-called normal.' And now Brockett's voice grew aggressive and bitter. 'I wouldn't go trying to force them to be friends—I'm not thinking so much of you now as of Mary; she's young, and the young are easily bruised. . . .'

He was perfectly sincere. He was trying to be helpful, spurred on by his curious affection for Stephen. At the moment he felt very friendly and anxious; there was nothing of the cynic left in him—at the moment. He was honestly advising according to his lights*—perhaps the only lights that the world had left him.

And Stephen could find very little to say. She was sick of denials and subterfuges, sick of tacit lies which outraged her own instincts and which seemed like insults thrust upon Mary; so she left Brockett's bolder statements unchallenged. As for the rest, she hedged a little, still vaguely mistrustful of Valérie Seymour. Yet she knew quite well that Brockett had been right—life these days must often be lonely for Mary. Why had she never thought of this before? She cursed herself for her lack of perception.

Then Brockett tactfully changed the subject; he was far too wise not to know when to stop. So now he told her about his new play, which for him was a very unusual proceeding. And as he talked on there came over Stephen a queer sense of relief at the thought that he knew. . . . Yes, she actually felt a sense of relief because this man knew of her relations with Mary; because there was no longer any need to behave as if those relations were shameful—at all events in the presence of Brockett. The world had at last found a chink in her armour.

6

'We must go and see Valérie Seymour one day,' Stephen remarked quite casually that evening. 'She's a very well-known woman in Paris. I believe she gives rather jolly parties. I think it's about time you had a few friends.'

'Oh, what fun! Yes, do let's—I'd love it!' exclaimed Mary.

Stephen thought that her voice sounded pleased and excited, and in spite of herself she sighed a little. But after all nothing really mattered except that Mary should keep well and happy. She would certainly take her to Valérie Seymour's—why not? She had probably been very foolish. Selfish too, sacrificing the girl to her cranks—

'Darling, of course we'll go,' she said quickly. 'I expect we'll find it awfully amusing.'

7

Three days later, Valérie, having seen Brockett, wrote a short but cordial invitation: 'Do come in on Wednesday if you possibly can—I mean both of you, of course. Brockett's promised to come, and one or two other interesting people. I'm so looking forward to renewing our acquaintance after all this long time, and to meeting Miss Llewellyn. But why have you never been to see me? I don't think that was very friendly of you! However, you can make up for past neglect by coming to my little party on Wednesday. . . .'

Stephen tossed the letter across to Mary. 'There you are!'

'How ripping—but will you go?'

'Do you want to?'

'Yes, of course. Only what about your work?'

'It will keep all right for one afternoon.'

'Are you sure?'

Stephen smiled. 'Yes, I'm quite sure, darling.'

CHAPTER 44

I

VALÉRIE'S rooms were already crowded when Stephen and Mary arrived at her reception, so crowded that at first they could not see their hostess and must stand rather awkwardly near the door—they had not been announced; one never was for some reason, when one went to Valérie Seymour's. People looked at Stephen curiously; her height, her clothes, the scar on her face, had immediately riveted their attention.

'Quel type!' murmured Dupont the sculptor to his neighbour, and promptly decided that he wished to model Stephen. 'It's a wonderful head; I adore the strong throat. And the mouth—is it chaste, is it ardent? I wonder. How would one model that intriguing mouth?' Then being Dupont, to whom all things were allowed for the sake of his art, he moved a step nearer and stared with embarrassing admiration, combing his greyish beard with his fingers.

His neighbour, who was also his latest mistress, a small fair-haired girl of a doll-like beauty, shrugged her shoulders. 'I am not very pleased with you, Dupont, your taste is becoming peculiar, mon ami—and yet you are still sufficiently virile. . . .'

He laughed. 'Be tranquil, my little hen, I am not proposing to give you a rival.' Then he started to tease. 'But what about you? I dislike the small horns that are covered with moss, even although they are no bigger than thimbles. They are irritating, those mossy horns, and exceedingly painful when they start to grow—like wisdom teeth, only even more foolish. Ah, yes, I too have my recollections. What is sauce for the gander is sauce for the goose,* as the English say—such a practical people!'

'You are dreaming, mon pauvre bougre,'* snapped the lady.

And now Valérie was making her way to the door. 'Miss Gordon! I'm most awfully glad to see you and Miss Llewellyn. Have you had any tea? No, of course not, I'm an abominable hostess! Come along to the table—where's that useless Brockett? Oh, here he is. Brockett, please be a man and get Miss Llewellyn and Miss Gordon some tea.'

Brockett sighed. 'You go first then, Stephen darling, you're so much more efficient than I am.' And he laid a soft white hand on her shoulder, thrusting her gently but firmly forward. When they reached the buffet, he calmly stood still. 'Do get me an ice—vanilla?' he murmured.

Every one seemed to know every one else, the atmosphere was familiar and easy. People hailed each other like intimate friends, and quite soon they were being charming to Stephen, and equally charming and kind to Mary.

Valérie was introducing her new guests with tactful allusions to Stephen's talent: 'This is Stephen Gordon—you know, the author; and Miss Llewellyn.'

Her manner was natural, and yet Stephen could not get rid of the feeling that every one knew about her and Mary, or that if they did not actually know, they guessed, and were eager to show themselves friendly.

She thought: 'Well, why not? I'm sick of lying.'

The erstwhile resentment that she had felt towards Valérie Seymour was fading completely. So pleasant it was to be made to feel welcome by all these clever and interesting people—and clever they were there was no denying; in Valérie's *salon* the percentage of brains was generally well above the average. For together with those who themselves being normal, had long put intellects above bodies, were writers, painters, musicians and scholars, men and women who, set apart from their birth, had determined to hack out a niche in existence. Many of them had already arrived, while some were still rather painfully hacking; not a few would fall by the way, it is true, but as they fell others would take their places. Over the bodies of prostrate comrades those others must fall in their turn or go on hacking—for them there was no compromise with life, they were lashed by the whip of self-preservation.* There was Pat who had lost her Arabella to the golden charms of Grigg and the Lido. Pat, who, originally hailing from Boston, still vaguely suggested a New England schoolmarm. Pat, whose libido apart from the flesh, flowed into entomological* channels—one had to look twice to discern that her ankles were too strong and too heavy for those of a female.

There was Jamie, very much more pronounced; Jamie who had come to Paris from the Highlands; a trifle unhinged because of the music that besieged her soul and fought for expression through her stiff and scholarly compositions. Loose limbed, raw boned and short-sighted she was; and since she could seldom afford new glasses, her eyes were red-rimmed and strained in expression, and she poked her head badly, for ever peering. Her tow-coloured* mop was bobbed by her friend, the fringe being only too often uneven.

There was Wanda, the struggling Polish painter; dark for a Pole with her short, stiff black hair, and her dusky skin, and her colourless lips; yet withal not unattractive, this Wanda. She had wonderful eyes that held fire in their depths, hell-fire at times, if she had been drinking; but at other times a more gentle flame, although never one that it was safe to play with. Wanda saw largely. All that she envisaged was immense, her pictures, her passions, her remorses. She craved with a wellnigh insatiable craving, she feared with a wellnigh intolerable terror—not the devil, she was brave with him when in her cups, but God in the person of Christ the Redeemer. Like a whipped cur she crawled to the foot of the Cross, without courage, without faith, without hope of mercy. Outraged by her body, she must ruthlessly scourge it—no good, the lust of the eye would betray her. Seeing she desired and desiring she drank, seeking to drown one lust in another. And then she would stand up before her tall easel, swaying a little but with hand always steady. The brandy went into her legs, not her hands; her hands would remain disconcertingly steady. She would start some gigantic and heart-broken daub,* struggling to lose herself in her picture, struggling to ease the ache of her passion by smearing the placid white face of the canvas with ungainly yet strangely arresting forms—according to Dupont, Wanda had genius. Neither eating nor sleeping she would grow very thin, so that everybody would know what had happened. They had seen it before, oh, but many times, and therefore for them the tragedy was lessened.

'Wanda's off again!' some one might say with a grin. 'She was tight* this morning; who is it this time?'

But Valérie, who hated drink like the plague, would grow angry; outraged she would feel by this Wanda.

There was Hortense, Comtesse de Kerguelen;* dignified and reserved, a very great lady, of a calm and rather old-fashioned beauty. When Valérie introduced her to Stephen, Stephen quite suddenly thought of Morton. And yet she had left all for Valérie Seymour; husband, children and home had she left; facing scandal, opprobrium, persecution. Greater than all these most vital things had been this woman's love for Valérie Seymour. An enigma she seemed, much in need of explaining. And now in the place of that outlawed love had come friendship; they were close friends, these one-time lovers.

There was Margaret Roland, the poetess, a woman whose work was alive with talent. The staunchest of allies, the most fickle of lovers, she seemed likely enough to end up in the workhouse, with her generous financial apologies which at moments made pretty large holes in her savings. It was almost impossible not to like her, since her only fault lay in being too earnest; every fresh love affair was the last while it lasted, though of course this was apt to be rather misleading. A costly business in money and tears; she genuinely suffered in heart as in pocket. There was nothing arresting in Margaret's appearance, sometimes she dressed well, sometimes she dressed badly, according to the influence of the moment. But she always wore ultra-feminine shoes, and frequently bought model gowns when in Paris. One might have said quite a womanly woman, unless the trained ear had been rendered suspicious by her voice which had something peculiar about it. It was like a boy's voice on the verge of breaking.

And then there was Brockett with his soft white hands; and several others there were, very like him. There was also Adolphe Blanc,* the designer—a master of colour whose primitive tints had practically revolutionized taste, bringing back to the eye the joy of the simple. Blanc stood in a little niche by himself, which at times must surely have been very lonely. A quiet, tawny man with the eyes of the Hebrew, in his youth he had been very deeply afflicted. He had spent his days going from doctor to doctor: 'What am I?' They had told him, pocketing their fees; not a few had unctuously set out to cure him. Cure him, good God! There was no cure for Blanc, he was, of all men, the most normal abnormal. He had known revolt, renouncing his God; he had known despair, the despair of the godless; he had known wild moments of dissipation; he had known long months of acute self-abasement. And then he had suddenly found his soul, and that finding had brought with it resignation, so that now he could stand in a niche by himself, a pitiful spectator of what, to him, often seemed a bewildering scheme of creation. For a living he designed many beautiful things—furniture, costumes and scenery for ballets, even women's gowns if the mood was upon him, but this he did for a physical living. To keep life in his desolate, long-suffering soul, he had stored his mind with much profound learning. So now many poor devils went to him for advice, which he never refused though he gave it sadly. It was always the same: 'Do the best you can, no man can do more—but never stop fighting. For us there is no sin so great as despair, and perhaps no virtue so vital as courage.' Yes, indeed, to this gentle and learned Jew went many a poor baptized Christian devil.

And such people frequented Valérie Seymour's, men and women who must carry God's mark on their foreheads. For Valérie, placid and self-assured, created an atmosphere of courage; every one felt very normal and brave when they gathered together at Valérie Seymour's. There she was, this charming and cultured woman, a kind of lighthouse in a storm-swept ocean. The waves had lashed round her feet in vain; winds had howled; clouds had spewed forth their hail and their lightning; torrents had deluged but had not destroyed her. The storms, gathering force, broke and drifted away, leaving behind them the shipwrecked, the drowning. But when they looked up, the poor spluttering victims, why what should they see but Valérie Seymour! Then a few would strike boldly out for the shore, at the sight of this indestructible creature.*

She did nothing, and at all times said very little, feeling no urge towards philanthropy. But this much she gave to her brethren, the freedom of her *salon*, the protection of her friendship; if it eased them to come to her monthly gatherings they were always welcome provided they were sober. Drink and drugs she abhorred because they were ugly—one drank tea, iced coffee, sirops and orangeade in that celebrated flat on the Quai Voltaire.

Oh, yes, a very strange company indeed if one analysed it for this or that stigma. Why, the grades were so numerous and so fine that they often defied the most careful observation. The timbre of a voice, the build of an ankle, the texture of a hand, a movement, a gesture—since few were as pronounced as Stephen Gordon, unless it were Wanda, the Polish painter. She, poor soul, never knew how to dress for the best. If she dressed like a woman she looked like a man, if she dressed like a man she looked like a woman!

2

And their love affairs, how strange, how bewildering—how difficult to classify degrees of attraction. For not always would they attract their own kind, very often they attracted quite ordinary people. Thus Pat's Arabella had suddenly married, having wearied of Grigg as of her predecessor. Rumour had it that she was now blatantly happy at the prospect of shortly becoming a mother. And then there was Jamie's friend

Barbara, a wisp of a girl very faithful and loving, but all woman as far as one could detect, with a woman's clinging dependence on Jamie.*

These two had been lovers from the days of their childhood, from the days when away in their Highland village the stronger child had protected the weaker at school or at play with their boisterous companions. They had grown up together like two wind-swept saplings on their bleak Scottish hill-side so starved of sunshine. For warmth and protection they had leaned to each other, until with the spring, at the time of mating, their branches had quietly intertwined. That was how it had been, the entwining of saplings, very simple, and to them very dear, having nothing mysterious or strange about it except inasmuch as all love is mysterious.

To themselves they had seemed like the other lovers for whom dawns were brighter and twilights more tender. Hand in hand they had strolled down the village street, pausing to listen to the piper at evening. And something in that sorrowful, outlandish music would arouse the musical soul in Jamie, so that great chords would surge up through her brain, very different indeed from the wails of the piper, yet born of the same mystic Highland nature.

Happy days; happy evenings when the glow of the summer lingered for hours above the grim hills, lingered on long after the flickering lamps had been lit in the cottage windows of Beedles.* The piper would at last decide to go home, but they two would wander away to the moorland, there to lie down for a space side by side among the short springy turf and the heather.

Children they had been, having small skill in words, or in life, or in love itself for that matter. Barbara, fragile and barely nineteen; the angular Jamie not yet quite twenty. They had talked because words will ease the full spirit; talked in abrupt, rather shy broken phrases. They had loved because love had come naturally to them up there on the soft springy turf and the heather. But after a while their dreams had been shattered, for such dreams as theirs had seemed strange to the village. Daft, the folk had thought them, mouching* round by themselves for hours, like a couple of lovers.

Barbara's grand-dame,* an austere old woman with whom she had lived since her earliest childhood—Barbara's grand-dame had mistrusted this friendship. 'I dinna richtly unnerstan' it,' she had frowned; 'her and that Jamie's unco throng. It's no richt for lass-bairns, an' it's no proaper!'*

And since she spoke with authority, having for years been the village post-mistress, her neighbours had wagged their heads and agreed. 'It's no richt; ye hae said it, Mrs. MacDonald!'

The gossip had reached the minister, Jamie's white-haired and gentle old father. He had looked at the girl with bewildered eyes—he had always been bewildered by his daughter. A poor housewife she was, and very untidy; if she cooked she mucked up the pots and the kitchen, and her hands were strangely unskilled with the needle; this he knew, since his heels suffered much from her darning. Remembering her mother he had shaken his head and sighed many times as he looked at Jamie. For her mother had been a soft, timorous woman,* and he himself was very retiring, but their Jamie loved striding over the hills in the teeth of a gale, an uncouth, boyish creature. As a child she had gone rabbit stalking with ferrets; had ridden a neighbour's farm-horse astride on a sack, without stirrup, saddle or bridle; had done all manner of outlandish things. And he, poor lonely, bewildered man, still mourning his wife, had been no match for her.

Yet even as a child she had sat at the piano and picked out little tunes of her own inventing. He had done his best; she had been taught to play by Miss Morrison of the next-door village, since music alone seemed able to tame her. And as Jamie had grown so her tunes had grown with her, gathering purpose and strength with her body. She would improvise for hours on the winter evenings, if Barbara would sit in their parlour and listen. He had always made Barbara welcome at the manse;* they had been so inseparable, those two, since childhood—and now? He had frowned, remembering the gossip.

Rather timidly he had spoken to Jamie. 'Listen, my dear, when you're always together, the lads don't get a chance to come courting, and Barbara's grandmother wants the lass married. Let her walk with a lad on Sabbath afternoons*—there's that young MacGregor, he's a fine, steady fellow, and they say he's in love with the little lass. . . .'

Jamie had stared at him, scowling darkly. 'She doesn't want to walk out with MacGregor!'

The minister had shaken his head yet again. In the hands of his child he was utterly helpless.

Then Jamie had gone to Inverness* in order the better to study music, but every week-end she had spent at the manse, there had been no real break in her friendship with Barbara; indeed they had seemed more devoted than ever, no doubt because of these forced separations.

Two years later the minister had suddenly died, leaving his little all to Jamie. She had had to turn out of the old, grey manse, and had taken a room in the village near Barbara. But antagonism, no longer restrained through respect for the gentle and child-like pastor, had made itself very acutely felt—hostile they had been, those good people, to Jamie.

Barbara had wept. 'Jamie, let's go away . . . they hate us. Let's go where nobody knows us. I'm twenty-one now, I can go where I like, they can't stop me. Take me away from them, Jamie!'

Miserable, angry, and sorely bewildered, Jamie had put her arm round the girl. 'Where can I take you, you poor little creature? You're not strong, and I'm terribly poor, remember.'

But Barbara had continued to plead. 'I'll work, I'll scrub floors, I'll do anything, Jamie, only let's get away where nobody knows us!'

So Jamie had turned to her music master in Inverness, and had begged him to help her. What could she do to earn her living? And because this man believed in her talent, he had helped her with advice and a small loan of money, urging her to go to Paris and study to complete her training in composition.

'You're really too good for me,' he had told her; 'and out there you could live considerably cheaper. For one thing the exchange would be in your favour. I'll write to the head of the Conservatoire* this evening.'

That had been shortly after the Armistice, and now here they were together in Paris.

As for Pat, she collected her moths and her beetles, and when fate was propitious an occasional woman. But fate was so seldom propitious to Pat—Arabella had put this down to the beetles. Poor Pat, having recently grown rather gloomy, had taken to quoting American history, speaking darkly of blood-tracks left on the snow by what she had christened: 'The miserable army.' Then too she seemed haunted by General Custer,* that gallant and very unfortunate hero. 'It's Custer's last ride, all the time,' she would say. 'No good talking, the whole darned world's out to scalp us!'

As for Margaret Roland, she was never attracted to anyone young and whole-hearted and free—she was, in fact, a congenital poacher.

While as for Wanda, her loves were so varied that no rule could be discovered by which to judge them. She loved wildly, without either chart or compass. A rudderless bark it was, Wanda's emotion, beaten now this way, now that, by the gale, veering first to the normal, then to the abnormal; a thing of torn sails and stricken masts, that never came within sight of a harbour.*

3

These, then, were the people to whom Stephen turned at last in her fear of isolation for Mary; to her own kind she turned and was made very welcome, for no bond is more binding than that of affliction. But her vision stretched beyond to the day when happier folk would also accept her, and through her this girl for whose happiness she and she alone would have to answer; to the day when through sheer force of tireless endeavour she would have built that harbour of refuge for Mary.

So now they were launched upon the stream that flows silent and deep through all great cities, gliding on between precipitous borders, away and away into no-man's-land—the most desolate country in all creation. Yet when they got home they felt no misgivings, even Stephen's doubts had been drugged for the moment, since just at first this curious stream will possess the balm of the waters of Lethe.*

She said to Mary: 'It was quite a good party; don't you think so?'

And Mary answered naïvely: 'I loved it because they were so nice to you. Brockett told me they think you're the coming writer. He said you were Valérie Seymour's lion;* I was bursting with pride—it made me so happy!'

For answer, Stephen stooped down and kissed her.

CHAPTER 45

I

By February Stephen's book was rewritten and in the hands of her publisher in England. This gave her the peaceful, yet exhilarated feeling that comes when a writer has given of his best and knows that that best is not unworthy. With a sigh of relief she metaphorically stretched, rubbed her eyes and started to look about her. She was in the mood that comes as a reaction from strain, and was glad enough of amusement; moreover the spring was again in the air, the year had turned, there were sudden bright days when the sun brought a few hours of warmth to Paris.

They were now no longer devoid of friends, no longer solely dependent upon Brockett on the one hand, and Mademoiselle Duphot on the other; Stephen's telephone would ring pretty often. There was now always somewhere for Mary to go; always people who were anxious to see her and Stephen, people with whom one got intimate quickly and was thus saved a lot of unnecessary trouble. Of them all, however, it was Barbara and Jamie for whom Mary developed a real affection; she and Barbara had formed a harmless alliance which at times was even a little pathetic. The one talking of Jamie, the other of Stephen, they would put their young heads together very gravely. 'Do you find Jamie goes off her food when she's working?' 'Do you find that Stephen sleeps badly? Is she careless of her health? Jamie's awfully worrying sometimes.'

Or perhaps they would be in a more flippant mood and would sit and whisper together, laughing; making tender fun of the creatures they loved, as women have been much inclined to do ever since that rib was demanded of Adam.* Then Jamie and Stephen would pretend to feel aggrieved, would pretend that they also must hang together, must be on their guard against feminine intrigues. Oh, yes, the whole business was rather pathetic.

Jamie and her Barbara were starvation-poor, so poor that a square meal came as a godsend. Stephen would feel ashamed to be rich, and, like Mary, was always anxious to feed them. Being idle at the moment, Stephen would insist upon frequently taking them out to dinner, and then she would order expensive viands—copper-green oysters straight from the Marennes,* caviare and other such costly things, to be followed by even more sumptuous dishes—and since they went short on most days in the week, these stomachic debauches would frequently upset them. Two glasses of wine would cause Jamie to flush, for her head had never been of the strongest, nor was it accustomed to such golden nectar. Her principal beverage was crême-de-menthe* because it kept out the cold in the winter, and because, being pepperminty and sweet, it reminded her of the bull's-eyes at Beedles.

They were not very easy to help, these two, for Jamie, pride-galled, was exceedingly touchy. She would never accept gifts of money or clothes, and was struggling to pay off the debt to her master. Even food gave offence unless it was shared by the donors, which though very praiseworthy was foolish. However, there it was, one just had to take her or leave her, there was no compromising with Jamie.

After dinner they would drift back to Jamie's abode, a studio in the old Rue Visconti.* They would climb innumerable dirty stone stairs to the top of what had once been a fine house but was now let off to such poor rats as Jamie. The concierge, an unsympathetic woman, long soured by the empty pockets of students, would peer out at them from her dark ground-floor kennel, with sceptical eyes.

'Bon soir, Madame Lambert.'

'Bon soir, mesdames,' she would growl impolitely.

Jamie's studio was large, bare, and swept by draughts. The stove was too small and at times it smelt vilely. The distempered grey walls were a mass of stains, for whenever it hailed or rained or snowed the windows and skylight would always start dripping. The furniture consisted of a few shaky chairs, a table, a divan and a hired grand piano. Nearly every one seated themselves on the floor, robbing the divan of its moth-eaten cushions. From the studio there led off a tiny room with an eye-shaped window that would not open. In this room had been placed a narrow camp-bed to which Jamie retired when she felt extra sleepless. For the rest, there was a sink with a leaky tap; a cupboard in which they kept crême-de-menthe, what remnants of food they possessed at the moment, Jamie's carpet slippers and blue jean jacket—minus which she could never compose a note—and the pail, cloths and brushes with which Barbara endeavoured to keep down the accumulating dirt and confusion. For Jamie with her tow-coloured head in the clouds, was not only short-sighted but intensely untidy. Dust meant little to her since she seldom saw it, while neatness was completely left out of her make-up; considering how limited were her possessions, the chaos they produced was truly amazing. Barbara would sigh and would quite often scold—when she scolded she reminded one of a wren who was struggling to discipline a large cuckoo.

'Jamie, your dirty shirt, give it to me—leaving it there on the piano, whatever!' Or, 'Jamie, come here and look at your hair-brush; if you haven't gone and put it next-door to the butter!'

Then Jamie would peer with her strained, red-rimmed eyes and would grumble: 'Oh, leave me in peace, do, lassie!'

But when Barbara laughed, as she must do quite often at the outrageous habits of the great loose-limbed creature, why then these days she would usually cough, and when Barbara started to cough she coughed badly. They had seen a doctor who had spoken about lungs and had shaken his head; not strong, he had told them. But neither of them had quite understood, for their French had remained very embryonic, and they could not afford the smart English doctor. All the same when Barbara coughed Jamie sweated, and her fear would produce an acute irritation.

'Here, drink this water! Don't sit there doing nothing but rack yourself to bits, it gets on my nerves. Go and order another bottle of that mixture. God, how can I work if you will go on coughing!' She would slouch to the piano and play mighty chords, pressing down the loud pedal to drown that coughing. But when it had subsided she would feel deep remorse. 'Oh, Barbara, you're so little—forgive me. It's all my fault for bringing you out here, you're not strong enough for this damnable life, you don't get the right food, or anything proper.'

In the end it would be Barbara who must console. 'We'll be rich some day when you've finished your opera—anyhow my cough isn't dangerous, Jamie.'

Sometimes Jamie's music would go all wrong, the opera would blankly refuse to get written. At the Conservatoire she would be very stupid, and when she got home she would be very silent, pushing her supper away with a frown, because coming upstairs she had heard that cough. Then Barbara would feel even more tired and weak than before, but would hide her weakness from Jamie. After supper they would undress in front of the stove if the weather was cold, would undress without speaking. Barbara could get out of her clothes quite neatly in no time, but Jamie must always dawdle, dropping first this and then that on the floor, or pausing to fill her little black pipe and to light it before putting on her pyjamas.

Barbara would fall on her knees by the divan and would start to say prayers like a child, very simply. 'Our Father,' she would say, and other prayers too, which always ended in: 'Please God, bless Jamie.' For believing in Jamie she must needs believe in God, and because she loved Jamie she must love God also—it had long been like this, ever since they were children. But sometimes she would shiver in her prim cotton nightgown, so that Jamie, grown anxious, would speak to her sharply:

'Oh, stop praying, do. You and all your prayers! Are you daft to kneel there when the room's fairly freezing? That's how you catch cold; now to-night you'll cough!'

But Barbara would not so much as turn round; she would calmly and earnestly go on with her praying. Her neck would look thin against the thick plait which hung neatly down between her bent shoulders; and the hands that covered her face would look thin—thin and transparent like the hands of a consumptive. Fuming inwardly, Jamie would stump off to bed in the tiny room with its eye-shaped window, and there she herself must mutter a prayer, especially if she heard Barbara coughing.

At times Jamie gave way to deep depression, hating the beautiful city of her exile. Homesick unto death she would suddenly feel for the dour little Highland village of Beedles. More even than for its dull bricks and mortar would she long for its dull and respectable spirit, for the sense of security common to Sabbaths, for the kirk* with its dull and respectable people. She would think with a tenderness bred by forced absence of the greengrocer's shop that stood on the corner, where they sold, side by side with the cabbages and onions, little neatly tied bunches of Scottish heather, little earthenware jars of opaque heather honey. She would think of the vast, stretching, windy moorlands; of the smell of the soil after rain in summer; of the piper with his weather-stained, agile fingers, of the wail of his sorrowful, outlandish music; of Barbara as she had been in the days when they strolled side by side down the narrow High Street. And then she would sit with her head in her hands, hating the sound and the smell of Paris, hating the sceptical eyes of the concierge, hating the bare and unhomely studio. Tears would well up from heaven alone knew what abyss of half-understood desolation, and would go splashing down upon her tweed skirt, or trickling back along her red wrists until they had wetted her frayed flannel wristbands. Coming home with their evening meal in a bag, this was how Barbara must sometimes find her.

2

Jamie was not always so full of desolation; there were days when she seemed to be in excellent spirits, and on one such occasion she rang Stephen up, asking her to bring Mary round after dinner. Every one was coming, Wanda and Pat, Brockett, and even Valérie Seymour; for she, Jamie, had persuaded a couple of negroes who were studying at the Conservatoire to come in and sing for them that evening—they had promised to sing Negro Spirituals, old slavery songs of the Southern plantations. They were very nice negroes, their name was Jones—Lincoln and Henry Jones, they were brothers. Lincoln and Jamie had become great friends; he was very interested in her opera. And Wanda would bring her mandolin—but the evening would be spoilt without Mary and Stephen.*

Mary promptly put on her hat; she must go and order them in some supper. As she and Stephen would be there to share it, Jamie's sensitive pride would be appeased. She would send them a very great deal of food so that they could go on eating and eating.

Stephen nodded: 'Yes, send them in tons of supper!'

3

At ten o'clock they arrived at the studio; at ten thirty Wanda came in with Brockett, then Blanc together with Valérie Seymour, then Pat wearing serviceable goloshes over her house-shoes because it was raining, then three or four fellow-students of Jamie's, and finally the two negro brothers.

They were very unlike each other,* these negroes; Lincoln, the elder, was paler in colour. He was short and inclined to be rather thick-set with a heavy but intellectual face—a strong face, much lined for a man of thirty. His eyes had the patient, questioning expression common to the eyes of most animals and to those of all slowly evolving races. He shook hands very quietly with Stephen and Mary. Henry was tall and as black as a coal; a fine, upstanding, but coarse-lipped young negro, with a roving glance and a self-assured manner.

He remarked: 'Glad to meet you, Miss Gordon—Miss Llewellyn,' and plumped himself down at Mary's side, where he started to make conversation, too glibly.

Valérie Seymour was soon talking to Lincoln with a friendliness that put him at his ease—just at first he had seemed a little self-conscious. But Pat was much more reserved in her manner, having hailed from abolitionist Boston.*

Wanda said abruptly: 'Can I have a drink, Jamie?' Brockett poured her out a stiff brandy and soda.

Adolphe Blanc sat on the floor hugging his knees; and presently Dupont the sculptor strolled in—being minus his mistress he migrated to Stephen.

Then Lincoln seated himself at the piano, touching the keys with firm, expert fingers, while Henry stood beside him very straight and long and lifted up his voice which was velvet smooth, yet as clear and insistent as the call of a clarion:

> 'Deep river, my home is over Jordan.
> Deep river—Lord, I want to cross over into camp ground,
> Lord, I want to cross over into camp ground,
> Lord, I want to cross over into camp ground,
> Lord, I want to cross over into camp ground. . . .'*

And all the hope of the utterly hopeless of this world, who must live by their ultimate salvation, all the terrible, aching, homesick hope that is born of the infinite pain of the spirit, seemed to break from this man and shake those who listened, so that they sat with bent heads and clasped hands—they who were also among the hopeless sat with bent heads and clasped hands as they listened. . . . Even Valérie Seymour forgot to be pagan.

He was not an exemplary young negro; indeed he could be the reverse very often. A crude animal Henry could be at times, with a taste for liquor and a lust for women—just a primitive force rendered dangerous by drink, rendered offensive by civilization. Yet as he sang his sins seemed to drop from him, leaving him pure, unashamed, triumphant. He sang to his God, to the God of his soul, Who would some day blot out all the sins of the world, and make vast reparation for every injustice: 'My home is over Jordan, Lord, I want to cross over into camp ground.'

Lincoln's deep bass voice kept up a low sobbing. From time to time only did he break into words; but as he played on he rocked his body: 'Lord, I want to cross over into camp ground. Lord, I want to cross over into camp ground.'

Once started they seemed unable to stop; carried away they were by their music, drunk with that desperate hope of the hopeless—far drunker than Henry would get on neat whisky. They went from one spiritual into another, while their listeners sat motionless, scarcely breathing. While Jamie's eyes ached from unshed tears quite as much as from her unsuitable glasses; while Adolphe Blanc, the gentle, the learned, grasped his knees and pondered many things deeply; while Pat remembered her Arabella and found but small consolation in beetles; while Brockett thought of certain brave deeds that he, even he had done out in Mespot—deeds that were not recorded in dispatches, unless in those of the recording angel;* while Wanda evolved an enormous canvas depicting the wrongs of all mankind; while Stephen suddenly found Mary's hand and held it in hers with a painful pressure; while Barbara's tired and childish brown eyes turned to rest rather anxiously on her Jamie. Not one of them all but was stirred to the depths by that queer, half-defiant, half-supplicating music.

And now there rang out a kind of challenge; imperious, loud, almost terrifying. They sang it together, those two black brethren,* and their voices suggested a multitude shouting. They seemed to be shouting a challenge to the world on behalf of themselves and of all the afflicted:

'Didn't my Lord deliver Daniel,
Daniel, Daniel!
Didn't my Lord deliver Daniel,
Then why not every man?'*

The eternal question, as yet unanswered for those who sat there spellbound and listened. . . . 'Didn't my Lord deliver Daniel, then why not every man?'

Why not? . . . Yes, but how long, O Lord, how long?

Lincoln got up from the piano abruptly, and he made a small bow which seemed strangely foolish, murmuring some stilted words of thanks on behalf of himself and his brother Henry: 'We are greatly obliged to you for your patience; we trust that we have satisfied you'; he murmured.

It was over. They were just two men with black skins and foreheads beaded with perspiration. Henry sidled away to the whisky, while Lincoln rubbed his pinkish palms on an elegant white silk handkerchief. Every one started to talk at once, to light cigarettes, to move about the studio.

Jamie said: 'Come on, people, it's time for supper,' and she swallowed a small glass of crême-de-menthe; but Wanda poured herself out some more brandy.

Quite suddenly they had all become merry, laughing at nothing, teasing each other; even Valérie unbent more than was her wont and did not look bored when Brockett chaffed her. The air grew heavy and stinging with smoke; the stove went out, but they scarcely noticed.

Henry Jones lost his head and pinched Pat's bony shoulder, then he rolled his eyes: 'Oh, boy! What a gang! Say, folks, aren't we having the hell of an evening? When any of you folk decide to come over to my little old New York, why, I'll show you around. Some burg!'* and he gulped a large mouthful of whisky.

After supper Jamie played the overture to her opera, and they loudly applauded the rather dull music—so scholarly, so dry, so painfully stiff, so utterly inexpressive of Jamie. Then Wanda produced her mandolin and insisted upon singing them Polish love-songs; this she did in a heavy contralto voice which was rendered distinctly unstable by brandy. She handled the tinkling instrument with skill, evolving some quite respectable chords, but her eyes were fierce, as was also her touch, so that presently a wire snapped with a ping, which appeared completely to upset her balance. She fell back and lay sprawled out upon the floor to be hauled up again by Dupont and Brockett.

Barbara had one of her bad fits of coughing: 'It's nothing . . .' she gasped, 'I swallowed the wrong way; don't fuss, Jamie . . . darling . . . I tell you it's . . . nothing.'

Jamie, flushed already, drank more crême-de-menthe. This time she poured it into a tumbler, tossing it off with a dash of soda. But Adolphe Blanc looked at Barbara gravely.

The party did not disperse until morning; not until four o'clock could they decide to go home. Everybody had stayed to the very last moment, everybody, that is, except Valérie Seymour—she had left immediately after supper. Brockett, as usual, was cynically sober, but

Jamie was blinking her eyes like an owl, while Pat stumbled over her own goloshes. As for Henry Jones, he started to sing at the top of his lungs in a high falsetto:

> 'Oh, my, help, help, ain't I nobody's baby?
> Oh, my, what a shame, I ain't nobody's baby.'*

'Shut your noise, you poor mutt!' commanded his brother, but Henry still continued to bawl: 'Oh, my, what a shame, I ain't nobody's baby.'

They left Wanda asleep on a heap of cushions—she would probably not wake up before mid-day.

CHAPTER 46

I

STEPHEN'S book, which made its appearance that May, met with a very sensational success* in England and in the United States, an even more marked success than *The Furrow*. Its sales were unexpectedly large considering its outstanding literary merit; the critics of two countries were loud in their praises, and old photographs of Stephen could be seen in the papers, together with very flattering captions. In a word, she woke up in Paris one morning to find herself, for the moment, quite famous.

Valérie, Brockett, indeed all her friends were whole-hearted in their congratulations; and David's tail kept up a great wagging. He knew well that something pleasant had happened: the whole atmosphere of the house was enough to inform a sagacious person like David. Even Mary's little bright-coloured birds seemed to take a firmer hold on existence; while out in the garden there was much ado on the part of the proudly parental pigeons—fledglings with huge heads and bleary eyes had arrived to contribute to the general celebration. Adèle went singing about her work, for Jean had recently been promised promotion, which meant that his savings, perhaps in a year, might have grown large enough for them to marry.

Pierre bragged to his friend, the neighbouring baker, anent Stephen's great eminence as a writer, and even Pauline cheered up a little.

When Mary impressively ordered the meals, ordered this or that delicacy for Stephen, Pauline would actually say with a smile: 'Mais oui, un grand génie doit nourrir le cerveau!'*

Mademoiselle Duphot gained a passing importance in the eyes of her pupils through having taught Stephen. She would nod her head and remark very wisely: 'I always declare she become a great author.' Then because she was truthful she would hastily add: 'I mean that I knowed she was someone unusual.'

Buisson admitted that perhaps, after all, it was well that Stephen had stuck to her writing. The book had been bought for translation into French, a fact which had deeply impressed Monsieur Buisson.

From Puddle came a long and triumphant letter: 'What did I tell you? I knew you'd do it! . . .'

Anna also wrote at some length to her daughter. And wonder of wonders, from Violet Peacock there arrived an embarrassingly gushing epistle. She would look Stephen up when next she was in Paris; she was longing, so she said, to renew their old friendship—after all, they two had been children together.

Gazing at Mary with very bright eyes, Stephen's thoughts must rush forward into the future. Puddle had been right, it was work that counted—clever, hard-headed, understanding old Puddle!

Then putting an arm round Mary's shoulder: 'Nothing shall ever hurt you,' she would promise, feeling wonderfully self-sufficient and strong, wonderfully capable of protecting.

2

That summer they drove into Italy with David sitting up proudly beside Burton. David barked at the peasants and challenged the dogs and generally assumed a grand air of importance. They decided to spend two months on Lake Como, and went to the Hotel Florence at Bellagio.* The hotel gardens ran down to the lake—it was all very sunny and soothing and peaceful. Their days were passed in making excursions, their evenings in drifting about on the water in a little boat with a gaily striped awning, which latter seemed a strange form of pleasure to David. Many of the guests at the Florence were English, and not a few scraped an acquaintance with Stephen, since nothing appears to succeed like success in a world that is principally made up of failure. The sight of her book left about in the lounge, or being devoured by some engrossed reader, would make Stephen feel almost childishly happy; she would point the phenomenon out to Mary.

'Look,' she would whisper, 'that man's reading my book!' For the child is never far to seek in the author.

Some of their acquaintances were country folk and she found that she was in sympathy with them. Their quiet and painstaking outlook on life, their love of the soil, their care for their homes, their traditions, were after all a part of herself, bequeathed to her by the founders of Morton. It gave her a very deep sense of pleasure to see Mary accepted and made to feel welcome by these grey-haired women and gentlemanly men; very seemly and fitting it appeared to Stephen.

And now, since to each of us come moments of respite when the mind refuses to face its problems, she resolutely thrust aside her misgivings, those misgivings that whispered: 'Supposing they knew—do you think they'd be so friendly to Mary?'

Of all those who sought them out that summer, the most cordial were Lady Massey and her daughter. Lady Massey was a delicate, elderly woman who, in spite of poor health and encroaching years, was untiring in her search for amusement—it amused her to make friends with celebrated people. She was restless, self-indulgent and not over sincere, a creature of whims and ephemeral fancies; yet for Stephen and Mary she appeared to evince a liking which was more than just on the surface. She would ask them up to her sitting-room, would want them to sit with her in the garden, and would sometimes insist upon communal meals, inviting them to dine at her table. Agnes, the daughter, a jolly, red-haired girl, had taken an immediate fancy to Mary, and their friendship ripened with celerity, as is often the way during idle summers. As for Lady Massey she petted Mary, and mothered her as though she were a child, and soon she was mothering Stephen also.

She would say: 'I seem to have found two new children,' and Stephen, who was in the mood to feel touched, grew quite attached to this ageing woman. Agnes was engaged to a Colonel Fitzmaurice who would probably join them that autumn in Paris. If he did so they must all foregather at once, she insisted—he greatly admired Stephen's book and had written that he was longing to meet her. But Lady Massey went further than this in her enthusiastic proffers of friendship—Stephen and Mary must stay with her in Cheshire; she was going to give a house party at Branscombe Court* for Christmas; they must certainly come to her for Christmas.

Mary, who seemed elated at the prospect, was for ever discussing this visit with Stephen: 'What sort of clothes shall I need, do you think? Agnes says it's going to be quite a big party. I suppose I'll want a few new evening dresses?' And one day she inquired: 'Stephen, when you were younger, did you ever go to Ascot or Goodwood?'*

Ascot and Goodwood, just names to Stephen; names that she had despised in her youth, yet which now seemed not devoid of importance since they stood for something beyond themselves—something that ought to belong to Mary. She would pick up a copy of *The Tatler* or *The Sketch*,* which Lady Massey received from England, and turning the pages would stare at the pictures of securely established, self-satisfied people—Miss this or that sitting on a shooting stick,* and beside her the man she would shortly marry; Lady so-and-so with her latest offspring; or perhaps some group at a country house. And quite suddenly Stephen would feel less assured because in her heart she must envy these people. Must envy these commonplace men and women with their rather ridiculous shooting sticks; their smiling fiancés; their husbands; their wives; their estates, and their well cared for, placid children.

Mary would sometimes look over her shoulder with a new and perhaps rather wistful interest. Then Stephen would close the paper abruptly: 'Let's go for a row on the lake,' she might say, 'it's no good wasting this glorious evening.'

But then she would remember the invitation to spend Christmas with Lady Massey in Cheshire, and would suddenly start to build castles in the air; supposing that she herself bought a small place near Branscombe Court—near these kind new friends who seemed to have grown so fond of Mary? Mary would also have her thoughts, would be thinking of girls like Agnes Massey for whom life was tranquil, easy and secure; girls to whom the world must seem blessedly friendly. And then, with a little stab of pain, she would suddenly remember her own exile from Morton. After such thoughts as these she must hold Stephen's hand, must always sit very close to Stephen.

3

That autumn they saw a good deal of the Masseys, who had taken their usual suite at the Ritz,* and who often asked Mary and Stephen to luncheon. Lady Massey, Agnes and Colonel Fitzmaurice, a pleasant enough man, came and dined several times at the quiet old house in the Rue Jacob, and those evenings were always exceedingly friendly, Stephen talking of books with Colonel Fitzmaurice, while Lady Massey enlarged upon Branscombe and her plans for the coming Christmas party. Sometimes Stephen and Mary sent flowers to the Ritz, hot-house plants or a large box of special roses—Lady Massey liked to have her rooms full of flowers sent by friends, it increased her sense of importance. By return would come loving letters of thanks; she would write: 'I do thank my two very dear children.'

In November she and Agnes returned to England, but the friendship was kept up by correspondence, for Lady Massey was prolific with her pen, indeed she was never more happy than when writing.

And now Mary bought the new evening dresses, and she dragged Stephen off to choose some new ties. As the visit to Branscombe Court drew near it was seldom out of their thoughts for a moment—to Stephen it appeared like the firstfruits* of toil; to Mary like the gateway into an existence that must be very safe and reassuring.

4

Stephen never knew what enemy had prepared the blow that was struck by Lady Massey. Perhaps it had been Colonel Fitzmaurice who might all the time have been hiding his suspicions; he must certainly have known a good deal about Stephen—he had friends who lived in the vicinity of Morton. Perhaps it had merely been unkind gossip connected with Brockett or Valérie Seymour, with the people whom Mary and Stephen knew, although, as it happened, Lady Massey had not met them. But after all, it mattered so little; what did it matter how the thing had come about? By comparison with the insult itself, its origin seemed very unimportant.

It was in December that the letter arrived, just a week before they were leaving for England. A long, rambling, pitifully tactless letter, full of awkward and deeply wounding excuses:

'If I hadn't grown so fond of you both,' wrote Lady Massey, 'this would be much less painful—as it is the whole thing has made me quite ill, but I must consider my position in the county. You see, the county looks to me for a lead—above all I must consider my daughter. The rumours that have reached me about you and Mary—certain things that I don't want to enter into—have simply forced me to break off our friendship and to say that I must ask you not to come here for Christmas. Of course a woman of my position with all eyes upon her has to be extra careful. It's too terribly upsetting and sad for me; if I hadn't been so fond of you both—but you know how attached I had grown to Mary . . .' and so it went on; a kind of wail full of self-importance combined with self-pity.

As Stephen read she went white to the lips, and Mary sprang up. 'What's that letter you're reading?'

'It's from Lady Massey. It's about . . . it's about . . .' Her voice failed.

'Show it to me,' persisted Mary.

Stephen shook her head: 'No—I'd rather not.'

Then Mary asked: 'Is it about our visit?'

Stephen nodded: 'We're not going to spend Christmas at Branscombe. Darling, it's all right—don't look like that . . .'

'But I want to know why we're not going to Branscombe.' And Mary reached out and snatched the letter.

She read it through to the very last word, then she sat down abruptly and burst out crying. She cried with the long, doleful sobs of a child whom some one has struck without rhyme or reason: 'Oh . . . and I thought they were fond of us . . .' she sobbed, 'I thought that perhaps . . . they understood, Stephen.'

Then it seemed to Stephen that all the pain that had so far been thrust upon her by existence, was as nothing to the unendurable pain which she must now bear to hear that sobbing, to see Mary thus wounded and utterly crushed, thus shamed and humbled for the sake of her love, thus bereft of all dignity and protection.

She felt strangely helpless: 'Don't—don't,' she implored; while tears of pity blurred her own eyes and went trickling slowly down her scarred face. She had lost for the moment all sense of proportion, of perspective, seeing in a vain, tactless woman a kind of gigantic destroying angel;* a kind of scourge laid upon her and Mary. Surely never before had Lady Massey loomed so large as she did in that hour to Stephen.

Mary's sobs gradually died away. She lay back in her chair, a small, desolate figure, catching her breath from time to time, until Stephen went to her and found her hand which she stroked with cold and trembling fingers—but she could not find words of consolation.

5

That night Stephen took the girl roughly in her arms.

'I love you—I love you so much . . .' she stammered; and she kissed Mary many times on the mouth, but cruelly so that her kisses were pain—the pain in her heart leapt out through her lips: 'God! It's too terrible to love like this—it's hell—there are times when I can't endure it!'

She was in the grip of strong nervous excitation; nothing seemed able any more to appease her. She seemed to be striving to obliterate, not only herself, but the whole hostile world through some strange and agonized merging with Mary. It was terrible indeed, very like unto death, and it left them both completely exhausted.

The world had achieved its first real victory.

CHAPTER 47

I

THEIR Christmas was naturally overshadowed, and so, as it were by a common impulse, they turned to such people as Barbara and Jamie, people who would neither despise nor insult them. It was Mary who suggested that Barbara and Jamie should be asked to share their Christmas dinner, while Stephen who must suddenly pity Wanda for a misjudged and very unfortunate genius, invited her also—after all why not? Wanda was more sinned against than sinning. She drank, oh, yes, Wanda drowned her sorrows; everybody knew that, and like Valérie Seymour, Stephen hated drink like the plague—but all the same she invited Wanda.

An ill wind it is that blows no one any good.* Barbara and Jamie accepted with rapture; but for Mary's most timely invitation, their funds being low at the end of the year, they two must have gone without Christmas dinner. Wanda also seemed glad enough to come, to leave her enormous, turbulent canvas for the orderly peace of the well-warmed house with its comfortable rooms and its friendly servants. All three of them arrived a good hour before dinner, which on this occasion would be in the evening.

Wanda had been up to Midnight Mass at the Sacré Cœur, she informed them gravely; and Stephen, reminded of Mademoiselle Duphot, regretted that she had not offered her the motor. No doubt she too had gone up to Montmartre for Midnight Mass—how queer, she and Wanda. Wanda was quiet, depressed and quite sober; she was wearing a straight-cut, simple black dress that somehow suggested a species of cassock. And as often happened when Wanda was sober, she repeated herself more than when she was drunk.

'I have been to the Sacré Cœur,' she repeated, 'for the Messe de Minuit; it was very lovely.'

But she did not reveal the tragic fact that her fear had suddenly laid hold upon her at the moment of approaching the altar rails, so that she had scuttled back to her seat, terrified of receiving the Christmas Communion.* Even a painfully detailed confession of intemperance, of the lusts of the eyes and the mind, of the very occasional sins of the body; even the absolution accorded by a white-haired old priest who had spoken gently and pitifully to his penitent, directing her prayers to the Sacred Heart from which his own heart had derived its compassion—even these things had failed to give Wanda courage when it came to the Christmas Communion. And now as she sat at Stephen's table she ate little and drank but three glasses of wine; nor did she ask for a cognac brandy when later they went to the study for coffee, but must talk of the mighty temple of her faith that watched day and night, night and day over Paris.

She said in her very perfect English: 'Is it not a great thing that France has done? From every town and village in France has come money to build that church at Montmartre. Many people have purchased the stones of the church, and their names are carved on those stones for ever. I am very much too hard up to do that—and yet I would like to own a small stone.* I would just say: "From Wanda," because of course one need not bother about the surname; mine is so long and so difficult to spell—yes, I would ask them to say: "From Wanda."'

Jamie and Barbara listened politely, yet without sympathy and without comprehension; while Mary must even smile a little at what seemed to her like mere superstition. But Stephen's imagination was touched, and she questioned Wanda about her religion. Then Wanda turned grateful eyes upon Stephen and suddenly wanted to win her friendship—she looked so reassuring and calm sitting there in her peaceful, book-lined study. A great writer she was, did not every one say so? And yet she was surely even as Wanda . . . Oh, but Stephen had got the better of her fate, had wrestled with her fate so that now it must serve her; that was fine, that was surely true courage, true greatness! For that Christmas none save Mary might know of the bitterness that was in Stephen's heart, least of all the impulsive, erratic Wanda.

Wanda needed no second invitation to talk, and very soon her eyes were aglow with the fire of the born religious fanatic as she told of the little town in Poland, with its churches, its bells that were always chiming—the Mass bells beginning at early dawn, the Angelus bells, the Vesperbells*—always calling, calling they were, said Wanda. Through the years of persecution and strife, of wars and the endless rumours of wars that had ravaged her most unhappy country, her people had clung to their ancient faith like true children of Mother Church,* said Wanda. She herself had three brothers, and all of them priests; her parents had been very pious people, they were both dead now, had been dead for some years; and Wanda signed her breast with the Cross, having regard for the souls of her parents. Then she tried to explain the meaning of her faith, but this she did exceedingly badly, finding that words are not always easy when they must encompass the things of the spirit, the things that she herself knew by instinct; and then, too, these days her brain was not clear, thanks to brandy, even when she was quite sober. The details of her coming to Paris she omitted, but Stephen thought she could easily guess them, for Wanda declared with a curious pride that her brothers were men of stone and of iron. Saints they all were, according to Wanda, uncompromising, fierce and relentless, seeing only the straight and narrow path on each side of which yawned the fiery chasm.

'I was not as they were, ah, no!' she declared, 'Nor was I as my father and mother; I was—I was . . .' She stopped speaking abruptly, gazing at Stephen with her burning eyes which said quite plainly: 'You know what I was, you understand.' And Stephen nodded, divining the reason of Wanda's exile.

But suddenly Mary began to grow restless, putting an end to this dissertation by starting the large, new gramophone which Stephen had given her for Christmas. The gramophone blared out the latest fox-trot,* and jumping up Barbara and Jamie started dancing, while Stephen and Wanda moved chairs and tables, rolled back rugs and explained to the barking David that he could not join in, but might, if he chose, sit and watch them dance from the divan. Then Wanda slipped an arm around Mary and they glided off, an incongruous couple, the one clad as sombrely as any priest, the other in her soft evening dress of blue chiffon. Mary lay gently against Wanda's arm, and she seemed to Stephen a very perfect dancer—lighting a cigarette, she watched them. The dance over, Mary put on a new record; she was flushed and her eyes were considerably brighter.

'Why did you never tell me?' Stephen murmured.

'Tell you what?'

'Why, that you danced so well.'

Mary hesitated, then she murmured back: 'You didn't dance, so what was the good?'

'Wanda, you must teach me to fox-trot,' smiled Stephen.

Jamie was blundering round the room with Barbara clasped to her untidy bosom; then she and Barbara started to sing the harmless, but foolish words of the fox-trot—if the servants were singing their old Breton hymns along in the kitchen, no one troubled to listen. Growing hilarious, Jamie sang louder, spinning with Barbara, gyrating wildly, until Barbara, between laughing and coughing, must implore her to stop, must beg for mercy.

Wanda said: 'You might have a lesson now, Stephen.'

Putting her hands on Stephen's shoulders, she began to explain the more simple steps, which did not appear at all hard to Stephen. The music seemed to have got into her feet so that her feet must follow its rhythm. She discovered to her own very great amazement that she liked this less formal modern dancing, and after a while she was clasping Mary quite firmly, and they moved away together while Wanda stood calling out her instructions:

'Take much longer steps! Keep your knees straight—straighter! Don't get so much to the side—look, it's this way—hold her this way; always stand square to your partner.'

The lesson went on for a good two hours, until even Mary seemed somewhat exhausted. She suddenly rang the bell for Pierre, who appeared with the tray of simple supper. Then Mary did an unusual thing—she poured herself out a whisky and soda.

'I'm tired,' she explained rather fretfully in answer to Stephen's look of surprise;* and she frowned as she turned her back abruptly. But Wanda shied away from the brandy as a frightened horse will shy from fire; she drank two large glasses of lemonade—an extremist she was in all things, this Wanda. Quite soon she announced that she must go home to bed, because of her latest picture which required every ounce of strength she had in her; but before she went she said eagerly to Stephen:

'Do let me show you the Sacré Cœur. You have seen it, of course, but only as a tourist; that is not really seeing it at all, you must come there with me.'

'All right,' agreed Stephen.

When Jamie and Barbara had departed in their turn, Stephen took Mary into her arms: 'Dearest . . . has it been a fairly nice Christmas after all?' she inquired almost timidly.

Mary kissed her: 'Of course it's been a nice Christmas.' Then her youthful face suddenly changed in expression, the grey eyes growing hard, the mouth resentful: 'Damn that woman for what she's done to us, Stephen—the insolence of it! But I've learnt my lesson; we've got plenty of friends without Lady Massey and Agnes, friends to whom we're not moral lepers.' And she laughed, a queer, little joyless laugh.

Stephen flinched, remembering Brockett's warning.

2

Wanda's chastened and temperate mood persisted for several weeks, and while it was on her she clung like a drowning man to Stephen, haunting the house from morning until night, dreading to be alone for a moment. It cannot be said that Stephen suffered her gladly, for now with the New Year she was working hard on a series of articles and short stories; unwilling to visualize defeat, she began once again to sharpen her weapon. But something in Wanda's poor efforts to keep sober, in her very dependence, was deeply appealing, so that Stephen would put aside her work, feeling loath to desert the unfortunate creature.

Several times they made a long pilgrimage on foot to the church of the Sacré Cœur; just they two, for Mary would never go with them; she was prejudiced against Wanda's religion.* They would climb the steep streets with their flights of steps, grey streets, grey steps leading up from the city. Wanda's eyes would always be fixed on their goal—pilgrim eyes they would often seem to Stephen. Arrived at the church she and Wanda would stand looking down between the tall, massive columns of the porch, on a Paris of domes and mists, only half revealed by the fitful sunshine. The air would seem pure up there on the height, pure and tenuous as a thing of the spirit. And something in that mighty temple of faith, that amazing thrust towards the sublime, that silent yet articulate cry of a nation to its God, would awaken a response in Stephen, so that she would seem to be brushing the hem of an age-old and rather terrible mystery—the eternal mystery of good and evil.

Inside the church would be brooding shadows, save where the wide lakes of amber fire spread out from the endless votive candles. Above the high altar the monstranced Host would gleam curiously white in the light of the candles. The sound of praying, monotonous, low, insistent, would come from those who prayed with extended arms, with crucified arms, all day and all night for the sins of Paris.

Wanda would make her way to the statue of the silver Christ* with one hand on His heart, and the other held out in supplication.

Kneeling down she would sign herself with His Cross, then cover her eyes and forget about Stephen. Standing quietly behind her Stephen would wonder what Wanda was saying to the silver Christ, what the silver Christ was saying to Wanda. She would think that He looked very weary, this Christ Who must listen to so many supplications. Queer, unbidden thoughts came to her at such moments; this Man Who was God, a God Who waited, could He answer the riddle of Wanda's existence, of her own existence? If she asked, could He answer? What if she were suddenly to cry out loudly: 'Look at us, we are two yet we stand for many. Our name is legion* and we also are waiting, we also are tired, oh, but terribly tired . . . Will You give us some hope of ultimate release? Will You tell us the secret of our salvation?'

Wanda would rise from her prayers rather stiffly to purchase a couple of votive candles, and when she had stuck them into the sconce she would touch the foot of the silver Christ as she bade Him farewell—a time-honoured custom. Then she and Stephen might turn again to the lake of fire that flowed round the monstrance.*

But one morning when they arrived at the church, the monstrance was not above the high altar. The altar had just been garnished and swept, so the Host was still in the Lady Chapel.* And while they stood there and gazed at the Host, came a priest and with him a grey-haired server; they would bear their God back again to His home, to the costly shrine of His endless vigil. The server must first light his little lantern suspended from a pole, and must then grasp his bell. The priest must lift his Lord from the monstrance and lay Him upon a silken cover, and carry Him as a man carries a child—protectively, gently, yet strongly withal, as though some frustrated paternal instinct were finding in this a divine expression. The lantern swung rhythmically to and fro, the bell rang out its imperative warning; then the careful priest followed after the server who cleared his path to the great high altar. And even as once very long ago, such a bell had been the herald of death in the putrefying hand of the leper: 'Unclean! Unclean!' death and putrefaction—the warning bell in the dreadful hand that might never again know the clasp of the healthful—so now the bell rang out the approach of supreme purity, of the Healer of lepers, earthbound through compassion; but compassion so vast, so urgent, that the small, white disc of the Host must contain the whole suffering universe. Thus the Prisoner of love Who could never break free while one spiritual leper remained to be healed, passed by on His patient way, heavy-laden.*

Wanda suddenly fell to her knees, striking her lean and unfruitful breast, for as always she very shamefully feared, and her fear was a bitter and most deadly insult. With downcast eyes and trembling hands she cowered at the sight of her own salvation. But Stephen stood upright and curiously still, staring into the empty Lady Chapel.

CHAPTER 48

*1**

THAT spring they made their first real acquaintance with the garish and tragic night life of Paris that lies open to such people as Stephen Gordon.

Until now they had never gone out much at night except to occasional studio parties, or occasional cafés of the milder sort for a cup of coffee with Barbara and Jamie; but that spring Mary seemed fanatically eager to proclaim her allegiance to Pat's miserable army. Deprived of the social intercourse which to her would have been both natural and welcome, she now strove to stand up to a hostile world by proving that she could get on without it. The spirit of adventure that had taken her to France, the pluck that had steadied her while in the Unit, the emotional, hot-headed nature of the Celt, these things must now work together in Mary to produce a state of great restlessness, a pitiful revolt against life's injustice. The blow struck by a weak and thoughtless hand had been even more deadly than Stephen had imagined; more deadly to them both, for that glancing blow coming at a time of apparent success, had torn from them every shred of illusion.

Stephen, who could see that the girl was fretting, would be seized with a kind of sick apprehension, a sick misery at her own powerlessness to provide a more normal and complete existence. So many innocent recreations, so many harmless social pleasures must Mary forego for the sake of their union—and she still young, still well under thirty. And now Stephen came face to face with the gulf that lies between warning and realization—all her painful warnings anent the world had not served to lessen the blow when it fell, had not served to make it more tolerable to Mary. Deeply humiliated Stephen would feel, when she thought of Mary's exile from Morton, when she thought of the insults this girl must endure because of her loyalty and her faith—all that Mary was losing that belonged to her youth, would rise up at this time to accuse and scourge Stephen. Her courage would flicker like a lamp in the wind, and would all but go out; she would feel less steadfast, less capable of continuing the war, that ceaseless war for the right to existence. Then the pen would slip from her nerveless fingers, no longer a sharp and purposeful weapon. Yes, that spring saw a weakening in Stephen herself—she felt tired, and sometimes very old for her age, in spite of her vigorous mind and body.

Calling Mary, she would need to be reassured; and one day she asked her: 'How much do you love me?'

Mary answered: 'So much that I'm growing to hate . . .' Bitter words to hear on such young lips as Mary's.

And now there were days when Stephen herself would long for some palliative, some distraction; when her erstwhile success seemed like Dead Sea fruit,* her will to succeed a grotesque presumption. Who was she to stand out against the whole world, against those ruthless, pursuing millions bent upon the destruction of her and her kind? And she but one poor, inadequate creature. She would start to pace up and down her study; up and down, up and down, a most desolate pacing; even as years ago her father had paced his quiet study at Morton. Then those treacherous nerves of hers would betray her, so that when Mary came in with David—he a little depressed, sensing something amiss—she would often turn on the girl and speak sharply.

'Where on earth have you been?'

'Only out for a walk. I walked round to Jamie's, Barbara's not well; I sent her in a few tins of Brand's jelly.'*

'You've no right to go off without letting me know where you're going—I've told you before I won't have it!' Her voice would be harsh, and Mary would flush, unaware of those nerves that were strained to breaking.

As though grasping at something that remained secure, they would go to see the kind Mademoiselle Duphot, but less often than they had done in the past, for a feeling of guilt would come upon Stephen. Looking at the gentle and foal-like face with its innocent eyes behind the strong glasses, she would think: 'We're here under false pretences. If she knew what we were, she'd have none of us, either. Brockett was right, we should stick to our kind.' So they went less and less to see Mademoiselle Duphot.

Mademoiselle said with her mild resignation: 'It is natural, for now our Stévenne is famous. Why should she waste her time upon us? I am more than content to have been her teacher.'

But the sightless Julie shook her head sadly: 'It is not like that; you mistake, my sister. I can feel a great desolation in Stévenne—and some of the youngness has gone from Mary. What can it be? My fingers grow blind when I ask them the cause of that desolation.'

'I will pray for them both to the Sacred Heart which comprehends all things,' said Mademoiselle Duphot.

And indeed her own heart would have tried to understand—but Stephen had grown very bitterly mistrustful.

And so now, in good earnest they turned to their kind, for as Puddle had truly divined in the past, it is 'like to like' for such people as Stephen. Thus when Pat walked in unexpectedly one day to invite them to join a party that night at the Ideal Bar,* Stephen did not oppose Mary's prompt and all too eager acceptance.

Pat said they were going to do the round. Wanda was coming and probably Brockett. Dickie West the American aviator* was in Paris, and she also had promised to join them. Oh, yes, and then there was Valérie Seymour—Valérie was being dug out of her hole by Jeanne Maurel, her most recent conquest. Pat supposed that Valérie would drink lemon squash and generally act as a douche of cold water, she was sure to grow sleepy or disapproving, she was no acquisition to this sort of party. But could they rely upon Stephen's car? In the cold, grey dawn of the morning after, taxis were sometimes scarce up at Montmartre. Stephen nodded, thinking how absurdly prim Pat looked to be talking of cold, grey dawns and all that they stood for up at Montmartre. After she had left, Stephen frowned a little.

2

The five women were seated at a table near the door when Mary and Stephen eventually joined them. Pat, looking gloomy, was sipping light beer. Wanda, with the fires of hell in her eyes, in the hell of a temper too, drank brandy. She had started to drink pretty heavily again, and had therefore been avoiding Stephen just lately. There were only two new faces at the table, that of Jeanne Maurel, and of Dickie West, the much discussed woman aviator.

Dickie was short, plump and very young; she could not have been more than twenty-one and she still looked considerably under twenty. She was wearing a little dark blue béret; round her neck was knotted an apache scarf*—for the rest she was dressed in a neat serge suit with a very well cut double-breasted jacket. Her face was honest, her teeth rather large, her lips chapped and her skin much weather-beaten. She looked like a pleasant and nice-minded schoolboy well soaped and scrubbed for some gala occasion. When she spoke her voice was a little too hearty. She belonged to the younger, and therefore more reckless, more aggressive and self-assured generation; a generation that was marching to battle with much swagger, much sounding of drums and trumpets, a generation that had come after war to wage a new war on a hostile creation. Being mentally very well clothed and well shod, they had as yet left no blood-stained footprints; they were hopeful as yet, refusing point-blank to believe in the existence of a miserable army. They said: 'We are as we are; what about it? We don't care a damn, in fact we're delighted!' And being what they were they must go to extremes, must quite often outdo men in their sinning; yet the sins that they had were the sins of youth, the sins of defiance born of oppression. But Dickie was in no way exceptionally vile—she lived her life much as a man would have lived it. And her heart was so loyal, so trustful, so kind that it caused her much shame and much secret blushing. Generous as a lover, she was even more so when there could not be any question of loving. Like the horseleech's daughter,* her friends cried: 'Give! Give!' and Dickie gave lavishly, asking no questions. An appeal never left her completely unmoved, and suspecting this, most people went on appealing. She drank wine in moderation, smoked Camel cigarettes* till her fingers were brown, and admired stage beauties. Her greatest defect was practical joking of the kind that passes all seemly limits. Her jokes were dangerous, even cruel at times—in her jokes Dickie quite lacked imagination.

Jeanne Maurel was tall, almost as tall as Stephen. An elegant person wearing pearls round her throat above a low cut white satin waistcoat. She was faultlessly tailored and faultlessly barbered; her dark, severe Eton crop fitted neatly. Her profile was Greek, her eyes a bright blue—altogether a very arresting young woman. So far she had had quite a busy life doing nothing in particular and everything in general. But now she was Valérie Seymour's lover, attaining at last to a certain distinction.

And Valérie was sitting there calm and aloof, her glance roving casually round the café, not too critically, yet as though she would say: 'Enfin,* the whole world has grown very ugly, but no doubt to some people this represents pleasure.'

From the stained bar counter at the end of the room came the sound of Monsieur Pujol's loud laughter. Monsieur Pujol was affable to his clients, oh, but very, indeed he was almost paternal. Yet nothing escaped his cold, black eyes—a great expert he was in his way, Monsieur Pujol. There are many collections that a man may indulge in; old china, glass, pictures, watches and bibelots;* rare editions, tapestries, priceless jewels. Monsieur Pujol snapped his fingers at such things, they lacked life—Monsieur Pujol collected inverts. Amazingly morbid of Monsieur Pujol, and he with the face of an ageing dragoon, and he just married en secondes noçes,* and already with six legitimate children. A fine, purposeful sire he had been and still was, with his young wife shortly expecting a baby. Oh, yes, the most aggressively normal of men, as none knew better than the poor Madame Pujol. Yet behind the bar was a small, stuffy sanctum in which this strange man catalogued his collection. The walls of the sanctum were thickly hung with signed photographs, and a good few sketches. At the back of each frame was a neat little number corresponding to that in a locked leather notebook—it had long been his custom to write up his notes before going home with the milk in the morning. People saw their own faces but not their numbers—no client suspected that locked leather notebook.*

To this room would come Monsieur Pujol's old cronies for a bock or a petit verre* before business; and sometimes, like many another collector, Monsieur Pujol would permit himself to grow prosy. His friends knew most of the pictures by heart; knew their histories too, almost as well as he did; but in spite of this fact he would weary his guests by repeating many a threadbare story.

'A fine lot, n'est-ce pas?' he would say with a grin, 'See that man? Ah, yes—a really great poet. He drank himself to death. In those days it was absinthe*—they liked it because it gave them such courage. That one would come here like a scared white rat, but Crénom!* when he left he would bellow like a bull—the absinthe, of course—it gave them great courage.' Or: 'That woman over there, what a curious head! I remember her very well, she was German. Else Weining, her name was—before the war she would come with a girl she'd picked up here in Paris, just a common whore,* a most curious business. They were deeply in love. They would sit at a table in the corner—I can show you their actual table. They never talked much and they drank very little; as far as the drink went those two were bad clients, but so interesting that I did not much mind—I grew almost attached to Else Weining. Sometimes she would come all alone, come early. "Pu," she would say in her hideous French; "Pu, she must never go back to that hell." Hell! Sacrénom—*she* to call it hell! Amazing they are, I tell you, these people. Well, the girl went back, naturally she went back, and Else drowned herself in the Seine. Amazing they are—ces invertis,* I tell you!'

But not all the histories were so tragic as this one; Monsieur Pujol found some of them quite amusing. Quarrels galore he was able to relate, and light infidelities by the dozen. He would mimic a manner of speech, a gesture, a walk—he was really quite a good mimic—and when he did this his friends were not bored; they would sit there and split their sides with amusement.

And now Monsieur Pujol was laughing himself, cracking jokes as he covertly watched his clients. From where she and Mary sat near the door, Stephen could hear his loud, jovial laughter.

'Lord,' sighed Pat, unenlivened as yet by the beer; 'some people do seem to feel real good this evening.'

Wanda, who disliked the ingratiating Pujol, and whose nerves were on edge, had begun to grow angry. She had caught a particularly gross blasphemy, gross even for this age of stupid blaspheming. 'Le salaud!'* she shouted, then, inflamed by drink, an epithet even less complimentary.

'Hush up, do!' exclaimed the scandalized Pat, hastily gripping Wanda's shoulder.

But Wanda was out to defend her faith, and she did it in somewhat peculiar language.

People had begun to turn round and stare; Wanda was causing quite a diversion. Dickie grinned and skilfully egged her on, not perceiving the tragedy that was Wanda. For in spite of her tender and generous heart, Dickie was still but a crude young creature, one who had not yet learnt how to shiver and shake, and had thus remained but a crude young creature. Stephen glanced anxiously at Mary, half deciding to break up this turbulent party; but Mary was sitting with her chin on her hand, quite unruffled, it seemed, by Wanda's outburst. When her eyes met Stephen's she actually smiled, then took the cigarette that Jeanne Maurel was offering; and something in this placid, self-assured indifference went so ill with her youth that it startled Stephen. She in her turn must quickly light a cigarette, while Pat still endeavoured to silence Wanda.

Valérie said with her enigmatic smile: 'Shall we now go on to our next entertainment?'

They paid the bill and persuaded Wanda to postpone her abuse of the ingratiating Pujol. Stephen took one arm, Dickie West the other, and between them they coaxed her into the motor; after which they all managed to squeeze themselves in—that is, all except Dickie, who sat by the driver in order to guide the innocent Burton.

3

At Le Narcisse* they surprised what at first appeared to be the most prosaic of family parties. It was late, yet the mean room was empty of clients, for Le Narcisse seldom opened its eyes until midnight had chimed from the church clocks of Paris. Seated at a table with a red and white cloth were the Patron and a lady with a courtesy title. 'Madame,' she was called. And with them was a girl, and a handsome young man with severely plucked eyebrows. Their relationship to each other was . . . well . . . all the same, they suggested a family party. As Stephen pushed open the shabby swing door, they were placidly engaged upon playing belotte.*

The walls of the room were hung with mirrors thickly painted with cupids, thickly sullied by flies. A faint blend of odours was wafted from the kitchen which stood in proximity to the toilet. The host rose at once and shook hands with his guests. Every bar had its social customs, it seemed. At the Ideal one must share Monsieur Pujol's lewd jokes; at Le Narcisse one must gravely shake hands with the Patron.

The Patron was tall and exceedingly thin—a clean-shaven man with the mouth of an ascetic. His cheeks were delicately tinted with rouge, his eyelids delicately shaded with kohl; but the eyes themselves were an infantile blue, reproachful and rather surprised in expression.

For the good of the house, Dickie ordered champagne; it was warm and sweet and unpleasantly heady. Only Jeanne and Mary and Dickie herself had the courage to sample this curious beverage. Wanda stuck to her brandy and Pat to her beer, while Stephen drank coffee; but Valérie Seymour caused some confusion by gently insisting on a lemon squash—to be made with fresh lemons. Presently the guests began to arrive in couples. Having seated themselves at the tables, they quickly became oblivious to the world, what with the sickly champagne and each other. From a hidden recess there emerged a woman with a basket full of protesting roses. The stout vendeuse* wore a wide wedding ring—for was she not a most virtuous person? But her glance was both calculating and shrewd as she pounced upon the more obvious couples; and Stephen watching her progress through the room, felt suddenly ashamed on behalf of the roses. And now at a nod from the host there was music; and now at a bray from the band there was dancing. Dickie and Wanda opened the ball—Dickie stodgy and firm, Wanda rather unsteady. Others followed. Then Mary leant over the table and whispered:

'Won't you dance with me, Stephen?'

Stephen hesitated, but only for a moment. Then she got up abruptly and danced with Mary.

The handsome young man with the tortured eyebrows was bowing politely before Valérie Seymour. Refused by her, he passed on to Pat, and to Jeanne's great amusement was promptly accepted.

Brockett arrived and sat down at the table. He was in his most prying and cynical humour. He watched Stephen with coldly observant eyes, watched Dickie guiding the swaying Wanda, watched Pat in the arms of the handsome young man, watched the whole bumping, jostling crowd of dancers.

The blended odours were becoming more active. Brockett lit a cigarette. 'Well, Valérie darling? You look like an outraged Elgin marble.* Be kind, dear, be kind; you must live and let live, this is life. . . .' And he waved his soft white hands. 'Observe it—it's very wonderful, darling. This is life, love, defiance, emancipation!'

Said Valérie with her calm little smile: 'I think I preferred it when we were all martyrs!'

The dancers drifted back to their seats and Brockett manœuvred to sit beside Stephen. 'You and Mary dance well together,' he murmured. 'Are you happy? Are you enjoying yourselves?'

Stephen, who hated this inquisitive mood, this mood that would feed upon her emotions, turned away as she answered him, rather coldly: 'Yes, thanks—we're not having at all a bad evening.'

And now the Patron was standing by their table; bowing slightly to Brockett he started singing. His voice was a high and sweet baritone; his song was of love that must end too soon, of life that in death is redeemed by ending. An extraordinary song to hear in such a place—melancholy, and very sentimental. Some of the couples had tears in their eyes—tears that had probably sprung from champagne quite as much as from that melancholy singing. Brockett ordered a fresh bottle to console the Patron. Then he waved him away with a gesture of impatience.

There ensued more dancing, more ordering of drinks, more dalliance by the amorous couples. The Patron's mood changed, and now he must sing a song of the lowest boites* in Paris. As he sang he skipped like a performing dog, grimacing, beating time with his hands, conducting the chorus that rose from the tables.

Brockett sighed as he shrugged his shoulders in disgust, and once again Stephen glanced at Mary; but Mary, she saw, had not understood that song with its inexcusable meaning. Valérie was talking to Jeanne Maurel, talking about her villa at St. Tropez; talking of the garden, the sea, the sky, the design she had drawn for a green marble fountain. Stephen could hear her charming voice, so cultured, so cool—itself cool as a fountain; and she marvelled at this woman's perfect poise, the genius she possessed for complete detachment; Valérie had closed her ears to that song, and not only her ears but her mind and spirit.

The place was becoming intolerably hot, the room too over-crowded for dancing. Lids drooped, mouths sagged, heads lay upon shoulders—there was kissing, much kissing at a table in the corner. The air was fœtid* with drink and all the rest; unbreathable it appeared to Stephen. Dickie yawned an enormous, uncovered yawn; she was still young enough to feel rather sleepy. But Wanda was being seduced by her eyes, the lust of the eye was heavy upon her, so that Pat must shake a lugubrious head and begin to murmur anent General Custer.

Brockett got up and paid the bill; he was sulky, it seemed, because Stephen had snubbed him. He had not spoken for quite half an hour, and refused point-blank to accompany them further. 'I'm going home to my bed, thanks—good morning,' he said crossly, as they crowded into the motor.

They drove to a couple more bars, but at these they remained for only a very few minutes. Dickie said they were dull and Jeanne Maurel agreed—she suggested that they should go on to Alec's.

Valérie lifted an eyebrow and groaned. She was terribly bored, she was terribly hungry. 'I do wish I could get some cold chicken,' she murmured.

4

As long as she lived Stephen never forgot her first impressions of the bar known as Alec's—that meeting-place of the most miserable of all those who comprised the miserable army. That merciless, drug-dealing, death-dealing haunt to which flocked the battered remnants of men whom their fellow-men had at last stamped under; who, despised of the world, must despise themselves beyond all hope, it seemed, of salvation. There they sat, closely herded together at the tables, creatures shabby yet tawdry, timid yet defiant—and their eyes, Stephen never forgot their eyes, those haunted, tormented eyes of the invert.

Of all ages, all degrees of despondency, all grades of mental and physical ill-being, they must yet laugh shrilly from time to time, must yet tap their feet to the rhythm of music, must yet dance together in response to the band—and that dance seemed the Dance of Death to Stephen.* On more than one hand was a large, ornate ring, on more than one wrist a conspicuous bracelet; they wore jewellery that might only be worn by these men when they were thus gathered together. At Alec's they could dare to give way to such tastes—what was left of themselves they became at Alec's.

Bereft of all social dignity, of all social charts contrived for man's guidance, of the fellowship that by right divine should belong to each breathing, living creature; abhorred, spat upon, from their earliest days the prey to a ceaseless persecution, they were now even lower than their enemies knew, and more hopeless than the veriest dregs of creation. For since all that to many of them had seemed fine, a fine, selfless and at times even noble emotion, had been covered with shame, called unholy and vile, so gradually they themselves had sunk down to the level upon which the world placed their emotions. And looking with abhorrence upon these men, drink-sodden, doped as were only too many, Stephen yet felt that some terrifying thing stalked abroad in that unhappy room at Alec's; terrifying because if there were a God His anger must rise at such vast injustice. More pitiful even than her lot was theirs, and because of them mighty should be the world's reckoning.

Alec the tempter, the vendor of dreams, the dispenser of illusions whiter than snow; Alec, who sold little packets of cocaine for large bundles of notes, was now opening wine, with a smile and a flourish, at the next-door table.

He set down the bottle: 'Et voilà, mes filles!'*

Stephen looked at the men; they seemed quite complacent.

Against the wall sat a bald, flabby man whose fingers crept over an amber chaplet.* His lips moved; God alone knew to whom he prayed, and God alone knew what prayers he was praying—horrible he was, sitting there all alone with that infamous chaplet between his fingers.

The band struck up a one-step.* Dickie still danced, but with Pat, for Wanda was now beyond dancing. But Stephen would not dance, not among these men, and she laid a restraining hand upon Mary. Despite her sense of their terrible affliction, she could not dance in this place with Mary.

A youth passed with a friend and the couple were blocked by the press of dancers in front of her table. He bent forward, this youth, until his face was almost on a level with Stephen's—a grey, drug-marred face with a mouth that trembled incessantly.

'Ma sœur,'* he whispered.

For a moment she wanted to strike that face with her naked fist, to obliterate it. Then all of a sudden she perceived the eyes, and the memory came of a hapless creature, distracted, bleeding from bursting lungs, hopelessly pursued, glancing this way, then that, as though looking for something, some refuge, some hope—and the thought: 'It's looking for God who made it.'*

Stephen shivered and stared at her tightly clenched hands; the nails whitened her flesh. 'Mon frère,' she muttered.

And now some one was making his way through the crowd, a quiet, tawny man with the eyes of the Hebrew; Adolphe Blanc, the gentle and learned Jew, sat down in Dickie's seat beside Stephen. And he patted her knee as though she were young, very young and in great need of consolation.

'I have seen you for quite a long time, Miss Gordon. I've been sitting just over there by the window.' Then he greeted the others, but the greeting over he appeared to forget their very existence; he had come, it seemed, only to talk to Stephen.

He said: 'This place—these poor men, they have shocked you. I've been watching you in between the dances. They are terrible, Miss Gordon, because they are those who have fallen but have not risen again—there is surely no sin so great for them, so unpardonable as the sin of despair; yet as surely you and I can forgive. . . .'

She was silent, not knowing what she should answer.

But he went on, in no way deterred by her silence. He spoke softly, as though for her ears alone, and yet as a man might speak when consumed by the flame of some urgent and desperate mission. 'I am glad that you have come to this place, because those who have courage have also a duty.'

She nodded without comprehending his meaning.

'Yes, I am glad that you have come here,' he repeated. 'In this little room, to-night, every night, there is so much misery, so much despair, that the walls seem almost too narrow to contain it—many have grown callous, many have grown vile, but these things in themselves are despair, Miss Gordon. Yet outside there are happy people who sleep the sleep of the so-called just and righteous. When they wake it will be to persecute those who, through no known fault of their own, have been set apart from the day of their birth, deprived of all sympathy, all understanding. They are thoughtless, these happy people who sleep—and who is there to make them think, Miss Gordon?'

'They can read,' she stammered, 'there are many books. . . .'

But he shook his head. 'Do you think they are students? Ah, but no, they will not read medical books; what do such people care for the doctors? And what doctor can know the entire truth? Many times they meet only the neurasthenics, those of us for whom life has proved too bitter. They are good, these doctors—some of them very good; they work hard trying to solve our problem, but half the time they must work in the dark—the whole truth is known only to the normal invert. The doctors cannot make the ignorant think, cannot hope to bring home the sufferings of millions; only one of ourselves can some day do that. . . . It will need great courage but it will be done, because all things must work toward ultimate good; there is no real wastage and no destruction.' He lit a cigarette and stared thoughtfully at her for a moment or two. Then he touched her hand. 'Do you comprehend? There is no destruction.'*

She said: 'When one comes to a place like this, one feels horribly sad and humiliated. One feels that the odds are too heavily against any real success, any real achievement. Where so many have failed who can hope to succeed? Perhaps this is the end.'

Adolphe Blanc met her eyes. 'You are wrong, very wrong—this is only the beginning. Many die, many kill their bodies and souls, but they cannot kill the justice of God, even they cannot kill the eternal spirit. From their very degradation that spirit will rise up to demand of the world compassion and justice.'

Strange—this man was actually speaking her thoughts, yet again she fell silent, unable to answer.

Dickie and Pat came back to the table, and Adolphe Blanc slipped quietly away; when Stephen glanced round his place was empty, nor could she perceive him crossing the room through the press and maze of those terrible dancers.

5

Dickie went sound asleep in the car with her head against Pat's inhospitable shoulder. When they got to her hotel she wriggled and stretched. 'Is it . . . is it time to get up?' she murmured.

Next came Valérie Seymour and Jeanne Maurel to be dropped at the flat on the Quai Voltaire; then Pat who lived a few streets away, and last but not least the drunken Wanda. Stephen had to lift her out of the car and then get her upstairs as best she could, assisted by Burton and followed by Mary. It took quite a long time, and arrived at the door, Stephen must hunt for a missing latch-key.

When they finally got home, Stephen sank into a chair. 'Good Lord, what a night—it was pretty awful.' She was filled with the deep depression and disgust that are apt to result from such excursions.

But Mary pretended to a callousness that in truth she was very far from feeling, for life had not yet dulled her finer instincts; so far it had only aroused her anger. She yawned. 'Well, at least we could dance together without being thought freaks; there was something in that. Beggars can't be choosers in this world, Stephen!'

CHAPTER 49

I

On a fine June day Adèle married her Jean in the church of Notre-Dame-des-Victoires*—that shrine of innumerable candles and prayers, of the bountiful Virgin who bestows many graces. From early dawn the quiet old house in the Rue Jacob had been in a flutter—Pauline preparing the déjeuner de noces,* Pierre garnishing and sweeping their sitting-room, and both of them pausing from time to time to embrace the flushed cheeks of their happy daughter.

Stephen had given the wedding dress, the wedding breakfast and a sum of money; Mary had given the bride her lace veil, her white satin shoes and her white silk stockings; David had given a large gilt clock, purchased for him in the Palais Royal;* while Burton's part was to drive the bride to the church, and the married pair to the station.

By nine o'clock the whole street was agog, for Pauline and Pierre were liked by their neighbours; and besides, as the baker remarked to his wife, from so grand a house it would be a fine business.

'They are after all generous, these English,' said he; 'and if Mademoiselle Gordon is strange in appearance, one should not forget that she served la France and must now wear a scar as well as a ribbon.' Then remembering his four sons slain in the war, he sighed—sons are sons to a king or a baker.

David, growing excited, rushed up and down stairs with offers to help which nobody wanted, least of all the flustered and anxious bride at the moment of putting on tight satin slippers.

'Va donc! Tu ne peux pas m'aider, mon chou, veux tu te taire, alors!'* implored Adèle.

In the end Mary had had to find collar and lead and tie David up to the desk in the study, where he brooded and sucked his white satin bow, deciding that only the four-legged were grateful. But at long last Adèle was arrayed to be wed, and must show herself shyly to Mary and Stephen. She looked very appealing with her good, honest face; with her round, bright eyes like those of a blackbird.* Stephen wished her well from the bottom of her heart, this girl who had waited so long for her mate—had so patiently and so faithfully waited.

2

In the church were a number of friends and relations; together with those who will journey for miles in order to attend a funeral or wedding. Poor Jean looked his worst in a cheap dress suit, and Stephen could smell the pomade on his hair; very greasy and warm it smelt, although scented. But his hand was unsteady as he groped for the ring, because he was feeling both proud and humble; because, loving much, he must love even more and conceive of himself as entirely unworthy. And something in that fumbling, unsteady hand, in that sleekly greased hair and those ill-fitting garments, touched Stephen, so that she longed to reassure, to tell him how great was the gift he offered—security, peace, and love with honour.

The young priest gravely repeated the prayers—ancient, primitive prayers, yet softened through custom. In her mauve silk dress Pauline wept as she knelt; but Pierre's handkerchief was spread out on the stool to preserve the knees of his new grey trousers. Next to Stephen were sitting Pauline's two brothers, one in uniform, the other retired and in mufti, but both wearing medals upon their breasts and thus worthily representing the army. The baker was there with his wife and three daughters, and since the latter were still unmarried, their eyes were more often fixed upon Jean in his shoddy dress suit than upon their Missals.* The greengrocer accompanied the lady whose chickens it was Pauline's habit to prod on their breastbones; while the cobbler who mended Pierre's boots and shoes, sat ogling the buxom and comely young laundress.

The Mass drew to its close. The priest asked that a blessing might be accomplished upon the couple; asked that these two might live to behold, not only their own but their children's children, even unto the third and fourth generation.* Then he spoke of their duty to God and to each other, and finally moistened their bowed young heads with a generous sprinkling of holy water. And so in the church of Notre-Dame-des-Victoires—that bountiful Virgin who bestows many graces—Jean and his Adèle were made one flesh in the eyes of their church, in the eyes of their God, and as one might confront the world without flinching.

Arm in arm they passed out through the heavy swing doors and into Stephen's waiting motor. Burton smiled above the white favour in his coat; the crowd, craning their necks, were also smiling. Arrived back at the house, Stephen, Mary, and Burton must drink the health of the bride and bridegroom. Then Pierre thanked his employer for all she had done in giving his daughter so splendid a wedding. But when that employer was no longer present, when Mary had followed her into the study, the baker's wife lifted quizzical eyebrows.

'Quel type! On dirait plutôt un homme; ce n'est pas celle-là qui trouvera un mari!'

The guests laughed. 'Mais oui, elle est joliment bizarre';* and they started to make little jokes about Stephen.

Pierre flushed as he leaped to Stephen's defence. 'She is good, she is kind, and I greatly respect her and so does my wife—while as for our daughter, Adèle here has very much cause to be grateful. Moreover she gained the Croix de Guerre through serving our wounded men in the trenches.'

The baker nodded. 'You are quite right, my friend—precisely what I myself said this morning.'

But Stephen's appearance was quickly forgotten in the jollification of so much fine feasting—a feasting for which her money had paid, for which her thoughtfulness had provided. Jokes there were, but no longer directed at her—they were harmless, well meant if slightly broad jokes made at the expense of the bashful bridegroom. Then before even Pauline had realized the time, there was Burton strolling into the kitchen, and Adèle must rush off to change her dress, while Jean must change also, but in the pantry.

Burton glanced at the clock. 'Faut dépêcher vous, 'urry, if you're going to catch that chemin de fer,' he announced as one having authority. 'It's a goodish way to the Guard de Lions.'*

3

That evening the old house seemed curiously thoughtful and curiously sad after all the merry-making. David's second white bow had come untied and was hanging in two limp ends from his collar. Pauline had gone to church to light candles; Pierre, together with Pauline's niece who would take Adèle's place, was preparing dinner. And the sadness of the house flowed out like a stream to mingle itself with the sadness in Stephen. Adèle and Jean, the simplicity of it . . . they loved, they married, and after a while they would care for each other all over again, renewing their youth and their love in their children. So orderly, placid and safe it seemed, this social scheme evolved from creation; this guarding of two young and ardent lives for the sake of the lives that might follow after. A fruitful and peaceful road it must be. The same road had been taken by those founders of Morton who had raised up children from father to son, from father to son until the advent of Stephen; and their blood was her blood—what they had found good in their day, seemed equally good to their descendant. Surely never was outlaw more law-abiding at heart, than this, the last of the Gordons.*

So now a great sadness took hold upon her, because she perceived both dignity and beauty in the coming together of Adèle and Jean, very simply and in accordance with custom. And this sadness mingling with that of the house, widened into a flood that compassed Mary and through her David, and they both went and sat very close to Stephen on the study divan. As the twilight gradually merged into dusk, these three must huddle even closer together—David with his head upon Mary's lap, Mary with her head against Stephen's shoulder.

CHAPTER 50

I

STEPHEN ought to have gone to England that summer; at Morton there had been a change of agent, and once again certain questions had arisen which required her careful personal attention. But time had not softened Anna's attitude to Mary, and time had not lessened Stephen's exasperation—the more so as Mary no longer hid the bitterness that she felt at this treatment. So Stephen tackled the business by writing a number of long and wearisome letters, unwilling to set foot again in the house where Mary Llewellyn would not be welcome. But as always the thought of England wounded, bringing with it the old familiar longing—home-sick she would feel as she sat at her desk writing those wearisome business letters. For even as Jamie must crave for the grey, wind-swept street and the wind-swept uplands of Beedles, so Stephen must crave for the curving hills, for the long green hedges and pastures of Morton. Jamie openly wept when such moods were upon her, but the easement of tears was denied to Stephen.

In August Jamie and Barbara joined them in a villa that Stephen had taken at Houlgate.* Mary hoped that the bathing would do Barbara good; she was not at all well. Jamie worried about her. And indeed the girl had grown very frail, so frail that the housework now tried her sorely; when alone she must sit down and hold her side for the pain that was never mentioned to Jamie. Then too, all was not well between them these days; poverty, even hunger at times, the sense of being unwanted outcasts, the knowledge that the people to whom they belonged—good and honest people—both abhorred and despised them, such things as these had proved very bad housemates for sensitive souls like Barbara and Jamie.

Large, helpless, untidy and intensely forlorn, Jamie would struggle to finish her opera; but quite often these days she would tear up her work, knowing that what she had written was unworthy. When this happened she would sigh and peer round the studio, vaguely conscious that something was not as it had been, vaguely distressed by the dirt of the place to which she herself had helped to contribute—Jamie, who had never before noticed dirt, would feel aggrieved by its noxious presence. Getting up she would wipe the keys of the piano with Barbara's one clean towel dipped in water.

'Can't play,' she would grumble, 'these keys are all sticky.'

'Oh, Jamie—my towel—go and fetch the duster!'

The quarrel that ensued would start Barbara's cough, which in turn would start Jamie's nerves vibrating. Then compassion, together with unreasoning anger and a sudden uprush of sex-frustration,* would make her feel wellnigh beside herself—since owing to Barbara's failing health, these two could be lovers now in name only. And this forced abstinence told on Jamie's work as well as her nerves, destroying her music, for those who maintain that the North is cold, might just as well tell us that hell is freezing. Yet she did her best, the poor uncouth creature, to subjugate the love of the flesh to the pure and more selfless love of the spirit—the flesh did not have it all its own way with Jamie.

That summer she made a great effort to talk, to unburden herself when alone with Stephen; and Stephen tried hard to console and advise, while knowing that she could help very little. All her offers of money to ease the strain were refused point-blank, sometimes almost with rudeness—she felt very anxious indeed about Jamie.

Mary in her turn was deeply concerned; her affection for Barbara had never wavered, and she sat for long hours in the garden with the girl who seemed too weak to bathe, and whom walking exhausted.

'Let us help,' she pleaded, stroking Barbara's thin hand, 'after all, we're much better off than you are. Aren't you two like ourselves? Then why mayn't we help?'

Barbara slowly shook her head: 'I'm all right—please don't talk about money to Jamie.'

But Mary could see that she was far from all right; the warm weather was proving of little avail, even care and good food and sunshine and rest seemed unable to ease that incessant coughing.

'You ought to see a specialist at once,' she told Barbara rather sharply one morning.

But Barbara shook her head yet again: 'Don't, Mary—don't, please . . . you'll be frightening Jamie.'

2

After their return to Paris in the autumn, Jamie sometimes joined the nocturnal parties; going rather grimly from bar to bar, and drinking too much of the crême-de-menthe that reminded her of the bull's-eyes at Beedles. She had never cared for these parties before, but now she was clumsily trying to escape, for a few hours at least, from the pain of existence. Barbara usually stayed at home or spent the evening with Stephen and Mary. But Stephen and Mary would not always be there, for now they also went out fairly often; and where was there to go to except the bars? Nowhere else could two women dance together without causing comment and ridicule, without being looked upon as freaks, argued Mary. So rather than let the girl go without her, Stephen would lay aside her work—she had recently started to write her fourth novel.

Sometimes, it is true, their friends came to them, a less sordid and far less exhausting business; but even at their own house the drink was too free: 'We can't be the only couple to refuse to give people a brandy and soda,' said Mary, 'Valérie's parties are awfully dull; that's because she's allowed herself to grow cranky!'

And thus, very gradually just at first, Mary's finer perceptions began to coarsen.

3

The months passed, and now more than a year had slipped by, yet Stephen's novel remained unfinished; for Mary's face stood between her and her work—surely the mouth and the eyes had hardened?

Still unwilling to let Mary go without her, she dragged wearily round to the bars and cafés, observing with growing anxiety that Mary now drank as did all the others—not too much perhaps, but quite enough to give her a cheerful outlook on existence.

The next morning she was often deeply depressed, in the grip of a rather tearful reaction: 'It's too beastly—why do we do it?' she would ask.

And Stephen would answer: 'God knows I don't want to, but I won't let you go to such places without me. Can't we give it all up? It's appallingly sordid!'

Then Mary would flare out with sudden anger, her mood changing as she felt a slight tug on the bridle. Were they to have no friends? she would ask. Were they to sit still and let the world crush them? If they were reduced to the bars of Paris, whose fault was that? Not hers and not Stephen's. Oh, no, it was the fault of the Lady Annas and the Lady Masseys who had closed their doors, so afraid were they of contamination!

Stephen would sit with her head on her hand, searching her sorely troubled mind for some ray of light, some adequate answer.

4

That winter Barbara fell very ill. Jamie rushed round to the house one morning, hatless, and with deeply tormented eyes: 'Mary, please come—Barbara can't get up, it's a pain in her side. Oh, my God—we quarrelled . . .' Her voice was shrill and she spoke very fast: 'Listen—last night—there was snow on the ground, it was cold—I was angry . . . I can't remember . . . but I know I was angry—I get like that. She went out—she stayed out for quite two hours, and when she came back she was shivering so. Oh, my God, but why did we quarrel, whatever? She can't move; it's an awful pain in her side . . .'

Stephen said quietly: 'We'll come almost at once, but first I'm going to ring up my own doctor.'

5

Barbara was lying in the tiny room with the eye-shaped window that would not open. The stove had gone out in the studio, and the air was heavy with cold and dampness. On the piano lay some remnants of manuscript music torn up on the previous evening by Jamie.

Barbara opened her eyes: 'Is that you, my bairn?'*

They had never heard Barbara call her that before—the great, lumbering, big-boned, long-legged Jamie.

'Yes, it's me.'

'Come here close . . .' The voice drifted away.

'I'm here—oh, I'm here! I've got hold of your hand. Look at me, open your eyes again—Barbara, listen, I'm here—don't you feel me?'

Stephen tried to restrain the shrill, agonized voice: 'Don't speak so loud, Jamie, perhaps she's sleeping'; but she knew very well that this was not so; the girl was not sleeping now, but unconscious.

Mary found some fuel and lighted the stove, then she started to tidy the disordered studio. Flakes of flue lay here and there on the floor; thick dust was filming the top of the piano. Barbara had been waging a losing fight—strange that so mean a thing as this dust should, in the end, have been able to conquer. Food there was none, and putting on her coat Mary finally went forth in quest of milk and other things likely to come in useful. At the foot of the stairs she was met by the concierge; the woman looked glum, as though deeply aggrieved by this sudden and very unreasonable illness. Mary thrust some money into her hand, then hurried away intent on her shopping.

When she returned the doctor was there; he was talking very gravely to Stephen: 'It's double pneumonia,* a pretty bad case—the girl's heart's so weak. I'll send in a nurse. What about the friend, will she be any good?'

'I'll help with the nursing if she isn't,' said Mary.

Stephen said: 'You do understand about the bills—the nurse and all that?'

The doctor nodded.

They forced Jamie to eat: 'For Barbara's sake . . . Jamie, we're with you, you're not alone, Jamie.'

She peered with her red-rimmed, short-sighted eyes, only half understanding, but she did as they told her. Then she got up without so much as a word, and went back to the room with the eye-shaped window. Still in silence she squatted on the floor by the bed, like a dumb faithful dog who endured without speaking. And they let her alone, let her have her poor way, for this was not their Calvary* but Jamie's.

The nurse arrived, a calm, practical woman: 'You'd better lie down for a bit,' she told Jamie, and in silence Jamie lay down on the floor.

'No, my dear—please go and lie down in the studio.'

She got up slowly to obey this new voice, lying down, with her face to the wall, on the divan.

The nurse turned to Stephen: 'Is she a relation?'

Stephen hesitated, then she shook her head.

'That's a pity, in a serious case like this I'd like to be in touch with some relation, some one who has a right to decide things. You know what I mean—it's double pneumonia.'

Stephen said dully: 'No—she's not a relation.'

'Just a friend?' the nurse queried.

'Just a friend,' muttered Stephen.

6

They went back that evening and stayed the night. Mary helped with the nursing; Stephen looked after Jamie.

'Is she a little—I mean the friend—is she mental at all, do you know?' The nurse whispered, 'I can't get her to speak—she's anxious, of course; still, all the same, it doesn't seem natural.'

Stephen said: 'No—it doesn't seem natural to you.' And she suddenly flushed to the roots of her hair. Dear God, the outrage of this for Jamie!

But Jamie seemed quite unconscious of outrage. From time to time she stood in the doorway peering over at Barbara's wasted face, listening to Barbara's painful breathing, and then she would turn her bewildered eyes on the nurse, on Mary, but above all on Stephen.

'Jamie—come back and sit down by the stove; Mary's there, it's all right.'

Came a queer, halting voice that spoke with an effort: 'But . . . Stephen . . . we quarrelled.'

'Come and sit by the stove—Mary's with her, my dear.'

'Hush, please,' said the nurse, 'you're disturbing my patient.'

7

Barbara's fight against death was so brief that it hardly seemed in the nature of a struggle. Life had left her no strength to repel this last foe—or perhaps it was that to her he seemed friendly. Just before her death she kissed Jamie's hand and tried to speak, but the words would not come—those words of forgiveness and love for Jamie.

Then Jamie flung herself down by the bed, and she clung there, still in that uncanny silence. Stephen never knew how they got her away while the nurse performed the last merciful duties.

But when flowers had been placed in Barbara's hands, and Mary had lighted a couple of candles, then Jamie went back and stared quietly down at the small, waxen face that lay on the pillow; and she turned to the nurse:

'Thank you so much,' she said, 'I think you've done all that there is to do—and now I suppose you'll want to be going?'

The nurse glanced at Stephen.

'It's all right, we'll stay. I think perhaps—if you don't mind, nurse . . .'

'Very well, it must be as you wish, Miss Gordon.'

When she had gone Jamie veered round abruptly and walked back into the empty studio. Then all in a moment the floodgates gave way and she wept and she wept like a creature demented. Bewailing the life of hardship and exile that had sapped Barbara's strength and weakened her spirit; bewailing the cruel dispensation of fate that had forced them to leave their home in the Highlands; bewailing the terrible thing that is death to those who, still loving, must look upon it. Yet all the exquisite pain of this parting seemed as nothing to an anguish that was far more subtle: 'I can't mourn her without bringing shame on her name—I can't go back home now and mourn her,' wailed Jamie; 'oh, and I want to go back to Beedles, I want to be home among our own people—I want them to know how much I loved her. Oh God, oh God! I can't even mourn her, and I want to grieve for her home there in Beedles.'

What could they speak but inadequate words: 'Jamie, don't, don't! You loved each other—isn't that something? Remember that, Jamie.' They could only speak the inadequate words that are given to people on such occasions.

But after a while the storm seemed to pass, Jamie seemed to grow suddenly calm and collected: 'You two,' she said gravely, 'I want to thank you for all you've been to Barbara and me.'

Mary started crying.

'Don't cry,' said Jamie.

The evening came. Stephen lighted the lamp, then she made up the stove while Mary laid the supper. Jamie ate a little, and she actually smiled when Stephen poured her out a weak whisky.

'Drink it, Jamie—it may help you to get some sleep.'

Jamie shook her head: 'I shall sleep without it—but I want to be left alone to-night, Stephen.'

Mary protested, but Jamie was firm: 'I want to be left alone with her, please—you do understand that, Stephen, don't you?'

Stephen hesitated, then she saw Jamie's face; it was full of a new and calm resolution: 'It's my right,' she was saying, 'I've a right to be alone with the woman I love before they—take her.'

Jamie held the lamp to light them downstairs—her hand, Stephen thought, seemed amazingly steady.

8

The next morning when they went to the studio quite early, they heard voices coming from the topmost landing. The concierge was standing outside Jamie's door, and with her was a young man, one of the tenants. The concierge had tried the door; it was locked and no one made any response to her knocking. She had brought Jamie up a cup of hot coffee—Stephen saw it, the coffee had slopped into the saucer. Either pity or the memory of Mary's large tips, had apparently touched the heart of this woman.

Stephen hammered loudly: 'Jamie!' she called, and then again and again: 'Jamie! Jamie!'

The young man set his shoulder to a panel, and all the while he pushed he was talking. He lived just underneath, but last night he was out, not returning until nearly six that morning. He had heard that one of the girls had died—the little one—she had always looked fragile.

Stephen added her strength to his; the woodwork was damp and rotten with age, the lock suddenly gave and the door swung inwards.

Then Stephen saw: 'Don't come here—go back, Mary!'

But Mary followed them into the studio.

So neat, so amazingly neat it was for Jamie, she who had always been so untidy, she who had always littered up the place with her large, awkward person and shabby possessions, she who had always been Barbara's despair . . . Just a drop or two of blood on the floor, just a neat little hole low down in her left side. She must have fired upwards with great foresight and skill—and they had not even known that she owned a revolver!

And so Jamie who dared not go home to Beedles for fear of shaming the woman she loved, Jamie who dared not openly mourn lest Barbara's name be defiled through her mourning, Jamie had dared to go home to God—to trust herself to His more perfect mercy, even as Barbara had gone home before her.*

CHAPTER 51

I

THE tragic deaths of Barbara and Jamie cast a gloom over every one who had known them, but especially over Mary and Stephen. Again and again Stephen blamed herself for having left Jamie on that fatal evening; if she had only insisted upon staying, the tragedy might never have happened, she might somehow have been able to impart to the girl the courage and strength to go on living. But great as the shock undoubtedly was to Stephen, to Mary it was even greater, for together with her very natural grief, was a new and quite unexpected emotion, the emotion of fear. She was suddenly afraid, and now this fear looked out of her eyes and crept into her voice when she spoke of Jamie.

'To end in that way, to have killed herself; Stephen, it's so awful that such things can happen—they were like you and me.' And then she would go over every sorrowful detail of Barbara's last illness, every detail of their finding of Jamie's body.

'Did it hurt, do you think, when she shot herself? When you shot that wounded horse at the front, he twitched such a lot, I shall never forget it—and Jamie was all alone that night, there was no one there to help in her pain. It's all so ghastly; supposing it hurt her!'

Useless for Stephen to quote the doctor who had said that death had been instantaneous; Mary was obsessed by the horror of the thing, and not only its physical horror either, but by the mental and spiritual suffering that must have strengthened the will to destruction.

'Such despair,' she would say, 'such utter despair . . . and that was the end of all their loving. I can't bear it!' And then she would hide her face against Stephen's strong and protective shoulder.

Oh, yes, there was now little room for doubt, the whole business was preying badly on Mary.

Sometimes strange, amorous moods would seize her, in which she must kiss Stephen rather wildly: 'Don't let go of me, darling—never let go. I'm afraid; I think it's because of what's happened.'

Her kisses would awaken a swift response, and so in these days that were shadowed by death, they clung very desperately to life with the passion they had felt when first they were lovers, as though only by constantly feeding that flame could they hope to ward off some unseen disaster.

2

At this time of shock, anxiety and strain, Stephen turned to Valérie Seymour as many another had done before her. This woman's great calm in the midst of storm was not only soothing but helpful to Stephen, so that now she often went to the flat on the Quai Voltaire; often went there alone, since Mary would seldom accompany her—for some reason she resented Valérie Seymour. But in spite of this resentment Stephen must go, for now an insistent urge was upon her, the urge to unburden her weary mind of the many problems surrounding inversion. Like most inverts she found a passing relief in discussing the intolerable situation; in dissecting it ruthlessly bit by bit, even though she arrived at no solution; but since Jamie's death it did not seem wise to dwell too much on this subject with Mary. On the other hand, Valérie was now quite free, having suddenly tired of Jeanne Maurel, and moreover she was always ready to listen. Thus it was that between them a real friendship sprang up—a friendship founded on mutual respect, if not always on mutual understanding.

Stephen would again and again go over those last heart-rending days with Barbara and Jamie, railing against the outrageous injustice that had led to their tragic and miserable ending. She would clench her hands in a kind of fury. How long was this persecution to continue? How long would God sit still and endure this insult offered to His creation? How long tolerate the preposterous statement that inversion was not a part of nature? For since it existed what else could it be? All things that existed were a part of nature!

But with equal bitterness she would speak of the wasted lives of such creatures as Wanda, who beaten down into the depths by the world, gave the world the very excuse it was seeking for pointing at them an accusing finger. Pretty bad examples they were, many of them, and yet—but for an unforeseen accident of birth, Wanda might even now have been a great painter.

And then she would discuss very different people whom she had been led to believe existed; hard-working, honourable men and women, not a few of them possessed of fine brains, yet lacking the courage to admit their inversion. Honourable, it seemed, in all things save this that the world had forced on them—this dishonourable lie whereby alone they could hope to find peace, could hope to stake out a claim on existence. And always these people must carry that lie like a poisonous asp pressed against their bosoms;* must unworthily hide and deny their love, which might well be the finest thing about them.

And what of the women who had worked in the war—those quiet, gaunt women she had seen about London? England had called them and they had come; for once, unabashed, they had faced the daylight. And now because they were not prepared to slink back and hide in their holes and corners, the very public whom they had served was the first to turn round and spit upon them; to cry: 'Away with this canker in our midst,* this nest of unrighteousness and corruption!' That was the gratitude they had received for the work they had done out of love for England!

And what of that curious craving for religion which so often went hand in hand with inversion?* Many such people were deeply religious, and this surely was one of their bitterest problems. They believed, and believing they craved a blessing on what to some of them seemed very sacred—a faithful and deeply devoted union. But the Church's blessing was not for them. Faithful they might be, leading orderly lives, harming no one, and yet the Church turned away; her blessings were strictly reserved for the normal.

Then Stephen would come to the thing of all others that to her was the most agonizing question. Youth, what of youth? Where could it turn for its natural and harmless recreations? There was Dickie West and many more like her, vigorous, courageous and kindhearted youngsters; yet shut away from so many of the pleasures that belonged by right to every young creature—and more pitiful still was the lot of a girl who, herself being normal, gave her love to an invert. The young had a right to their innocent pleasures, a right to social companionship; had a right, indeed, to resent isolation. But here, as in all the great cities of the world, they were isolated until they went under; until, in their ignorance and resentment, they turned to the only communal life that a world bent upon their destruction had left them; turned to the worst elements of their kind, to those who haunted the bars of Paris. Their lovers were helpless, for what could they do? Empty-handed they were, having nothing to offer. And even the tolerant normal were helpless—those who went to Valérie's parties, for instance. If they had sons and daughters, they left them at home; and considering all things, who could blame them? While as for themselves, they were far too old—only tolerant, no doubt, because they were ageing. They could not provide the frivolities for which youth had a perfectly natural craving.

In spite of herself, Stephen's voice would tremble, and Valérie would know that she was thinking of Mary.

Valérie would genuinely want to be helpful, but would find very little to say that was consoling. It was hard on the young, she had thought so herself, but some came through all right, though a few might go under. Nature was trying to do her bit; inverts were being born in increasing numbers,* and after a while their numbers would tell, even with the fools who still ignored Nature. They must just bide their time—recognition was coming. But meanwhile they should all cultivate more pride, should learn to be proud of their isolation. She found little excuse for poor fools like Pat, and even less for drunkards like Wanda.

As for those who were ashamed to declare themselves, lying low for the sake of a peaceful existence, she utterly despised such of them as had brains; they were traitors to themselves and their fellows, she insisted. For the sooner the world came to realize that fine brains very frequently went with inversion, the sooner it would have to withdraw its ban, and the sooner would cease this persecution. Persecution was always a hideous thing, breeding hideous thoughts—and such thoughts were dangerous.

As for the women who had worked in the war, they had set an example to the next generation, and that in itself should be a reward. She had heard that in England many such women had taken to breeding dogs in the country. Well, why not? Dogs were very nice people to breed. 'Plus je connais les hommes, plus j'aime les chiens.'* There were worse things than breeding dogs in the country.

It was quite true that inverts were often religious, but church-going in them was a form of weakness; they must be a religion unto themselves if they felt that they really needed religion. As for blessings, they profited the churches no doubt, apart from which they were just superstition. But then of course she herself was a pagan, acknowledging only the god of beauty; and since the whole world was so ugly these days, she was only too thankful to let it ignore her. Perhaps that was lazy—she was rather lazy. She had never achieved all she might have with her writing. But humanity was divided into two separate classes, those who did things and those who looked on at their doings. Stephen was one of the kind that did things—under different conditions of environment and birth she might very well have become a reformer.

They would argue for hours, these two curious friends whose points of view were so widely divergent, and although they seldom if ever agreed, they managed to remain both courteous and friendly.

Valérie seemed wellnigh inhuman at times, completely detached from all personal interest. But one day she remarked to Stephen abruptly: 'I really know very little about you, but this I do know—you're a bird of passage, you don't belong to the life here in Paris.' Then as Stephen was silent, she went on more gravely: 'You're rather a terrible combination: you've the nerves of the abnormal with all that they stand for—you're appallingly over-sensitive, Stephen—well, and then we get le revers de la médaille;* you've all the respectable county instincts of the man who cultivates children and acres—any gaps in your fences would always disturb you; one side of your mind is so aggressively tidy. I can't see your future, but I feel you'll succeed; though I must say, of all the improbable people . . . But supposing you could bring the two sides of your nature into some sort of friendly amalgamation and compel them to serve you and through you your work—well then I really don't see what's to stop you. The question is, can you ever bring them together?' She smiled. 'If you climb to the highest peak, Valérie Seymour won't be there to see you. It's a charming friendship that we two have found, but it's passing, like so many charming things; however, my dear, let's enjoy it while it lasts, and . . . remember me when you come into your kingdom.'*

Stephen said: 'When we first met I almost disliked you. I thought your interest was purely scientific or purely morbid. I said so to Puddle—you remember Puddle, I think you once met her. I want to apologize to you now; to tell you how grateful I am for your kindness. You're so patient when I come here and talk for hours, and it's such a relief; you'll never know the relief it is to have some one to talk to.' She hesitated. 'You see it's not fair to make Mary listen to all my worries—she's still pretty young, and the road's damned hard . . . then there's been that horrible business of Jamie.'

'Come as often as you feel like it,' Valérie told her; 'and if ever you should want my help or advice, here I am. But do try to remember this: even the world's not so black as it's painted.'

CHAPTER 52

I

ONE morning a very young cherry-tree* that Mary herself had planted in the garden was doing the most delightful things—it was pushing out leaves and tight pink buds along the whole length of its childish branches. Stephen made a note of it in her diary: 'To-day Mary's cherry-tree started to blossom.' This is why she never forgot the date on which she received Martin Hallam's letter.

The letter had been redirected from Morton; she recognized Puddle's scholastic handwriting. And the other writing—large, rather untidy, but with strong black down-strokes and firmly crossed T's—she stared at it thoughtfully, puckering her brows. Surely that writing, too, was familiar? Then she noticed a Paris postmark in the corner—that was strange. She tore open the envelope.

Martin wrote very simply: 'Stephen, my dear. After all these years I am sending you a letter, just in case you have not completely forgotten the existence of a man called Martin Hallam.

'I've been in Paris for the past two months. I had to come across to have my eye seen to; I stopped a bullet with my head here in France—it affected the optic nerve rather badly. But the point is: if I fly over to England as I'm thinking of doing, may I come and see you? I'm a very poor hand at expressing myself—can't do it at all when I put pen to paper—in addition to which I'm feeling nervous because you've become such a wonderful writer. But I do want to try and make you understand how desperately I've regretted our friendship—that perfect early friendship of ours seems to me now a thing well worth regretting. Believe me or not, I've thought of it for years; and the fault was all mine for not understanding. I was just an ignorant cub in those days. Well, anyhow, please will you see me, Stephen? I'm a lonely sort of fellow, so if you're kind-hearted you'll invite me to motor down to Morton, supposing you're there; and then if you like me, we'll take up our friendship just where it left off. We'll pretend that we're very young again, walking over the hills and jawing about life. Lord, what splendid companions we were in those early days—like a couple of brothers!

'Do you think it's queer that I'm writing all this? It does seem queer, yet I'd have written it before if I'd ever come over to stay in England; but except when I rushed across to join up, I've pretty well stuck to British Columbia. I don't even know exactly where you are, for I've not met a soul who knows you for ages. I heard of your father's death of course, and was terribly sorry—beyond that I've heard nothing; still, I fancy I'm quite safe in sending this to Morton.

'I'm staying with my aunt, the Comtesse de Mirac; she's English, twice married and once more a widow. She's been a perfect angel to me. I've been staying with her ever since I came to Paris. Well, my dear, if you've forgiven my mistake—and please say you have, we were both very young—then write to me at Aunt Sarah's address, and if you write don't forget to put "Passy." The posts are so erratic in France, and I'd hate to think that they'd lost your letter. Your very sincere friend, MARTIN HALLAM.'

Stephen glanced through the window. Mary was in the garden still admiring her brave little cherry-tree; in a minute or two she would feed the pigeons—yes, she was starting to cross the lawn to the shed in which she kept pigeon-mixture—but presently she would be coming in. Stephen sat down and began to think quickly.

Martin Hallam—he must be about thirty-nine. He had fought in the war and been badly wounded—she had thought of him during that terrible advance, the smitten trees had been a reminder. . . . He must often have been very near her then; he was very near now, just out at Passy, and he wanted to see her; he offered his friendship.

She closed her eyes the better to consider, but now her mind must conjure up pictures. A very young man at the Antrims' dance—oh, but very young—with a bony face that glowed when he talked of the beauty of trees, of their goodness . . . a tall, loose-limbed young man who slouched when he walked, as though from much riding. The hills . . . winter hills rust-coloured by bracken . . . Martin touching the ancient thorns with kind fingers. 'Look, Stephen—the courage of these old fellows!' How clearly she remembered his actual words after all these years, and her own she remembered: 'You're the only real friend I've ever had except Father—our friendship's so wonderful somehow. . . .' And his answer: 'I know, a wonderful friendship.' A great sense of companionship, of comfort—it had been so good to have him beside her; she had liked his quiet and careful voice, and his thoughtful blue eyes that moved rather slowly. He had filled a real need that had always been hers and still was, a need for the friendship of men—how very completely Martin had filled it, until . . . But she resolutely closed her mind, refusing to visualize that last picture. He knew now that it had been a ghastly mistake—he understood—he practically said so. Could they take up their friendship where they had left it? If only they could . . .

She got up abruptly and went to the telephone on her desk. Glancing at his letter, she rang up a number.

'Hallo—yes?'

She recognized his voice at once.

'Is that you, Martin? It's Stephen speaking.'

'Stephen . . . oh, I'm so glad! But where on earth are you?'

'At my house in Paris—35, Rue Jacob.'

'But I don't understand, I thought . . .'

'Yes, I know, but I've lived here for ages—since before the war. I've just got your letter, sent back from England. Funny, isn't it? Why not come to dinner to-night if you're free—eight o'clock.'

'I say! May I really?'

'Of course . . . come and dine with my friend and me.'

'What number?'

'Thirty-five—35 Rue Jacob.'

'I'll be there on the actual stroke of eight!'

'That's right—good-bye, Martin.'

'Good-bye, and thanks, Stephen.'

She hung up the receiver and opened the window.

Mary saw her and called: 'Stephen, please speak to David. He's just bitten off and swallowed a crocus! Oh, and do come here: the scyllas* are out, I never saw anything like their blueness. I think I shall go and fetch my birds, it's quite warm in the sun over there by the wall. David, stop it; *will* you get off that border!'

David wagged a bald but ingratiating tail. Then he thrust out his nose and sniffed at the pigeons. Oh, hang it all, why should the coming of spring be just one colossal smell of temptation! And why was there nothing really exciting that a spaniel might do and yet remain lawful? Sighing, he turned amber eyes of entreaty first on Stephen, and then on his goddess, Mary.

She forgave him the crocus and patted his head. 'Darling, you get more than a pound of raw meat for your dinner; you mustn't be so untruthful. Of course you're not hungry—it was just pure mischief.'

He barked, trying desperately hard to explain. 'It's the spring; it's got into my blood, oh, Goddess! Oh, Gentle Purveyor of all Good Things, let me dig till I've rooted up every damned crocus; just this once let me sin for the joy of life, for the ancient and exquisite joy of sinning!'

But Mary shook her head. 'You must be a nice dog; and nice dogs never look at white fantail pigeons, or walk on the borders, or bite off the flowers—do they, Stephen?'

Stephen smiled. 'I'm afraid they don't, David.' Then she said: 'Mary, listen—about this evening. I've just heard from a very old friend of mine, a man called Hallam that I knew in England. He's in Paris; it's too queer. He wrote to Morton and his letter has been sent back by Puddle. I've rung him up, and he's coming to dinner. Better tell Pauline at once, will you, darling?'

But Mary must naturally ask a few questions. What was he like? Where had Stephen known him?—she had never mentioned a man called Hallam—where had she known him, in London or at Morton? And finally: 'How old were you when you knew him?'

'Let me think—I must have been just eighteen.'

'How old was he?'

'Twenty-two—very young—I only knew him for quite a short time; after that he went back to British Columbia. But I liked him so much—we were very great friends—so I'm hoping that you're going to like him too, darling.'

'Stephen, you are strange. Why haven't you told me that you once had a very great friend—a man? I've always thought that you didn't like men.'

'On the contrary, I like them very much. But I haven't seen Martin for years and years. I've hardly ever thought about him until I got his letter this morning. Now, sweetheart, we don't want the poor man to starve—you really must go off and try to find Pauline.'

When she had gone Stephen rubbed her chin with thoughtful and rather uncertain fingers.

2

He came. Amazing how little he had changed. He was just the same clean-shaven, bony-faced Martin, with the slow blue eyes and the charming expression, and the loose-limbed figure that slouched from much riding; only now there were a few faint lines round his eyes, and the hair had gone snow-white on his temples. Just beside the right temple was a deep little scar—it must have been a near thing, that bullet.

He said: 'My dear, it is good to see you.' And he held Stephen's hand in his own thin brown ones.

She felt the warm, friendly grip of his fingers, and the years dropped away. 'I'm so glad you wrote, Martin.'

'So am I. I can't tell you how glad I am. And all the time we were both in Paris, and we never knew. Well, now that I've found you, we'll cling like grim death, if you don't mind, Stephen.'

As Mary came into the room they were laughing.

She looked less tired, Stephen thought with satisfaction, or perhaps it was that her dress became her—she was always at her best in the evening.

Stephen said quite simply: 'This is Martin, Mary.'

They shook hands, and as they did so they smiled. Then they stared at each other for a moment, almost gravely.

He proved to be wonderfully easy to talk to. He did not seem surprised that Mary Llewellyn was installed as the mistress of Stephen's home; he just accepted the thing as he found it. Yet he let it be tacitly understood that he had grasped the exact situation.

After dinner Stephen inquired about his sight: was it badly injured? His eyes looked so normal. Then he told them the history of the trouble at full length, going into details with the confidence displayed by most children and lonely people.

He had got his knock-out in 1918. The bullet had grazed the optic nerve. At first he had gone to a base hospital, but as soon as he could he had come to Paris to be treated by a very celebrated man. He had been in danger of losing the sight of the right eye; it had scared him to death, he told them. But after three months he had had to go home; things had gone wrong on some of his farms owing to the mismanagement of a bailiff. The oculist had warned him that the trouble might recur, that he ought to have remained under observation. Well, it had recurred about four months ago. He had got the wind up and rushed back to Paris. For three weeks he had lain in a darkened room, not daring to think of the possible verdict. Eyes were so tiresomely sympathetic: if the one went the other might easily follow. But, thank God, it had proved to be less serious than the oculist had feared. His sight was saved, but he had to go slow, and was still under treatment. The eye would have to be watched for some time; so here he was with Aunt Sarah at Passy.

'You must see my Aunt Sarah, you two; she's a darling. She's my father's sister. I know you'll like her. She's become very French since her second marriage, a little too Faubourg St. Germain* perhaps, but so kind—I want you to meet her at once. She's quite a well-known hostess at Passy.'

They talked on until well after twelve o'clock—very happy they were together that evening, and he left with a promise to ring them up on the following morning about lunch with Aunt Sarah.

'Well,' said Stephen, 'what do you think of my friend?'

'I think he's most awfully nice,' said Mary.

3

Aunt Sarah lived in the palatial house that a grateful second husband had left her. For years she had borne with his peccadilloes, keeping her temper and making no scandal. The result was that everything he possessed apart from what had gone to her stepson—and the Comte de Mirac had been very wealthy—had found its way to the patient Aunt Sarah. She was one of those survivals who look upon men as a race of especially privileged beings. Her judgment of women was more severe, influenced no doubt by the ancien régime,* for now she was even more French than the French whose language she spoke like a born Parisian.

She was sixty-five, tall, had an aquiline nose, and her iron-grey hair was dressed to perfection; for the rest she had Martin's slow blue eyes and thin face, though she lacked his charming expression. She bred Japanese spaniels, was kind to young girls who conformed in all things to the will of their parents, was particularly gracious to good-looking men, and adored her only surviving nephew. In her opinion he could do no wrong, though she wished that he would settle down in Paris. As Stephen and Mary were her nephew's friends, she was predisposed to consider them charming, the more so as the former's antecedents left little or nothing to be desired, and her parents had shown great kindness to Martin. He had told his aunt just what he wished her to know and not one word more about the old days at Morton. She was therefore quite unprepared for Stephen.

Aunt Sarah was a very courteous old dame, and those who broke bread at her table were sacred, at all events while they remained her guests. But Stephen was miserably telepathic, and before the déjeuner was half-way through, she was conscious of the deep antagonism that she had aroused in Martin's Aunt Sarah. Not by so much as a word or a look did the Comtesse de Mirac betray her feelings; she was gravely polite, she discussed literature as being a supposedly congenial subject, she praised Stephen's books, and asked no questions as to why she was living apart from her mother. Martin could have sworn that these two would be friends—but good manners could not any more deceive Stephen.

And true it was that the Comtesse de Mirac saw in Stephen the type that she most mistrusted, saw only an unsexed creature of pose, whose cropped head and whose dress were pure affectation; a creature who aping the prerogatives of men, had lost all the charm and the grace of a woman. An intelligent person in nearly all else, the Comtesse would never have admitted of inversion as a fact in nature. She had heard things whispered, it is true, but had scarcely grasped their full meaning. She was innocent and stubborn; and this being so, it was not Stephen's morals that she suspected, but her obvious desire to ape what she was not—in the Comtesse's set, as at county dinners, there was firm insistence upon sex-distinction.

On the other hand, she took a great fancy to Mary, whom she quickly discovered to be an orphan. In a very short time she had learnt quite a lot about Mary's life before the war and about her meeting with Stephen in the Unit; had learnt also that she was quite penniless—since Mary was eager that every one should know that she owed her prosperity entirely to Stephen.

Aunt Sarah secretly pitied the girl who must surely be living a dull existence, bound, no doubt, by a false sense of gratitude to this freakish and masterful-looking woman—pretty girls should find husbands and homes of their own, and this one she considered excessively pretty. Thus it was that while Mary in all loyalty and love was doing her best to extol Stephen's virtues, to convey an impression of her own happiness, of the privilege it was to serve so great a writer by caring for her house and her personal needs, she was only succeeding in getting herself pitied. But as good luck would have it, she was blissfully unconscious of the sympathy that her words were arousing; indeed she was finding it very pleasant at Aunt Sarah's hospitable house in Passy.

As for Martin, he had never been very subtle, and just now he must rejoice in a long-lost friendship—to him it appeared a delightful luncheon. Even after the guests had said good-bye, he remained in the very highest of spirits, for the Comtesse was capable of unexpected tact, and while praising Mary's prettiness and charm, she was careful in no way to disparage Stephen.

'Oh, yes, undoubtedly a brilliant writer, I agree with you, Martin.' And so she did. But books were one thing and their scribes another; she saw no reason to change her opinion with regard to this author's unpleasant affectation, while she saw every reason to be tactful with her nephew.

4

On the drive home Mary held Stephen's hand. 'I enjoyed myself awfully, didn't you? Only—' and she frowned; 'only will it last? I mean, we mustn't forget Lady Massey. But he's so nice, and I liked the old aunt . . .'

Stephen said firmly: 'Of course it will last.' Then she lied. 'I enjoyed it very much too.'

And even as she lied she came to a resolve which seemed so strange that she flinched a little, for never before since they had been lovers, had she thought of this girl as apart from herself. Yet now she resolved that Mary should go to Passy again—but should go without her. Sitting back in the car she half closed her eyes; just at that moment she did not want to speak lest her voice should betray that flinching to Mary.

CHAPTER 53

I

WITH Martin's return Stephen realized how very deeply she had missed him; how much she still needed the thing he now offered, how long indeed she had starved for just this—the friendship of a normal and sympathetic man whose mentality being very much her own, was not only welcome but reassuring. Yes, strange though it was, with this normal man she was far more at ease than with Jonathan Brockett, far more at one with all his ideas, and at times far less conscious of her own inversion; though it seemed that Martin had not only read, but had thought a great deal about the subject. He spoke very little of his studies, however, just accepting her now for the thing that she was, without question, and accepting most of her friends with a courtesy as innocent of patronage as of any suspicion of morbid interest. And thus it was that in these first days they appeared to have achieved a complete reunion. Only sometimes, when Mary would talk to him freely as she did very often of such people as Wanda, of the night life of the cafés and bars of Paris—most of which it transpired he himself had been to—of the tragedy of Barbara and Jamie that was never very far from her thoughts, even although a most perfect spring was hurrying forward towards the summer—when Mary would talk to him of these things, Martin would look rather gravely at Stephen.

But now they seldom went to the bars, for Martin provided recreations that were really much more to Mary's liking. Martin the kindly, the thoroughly normal, seemed never at a loss as to what they should do or where they should go when in search of pleasure. By now he knew Paris extremely well, and the Paris he showed them during that spring came as a complete revelation to Mary. He would often take them to dine in the Bois. At the neighbouring tables would be men and women; neat, well-tailored men; pretty, smartly dressed women who laughed and talked very conscious of sex and its vast importance—in a word, normal women. Or perhaps they would go to Claridge's for tea or to Ciro's* for dinner, and then on to supper at an equally fashionable restaurant, of which Mary discovered there were many in Paris. And although people still stared a little at Stephen, Mary fancied that they did so much less, because of the protective presence of Martin.

At such places of course, it was out of the question for a couple of women to dance together, and yet every one danced, so that in the end Mary must get up and dance with Martin.

He had said: 'You don't mind, do you, Stephen?'

She had shaken her head: 'No, of course I don't mind.' And indeed she had been very glad to know that Mary had a good partner to dance with.

But now when she sat alone at their table, lighting one cigarette from another, uncomfortably conscious of the interest she aroused by reason of her clothes and her isolation—when she glimpsed the girl in Martin's arms, and heard her laugh for a moment in passing, Stephen would know a queer tightening of her heart, as though a mailed fist had closed down upon it. What was it? Good God, surely not resentment? Horrified she would feel at this possible betrayal of friendship, of her fine, honest friendship for Martin. And when they came back, Mary smiling and flushed, Stephen would force herself to smile also.

She would say: 'I've been thinking how well you two dance—'

And when Mary once asked rather timidly: 'Are you sure you're not bored, sitting there by yourself?'

Stephen answered: 'Don't be so silly, darling; of course I'm not bored—go on dancing with Martin.'

But that night she took Mary in her arms—the relentless, compelling arms of a lover.

On warm days they would all drive into the country, as Mary and she had so frequently done during their first spring months in Paris. Very often now it would be Barbizon,* for Martin loved to walk in the forest. And there he must start to talk about trees, his face glowing with its curious inner light, while Mary listened half fascinated.

One evening she said: 'But these trees are so small—you make me long to see real forests, Martin.'

David loved these excursions—he also loved Martin, not being exactly disloyal to Stephen, but discerning in the man a more perfect thing, a more entirely fulfilling companion. And this little betrayal, though slight in itself, had the power to wound out of all proportion, so that Stephen would feel very much as she had done when ignored years ago by the swan called Peter. She had thought then: 'Perhaps he thinks I'm a freak,' and now she must sometimes think the same thing as she watched Martin hurling huge sticks for David—it was strange what a number of ridiculous trifles had lately acquired the power to hurt her. And yet she clung desperately to Martin's friendship, feeling herself to be all unworthy if she harboured so much as a moment's doubt; indeed they both loyally clung to their friendship.

He would beg her to accept his aunt's invitations, to accompany Mary when she went to Passy:

'Don't you like the old thing? Mary likes her all right—why won't you come? It's so mean of you, Stephen. It's not half as much fun when you're not there.' He would honestly think that he was speaking the truth, that the party or the luncheon or whatever it might be, was not half as much fun for him without Stephen.

But Stephen always made her work an excuse: 'My dear, I'm trying to finish a novel. I seem to have been at it for years and years; it's growing hoary like Rip Van Winkle.'*

2

There were times when their friendship seemed well nigh perfect, the perfect thing that they would have it to be, and on such a day of complete understanding, Stephen suddenly spoke to Martin about Morton.

They two were alone together in her study, and she said: 'There's something I want to tell you—you must often have wondered why I left my home.'

He nodded: 'I've never quite liked to ask, because I know how you loved the place, how you love it still . . .'

'Yes, I love it,' she answered.

Then she let every barrier go down before him, blissfully conscious of what she was doing. Not since Puddle had left her had she been able to talk without restraint of her exile. And once launched she had not the least wish to stop, but must tell him all, omitting no detail save one that honour forbade her to give—she withheld the name of Angela Crossby.

'It's so terribly hard on Mary,' she finished; 'think of it, Mary's never seen Morton; she's not even met Puddle in all these years! Of course Puddle can't very well come here to stay—how can she and then go back to Morton? And yet I want her to live with my mother . . . But the whole thing seems so outrageous for Mary.' She went on to talk to him of her father: 'If my father had lived, I know he'd have helped me. He loved me so much, and he understood—I found out that my father knew all about me, only—' She hesitated, and then: 'Perhaps he loved me too much to tell me.'

Martin said nothing for quite a long time, and when he did speak it was very gravely: 'Mary—how much does she know of all this?'

'As little as I could possibly tell her. She knows that I can't get on with my mother, and that my mother won't ask her to Morton; but she doesn't know that I had to leave home because of a woman, that I was turned out—I've wanted to spare her all I could.'

'Do you think you were right?'

'Yes, a thousand times.'

'Well, only you can judge of that, Stephen.' He looked down at the carpet, then he asked abruptly: 'Does she know about you and me, about . . .'

Stephen shook her head: 'No, she's no idea. She thinks you were just my very good friend as you are to-day. I don't want her to know.'

'For my sake?' he demanded.

And she answered slowly: 'Well, yes, I suppose so . . . for your sake, Martin.'

Then an unexpected, and to her very moving thing happened; his eyes filled with pitiful tears: 'Lord,' he muttered, 'why need this have come upon you—this incomprehensible dispensation? It's enough to make one deny God's existence!'

She felt a great need to reassure him. At that moment he seemed so much younger than she was as he stood there with his eyes full of pitiful tears, doubting God, because of his human compassion: 'There are still the trees. Don't forget the trees, Martin—because of them you used to believe.'

'Have you come to believe in a God then?' he muttered.

'Yes,' she told him, 'it's strange, but I know now I must—lots of us feel that way in the end. I'm not really religious like some of the others, but I've got to acknowledge God's existence, though at times I still think: "Can He really exist?" One can't help it, when one's seen what I have here in Paris. But unless there's a God, where do some of us find even the little courage we possess?'

Martin stared out of the window in silence.

3

Mary was growing gentle again; infinitely gentle she now was at times, for happiness makes for gentleness, and in these days Mary was strangely happy. Reassured by the presence of Martin Hallam, re-established in pride and self-respect, she was able to contemplate the world without her erstwhile sense of isolation, was able for the moment to sheathe her sword, and this respite brought her a sense of well-being. She discovered that at heart she was neither so courageous nor so defiant as she had imagined, that like many another woman before her, she was well content to feel herself protected; and gradually as the weeks went by, she began to forget her bitter resentment.

One thing only distressed her, and this was Stephen's refusal to accompany her when she went to Passy; she could not understand it, so must put it down to the influence of Valérie Seymour who had met and disliked Martin's aunt at one time, indeed the dislike, it seemed, had been mutual. Thus the vague resentment that Valérie had inspired in the girl, began to grow much less vague, until Stephen realized with a shock of surprise that Mary was jealous of Valérie Seymour. But this seemed so absurd and preposterous a thing, that Stephen decided it could only be passing, nor did it loom very large in these days that were so fully taken up by Martin. For now that his eyesight was quite restored he was talking of going home in the autumn, and every free moment that he could steal from his aunt, he wanted to spend with Stephen and Mary. When he spoke of his departure, Stephen sometimes fancied that a shade of sadness crept into Mary's face, and her heart misgave her, though she told herself that naturally both of them would miss Martin. Then, too, never had Mary been more loyal and devoted, more obviously anxious to prove her love by a thousand little acts of devotion. There would even be times when by contrast her manner would appear abrupt and unfriendly to Martin, when she argued with him over every trifle, backing up her opinion by quoting Stephen—yes, in spite of her newly restored gentleness, there were times when she would not be gentle with Martin. And these sudden and unforeseen changes of mood would leave Stephen feeling uneasy and bewildered, so that one night she spoke rather anxiously:

'Why were you so beastly to Martin this evening?'

But Mary pretended not to understand her: 'How was I beastly? I was just as usual.' And when Stephen persisted, Mary kissed her scar: 'Darling, don't start working now, it's so late, and besides . . .'

Stephen put away her work, then she suddenly caught the girl to her roughly: 'How much do you love me? Tell me quickly, quickly!' Her voice shook with something very like fear.

'Stephen, you're hurting me—don't, you're hurting! You know how I love you—more than life.'

'You are my life . . . all my life,' muttered Stephen.

CHAPTER 54

I

FATE, which by now had them well in its grip, began to play the game out more quickly. That summer they went to Pontresina* since Mary had never seen Switzerland; but the Comtesse must make a double cure,* first at Vichy and afterwards at Bagnoles de l'Orne, which fact left Martin quite free to join them. Then it was that Stephen perceived for the first time that all was not well with Martin Hallam.

Try as he might he could not deceive her, for this man was almost painfully honest, and any deception became him so ill that it seemed to stand out like a badly fitting garment. Yet now there were times when he avoided her eyes, when he grew very silent and awkward with Stephen, as though something inevitable and unhappy had obtruded itself upon their friendship; something, moreover, that he feared to tell her. Then one day in a blinding flash of insight she suddenly knew what this was—it was Mary.

Like a blow that is struck full between the eyes, the thing stunned her, so that at first she groped blindly. Martin, her friend . . . But what did it mean? And Mary . . . The incredible misery of it if it were true. But was it true that Martin Hallam had grown to love Mary? And the other thought, more incredible still—had Mary in her turn grown to love Martin?

The mist gradually cleared; Stephen grew cold as steel, her perceptions becoming as sharp as daggers—daggers that thrust themselves into her soul, draining the blood from her innermost being. And she watched. To herself she seemed all eyes and ears, a monstrous thing, a complete degradation, yet endowed with an almost unbearable skill, with a subtlety passing her own understanding.

And Martin was no match for this thing that was Stephen. He, the lover, could not hide his betraying eyes from her eyes that were also those of a lover; could not stifle the tone that crept into his voice at times when he was talking to Mary. Since all that he felt was a part of herself, how could he hope to hide it from Stephen? And he knew that she had discovered the truth, while she in her turn perceived that he knew this, yet neither of them spoke—in a deathly silence she watched, and in silence he endured her watching.

It was rather a terrible summer for them all, the more so as they were surrounded by beauty, and great peace when the evening came down on the snows, turning the white, unfurrowed peaks to sapphire and then to a purple darkness; hanging out large, incredible stars above the wide slope of the Roseg Glacier. For their hearts were full of unspoken dread, of clamorous passions, of bewilderment that went very ill with the quiet fulfilments, with the placid and smiling contentment of nature—and not the least bewildered was Mary. Her respite, it seemed, had been pitifully fleeting; now she was torn by conflicting emotions; terrified and amazed at her realization that Martin meant more to her than a friend, yet less, oh, surely much less than Stephen. Like a barrier of fire her passion for the woman flared up to forbid her love of the man; for as great as the mystery of virginity itself, is sometimes the power of the one who has destroyed it, and that power still remained in these days, with Stephen.*

Alone in his bare little hotel bedroom, Martin would wrestle with his soul-sickening problem, convinced in his heart that but for Stephen, Mary Llewellyn would grow to love him, nay more, that she had grown to love him already. Yet Stephen was his friend—he had sought her out, had all but forced his friendship upon her; had forced his way into her life, her home, her confidence; she had trusted his honour. And now he must either utterly betray her or through loyalty to their friendship, betray Mary.

And he felt that he knew, and knew only too well, what life would do to Mary Llewellyn, what it had done to her already; for had he not seen the bitterness in her, the resentment that could only lead to despair, the defiance that could only lead to disaster? She was setting her weakness against the whole world, and slowly but surely the world would close in until in the end it had utterly crushed her. In her very normality lay her danger. Mary, all woman, was less of a match for life than if she had been as was Stephen. Oh, most pitiful bond, so strong yet so helpless; so fruitful of passion yet so bitterly sterile; despairing, heart-breaking, yet courageous bond that was even now holding them ruthlessly together. But if he should break it by taking the girl away into peace and security, by winning for her the world's approbation so that never again need her back feel the scourge and her heart grow faint from the pain of that scourging—if he, Martin Hallam, should do this thing, what would happen, in that day of his victory, to Stephen? Would she still have the courage to continue the fight? Or would she, in her turn, be forced to surrender? God help him, he could not betray her like this, he could not bring about Stephen's destruction—and yet if he spared her, he might destroy Mary.

Night after night alone in his bedroom during the miserable weeks of that summer, Martin struggled to discover some ray of hope in what seemed a wellnigh hopeless situation. And night after night Stephen's masterful arms would enfold the warm softness of Mary's body, the while she would be shaken as though with great cold. Lying there she would shiver with terror and love, and this torment of hers would envelop Mary so that sometimes she wept for the pain of it all, yet neither would give a name to that torment.

'Stephen, why are you shivering?'

'I don't know, my darling.'

'Mary, why are you crying?'

'I don't know, Stephen.'

Thus the bitter nights slipped into the days, and the anxious days slipped back into the nights, bringing to that curious trinity neither helpful counsel nor consolation.

2

It was after they had all returned to Paris that Martin found Stephen alone one morning.

He said: 'I want to speak to you—I must.'

She put down her pen and looked into his eyes: 'Well, Martin, what is it?' But she knew already.

He answered her very simply: 'It's Mary.' Then he said: 'I'm going because I'm your friend and I love her . . . I must go because of our friendship, and because I think Mary's grown to care for me.'

He thought Mary cared . . . Stephen got up slowly, and all of a sudden she was no more herself but the whole of her kind out to combat this man, out to vindicate their right to possess, out to prove that their courage was unshakable, that they neither admitted of nor feared any rival.

She said coldly: 'If you're going because of me, because you imagine that I'm frightened—then stay. I assure you I'm not in the least afraid; here and now I defy you to take her from me!' And even as she said this she marvelled at herself, for she was afraid, terribly afraid of Martin.

He flushed at the quiet contempt in her voice, which roused all the combative manhood in him: 'You think that Mary doesn't love me, but you're wrong.'

'Very well then, prove that I'm wrong!' she told him.

They stared at each other in bitter hostility for a moment, then Stephen said more gently: 'You don't mean to insult me by what you propose, but I won't consent to your going, Martin. You think that I can't hold the woman I love against you, because you've got an advantage over me and over the whole of my kind. I accept that challenge—I must accept it if I'm to remain at all worthy of Mary.'

He bowed his head: 'It must be as you wish.' Then he suddenly began to talk rather quickly: 'Stephen, listen, I hate what I'm going to say, but by God, it's got to be said to you somehow! You're courageous and fine and you mean to make good, but life with you is spiritually murdering Mary. Can't you see it? Can't you realize that she needs all the things that it's not in your power to give her? Children, protection, friends whom she can respect and who'll respect her—don't you realize this, Stephen? A few may survive such relationships as yours, but Mary Llewellyn won't be among them. She's not strong enough to fight the whole world, to stand up against persecution and insult; it will drive her down, it's begun to already—already she's been forced to turn to people like Wanda. I know what I'm saying, I've seen the thing—the bars, the drinking, the pitiful defiance, the horrible, useless wastage of lives—well, I tell you it's spiritual murder for Mary. I'd have gone away because you're my friend, but before I went I'd have said all this to you; I'd have begged and implored you to set Mary free if you love her. I'd have gone on my knees to you, Stephen . . .'

He paused, and she heard herself saying quite calmly: 'You don't understand, I have faith in my writing, great faith; some day I shall climb to the top and that will compel the world to accept me for what I am. It's a matter of time, but I mean to succeed for Mary's sake.'

'God pity you!' he suddenly blurted out. 'Your triumph, if it comes, will come too late for Mary.'

She stared at him aghast: 'How dare you!' she stammered, 'How dare you try to undermine my courage! You call yourself my friend and you say things like that . . .'

'It's your courage that I appeal to,' he answered. He began to speak very quietly again: 'Stephen, if I stay I'm going to fight you. Do you understand? We'll fight this thing out until one of us has to admit that he's beaten. I'll do all in my power to take Mary from you—all that's honourable, that is—for I mean to play straight, because whatever you may think I'm your friend, only, you see—I love Mary Llewellyn.'

And now she struck back. She said rather slowly, watching his sensitive face as she did so: 'You seem to have thought it all out very well, but then of course our friendship has given you time . . .'

He flinched and she smiled, knowing how she could wound: 'Perhaps,' she went on, 'you'll tell me your plans. Supposing you win, do I give the wedding? Is Mary to marry you from my house,* or would that be a grave social disadvantage? And supposing she should want to leave me quite soon for love of you—where would you take her, Martin? To your aunt's for respectability's sake?'

'Don't, Stephen!'

'But why not? I've a right to know because, you see, I also love Mary, I also consider her reputation. Yes, I think on the whole we'll discuss your plans.'

'She'd always be welcome at my aunt's,' he said firmly.

'And you'll take her there if she runs away to you? One never knows what may happen, does one? You say that she cares for you already . . .'

His eyes hardened: 'If Mary will have me, Stephen, I shall take her first to my aunt's house in Passy.'

'And then?' she mocked.

'I shall marry her from there.'

'And then?'

'I shall take her back to my home.'

'To Canada—I see—a safe distance of course.'

He held out his hand: 'Oh, for God's sake, don't! It's so horrible somehow—be merciful, Stephen.'

She laughed bitterly: 'Why should I be merciful to you? Isn't it enough that I accept your challenge, that I offer you the freedom of my house, that I don't turn you out and forbid you to come here? Come by all means, whenever you like. You may even repeat our conversation to Mary; I shall not do so, but don't let that stop you if you think you may possibly gain some advantage.'

He shook his head: 'No, I shan't repeat it.'

'Oh, well, that must be as you think best. *I* propose to behave as though nothing had happened—and now I must get along with my work.'

He hesitated: 'Won't you shake hands?'

'Of course,' she smiled; 'aren't you my very good friend? But you know, you really must leave me now, Martin.'

3

After he had gone she lit a cigarette; the action was purely automatic. She felt strangely excited yet strangely numb—a most curious synthesis of sensations; then she suddenly felt deathly sick and giddy. Going up to her bedroom she bathed her face, sat down on the bed and tried to think, conscious that her mind was completely blank. She was thinking of nothing—not even of Mary.

CHAPTER 55

I

A BITTER and most curious warfare it was that must now be waged between Martin and Stephen, but secretly waged, lest because of them the creature they loved should be brought to suffer; not the least strange aspect being that these two must quite often take care to protect each other, setting a guard upon eyes and lips when they found themselves together with Mary. For the sake of the girl whom they sought to protect, they must actually often protect each other. Neither would stoop to detraction or malice: though they fought in secret, they did so with honour. And all the while their hearts cried out loudly against this cruel and insidious thing that had laid its hand upon their doomed friendship—verily a bitter and most curious warfare.

And now Stephen, brought suddenly face to face with the menace of infinite desolation, fell back upon her every available weapon in the struggle to assert her right to possession. Every link that the years had forged between her and Mary, every tender and passionate memory that bound their past to their ardent present, every moment of joy—aye, and even of sorrow, she used in sheer self-defence against Martin. And not the least powerful of all her weapons, was the perfect companionship and understanding that constitutes the great strength of such unions. Well armed she was, thanks to both present and past—but Martin's sole weapon lay in the future.

With a new subtlety that was born of his love, he must lead the girl's thoughts very gently forward towards a life of security and peace; such a life as marriage with him would offer. In a thousand little ways must redouble his efforts to make himself indispensable to her, to surround her with the warm, happy cloak of protection that made even a hostile world seem friendly. And although he forbore to speak openly as yet, playing his hand with much skill and patience—although before speaking he wished to be certain that Mary Llewellyn, of her own free will, would come when he called her, because she loved him—yet nevertheless she divined his love, for men cannot hide such knowledge from women.

Very pitiful Mary was in these days, torn between the two warring forces; haunted by a sense of disloyalty if she thought with unhappiness of losing Martin, hating herself for a treacherous coward if she sometimes longed for the life he could offer, above all intensely afraid of this man who was creeping in between her and Stephen. And the very fact of this fear made her yield to the woman with a new and more desperate ardour, so that the bond held as never before—the days might be Martin's, but the nights were Stephen's. And yet, lying awake far into the dawn, Stephen's victory would take on the semblance of defeat, turned to ashes by the memory of Martin's words: 'Your triumph, if it comes, will come too late for Mary.' In the morning she would go to her desk and write, working with something very like frenzy, as though it were now a neck-to-neck race between the world and her ultimate achievement. Never before had she worked like this; she would feel that her pen was dipped in blood, that with every word she wrote, she was bleeding!

2

Christmas came and went, giving place to the New Year, and Martin fought on but he fought more grimly. He was haunted these days by the spectre of defeat, painfully conscious that do what he might, nearly every advantage lay with Stephen. All that he loved and admired most in Mary, her frankness, her tender and loyal spirit, her compassion towards suffering of any kind, these very attributes told against him, serving as they did to bind her more firmly to the creature to whom she had given devotion. One thing only sustained the man at this time, and that was his conviction that in spite of it all, Mary Llewellyn had grown to love him.

So careful she was when they were together, so guarded lest she should betray her feelings, so pitifully insistent that all was yet well—that life had in no way lessened her courage. But Martin was not deceived by these protests, knowing how she clung to what he could offer, how gladly she turned to the simple things that so easily come to those who are normal. Under all her parade of gallantry he divined a great weariness of spirit, a great longing to be at peace with the world, to be able to face her fellow-men with the comforting knowledge that she need not fear them, that their friendship would be hers for the asking, that their laws and their codes would be her protection. All this Martin perceived; but Stephen's perceptions were even more accurate and far-reaching, for to her there had come the despairing knowledge that the woman she loved was deeply unhappy. At first she had blinded herself to this truth, sustained by the passionate stress of the battle, by her power to hold in despite of the man, by the eager response that she had awakened. Yet the day came when she was no longer blind, when nothing counted in all the world except this grievous unhappiness that was being silently borne by Mary.

Martin, if he had wished for revenge, might have taken his fill of it now from Stephen. Little did he know how, one by one, Mary was weakening her defences; gradually undermining her will, her fierce determination to hold, the arrogance of the male that was in her. All this the man was never to know; it was Stephen's secret, and she knew how to keep it. But one night she suddenly pushed Mary away, blindly, scarcely knowing what she was doing; conscious only that the weapon she thus laid aside had become a thing altogether unworthy, an outrage upon her love for this girl. And that night there followed the terrible thought that her love itself was a kind of outrage.

And now she must pay very dearly indeed for that inherent respect of the normal which nothing had ever been able to destroy, not even the long years of persecution—an added burden it was, handed down by the silent but watchful founders of Morton. She must pay for the instinct which, in earliest childhood, had made her feel something akin to worship for the perfect thing which she had divined in the love that existed between her parents. Never before had she seen so clearly all that was lacking to Mary Llewellyn, all that would pass from her faltering grasp, perhaps never to return, with the passing of Martin—children, a home that the world would respect, ties of affection that the world would hold sacred, the blessèd security and the peace of being released from the world's persecution. And suddenly Martin appeared to Stephen as a creature endowed with incalculable bounty, having in his hands all those priceless gifts which she, love's mendicant,* could never offer. Only one gift could she offer to love, to Mary, and that was the gift of Martin.

In a kind of dream she perceived these things. In a dream she now moved and had her being; scarcely conscious of whither this dream would lead, the while her every perception was quickened. And this dream of hers was immensely compelling, so that all that she did seemed clearly predestined; she could not have acted otherwise, nor could she have made a false step, although dreaming. Like those who in sleep tread the edge of a chasm unappalled, having lost all sense of danger, so now

Stephen walked on the brink of her fate, having only one fear; a nightmare fear of what she must do to give Mary her freedom.

In obedience to the mighty but unseen will that had taken control of this vivid dreaming, she ceased to respond to the girl's tenderness, nor would she consent that they two should be lovers. Ruthless as the world itself she became, and almost as cruel in this ceaseless wounding. For in spite of Mary's obvious misgivings, she went more and more often to see Valérie Seymour, so that gradually, as the days slipped by, Mary's mind became a prey to suspicion. Yet Stephen struck at her again and again, desperately wounding herself in the process, though scarcely feeling the pain of her wounds for the misery of what she was doing to Mary. But even as she struck the bonds seemed to tighten, with each fresh blow to bind more securely. Mary now clung with every fibre of her sorely distressed and outraged being; with every memory that Stephen had stirred; with every passion that Stephen had fostered; with every instinct of loyalty that Stephen had aroused to do battle with Martin. The hand that had loaded Mary with chains was powerless, it seemed, to strike them from her.

Came the day when Mary refused to see Martin, when she turned upon Stephen, pale and accusing: 'Can't you understand? Are you utterly blind—have you only got eyes now for Valérie Seymour?'

And as though she were suddenly smitten dumb, Stephen's lips remained closed and she answered nothing.

Then Mary wept and cried out against her: 'I won't let you go—I won't let you, I tell you! It's your fault if I love you the way I do. I can't do without you, you've taught me to need you, and now . . .' In half-shamed, half-defiant words she must stand there and plead for what Stephen withheld, and Stephen must listen to such pleading from Mary. Then before the girl realized it she had said: 'But for you, I could have loved Martin Hallam!'

Stephen heard her own voice a long way away: 'But for me, you could have loved Martin Hallam.'

Mary flung despairing arms round her neck: 'No, no! Not that, I don't know what I'm saying.'

3

The first faint breath of spring was in the air, bringing daffodils to the flower-stalls of Paris. Once again Mary's young cherry tree in the garden was pushing out leaves and tiny pink buds along the whole length of its childish branches.

Then Martin wrote: 'Stephen, where can I see you? It must be alone. Better not at your house, I think, if you don't mind, because of Mary.'

She appointed the place. They would meet at the Auberge du Vieux Logis* in the Rue Lepic. They two would meet there on the following evening. When she left the house without saying a word, Mary thought she was going to Valérie Seymour.

Stephen sat down at a table in the corner to await Martin's coming—she herself was early. The table was gay with a new check cloth—red and white, white and red, she counted the squares, tracing them carefully out with her finger. The woman behind the bar nudged her companion: 'En voilà une originale—et quelle cicatrice, bon Dieu!'* The scar across Stephen's pale face stood out livid.

Martin came and sat quietly down at her side, ordering some coffee for appearances' sake. For appearances' sake, until it was brought, they smiled at each other and made conversation. But when the waiter had turned away, Martin said: 'It's all over—you've beaten me, Stephen . . . The bond was too strong.'

Their unhappy eyes met as she answered: 'I tried to strengthen that bond.'

He nodded: 'I know . . . Well, my dear, you succeeded.' Then he said: 'I'm leaving Paris next week'; and in spite of his effort to be calm his voice broke, 'Stephen . . . do what you can to take care of Mary . . .'

She found that she was holding his hand. Or was it some one else who sat there beside him, who looked into his sensitive, troubled face, who spoke such queer words?

'No, don't go—not yet.'

'But I don't understand . . .'

'You must trust me, Martin.' And now she heard herself speaking very gravely: 'Would you trust me enough to do anything I asked, even although it seemed rather strange? Would you trust me if I said that I asked it for Mary, for her happiness?'

His fingers tightened: 'Before God, yes. You know that I'd trust you!'

'Very well then, don't leave Paris—not now.'

'You really want me to stay on, Stephen?'

'Yes, I can't explain.'

He hesitated, then he suddenly seemed to come to a decision: 'All right . . . I'll do whatever you ask me.'

They paid for their coffee and got up to leave: 'Let me come as far as the house,' he pleaded.

But she shook her head: 'No, no, not now. I'll write to you . . . very soon . . . Good-bye, Martin.'

She watched him hurrying down the street, and when he was finally lost in its shadows, she turned slowly and made her own way up the hill, past the garish lights of the Moulin de la Galette.* Its pitiful sails revolved in the wind, eternally grinding out petty sins—dry chaff blown in from the gutters of Paris. And after a while, having breasted the hill, she must climb a dusty flight of stone steps, and push open a heavy, slow-moving door; the door of the mighty temple of faith* that keeps its anxious but tireless vigil.

She had no idea why she was doing this thing, or what she would say to the silver Christ with one hand on His heart and the other held out in a patient gesture of supplication. The sound of praying, monotonous, low, insistent, rose up from those who prayed with extended arms, with crucified arms—like the tides of an ocean it swelled and receded and swelled again, bathing the shores of heaven.

They were calling upon the Mother of God: 'Sainte Marie, Mère de Dieu, priez pour nous, pauvres pêcheurs, maintenant et à l'heure de notre mort.'*

'Et à l'heure de notre mort,' Stephen heard herself repeating.

He looked terribly weary, the silver Christ: 'But then He always looks tired,' she thought vaguely; and she stood there without finding anything to say, embarrassed as one so frequently is in the presence of somebody else's sorrow. For herself she felt nothing, neither pity nor regret; she was curiously empty of all sensation, and after a little she left the church, to walk on through the wind-swept streets of Montmartre.

CHAPTER 56

1

VALÉRIE stared at Stephen in amazement: 'But . . . it's such an extraordinary thing you're asking! Are you sure you're right to take such a step? For myself I care nothing; why should I care? If you want to pretend that you're my lover, well, my dear, to be quite frank, I wish it were true—I feel certain you'd make a most charming lover. All the same,' and now her voice sounded anxious, 'this is not a thing to be done lightly, Stephen. Aren't you being absurdly self-sacrificing? You can give the girl a very great deal.'

Stephen shook her head: 'I can't give her protection or happiness, and yet she won't leave me. There's only one way . . .'

Then Valérie Seymour, who had always shunned tragedy like the plague, flared out in something very like temper: 'Protection! Protection! I'm sick of the word. Let her do without it; aren't you enough for her? Good heavens, you're worth twenty Mary Llewellyns! Stephen, think it over before you decide—it seems mad to me. For God's sake keep the girl, and get what happiness you can out of life.'

'No, I can't do that,' said Stephen dully.

Valérie got up: 'Being what you are, I suppose you can't—you were made for a martyr! Very well, I agree'; she finished abruptly, 'though of all the curious situations that I've ever been in, this one beats the lot!'

That night Stephen wrote to Martin Hallam.

2

Two days later as she crossed the street to her house, Stephen saw Martin in the shadow of the archway. He stepped out and they faced each other on the pavement. He had kept his word; it was just ten o'clock.

He said: 'I've come. Why did you send for me, Stephen?'

She answered heavily: 'Because of Mary.'

And something in her face made him catch his breath, so that the questions died on his lips: 'I'll do whatever you want,' he murmured.

'It's so simple,' she told him, 'it's all perfectly simple. I want you to wait just under this arch—just here where you can't be seen from the house. I want you to wait until Mary needs you, as I think she will . . . it may not be long . . . Can I count on your being here if she needs you?'

He nodded: 'Yes—yes!' He was utterly bewildered, scared too by the curious look in her eyes; but he allowed her to pass him and enter the courtyard.

3

SHE let herself into the house with her latch-key. The place seemed full of an articulate silence that leapt out shouting from every corner—a jibing, grimacing, vindictive silence. She brushed it aside with a sweep of her hand, as though it were some sort of physical presence.

But who was it who brushed that silence aside? Not Stephen Gordon . . . oh, no, surely not . . . Stephen Gordon was dead; she had died last night: 'A l'heure de notre mort . . .' Many people had spoken those prophetic words quite a short time ago—perhaps they had been thinking of Stephen Gordon.

Yet now some one was slowly climbing the stairs, then pausing upon the landing to listen, then opening the door of Mary's bedroom, then standing quite still and staring at Mary. It was some one whom David knew and loved well; he sprang forward with a sharp little bark of welcome. But Mary shrank back as though she had been struck—Mary pale and red-eyed from sleeplessness—or was it because of excessive weeping?

When she spoke her voice sounded unfamiliar: 'Where were you last night?'

'With Valérie Seymour. I thought you'd know somehow . . . It's better to be frank . . . we both hate lies . . .'

Came that queer voice again: 'Good God—and I've tried so hard not to believe it! Tell me you're lying to me now; say it, Stephen!'

Stephen—then she wasn't dead after all; or was she? But now Mary was clinging—clinging.

'Stephen, I can't believe this thing—Valérie! Is that why you always repulse me . . . why you never want to come near me these days? Stephen, answer me; are you her lover? Say something, for Christ's sake! Don't stand there dumb . . .'

A mist closing down, a thick black mist. Some one pushing the girl away, without speaking. Mary's queer voice coming out of the gloom, muffled by the folds of that thick black mist, only a word here and there getting through: 'All my life I've given . . . you've killed . . . I loved you . . . Cruel, oh, cruel! You're unspeakably cruel . . .' Then the sound of rough and pitiful sobbing.

No, assuredly this was not Stephen Gordon who stood there unmoved by such pitiful sobbing. But what was the figure doing in the mist? It was moving about, distractedly, wildly. All the while it sobbed it was moving about: 'I'm going . . .'

Going? But where could it go? Somewhere out of the mist, somewhere into the light? Who was it that had said . . . wait, what were the words? 'To give light to them that sit in darkness . . .'*

No one was moving about any more—there was only a dog, a dog called David. Something had to be done. Go into the bedroom, Stephen Gordon's bedroom that faced on the courtyard . . . just a few short steps and then the window. A girl, hatless, with the sun falling full on her hair . . . she was almost running . . . she stumbled a little. But now there were two people down in the courtyard—a man had his hands on the girl's bowed shoulders. He questioned her, yes, that was it, he questioned; and the girl was telling him why she was there, why she had fled from that thick, awful darkness. He was looking at the house, incredulous, amazed; hesitating as though he were coming in; but the girl went on and the man turned to follow . . . They were side by side, he was gripping her arm . . . They were gone; they had passed out under the archway.

Then all in a moment the stillness was shattered; 'Mary, come back! Come back to me, Mary!'

David crouched and trembled. He had crawled to the bed, and he lay there watching with his eyes of amber; trembling because such an anguish as this struck across him like the lash of a whip, and what could he do, the poor beast, in his dumbness?

She turned and saw him, but only for a moment, for now the room seemed to be thronging with people. Who were they, these strangers with the miserable eyes? And yet, were they all strangers? Surely that was Wanda? And some one with a neat little hole in her side—Jamie clasping Barbara by the hand; Barbara with the white flowers of death on her bosom. Oh, but they were many, these unbidden guests, and they called very softly at first and then louder.

They were calling her by name, saying: 'Stephen, Stephen!' The quick, the dead, and the yet unborn—all calling her, softly at first and then louder. Aye, and those lost and terrible brothers from Alec's, they were here, and they also were calling: 'Stephen, Stephen, speak with your God and ask Him why He has left us forsaken!' She could see their marred and reproachful faces with the haunted, melancholy eyes of the invert—eyes that had looked too long on a world that lacked all pity and all understanding: 'Stephen, Stephen, speak with your God and ask Him why He has left us forsaken!' And these terrible ones started pointing at her with their shaking, white-skinned, effeminate fingers: 'You and your kind have stolen our birthright; you have taken our strength and have given us your weakness!' They were pointing at her with white, shaking fingers.

Rockets of pain, burning rockets of pain—their pain, her pain, all welded together into one great consuming agony. Rockets of pain that shot up and burst, dropping scorching tears of fire on the spirit—her pain, their pain . . . all the misery at Alec's. And the press and the clamour of those countless others—they fought, they trampled, they were getting her under. In their madness to become articulate through her, they were tearing her to pieces, getting her under. They were everywhere now, cutting off her retreat; neither bolts nor bars would avail to save her. The walls fell down and crumbled before them; at the cry of their suffering the walls fell and crumbled: 'We are coming, Stephen—we are still coming on, and our name is legion*—you dare not disown us!' She raised her arms, trying to ward them off, but they closed in and in: 'You dare not disown us!'

They possessed her. Her barren womb became fruitful—it ached with its fearful and sterile burden. It ached with the fierce yet helpless children who would clamour in vain for their right to salvation. They would turn first to God, and then to the world, and then to her. They would cry out accusing: 'We have asked for bread; will you give us a stone? Answer us: will you give us a stone? You, God, in Whom we, the outcast, believe; you, world, into which we are pitilessly born; you, Stephen, who have drained our cup to the dregs—we have asked for bread; will you give us a stone?'*

And now there was only one voice, one demand; her own voice into which those millions had entered. A voice like the awful, deep rolling of thunder; a demand like the gathering together of great waters.

A terrifying voice that made her ears throb, that made her brain throb, that shook her very entrails, until she must stagger and all but fall beneath this appalling burden of sound that strangled her in its will to be uttered.

'God,' she gasped, 'we believe; we have told You we believe . . . We have not denied You, then rise up and defend us. Acknowledge us, oh God, before the whole world. Give us also the right to our existence!'

THE END

APPENDIX

THIS Appendix includes selected extracts from Radclyffe Hall's drafts of *The Well of Loneliness*, housed in the Radclyffe Hall and Una Vincenzo, Lady Troubridge Papers at the Harry Ransom Center, University of Texas at Austin (hereafter Hall–Troubridge Papers: container numbers from the archive are provided in brackets in the heading for each extract). Unless stated otherwise, extracts are from RH's handwritten notebooks. Signposts to the relevant points in this Appendix are included in the Explanatory Notes. It has not always been possible to decipher Hall's handwriting, and any illegible words in the notes are represented by '[?]'. Hall's idiosyncratic spellings have either been marked with '[*sic*]' or corrected in square brackets.

1.1 (Hall–Troubridge Papers, 13.2)

Anna is 'deeply disturbed and anxious about Stephen, who although seventeen was not yet a woman':

> Came the day when Anna spoke shyly to Stephen, explaining what she felt should be explained, prepairing [*sic*] the girl for the coming of womanhood and blushing deeply the while she did so. Nor did Stephen assist this halting explanation, but rather she hindered by her ominous silence, by the gloom on her brough [*sic*], and the look of deep depression that gathered in her brooding eyes.
>
> 'So you see, my darling,' concluded Anna finally, 'Nature is a wonderful thing after all.'
>
> Stephen said nothing, but later, in the schoolroom, she took Puddle by the shoulders and shook her to attention.
>
> 'I can't bear it,' she told her. 'It's all Hell, Puddle, but perhaps it's not going to happen—not to me.'

Stephen continues to seek solace in Puddle, who tells her that she 'fail[s] to see why you should be exempt, come to think of it, any more than I was, Stephen.'

> 'You!' gasped Stephen, 'but Puddle your [*sic*] different, your [sic] different to me—your [*sic*] a woman, a real woman I mean.'

1.2 (Hall–Troubridge Papers, 13.2)

In an early draft of Chapter 9, RH writes:

> Mrs Antrim had taken to saying quite lately, 'I can't stand these masculine girls—they're so odd'. She was always most careful to speak in the plural—to hear her was to think that the county had an army of unsexed young females, yet somehow or other when ever she said this people[']s

thoughts turned to Stephen, not exactly unkindly but with a new interest that was very slightly suspicious. [. . .] Thus it was that they grew to look upon Stephen as a kind of affliction, and they dreaded afflictions. They were very polight [*sic*] as one is to a cripple, while avoiding the appearance of too intimate a knowledge.

1.3 (Hall–Troubridge Papers, 12.4)

The draft provides more detail about Anna's hopes for Stephen's future with Martin:

> He and Stephen could go in for pedigree cattle, Tenley Court had three farms and some excellent pasture. Or why not breed hunters? There'd be plenty of money, Martin Hallam was rich, a Hallam, they were all very rich.

2.1 (Hall–Troubridge Papers, 13.3)

> 'I love you—you hurt me terribly Morton, because you make me remember, and yet I adore you. I shall never leave you as long as you need me, as long as you'll have me.' She would talk to Morton as though it had ears and a heart that grieved with a great understanding, imagining in its very dumbness an appeal: 'Stephen, Stephen, don[']t leave me Stephen!' 'Why should I leave you?' she would answer gently, 'he loved you, my father, he taught me to love you.'

2.2 (Hall–Troubridge Papers, 13.3)

> A tearless woman because by his going, Sir Philip had taken a part of her with him, the part of her woman[']s soul that could weap [*sic*] he had taken away by his going. Dry eyed and calm, with a terrible calmness she moved about Morton caring for its wellfair [*sic*]. And sometimes she would seem more dead to her child than the father who lay still under his gravestone [. . .] And another torment must Anna endure, the knowledge of complete and soul-sickening failiour [*sic*] when it came to the making of reparation to the man she loved by loving his child. She would sometimes cry out to him in the night time: 'Phillip [*sic*]—God help me, I cannot love her. Phillip [*sic*] forgive me don[']t love me less Phillip [*sic*], I can't help myself, only God can help me. Philip listen—it's something about her, it[']s stronger than I am, what is it, what is it?'

2.3 (Hall–Troubridge Papers, 13.3)

This is partially crossed out:

> Someone was riding not very far ahead, a woman wearing a dark brown habit. Stephen stared at her back with curious eyes—it was slender,

a straight, prepossessing looking back but strange; she did not recognise the habit, she thought: 'I wonder if that[']s Mrs Crosby [*sic*] whose [*sic*] just taken Glen House the other side of Upton,['] then she shrugged her shoulders and quickly lost interest. [. . .] But what on Earth was the woman about? She was actually putting her horse at a ditch, an old riding school hack it was, hired from Malvern, Stephen knew the beast well, it had one wall eye. Good Lord! She was pulling its head round crooked, and trying to kick it into a gallop. [. . .] The horse was no fool and he stopped abruptly, shooting his rider with great precision and [?] over his shoulder; Stephen started to laugh, she simply could not help it, it was such a thoroughly well merited toss, and there stood the horse looking down quite demurely for a moment, then he quietly started grazing—only why did the woman lie there like a dummy, why didn't she get up again? Was she hurt? Stephen kicked Raftery into a canter, then she quickly dismounted.

2.4 *(Hall–Troubridge Papers, 13.3)*

And that kiss paved the way to another, and another, as the hot blood of youth began to surge quickly, then the vast sea of love became Angela['s] lips, as they eagerly gave kiss for kiss back to Stephen.

2.5 *(Hall–Troubridge Papers, 13.3)*

In her own mind convinced she felt that Stephen was suffering all hell because of Angela Crossby. Their inseparable friendship and now this break—it seemed only too terribly clear to Puddle. But what was not clear was how far things had gone, and this vital question she dared not ask Stephen. Oh, but she had prayed that it might never happen, that the girl might be spared a full knowledge of herself. She had prayed on her knees, had argued with God about it: 'You know what it means', she had argued, 'you must know, since you made us—I can't bear it for Stephen, she[']s so strong yet so helpless—she'd be utterly helpless if it came.' [. . .] Puddle in her great perturbation grew desperate, and now she imagined all sorts of horrors. Suppose the girl should take her own life? It had been done before—she knew of a case [*originally:* there had been that girl at Oxford]—what aught she to do, what aught she to say?

2.6 *(Hall–Troubridge Papers, 13.4)*

Stephen takes Angela for a drive in the Malvern Hills and almost crashes the car during a fit of jealous passion.

Every cruel and primitive instinct known to man [. . .] had suddenly lept [*sic*] up fully armed and agressive [*sic*] in this creature that had so long endure[d] frustration.

Stephen's 'madness' behind the wheel leads to a moment of intimacy:

> 'Come close to my body and it will warm you, I'm terribly ashamed—it was vile of me darling, perfectly vile—I don't know what possessed me to do it.' [. . .] They sat on together in the soft summer evening, Angela said: 'You made me afraid'; And so queer and complex is woman, that her voice had a note of [?] and respect, and of something else, too, could Stephen have heard it—a note of excitement, and she caught Stephen[']s hand and laid it against her breast—over her heart.
>
> 'Feel my heart, how heavily it[']s beating, Stephen.'
>
> But Stephen[']s needs were dulled by contrition—so she let the moment passed [*sic*] by her, unheeded.

2.7 *(Hall–Troubridge Papers, 13.4)*

RH considers a different ending to Ralph's letter:

> Miss Gordon is young, I believe not more than twenty two, and of course you being her mother have a right to know of this deplorable thing that has happened—you may be able to guid [*sic*] her into healthier and more normal habits of mind.

2.8 *(Hall–Troubridge Papers, 13.4)*

> She selected one [of the books] at random. Karl Ulrichs she read. She had never heard of the author, and the book was in German—some sort of textbook perhaps, her father had often read German, and she also was quite a good German scollar [*sic*].

The draft includes more detailed information about Philip's annotations:

> Page 60—Stephen—her leaning towards sport.
> Physical appearance—not woman[.]
> Certain characteristic movements.

The decision to replace German lawyer, journalist, and writer Karl Heinrich Ulrichs (1825–95) with German sexologist and psychiatrist Richard von Krafft-Ebing (1840–1902) in the published novel is significant, since Ulrichs's works were not primarily written through a medicalizing lens. Ulrichs did, however, lack Krafft-Ebing's psychiatric authority.

3.1 *(Hall–Troubridge Papers, 13.4)*

Stephen and Puddle read reviews of Stephen's novel, all but one of which offer 'high praise'. 'Your book's had a simply phenomenal press,' declares Puddle. 'Your London press has been wonderful to you—and so have most of the provincial papers.' While one reader observes that the novel's style 'is quite free from all affectation', the negative review in 'an unimportant paper' draws attention to the 'ostentatious style of the writing'—a criticism that has since been levelled at *The Well.* To Puddle's frustration, Stephen struggles to see beyond this review and its claim that the novel is somehow inauthentic ('this writer has never really lived in the countryside of which she writes at some length').

3.2 (Hall–Troubridge Papers, 13.4)

The reviewer of Stephen's *The Furrow* who criticizes the novel's ostentatious style and its author's inexperience (see 3.1, above) acknowledges that 'there are one or two fine things in the book, as for instance the description of the old stud groom Pickford who "gets religion", and of "Lizzy" his wife who mothers him in his second childhood'. *The Well*'s old stud groom Williams, returning to the novel in a bath chair—a hooded wheelchair—evidently bears some similarity to *The Furrow*'s Pickford. (Williams, whom we know has been cared for by his forbearing wife, discusses religion with Stephen in Chapter 22.) RH's sense of *The Furrow*'s emotional appeal would prove strangely prescient. On 2 September 1928, Woolf shared her thoughts on *The Well* with Vanessa Bell:

> I think much of Miss Radclyffe Hall[']s book is very beautiful. There is the old horse—that is wonderful—when she has to shoot the old horse after every vet. has been to see it; but it has grown to be so old they can do nothing. It is too old for them to do anything. And so she shoots the horse herself. That is beautiful. And William[s] is a splendid character. He is the old groom. All that about the old horse and the old groom is very beautiful. But the rest of the book I did not care for. (*A Change of Perspective: The Letters of Virginia Woolf*, iii. *1923–1928*, ed. Nigel Nicolson and Joanne Trautmann (London: Hogarth Press, 1977), 526)

3.3 (Hall–Troubridge Papers, 13.4)

The narrator introduces Jonathan Brockett as 'young Humphrey Brock the playwrite [*sic*]'. Humphrey informs Stephen that 'your friend [Tom Ramsay *in the typed draft*] was my Cousin—he left me The Grange but of course I sold it—I sold the place to some people called Crossby—I expect you came across them down there—pretty woman, but the man was a deadly person. I believe my mother once met your father before the flood'. Stephen and Humphrey have an amusing yet revelatory conversation:

> One day when they were alone together he suddenly asked ~~an impertinent outrageous~~ her a blatant question:
>
> 'Are you a Lesbian?' he had enquired.
>
> 'No—I'm English on my father[']s side and Irish on my mother[']s.' Stephen had told him, smiling.

In a typed draft with handwritten annotations, Stephen responds simply:

> 'Oh, no, I'm English.'

RH adds:

> and she smiled her quiet, cowering smile that he found so disconcerting. But she did not appear to resent his question. Indeed it was hard to resent Humphrey Brock, he could say the worst, truely [*sic*] presperous [preposterous] things without any offence—no doubt because he himself saw no offence in them.

3.4 (Hall–Troubridge Papers, 13.5)

A note written on paper from Brighton's Royal Crescent Hotel explains that Stephen 'Meets Valerie beginning July 1913'. In a crossed-out section, the following conversation between Stephen and Jonathan, in which RH revisits and rewrites the 'Lesbian' question (3.3 above), precedes the first meeting with Valerie:

> Came the day when he took her to see Valerie Seymour [. . .] 'You'll meet all sorts of people at Valerie[']s if you two become friends—all sorts of [?] people like yourself—men and women not made to pattern. She[']s one of the best known Lesbians in Paris, and my God she[']s had a tough bullet to chew in her time, that[']s why I admire her courage. By the way Stephen, are you a Lesbian?'
>
> Stephen smiled her quiet, cowering smile—'Oh no,' she told him, 'I'm English.'
>
> The unusual question had not really made her angry, outrageous though it was, for Jonathan Brockett could often say preposterous things quite without offence—perhaps because he himself saw no offence in them.
>
> 'Well,' he said, placidly accepting her snub. 'I want you to be just a little bit weary [wary] at Valerie[']'s. All is not gold that glitters—in other words all is not poetry in Lesbos—far from it, there[']s any amount of dogral [doggerel].'
>
> 'Thank you Brockett—I'll remember what you say[,]' she said calmly.

3.5 (Hall–Troubridge Papers, 13.5)

The following is crossed out:

> On the pannells [*sic*] were one or two priceless pictures. A Canaletto, a [Francesco] Francia Madonna, together with some brilliant pencil sketches by a modern artist already quite famous—sketches these, of Valerie [*sic*] Seymour herself, before she had put her clothes on.

3.6 (Hall–Troubridge Papers, 13.5)

The following is crossed out:

> What you do with your life? I say nothing. You should be a champion fencer. You are not like others[,] you should not be afraid to show that

you are not like all the others. Others can write, who have not got your muscles—you should be willing to be what you are instead of, what is the word you say—skulking.

3.7 (Hall–Troubridge Papers, 13.5)

RH adds:

When it came to the nursing of the wounded they [female sexual inverts] failed, for like Stephen's, their hands were inclined to be clumsy. Willing hands, they yet lacked the fine intuition that has always made nursing a profession for the female. Their usefulness lay outside the walls of hospitals, as did their tasks for the wounded.

4.1 (Hall–Troubridge Papers, 14.1)

The war scenes are extended in the draft, as a raid forces Stephen and Mary to take shelter in a dark cellar:

'Stephen, does this mean we're going to die?'

'I think so.' She would not insult the girl[']s courage by evasion or lies, her courage was too fine.

But now as they sat there their bodies were touching. Then, it may have been the nearness of death, their bodies grew suddenly terribly alive, seemed to quicken into an agonised living, so that they felt the throb of their bodies in each separate nerve and fibre of muscle.

'Stephen, hold me to you—closer—I love you ~~so much~~ . . .'

'Mary—Oh, God help me!' They had found each other[']s lips there in that shell wracked darkness.

This then was the surging up of their love, having something urgent and fierce about it; having in it the terror and blood of battle, the thirst of a man long lost in the desert, the fearful urge of Creation to create, the mad urge to fructify that sweeps in through the flood gates, flooding the sterile channells [*sic*] along whose borders no life may blossom, no desire can come to perfect fruition.

The hours slipped by while they clung together.

Blind, senseless, [bemused?] except for each other. Death came near and passed by, then came near once again, as though fascinated by such strange lovers.

5.1 (Hall–Troubridge Papers, 14.1)

RH adds:

A thing terrible yet gentle as God himself, the pure and eternal spring of such loving. But the moment passed and they drew together—their eyes met, beholding only the flesh, symbol of their physical bondage.

Another crossed-out section extends the passage further:

> Very gravely they clasped each other[']s hands and Stephen said: 'This is for always Mary.'
>
> Mary answered ne'er a word, but she moved a step nearer, so that her breath touched Stephen[']s cheek—and at that moment of contact the vision faded.
>
> Then Stephen gathered Mary with her arms, pressing her close, against her body—stammering like a creature bewildered—only half conscious of what she was saying, blinded for the moment by that sudden brightness that had come and passed, leaving them utterly helpless, a pray [*sic*] to their earthly passion.
>
> And Mary answered: 'It has always been—' without fully understanding the words, but she moved a little nearer to Stephen.
>
> Her breath touched Stephen[']s cheek, their eyes met, they saw only each other clothed in the flesh, in symbol of their physical servitude, for at that moment the vision had faded. Stephen's arms went round her, masterful possessive, crushing the girl against her own body. And they stammered like two bewildered creatures, only half conscious of what they were saying, smitten by that brightness that had come and passed, leaving them standing there utterly helpless.

5.2 *(Hall–Troubridge Papers, 14.1)*

In a crossed-out section, Stephen and Mary look at old photographs of Stephen, Sir Philip, Puddle, and Raftery at Morton, prompting Mary to ask: 'When will you take me to see your real home?' The chapter concludes with Stephen wondering: 'Ought she to tell this girl the facts, to tell her that she had been turned out of Morton—that never as long as her mother lived could she take Mary home.'

5.3 *(Hall–Troubridge Papers, 14.1)*

The draft states yet more explicitly:

> We must lie and lie both in words and actions. Must behave as though we were utterly vile; two degenerates, hiding their degredation [*sic*]—that's what our love would mean to us at Morton!

5.4 *(Hall–Troubridge Papers, 14.1)*

Mary remembers a sentence from American author James Lane Allen's (1849–1925) novel *Kentucky Cardinal* (1894), which she and Stephen have 'read together times without number': 'Happy, happy night to come when one short candle will do for us both.' The novel describes the romance between a naturalist, Adam Moss, and his alluring neighbour Georgianna. In the sequel, *Aftermath* (1895), the couple's idyllic marriage ends when

Georgianna passes away during childbirth, leaving Adam to seek refuge in nature.

5.5 (Hall–Troubridge Papers, 14.1)

RH emphasizes Mary's Welsh heritage:

> as she sat there, her heart seemed to swell within her as though in response to some mighty challenge and the blood handed down from the past generations of men who had died in defence of their mountains—rose up in defense [*sic*] of herself, of Stephen.

5.6 (Hall–Troubridge Papers, 14.1)

RH provides more detail about Stephen's novel:

> Good it had been, but not good enough, for she now saw life from a far wider angle. This book must surpass 'The Furrow' in merit, must be the finest thing she had written—was she not writing this book for Mary?
>
> The story like its predecessors was simple, for her mind still clung to the country round Morton, but perhaps few things are as simple as love and the longing of all mankind for fulfilment—and now she could write of these things with knowledge, it would be a far finer book than 'The Furrow'.

5.7 (Hall–Troubridge Papers, 14.1)

Stephen is not too tired to respond to Mary's desire (this passage is crossed out):

> She [Mary] would cling very close, and once she asked: 'Do you think you love me any less than you did out in Orotava? Do you remember the singing[,] Stephen?' And Stephen, catching fire from her nearness, let the manuscript slip onto the ground, where it lay a forgotten heap of papers. There was no more reading aloud that evening.

5.8 (Hall–Troubridge Papers, 14.1)

Brockett states:

> 'if you were a man she[']d have all these things—trouble is, my dear, she[']s in love with an invert, and the lot of all inverts is horribly lonely unless they get out in the world and hustle, and those who love them are apt to be lonely—'.

5.9 (Hall–Troubridge Papers, 17.1)

The typed draft includes the following crossed-out paragraph:

> No wonder that these folk with God's mark on their foreheads fled for information to the writers of text-books; to Ulrichs, Kraft Ebing [*sic*],

> Moll, Carpenter, Freud, Havelock Ellis, Weininger and Ferenczi. And no wonder that one of these experts even, appalled at the insurmountable problems, had decided that death was better than life, much less of a gamble, and he just over twenty! Idioplasm, arrhenoplasm, thelyplasm, organotherapy; internal secretions, and the endocrine glands. Dear Lord, what a truly appalling muddle! So many high-sounding, jaw-breaking names to explain the matter of sexual attraction. Was it strange that these folk with God's mark on their foreheads, often turned in despair from their erudite text-books; or like Weininger sometimes preferred death to life, since life seemed to offer no sane solution? Yet Valérie Seymour and Adolphe Blanc had arrived in their separate ways at a state that was very nearly approaching peace; the one through her dreams of a bygone age, the other through his learning and resignation.

Albert Moll (1862–1939) was a German neurologist and psychologist whose work on hypnosis UT read in 1913 (see Introduction, p. xxi). In place of English sexologist, writer, and social reformer Henry Havelock Ellis (1859–1939), the handwritten draft mentions 'Young [*sic*]', i.e. Austrian psychiatrist and psychoanalyst Carl Gustav Jung (1875-1961), and it describes Hungarian psychoanalyst Sándor Ferenczi (1873–1933) as 'terrible' (Hall–Troubridge Papers, 14.2; see p. 289 with note). RH may have been aware of Ferenczi's belief that 'obsessional homo-erotism will be just as curable by means of the psycho-analytic method as the other forms of obsessional neurosis' (Sandór Ferenczi, 'The Nosology of Male Homosexuality (Homoerotism)', in *First Contributions to Psycho-Analysis* (London: Hogarth Press, 1952), 296–318 (311)). The technical terms are taken from Austrian philosopher Otto Weininger's (1880–1903) *Sex and Character* (see note to p. 327). Organotherapy is a medical treatment utilizing extracts from human and non-human animal organs, especially glands, often associated with the work of French-American physiologist and neurologist Charles-Édouard Brown-Séquard (1817–94). Although the efficacy of organotherapy was disputed, it did serve as a forerunner to hormonal treatments that gained popularity with the rise of endocrinology in the early twentieth century.

5.10 (Hall–Troubridge Papers, 14.2)

Lincoln and Henry begin the concert by singing the song 'By An' By', which was included in the *The Book of American Negro Spirituals* (1925) in an arrangement by J. Rosamond Johnson:

> O, by an' by, by an' by,
> I'm gwinter [going to] lay down my heavy load.
> I know my robes winter fit me well;

I tried it on at the gates of hell.
I'm gwinter lay down my heavy load.
O, hell is deep an' a dark despair.
I'm gwinter lay down my heavy load.
O, stop po' sinner, an' don't go dere.
I'm gwinter lay down my heavy laid.
O, by an' by, by an' by,
I'm gwinter lay down my heavy load.

EXPLANATORY NOTES

ALL references to the Bible are to the Oxford World's Classics edition *The Bible: Authorized King James Version with Apocrypha*, ed. Robert Carroll and Stephen Prickett (Oxford: Oxford University Press, 2008). A convention of the Authorized Version is that 'words and phrases which appear in italics in the translation represent words and phrases *not* found in the original language texts and does not indicate emphasis' (323).

Unless stated otherwise, translations are the editors' own.

ABBREVIATIONS

AB	*Adam's Breed* (1926; London: Virago Press, 1985)
AWCJ	Sally Cline, *Radclyffe Hall: A Woman Called John* (London: John Murray, 1997)
Hall–Troubridge Papers	Radclyffe Hall and Una Vincenzo, Lady Troubridge Papers, Harry Ransom Center, University of Texas at Austin (MS-01793)
LaD	Una, Lady Troubridge, *The Life and Death of Radclyffe Hall* (London: Hammond, Hammond and Co., 1961)
Ladye	Mabel Veronica Batten (1856–1916)
MO	Radclyffe Hall, *Miss Ogilvy Finds Herself* (London: William Heinemann, 1934)
OED	Oxford English Dictionary, electronic edition
PP	Laura Doan and Jay Prosser (eds.), *Palatable Poison: Critical Perspectives on The Well of Loneliness* (New York: Columbia University Press, 2001)
PS	Richard von Krafft-Ebing, *Psychopathia Sexualis: mit besonderer Berücksichtigung der Contraeren Sexualempfindung* (1886; 7th edn., Stuttgart: Ferdinand Enke, 1892)
RH	Radclyffe Hall (1880–1943)
SI	Havelock Ellis, *Sexual Inversion* (1897; 3rd edn., Philadelphia: F.A. Davis, 1915)
Songs	Marguerite Radclyffe-Hall, *Songs of Three Counties and Other Poems* (London: Chapman & Hall, 1913)
TIS	Edward Carpenter, *The Intermediate Sex: A Study of Some Transitional Types of Men and Women* (London: Swan Sonnenschein & Co., 1908)
TW	*'The World' and Other Unpublished Works of Radclyffe Hall*, ed. Jana Funke (Manchester: Manchester University Press, 2016)

TWoL	*The Well of Loneliness*
UL	*The Unlit Lamp* (1924; London: Virago Press, 1983)
UT	Una Vincenzo, Lady Troubridge (1887–1963)

3 '. . . *nothing . . . malice*': from Shakespeare's *Othello* (V. ii. 341–2).

5 *OUR THREE SELVES*: UT provides the following explanation: 'The Three Selves referred to in the dedication were Ladye, who had encouraged her first efforts in prose and of whose continued interest she was firmly convinced; myself, whose glad and humble service to her talent she chose thus to acknowledge and honour and . . . Radclyffe Hall, since, generous as she was in her tribute to Ladye's influence and to my service, she could not deny that the books were her own creation' (*LaD*, 80). The dedication to 'Our Three Selves' appears in all of RH's works from *Adam's Breed* (1926) onwards. *The Unlit Lamp* (1924) was dedicated to 'Mabel Veronica Batten in deep affection, gratitude, and respect'; *A Saturday Life* (1925) was dedicated to 'Myself'.

7 *COMMENTARY*: Henry Havelock Ellis (1859–1939) was a leading English sexologist, writer, and social reformer. Though a qualified physician, Ellis devoted his time not to the practice of medicine but to a range of intellectual pursuits and, from the early 1890s, to sexological study. Ellis was no stranger to literary culture: his publications include a respected article on 'The Novels of Thomas Hardy' (1883) for the *Westminster Review*, and he served as general editor of the pioneering Mermaid Series launched by Henry Vizetelly (1820–94) in 1887, publishing reprints of Elizabethan, Jacobean, and Restoration drama. With the poet and Renaissance scholar John Addington Symonds (1840–93), Ellis co-authored *Sexual Inversion*, the first English book-length study of 'sexual instinct turned by inborn constitutional abnormality toward persons of the same sex' (*SI*, 1). After first appearing in a German translation in 1896, *Sexual Inversion* was published in English in 1897 and included in Ellis's seven-volume *Studies in the Psychology of Sex* (1897–1928). In 1898, London bookseller George Bedborough was arrested for selling a copy of *Sexual Inversion* and charged with 'publishing an obscene libel with the intention of corrupting the morals of Her Majesty's Subjects'; see Ellis, *A Note on the Bedborough Trial* (Watford: University Press, 1898). The trial led to the withdrawal of the book from sale and forced Ellis to publish the remaining *Studies* in the US. RH wrote to Ellis personally to ask him to provide a preface to *TWoL*. In an earlier draft, Ellis referred directly to 'various aspects of sexual inversion', but RH's 'agitated' publisher, Jonathan Cape, changed it to 'a particular aspect of sexual life' (*AWCJ*, 237–8; in *PP*, 3). Ellis was one of a number of early twentieth-century sexologists who was invested in eugenicist ideas; he served as vice president of the Eugenics Society from 1909 to 1912.

8 *A motor ambulance unit of British women drivers*: RH drew heavily on the experiences of her friend May 'Toupie' Lowther (1874–1944), leader of an all-women team of ambulance drivers close to the front at Compiègne.

Lowther's work in the Hackett Lowther Unit also informed RH's short stories 'Miss Ogilvy Finds Herself' (*MO*, 3–34), and 'Malise' (*TW*, 183–92); in the 'Author's Forenote' to the *Miss Ogilvy Finds Herself* collection (1934), RH notes that 'those who have read *The Well of Loneliness* will find in the earlier part of the story the nucleus of those sections of my novel which deal with Stephen Gordon's childhood and girlhood, and with the noble and selfless work done by hundreds of sexually inverted women during the Great War' (*MO*, n.p.). RH kept detailed notes about the daily lives and experiences of the Unit (Hall–Troubridge Papers, 12.5). Sir Chartres Biron (1863–1940), chief magistrate in the British obscenity trial, drew the court's attention to the novel's suggestion that 'a number of women of position and admirable character, who were engaged in driving ambulances in the course of the war, were addicted to this vice [of sexual inversion]' (in *PP*, 45).

9 *Upton-on-Severn . . . Malvern Hills*: Upton-upon-Severn is a small riverside town, once a bustling inland port, in the Malvern Hills District of Worcestershire in the English West Midlands. Highfield House, now Haslington House, where RH wrote her early romantic and pastoral poems, is located 6 miles west of Upton and 2 miles south of Great Malvern on the eastern slopes of the Malvern Hills. 'The Malvern Hills' appears in RH's fourth volume and opens thus: 'The Malvern Hills be green some days. | And some days purple-blue, | There never was the like of them | The whole of England through' (*Songs*, p. 9, ll. 1–4). 'The Hills', in the same collection, begins 'When I the hills of Malvern see, | There comes a sadness over me' (*Songs*, p. 7, ll. 1–2).

Morton Hall: the Grade II-listed Morton Hall in the Worcestershire parish of Inkberrow, some 20 miles north-east of Upton, is of Georgian red brick. RH may have taken its name, charm, and extensive grounds, if not its location.

Anna Molloy, the slim virgin thing: Margot Gayle Backus argues that such 'inverted' sentence patterns 'explicitly mimic constructions typical of Anglo-Irish syntax'. See 'Sexual Orientation in the (Post)Imperial Nation: Celticism and Inversion Theory in Radclyffe Hall's *The Well of Loneliness*', *Tulsa Studies in Women's Literature*, 15/2 (Autumn 1996), 253–66 (259). We later learn that Sir Philip and Anna are 29 and 20 respectively when they meet in County Clare, western Ireland (p. 9).

10 *he admired the pluck of that Saint*: the first martyr of Christianity, St Stephen (*c.* AD 5–34) was stoned to death after being accused of 'blasphemous words against Moses, and *against* God' (Acts 6:11). Stephen and Philip the Evangelist, not to be confused with Philip the Apostle, had been selected as two of 'seven men of honest report, full of the Holy Ghost and wisdom' (Acts 6:3) who would minister to the physical and spiritual needs of the poor. The theme of martyrdom drives *TWoL* from the outset (see Introduction, p. xv), and Stephen and Philip will be brethren of sorts. At the beginning of the handwritten draft, Sir Philip is named Sir Stephen

(Hall–Troubridge Papers, 13.1). RH's conversion to Roman Catholicism was solemnized by Father Henry Sebastian Bowden, who almost converted Oscar Wilde (1854–1900) in April 1878, at London's fashionable Brompton Oratory on 5 February 1912.

10 *put Stephen down for Harrow*: Harrow School, founded in 1572, is an elite full-boarding school in London for boys aged 13–18.

11 *'Man proposes—God disposes'*: a translation of the medieval Latin phrase 'Homo proponit, sed Deus disponit' from Thomas à Kempis's *De Imitatione Christi* (*The Imitation of Christ*, *c.*1418–27). *Man Proposes, God Disposes* is also the title of an 1846 oil painting by Sir Edwin Landseer (1802–73), sculptor of Trafalgar Square's lions.

on Christmas Eve: St Stephen's Day is two days later. It is significant that Stephen is born on Christmas Eve: as we shall see, Stephen's martyrdom extends to an identification with Jesus Christ. As Stephen turns 27 in 1913 (p. 246), we know that the year is 1886—the same year as the first publication of German sexologist and psychiatrist Richard von Krafft-Ebing's (1840–1902) *Psychopathia Sexualis* (see note to p. 203). RH recorded key dates in Stephen's life in a notebook (Hall–Troubridge Papers, 12.5). According to UT, at one time RH 'had thought of making [*TWoL*] a "period" book, built round an actual personality of the early nineteenth century' (*LaD*, 81).

12 *well corned up*: (of a horse) lively and unruly, presumably after consuming too much corn.

It cannot . . . surroundings: the narrator adopts the style and tone of a sexologist or psychoanalyst.

sudden fits of hot temper: discussing RH's absent father, Radclyffe Radclyffe-Hall (1849–98), known appropriately as Rat, UT notes that his temper 'is said to have been quite uncontrollably violent (a temper inherited by his daughter who, however, learned to control it)' (*LaD*, 11).

13 *an unnatural mother*: in contrast to those 'great green-girdled mothers of splendid sons' (p. 10), the Malvern Hills. RH's *The Unlit Lamp* explores an unhealthy mother–daughter relationship in which the overbearing mother is 'almost lover-like' (*UL*, 66) in her behaviour towards her daughter, and the daughter's overwhelming sense of duty appears 'unnatural', 'abnormal', and 'no ordinary thing' (*UL*, 70–2). RH's relationship with her own mother was far from happy (see *LaD*, 13–17, and *AWCJ*, 11–36).

a blemished, unworthy, maimed reproduction: see p. 203 with note. Although causes of sexual inversion were widely debated, sexologists including Krafft-Ebing and Ellis identified a 'hereditary taint' in a number of their subjects (see, for example, *PS*, 226). Ellis cites an 'American case': 'He stated that he believed there was an element of heredity in his case, his father having been a dipsomaniac and one brother having died insane. He nevertheless stated it to be his opinion that, notwithstanding the hereditary taint, he would have been perfectly normal from a sexual standpoint had it not been for acquired impressions at or about the period of puberty' (*SI*, 273–4). The sixth case history in Ellis's chapter on 'Sexual Inversion in Men', identified as 'E.S., physician, aged 50', places himself 'under the despised and tainted category' (*SI*, 106). For RH, inversion was simply 'a fact in Nature' (Hall–Troubridge Papers, 17.3).

15 *'second of three'*: the second in rank of three housemaids employed by the Gordons. In the hierarchy of domestic service in 1890s country houses, housemaids were on the lower tier—below the butler, housekeeper, lady's maid, and cook. Though the officious Mrs Bingham is clearly superior to Collins in both age and status, both characters' poor grammar denotes their low social standing. In the Holy Trinity, Christ is the second of three.

full-bosomed: like the Malvern Hills as described in Chapter 1.

a staggering revelation!: a number of sexological case histories report a sexual awakening at or around the age of 7, with some subjects experiencing desire for a member of household staff. In Krafft-Ebing, 'The patient states that, when only seven years old, he had a peculiar inclination for male persons. It was particularly coachmen and servants with moustaches for whom he showed partiality at that time. He experienced a peculiar delightful sensation when he was able to nestle against such persons' (*PS*, 341). In Ellis, 'At 7 years of age, while staying in the country, a very good-looking groom, about 25 years of age, misbehaved himself with me. I often used to visit him in the stables, as this man had a strange attraction for me' (*SI*, 130). 'Give me a child until he is seven and I will show you the man' is variously attributed to Aristotle (384–322 BC), St Ignatius of Loyola (1491–1556), and St Francis Xavier (1506–52).

16 *found no name for*: 'the love that dare not speak its name' is the final line of 'Two Loves', a poem by Wilde's lover Lord Alfred Douglas ('Bosie', 1870–1945) written in September 1892 and published in *The Chameleon* in 1894.

17 *sitz-bath*: from the German verb *sitzen* (to sit), a sitz or hip bath is a shallow, upright tub. The sitz bath has a Great Malvern connection: it was introduced as part of the Malvern Water Cure in 1842.

William Tell, or Nelson, or the whole Charge of Balaclava: according to legend, Swiss hero and freedom fighter William Tell evaded death by successfully shooting an apple off his son's head. Vice Admiral Horatio Nelson, 1st Viscount Nelson (1758–1805), led the British to naval victories in the French Revolutionary and Napoleonic wars. The Charge of Balaclava, memorialized in Alfred Lord Tennyson's 'The Charge of the Light Brigade' (1854), was a failed assault by British cavalry on Russian armies at the Battle of Balaclava (25 October 1854) during the Crimean War. In *The Unlit Lamp*, Mary Ogden believes her ancestor Admiral Sir William Routledge to have been 'Nelson's darling' (*UL*, 16), and she takes a motherly pride in her 'Nelson chair' (*UL*, 33).

18 *"What is fear?"*: the young Nelson apparently uttered these words to his grandmother after returning home late from a long and dangerous ramble.

Asked whether he had been afraid, Nelson replied, 'Fear! grandmamma, I never saw fear: what is it?' (Robert Southey, *The Life of Nelson* (London: George Routledge and Sons, 1886), 11). Later, Philip will ask Stephen 'What is honour?' (p. 61).

18 *a queer kid*: in RH's *Adam's Breed*, Gian-Luca's first crush calls him 'a queer child' (*AB*, 128); in *A Saturday Life* (1925; London: Virago Press, 1987), Frances Reide describes the young Sidonia Shore as 'a queer fish' (33); *The Unlit Lamp*'s Joan Ogden is repeatedly described as queer in childhood and beyond. In a letter of 24 October 1934 to Evguenia Souline (1904–58), the Belarusian nurse with whom she conducted a nine-year love affair until her death in 1943, RH writes: 'I have been called the writer of "misfits." And it may be that being myself a "misfit," for as you know, beloved, I am a born invert, it may be that I am a writer of "misfits" in one form or another—I think I understand them—their joys & their sorrows, indeed I know I do, and all the misfits of this world are lonely, being conscious that they differ from the rank and file' (Hall–Troubridge Papers, 46.6). The *OED*'s first recorded use of 'queer' as a noun referring to a homosexual man is in the phrase 'The Snob Queers', in an 1894 letter written by John Sholto Douglas (1844–1900), 9th Marquess of Queensberry and father of 'Bosie'.

garments she hated: Ellis notes 'a very pronounced tendency among sexually inverted women to adopt male attire when practicable. In such cases male garments are not usually regarded as desirable chiefly on account of practical convenience, nor even in order to make an impression on other women, but because the wearer feels more at home in them' (*SI*, 245).

free and comfortable in breeches: the eponymous protagonist of Virginia Woolf's (1882–1941) *Orlando* (1928) also wears breeches. Vita Sackville-West (1892–1962), the real-life inspiration for Orlando, recalls her first time wearing 'clothes like women-on-the-land were wearing' in April 1918: 'in the unaccustomed freedom of breeches and gaiters I went into wild spirits; I ran, I shouted, I jumped, I climbed, I vaulted over gates, I felt like a schoolboy let out on a holiday' (in Nigel Nicolson, *Portrait of a Marriage* (London: George Weidenfeld and Nicolson, 1973), 105). Remembering a happy time in her relationship with RH, UT writes: 'I see her in breeches or jodhpurs and a bérèt [*sic*]' (*LaD*, 180).

dolls: Krafft-Ebing says of 'the female urning' (or female homosexual) that her 'favourite place is the play-ground of boys. She seeks to rival them in their games. The girl will have nothing to do with dolls; her passion is for playing horse, soldier, and robber' (*PS*, 280). In Ellis's chapter on 'Sexual Inversion in Women', one subject (History XXXVI) 'never cared to play with dolls, and in her games always took the part of a man. Her first rudimentary sex-feelings appeared at the age of 8 or 9, and were associated with dreams of whipping and being whipped' (*SI*, 224). UT claims that the young RH 'hated dolls, loved drums and noisy toys, but such tastes are common to many girl children and might seem to have had little if any significance had the future not confirmed the fact of her sexual inversion' (*LaD*, 19).

19 *housemaid's knee*: common name for prepatellar bursitis, a painful inflammation of the sac above the kneecap often caused by kneeling on hard surfaces for sustained periods.

Jesus was hurt for sinners: 'Who his own self bare our sins in his own body on the tree, that we, being dead to sins, should live unto righteousness: by whose stripes ye were healed' (Peter 2:24). We might note how both Philip and Collins have drawn attention to the nails on Stephen's hands (pp. 11 and 15).

Child's Book of Scripture Stories: we could not locate a book with this exact title. A number of illustrated children's or family Bibles would have been available in the 1890s.

barked her shins: 'To scrape or rub off the skin (esp. from the shins and joints); to graze, abrade' (*OED*).

20 *wash Collins in my blood*: to be 'washed in the blood' is to be redeemed through Christ's sacrifice, as in 'him that loved us, and washed us from our sins in his own blood' (Revelation 1:5).

The dream: Jay Prosser reads Stephen's 'dream of transferable flesh' as a 'reassignment dream' that reveals Stephen's transgender desire for physical transformation (in *PP*, 140).

21 *Battle of Trafalgar*: the British Royal Navy famously defeated the combined fleets of France and Spain at this decisive Napoleonic battle on 21 October 1805. Nelson was shot by a French sniper and lost his life. Nelson's dying request to close friend and flag captain Sir Thomas Masterman Hardy, 'Kiss me, Hardy', has fuelled speculation about his sexuality.

On the eighth day: in early Christianity, the eighth day symbolized God's new creation in the resurrection of Christ: 'I shall make a beginning of the eighth day, that is, a beginning of another world. Wherefore, also, we keep the eighth day with joyfulness, the day also on which Jesus rose again from the dead' (Epistle of Barnabas, AD 70–132). In the Bible, the eighth day is significant as the day of Christ's circumcision ('And in the eighth day the flesh of his foreskin shall be circumcised', Leviticus 12:3) and as a Sabbath day where there would be 'no servile work' (Leviticus 23:35–6; Numbers 29:35). Aaron and his sons are consecrated for seven days before making a sacrifice on the eighth day (Leviticus 8–9); the Nazirites undergo seven days of cleansing before offering sacrifices (Numbers 6). After four weeks of prayer and seven days of painful kneeling, Stephen ends her period of 'servile work' and offers her 'scarified' (not quite sacrificed) knees up to Collins.

22 *a caution!*: a slang term, of US origin, for 'an extraordinary thing or person' (*OED*). RH may have inherited American colloquialisms from her Philadelphia-born mother, Mary Jane Diehl (later Visetti; 1854–1945).

Love's young dream: the title of a poem by Irish writer Thomas Moore (1779–1852).

23 *leg-of-mutton . . . story*: a leg-of-mutton sail is a simple triangular sail, typically on a small boat. A number of popular fairy stories feature small sailing boats that would fit RH's description.

24 *Karl Heinrich Ulrichs*: a lawyer, journalist, and writer, Ulrichs (1825–95) was a pioneer of sexological science and is remembered as a remarkably courageous early gay-rights activist. Ulrichs announced to his family that he was a 'Uranian' (*Uranier* in German) in 1862 and spoke out publicly against sodomy laws at the Congress of German Jurists on 29 August 1867. He had coined the term 'Uranian' (later 'Urning') in reference to Pausanias' speech in Plato's *Symposium*, which celebrates the 'Celestial' Aphrodite, the daughter of Uranus, who inspires a spiritual and noble form of love between men (*Symposium*, ed. Robin Waterfield (Oxford: Oxford University Press, 1998), 13). The terms *Uranier* and 'Urning' are usually translated as 'homosexual man', though this identity category was not yet available to Ulrichs in the 1860s. His 1864 short works *Vindex* and *Inclusa*, which presented same-sex love as natural and innate, were banned throughout Prussia in September 1864. In *Vindex*, Ulrichs described Urnings as '*similar to hermaphrodites*. As a *third sex*, we are on the same level as the male or female sex, but we are independent of the male or female sex, fully separate from both. We are not fully men or women, but by nature we are different' (in Ulrichs, *The Riddle of Man-Manly Love: The Pioneering Work on Male Homosexuality*, 2 vols., trans. Michael A. Lombardi-Nash (New York: Prometheus Books, 1994), i. 3, emphases in original). Twelve of Ulrichs's tracts were collected as *Forschungen über das Rätsel der mannmännlichen Liebe* (*Research on the Riddle of Man-Manly Love*) between 1864 and 1880. English audiences were introduced to Ulrichs's terminology by Symonds's privately published *A Problem in Modern Ethics* (1891) and English socialist campaigner and author Edward Carpenter's (1844–1929) more widely read *The Intermediate Sex* (1908). Ulrichs is often described as the first gay man in history, and there are streets named after him in Berlin, Bremen, Hanover, and Munich.

25 *Millais*: Sir John Everett Millais (1829–96), renowned painter and illustrator whose *Christ in the House of His Parents* (1849–50) offended nineteenth-century audiences with its depiction of a startlingly ordinary Holy Family in Joseph's disordered workshop. RH's next novel, *The Master of the House* (London: Jonathan Cape, 1932), takes a similar approach to its holy subjects: Christophe Bénédit's father, Jóusè, is a carpenter who spits upon his rough palms and pauses in his work 'to exchange the time of day or some crude but harmless joke with a neighbour' (29). In Chapter 6 of *TWoL*, Stephen considers St Joseph as depicted on a piety card to look 'very respectable and kind, like the fishmonger in Great Malvern' (p. 62).

bull's-eyes: hard-boiled peppermint sweets, spherical in shape with black and white stripes.

26 *Gregory powder*: Dr Gregory's stomachic powder 'for Gout, Indigestion, Acidity, &c., composed of Turkey Rhubarb, Aroma of Jamaica Ginger, and

pure Calcined Magnesia', a laxative or purgative medicine that may be taken 'without any restraint whatever' (*J. Davies & Co.'s Catalogue of Drugs, Chemicals, &c.*, 1835).

30 *speechless through shyness*: Stephen is repeatedly described as shy and self-conscious. UT maintained that RH 'was intensely shy by nature' (*LaD*, 95).

The scents . . . hedges: dog daisies (or ox-eye daisies), buttercups, and meadowsweet (mead wort, or 'queen of the meadow') are early summer wildflowers. The scent of meadowsweet, as the name suggests, is intensely sweet; it is later described as 'queerly unbearable' (p. 34). Dog daisies are not to be confused with dog roses—scrambling pink or white wild roses that commonly grow in hedgerows, as we see on pp. 33 and 42.

31 *Great Malvern*: one of the three 'centres' of the Victorian spa town of Malvern, Worcestershire, at the foot of the Malvern Hills. RH's time in Malvern is discussed in the Introduction (p. xviii). The Abbey Hotel, where Anna and Stephen have lunch, was built in 1848 and still welcomes guests today.

32 *as strong as a lion*: when pregnant with Stephen in Chapter 1, Anna believed that her child would have 'the courage of a lion in his heart!' (p. 10).

Very protective: protection will become a key theme of the novel. UT recalls RH's 'protection mania', which 'flowered in every book she wrote and in her every thought and act to man and beast' (*LaD*, 16). She describes RH's protective instinct towards her grandmother: 'as a very little girl indeed when crossing London streets she would put her hand on the elderly lady's arm and say: "Hold on to me, granny, and I'll take you across. Don't be afraid . . ."' (*LaD*, 15).

brougham: a four-wheeled closed carriage, usually pulled by one horse or two ponies. Here, the Gordons' brougham is drawn by two cobs or stout ponies.

33 *Leghorn*: a ladies' straw hat or bonnet, often decorated with ribbon, muslin, or artificial flowers, and named after the straw- and hat-producing Tuscan port city of Leghorn or Livorno. Stephen is envious of the ordinary men who may doff their bowler hats to women as a sign of respect.

34 *orris-root*: (also Queen Elizabeth Root) from the rhizome of the iris flower, and often used as an expensive ingredient in perfumes, powders, and other cosmetics. Its fragrance is reminiscent of violets.

35 *narrow-hipped and wide-shouldered*: Stephen is described as 'a narrow-hipped, wide-shouldered little tadpole of a baby' upon her birth in Chapter 1 (p. 11). This description will appear again on p. 140.

37 *Saul and a witch . . . like*: in the Old Testament, King Saul of Israel disguises himself in order to seek the services of the Witch of Endor, who conjures the spirit of Samuel (1 Samuel 28:7–25).

38 *riding astride*: i.e. as a man or boy would ride, not side-saddle as befitting a young lady.

38 *fetlock*: 'That part of a horse's leg where the tuft of hair grows behind the pastern-joint [i.e. just above the hoof]; the tuft itself' (*OED*).

Erasmic: the Erasmic Company, a subsidiary of soap manufacturers Joseph Crosfield & Sons, produced a range of perfumes with names like 'Duchess' and 'La Belle'.

transmigrated: to transmigrate can simply mean 'to remove or pass from one place to another' (*OED*), but here the suggestion is that Collins's soul has passed into the horse's body as though after a death. Metempsychosis, the transmigration of souls, is famously discussed in the fourth chapter of James Joyce's *Ulysses* (1922): 'Metempsychosis, he said, is what the ancient Greeks called it. They used to believe you could be changed into an animal or a tree, for instance' (*Ulysses*, ed. Hans Walter Gabler (London: Bodley Head, 1986 edn.), 4. 375–6).

39 *meet*: another word for a hunt. The fox-hunting season traditionally runs from November to March. Under the Hunting Act 2004, it is now illegal to hunt wild mammals with dogs in the UK.

40 *four-legged Amazons*: an Amazon is a tall, strong, often masculine woman, after the formidable female warriors in Greek mythology. Mademoiselle Duphot will describe Stephen as 'une vraie petite Amazone' (p. 54).

giving tongue: 'tongue' in this context is 'the hunting-cry or "music" of a hound in pursuit of game' (*OED*); when the hound 'gives tongue', it is 'on a line' (i.e. chasing a fox).

41 *hunter*: not a particular breed but rather any horse with the strength, endurance, and temperament to perform well in the hunt.

brush: the fox's tail, the hunting trophy.

42 *the Croome*: the Croome Hunt (now the Croome and West Warwickshire Hunt, still known as 'The Croome') was established by the 9th Earl of Coventry in 1874. RH's first house in Malvern Wells, Highfield House, was 'in a situation that enabled her to hunt with three packs' (*LaD*, 31), including the Croome.

frost rime: also rime ice, 'Frost formed by the rapid freezing of supercooled water droplets in cloud or fog when they make contact with a cold object' (*OED*).

43 *loose-box*: a compartment in a stable in which a horse may move around freely.

45 *promoted to Etons*: an Eton suit was often the first suit a boy wore after growing out of tunics, sailor suits, and other boyish outfits, usually at around the age of 10. The Eton jacket—short, black, with wide lapels and an open front—was so named as it forms part of the uniform at Eton College, an elite public school for boys aged 13–18 near Windsor, Berkshire, founded in 1440 by Henry VI. We later learn that Sir Philip was a pupil at Eton (p. 166). There is a long-standing rivalry between Eton and Harrow, which could have been Stephen's school had she been a boy (p. 10). The protagonist of RH's first published novel *The Forge* (1924),

Hilary Brent, is an Eton alumnus. RH's father, in UT's words, 'seems to have scrambled through Eton and Oxford' (*LaD*, 11).

47 *Ledbury*: a small town in Herefordshire, west of the Malvern Hills. RH's poem 'Sunlight on Distant Hills', in her first collection, is subtitled '(Ledbury)' (Marguerite Radclyffe-Hall, *'Twixt Earth and Stars* (London: John and Edward Bumpus, 1906), 19).

dog-cart: a light, two-wheeled, horse-drawn vehicle, originally used to transport hunting dogs.

British Camp: an Iron Age hill fort at the top of Herefordshire Beacon, one of the highest peaks of the Malvern Hills.

48 *woods of Eastnor*: RH's 'Primrose Flowers' opens thus: 'I rode through Eastnor woods to-day. | And all the air did promise May, | Did promise May till every tree | Found voice to make much melody' (*Songs*, p. 29, ll. 1–4).

She began to whistle . . . pride: 'inverted women are very often good whistlers; [German sexologist Magnus] Hirschfeld [1868–1935] even knows two who are public performers in whistling' (*SI*, 256). Whistling was considered a marker of masculinity in inverted women; correspondingly, male inverts did not make good whistlers. The question 'How can you whistle?' appears in Hirschfeld's 1899 psychobiological questionnaire for 'the objective diagnosis of homosexuality' ('Die objektive Diagnose der Homoseksualität [*sic*]', *Jahrbuch für sexuelle Zwischenstufen unter besonderer Berücksichtigung der Homosexualität*, 1 (1899), 4–35 (29)).

50 *grampus*: a cetacean of the dolphin family, and—as RH is using it here—once a popular name for a killer whale. 'Coughing like a grampus' appears in Charles Dickens's *Dombey and Son* (1848), ed. Alan Horsman and Dennis Walder (Oxford: Oxford University Press, 2008), 62.

thrown his sprat and had landed his mackerel: the phrase 'a sprat to catch a mackerel' refers to 'a small outlay or risk ventured in the hope or expectation of a significant return', recorded from 1747 (*OED*).

51 *Liberty smock*: a loose-fitting dress with a gathered front made by Liberty & Co. (now Liberty London), specialists in luxurious imported materials and leading purveyors of art nouveau (*stile Liberty* in Italian) fashions and furnishings. The first Liberty shop opened on London's Regent Street in 1875. Stephen's 'Liberty smock' would have been part of the 'Artistic Dress for Children' range, inspired by the Regency-style illustrations of artist and writer Kate Greenaway (1846–1901).

53 *bluestocking*: an educated woman with intellectual interests. The Blue Stocking Society of England was a literary salon founded and hosted by a group of society ladies in the early 1750s. 'Bluestocking' was originally 'used neutrally to refer to a woman engaged in the literary pursuits of the bluestocking circle, but later was applied to intellectual women in general, with derogatory connotations. The depreciative usage was common throughout the 19th century, but died out as attitudes to women's education changed in the 20th century' (*OED*). Philip is clearly using the term

positively: he wishes for Stephen to be given a fine education by 'some woman who's been to Oxford'. Women had studied at Oxford since 1878 but were not permitted to take degrees until 1920. *The Unlit Lamp*'s Elizabeth Rodney is 'just down from Cambridge' (*UL*, 18) when she takes on the role of governess, much to the distaste of the 22-year-old Lawrence Benson: 'But surely a woman doesn't need to go to Cambridge to be charming? Personally I think it's a great mistake, this education craze; I don't believe men really care for such things in women' (*UL*, 59). Joan Ogden's plans to study at Cambridge, where women had been admitted since 1869 but would not be awarded degrees until 1948, are stymied by her stifling mother.

54 *'Comme . . . cœur'*: 'How kind she is, this funny little girl; she has such a good heart.'

anent splints and spavins, cow hocks and colic: anent is an archaic form of 'about'; splints and spavins are bony growths, the former often the result of an injury or overuse and the latter a sign of arthritis, on a horse's leg; cow hocks are a deformity of the hind legs; colic is a pain in the abdomen, usually caused by problems in the gastrointestinal tract.

'Mais quel type, quel type!' . . . 'N'est-ce pas?': 'But what a character, what a character [*or* what a one]! You're already a real little Amazon, Stephen.' 'Isn't that so?' The French *type* is also an informal term for a man, similar to 'bloke' or 'chap' in English. As a member of household staff, Mademoiselle Duphot addresses Stephen with the formal and respectful subject pronoun *vous*.

Bibliothèque Rose: the *Bibliothèque Rose Illustrée* (or *The Illustrated Pink Library*) was a range of children's books launched by Hachette in 1856. Mademoiselle Duphot's *Bibliothèque Rose* is evidently a single volume that contains a number of stories; the 'long, foolish dictées' are dictations from it.

55 *'"Les Petites Filles Modèles,"' . . . '"Comment . . . Mme. de Fleurville!"'*: La Comtesse de Ségur's (1799–1874) *Les Petites Filles Modèles* was published in 1858. At this point in the story, the mischievous and greedy Sophie has been confined to Madame de Fleurville's *cabinet de pénitence* (a penance closet, but in this case a spare bedroom) after a fight with Marguerite: '"The Perfect Little Girls,"' Mademoiselle would announce, while Stephen yawned out her ineffable boredom; 'Now we are going to rejoin Sophie [. . .]: "This evidence of trust touched Sophie and further increased her regret at having been so naughty." "How, she asked herself, could I have given in to such anger? How could I have been so horrible to such good friends as I have here, and so impudent towards someone as gentle and as loving as Madame de Fleurville!"'

'Les Bons Enfants': 'The Good Children', another children's story by La Comtesse de Ségur, published in 1862 and included in the *Bibliothèque Rose Illustrée*.

'La Maman. Donne-lui ton cœur,' . . . '—Mon cœur? . . . couteau': *The Mother* [speaking]: 'Give her your heart, my Henri. That's the nicest thing

you could give her.' '—My heart?' Henri said, unbuttoning his coat and opening his shirt. 'But how would I do that? I would need a knife.'

shamming: pretending; putting it on.

'Bon Dieu . . . au moins—': 'Good Lord, one has to live—one has to eat, at least—'

Petite Marmite: a hearty broth made of stock (chicken stock, in this case) and various meats and vegetables. *Petite marmite* translates as 'little pot', but the phrase generally refers to the broth rather than the vessel.

56 *'Mais . . . la vie!'*: 'But it's hard—life is terribly hard!'

'Est-elle heureuse . . . Qui sait!': 'Is she happy, this strange little being? Will she be happy later on? Who knows!'

fencing: Krafft-Ebing's *Psychopathia Sexualis* includes the case history of the Hungarian Countess Sarolta V/Count Sandor V (Sándor Vay), 'a very skillful fencer' (*PS*, 311). The similarities between Sándor and Stephen are striking: 'One of her father's foibles was that he brought S. up entirely as a boy, allowed her to ride, drive, and hunt, admiring her masculine energy, calling her Sandor' (*PS*, 311). Ellis describes Sándor's case as the 'most fully investigated case of sexual inversion in a woman in modern times' (*SI*, 195).

Sandowing: Eugen Sandow (1867–1925) was a world-famous strongman, showman, and sex symbol who wowed fin-de-siècle audiences with his Olympian physique and feats of extraordinary strength. A key proponent of the physical culture movement, and founder of *Sandow's Magazine of Physical Culture* (1898, initially *Physical Culture*), Sandow was considered a figure of perfect masculinity and is often described as the father of modern bodybuilding. Authoring a series of books including *Sandow's System of Physical Training* (1894) and *Strength and How to Obtain It* (1897), Sandow inspired men, women, and children to adopt his 'system' of regular strength-building exercise. Contrary to Mademoiselle Duphot's fears, in a chapter on 'Physical Culture for Women' in the second edition of *Strength and How to Obtain It* (Aldershot: Gale and Polden, 1901), Sandow advises that 'improper, violent and one-sided exercise will naturally result in making a woman clumsy, heavy, and ungraceful, but proper exercise, having for its object symmetrical and perfect development, will have an exactly contrary effect' (24). In Joyce's *Ulysses*, Leopold Bloom reflects on his ageing body and thinks: 'Must begin again those Sandow's exercises' (4. 234). The narrator draws our attention to the curious phrasing of 'I want to go in for Sandowing'; having just been introduced to ex-Sargeant Smylie, readers might expect 'go in for Sandhurst'—the Royal Military College established in 1802 (later the Royal Military Academy, where women could not train until 1984).

Samson wrecking the house of the Philistines: imprisoned by the Philistines, the enfeebled and blinded Samson calls out to God for the strength to avenge himself. He takes hold of the pillars of the temple of Dagon and brings the whole building down, killing everyone inside including himself (Judges 16).

56 *cut off my hair*: a reference to the source of Samson's legendary strength. When Samson informs Delilah that 'if I be shaven, then my strength will go from me, and I shall become weak, and be like any other man' (Judges 16:17), Delilah famously orders for Samson's head to be shaved. 'Virile strength', writes Ellis, 'has always been associated with hair, as the story of Samson bears witness' (*SI*, 254). Here, however, Stephen presumably expresses a wish to cut off her hair in order to be like any other man. One of Ellis's cases of female inversion, 'Miss V.' (History XXXVIII), recalls that when her hair was clipped in childhood, she 'was delighted and made everyone call me "John"' (*SI*, 229–30).

57 *diapan muscles*: a misunderstanding or mispronunciation of 'diaphragm muscles'.

'Bon Dieu, soyez clément!': 'Good Lord, have mercy!'

its strength could rejoice her: to quote Ellis on 'Sexual Inversion in Women': 'The muscles tend to be everywhere firm, with a comparative absence of soft connective tissue; so that an inverted woman may give an unfeminine impression to the sense of touch. A certain tonicity of the muscles has indeed often been observed in homosexual women. Hirschfeld found that two-thirds of inverted women are more muscular than normal women, while, on the other hand, he found that among inverted men the musculature was often weak' (*SI*, 255).

cold baths were forbidden: Stephen is evidently not 'going in for Sandowing' here: in a chapter of *Strength and How to Obtain It* (1897) on 'The Secret of the Cold Bath', later revised as 'The Magic Cold Bath' (1901), Sandow extols the benefits of a brisk cold bath immediately after exercise.

58 *Raftery, after the poet*: Antoine Ó Raifteirí (1779–1835), also Anthony Raftery, celebrated Irish-language poet and fiddle-playing 'wandering bard' whose verse is still taught in Irish schools. Ó Raifteirí, who became blind after contracting smallpox as a child, is remembered in W. B. Yeats's 'The Tower' (1927): 'Strange, but the man who made the song was blind; | Yet, now I have considered it, I find | That nothing strange; the tragedy began | With Homer that was a blind man' (ll. 50–3).

It was love . . . more than words: RH explores communication with animals elsewhere in her work. In 'To My Collie', in *Poems of the Past & Present* (London: Chapman and Hall, 1910), the speaker and their 'silent friend' converse with their eyes (p. 30, l.1). In the short story 'The Scarecrow', a scarecrow engages in conversation with a mouse, an owl, and a sheepdog, and a young girl 'hear[s] the words of all beasts' (*TW*, 102–6 (105)).

a-hunting: 'A-Hunting We Will Go' is a well-known folk-song and nursery rhyme composed by Thomas Arne in 1777.

Bellerophon: in Greek mythology, Bellerophon successfully captures and rides the winged horse Pegasus. Angered by Bellerophon's nerve in riding

Pegasus to Mount Olympus, home of the gods, Zeus sends a gadfly that stings Pegasus and causes Bellerophon to fall. Zeus welcomes Pegasus to Mount Olympus while Bellerophon is left injured and blinded, searching in vain for his steed until the end of his life.

59 *all play and no work will make a dull Stephen*: an inversion of 'All work and no play makes Jack a dull boy', first recorded in James Howell's *Proverbs* (1659). UT reflects on RH's early indolence: 'Throughout her adolescence and her maturity until the age of thirty-four, she was idle, bone idle, spending her days, as soon as she became mistress of her own time, in pleasure; in hunting, travelling, writing an occasional poem, in entertaining and being entertained' (*LaD*, 18).

mouthing: in child development, when an infant brings objects to their mouth; to mouth is also to 'train the mouth of (a horse); to accustom to the use of the bit' (*OED*).

61 *'Chérie . . . petit chou!'*: 'Darling—my baby, little pet!' *Chou*, which literally translates as 'cabbage', is a common French endearment. *Chou* is also short for *chou à la crème*, a cream puff.

tippet: a scarf- or stole-like garment, usually made of fur or wool, that covers the shoulders.

fly: a light horse-drawn vehicle used to convey public passengers; a cab or hansom.

62 *pink blotting pad*: sheets from RH's own pink blotting pads may be found among the Hall–Troubridge Papers; see e.g. 13.3.

unchidden: without being scolded.

Chock-a-block: here and elsewhere in the novel (p. 65), RH uses 'chock-a-block' to refer to objects placed closely together rather than a place that is full or crowded.

'Priez pour ma petite Stévenne': 'Pray for my little Stephen.' Mademoiselle Duphot, a Catholic, has evidently been praying to St Joseph, patron and protector of the Universal Church, the exiled, and the afflicted.

'Grand manque d'attention': 'Serious lack of attention'—a comment on Stephen's engagement with her work.

63 *box-sofa*: a settee or daybed with room for storage beneath the hinged seat; a combination of a chaise longue and an ottoman. The box-sofa is later referred to as a 'box lounge' (p. 67).

64 *Panhard*: leading French automobile manufacturer Panhard et Levassor, established in 1887, whose *Système Panhard* model (1891) shaped motor-car history with the introduction of a front-mounted engine, rear-wheel drive, and sliding gears. As Stephen has recently turned 14, we know that the year is 1901; RH marks the end of Victoria's reign with the arrival of modernity at Morton.

dyspepsia: indigestion (here used figuratively).

French victorias: a victoria is 'A light, low, four-wheeled carriage having a collapsible hood, with seats (usually) for two persons and an elevated seat in front for the driver' (*OED*). Named after the Queen, the elegant victoria was popular among wealthy women.

65 *phaeton*: a fast, sporty, often dangerous open carriage that took its name from the mythological Phaethon who failed to control the chariot of the sun.

gees . . . shovver: 'gee-gee' is a colloquial term for a horse; 'shovver' is a jocular alteration of 'chauffeur'.

67 *queer little woman*: Miss Puddleton, who was educated at Oxford (see note to p. 53), is not the first queer-coded governess in RH's fiction. *The Unlit Lamp*'s Cambridge-educated, unmarried Elizabeth Rodney introduces new professional and personal opportunities for Joan Ogden. Though not a governess, *A Saturday Life*'s Frances Reide—who sports a tortoiseshell eyeglass and smokes cigarettes—acts as mentor to Sidonia Shore before setting up home with Sidonia's mother, Lady Prudence. Cline has observed that the 'grey' and 'square' Miss Puddleton is modelled on RH's maternal grandmother, 'Granny' Sarah Diehl (*AWCJ*, 29).

68 *run between shafts*: shafts are the two long bars with which a horse is harnessed to a vehicle. In his preface to Lady Augusta Gregory's (1852–1932) retelling of the Celtic legends of Cú Chulainn, *Cuchulain of Muirthemne* (1902; London: John Murray, 1903), Yeats describes 'the world of the Irish country-people': 'Its events, and things, and people are wild, and are like unbroken horses, that are so much more beautiful than horses that have learned to run between shafts', pp. vii–xvii (xiv).

69 *the first cuckoo*: the title of one of RH's poems, which follows 'The Malvern Hills' in *Songs* (11). In 'The First Cuckoo', the cuckoo's song is associated with melancholy and unfulfilled romance.

I'm Stephen . . . nothing—: there are direct parallels between Stephen and *Adam's Breed*'s Gian-Luca, RH's earlier writer-protagonist. Where Stephen reflects that 'I'm Stephen—but that's being nothing', Gian-Luca feels that he is 'not anything at all—I am just Gian-Luca' (*AB*, 86). Gian-Luca feels 'shy and shamefaced' (*AB*, 86) at the thought of writing poetry, but Stephen (in the next paragraph) finds that she 'could say things in writing without feeling self-conscious, without feeling shy and ashamed and foolish'; as a writer, in Hannah Roche's words, '*Adam's Breed*'s "queer child" reaches maturity in *The Well*' ('Strange Soil and Novel Ground: Radclyffe Hall's Romance Plots', in Roche, *The Outside Thing: Modernist Lesbian Romance* (New York: Columbia University Press, 2019), 98).

70 *Adeimantus . . . Plato*: the reference that Philip is looking for is from Plato's *Republic* (*c.*375 BC): 'For he, Adeimantus, whose mind is fixed upon true being, has surely no time to look down upon the affairs of earth, or to be filled with malice and envy, warring against men' (*The Republic of Plato*, trans. Benjamin Jowett (2nd edn., Oxford: Clarendon Press, 1881), 193–4). Adeimantus of Collytus (*c.*432–382 BC) was Plato's brother.

71 *stays*: generally used interchangeably with 'corset' or 'a pair of stays', a stiff, structured undergarment worn to support and shape a woman's

figure. Tight and restrictive, stays and corsets have long been considered symbols of women's oppression.

flat: Ellis's chapter on 'Sexual Inversion in Women' makes reference to a number of young girls with small or 'atrophic' breasts and a 35-year-old inverted woman whose 'breasts are little developed' (*SI*, 254, 250).

But in spite of all this . . . softening to the features: Ellis writes of inverted women: 'When they still retain female garments, these usually show some traits of masculine simplicity, and there is nearly always a disdain for the petty feminine artifices of the toilet. Even when this is not obvious, there are all sorts of instinctive gestures and habits which may suggest to female acquaintances the remark that such a person "ought to have been a man." The brusque, energetic movements, the attitude of the arms, the direct speech, the inflexions of the voice, the masculine straightforwardness and sense of honor, and especially the attitude toward men, free from any suggestion either of shyness or audacity, will often suggest the underlying psychic abnormality to a keen observer' (*SI*, 250).

73 *presented*: introduced to society, usually with a view to securing a marriage.

74 *surely every one . . . at certain times*: common myths or old wives' tales about menstruation. 'During the existence of the "turns" or "monthlies," as they are often called,' advises American physician Charles Knowlton (1800–50) in his popular pamphlet *Fruits of Philosophy* (1832; 2nd edn., Rotterdam: Van de Hoeven and Buys, 1878), 'indigestible food, dancing in warm rooms, sudden exposure to cold or wet, and mental agitations should be avoided as much as possible' (24). In the case of Sándor Vay (see note to p. 56), 'The menses began at seventeen, but were always scanty, and without pain. It was plain to be seen that S. had a horror of speaking of menstruation; that it was a thing repugnant to her masculine consciousness and feeling' (*PS*, 314). Ellis refers to sexually inverted women for whom menstruation was 'scanty' (*SI*, 235) or 'absent' (*SI*, 255). See Appendix, p. 429 (1.1).

76 *male and female created He them!*: 'So God created man in his *own* image, in the image of God created he him; male and female created he them' (Genesis 1:27; see also 5:2).

77 *no real abiding city*: 'For here have we no continuing [*elsewhere translated as* abiding] city, but we seek one to come' (Hebrews 13:14). The hymn known as 'We've No Abiding City Here' (*c.*1804), by Irish evangelical Thomas Kelly (1769–1855), includes the lines '"We've no abiding city here" | Sad truth, were this to be our home; | But let the thought our spirits cheer, | "We seek a city yet to come"' (in *Hymns on Various Passages of Scripture* (Dublin: Marcus Moses, 1853), p. 266, ll. 5–8.

no-man's-land of sex: Hirschfeld's doctrine of *Sexuelle Zwischenstufen* (sexual intermediaries) proposes that intersecting variations of physical sex, sexual orientation, and gender identification are part of nature: 'in all mental and physical aspects there are only gradual, quantitative differences between man and woman; there is an extraordinary variety of mixed forms in all directions between them, at the extremes of which, as paradoxically it might sound, men with female and women with male genitals exist. Here, as elsewhere, nature has not deviated from her general rule that she operates in gradations and not in leaps' ('Die objektive Diagnose der Homoseksualität [*sic*]', 4). Carpenter observes that 'the number of persons occupying an intermediate position between the two sexes is very great, that they play a considerable part in general society, and that they necessarily present and embody many problems which, both for their own sakes and that of society, demand solution' (*TIS*, 9). Carpenter's work had a profound impact on First World War poets Robert Graves (1895–1985) and Siegfried Sassoon (1886–1967).

78 *a seed in deep soil*: Ed Madden argues that Ellis repeatedly alludes to the biblical parable of the sower 'to support his argument for the congenital nature of homosexuality' (e.g. 'The seed of suggestion can only develop when it falls on a suitable soil', *SI*, 270). See Madden, '*The Well of Loneliness*, or The Gospel According to Radclyffe Hall', *Journal of Homosexuality*, 33/3–4 (1997), 163–86 (168–9). RH calls on similar metaphors; see note to p. 211.

Erasmus: Erasmus of Rotterdam (1466–1536), Dutch philosopher and Roman Catholic theologian. While his contemporary Martin Luther (1483–1546) advanced the doctrine of divine predestination (i.e. that all events are predetermined by God), Erasmus maintained that humans may exercise free will.

79 *gibing*: usually 'jibing': 'To speak sneeringly; to utter taunts; to jeer, flout, scoff. Also *dialect* to scold' (*OED*).

how to love my own child: 'That they may teach the young women to be sober, to love their husbands, to love their children' (Titus 2:4).

81 *flesh of their flesh*: 'And Adam said, This *is* now bone of my bones, and flesh of my flesh: she shall be called Woman, because she was taken out of Man' (Genesis 2:23).

82 *holy of holies*: in the Hebrew Bible, the Holy of Holies is the inner sanctum of the tabernacle, inaccessible to all but God and the high priest (see Exodus 26:31–4 and Leviticus 16:2). The phrase is used figuratively here to refer to 'a place of special sacredness, an innermost shrine' (*OED*).

'When I was a child . . . I thought as a child': 'When I was a child, I spake as a child, I understood as I child, I thought as a child: but when I became a man, I put away childish things' (1 Corinthians 13:11). Like the verse from Titus above (see note to p. 79), these words are from the Epistles of Paul the Apostle, or St Paul.

84 *hand in hand*: there are obvious allusions to Adam and Eve in these paragraphs ('her father a man, her mother a woman, with their destiny already upon them'). In John Milton's (1608–74) epic *Paradise Lost* (1667), Adam and Eve walk hand in hand through the Garden of Eden—'So hand in hand they passed, the loveliest pair, | That ever since in love's embraces

met' (iv. 321–2)—and remain so after the Fall: 'hand in hand, with wandering steps and slow, | Through Eden took their solitary way' (xii. 648–9).

one flesh, one spirit: the phrase 'one flesh' first appears in Genesis ('Therefore shall a man leave his father and mother, and shall cleave unto his wife: and they shall be one flesh', 2:24). As Stephen has been reflecting on St Paul, we might also think of 1 Corinthians—'know ye not that he which is joined to a harlot is one body? For two, saith he, shall be one flesh. But he that is joined unto the Lord is one spirit' (6:16–17)—where Paul condemns a number of 'unrighteous' sexual acts including, apparently, homosexuality between men ('nor effeminate, nor abusers of themselves with mankind', 6:9).

85 *take that stiff timber*: successfully clear a fence or fallen tree.

going in the wind: losing lung capacity.

Then the thought . . . 'He . . . whose?': RH draws attention to Philip's 'purposeful back' (p. 41) from Stephen's early childhood onwards (when she 'clambered on to his back', p. 12). The implication here is that Philip is like St Christopher, carrying the increasingly heavy burden of Christ.

86 *old German custom*: Germany is usually credited as the home of the Christmas tree (*Tannenbaum*), with records indicating a Christmas tree in Strasbourg Cathedral in 1539, but both Latvia and Estonia have laid claim to the tradition.

anxious-faced eagle: the lectern is in the shape of an eagle, a symbol of John the Evangelist, with the Bible resting on its wings. Eagle lecterns are common in Anglican churches.

87 *Then Stephen sang . . . 'While shepherds . . . night'*: it is unsurprising that Stephen sings in a 'husky' voice. To quote Ellis: 'Not only is the tone of the voice often different [in female inverts], but there is reason to suppose that this rests on a basis of anatomical modification' (*SI*, 255). The words of the Christmas carol 'While Shepherds Watched Their Flocks' are believed to have been written by Irish poet Nahum Tate (1652–1715), appointed Poet Laureate of the Kingdom of England in 1692.

Lady-apples: small light-green apples with a red blush, traditionally used to decorate Christmas trees and wreaths.

in mufti: not in uniform. The Gordons' staff have evidently dressed smartly for Christmas.

88 *ills that all grape-flesh is heir to*: a play on 'the ills that flesh is heir to', adapted from 'The heartache and the thousand natural shocks | That flesh is heir to' from Hamlet's soliloquy (Shakespeare, *Hamlet*, III. i. 70–1).

Kew Gardens: world-famous Royal Botanic Gardens in Richmond upon Thames, south-west London, first opened to the public in 1840. When *Adam's Breed*'s characters visit Kew, which 'lay like a jewel in the sun, the grass green and gleaming as an emerald' (*AB*, 76), Gian-Luca empathizes with the 'tall, anxious trees, always doomed to look through windows' (*AB*, 79) in the stifling hothouses. Woolf's short story 'Kew Gardens' was first published in 1919.

89 *'Noël, Noël—'*: the children are singing 'The First Noël', a Christmas carol of Cornish origin first published in its current form in 1823.

Sandhurst: Royal Military College, Sandhurst, established in 1802 (later the Royal Military Academy, where women could not train until 1984).

Could . . . declared Mrs. Antrim: see Appendix, p. 429 (1.2).

90 *Margate*: seaside holiday town with a sandy beach in Kent, south-east England. Donkey rides on the beach are a traditional British childhood holiday activity.

Martin Hallam: a similar name to 'Morton Hall'.

British Columbia: Canada's westernmost province. British citizens emigrated to Canada in their droves in the early 1900s: in 1903 the number of Britons in Canada increased to 42,198 (30 per cent of the population) from 17,275 the previous year. From 1896, the liberal Canadian government had sustained a successful campaign for immigration from Britain and the United States, promoting the country's vast prairies and agricultural possibilities. Among RH's favourite books (*AWCJ*, 323) were Canadian writer Mazo de la Roche's *Jalna* novels, also known as the *Whiteoaks Chronicles* (1927–60), which centre on a British and Irish family in Ontario, Canada. De la Roche (1879–1961) raised two orphaned children with her cousin and lifelong partner Caroline Clement.

92 *A queer, sensitive fellow*: Laura Doan has observed that Martin 'compares favourably with Carpenter's description of "the more normal type of the Uranian man" who, "while possessing thoroughly masculine powers of mind and body, combines them with the tenderer and more emotional soul-nature of the woman"' (*Fashioning Sapphism: The Origins of a Modern English Lesbian Subculture* (New York: Columbia University Press, 2001), 158). Doan is quoting *TIS*, 32.

Castle Morton: the village and civil parish of Castlemorton lies 5 miles south-west of Upton-upon-Severn and 7 miles south of Great Malvern.

93 *Bromsberrow . . . Eastnor*: the timber-framed Clencher's (or Clenchers) Mill, located between the villages of Eastnor and Bromsberrow, is part of the Eastnor Castle Estate. RH's misspelling also appears in her poem 'Sunday Evening' (*Songs*, p. 20, l. 4). Eastnor in springtime provides the setting of 'Eastnor Churchyard' and 'Primrose Flowers', both in *Songs*.

Worcestershire Beacon: a hill with a summit at 425 metres, the highest point of the Malvern Hills and the county of Worcestershire. 'Worcester Beacon bold' features in RH's 'The Malvern Hills' (*Songs*, p. 9, l. 12).

Raggedstone . . . legend: RH provides an explanatory note to her poem 'The Shadow of Raggedstone': 'A legend is attached to Raggedstone Hill in Worcestershire. The Hill was cursed by a Benedictine Monk. From time to time a great shadow rises up from it, spreading across the surrounding country. Woe betide those on whom the shadow falls, as it brings with it terrible misfortune! Many of the people living near Raggedstone still firmly believe in this legend' (*Songs*, 4).

"And in death they were not divided": Saul and his eldest son Jonathan '*were* lovely and pleasant in their lives, and in their death they were not divided: they were swifter than eagles, they were stronger than lions' (2 Samuel 1:23). The love between Jonathan and David, which 'was wonderful, passing the love of women' (2 Samuel 1:26), has been read as homosexual—see, for instance, Symonds's poem 'The Meeting of David and Jonathan' (1878). Ladye gave RH the pet name John, 'reserving to herself the name Jonathan as a reminder of the biblical bond between David and Jonathan' (*AWCJ*, 66). In *TWoL*, characters either stand 'divided' (Stephen and Anna, p. 121) or 'undivided' (Williams and his wife, p. 170).

poor, blind Stephen!: in the New Testament, blindness is often spiritual rather than physical, as in 'And Jesus said, For judgment I am come into this world, that they which see not might see; and that they which see might be made blind' (John 9:39).

94 *calling*: in RH's 'The First Cuckoo' (see note to p. 69), the cuckoo's call portends a broken engagement.

roof-tree: 'The main beam or ridge pole of a roof [. . .]; (by extension) a home' (*OED*).

95 *Tenley Court*: fictional, but a number of country houses around Upton-upon-Severn fit RH's description. Ham Court, for instance, advertised to be let in *The Field* newspaper on 2 November 1907, offered a 'southern aspect', 'home farm of about 200 acres', and possibilities for 'hunting with several packs'. See Appendix, p. 430 (1.3).

96 *Ross*: Ross-on-Wye, a market town in Herefordshire, near the Welsh border.

hornbeam: a hardwood hedging tree that produces lush green leaves in spring. The descriptions of springtime flora here obviously imply fertility and new growth, but we might remember that Martin's adored trees are 'twisted and crippled' with the 'enormous courage' to withstand the life that God has given them (p. 93). Martin's trees are insistently masculine: the 'erect, towering firs' are 'many centuries old and their girth that of giants' (p. 94), and the red pines are coveted for their 'tough, manly wood' (p. 94).

99 *two men, companions, sharing each other's interests*: Of 'Miss H.' (History XXXVI), Ellis writes: 'Her feeling toward men is friendly, but she has never had sexual attraction toward a man. She likes them as good comrades, as men like each other. She enjoys the society of men on account of their intellectual attraction. She is herself very active in social and intellectual work. Her feeling toward marriage has always been one of repugnance. She can, however, imagine a man whom she could love or marry' (*SI*, 225). 'Miss H.' is widely believed to be writer and women's rights activist Edith Ellis (née Lees, 1861–1916), who married Ellis in 1891.

102 *Drat*: a mild expression of annoyance or frustration.

roan: 'Of a horse: having a coat in which the prevailing colour (usually bay, sorrel, or chestnut) is thickly interspersed with white or grey, typically producing a dull red or reddish-grey. Also (and in earliest use) designating the overall colour itself' (*OED*).

102 *gall*: an open sore on a horse's skin caused by friction with a poorly fitting saddle.

104 *an intolerable pity*: RH repeatedly draws attention to Philip's feelings of pity (pp. 112, 203) for both Stephen and Anna. Where Anna fails to feel 'mother-pity' (p. 80) for her teenage daughter, the sensitive Philip is overcome with pity and tenderness. Carpenter's 'more normal type of the Uranian man' (see note to p. 92) is emotionally 'extremely complex, tender, sensitive, pitiful and loving' and 'often a dreamer, of brooding, reserved habits' (*TIS*, 33). We have already learned that Philip is 'a dreamer and a lover' (p. 10).

Unto the third and fourth generations . . . .: in Exodus 34:7, God speaks the following words to Moses: 'Keeping mercy for thousands, forgiving iniquity and transgression and sin, and that will by no means clear *the guilty*; visiting the iniquity of the fathers upon the children, and upon the children's children, unto the third and to the fourth *generation*.'

gall: a different meaning from 'gall' above. As the Roman soldiers were preparing to crucify Jesus, they gave him 'vinegar to drink mingled with gall: and when he had tasted *thereof*, he would not drink' (Matthew 27:34). Scholars disagree on the specific meaning and make-up of 'gall', but it is evidently a bitter-tasting plant-based substance, probably of wormwood or myrrh, that may be mixed with wine to produce a sedative or desensitizing effect.

107 *dignity . . . ostentation*: an echo of the novel's second paragraph (p. 9).

When hounds checked and the field collected together: in hunting terminology, a 'check' occurs when the hounds have temporarily lost the scent, and 'the field' is the collective term for the mounted followers; RH is describing a pause in the hunt.

loves a good bit of timber: Raftery enjoys and is good at jumping over obstacles.

'If some bloody fools . . . farmers': Colonel Antrim is unhappy about having to pay compensation to farmers for the hunt's damage to their land. More skilled riders like Stephen, he thinks, would incur fewer costs.

108 *the 'Pink 'Un'*: *The Sporting Times (The Pink 'Un)* (1865–1932) was a British weekly newspaper, printed on salmon-coloured paper and published on Saturdays. A 1928 edition discussed James Douglas's (1867–1940) attack on *TWoL*: 'the stunt press has stunted the book into enormous popularity. A friend asked for it at Hatchard's and another Piccadilly bookshop, and at each was told that the book was out of stock, and no copies would be available until next week. Which all goes to show that if a book is pronounced unfit to read people will buy it to see what makes it so' ('The Well of Loneliness: A Sequel', *Sporting Times*, 25 Aug. 1928, 3). Though *The Pink 'Un* was mostly devoted to sport, its interest in gossip,

scandal, and salacious fiction—the same edition advertises 'Breezy French Novels in English' including *The Awful Disclosures of Maria Monk* (1836) and Daniel Defoe's *Moll Flanders* (1722) on its back page—makes it 'anathema because of Violet' (see Introduction, p. xv).

'Oh come, let us sing unto the Lord': 'O come, let us sing unto the LORD: let us make a joyful noise to the rock of our salvation' (Psalm 95:1).

109 *unclean . . . wicked*: 'When the unclean spirit is gone out of a man, he walketh through dry places, seeking rest, and findeth none. Then he saith, I will return into my house from whence I came out; and when he is come, he findeth *it* empty, swept, and garnished. Then goeth he, and taketh with himself seven other spirits more wicked than himself, and they enter in and dwell there: and the last *state* of that man is worse than the first. Even so shall it be also unto this wicked generation' (Matthew 12:43–5).

111 *life's not all beer and skittles*: an idiom common from at least the early nineteenth century, used to point out that life (or a particular situation) is not always amusing or enjoyable. 'That it should not be all beer and skittles with us, and therefore apt to pall, my cousins and I had to work pretty hard' appears in George du Maurier's *Peter Ibbetson* (1891; New York and London: Harper and Brothers, 1919), 47, which Stephen will read on p. 319.

a drowning man will cling to a spar: similar to the proverb 'a drowning man will clutch at a straw', an early version of which appears in Thomas More's (1478–1535) *Dialogue of Comfort Against Tribulation* (written 1534). A spar is a pole used to support the rigging and sails of a ship.

113 *cedar*: just before Martin's proposal in Chapter 11, the cedar 'grew reddish pink tips to its elegant fingers' (p. 96).

galled: a gall here is an 'excrescence [growth] produced on trees, especially the oak, by the action of insects' (*OED*). A heavy or prolonged gall infestation may weaken a tree.

116 *the shadow of the valley of death*: 'Yea, though I walk through the valley of the shadow of death, I will fear no evil: for thou *art* with me; thy rod and thy staff they comfort me' (Psalm 23:4).

farthing: a former monetary unit and coin worth a quarter of an old penny; here used figuratively to show that Philip must pay for the 'sin of his anxious and pitiful heart' by expending every possible effort to speak. In his Sermon on the Mount, Jesus declares: 'Verily I say unto thee, Thou shalt by no means come out thence, till thou hast paid the uttermost farthing' (Matthew 5:26–8).

117 *God of love*: 'He that loveth not knoweth not God; for God is love' (1 John 4:8).

the quick and the dead: 'quick' here means 'living'. RH is alluding to the Day of Judgement, when all of the living and the dead would 'appear before the judgment seat of Christ; that every one may receive the things *done* in *his* body, according to that he hath done, whether *it be* good or bad' (2 Corinthians 5:10). The phrase 'quick and dead' is found in Acts 10:42:

'And he commanded us to preach unto the people, and to testify that it is he which was ordained of God *to be* the Judge of quick and dead.' The cadence of Book One's emphatic closing sentence brings to mind the final line of James Joyce's 'The Dead' (1914): 'His soul swooned softly as he heard the snow falling faintly through the universe and faintly falling, like the descent of their last end, upon all the living and the dead' (in *Dubliners*, ed. Jeri Johnson (Oxford: Oxford University Press, 2000), 176). 'The quick, the dead, and the yet unborn' will appear in the novel's final chapter (p. 427).

119 *BOOK TWO*: 'Stephen is 19 when this book opens' (Hall–Troubridge Papers, 13.3; the notebook in 13.3 contains more than one false start to Book Two).

120 *Morton had become . . . for comfort*: in the handwritten draft, Stephen addresses Morton directly here. See Appendix, p. 430 (2.1).

quite a considerable income: RH received an inheritance from her paternal grandfather, Dr Charles Radclyffe Hall (1820–79), physician and author of *Torquay in Its Medical Aspects* (1857) and *Is Torquay Relaxing?* (1874), at the age of 21 (*AWCJ*, 24).

121 *But Anna . . . insidious barrier*: the handwritten draft provides further detail. See Appendix, p. 430 (2.2).

crafty old ostrich of a world: the phrase 'to bury one's head in the sand' is based on the legendary belief that an ostrich buries its head in sand when threatened (*OED*). The following sentences refer to the proverbial 'seeing is believing' and 'silence is golden'.

122 *like a woebegone child*: the adult Stephen is frequently likened to a child and described as childish (pp. 156 and 162). Sexological and psychoanalytic writers turned to the concept of arrested development to account for sexual inversion and other non-normative sexualities and gender expressions. Ellis maintains that 'there is more or less arrested development and infantilism' present in 'all three of the cases [of female sexual inversion] concerning whom I have precise information' (*SI*, 256).

a mighty fine doer: 'A horse or other animal that "does" or thrives' (*OED*); one that maintains a good weight on a minimum amount of food.

123 *chestnut*: a chestnut-coloured horse; Stephen's hair is also chestnut (p. 135).

'If we find . . . every man's hand against us': 'to find' here is to sniff out the fox. In Genesis, the angel of the Lord informs Hagar, Sarai's maid, that she will bear a son named Ishmael: 'And he will be a wild man; his hand *will be* against every man, and every man's hand against him' (16:12).

cover: a cover or covert is 'A place which gives shelter to wild animals or game [in this case, the hunted fox]; esp. a thicket' (*OED*).

124 *'It's looking for God Who made it'*: RH explores the relationship between animals and God in several other works, often demonstrating an inclusive religious approach that accommodates human and non-human animals. In her short story 'Saint Ethelflaeda', a medieval abbess calls for a hare to be

accepted into the Christian community, believing that the hare 'may very well say little prayers' (*TW*, 96–101 (99)).

125 *We'll never hunt any more, we two, Raftery*: UT describes how RH lost her appetite for hunting after a sporting injury, which coincided with a growing 'horror of killing' (*LaD*, 32). By the time UT and RH began their intimate relationship in 1915, 'hunting was a distant memory' (*LaD*, 32).

127 *dressed in tailor-made clothes*: in UT's words, RH wore 'very simple tailor-made clothes' (*LaD*, 43). RH's sartorial flair is discussed in the Introduction (p. xxiv).

old rip of an Airedale: used colloquially, a 'rip' or 'old rip' describes both a 'worthless or worn-out horse; one that is of inferior quality' and a 'disreputable, dissolute, or immoral man' (*OED*). Airedales are the largest of the British terriers.

128 *carbolic*: an acid, especially phenol, used as a disinfectant.

Angela Crossby: in the handwritten draft, Stephen first meets Angela while they are both out riding, and it is Angela rather than Tony who is injured. See Appendix, p. 430 (2.3).

129 *like a mediæval page*: the pageboy cut was one of the fashionable bob hairstyles of the 1920s, popularized by American film actresses Louise Brooks (1906–85) and Colleen Moore (1899–1988) and associated with female independence and modernity.

a very bad asset: the English upper-class circles to which Stephen and her family belong judge Angela for being American and having worked as a vaudeville performer prior to her marriage. Richard Dellamora observes that RH 'had money but not class', as her social status was defined by her American mother rather than her absent English father (*Radclyffe Hall: A Life in the Writing* (Philadelphia: University of Pennsylvania Press, 2011), 86).

he bounded: similar to a cad, a bounder is 'A man of objectionable manners or antisocial behaviour; a man who behaves dishonourably, esp. towards a woman' (*OED*).

His subscription . . . five guineas: unlike other Malvern landowners, the unpardonably mean Crossby contributes only five guineas towards the Hunt. The guinea, worth £1. 1*s* (one pound and one shilling), was considered a gentlemanly unit of currency; luxury items including cars, horses, and works of art were priced in guineas. To this day, bids for racehorses at auction are made in guineas. In the next sentence, we learn that Crossby's lack of generosity extends to an unwillingness to allow access to his land: he hopes that the Hunt will keep clear of his covers (see note to p. 123).

130 *queer flower*: RH's 'queer flower' nods to Charles Baudelaire's (1821–67) poetry collection *Les Fleurs du Mal* (*The Flowers of Evil*, 1857), originally titled *Les Lesbiennes*, which was targeted by French prosecutor Ernest Pinard (1822–1909) in August 1857. The court banned six of Baudelaire's

erotic poems, two of which were on lesbian themes. RH's description of Angela as 'like some rare, pale flower without blemish or stain' also echoes queer American poet Amy Lowell's (1874–1925) 'The Weather-Cock Points South', where the feminine beloved is presented as a 'White flower, | Flower of wax, of jade, of unstreaked agate; | Flower with surfaces of ice' (in *Pictures of the Floating World* (Boston and New York: Houghton Mifflin, 1919), pp. 51–2, ll. 11–13). Like the leaves around Lowell's flower, which are 'veined with purple' (l. 5), Angela's eyes 'almost seemed to be tinted with purple'. The 'queer flower' stands in contrast to the carefully classified roses that Angela's husband grows in his English garden (p. 157).

132 *rang up The Grange*: the Post Office opened the first automatic telephone exchange in May 1912, but it took decades for automatic dialling to roll out across the country. In small towns like Upton, the telephone switchboard would usually have been operated by a single individual, who would have been able to listen in on private conversations. Telephone calls were insecure communications, vulnerable to eavesdropping and gossip.

134 *the songs of blackbirds and thrushes*: this line is repeated verbatim at the end of the next paragraph, giving the passage a rhythmical quality that echoes the natural rhythms Stephen is observing here.

136 *'Pop goes the weasel'*: popular English and American song, country dance, and nursery rhyme dating to the mid-nineteenth century.

137 *the Prickly Cradle:* it is not clear why RH capitalizes this phrase (here and at the end of the next paragraph), which most often appears in botanical or zoological contexts (e.g. 'you'll always find at least one yellow gorse-bud, peeking out from its prickly cradle', *Leeds Mercury*, 18 Sept. 1923, 5; '[kingfisher] parents [. . .] form a prickly cradle for the unhappy fledglings', Neltje Blanchan, *Bird Neighbours: An Introductory Acquaintance With One Hundred and Fifty Birds Commonly Found in the Gardens, Meadows, and Woods About Our Homes* (New York: Doubleday, 1903), 104.

'O, Tannebaum, O Tannebaum [sic], wie grün sind Deine Blätter': 'O, Tannenbaum' is a traditional German Christmas song, known in English as 'O Christmas Tree'. The modern German lyrics were written in 1824. The lines sung here literally translate as: 'O Christmas Tree, O Christmas Tree, how green your branches are.' The song describes the fir as a symbol of loyalty and faithfulness due to it being an evergreen.

138 *three lumps*: Stephen favours sweet drinks; Puddle later prepares cocoa with four lumps of sugar to raise her spirits (p. 154). We have already learned of Stephen's ability to consume large quantities of plum cake, which is considered unfeminine (p. 47). The novel's other sugar-guzzling character is the 'fat, aged Collins' (pp. 88 and 167).

dissemble: disguise or conceal one's true feelings or intentions.

a visitation: in this context, 'A prolonged visit, or one which is disagreeable to the recipient' (*OED*).

139 *king-cups*: perennial herbaceous plants of the buttercup family, which flower between April and August.

140 *narrow-hipped and wide shouldered*: the phrase is used for the third time to describe Stephen's body (see pp. 11 and 35). It takes on more favourable connotations here, since Angela admires Stephen's athleticism and strength.

143 *Kismet*: destiny, fate (Turkish, from the Arabic *qisma* meaning lot or division).

Hand in hand: see note to p. 84.

the swan called Peter: the handwritten draft states that 'Peter's the spirit of Morton' (Hall–Troubridge Papers, 13.3). Swans are predominantly monogamous and often spend several years or even a lifetime with a single mate.

144 *we're happy, happy*: Stephen frequently uses repetition (often epizeuxis) when trying to explain or justify the positive qualities of same-sex relationships to others (see 'we're perfect, a perfect thing' two paragraphs below).

not two separate people but one: this phrasing echoes biblical depictions of marriage, e.g. 'Therefore shall a man [. . .] cleave unto his wife: and they shall be one flesh' (Genesis 2:24). In the New Testament, Jesus makes a case against divorce, arguing: 'Have ye not read, that he which made *them* at the beginning made them male and female, and said, For this cause [marriage] shall a man leave father and mother, and shall cleave to his wife: and they twain shall be one flesh? Wherefore they are no more twain, but one flesh. What therefore God hath joined together, let no man put asunder' (Matthew 19:4–6).

she kissed her full on the lips, as a lover: a repetition of the scene between Henry and Collins in Chapter 2: 'he kissed her full on the lips' (p. 26). RH clearly struggled to decide on the wording of this emphatic final line of the chapter: the handwritten draft includes 'she stooped and kissed her on the mouth, as a lover', and 'Stephen gathered her into her arms, and kissed Angela full on the lips, as a lover', among other slight variations (Hall–Troubridge Papers, 13.3).

145 *a fine, selfless thing*: Krafft-Ebing suggests that the sexual impulse is an evolutionary mechanism that does not only serve biological reproduction but can also awaken 'higher, nobler feelings' resulting in a 'world of beauty, sublimity, and morality' (*PS*, 1). In his final judgement in the UK obscenity trial, Biron condemned this passage for presenting 'horrible practices' in affirmative terms (in *PP*, 43). Later, Stephen's 'fine instinct of utterly selfless protection' is contrasted with Angela's 'primitive instinct of self-preservation' (p. 196).

146 *humble . . . beast:* in Genesis, God curses the serpent for seducing Eve: 'above every beast of the field; upon thy belly shalt thou go, and dust shalt thou eat all the days of thy life' (Genesis 3:14).

146 *painful and terribly sterile kisses*: RH repeatedly laments the sterility of same-sex relationships. Cline notes that she 'may have wanted children' of her own with UT (*AWCJ*, 139–140, 352); UT's diary reveals how, on an extended stay in Florence in 1921–2, the couple visited an orphanage where RH was 'sorely tempted to buy a baby' (quoted in Richard Ormrod, *Una Troubridge: The Friend of Radclyffe Hall* (London: Jonathan Cape, 1984), 145).

147 *I'm of the earth earthy*: a reference to Adam, the first man made of the earth: 'he that is of the earth is earthly, and speaketh of the earth: he that cometh from the heaven is above all' (John 3:31); 'The first man *is* of the earth earthy; the second man *is* the Lord from heaven' (1 Corinthians 15:47). Angela insists on the embodied and sensual nature of her desires, which contrast with Stephen's elevated and spiritual feelings for her.

So Stephen . . . took kisses: see Appendix, p. 431 (2.4), for an earlier version of this sentence.

Tewkesbury . . . abbey: Tewkesbury Abbey, or the Abbey Church of St Mary the Virgin, is located in Gloucestershire, south-west England.

carburettor: part of the internal combustion engine of a car, which supplies a mixture of fuel and air.

Egypt: Egyptomania, the appropriation and exploitation of Egyptian history and culture, took hold of Europe in the early nineteenth century, and interest was renewed after the discovery of Tutankhamun's (*c.*1341–1323 BC) tomb in 1922. Some writers constructed Egypt as a space of sexual transgression. Wilde's 174-line poem 'The Sphinx' (1894), for instance, features a young man asking the Sphinx 'Who were your lovers?' and speculating about her sexual adventures before accusing her of waking 'foul dreams of sensual life' and turning to his crucifix and Christian faith. See *Selected Poems* (London: Phoenix, 2010), 76–88 (79, 88). Hirschfeld includes Hatshepsut (*c.*1507–1458 BC), the fifth Pharaoh of the Eighteenth Dynasty of Egypt, in a chapter on 'The History of Homosexuality' (*Die Homosexualität des Mannes und des Weibes* (Berlin: Louis Marcus, 1914), 739). Ellis includes her as an example of 'Sexual Inversion in Women' (*SI*, 196). In RH's *A Saturday Life*, Sidonia Shore's parents are Egyptologists.

148 *cur*: a contemptuous term for a worthless or low-bred dog; also 'a term of contempt: a surly, ill-bred, low, or cowardly fellow' (*OED*).

149 *some curious, primitive thing conceived in a turbulent age of transition*: a paradoxical description of Stephen as both primitive and a product of modernity (see Introduction, p. xxviii), and a direct echo of Chapter 5. As she prepares to fight Roger Antrim in her Liberty smock, Stephen appears 'grotesque and splendid, like some primitive thing conceived in a turbulent age of transition' (p. 51). Carpenter's *Intermediate Types among Primitive Folk* was published in 1914.

'Could you marry me, Stephen?': RH considered herself married to UT (*AWCJ*, 137). In a 1934 statement about *TWoL* written in response to an

enquiry from literary critic Gorham Munson (1896–1969), RH anticipated that sexual inverts would one day be given the option to legalize their unions: 'Like their more normal brethren they are honest, simple souls who long to live honestly and to live as themselves, they desire to form a part of the social scheme, to conform in all ways to the social code as it exists at present. Because, though they see its imperfections as every intelligent person must, they realise that, on the whole, this code as it is—save for its injustice towards themselves—is a workable and necessary proposition unless we are to fall into chaos. Such inverts desire to legalise their unions. Preposterous, do you say? And yet it may come, though I may not be here to welcome its coming' (Hall–Troubridge Papers, 17.3).

150 *'Littera scripta manet'*: 'The written word remains', extracted from 'Vox audita perit, littera scripta manet', meaning 'The spoken word perishes, but the written word remains'.

freak: the term is used eight times in *TWoL* to refer to Stephen and other sexual inverts (p. 263). Gaining currency in the early nineteenth century, the noun described 'a person, plant, or animal with an unusual physical abnormality' (*OED*).

putting down at birth: Ralph uses eugenic rhetoric to call for the extinction of sexually inverted people like Stephen.

151 *make feeble love*: (see also 'love-making', p. 189), not to have sex but to make amorous advances.

abomination: the term is repeatedly used in Leviticus, Deuteronomy, and other parts of the Bible to describe loathsome behaviour and offences against God. In Leviticus: 'If a man also lie with mankind, as he lieth with a woman, both of them have committed an abomination: they shall surely be put to death; their blood *shall be* upon them' (20:13).

152 *'Why am I as I am—and what am I?'*: Stephen's struggle to understand or define herself and her desire, here and elsewhere in the novel, echoes sexological case studies. In *Sexual Inversion,* for instance, a male sexual invert (Case V) states that 'My own sexual nature was a mystery to me' (*SI*, 132). A crossed-out section of the handwritten draft provides more detail about Stephen's dawning self-awareness: 'It had seemed so natural, this falling in love, that at first she had not realised its strangeness. It had come, that was all, and she had accepted its coming with joy, as a thing almost holy, as a thing that was greater and finer than she was, not stopping to think of its strangeness. Had this thing ever happened to anyone before? She remembered half understood allusions in the Classics. Puddle had never dwelt on those allusions—nor had she. They had not seemed to matter much—it was all such a very long time ago—everything was that happened in the Classics. Still she would read up those curious allusions. Oh, but she wanted something more concrete than were Classical allusions, yet where could she find it? To whom could she turn for enlightenment, advice—her father was dead' (Hall–Troubridge Papers, 13.3). In E. M. Forster's (1879–1970) *Maurice* (written 1913–14;

published 1971), Plato's *Symposium* plays a vital role in making two of the main characters, Maurice and Clive, aware of the possibility of male–male intimacy. The first edition of *Sexual Inversion* included a long appendix by Symonds, titled 'A Problem in Greek Ethics', which discussed (predominantly male) same-sex desire in classical Greek literature and culture. Symonds described in his *Memoirs* how the discovery of Plato's work (specifically the *Phaedrus* and *Symposium*) was a sexual 'revelation' that allowed him to understand his own sexuality as a young man (*The Memoirs of John Addington Symonds: A Critical Edition*, ed. Amber K. Regis (Basingstoke: Palgrave, 2016), 152).

152 *execration*: an archaic term, meaning to utter or to lay someone under a curse; also, as is the case here, 'utter detestation; intense abhorrence' (*OED*). The term is used in the Bible: 'ye shall be an execration, and an astonishment, and a curse, and a reproach' (Jeremiah 42:18).

153 *She was frightened . . . wounded*: like the hunted fox, 'with the desperate eyes of the hopelessly pursued, bright with terror and glancing now this way now that as though looking for something; and the thought came to Stephen: "It's looking for God Who made it"' (p. 124).

'I know . . . great life-work, Stephen': Puddle's unspoken words offer readers an affirmative framework for understanding Stephen. Puddle's claim that Stephen is a part of nature and neither morally corrupt nor 'mad' aligns with ideas presented by reform-oriented sexologists including Carpenter, Ellis, Hirschfeld, and Ulrichs (see Introduction, p. xxiii). In a letter to Souline dated 20 August 1934, RH writes: 'I am an invert, and all the world knows precisely what I am—and all the world is accepting the fact we people have got our nitch [*sic*] in nature, and my book: The Well of Loneliness, has helped this on by bringing about a better understanding' (Hall–Troubridge Papers, 46.5).

154 *For none knew better*: another indirect reference (see 'old sorrows, old miseries, long decently buried but now disinterred by this pitiful Stephen', p. 111) to Puddle's own sexual inversion. See Appendix, p. 431 (2.5), where Puddle's concerns for Stephen are graver still.

the terrible nerves of the invert: RH supported the view that a 'highly sensitized nervous system' was 'characteristic of inversion' (Hall–Troubridge Papers, 17.3). Krafft-Ebing and other late nineteenth-century sexologists claimed that sexual inversion was caused by an 'inherited pathological constitution of the central nervous system' (*PS*, 34). While these differences were often described in stigmatizing terms, they were also linked to a heightened sensitivity towards external stimuli that could result in profound imaginative and creative talents. In *Sexual Inversion*, the invert 'is specially liable to suffer from a high degree of neurasthenia, often involving much nervous weakness and irritability' (*SI*, 332), but their nervous temperament could lead to an increased ability to connect sensorially to the world: 'the congenitally inverted may, I believe, be looked upon as a class of individuals exhibiting nervous characters which to some extent approximate them to persons of artistic genius' (*SI*, 296). Carpenter approvingly cited sexologist Otto de Joux, arguing that the 'nerve-system of many an Urning is the finest and the most complicated musical instrument' (*TIS*, 34). This nervous predisposition, de Joux suggested, allowed the Urning to experience heightened 'emotion and sympathy' (*TIS*, 33). We have already learned that Stephen is 'painfully hyper-sensitive' (p. 45).

seven-league boots: translated from the French *bottes de sept lieues*, popularized by Charles Perrault's (1628–1703) fairy tales. The legendary boots allow the wearer to take individual strides of seven leagues.

157 *Mrs. John Laing . . . Frau Karl Druschki*: different varieties of roses. The Frau Karl Druschki rose, which reminds Ralph of Angela, is also known as the Snow Queen. Ralph and Stephen are binding Mrs John Laing with bass, a kind of gardener's twine.

159 *Watergate Bay*: the Watergate Bay Hotel, built in 1900, is near the coastal town of Newquay in North Cornwall. The 1928 *Great Western Railway Guide* describes the hotel as being 'in one of the most charming positions in the Cornish Riviera, and within 20 yards of the Atlantic Ocean. Magnificent views of Cliffs, Sands and Ocean from Hotel Grounds'. RH, UT, and Ladye stayed at Watergate Bay in 1915 (*AWCJ*, 121). 'There,' recalls UT, 'my intimacy with John developed in the course of long walks and talks and drives in the local jingles' (*LaD*, 48).

160 *'Have you noticed . . . I sometimes feel sorry for her'*: *The Unlit Lamp* features a mother–daughter hotel stay in Lynton, North Devon, where Joan Ogden's unusual appearance attracts attention. Two young girls 'with bobbed hair and tailored clothes' describe Joan as 'a funny old thing' and a 'forerunner, a kind of pioneer that's got left behind' (*UL*, 284). The scene—and the novel itself—was prompted by the sight of a 'maiden daughter' attending to her elderly mother during a holiday at the Lynton Cottage Hotel: RH apparently turned to UT and said, 'Isn't it ghastly to see these unmarried daughters who are just unpaid servants and the old people sucking the very life out of them like octopi!' UT describes RH's sudden urge to write *Octopi*, her first novel (published as *The Unlit Lamp*), as 'the most important decision of her life' (*LaD*, 69).

shoot: a shooting party. We later learn that Ralph is 'a wonderful shot' (p. 172).

161 *her mother's deep eyes*: while Anna has 'blue Irish eyes' (p. 64), Stephen has inherited the 'brave hazel eyes' of her father (p. 13).

And one evening . . . quickened: in Chapter 2, Stephen decides not to 'discuss her affection for Collins' with her mother (p. 28). RH's work often idealizes mothers and motherhood while at the same time presenting fraught relationships between mothers and children. In *The Unlit Lamp*, Joan Ogden considers 'the ideal mother-love; it never waned, but it never exacted. It was a beautiful thing [. . .]. It was a love that kissed you quietly on both cheeks, too sure of itself to need undue demonstration' (*UL*, 141).

161 *all the bitterness, all the sweetness of her*: Sappho used the word *glukupikron* ('bittersweet') to describe Eros. See Anne Carson, *Eros the Bittersweet: An Essay* (Princeton: Princeton University Press, 1986). In Chapter 3, the 'white smell' (p. 30) of the wildflowers that so overwhelms Stephen is at once pungent and sweet. In the Book of Revelation, when John eats the angel's 'little book', he finds that 'it was in my mouth sweet as honey: and as soon as I had eaten it, my belly was bitter' (10:10).

162 *fagged*: 'to decline in vigour or strength [. . .]; to tire or flag after exertion' (*OED*).

163 *hunger of the eyes*: this phrase, which appears twice here and again in Chapter 23 (p. 174), is also found in Algernon Charles Swinburne's (1837–1909) essay 'The Portrait' (written in 1861; privately printed in 1909). Swinburne was an English poet, novelist, and critic whose work engaged with taboo topics including lesbian desire (see 'Sapphics', in *Poems and Ballads: First Series*, 1866). RH's early poetry was inspired by Swinburne, and she published an 'Ode to Swinburne' in *Poems of the Past and Present* (1910) to mark his death. In Dellamora's words, RH's poem 'sutures Hall's Sapphism with the tradition of male Aestheticism and Decadence' (*Radclyffe Hall: A Life in the Writing*, 45). In 'The Portrait', Swinburne expresses a sensuous synaesthetic view of art, stating that the artwork must satisfy 'not the wonder and hunger of the eyes only, but also the mouth and the ears' (Algernon Charles Swinburne, 'The Portrait', in *Major Poems and Selected Prose*, ed. Jerome McGann and Charles L. Sligh (New Haven: Yale University Press, 2004), 437–9 (438)).

diadems worthy of Cleopatra: Cleopatra VII Philopator (69–30 BC) was queen of the Ptolemaic Kingdom of Egypt from 51 to 30 BC. She is usually depicted wearing a royal diadem (a headband-like crown) as a sign of her sovereignty and power.

Bond Street: located in Mayfair in the West End of London, Bond Street connects Piccadilly and Oxford Street and is often described as the home of luxury shopping. A number of the high-end Bond Street jewellers available to Stephen still operate today: Beards, established in 1804, is one of the oldest jewellery houses in England. The experience of shopping on Bond Street is described in Virginia Woolf's 'Mrs Dalloway on Bond Street' (1923).

164 *Pearls*: we might read Stephen's search for 'one pearl' against the Parable of the Pearl (Matthew 13:45–6). In the Bible, pearls symbolize purity, wisdom, the heavenly (Revelation 21:21; Stephen goes on to describe the pearl as 'some sort of celestial marble'), and, by contrast, feminine immodesty (Revelation 17:3–5; 1 Timothy 2:9). RH's poem 'A Pearl Necklace' (1908), inspired by a gift she gave to Violet Hunt (*AWCJ*, 55), appears in *A Sheaf of Verses* (London: John and Edward Bumpus, 1908), 81. The likeness of a pearl to a clitoris has led to its exploration in erotic lesbian poetry and fiction: see e.g. Carol Ann Duffy's 'Warming Her Pearls' (1987) and Sarah Waters's *Tipping the Velvet* (1998) and *Fingersmith* (2002).

166 *dandy*: one of a number of hints (see also 'he had sown no few wild oats', p. 10) that Philip has had an interesting past. Connotations of dandyism changed over the nineteenth century and would have been different for Philip and Stephen in their twenties: the jeweller may simply be referring to Philip's taste for high fashion, whereas Stephen would associate the dandy with the Decadent movement of the late nineteenth century and, by extension, with sexual and gender transgression. RH much admired Wilde, and she read his work as part of her research towards *TWoL* (*AWCJ*, 229). Dellamora argues that 'Hall's gender-crossing ways are [best] understood as the expression of a self-consciously modern, female dandyism' (*Radclyffe Hall: A Life in the Writing*, 86).

reference: a guarantee that the cheque will clear, i.e. that Stephen has sufficient funds to purchase the ring.

167 *good with the goodness of home*: 'good with the goodness of danger' is how Stephen imagines the 'man's life' that is available to Martin (p. 100).

168 *cup of pleasure*: the Roman statesman and philosopher Cicero (106–43 BC) writes in *Tusculan Disputations V* (*c.*45 BC): 'where we see a man passionately stirred with the madness of lust, desiring all things in a fury of unsatisfied longing, and the more copiously he drains the cup of pleasure wherever offered, the deeper and more consuming his thirst, would you not rightly pronounce him utterly wretched?' (Loeb Classical Library (Cambridge, MA: Harvard University Press, 2014), 441). Whereas humans struggle to moderate their passions, Raftery's cup of pleasure is 'innocent'.

mumbling from Revelation: 'And the heads . . . brimstone': Williams is reading from the final book of the New Testament: 'And thus I saw the horses in the vision, and them that sat on them, having breastplates of fire, and of jacinth, and brimstone: and the heads of the horses *were* as the heads of lions; and out of their mouths issued fire and smoke and brimstone' (Revelation 9:17).

170 *Saint John*: the author of the Book of Revelation refers to himself as 'John', but his identity is disputed. RH suggests that the name refers to John the Apostle, also known as St John the Beloved, one of the Twelve Apostles of Jesus.

171 *'and the ice . . . and our home is Morton. . . .'*: Stephen is reciting the words she spoke during Angela's first visit to Morton (p. 144). The hopeful vision of a shared future has not come to pass. Stephen will revisit this memory again in Chapter 27 (p. 200).

172 *the manner of sixty*: presumably with the manner of a 60-year-old woman; Violet is very condescending towards Stephen.

ironmonger: we have previously learned that Ralph is an 'important Birmingham magnate who had lately retired from some hardware concern' (p. 129). He is wealthy but not of the landed gentry like Violet and Stephen; he later jokes that he is 'just a plain tradesman' (p. 182).

174 *crêpe de Chine*: a luxurious thin and transparent gauze-like fabric, usually made of raw silk.

176 *She seemed . . . strength of a woman*: the idea that sexual inverts combined conventionally masculine and feminine traits in beneficial ways was articulated by Carpenter (see Introduction, p. xxiii).

177 *If our love is a sin*: reform-oriented sexologists tended to reject the association of same-sex desire with sin. Later editions of *Psychopathia Sexualis* include 'the memorial of an urning' who is 'a man of high position in London' and who reports: 'some [urnings] at last come to the knowledge that the powerful instinct born in them cannot possibly be sinful, and, therefore they cease to try to do the impossible—the repression of the instinct' (*PS*, 410–11).

weary unto death: Christ is 'weary unto death' before his crucifixion (Matthew 26:38; appears as 'My soul is exceeding sorrowful, even unto death' in the Authorized King James Version).

Colonial home . . . Potomac River: Angela's family home in the south-eastern state of Virginia is described as Colonial, a style of architecture combining Old and New World features that emerged during the colonial period of North America (1492–1763). The house is situated near the Potomac River, which flows to the Chesapeake Bay, one of the main entry points for enslaved people who had forcibly been brought to the US. We learn that Angela's ancestors belonged to the so-called 'Southern gentry' and profited from the institution of slavery, which was formally ended as a result of the American Civil War (1861–5). RH visited her mother's homeland of America several times as a child and spent a year there in her twenties, staying mainly in the Washington DC area (*AWCJ*, 19, 44). A number of her early poems describe locations on the American East coast—see 'Georgetown, U.S.A.' and 'On the Potomac River U.S.A.' (*Songs*, 61–4).

179 *'Have you understood me?'*: Angela is making sure Stephen has understood that she has had sex before marriage. In the handwritten draft, Angela is more direct: 'Stephen I gave in—for a while I was that man[']s mistress' (Hall–Troubridge Papers, 13.4).

crocked up: also 'crocking' (p. 180), 'to become feeble, collapse, give way, break down' (*OED*).

180 *pound of flesh*: from Shakespeare's *Merchant of Venice* (e.g. III. iii. 33); 'something strictly or legally due, but which it is ruthless or inhuman to demand' (*OED*).

cinch: a strap that holds a saddle on a horse; used figuratively to describe 'a sure, safe, or easy thing; a dead certainty' (*OED*).

183 *argue with God like Job*: in the Bible, Job is a prosperous and devout man whose piety is tested when a series of disasters, orchestrated by Satan, besets him and his family. When Job questions God, God responds directly (the Divine Speeches, Job 38–41) and ultimately restores Job's

faith. The Book of Job engages with the problem of divine justice and asks why righteous people are made to suffer. Puddle pleads with God on Stephen's behalf, quoting Job 10:8. These words will be repeated in Chapter 28 (p. 213).

congenital unsoundness: like Ralph, Roger judges Stephen through a eugenicist lens: a horse would not be bred if it showed inheritable signs of disease. Ellis uses the term 'congenital inversion' to signal that most forms of sexual inversion are inborn and firmly established from birth (see Introduction, p. xxiii). Douglas of the *Sunday Express* called into question *TWoL*'s model of inborn inversion: 'These moral derelicts are not cursed from their birth. Their downfall is caused by their own act and their own will. They are damned because they choose to be damned, not because they are doomed from the beginning' (in *PP*, 38).

185 *shedding tears as of blood*: an allusion to Jesus in the Garden of Gethsemane before his crucifixion: 'And being in an agony he prayed more earnestly: and his sweat was as it were great drops of blood falling down to the ground' (Luke 22:44).

186 *West End tailor's*: London's West End is home to Savile Row, famous for bespoke men's tailoring.

Métallurgique: a car manufactured by Société Anonyme L'Auto Métallurgique in Marchienne-au-Pont, Belgium, between 1898 and 1928.

brocade: a luxurious, patterned, woven fabric. In August 1920, RH's tailor fitted her with a brocade smoking jacket, which she wore in several photographs (*AWCJ*, 151–2). The smoking jacket became part of RH's signature look.

carnations: Oscar Wilde made the dyed green carnation a symbol of homosexuality and decadence. The actor playing dandy Cecil Graham in Wilde's play *Lady Windermere's Fan* sported a green carnation on opening night in 1892; Wilde apparently encouraged his followers to wear the flower, which represented a combination of nature and artifice, on their lapels. In 1894, Robert Hitchens anonymously published a satirical novel about Wilde and the Decadent movement titled *The Green Carnation*. The flower also features in Noël Coward's (1899–1973) song 'We All Wear a Green Carnation' from his operetta *Bitter Sweet* (1929; see note to p. 221).

stared at herself in the glass: Prosser argues that the mirror scene expresses Stephen's trans identity, since her body in this moment is felt to be 'uninhabitable in its femaleness' (in *PP*, 138). He draws particular attention to the 'thrice repetition of the "yet" in this short passage' (*PP*, 138), which signals the ambivalence that Stephen feels towards her body.

groped for the God who had fashioned her: like the hunted fox, 'looking for God Who made it' (p. 124).

187 *'A perfect duck of a house in Belgravia'*: 'What a jolly little duck of a house!' appears in John Galsworthy's (1867–1933) *To Let* (1921), the third and final novel in *The Forsyte Saga*. Among London's most desirable districts,

Belgravia has long been home to the rich and famous. Stanley Baldwin (1867–1947), prime minister at the time of *TWoL*'s composition and publication, purchased a house in Belgravia in 1913.

187 *Apostle teaspoons . . . salver from . . . tenants*: Violet and Alec have received gifts for their new household as a married couple. Apostle teaspoons are so named because the top of the handle is shaped like an apostle or saint; a salver is a tray for serving refreshments or presenting visiting cards or letters.

188 *how straight can run the path of true love*: adapted from Shakespeare's *A Midsummer Night's Dream*: 'The course of true love never did run smooth' (I. i. 134).

pariah, hiding her sores: a pariah is a member of a low caste or an outcast; a despised person. In the Bible, Lazarus is described as a 'beggar [. . .] full of sores' (Luke 16:20). In the Gospel of John (11–12), Jesus performs a miracle by bringing Lazarus back to life four days after his death.

forging: RH's first published novel was *The Forge* (1924).

The splendid new motor: see Appendix, p. 431 (2.6).

189 *foil*: 'a light weapon used in fencing; a kind of small-sword with a blunt edge and a button at the point' (*OED*).

190 *Black Mountains*: Stephen and Angela are driving westward from the Malvern Hills towards the Wye Valley and the Welsh border. In the distance, they can see the Black Mountains, which form part of the Bannau Brycheiniog (formerly Brecon Beacons) National Park in South Wales. Pen Cerrig-calch and Pen y Gadair Fawr ('Gadrfaer') are the highest and second-highest peaks in the Black Mountains.

191 *Symond's Yat*: Stephen is planning to drive westward towards Symonds Yat, a picturesque village in the Wye Valley, and cross over into Wales. The market town of Abergavenny is often described as the gateway to Wales.

192 *cachet*: a wafer or capsule enclosing a dose of medicine, introduced by Limousin of Paris in the 1870s.

196 *God's mistake*: in *Psychopathia Sexualis*, Countess Sarolta V/Count Sandor V (see note to p. 56) declares that their desires are God-given: 'Love led me to take the step I took; all my deeds were conditioned by it. God put it in my heart. If he created me so, and not otherwise, am I then guilty; or is it the eternally incomprehensible way of fate?' (*PS*, 313).

197 *pervert . . . degenerate creature*: the defence lawyer in the UK obscenity trial, Norman Birkett (1883–1962), differentiated between 'perverts' and 'inverts' on the grounds that the former chose to engage in same-sex practices whereas the latter were born with these desires and therefore not responsible for their actions (in *PP*, 40). Similar distinctions can be found in sexological writings including *Psychopathia Sexualis* (56). The term 'degenerate' describes a person 'who has lost, or has become deficient in, the qualities considered proper to the race or kind; [. . .] a person of

debased physical or mental constitution' (*OED*). The suggestion of a relationship between homosexuality and degeneracy is dismissed by a number of sexologists: Carpenter cites German psychiatrist Paul Naecke (1851–1913) in *Der Tag* on 26 October 1907, who observes that 'the best experts in the subject have so far not discovered more psychic abnormalities among homosexuals than among heterosexuals—nor more degeneracy or signs of degeneracy' (*TIS*, 161). At the turn of the twentieth century, the idea of degeneracy was famously popularized in German physician Max Nordau's (1849–1923) *Degeneration* (published in German as *Entartung* in 1892 and in English in February 1895, just months before Wilde's conviction for gross indecency on 25 May 1895). Nordau's succès de scandale takes aim at Decadence: Wilde is presented as an idle egotist who 'despises Nature' and 'apparently admires immorality, sin and crime' (*Degeneration* (London: William Heinemann, 1895), 319, 320).

Lamb of God stuff: Jesus is described as the 'Lamb of God, which taketh away the sin of the world' (John 1:29).

198 *flesh of flesh*: in Genesis (2:23), God creates Eve out of Adam's rib: 'And Adam said, This *is* now bone of my bones, and flesh of my flesh: she shall be called Woman, because she was taken out of Man.'

Dear Lady Anna . . . Ralph Crossby: see Appendix, p. 432 (2.7). When Stephen reads Ralph's letter, she stands as though 'turned to stone'; in Genesis 19:26, Lot's disobedient wife is turned into 'a pillar of salt' for looking back upon the destruction of Sodom and Gomorrah. The phrase is repeated in Chapter 37 (p. 291).

199 *My gorge rises*: 'gorge' is an archaic term for the throat or stomach; to make someone's gorge rise is to make them sick. Used figuratively, a rising or risen gorge is a sign of 'extreme disgust or [. . .] violent resentment' (*OED*), as in Shakespeare's *Hamlet*: 'How abhorred in my imagination it is: my gorge rises at it' (V. i. 178–9).

200 *good, good, good*: in his final judgement in the UK censorship trial, Biron discussed this paragraph at length: 'repeated three times, the last "good" emphasized in order that one may make no mistake about what is meant in this book. [. . .] I am asked to say that this book is in no sense a defence of unnatural practices between women, or a glorification of them, or a praise of them, to put it perhaps not quite so strongly. "Natural" and "Sacred"! "Good" repeated three times' (in *PP*, 44). As we have seen, RH often uses the rhetorical device of epizeuxis (see 'home, home, home', p. 167).

201 *rent-rolls*: 'A roll or register of rents; a list of lands and buildings owned by a person, together with the rents due from them; (also) the sum of a person's income from the rents that are due to him or her' (*OED*).

202 *her father's locked book-case*: Philip's decision to hide his collection of sexological texts behind another row of books and in a locked cabinet is indicative of wider fears regarding the circulation of sexological knowledge in the late nineteenth and early twentieth centuries (see note to p. 7). While many British libraries collected sexological publications, they established

strict access regimes: students wishing to read sexological materials in the Phi Collections at Oxford's Bodleian Library and the Arcana Collections at Cambridge's University Library, for instance, needed to produce a written endorsement from a tutor. Sexological texts were included in the British Museum's private case alongside other allegedly obscene publications. See Lloyd (Meadhbh) Houston, 'Towards a History of the Phi Collection, 1882–1945', *Bodleian Library Record*, 28/2 (Oct. 2015), 179–94, and Liam Sims, '"Scandalous and Libellous Books": the Arc Collection at Cambridge University Library', *Transactions of the Cambridge Bibliographical Society*, 15/4 (2015), 625–45.

202 *the action seemed curiously automatic*: Valerie Rohy interprets this as a scene of 'automatic reading', since Stephen is guided to the study and the sexological books with an 'uncanny sense of somnambulist inevitability' ('Desire and the Scene of Reading', in *Lost Causes: Narrative, Etiology, and Queer Theory* (Oxford: Oxford University Press, 2015), 121).

203 *Krafft Ebing*: Krafft-Ebing practised as a psychiatrist in different German and Austrian hospitals and asylums and later became a professor of psychiatry in Austria. His major work was *Psychopathia Sexualis* (1886), widely recognized as a foundational work of sexology. The book discussed various forms of gender and sexual nonconformity, including homosexuality, sadism, and masochism. It is known for its detailed case studies, many of which give vivid and moving accounts of individual struggles and experiences. Early editions of the work presented same-sex desires in pathological and degenerative terms, but Krafft-Ebing later began to see (some forms of) homosexuality as natural variations (see Introduction, p. xxiii). It is not possible to tell which edition of the book Stephen reads in her father's study. Stephen's sense of relief at learning that she is part of a community of sexual inverts was shared by many readers of *Psychopathia Sexualis*. In 1900, a young nobleman, Von R., wrote to Krafft-Ebing, stating that the book made him realize that 'I am not the only "step-child of nature"' (cited in Harry Oosterhuis, *Stepchildren of Nature: Krafft-Ebing, Psychiatry, and the Making of Sexual Identity* (Chicago: Chicago University Press, 2000), 69). See Appendix, p. 432 (2.8), where Stephen finds a book by Ulrichs (see note to p. 24) instead.

Cain: the firstborn son of Adam and Eve. In Genesis, Cain murders his brother, Abel, who is favoured by God. In response, God condemns Cain to a life of endless wandering, setting a mark on him to prevent him from being killed: 'And Cain said unto the LORD, My punishment *is* greater than I can bear. Behold, thou hast driven me out this day from the face of the earth; and from thy face shall I be hid; and I shall be a fugitive and a vagabond in the earth; and it shall come to pass, *that* every one that findeth me shall slay me. And the LORD said unto him, Therefore whosoever slayeth Cain, vengeance shall be taken on him sevenfold. And the LORD set a mark upon Cain, lest any finding him should kill him' (Genesis 4:13–15). The precise nature of the mark has been widely debated, and some Bible scholars interpret it as a physical blemish.

Where you go, I go, Stephen: the biblical Ruth remains with her husband's mother, Naomi, after both women have been widowed. When Naomi urges Ruth to return to her family, Ruth pleads: 'Intreat me not to leave thee, *or* to return from following after thee: for whither thou goest, I will go; and where thou lodgest, I will lodge' (Ruth 1:16). Ruth has become a symbol of abiding loyalty and devotion.

204 *You've got work to do*: while Puddle's encouraging words and emphasis on Stephen's 'curious double insight' echo sexologists' discussions of inverts' creative talents (see note to p. 154), RH is clear that other inverts are 'less strong and less gifted' than Stephen. Puddle's reassuring claim that sexual inverts are 'all part of nature', like RH's reading of inversion as 'a fact in Nature' (Hall–Troubridge Papers, 17.3), aligns more closely with certain sexological frameworks (see Introduction, p. xxiii).

'I'm here to help you to do it, Stephen': RH adds a note to her handwritten draft: 'At end of Book 2 she is turned out of Morton. In June, aged 22½. Date 1910' (Hall–Troubridge Papers, 12.5).

205 *BOOK THREE*: RH adds notes to her handwritten draft: 'At end Book II Stephen is 22½ when she leaves Morton in June 1910. (that Xmas she was 23.) Raftery is 7 years younger than Stephen' (Hall–Troubridge Papers, 13.4); 'Date 1912 (March). Age 24 + 3 months. Raftery is 17. (Williams is 82)' (Hall–Troubridge Papers, 13.4).

harrow: 'A heavy frame of timber (or iron) set with iron teeth or tines, which is dragged over ploughed land to break clods, pulverize and stir the soil, root up weeds, or cover in the seed' (*OED*).

Chelsea Embankment: a road and walkway on the north bank of the Thames, constructed in 1874. The 200-acre Battersea Park, built between 1854 and 1870, is on the opposite side of the river (or, as we see at the end of this paragraph, 'across the stream'). In early 1909, RH and Granny Diehl moved into an apartment at Shelley Court, 56 Tite Street, close to Ladye's house at Tedworth Square. Tite Street, which was built in 1877 to provide access to the Chelsea Embankment, has a notable queer history: Oscar Wilde lived and wrote at number 34 from January 1885 until his imprisonment ten years later, and number 50 was the home and studio of artist Romaine Brooks (1874–1970) from 1904 to 1905. See Devon Cox, *The Street of Wonderful Possibilities: Whistler, Wilde and Sargent in Tite Street* (London: Frances Lincoln, 2015). RH lived further north of the Thames, at 37 Holland Street, Kensington, when she wrote *TWoL*.

206 *a voracious smoker*: 'In the habits [of the inverted woman] not only is there frequently a pronounced taste for smoking cigarettes, often found in quite feminine women, but also a decided taste and toleration for cigars. There is also a dislike and sometimes incapacity for needle-work and other domestic occupations, while there is often some capacity for athletics' (*SI*, 250). Doan, however, warns that 'we should be cautious in pinning down the cultural significance of monocles, short hair, and cigarettes to any one effect. [. . .] No manner of smoking (the cigarette in its holder, a pipe or

cigar) signaled sexual preference, for all such signs were up for grabs' (*Fashioning Sapphism*, 97, 107).

206 *unmarred by the stiff clumpy plait in the nape of her neck*: RH did not crop her own waist-length hair until 17 December 1920, at the age of 40; the younger RH usually wore her hair 'in tight plaits closely twisted round her small and admirably shaped head' (*LaD*, 45). After the publication of *Adam's Breed*, RH's 'Eton crop' hairstyle attracted attention in newspapers across the world.

Vestal Virgin: in ancient Rome, the six Vestal Virgins were charged with the task of keeping the fire burning in the Temple of Vesta.

Jackson's or Fortnum and Mason: Jacksons of Piccadilly (founded 1700, now owned by Twinings) was a tea house, wine merchant, and high-end department store; Fortnum & Mason (founded 1707), also in London's Piccadilly, is a luxury department store and purveyor of gourmet goods. The other Jackson's in the novel (pp. 31, 68) is evidently a bookshop in Great Malvern.

Brand's Essence: created in 1835 by Henderson William Brand (1805–93) Brand's Essence of Beef or Chicken was marketed as a food supplement and natural stimulant that would 'invigorate the heart and brain immediately'. In Irish writer L. T. Meade's (b. Elizabeth Thomasina Meade, 1844–1914) novel *A Ring of Rubies* (New York: Grosset and Dunlap, 1892), a female character 'in almost the last extremity of weakness' consumes a spoonful of Brand's meat jelly, which 'act[s] as a stimulant at once' (85). Brand's original Essence of Chicken is still available today.

207 *Every morning she rode very early in the park*: in the early days of her relationship with Ladye, RH would transport her horses from Malvern to London and ride on 'the Row' (also known as 'Rotten Row'), the sandy bridleway in Hyde Park connecting Kensington Palace and St James's Palace. 'There was a very handsome cob, Grey Dawn, which she sometimes brought to London and rode in the Row. There was a beloved and very wise hunter, Joseph, who was also sometimes brought to London' (*LaD*, 31–2).

208 *Mothers' Meetings*: though the phrase is now used colloquially to refer to a group of people engaged in chatter, mothers' meetings were regular social gatherings of women connected with a parish or congregation. It would not have been unusual for the 'childless' Mrs Carson to have attended a mothers' meeting. See F. Prochaska, 'A Mother's Country: Mothers' Meetings and Family Welfare in Britain, 1850–1950', *History*, 74/242 (Oct. 1989), 379–99.

Malta: after becoming a British colony in 1814, Malta served as a military base for the British armed forces. The country gained independence in 1964.

'I'm so glad your book has succeeded, Stephen': RH's mother responded to the publication of RH's first published novel, *The Forge*, with similar

indifference: 'Whatever praise or affection she was hoping for she did not receive. Her mother took the book and said nothing. Whether she ever read it, John never knew' (*AWCJ*, 188).

210 *great final expiation*: see note to p. 20. In the Bible, expiation is the removal or cleansing of sin.

a tinker's darn: a tiny amount, or the slightest heed. The *OED* traces the first use of 'tinker's damn' to 1839.

The Literary Monthly: a fictional name for a literary magazine. RH's *The Forge* received positive reviews (*AWCJ*, 188–9). See Appendix, p. 432 (3.1).

make shift: 'To do one's best *with* (inferior means), to be content *with*, put up *with*' (*OED*).

211 *The Furrow*: in Chapter 7, when Stephen first puts pen to paper, she finds herself 'able to write many things that had long lain dormant in her heart—[. . .] those rides home from hunting together with her father—bare furrows, the meaning of those bare furrows. And later, how many queer hopes and queer longings, queer joys and even more curious frustrations' (p. 69). In the handwritten draft of Book Three, Puddle advises an anxious and exhausted Stephen that 'those who set their hand to the plough must go on ploughing up the ground for others' (Hall–Troubridge Papers, 13.4). RH would return to the metaphor in her 1933 lecture on 'The Writing of Novels': 'Persecution is very often the road by which a goal is ultimately reached—the field must submit to being torn by the plough before it can hope to bear a rich harvest' (Hall–Troubridge Papers, 22.3).

212 *'I must work when the spirit moves me'*: Stephen's irregular working hours are similar to RH's own. UT recalls seeing RH 'grey with exhaustion when, determined to dispose of some situation, to complete some section or chapter, she has wrestled vainly, hour after hour, against an inspirational blackout'. UT presents herself as a supportive Puddle-like figure who 'many times implored her to desist, to wait until the spirit really moved her' (*LaD*, 70). RH also 'put a blue pencil through' dissatisfying drafts (see e.g. Hall–Troubridge Papers, 13.4).

213 *It's unfair . . . unnatural repression?*: Stephen's fear that sexual repression may hinder her creativity stands in contrast to the psychoanalytic theory of sublimation—the idea that the sexual drive or libido may be transformed into socially useful activities and achievements. In his 1910 case history of Leonardo da Vinci (1452–1519), Sigmund Freud (1856–1939) argues that the Italian Renaissance polymath's 'cool repudiation of sexuality' was indicative of 'ideal (sublimated) homosexuality' and closely tied to his artistic and intellectual genius. See 'Leonardo da Vinci and a Memory of His Childhood', in *The Standard Edition of the Complete Psychological Works of Sigmund Freud*, xi. *1910*, trans. James Strachey (London: Hogarth Press, 1957), 63–137 (69, 80). Stephen's views align more closely with those expressed by Ellis: 'The method of self-restraint and self-culture, without self-repression, seems to be the most rational method of dealing with sexual inversion when that condition is really organic and

deeply rooted. It is better that a man should be enabled to make the best of his own strong natural instincts, with all their disadvantages, than that he should be unsexed and perverted, crushed into a position which he has no natural aptitude to occupy' (*SI*, 341). Several case histories included in *Sexual Inversion* highlight the harmful impact of sexual repression. Miss H. (History XXXVI), for instance, maintains that 'The effect on her of loving women is distinctly good, [. . .] both spiritually and physically, while repression leads to morbidity and hysteria' (*SI*, 226).

213 *'Thine hands . . . destroy me'*: spoken by Job (10:8; see note to p. 183) when his faith is tested by God.

214 *the heart of the Author knoweth its own sorrows*: 'The heart knoweth his own bitterness; and a stranger does not intermeddle with his joy' (Proverbs 14:10).

the tan of the Row: a reference to the sandy colour of Hyde Park's Rotten Row (see note to p. 207). The hard surface has taken its toll on Raftery's legs.

Professor Hobday: Sir Frederick Thomas George Hobday (1870–1939), celebrated veterinary surgeon and principal of the Royal Veterinary College, London, from 1927 to 1937. A pioneering specialist in the use of anaesthesia beyond the laboratory, Hobday published *Anaesthesia and Narcosis of Animals and Birds* in 1915. From 1912 until his death, Hobday was honorary veterinary surgeon to Alexandra of Denmark (1844–1925), mother of George V (1865–1936).

218 *And there . . . almost childish*: see Appendix, p. 433 (3.2).

219 *'Bury him here,' she said briefly*: in UT's words, RH's 'beloved and very wise hunter' Joseph lived 'until old age brought infirmity and, like Raftery in *The Well of Loneliness*, of whom he was to some extent the prototype, he was shot in her presence' (*LaD*, 32). In an article for the *Irish Times* in 2019, Frank McNally observes that 'by some accounts, the death of a horse was also a pivotal event in the two-legged Raftery's life' ('Raftery Remembered—Frank McNally on two contrasting tributes to the Bard of Kiltimagh', 31 Jan. 2019).

stud-book: an official record of the pedigree of purebred animals.

curry comb: used for removing mud and loose hair from a horse's coat, and for cleaning other brushes. The verb 'curry' means 'to rub down or dress (a horse, ass, etc.) with a comb' (*OED*).

221 *Jonathan Brockett, the playwright*: as Terry Castle has shown, Jonathan Brockett was likely modelled on gay playwright, composer, director, actor, and singer Noël Coward. RH and UT, keen theatre-goers and 'first night-ers', had met Coward 'through shared friends in the theater—probably the playwright Gabrielle Enthoven [1868–1950] or the American [Argentine] singer-actress Teddie Gerard [1890–1942]' in the mid-1920s. In the run-up to *TWoL*'s trial, Coward would provide 'much-needed behind-the-scenes moral support'. See Castle, *Noël Coward and Radclyffe*

Hall: Kindred Spirits (New York: Columbia University Press, 1996), 20, 22, 38–55. RH's lecture 'The "First Night"', where she discusses 'the charm, the allure of "first nights," their irresistible attraction', is in Hall–Troubridge Papers, 22.2 (1). See Appendix, p. 433 (3.3), where an earlier version of Brockett asks Stephen a direct question about her sexuality.

any port in a storm: used to suggest that any refuge, however unappealing, will suffice in times of trouble; first recorded in John Cleland's (*c.* 1709–89) *Fanny Hill, or Memoirs of a Woman of Pleasure* (1748–9).

his hands: 'The physical resemblance to Coward is strong—even down to the insinuating "feminine" hands. [. . .] Coward's white hands, languidly supporting a cigarette, were of course an essential part of his visual mystique—and "womanly" enough to make his occasional drag appearances fairly unnerving' (Castle, *Noël Coward and Radclyffe Hall*, 40–2; see note above). In the handwritten draft, RH notes that 'he seemed completely a-sexsual [*sic*], so that on that score she did not fear him—but her gorge rose when ever she looked at his hands' (Hall–Troubridge Papers, 13.4).

222 *Seven Dials*: an area of London's West End, to the north-west of Covent Garden, where seven roads converge at a circular junction. The New Theatre (now the Noël Coward Theatre), where Coward made his West End debut in his own play *I'll Leave It to You: A Light Comedy in Three Acts* (1920), is on St Martin's Lane, Seven Dials.

thistledown: the soft, thin, white threads that are attached to thistle seeds, allowing them to be blown through the air.

223 *The Good Housewife*: given Stephen's apparent lack of interest in domestic affairs, the title of this fictional women's magazine might raise a smile. The American *Good Housekeeping* was launched in May 1885, with the first British edition appearing in March 1922. As Mike Ashley observes, before its wartime shift 'to more sentimental stories', *Good Housekeeping* was 'one of the premier fiction-carrying magazines in Britain' (*The Age of the Storytellers: British Popular Fiction Magazines, 1880–1950* (London: British Library, 2006), 254). The day before *TWoL*'s publication, a 'good housekeeping' interview with RH was printed in the *Daily Mail* (Evelyn Irons, 'Woman's Place *Is* the Home', 26 July 1928; an earlier interview, 'How Other Women Run Their Homes', had been published in the same newspaper on 11 May 1927). RH presented herself as a committed home-maker, informing readers of her 'housemaid's seeing eye' and 'perfect mania for cleanliness'. Doan describes RH as 'a clever tactician in seizing on the eve of the novel's publication the opportunity to reassure readers that she was by no means radical and that, on the contrary, she was eager to endorse the social values of the dominant culture'; Susan Fraiman has been 'far more willing to be seduced by Hall's housekeeping language' in the interviews. See Doan, '"Woman's Place *Is* the Home": Conservative Sapphic Modernity', in Doan and Jane Garrity (eds.), *Sapphic Modernities: Sexuality, Women and National Culture* (Basingstoke: Palgrave Macmillan,

2006), 91–105 (104), and Susan Fraiman, *Extreme Domesticity: A View from the Margins* (New York: Columbia University Press, 2017), 205 n. 27.

223 *beef-tea*: 'The juice of beef extracted by prolonged simmering in a very little water, used as a nutritious food for invalids' (*OED*); a type of restorative broth.

224 *reindeer gloves*: a 1910 *Vogue* article on 'The Well-Dressed Man' suggests grey reindeer gloves for afternoon wear (36/9 (Nov. 1910), 61).

baronia: presumably *Boronia megastigma*, commonly known as brown boronia, a sweet-scented evergreen shrub.

pâté de foie gras . . . Rose's lime-juice: pâté de foie gras is a rich delicacy, often served as an appetizer, made from the enlarged liver of a goose or duck. We go on to learn that Brockett's pâté from Fortnum & Mason contains truffles, making it even more of a speciality. The production of foie gras involves the cruel force-feeding of the bird in order to fatten its liver, hence Brockett's feeling 'so sorry for the geese' (p. 225). Huntley & Palmers Rich Mixed Biscuits were 'a delicious assortment including twenty-four different kinds of Huntley & Palmers['] most popular biscuits' (advertisement in the *Illustrated Sporting and Dramatic News*, 5 Dec. 1908, 567). Rose's lime juice was the first commercially produced concentrate fruit juice, patented in 1867, and advertised as the 'original and still the best lime juice in the World' (in *Country Life*, 25 Jan. 1913, 27).

225 *From time to time . . . tropical fever*: as Brockett has been in Paris, it is likely that his 'gross' yellow cigarettes are Gitanes Maïs (launched in 1918, eight years after the original Gitanes): small, strong-smelling cigarettes made of dark tobacco encased in corn paper. With a name meaning 'Gypsy woman', intended to evoke Spain, Gitanes were considered a classier alternative to the working man's Gauloises. Though 1920s advertisements for Gitanes emphasized exoticism, they were produced not on 'an unpropitious island' but in France. Small yellow cigarettes serve as markers of luxury and effeminacy in Guy Thorne's bestselling novel *When It Was Dark: The Story of a Great Conspiracy* (1903; Bath: Cedric Chivers, 1974): Professor Robert Llwellyn—whose dressing room 'suggests a man about town, a dandy with many sartorial interests'—smokes 'tiny yellow cigarettes', identified as Greek Salonikas (58).

226 *Ogilvy*: 'Miss Ogilvy Finds Herself' is the title of RH's best-known short story and only collection of short fiction, published in 1934. In the 'Author's Forenote' to the collection, RH states that the story was written in July 1926, 'shortly before I definitely decided to write my serious study of congenital sexual inversion, *The Well of Loneliness*' (*MO*, n.p.). Jana Funke has drawn attention to an alternative draft with a 'strikingly different' ending (*TW*, 30). *Miss Ogilvy Finds Herself* received poor reviews (*AWCJ*, 307–8).

227 *bran-pie*: 'A tub full of bran with small gifts hidden in it to be drawn out at random, as part of festivities at Christmas, etc.' (*OED*); a lucky dip. We will meet Valérie Seymour in Chapter 31.

229 *Moloch*: generally understood to be a Canaanite deity to whom children were sacrificed, though this has been subject to debate. In the handwritten draft, RH writes and crosses out 'the flesh of babies' before ending the sentence 'live flesh and blood' (Hall–Troubridge Papers, 13.5). In the New Testament, Stephen names Moloch as he denounces his accusers and their ancestors, quoting the Book of Amos (5:26–7): 'Yea, ye took up the tabernacle of Moloch, and the star of your god Remphan, figures which ye made to worship them : and I will carry you away beyond Babylon' (Acts 7:43).

230 *At Morton . . . distance*: we might read this sentence, written in the style of a children's story, against the opening line of the novel's third paragraph.

Like a vine: 'Thy mother *is* like a vine in thy blood, planted by the waters: she was fruitful and full of branches by reason of many waters' (Ezekiel 19:10).

231 *cried out for light in His darkness*: in this paragraph, Philip is both God the creator ('Let there be light', Genesis 1:2–3) and St Christopher, with 'a patient, protective back, bowed as though bearing another's burden' (see p. 85 with note; see also p. 216). Stephen is once again identified with the martyred Christ: 'Now from the sixth hour there was darkness over all the land unto the ninth hour. And about the ninth hour Jesus cried with a loud voice, saying, Eli, Eli, lama sabachthani? that is to say, My God, my God, why hast thou forsaken me?' (Matthew 27:45–6). The New Testament is rich in light/darkness symbolism, e.g. 'I am come a light into the world, that whomsoever believeth on me should not abide in darkness' (John 12:46).

yoke: 'a device fitted to the neck of a pair of draught animals to enable them to pull a plough, cart, etc., together; a similar device fitted to a single draught animal for the same purpose' (*OED*). In the Bible, 'yoke' is used both literally and metaphorically ('Take my yoke upon you, and learn of me [. . .] For my yoke *is* easy, and my burden is light', Matthew 11:29–30).

232 *large, brown hands*: in stark contrast to Brockett's 'soft white hands' (p. 229). Martin Hallam has 'bony, brown hands with spatulate fingers' (p. 91).

Thus was Anna Gordon baptized . . . salvation: 'I indeed baptize you with water unto repentance: but he that cometh after me is mightier than I, whose shoes I am not worthy to bear: he shall baptize you with the Holy Ghost, and *with* fire' (spoken by John the Baptist in Matthew 3:11).

233 *Rue St. Roch*: a street in the first arrondissement of Paris, near to the Musée du Louvre and the Jardin des Tuileries.

Turkish cigarettes: tobacco produced in the Ottoman Empire enjoyed enormous popularity in the years before the First World War. Widely advertised brands included Matinée, Pera, and the 'high-class' El Hamur, marketed as 'the tobacco of tobaccos' (*The Tatler*, 9 Feb. 1910, 11).

Meurice: a palace hotel opposite the Jardin des Tuileries (in its current location since 1835), designed to appeal to British high society and often referred to as 'l'Hôtel des Rois' (the Hotel of Kings) thanks to its many royal guests.

233 *Versailles*: the seventeenth-century Palace of Versailles opened as a museum in 1837. The Treaty of Versailles, signed on 28 June 1919, is known to RH but not to her characters: the First World War is yet to come. Versailles is 12.5 miles south-west of Paris.

Does he remember . . . the right . . . the left?': 'The custom of driving on the right dates from the French Revolution. The revolutionary wars and Napoleon's [1769–1821] subsequent conquests spread the new rightism to the Low Countries, Switzerland, Germany, Italy, Poland, and Spain. The states that had resisted Napoleon kept broadly left—Britain, the Austro-Hungarian Empire, Russia and Portugal. [. . .] This European division, between the left- and right-hand nations[,] remained fixed for more than 100 years, until after the First World War' (Mick Hamer, 'Left is Right on the Road', *New Scientist*, 25 Dec. 1986–1 Jan. 1987, 16–18).

the Hotel des Reservoirs: built in 1751 for Madame de Pompadour (1721–64), and originally connected by corridor to the Palace of Versailles, the building was transformed into a luxury hotel in 1875.

'Oui, monsieur, tout de suite—à l'instant, monsieur!': 'Yes, sir, right away—right this minute, sir!'

234 *Roi Soleil*: literally 'Sun King', Louis XIV (1638–1715), King of France from 1643. From the beginning of his personal rule in 1661, Louis XIV vastly expanded the small château at Versailles into a grand palace and gardens, installing the royal court and government there in 1682.

Galerie des Glaces: a symbol of Louis XIV's absolutist power, the Hall of Mirrors—a long gallery with seventeen windows facing seventeen mirror-clad arches, and a vaulted ceiling featuring thirty paintings (by Charles Le Brun, 1619–90) depicting Louis XIV's successes—was constructed between 1678 and 1684.

the luckless queen: Marie Antoinette (1755–93), the last queen of France before the Revolution (consort of Louis XVI, 1754–93, r. from 1774). The 'small, humble rooms which the queen had chosen' are a suite of private chambers, laid out around two inner courtyards, reserved for Marie Antoinette and her ladies-in-waiting.

235 *Madame de Lamballe*: Marie Thérèse Louise of Savoy, Princesse de Lamballe (1749–92), Superintendent of the Queen's Household from 1774. As Castle points out, this episode is 'incomprehensible without some knowledge of the homoerotic biographical traditions surrounding the queen in the later nineteenth century. Clearly Hall expected her lesbian readers to understand the reference to "Madame de Lamballe" and to find in Brockett's cryptic history lesson a consoling, if melancholy, image of homosexual communion'. Rumours about Marie Antoinette's love of women had circulated from as early as 1776, with anti-royalist pamphleteers in the 1780s and 1790s insisting on the Queen's 'depraved' sexual appetites. See Castle, 'Marie-Antoinette Obsession', *Representations*, 38 (Spring 1992), 1–38 (27), and Nancy N. Barker, '"Let Them Eat

Cake": The Mythical Marie Antoinette and the French Revolution', *The Historian*, 55/4 (Summer 1993), 709–24.

the Tapis Vert: literally 'the Green Carpet', a long lawn lined with statues. The 'straight, lovely line of water' is the Grand Canal.

the Temple d'Amour . . . Hameau: 'the Temple of Love', built 1777–8, is a folly in the English garden of the Petit Trianon, Marie Antoinette's private château on the Versailles estate. Le Hameau de la Reine ('the Queen's Hamlet'), another folly, was built for Marie Antoinette between 1783 and 1786. This ornamental hamlet, complete with a dairy, a windmill, a working farm, and farmers' cottages, allowed the queen to sample the pleasures but not the poverty of rustic life. As the narrator observes, the cottages were 'badly in need of repair' at the time of Stephen and Brockett's visit; the hamlet was not restored until the 1930s.

the Conciergerie: former courthouse and prison where Marie Antoinette was detained and sentenced to death in 1793. La Conciergerie was listed as a national historical monument and opened to the public in 1914.

236 *tread delicately, like Agag*: in the Old Testament, Agag is executed by the prophet Samuel: 'And Samuel said, Bring ye hither to me Agag the king of the Amalekites. And Agag came unto him delicately' (1 Samuel 15:32). Samuel then 'hewed Agag in pieces before the LORD' (15:33).

237 *Rue de la Paix . . . Montmartre*: Rue de la Paix is a fashionable shopping street in the second arrondissement. Montmartre is a hill and surrounding district in the eighteenth arrondissement; the Roman Catholic Basilica of Sacré-Cœur de Montmartre, or simply Sacré-Cœur, is at its summit. Montmartre, meaning 'the mountain of the martyr', takes its name from the third-century martyr St Denis de Paris, believed to have been decapitated in Montmartre around AD 250. In the early twentieth century, Montmartre was a hub of bohemian and avant-garde art and entertainment: Puddle could have passed Pablo Picasso's (1881–1973) studio, the famous Bateau-Lavoir, and the Moulin Rouge cabaret (est. 1889), birthplace of the cancan. In Sue Roe's words, 'the leading artists of the twentieth century spent their early years living among acrobats, dancers, prostitutes and clowns' (*In Montmartre: Picasso, Matisse and Modernism in Paris 1900–1910* (London: Penguin, 2015), p. xiii).

238 *Sufficient unto the day was the evil thereof*: 'Take therefore no thought for the morrow: for the morrow shall take thought for the things of itself. Sufficient unto the day is the evil thereof' (Matthew 6:34).

Valérie Seymour's: closely modelled on RH and UT's friend Natalie Clifford Barney (1876–1972). Born to wealthy parents in Dayton, Ohio, in the American Midwest, Barney was bilingual from childhood, and she would later publish in both English and French. She attended the Les Ruches boarding school in Fontainebleau, France, which featured in Dorothy Strachey's (later Bussy; 1865–1960) autobiographical lesbian novel *Olivia* (1949), and settled permanently in Paris at the turn of the century (see Karla Jay, *The Amazon and the Page: Natalie Clifford Barney and Renée Vivien* (Bloomington: Indiana University Press, 1988), 2–3). Barney was a prolific writer, producing more than twenty volumes of poems, plays, epigrams, portraits of her contemporaries, and one novel. She also gained fame as the hostess of one of the most influential literary salons of the modernist period: her friends and acquaintances included Colette (1873–1954), Djuna Barnes (1892–1982), T. S. Eliot (1888–1965), Janet Flanner (1892–1978), James Joyce (1882–1941), Ezra Pound (1885–1972), Gertrude Stein (1874–1946), Alice B. Toklas (1877–1967), and Paul Valéry (1871–1945). In 1902, Barney was briefly engaged to Oscar Wilde's former lover, Lord Alfred Douglas (Bosie). In addition to her enduring friendships, Barney is known for her romantic and sexual relationships and affairs. Partners included the heiress Eva Palmer (1874–1952), the dancer Liane de Pougy (1869–1950), the poet Renée Vivien (1877–1909), and the painter Romaine Brooks. Barney and Brooks—'both American, rich and grandly lesbian'—met in Paris in 1915; their open relationship lasted more than fifty years (Diana Souhami, *Wild Girls—Paris, Sappho & Art: The Lives and Loves of Natalie Barney & Romaine Brooks* (London: Weidenfeld and Nicolson, 2004), 1). Barney's romantic prowess and circle of sapphic friends are remembered in Barnes's satirical *Ladies Almanack* (1928), which features Barney as Dame Evangeline Musset alongside RH as Tilly Tweed-in-Blood and UT as Lady Buck-and-Balk. RH's deep friendship with Barney began after the two were introduced by Brooks in Paris in January 1922 (*AWCJ*, 193–4). RH's portrayal of her friend as Valérie Seymour in *TWoL* not only reflects the circumstances of Barney's life as a bilingual American socialite living in Paris but also captures 'her charming voice', 'her wit, her literary talent', her abundant 'love affairs', and her appreciation of 'beauty in all its forms'. See Appendix, p. 434 (3.4).

238 *St. Tropez*: a coastal town on the French Riviera. Barney's friend Colette owned a villa in Saint-Tropez, which RH and UT visited in the early 1930s (*AWCJ*, 281). RH also spent time with Brooks and Barney in Saint-Tropez and fictionalized the town as St Loup-sur-Mer in *The Master of the House*.

239 *Quai Voltaire*: a street in the seventh arrondissement of Paris known for its large number of booksellers and antique shops. The street is named after the Enlightenment philosopher Voltaire (François-Marie Arouet; 1694–1778), who died there while staying in the home of his wealthy protégé, the Marquis de Villette (1736–93), who was known to be attracted to other men.

Greek mœurs: Greek customs or practices. From the beginning of her writing career, Barney drew inspiration from the life and work of Greek lyrical poet Sappho (*c.*630–570 BC), helping to consolidate the association of Sappho with female-centric creativity and desire between women. In *Cinq petits dialogues grecs* (*Five Short Greek Dialogues*, 1901), published under the Greek pseudonym Tryphé, Barney describes Sappho as 'more faithful in her inconstancy than others in their fidelity' (quoted in George Wickes, *Amazon of Letters: The Life and Loves of Natalie Barney* (New York: Popular Library, 1978), 59). Barney and Vivièn visited Lesbos, the island on which Sappho had lived, and Barney's 'Académie des Femmes' was modelled on Sappho's possible work as a schoolmistress teaching younger women and girls (Jay, *The Amazon and the Page*, 15, 33). Barney contributed a chapter to her lover Liane de Pougy's lesbian roman-à-clef *Idylle Saphique* (*Sapphic Idyll*) in 1901, and she wrote a play that revised the legend of Sappho's death, *Epivoque* (*Ambiguity*) in 1905/6. Ellis observes that 'Sappho [. . .] has left a name which is permanently associated with homosexuality' (*SI*, 197).

libre penseuse: a free thinker.

The first thing: see Appendix, p. 434 (3.5), where RH provides some detail about the artwork in Valérie's flat.

240 *tuberoses . . . broken*: the details in this scene are highly suggestive of decadent self-indulgence. In a chapter on 'Carnal Flowers, Charnel Flowers: Tuberose in Late Victorian Poetry', Catherine Maxwell shows how the scent of the tuberose, an exotic hothouse flower strongly associated with Victorian decadence, is 'bound up with dangerous or voluptuous pleasures, with love, eroticism, criminality, and death' (in *Scents and Sensibility: Perfume in Victorian Literary Culture* (Oxford: Oxford University Press, 2017), 182–200). The chocolate-covered peppermint creams, which Valérie has evidently been enjoying on her divan, were sold in characteristic green boxes by London-based confectioner Fuller's (established *c.*1899). Artists and writers often depict Sappho playing a lute or a lyre; see, for instance, Letitia Elizabeth Landon's (1802–38) poem 'Sappho's Song' (1824). In her interpretation of this scene, Deborah Longworth notes that 'no new poet can sing Sappho's songs of love because the strings are broken' ('The Gender of Decadence: Paris-Lesbos from the Fin de Siècle to the Interwar Era', in Jane Desmarais and David Weir (eds.), *Decadence and Literature* (Cambridge: Cambridge University Press, 2019), 362–378 (374)).

Capri: in Italy's Bay of Naples, an island that offered refuge to queer artists in the early twentieth century. Romaine Brooks owned a house, Villa Cercola, on Capri and invited RH and UT to visit her there in 1921 (*AWCJ*, 192–3). Brooks had previously studied painting on the island and met her husband, the gay English poet John Ellingham Brooks (1863–1929), there in 1899. Compton Mackenzie's satirical lesbian novel *Extraordinary Women* (1928), published in the wake of the British censorship trial of *TWoL*, is set on the island of Sirene, a fictionalized version of Capri. Mackenzie had previously visited the island and stayed with Louisa, Marchesa Casati (1881–1957), an eccentric Italian heiress and patron of the arts. Mimi Franchetti (1893–1943), one of Barney's lovers, lived on Capri and was fictionalized in *Extraordinary Women* alongside RH and Brooks. Wilde and Douglas stayed at the island's Grand Hotel Quisisana in 1897. Capri was also the site of one of the most notorious gay scandals of the early twentieth century: in 1902, Friedrich Alfred Krupp (1854–1902), a wealthy German steel magnate and influential politician with direct ties to the Kaiser, was accused of having sexual relations with local boys and men on the island. The English writer Norman Douglas (1868–1952), who was friends with queer modernists H.D. (1886–1961) and Bryher (1894–1983), also lived on Capri. The Blue Grotto is a sea cave and popular tourist attraction on the north-western coast of the island.

240 *take the veil*: to become a nun.

Lido: though the term can be used generically to describe a public open-air swimming pool, RH may well be referring to Le Lido des Champs-Élysées, which opened in Paris in 1928 as she was completing *TWoL*. Located in the basement of 78 Avenue des Champs-Élysées, Le Lido provided amusement in the form of an underground pool, a casino, musical performances, and a cocktail bar until it closed in 1933.

241 *stigmata of the abnormal*: according to Catholic faith, stigmata are bodily wounds or scars corresponding to marks left on Christ's body by the Crucifixion. Stigmata have allegedly appeared on the hands, wrists, or feet of various saints, including St Francis of Assisi (*c.*1181–1226) and St Padre Pio (1887–1968). When writing *The Master of the House*, RH engaged in 'intensive study of the Passion of Christ' and apparently developed 'an angry-looking red stain' at the centre of each palm (*LaD*, 104–5).

libertine: first coined by sixteenth-century French Protestant theologian and reformer John Calvin (1509–64) to describe those who opposed his doctrines. In the seventeenth and eighteenth centuries, libertinism came to be associated with the free operation of sexual desire along with anti-establishment and anticlerical thought. The eighteenth century witnessed the rise of the libertine novel, led by French writers including Cyrano de Bergerac (1619–55), Choderlos de Laclos (1741–1803), and the Marquis de Sade (1740–1814). These elite male writers opposed or renegotiated moral, religious, and civil expectations to claim forms of sexualized freedom that were deemed scandalous and obscene by some of their contemporaries. Carpenter would later state that 'to confuse Uranians (as is so often done) with libertines having no law but curiosity in self-indulgence is to do them a great wrong' (*TIS*, 26).

pagan: Barney and Vivien rejected the Christian faith and, in Jay's words, 'took Sappho's "Ode to Aphrodite" and from it recreated a pagan cult with Aphrodite as its chief goddess' (*The Amazon and the Page*, 67). Their pagan practices revolved around the sensuous appreciation of pleasure and beauty, and the celebration of the nude female body. Whereas Vivien is believed to have converted to Catholicism shortly before her death by suicide, Barney remained committed to paganism.

Pierre Louÿs . . . 'Le monde . . . laideur': Pierre Louÿs (1870–1925) was a French poet and classical Greek scholar. His collection of lesbian erotic prose poems *Les Chansons de Bilitis* (*Songs of Bilitis*, 1894) was a literary hoax: Louÿs claimed to have translated poems written by a contemporary of Sappho. Barney and Vivien read and greatly admired the collection in 1899 or 1900 (Jay, *The Amazon and the Page*, 62); Louÿs later became a mentor for both women and often attended Barney's salon. Ellis discusses Louÿs's work in his chapter on 'Sexual Inversion in Women', criticizing the poet's 'inadequate knowledge of Greek antiquity' (*SI*, 200). 'Le monde moderne succombe sous un envahissement de laideur' ('The modern world is succumbing to an invasion of ugliness') is taken from the preface to Louÿs's 1896 novel *Aphrodite: Mœurs antiques*, ed. Jean-Paul Goujon (Paris: Gallimard, 1992), 39.

Rue Jacob: Barney moved to 20 Rue Jacob in the sixth arrondissement in 1909 and stayed there for over half a century. The 'semicircular temple' (p. 244) in Stephen's garden evokes the small Doric temple on Barney's property, the Temple of Friendship ('à l'Amitié' is inscribed above its door), which served as the background for amateur theatricals and performances. Rue Jacob is situated on the 'Rive Gauche', the Left Bank, on the southern side of the river Seine. The area was home to modernist artists and writers and has come to be associated with feminist, queer, and lesbian modernist countercultures. See Shari Benstock, *Women of the Left Bank* (Austin: University of Texas Press, 1986), and Andrea Weiss, *Paris Was a Woman: Portraits from the Left Bank* (Berkeley: Counterpoint Press, 1995).

242 *phenacetin*: an analgesic and fever-reducing drug introduced in 1887 and withdrawn from medical use in the 1970s.

'O Sole Mio': a well-known Neapolitan song written in 1898. The title literally translates as 'O My Sun'.

243 *Buisson's*: François-Auguste Brun-Buisson (dates unknown) was a professional French fencer who participated in the 1900 Summer Olympics in Paris.

because she thought me: a crossed-out section of the handwritten draft states explicitly: 'I couldn't help feeling that she liked me because she thought me a freak, because she thought me—well—what I am, Puddle' (Hall–Troubridge Papers, 13.5).

244 *salle à manger*: dining room.

245 *Caporals*: caporal is a type of strong tobacco used in Gauloises Caporal among other cigarette brands (see note to p. 225).

thickly powdered: though Stephen's hair and 'neat blue serge shoulders'—in a jacket of twilled wool or worsted—have simply been covered in dust, we are reminded of Marie Antoinette, who wore elaborate Rococo wigs treated with grey or white powder.

Empire study . . . first Napoleon: the Empire style of furniture design, which favoured ornate symmetry and ancient Egyptian, Greek, and Roman motifs, flourished in France in the time of the First Empire (1804–14). As a teenager, UT idolized Emperor Napoleon (*AWCJ*, 110); RH wrote a short story entitled 'Bonaparte' set on the French island of Corsica, where Napoleon was born (*TW*, 75–83).

245 *yellow, to give the illusion of sunshine*: in the 'How Other Women Run Their Homes' interview (*Daily Mail*, 11 May 1927; see note to p. 223), RH shares her thoughts on interior design. '"I think yellow is the best colour for walls," Miss Radclyffe Hall explained; "it's so warm and sunshiny."'

Austrian Tyrol: Noël Coward, who inspired the character of Brockett (see note to p. 221), starred in the popular 1926 West End stage production of *The Constant Nymph*. The play was based on the bestselling 1924 bohemian novel by English author Margaret Kennedy (1896–1967), which is set in the western Austrian state of Tyrol.

whistling as she drove her car: both whistling and driving are markers of masculinity (see note to p. 48). RH was a keen driver and shared a passion for cars with Lowther (AWCJ, 153; see note to p. 8). In 'Miss Ogilvy Finds Herself', RH describes the close bond between the protagonist and the car she has driven while serving in an ambulance unit during the First World War. Here, Stephen drives back to an auberge, an inn or tavern.

246 *Magasin de Blanc*: a shop selling linens.

batterie de cuisine: kitchenware; pots and pans.

Breton ménage: a Breton household. Bretons are natives or inhabitants of Brittany in north-western France. Brittany is among the six Celtic nations; the Breton language is akin to Cornish and Welsh.

en brosse: literally 'resembling a brush'; a closely cropped haircut in which the hair sticks upwards, bristle-like; a crew cut.

247 *as though He were looking for His presents*: an echo of Chapter 10 (p. 86).

'Oh, comme c'est beau, l'arbre de Noël!': 'Oh, how beautiful it is, the Christmas tree!'

Poilus: literally 'the hairy ones', referring to rustic virility; an informal term for a French soldier, widely used as a term of endearment for the French infantry during the First World War.

248 *trod on the necks*: during the conquest of Canaan, Joshua 'called for all the men of Israel, and said unto the captains of the men of war which went with him, Come near, put your feet upon the necks of these kings. And they came near, and put their feet upon the necks of them' (Joshua 10:24).

250 *'Mais comment ferez-vous . . . bénirai double!'*: the lyrics are based on 'La Messe en Mer' ('The Mass at Sea', 1793) by Breton composer, singer, and poet Jean-Baptiste-Théodore-Marie Botrel (1868–1925), official 'Bard of the Armies' during the First World War. The song title references an 1864 oil painting by French painter Lois-Jean-Noël Duveau (1818–67), *Une messe en mer, 1793*, which depicts a Catholic priest and his congregation, most likely Bretons, holding Mass off the coast of France at night to escape prosecution during the French Revolution. The song was included in Botrel's 1912 collection *Chansons en Sabots*, which celebrates rural life in

Brittany. *Chansons en Sabots* literally translates as 'clog songs' and refers to the simple wooden shoes worn by Breton peasants. ('Ma Doué' is Breton for 'Mon Dieu'.)

'But what will you do, Father,
My God?
But what will you do, Father,
To say Mass for us?'
'When the night has fallen,
I will keep my promise.'

'But what will you do, Father,
My God,
But what will you do, Father,
Without a layer of fine cloth?'
'Our Sweet Lord will lie
On a piece of sail cloth.'

'But what will you do, Father,
My God,
But what will you do, Father,
Without candle and taper?'
'The stars will be lit
By the Virgin Mary.'

'But what will you do, Father,
My God,
But what will you do, Father,
Without a resonant organ?'
'Jesus will play the keys
of the roaring waves.'

'But what will you do, Father,
My God,
But what will you do, Father,
If the enemy troubles us?'
'I will bless you once,
I will bless the Blues [France] twice.'

251 *'à bientôt'*: 'see you soon'.

gathering in the shekels: Brockett's plays are making money. A shekel is originally a 'unit of weight of the Babylonians, and hence of the Phoenicians, Hebrews and others' (*OED*); the term is frequently used to describe a coin of this weight in the Bible.

'Hideous, affreux, horriblement English!': 'Hideous, awful, horribly English!' See Appendix, p. 434 (3.6), where Buisson scolds Stephen even more harshly.

252 *'Tiens, tiens!'*: from the verb 'to hold'; two *tiens* in quick succession are often used to express surprise. Here, Buisson is saying 'well, well' or 'how about that' in reference to Stephen's strong and youthful muscles.

make the long nose: *'faire un long nez'* is to show one's discontent or disappointment.

the Bois: the Bois de Boulogne, a large public park along the western edge of the sixteenth arrondissement. Barney apparently rode in the Bois de Boulogne 'every morning, carrying a cane, dressed in a bowler hat and a black bow tie' (*AWCJ*, 194). One of RH and UT's dogs, Fido—'an outsize white poodle of unknown age and origin', purchased in Florence's Via Tornabuoni—boarded with the head keeper in the Bois de Boulogne for several months during the First World War (*LaD*, 147–8). The wood in the title of Barnes's modernist classic *Nightwood* (1936) is both Thelma Wood (1901–70), Barnes's partner, and the Bois de Boulogne, 'the sweet woods of Paris', toured by carriage at midnight in chapter 4 (*Nightwood* (London: Faber and Faber, 2007 edn.), 66).

Quarter . . . Rue des Saints Pères: Stephen is exploring the area around her home on Rue Jacob on the Left Bank. The Latin Quarter, or the fifth arrondissement, is home to the Sorbonne, the historic University of Paris. Rue des Saints-Pères crosses Rue Jacob in the adjacent sixth arrondissement.

Pont des Arts . . . Passage Choiseul: the Pont des Arts is a pedestrian bridge crossing the Seine and connecting the Left Bank with the Right Bank, or Rive Droite, on the northern side of the river. The Rue des Petits Champs is in the first and second arrondissements, north of the Seine. It is home to the Passage Choiseul, one of the longest covered shopping arcades in Paris, built in 1827. A notebook kept by RH when writing *TWoL* contains detailed notes about Passage Choiseul (Hall–Troubridge Papers, 12.5). The names of businesses given here are real, though the art supply and stationery shop Lavrut opened in 1922, eight years after Stephen's visit. In addition to purchasing caoutchouc (or natural rubber) bands by weight, customers can pick up 'Gomme Onyx' erasers, so named as they resembled black marble. 'Lemerre' refers to a library owned by publisher and editor Alphonse Lemerre (1838–1912), who published most of Vivien's poetry alongside other Decadent and Parnassian works. Stephen admires the 'splendid display of yellow bindings': in turn-of-the-century France, books with illicit or lascivious content were often wrapped in yellow paper. In Wilde's novel *The Picture of Dorian Gray* (1890), Dorian is famously corrupted by a 'yellow book'; the fashionable London magazine *The Yellow Book*, which ran from 1894 to 1897, took its name from the notorious French coverings. Wilde himself was allegedly carrying a yellow-bound copy of Louÿs's *Aphrodite* (1896) when he was arrested for gross indecency. Although RH does not mention the name of the taxidermist in either the notebook or the novel, taxidermy specimens by 'F. Antoine, Naturaliste', who owned a shop in Passage Choiseul in the early twentieth century, are still on the market today. Stephen is a kind of modern flâneur here, though she is interested in making purchases, and the succession of 'Where' fragments reads almost like advertising copy (see Introduction, p. xix). The final sentence of the paragraph ('wares [that] do not figure in school manuals on the practical uses of rubber') provides a playful and suitably oblique reference to contraception.

253 *Comédie Française*: founded in 1680, the Comédie-Française is the oldest active theatre company in the world. Its primary venue is the magnificent Salle Richelieu in the Palais-Royal in the first arrondissement of Paris.

pince-nez: a style of spectacles clipped to the wearer's nose.

254 *'Ah, quelle joie! Quelle joie!'*: 'Oh, what joy! What joy!' Mademoiselle Duphot prophesies this reunion upon her departure from Morton in Chapter 6: '"It's not farewell, it shall not be for ever—" she sobbed. "You come, but I feel it, to Paris. We meet once more, Stévenne, my poor little baby, when you grow up bigger, we two meet once more—"' (p. 61).

Avenue de la Grande Armée: an avenue between the sixteenth and seventeenth arrondissement, close to the Bois de Boulogne.

255 *marron glacé*: a candied chestnut, a French confection.

257 *Bouguereaus*: William-Adolphe Bouguereau (1825–1905), a leading French painter in the academic tradition who regularly exhibited at the Paris Salon. Mademoiselle Duphot's artistic tastes have not moved with the times: Bouguereau's interpretations of classical subjects and realist portraits were generally considered outdated and sentimental by the 1910s. Mademoiselle Duphot's treasured Bouguereau prints are in keeping with both her character and the 'mementoes' on her table.

258 *our little Thérèse . . . fingers*: Thérèse of Lisieux (1873–97), known as 'la petite Thérèse' (little Thérèse), was a French Catholic Discalced Carmelite nun. She aspired to martyrdom and wrote two plays in honour of Joan of Arc (*c.*1412–31); in her 1898 memoir, *Histoire d'une âme* (*The Story of a Soul*), she claimed that she 'should like to accomplish the most heroic deeds—the spirit of the Crusader burns within me, and I long to die on the field of battle in defense of Holy Church' (*The Story of the Soul*, trans. Thomas N. Taylor (New York: Cosimo, 2007), 159). Thérèse died of tuberculosis at the age of 24. 'The Very Reverend Father Rodrigo' presented the Cause for beatification in 1909, and Thérèse was canonized in 1925, twelve years after Stephen's visit to Mademoiselle Duphot's home. Thérèse referred to herself as the 'Little Flower of Jesus' and, as we see in this passage, used roses as metaphors for blessings or acts of love and grace. The 'miracles for all those who ask her' are spontaneous cures apparently unexplained by medical treatment, which led to her canonization. UT and RH visited Lisieux in September 1927: 'It was before the building of the new Basilica (begun in 1929 and completed in 1954) and the tinted and clothed marble effigy of Thérèse still lay in the chapel of the Carmel with the Holy Father's Golden Rose in her hand. But already it was one of the greatest pilgrimages in France, masses were said daily at

a dozen altars, from five in the morning until noon or later, and pilgrims came from all over the world to pay homage to the Alençon jeweller's daughter who had been so certain of the road to heaven. Blatant vulgarity was already enthroned and at High Mass when the bell rang for the Elevation, electric lights surrounding the tinted marble altarpiece spelt out: "*Je ferai tomber une pluie de roses*" (I will let fall a shower of roses)' (*LaD*, 88).

260 *War*: after a decade of increasing diplomatic tension across Europe, the conflict that culminated in the First World War started with the assassination of Archduke Franz Ferdinand (1863–1914), who was heir to the Austro-Hungarian Empire, on 28 June 1914. Austria-Hungary deemed Serbia responsible and declared war a month later. By early August, Germany, France, Britain, and Russia had joined the conflict. RH extensively explored the impact and aftermath of the First World War in her writing: in *Adam's Breed*, 'Youth 1914–1918' (Hall–Troubridge Papers, 21.5), 'The Rest Cure—1932' (*MO*, 181–201), and 'The World' (*TW*, 115–70), she offers thoughtful portrayals of male characters who have been spiritually and psychologically broken by the war. Her work reveals a particular preoccupation with men who were not permitted to sign up for active duty on grounds of nationality or because they were deemed 'unfit'. *TWoL* also expresses the frustration felt by female sexual inverts who were excluded from military service. RH 'said frequently that had she been a man she would have enlisted at once' (*AWCJ*, 96); instead, she 'occupied herself by writing recruiting leaflets, running enlistment campaigns, and giving speeches on the importance of joining up' (*AWCJ*, 97).

'C'est la guerre! C'est la guerre!': 'It's war! It's war!'

Champs Elysées: a famous (and famously desirable) tree-lined avenue in the eighth arrondissement, stretching from the Place de la Concorde in the east to the Arc de Triomphe in the centre of Place Charles de Gaulle in the west. The Champs-Élysées is the site of major public events, protests, celebrations, and military victory parades.

German names: RH, who had studied literature for a year in Dresden, was sympathetic to the experiences of Germans living in Allied countries during the First World War (*AWCJ*, 30). Her short story 'Fräulein Schwartz' (*MO*, 137–77) explores the profound isolation of a middle-aged German immigrant living in England after the outbreak of war.

261 *offered Morton to the Red Cross*: the British Red Cross, a humanitarian organization founded in 1870 as part of the International Red Cross Movement, set up hospitals for the war wounded in Malvern during the First World War. As Cline writes, 'John and Ladye attended ambulance lectures, bandaging classes, and home nursing tutorials. They made two rooms of the White Cottage available for wounded soldiers, even Germans' (*AWCJ*, 96).

262 *Flying Corps*: during the First World War, the Royal Flying Corps was the air arm of the British army. It preceded the formation of the Royal Air

Force in 1918, which merged the Royal Flying Corps and the Royal Naval Air Service.

jingo plays . . . "Business as Usual!": Brockett jokes that it is now inappropriate for him to write patriotic (jingoistic) plays. 'Business as usual' was a British government policy in the early years of the war.

263 *her bony masculine hands*: see Appendix, p. 435 (3.7).

264 *greasing his foils*: a foil is a weapon used in fencing; Buisson is applying grease to protect the steel from corrosion. After the next reference to Buisson 'greasing his foils', the handwritten draft adds: 'Poor Buisson[,] he would soon be sitting knee deep in the mud and the slime of the trenches' (Hall–Troubridge Papers, 13.5).

Parbleu!: a corruption of 'Par Dieu!', meaning 'By God!'; a minced oath.

265 *horrible Birmingham chimneys*: we might be reminded of Ralph Crossby, who 'had been an important Birmingham magnate' (p. 129).

Mitylene: the capital of the Greek island of Lesbos, home of Sappho.

War . . . microbes: Buisson is expressing the eugenicist view that war may have the beneficial impact of reducing a population grown too large due to advances in modern medicine.

Havre: a major port city in the Normandy region of northern France.

The London Ambulance Column: a voluntary civilian organization, established soon after the outbreak of war, responsible for meeting trains arriving at London stations and transporting soldiers to hospitals in and around the city.

266 *An ambulance . . . very fine service:* see note to p. 8. The British writer May Sinclair (1863–1946), an acquaintance of RH's, volunteered as a reporter with the Munro Ambulance Corps aiding Belgian soldiers on the Western Front; she wrote about her experiences in *A Journal of Impressions in Belgium* (1915). Reluctant to leave the side of her ailing partner Ladye, RH felt unable to choose a similar course of action (*AWCJ*, 96–7).

And England had taken her: the idea that war offered new opportunities and a national 'home' for female inverts has been explored by both novelists and critics: see, for example, Sarah Waters's *The Night Watch* (2006), and Claire Buck's '"Still Some Obstinate Emotion Remains": Radclyffe Hall and the Meanings of Service', in Suzanne Raitt and Trudi Tate (eds.), *Women's Fiction and the Great War* (Oxford: Clarendon Press, 1997), 174–96 (176)). Laura Doan observes that RH's fiction played a significant role in forging a retrospective association between women 'who donned mannish uniforms and joined their female comrades to drive ambulances near the fighting at the front' and the sexological type of the sexual invert (*Disturbing Practices: History, Sexuality and Women's Experience of Modern War* (Chicago: Chicago University Press, 2015), 128). In a crossed-out section of the handwritten draft, Stephen hails the 'unmistakable figures' as 'companions and sisters' (Hall–Troubridge Papers, 13.5). We might read this passage, where women like Stephen have 'crept out of [their] hole[s] and come into the daylight', against Woolf's later *A Room of One's Own* (1929), an extended essay based on two lectures delivered in October 1928: 'what happens when Olivia—this organism that has been under the shadow of the rock these million years—feels the light fall on it, and sees coming her way a piece of strange food—knowledge, adventure, art' (*A Room of One's Own* (London: Hogarth Press, 1935 edn.), 127).

266 *breeding dogs in the country*: in the early 1920s, RH and UT were celebrated breeders of champion dachshunds. 'In the world of dog shows,' writes UT, 'though we had many good friends and incidentally were very successful, there were also some who thought us cranks' (*LaD*, 50). For the couple's Kennel Club registration certificates (1914–26) and dog-show clippings (1922–3), see Hall–Troubridge Papers, 25. Cline notes that RH's appearance at dog shows was 'defiantly masculine' (*AWCJ*, 151): she wore trousers to Crufts in 1923.

Miss Oliphant: 'Miss Ogilvy' in the handwritten draft (Hall–Troubridge Papers, 13.5), the name of the protagonist of RH's short story 'Miss Ogilvy Finds Herself'.

Sam Browne belt: 'A leather belt with a supporting strap that passes diagonally over the right shoulder' (*OED*), named after Sir Samuel J. Browne (1824–1901), a British Indian Army general.

their nerves were not at all weak . . . God's good people: though RH insists on 'the terrible nerves of the invert' (see note to p. 154), here the narrator observes that female sexual inverts are particularly well equipped to withstand the shock of military activity. Sexual inverts, RH reminds us, are troubled not by bombs but by the regular hostilities that they face, often described in the language of warfare: 'the guns of Bond Street' (p. 165), for instance, or 'the war of existence' (p. 322).

267 *British Warm*: 'a warm short overcoat worn especially by officers of the army' (*OED*).

Later on would come bitterness, disillusion: in 'Miss Ogilvy Finds Herself', and in a manuscript entitled 'Ghosts' (Hall–Troubridge Papers, 18.8), RH explores the bleak experiences of demobilized sexual inverts whose accomplishments were quickly forgotten in post-war England.

And now he was asking for Houbigant . . . Truefitt's: Brockett's requests once again reveal a taste for luxury. La Maison Houbigant is an exclusive French perfumery, founded in 1775. Eau Athénienne (Athenian Water) is a traditional hair lotion produced by famous Mayfair barber shop Truefitt & Hill, founded in 1805 and granted its first royal warrant under George III (1738–1820). 'At Mr. Truefitt's, the excellent hairdresser's, they are learning French to beguile the time', writes Dickens in *The Uncommercial Traveller* (1861).

Mesopotamia: the Ottoman entry into the First World War in October 1914 threatened British interests in the Middle East. In response, Britain sent troops to Mesopotamia (now Iraq) to protect its access to valuable oil supplies in the region. The military campaign lasted for four years and involved many setbacks and mass casualties for the British forces.

268 *V.A.D.*: Voluntary Aid Detachments were voluntary units of civilians providing humanitarian aid and nursing care for naval and military forces in the United Kingdom and abroad. VADs were formed in 1909 by the British Red Cross and the Order of St John at the request of the War Office. Over 90,000 volunteers worked as VADs during the First World War.

capons: a capon is a castrated cockerel. Along with a rich diet, a lack of testosterone is intended to make the meat more tender and flavourful.

burning Zeppelin: the German military made extensive use of Zeppelins to bomb British cities during the First World War. Since Zeppelins were filled with hydrogen, a highly flammable gas, they were extremely vulnerable to explosive shells and would catch fire, often in spectacular fashion, when shot down by the British defences.

Military Cross: until 1993, the Military Cross was the second-level military decoration awarded to captains or officers of lower rank (up to warrant officers) of the British Armed Forces. It was introduced by George V (1865–1936) in December 1914.

269 *BOOK FOUR*: RH adds a note to her handwritten draft: 'We take her up again after she has been with the Breakspeare Unit for 6 months—it is now March 1918 in Compiègne' (Hall–Troubridge Papers, 13.5).

Compiègne: a town and *commune* in the Oise department of northern France, and a target of the German Spring Offensive (*Kaiserschlacht*) of 1918.

Breakspeare Unit: see note to p. 8. The Hackett Lowther Canteen and Ambulance Unit (with the canteen service run by Norah Desmond Hackett, 1886–1940) was incorporated into the French Army as part of the Section de Sanitaire. See Michael Baker, *Our Three Selves: The Life of Radclyffe Hall* (New York: William Morrow and Co., 1985), 125–7, and Val Brown, *Toupie Lowther: Her Life* (Leicester: Matador, 2017). In the handwritten draft (Hall–Troubridge Papers, 13.5), Stephen is interviewed by Mrs Breakspeare for her place in the Unit.

Jaeger: premium London fashion brand (founded 1884) known for its use of high-quality natural fibres. Jaeger contributed to the war effort by producing underwear, blankets, and—as we see here—sleeping bags.

270 *shell-shock*: a diagnostic category used to describe an array of symptoms displayed by soldiers in response to the experience of war, including trembling, headache, tinnitus, dizziness, confusion, and loss of memory. The term was introduced to medical literature by physician and psychologist Charles S. Myers (1873–1946) of the Royal Army Medical Corps in a 1915 article in *The Lancet*, which offers 'an account of three cases of loss of memory, vision, smell, and taste' ('A Contribution to the Study of Shell Shock', *The Lancet*, 13 Feb. 1915, 316–20). Early medical opinion suggested

that the damage was caused by hidden physical injuries to the brain caused by exploding shells. However, by 1916, military and medical authorities observed that many patients suffering from shell shock had not been near exploding shells. Shell shock was increasingly understood as a form of nervous weakness akin to hysteria and neurasthenia (see note to p. 334). In 1919, physician and psychiatrist Hugh Crichton-Miller (1877–1959), who was first consulted by UT in 1913 (see Introduction, p. xxi), explored treatment options for shell shock in his edited collection *Functional Nerve Disease: An Epitome of War Experience for the Practitioner* (1920). The chapter by neurologist and psychiatrist Maurice Nicoll (1884–1953) examines the symptom of regression, 'a psychic act' that constitutes 'a movement away from the adaptations of life back towards that condition of security which the infant experiences in its mother's arms' (*Functional Nerve Disease*, 100–1). Later in the chapter, one of the wounded soldiers transported by Stephen and Mary speaks with 'the voice of a child demanding its mother' (p. 274). The protagonist of 'Miss Ogilvy Finds Herself' wonders whether she suffers from shell shock (*MO*, 23). Characters experience shell shock in several modernist texts, including Rebecca West's (1892–1983) *The Return of the Soldier* (1918), Ford Madox Ford's (1873–1939) *Parade's End* (1924–8), and Woolf's *Mrs Dalloway* (1925).

270 *Boches*: a derisive term for Germans or the German Army.

blue-clad figures: convalescent soldiers in military hospitals wore blue flannelette uniforms known as 'hospital blues'.

272 *Uhlan's*: an uhlan was a type of cavalryman armed with a lance. Originating in Lithuania and Poland, uhlan regiments became common to a number of European armies; at the beginning of the First World War, there were twenty-six uhlan regiments in the Imperial German Army. Uhlans wore distinctive square-topped caps (*czapkas*) on their close-cropped heads. There was a tendency among British and French armies to describe all German cavalry units as uhlans.

Poste: short for *le Poste de Secours*, a dressing station where emergency aid would be administered before patients were transferred to a field hospital.

273 *Militaires!*: Servicewomen!

'Il faut vivre': 'One must live.'

274 *Ford ambulances*: the American Ford Motor Company (founded in Michigan in 1903) built 5,745 ambulances for the Allied armies during the First World War, and another 107 for the Red Cross. In their war work for the American Fund for French Wounded, Gertrude Stein and Alice B. Toklas drove a Ford truck that they fondly nicknamed 'Auntie' after Stein's dependable Auntie Pauline.

279 *Blakeney looked more like a monkey than ever*: Blakeney bears a close resemblance to the protagonist of 'Miss Ogilvy Finds Herself', a similarly

monosyllabic character with an affinity for cars. Miss Ogilvy is also described in simian terms, with 'sad brown eyes like those of a monkey' (*MO*, 26).

Pinard: low-quality wine issued to French troops. In the popular imagination, the figure of the *poilu* (see note to p. 247) was never far from his *pinard*.

280 *Louis Quinze*: a style of architecture, furniture, and decorative arts popular during the reign of Louis XV (1710–74), ruler of France from 1715. The Louis XV style of interior decoration was initially ornate and extravagant but became more restrained from around 1750.

281 *schoolroom*: a number of sexologists agreed that even people who were not inborn inverts could develop same-sex attachments, especially in the impressionable years of youth. In 'Appendix B.: The School-Friendships of Girls', Ellis discusses schoolroom 'flames', or friendships with a 'note of passion', which 'cannot be regarded as an absolute expression of real congenital perversion of the sex-instinct' (*SI*, 368). One of Ellis's informants reports that 'attachments to [female] teachers are far commoner than between two girls' (*SI*, 378). In the words of feminist critic Elaine Marks, the girls' school 'ruled by the seductive or seducing teacher has become, since the eighteenth century, the preferred locus for most fictions about women loving women' ('Lesbian Intertextuality', in George Stambolian and Elaine Marks (eds.), *Homosexualities and French Literature: Cultural Contexts, Critical Texts* (Ithaca, NY: Cornell University Press, 1979), 353–77 (357)); we might think of Clemence Dane's (b. Winifred Ashton, 1888–1965) *Regiment of Women* (1917), which RH read in December 1919 (*AWCJ*, 147), or Muriel Spark's (1918–2006) *The Prime of Miss Jean Brodie* (1961). In 1931, Leontine Sagan (1889–1974) directed *Girls in Uniform*, the film adaptation of Christa Winsloe's (1888–1944) play *Yesterday and Today* (1929). RH saw the film, which featured an on-screen kiss between a teenage girl and her female teacher, in 1932 (*AWCJ*, 300).

great child-nation: the United States of America, founded in 1776 and thus a comparatively 'young' country, declared war on the German Empire on 6 April 1917. On p. 283, RH writes: 'it was not their war, yet they helped to fight it because they were young and their nation was young'.

282 *V.C.*: the Victoria Cross, the highest British military honour.

283 *In July came the Allied counter-offensive*: the last of the German offensives, the Second Battle of the Marne, was launched on 15 July 1918; the Allied armies responded with a successful counter-attack three days later.

orgy of destruction: on their retreat from Operation Alberich (February–March 1917), German troops felled trees, poisoned wells, planted landmines, and demolished buildings, bridges, and roads in northern France.

284 *Near by . . . revolver*: the second time that Stephen has had to shoot a horse (p. 217). In 'Malise', a short story written between 1925 and 1928, Malise Gordon—an early version of Stephen—is forced to shoot an injured mule

with her automatic, leading to tears from her beloved Pamela Wentworth (*TW*, 184).

284 *an honourable scar*: see 'And the Lord set a mark upon Cain' (p. 203 with note). In RH's poem 'The Scar', the scar 'seems to beautify, not mar | My inner self, for from that deep wound leads | A path to gained respect' (in *A Sheaf of Verses*, p. 108, ll. 5–7).

Croix de Guerre: a French military honour first awarded during the First World War. Toupie Lowther and members of the Hackett Lowther Unit were 'decorated with the Croix de Guerre Bronze star, with the right to display a fanion (a small flag) depicting the Croix de Guerre medal on the side of the ambulances. Colonel Meyer—the "Directeur du Service de Santé"—did the honours, and as he did so an aeroplane from the nearby aerodrome swooped around in salute overhead' (Brown, *Toupie Lowther: Her Life*, 77).

285 *Aces*: (or flying aces), fighter pilots who have successfully shot down enemy planes.

a mention in despatches: a commendation in an official report written by a superior officer.

Then she said very slowly: 'After the war . . . Mary': see Appendix, p. 435 (4.1).

286 *St. Quentin*: a city in the Aisne department of northern France, about halfway between Paris and Brussels. Saint-Quentin was under German occupation from August 1914 until October 1918 and, as part of the Hindenburg Line (from 1917), was all but destroyed.

'Eh bien, mesdames, c'est l'Armistice': 'Well, ladies, it's the Armistice.' The Armistice of Compiègne, which ended the First World War, was signed on 11 November 1918.

287 *en fête*: literally 'in festival'; prepared for a celebration. The tricolour, the French flag, is flying.

immortelles: 'A name for various composite flowers of papery texture (esp. *Helichrysum orientale*, and other species of *Helichrysum*, *Xeranthemum*, etc.) which retain their colour after being dried' (*OED*); so-called 'everlasting' flowers.

'Oh, la pauvre! . . . un vrai désastre!': 'Oh, poor thing! For a lady, this is a real disaster!'

288 *Orotava*: La Orotava, a hillside town and municipality on the north of the island of Tenerife, where RH enjoyed 'rapturous' holidays with Ladye (*AWCJ*, 63). During their stay in the port city of Santa Cruz de Tenerife in 1910, writes Diana Souhami, the couple 'rode on pack mules into the mountains, bought a parrot they called Mr Povey, sang island songs and picnicked overlooking a ravine. Ladye worked on John's poems and read them aloud. Both declared they had never been as happy in their lives before and that this was their one great love' (Souhami, *The Trials of Radclyffe Hall* (London: Weidenfeld & Nicolson, 1998), 48). For UT, it

was 'obvious that, particularly after their voyage to Orotava, in John herself brawn was giving way to brain and she was eager for more voyages and exploration of pastures new' (*LaD*, 34). La Orotava also provides the setting of RH's short story 'Poor Miss Briggs' (*TW*, 84–6).

289 *beard*: 'To oppose or confront (a person) openly, boldly, or insolently; to defy, defeat, affront' (*OED*).

demobilization: the complex process of demobilization—the release of troops from active service—continued long after the signing of the Armistice. Winston Churchill (1874–1965), as new Secretary of State for War, responded to outbreaks of unrest among troops and ex-servicemen by introducing a new and mostly successful demobilization scheme in January 1919.

worse still a complex . . . better read Ferenczi!: first theorized by Austrian psychiatrist and psychoanalyst Carl Gustav Jung (1875–1961), a 'complex' describes 'the image of a certain psychic situation which is strongly accentuated emotionally and is, moreover, incompatible with the habitual attitude of consciousness' ('A Review of the Complex Theory', in *The Collected Works of C.G. Jung*, viii (Princeton: Princeton University Press, 1970), 92–104 (96)). In 1926, Hirschfeld noted that the term was being used excessively as a 'fashionable buzzword' that 'had not contributed to solving sexual scientific problems' (*Geschlechtskunde*, i (Stuttgart: Julius Püttman, 1926), 240–1). RH takes particular aim at Hungarian psychoanalyst Sándor Ferenczi (1873–1933) (see Appendix, pp. 437–8 (5.9). Prosser claims that RH 'takes care in *The Well* to mock psychoanalysis, in one brief reference to Sándor Ferenczi, showing that she knows it and doesn't need it' (in *PP*, 141).

291 *Men—they were selfish, arrogant, possessive . . . Mary . . . the belovèd*: in 'Malise', Malise Gordon and Pamela Wentworth—prototypes of Stephen and Mary—'would play with the idea of marriage, would talk of their children, these unborn children who wanted so much to be borne [*sic*], they had decided' (*TW*, 189). Unlike Malise, who had 'always wanted a child' (*TW*, 190), Stephen is able to envision 'the amazing completeness' of a relationship with Mary (who, as we have seen, is at once 'child' and belovèd to Stephen). Though Carpenter notes the possibility that intermediate types 'may have an important part to play in the evolution of the race' (*TIS*, 24), he laments the 'painful fact that—in consequence of their peculiar temperament—[women of the intermediate type] are, though fond of children, not in the position to found a family' (*TIS*, 29).

292 *What is honour, my daughter?*: Sir Philip speaks these words in Chapter 6 (p. 61).

293 *Viyella*: the first branded fabric in history (registered as a trademark in 1894), made from a blend of wool and cotton.

'Not quite twenty-two': the novel's repeated emphasis on Mary's youth ('the immature figure', p. 270; 'the girl'; 'the child') made it easy for *TWoL*'s denouncers to claim that she was seduced and corrupted by Stephen. In his

scathing attack on *TWoL*, Douglas claimed that the 'pestilence' of 'sexual inversion and perversion' was 'devastating younger generations', 'wrecking young lives', and 'defiling young souls' (in *PP*, 37). Addressing the court, Biron presented Mary as 'a perfectly innocent girl' whom Stephen 'debauches' (in *PP*, 46). Revealingly, a timeline of the novel written in pencil at the beginning of the handwritten draft of Book One begins 'Seduction at 19' and goes on to note: 'War from 1914 to 18 (4 years). Someone ill and Barbara [Mary] who is 20 joins Unit in their place in 1917—last years of war. Seduction of Barbara' (Hall–Troubridge Papers, 13.1).

295 *I'm trying to play straight*: to behave with sincerity and integrity. 'Straight' was not used as a slang term for 'heterosexual' until over a decade later; one of its earliest appearances is in American psychiatrist George W. Henry's (1889–1964) *Sex Variants: A Study of Homosexual Patterns* (1941).

296 *The Villa del Ciprés . . . Puerto*: *Ciprés* is cypress in Spanish; *Puerto* is port. The sixteenth-century town of La Orotava is just over 2 miles inland from the city of Puerto de la Cruz, named Puerto de La Orotava until 1808.

297 *a veritable Eden*: Sarah E. Chinn argues that the primitivist landscape of Tenerife serves as counterpart to the 'always-already lost Eden' of Morton. The island offers 'an escape from the modernity of Europe' and allows for 'the expression of an untroubled lesbian sexuality' (in *PP*, 303, 301). In 'Miss Ogilvy Finds Herself', an English island (inspired by Burgh Island off the coast of south Devon) provides a space of queer possibility.

Santa Cruz: Santa Cruz de Tenerife, capital city of Tenerife and sole capital of the Canary Islands from 1833 to 1927, is 22 miles east of La Orotava. See note to p. 288.

298 *per Dios*: by God (a mild oath, used to intensify a statement).

santa noche: presumably *cestrum nocturnum*, night-blooming jasmine.

tabachero: a name used in the Canary Islands for *Wigandia macrophylla*, a shrub with purple flowers.

299 *soft yellow wine*: Tenerife has produced white wine since the fifteenth century; the island's popular Malvasía wine is pale yellow with a fruity taste.

heliotrope and datura: poisonous night-blooming plants; white datura flowers are known as 'devil's trumpets' and 'hell's bells'.

300 *postigos*: the traditional 'green latticed shutters' (p. 296) that characterize the town's windows and doors.

trailing arbutus: also 'madrones', from the Spanish *madroño* or strawberry tree, small trees or shrubs with edible red berries.

'Vaya . . . boo!': 'Go on, donkey! Celestino, giddy up! Giddy up—boo!'

301 *Teide*: (or *Pico del Teide*, Peak of Teide), an active volcano that last erupted in 1909. Teide is the third highest volcanic structure in the world and the highest point in Spain.

'A-a-a-y! . . . at peace': revisions to the handwritten draft suggest that these lyrics are RH's own (Hall–Troubridge Papers, 14.1). RH's handwritten book of 'Canary Island Songs' is in Hall–Troubridge Papers, 23.3.

303 *pay to the uttermost farthing*: see p. 116 with note.

304 *that night they were not divided*: an echo of 'And in death they were not divided' (see p. 93 with note).

305 *A STRANGE . . . to Mary and Stephen*: in his judgement on the novel, Biron quoted these two sentences and selected passages from this chapter as evidence of 'two people living in filthy sin at Orotava' (in *PP*, 46), arguing that these scenes contradicted the defence's claim 'that there is nothing in this book which in any way is a defense of or appreciation of these practices [of same-sex love]' (*PP*, 46).

For now . . . channels: see Appendix, p. 435 (4.1). The opening line of RH's short story 'Malise' reads: 'This then was the surging up of their love, having something fierce and urgent about it, as the terror and joy and blood of battle, as the thirst of a man who is lost in the desert, as the fearful urge of creation to create, even through sterile channels' (*TW*, 183).

beggars would come . . . heart of the island: a direct echo of p. 301; as before, the lyrics likely spring not from the heart of the island but from RH's pen.

306 *Mary, because she was perfect woman*: Mary's relationship to inversion is unclear: Brockett later describes her as 'a perfectly normal young woman' (p. 334), and the narrator twice notes her normality (pp. 334 and 413) and presents her as 'all woman' (p. 413). In her letters to Souline, RH refers to 'normal love between men and women' (11 Sept. 1935; Hall–Troubridge Papers, 47.3) but also draws on sexological and psychoanalytic theories to argue that 'the bi-sexual is the true normal' (19 Aug. 1934, Hall–Troubridge Papers, 46.5). The phrase 'normal invert' will later appear in *TWoL* (p. 379). Mary's contested identity is discussed in the Introduction (p. xxvii).

307 *amighita*: a misspelling of *amiguita*, meaning girlfriend (literally 'little friend').

Quien sabe?: Who knows?

pesetas: the currency of Spain between 1868 and 2002.

309 *This second home-coming . . . a little glow of pleasure*: in Chapter 9, Stephen imagines how her mother 'passed for the first time through the heavy white doorway' of Morton after marrying Philip (p. 83). In Chapter 15, Stephen finds traces of her father's memory in 'the little inanimate objects' that remain in the house after his death (p. 119).

310 *Invisible Mending people*: a number of companies advertised 'invisible mending' services in the 1910s and 1920s. To provide one example: 'The Invisible Mending Co., 88 Westbourne-grove, by a special process mend all kinds of damaged clothing in such a way that instead of a patch, which however well-pressed can be detected, the hole or tear, or whatever it may be, is mended and is invisible' (*Hampstead News*, 13 July 1913, 2). To 'pick up a ladder' here is to repair a tear in a stocking.

311 *But the moment passed and they drew together. . . .*: 'In order that there be no mistake what is meant by that passage', stated Biron in his judgement,

'there are four asterisks placed directly after it' (in *PP*, 47). See Appendix, p. 435 (5.1).

312 *Bateaux de Location*: rental boats.

bocks, groseille, limonade: beer, redcurrant juice, lemonade.

the Madeleine: the Église Sainte-Marie-Madeleine, a Catholic church on Place de la Madeleine in the eighth arrondissement. Built in neoclassical style, the church imitates the external form of an ancient temple with classical columns on all four sides of the building. The Place de la Madeleine hosts one of the busiest flower markets in Paris.

dray-horses: large horses bred as working animals to pull heavy loads, including carts and carriages carrying passengers.

313 *Lapérouse*: one of the oldest and most elite restaurants in Paris, founded in 1766 and located at 51 Quai de Grands Augustins on the south bank of the Seine. Frequented by writers and artists including Baudelaire, Colette, Marcel Proust (1871–1922), and Émile Zola (1840–1902), in 1933 it became the first restaurant to be awarded three Michelin stars. Though the term 'epicurean' is used to describe a love of sensual pleasure and enjoyment of good food and drink, ancient Greek philosopher Epicurus (341–270 BC) saw modest and sustainable pleasure, enjoyed prudently and in moderation, as the ultimate good.

Mary loved Prunier's . . . English stomachs: Prunier's was a premier seafood restaurant at 9 Rue Duphot, close to the Place de la Madeleine. Founded in 1872, it invented the oyster bar and was the first establishment to sell French caviar (in 1921). Mary enjoys sea urchins (*oursins*), winkles (*bigorneaux*), and smoked eels (*anguilles fumées*).

314 *'Mais regardez moi ça! Elle est belle, la petite; comme c'est rigolo!'*: 'But look at that! She is beautiful, the little one; how funny!'

ils en ont vu bien d'autres: they have seen many others.

Sulka's: A. Sulka & Company, founded in 1895, was a luxury American menswear retailer with shops in New York, Chicago, London, and Paris.

Down the Rue de Rivoli . . . church of St. Germain . . . bloody slaying: named after the Battle of Rivoli at which Napoleon defeated the Austrian army in 1797, the Rue de Rivoli is a fashionable shopping street in the first and fourth arrondissements. The Roman Catholic church Saint-Germain-l'Auxerrois is located south of Rue de Rivoli, directly opposite the Louvre. The ringing of the church bell on the night of 23 August 1572, during the French Wars of Religion (1562–98), is said to have initiated the St Bartholomew's Day Massacre. A violent Catholic mob killed thousands of Huguenots, who were visiting Paris to attend a royal wedding.

315 *the poor Henri*: a character in 'Les Bons Enfants' (see p. 55 with note).

A happy and pleasant visit . . . evening: see Appendix, p. 436 (5.2), where the evening ends on a more melancholy note.

316 *the Worcesters*: the Worcestershire Regiment, an infantry unit raised during the British Army reforms of 1881. Its members served in all of the main theatres of war in the First World War, winning nine Victoria Crosses.

Stephen bought a touring Renault and a . . . landaulette for Mary: a 'touring' car would usually seat four or more passengers; Stephen has purchased hers from French manufacturer Renault (est. 1899). The landaulette motor car takes its name from horse-drawn carriages called landaus, which had a similar design; passengers travelling in the rear of a landaulette would usually be separated from the chauffeur by a division and covered by a convertible top.

swank: 'ostentatious or pretentious behaviour or talk; swagger; pretence' (*OED*).

We're happy, Stephen!: an echo of the birdsong heard after Martin's departure (p. 100) and during Angela's visit to Morton (p. 143).

'Mais voyons, voyons!': 'Come on, come on!', uttered as an expression of disbelief or false indignation.

317 *'More than seventy francs . . . spit in our faces!'*: Buisson is complaining about the long-term impact of the First World War on the French economy, alluding to inflation and reconstruction debt. Germany had begun to default on war reparations soon after the 1919 Treaty of Versailles. 'Sacre Nom!' (literally 'Holy Name!') is an oath, similar to 'For God's sake!' or 'Bloody hell!'

318 *Avenue Victor Hugo*: a prestigious avenue in the sixteenth arrondissement named after the French novelist (1802–85), most famous for his novels *Notre-Dame de Paris* (1831) and *Les Misérables* (1862).

Deauville: a civil parish and fashionable seaside resort in the Normandy region of northern France. Since the mid-nineteenth century, Deauville has been a popular destination for the wealthy. Proust's seven-volume novel *A la recherche du temps perdu* (*In Search of Lost Time*, 1913–27) is set in this area of Normandy.

Stephen . . . daughter: building on ancient Greek pederastic models, some of RH's contemporaries, including Carpenter, presented same-sex relationships with an age gap as potentially beneficial to both parties (*TIS*, 83–106). Though these arguments focused mainly on male–male relationships, the imaginative engagement with Sappho as a teacher of younger female students opened up similar possibilities for lesbian partnerships (Marks, 'Lesbian Intertextuality', 357–8). Martha Vicinus observes that age-unequal relationships between women could also be modelled on mother–daughter bonds (*Intimate Friends: Women Who Loved Women, 1778–1928* (Chicago: Chicago University Press, 2004), 113–42); RH adapts this model by presenting Stephen in the role of her father. RH herself may have benefited from the pedagogical influence of Ladye, who was twenty-four years her senior: in UT's words, Batten saw RH as 'a half-educated young cub who ignored all the important aspects of a civilised existence and preferred hunting to literature, music or the arts' when they first met (*LaD*, 30).

319 *Peter Ibbetson*: 1891 novel by Franco-British writer and cartoonist George du Maurier (1834–96), grandfather of novelist Daphne du Maurier (1907–89). It tells the story of two lovers who are separated in childhood and reunited years later. When Peter is wrongly convicted of murder, the couple discover that they can enter each other's consciousness through a psychological process called 'dreaming true', allowing them to live their lives together even when they are physically separated. UT includes du Maurier's novel in a list of books RH enjoyed due to their 'other-worldly' qualities, which 'seemed to fulfil something in her nature that was dissatisfied with material life; the something that would occasionally make her say that she was feeling happy because for the moment she had a sensation that the veil between this world and another was very tenuous indeed' (*LaD*, 149).

married couples of white fantail pigeons: like the swans at Morton, fantail pigeons are monogamous and will typically keep the same mate for life. Mary makes a request for 'pigeons with wide, white tails' in Chapter 37 (p. 289).

320 *Irish water-spaniel*: the Irish Water Spaniel is instantly recognizable by its densely curled liver-coloured coat, tapering smooth tail, and cleanly chiselled head. Bred for hunting, Irish Water Spaniels are known to be alert, inquisitive, playfully affectionate, and excellent at swimming.

"We . . . Ireland. . . .": the Laws of Hywel Dda (anglicized as 'Howell Dda') are a system of native Welsh laws named after medieval king Hywel Dda (d. 950). The exact origins of Irish Water Spaniels are obscure: the modern breed first appeared in Ireland in the 1830s, but Water Spaniels have a much longer lineage. One suggestion is that Water Spaniels evolved from dogs that originated in Persia and were brought to Ireland via Spain, hence the reference to Iberians introducing the breed.

321 *'David'*: St David (Dewi Sant, *c.* AD 500–89) is the patron saint of Wales.

322 *Oh, but she knew . . . 'Mary . . . remember my mother'*: see Appendix, p. 436 (5.3).

323 *'I would rather see you dead at my feet. . . .'*: Anna speaks these words in Chapter 27 (p. 199).

324 *Yet now as she sat in the empty study*: see Appendix, p. 436 (5.4).

He wanted to make an enormous noise . . . old French colonel: the narrator imagines David's mother's owner to have been a high-ranking official in the French military, possibly stationed in so-called French West Africa (1895–1958), a federation of colonial territories.

325 *'Could you marry me, Stephen?'*: Stephen remembers Angela posing the question in Chapter 19 (p. 149 with note).

326 *some mighty challenge*: see Appendix, p. 437 (5.5).

327 *depends on the sexual mixture*: the Austrian philosopher Otto Weininger (1880–1903) argued in his influential study *Sex and Character* (*Geschlecht und Charakter*, 1903) that masculinity and femininity were mixed in every individual: 'every cell in a multi-cellular organism possesses a combination of the characters of its species and race'. Weininger used the term

'Idioplasm' to describe the 'bearer of the specific characters' and differentiated between 'Arrhenoplasm' (male plasm) and 'Thelyplasm' (female plasm), concluding that 'every single cell possesses a sexuality lying somewhere between arrhenoplasm and thelyplasm' (*Sex and Character* (London: Heinemann, 1906), 16–17). Although Weininger was Jewish, the book was deeply anti-Semitic, denouncing Judaism as 'saturated with femininity' and incapable of distinguishing between 'good and evil' (*Sex and Character*, 306, 309). Weininger's work gained popularity after his death by suicide at the age of 23. Carpenter chose a quote from *Sex and Character* as the epigraph of *TIS*: 'There are transitional forms between the metals and non-metals, between chemical combinations and simple mixtures, between animals and plants, between phanerogams and cryptograms [plants with and without seeds], and between mammals and birds. . . . The improbability may henceforth be taken for granted of finding in Nature a sharp cleavage between all that is masculine on the one side and all that is feminine on the other; or that any living being is so simple in this respect that it can be put wholly on one side, or wholly on the other, of the line' (*TIS*, 6; from *Sex and Character*, 2–3). Weininger's work was also discussed by Hirschfeld (see e.g. *Die Homosexualität des Mannes und des Weibes*, 388–9). RH's contemporary Vita Sackville-West studied *Sex and Character* alongside *The Intermediate Sex* and Ellis's *Studies in the Psychology of Sex*, arriving at the conclusion that 'cases of dual personality do exist, in which the feminine and the masculine elements alternately preponderate. I advance this in an impersonal and scientific spirit, and claim that I am qualified to speak with the intimacy a professional scientist could acquire only after years of study and indirect information, because I have the object of study always to hand, in my own heart, and can gauge the exact truthfulness of what my own experience tells me' (Nicolson, *Portrait of a Marriage*, 106).

bailiff and agent: staff employed to act as stewards and manage the estate, for instance by collecting rent.

328 *jibs*: 'Of a horse or other animal in harness: To stop and refuse to go on [. . .]; to balk stubbornly' (*OED*), used figuratively here. An example of Stephen's frequent use of language related to horsemanship.

2: RH adds a note to her handwritten draft: 'France October 1919' (Hall–Troubridge Papers, 14.1).

329 *Passy*: an area of Paris, located in the sixteenth arrondissement, on the Right Bank.

For although his heart . . . Mary: Mary is likened to her namesake, the Mother of God, who dispenses salvation by giving birth to Christ. David's desire for Stephen's company is aligned with the homosocial male culture of gentlemen's clubs. The most distinguishing feature of White's, the oldest gentlemen's club in London (founded in 1693 and relocated to new premises on St James's Street in 1778), was the famous Bow (or Beau) Window on its ground floor. The table directly in front of the window became a seat of distinction for socially influential men in the club who wished to be seen together.

330 *'Quel drôle de chien, mais regardez sa queue!'*: 'What a funny dog, but look at its tail!'

the Celt in his blood: see the description of 'the Celtic soul' in Chapter 36 (p. 276). Stephen, like Mary and Anna, has 'in her veins the warm Celtic blood' (p. 31). Discussing RH's lineage, UT observes that 'there was plenty of Celtic blood in her maternal ancestry to account for her creative imagination' (*LaD*, 9).

Stephen was working . . . hem of greatness: see Appendix, p. 437 (5.6).

331 *If only Stephen had confided in her*: in the handwritten draft, as in Chapter 36 (p. 280), RH uses a racist simile to describe hard work: 'Don't you know that I'm working like a gall[e]y n***** because I love you?' (Hall–Troubridge Papers, 14.1).

serving two masters: 'No man can serve two masters: for either he will hate the one, and love the other; or else he will hold to the one, and despise the other. Ye cannot serve God and mammon' (Matthew 6:24).

far into the night: UT provides a detailed account of RH's own writing habits, recalling that 'she did not at first work at night; her bad habits grew with the years' (*LaD*, 69).

332 *But Mary would not sleep . . . windows*: see Appendix, p. 437 (5.7).

333 *books that intend to get born:* 'It certainly does not seem impossible to suppose that as the ordinary love has a special function in the propagation of the race, so the other has its special function in social and heroic work, and in the generation—not of bodily children—but of those children of the mind, the philosophical concepts and ideals which transform our lives and those of society' (*TIS*, 70). This line of argument can be traced back to Plato's *Symposium*, which suggests that male same-sex desire is likely to produce 'offspring you might expect a mind to bear', including 'creations brought into the world by the poets' (*Symposium*, 52). Stephen's characters are compared to 'infants' that 'sucked at her breasts of inspiration' in Chapter 28 (p. 209).

What wonderful lilac!: from the time of Sappho, lilacs, lavender, violets, and other purple flowers have had queer connotations. In her poem 'To the Friend of My Youth: To Kitty' (1900), for example, American writer Kate Chopin (1850–1904) compares her love for her female friend Kitty Garesché to a 'mystic garland which the spring did twine | Of scented lilac and new-blown rose' (*The Complete Works of Kate Chopin* (Baton Rouge: Louisiana State University Press, 1969), 735–6 (735)). Jonathan may have purchased the more unusual 'faintly perfumed ascetic white lilac' sold at the flower market on the Place de la Madeleine (p. 312).

334 *neurasthenia*: from the ancient Greek *neuron* ('nerves') and *asthenés* ('weak'), a loosely defined diagnostic category popularized by American neurologist George Miller Beard (1839–83) around 1869. The condition

was believed to be caused by the exhaustion of the central nervous system's energy reserves. Beard's *A Practical Treatise on Nervous Exhaustion (Neurasthenia)* (New York: William Wood & Company, 1880) includes a long list of symptoms ranging from '*Tenderness of the Scalp*' to '*Sick Headache and Various Forms of Head Pain*', '*Hopelessness*', and '*Insomnia*' (15–44). In a posthumous 1884 publication, Beard introduced the term 'sexual neurasthenia (sexual exhaustion)', arguing that this clinical variety of neurasthenia was caused by a range of factors, including 'evil habits, excesses, tobacco, alcohol, worry and special excitements, even climate itself—all the familiar excitants being secondary to the one great predisposing cause—civilization' (George Miller Beard, *Sexual Neurasthenia (Nervous Exhaustion)* (New York: E. B. Treat, 1884), 43, 15). Beard maintained that neurasthenia often affected 'The sensitive white woman [. . .] living in-doors; torn and crossed by happy or unhappy love; subsisting on fiction, journals, receptions; waylaid at all hours by the cruellest of robbers, worry and ambition, that seize the last unit of her force' (*Sexual Neurasthenia*, 59–60). During the First World War, neurasthenia was frequently mentioned (alongside hysteria) in discussions of shell shock (see note to p. 270). Virginia Woolf was first diagnosed as neurasthenic by her family doctor, the prominent English psychiatrist Sir George Henry Savage (1852–1921), who oversaw her health from childhood until her 1913 breakdown. Woolf describes her experience of the rest cure in her essay *On Being Ill* (1926). Neurasthenia remained a common medical diagnosis well into the twentieth century.

But if you were a man: see Appendix, p. 437 (5.8).

335 *according to his lights*: in line with his idea of what is right.

337 *What is sauce for the gander is sauce for the goose*: though generally used to mean that what is acceptable for one person should also be acceptable for another, 'what is sauce for the goose is sauce for the gander' (inverted here by RH) hinges on sex. Similar expressions can be traced back to the Tudor period, e.g. 'But *as deepe drinketh the goose as the gander*' from *The Proverbs of John Heywood* (1546; London: George Bell and Sons, 1874), 143.

mon pauvre bougre: 'my poor bugger'. In her recollections on 'Old Bloomsbury', read to the Memoir Club on 4 July 1928, Woolf famously reveals that 'The word bugger was never very far from our lips' (in *Moments of Being*, ed. Jeanne Schulkind (2nd edn., San Diego: Harcourt Brace Jovanovich, 1985), 179–201 (196)). RH softens the word by including it in French.

338 *For together with those . . . the whip of self-preservation*: the evolutionary argument that sexual inverts must 'hack out a niche in existence' echoes Puddle's thoughts on Stephen's 'niche in creation' in Chapter 20 (p. 153). Carpenter asserted that 'a vast number of intermediates do actually perform most valuable social work, and that they do so partly on account and by reason of their special temperament' (*TIS*, 107). The term 'comrade' to describe kinship between sexual inverts is also taken from Carpenter,

who drew inspiration from Walt Whitman (1819–92; see *TIS*, 75–6). The remainder of the chapter presents a series of sexological case histories, mapping different 'grades' of sexual inversion based on psychological and physiological traits, including 'The timbre of a voice, the build of an ankle, the texture of a hand, a movement, a gesture' (p. 341).

338 *entomological*: entomology is the study of insects.

339 *tow-coloured*: very light blonde.

daub: although the term 'daub' implies that Wanda's work is 'coarsely executed, [and] inartistic' (*OED*), the fact that she smears the canvas with abstract forms suggests that she has developed a modern and non-naturalistic style.

tight: drunk (like 'in her cups' above).

Comtesse de Kerguelen: although the Comtesse de Kerguelen is a little-known historical figure, the character was likely modelled on one of Barney's lovers, the French aristocrat and writer Élisabeth de Gramont, Duchesse de Clermont-Tonnerre (1875–1954). De Gramont was unhappily married to Aimé-François Philibert, Duc de Clermont-Tonnerre (1871–1940), and divorced him in 1920. She had met Barney in 1909 and remained committed to her for life. The handwritten draft describes the Comtesse as 'brave, as brave as a lion. She said: "It is not I who made the world—nor had I the least wish to love this woman but since it has happened—I respect my love, I will fall or stand by it. I am not a coward"' (Hall–Troubridge Papers, 14.2). Lisa Walker argues that the Comtesse de Kerguelen is 'from old money [. . . and] clearly recalls Anna, Stephen's mother. [. . .] The Comtesse represents the puzzle of the upper-class femme with traditional values, the "womanly woman" who has society's approval to lose for identifying as a lesbian, but the strength to leave it all behind' ('Martyred Butches and Impossible Femmes: Radclyffe Hall and the Modern Lesbian', in Walker, *Looking Like What You Are: Sexual Style, Race, and Lesbian Identity* (New York: New York University Press), 53). The subantarctic Kerguelen Islands, also known as the Desolation Islands, are among the most isolated places on Earth.

340 *Adolphe Blanc:* not to be confused with the French violinist and composer (1828–85). There are parallels between Blanc's failed efforts to seek a 'cure' for his homosexuality and Forster's *Maurice*, in which the protagonist consults an American hypnotist, Dr Lasker Jones, to try to rid himself of his desire for men. As with Blanc, Maurice's encounter with the doctor only serves to affirm his identity as an 'invert' who is diagnosed with 'Congenital homosexuality'. See E. M. Forster, *Maurice* (London: Penguin, 2005), 190, 160. Although the portrayal of Blanc is largely sympathetic, RH held strongly antisemitic views (*AWCJ*, 361).

341 *And such people . . . this indestructible creature*: Barnes's *Ladies Almanack* (1928; New York: New York University Press, 1992) opens with an amusing illustration of Dame Evangeline Musset, a fictionalized version of

Barney, 'carrying a pole and muff' to save women from 'sinking' in a frozen pond (iv).

342 *And their love affairs, how strange, how bewildering . . . a woman's clinging dependence on Jamie*: Ellis acknowledged that female sexual inverts were often attracted to women whose sexuality was more difficult to categorize: 'A class in which homosexuality, while fairly distinct, is only slightly marked, is formed by the women to whom the actively inverted woman is most attracted. [. . .] So far as they may be said to constitute a class, they seem to possess a genuine, though not precisely sexual, preference for women over men, and it is this coldness, rather than lack of charm, which often renders men rather indifferent to them. The actively inverted woman usually differs from the woman of the class just mentioned in one fairly essential character: a more or less distinct trace of masculinity' (*SI*, 222).

Beedles: most likely a fictional village in the Scottish Highlands. The similar-sounding Peebles is a town in the Scottish Borders.

mouching: presumably an alternative spelling of 'mooching'.

grand-dame: grandmother.

'I dinna . . . no proaper!': 'I don't fully understand it, [. . .] her and that Jamie's odd relationship. It's not right for a girl-child, and it's not proper!' The Scottish term 'throng' can also refer to 'Company, intimacy, close friendship' (*OED*).

343 *a soft, timorous woman*: 'Wee, sleekit, cowrin, tim'rous beastie, | O, what a panic's in thy breastie!' are the opening lines of Scottish Bard Robert Burns's (1759–96) 'To a Mouse, on Turning Her Up in Her Nest With the Plough' (1785).

manse: 'a house allocated to or occupied by a minister of certain Nonconformist or non-episcopal Churches, esp. the Church of Scotland' (*OED*).

Sabbath afternoons: 'Remember the sabbath day, to keep it holy' (Exodus 20:8) is one of the ten commandments. In 1918, the Church of Scotland defended Sabbatarianism, arguing that 'Scotland should determine to abide by its Sabbath-keeping character' (William Speirs Bruce, 'The Decline of Discipline', in William Paterson and David Watson (eds.), *Social Evils and Problems: Edited for the Church of Scotland Commission on the War* (Edinburgh: W. Blackwood, 1918), 156).

Inverness: a town (now a city) on the north-east coast of Scotland, often considered the capital of the Highlands.

344 *Conservatoire*: the Conservatoire de Paris, a world-famous college of music and dance founded in 1795.

General Custer: George Armstrong Custer (1839–76), a United States Army officer and cavalry commander. Pat is referring to the Battle of the Little Bighorn (25–6 June 1876), often described as Custer's Last Stand or Ride. Adding to the long-standing settler-colonial violence against Indigenous people, Custer and his troops broke the Sioux Treaty of 1868 and attacked an encampment of Lakota, Cheyenne, and Arapaho people in the region. The combined forces of these tribes achieved an overwhelming victory over the US army, killing 268 of its members, including Custer himself. UT fantasized that RH's 'face and features' were 'distinctly reminiscent of the North American Indian' (*LaD*, 9). The phrase 'miserable army' is used on three further occasions to refer to sexual inverts (pp. 368, 371, 377).

345 *sight of a harbour*: see Appendix, p. 437 (5.9), where this section concludes with a brief discussion of sexological and psychoanalytical theories.

Lethe: in Greek mythology, the Lethe is one of the rivers of the underworld. The dead could drink from the river to erase memories from their previous life. In Classical Greek, the word 'lethe' means 'oblivion' or 'forgetfulness'.

Valérie Seymour's lion: Valérie sees Stephen as a 'person of note or celebrity' (*OED*).

346 *since that rib was demanded of Adam*: 'And the LORD God caused a deep sleep to fall upon Adam, and he slept: and he took one of his ribs, and closed up the flesh instead thereof; And the rib, which the LORD God had taken from man, made he a woman, and brought her unto the man' (Genesis 2: 21–2).

347 *the Marennes*: a coastal area in the Nouvelle-Aquitaine region of eastern France, famous for its oyster farms.

crême-de-menthe: crème de menthe is a sweet, mint-flavoured liqueur invented by French pharmacist Emile Giffard (1842–1901) in 1885.

Rue Visconti: named after Louis Visconti (1791–1853), the designer of Napoleon's tomb. The street is near to Stephen and Mary's apartment in the sixth arrondissement.

349 *kirk*: church (Scottish).

350 *Every one was coming . . . the evening would be spoilt without Mary and Stephen*: the scene is inspired by a private concert by American singers Taylor Gordon (1893–1971) and J. Rosamond Johnson (1873–1954) at RH and UT's Kensington home (see Introduction, p. xxx). Gordon and Johnson achieved fame as a singing duo, touring the US, France, and England together in the late 1920s. Gordon and Johnson were acclaimed for their performance of spirituals in private houses and public venues, including New York's Carnegie Hall and London's Coliseum and Wigmore Hall. The concert at RH and UT's home was attended by members of London's literary establishment, including Gabrielle Enthoven (1868–1950), John Galsworthy, Violet Hunt (1862–1942), Margaret Irwin (1889–1967), Sheila Kaye-Smith (1887–1956), and Lowther (*AWCJ*, 220–1). Johnson composed the spiritual 'Lift Every Voice and Song' and compiled the classic *Book of American Negro Spirituals* (1925) together with his brother, the writer James Weldon Johnson (1871–1938), who observed that the book honours 'the unknown black bards' who created the Black

spiritual tradition: 'As many as survived the passage [across the Atlantic] were immediately thrown into slavery. [. . .] [I]t was from these people this mass of noble music sprang; this music which is America's only folk music and, up to this time, the finest distinctive artistic contribution she has to offer the world' (James Weldon Johnson and J. Rosamond Johnson (eds.), *The Book of American Negro Spirituals* (New York: Viking Press, 1925), 12–13). Jean Walton reads the concert scene as indicative of RH's attempt to articulate a sense of 'alliance' with Black people while also foregrounding its racist politics (in *PP*, 298).

They were very unlike each other: Walton highlights the racist dynamics expressed in the description of the two brothers: 'the lightness of Lincoln's skin is an indication of his relative position on an evolutionary scale; [. . .] it is because the white admixture in his blood has brought him to an evolutionary stage that is nearer than Henry's to that of his white audience members' (in *PP*, 283). In the handwritten draft, RH describes Henry as a 'coarse[-]lipped young n*****' (Hall–Troubridge Papers, 14.2).

351 *abolitionist Boston*: the capital of Massachusetts was a hub of anti-slavery activity. The city's abolitionist movement emerged from a long-settled free Black population and included such organizations as the New England Anti-Slavery Society, founded in 1832. Pat's reservations towards Henry and Lincoln indicate concerns about Black emancipation. Similar racist sentiments can be found elsewhere in RH's work and life. The early short story 'The Career of Mark Anthony Brakes' (*c.*1914–15) reinforces anti-Black ideologies according to which free, educated, and socially mobile Black men pose a threat to white women. Describing a year that RH spent in the US in her twenties, UT claims that she 'drove her cousin Jane Randolph (later Caruth) all over the States in a primitive car with one spark-plug at the back and a revolver handy for obstreperous negroes' (*LaD*, 19).

'Deep river . . . camp ground. . . .': 'Deep River' is an anonymously written African American spiritual. The song was performed in 1875 by the Fisk Jubilee Singers—a group of African American singers made up of students from the historically Black Fisk University in Nashville, Tennessee, who toured the US and Europe—and popularized by American composer and singer Henry Thacker Burleigh (1866–1949) in his 1916 collection *Jubilee Songs of the USA*. Like other Black spirituals composed in conditions of slavery, the song draws heavily on metaphor and double meaning. 'Camp ground' refers to a temporary dwelling on a journey; the term 'camp' appears frequently in Exodus, which narrates the Israelites' escape from slavery in Egypt. A home 'over Jordan' is a reference to the miraculous crossing of the river Jordan in the Bible, where God parts the waters to allow the Israelites to enter the promised land after forty years in the desert (Joshua 3). American audiences would have been reminded of the Ohio River, which represented a pronounced dividing line between the American North and South, and between freedom and enslavement. A home over Jordan also evokes a journey towards a heavenly home and

place of deliverance (e.g. Deuteronomy 12:10) and towards a lost home across the Atlantic on the African continent. See Appendix, p. 438 (5.10), where the concert opens differently.

352 *the recording angel*: angels assigned with the task of recording the actions of each individual, including their sins and good deeds. In 1915, RH wrote a short story titled 'The Rechording [*sic*] Angel' (Hall–Troubridge Papers, 20.6).

brethren: in Walton's reading, the use of the term 'brethren' instead of 'brothers' here suggests that the 'rules of kinship' must be extended beyond blood relations (in *PP*, 287).

'Didn't my Lord . . . every man?': another spiritual of unknown origin included in the Fisk Jubilee Singers' repertoire in 1875. The lyrics refer to the biblical Daniel who is thrown into a lion's den and saved through divine intervention (Daniel 6:16–24).

353 *burg*: colloquial American English for 'city'. In the handwritten draft, Henry starts 'to dance in the manner of Harlem' after making the invitation (Hall–Troubridge Papers, 14.2).

354 *'Oh, my, . . . nobody's baby'*: a fragment of the song 'I'm Nobody's Baby', first recorded by American singer Aileen Stanley (1893–1982) in 1921. In contrast to the spirituals sung earlier in the evening, the song is popular and secular, ostensibly expressing the singer's longing for a lover. Walton reads Henry's 'high falsetto' as a sign of his inversion (in *PP*, 293).

355 *a very sensational success*: a timeline included in a notebook suggests that Stephen's second novel is published in May 1920 (Hall–Troubridge Papers, 14.2). RH's fourth novel, *Adam's Breed*, published two years before *TWoL*, was an international success and translated into several languages (see Introduction, p. xi).

'Mais oui, un grand génie doit nourrir le cerveau!': 'Yes, a great genius must feed their brain!'

356 *Lake Como . . . Hotel Florence at Bellagio*: founded in 1864, the Hotel Florence is located in the *comune* of Bellagio on Lake Como in northern Italy's Lombardy region.

357 *Branscombe Court*: fictional, but RH may have drawn inspiration from Dunham Massey, a historic seventeenth-century Georgian house surrounded by a 300-acre deer park and located between Manchester and the beginnings of rural Cheshire. RH's paternal great-grandfather, John Radcliffe Hall (1785–1861), established family estates in Congleton, Cheshire (*AWCJ*, 12–13).

Ascot or Goodwood: the famous Ascot Racecourse is in Berkshire, England, on land leased from the Crown Estate and in close proximity to Windsor Castle. Founded by Queen Anne in 1711, the racecourse hosts Royal Ascot, a week of races attended by the Royal Family. Goodwood Racecourse is on the Goodwood Estate, owned by the family of the Duke of Richmond, in East Sussex. Stephen evidently 'despises' the social character and 'self-satisfied' snobbery of the upper classes.

The Tatler or The Sketch: *The Tatler* (later *Tatler*) was introduced in 1901, taking its name from the society journal founded by Anglo-Irish writer and politician Richard Steele (1671–1729) in 1709. Aimed at an upper-middle- and upper-class readership, *The Tatler* primarily covered high society events, fashion, and gossip. *The Sketch* was a British illustrated weekly journal that ran between 1893 and 1959, discussing royalty, aristocracy, and high society, and featuring photographs and reports of society ladies and their children. Both journals were founded by British journalist and literary critic Clement King Shorter (1857–1926). RH and UT made multiple appearances in *The Tatler*, both with and without their dachshunds; they were caricatured in a cartoon captioned 'At Any First Night In Any London Theatre' in the 30 November 1928 edition, just weeks after the end of the British censorship trial.

358 *shooting stick*: 'a walking-stick with a handle that may be opened to form an impromptu seat, first used by shooters' (*OED*).

the Ritz: the Ritz Paris was founded in 1898 by Swiss hotelier César Ritz (1850–1918) on Place Vendôme in the first arrondissement. Considered one of the most luxurious hotels in the world, it featured in Noël Coward's play *Semi-Monde* (written in 1926, but not produced until 1977).

359 *firstfruits*: 'The earliest products or results of anything; the first products of a person's work or endeavour' (*OED*). See also: 'Honour the LORD with thy substance, and with the firstfruits of all thine increase: so shall thy barns be filled with plenty, and thy presses shall burst out with new wine' (Proverbs 3:9–10).

360 *a kind of gigantic destroying angel*: 'So the LORD sent pestilence upon Israel: and there fell of Israel seventy thousand men. And God sent an angel unto Jerusalem to destroy it: and as he was destroying, the LORD beheld, and he repented him of the evil, and said to the angel that destroyed, It is enough, stay now thine hand' (1 Chronicles 21:14–15).

361 *An ill wind . . . good*: adapted from 'Ill blows the wind that profits nobody' (Shakespeare, *3 Henry VI*, II. v. 55), meaning that one person's misfortune is often another's good luck.

terrified of receiving the Christmas Communion: in the Catholic faith, worshippers must not receive Holy Communion until they have been delivered of their mortal sin.

362 *From every town and village . . . small stone*: the construction of the Sacré-Cœur began in 1875 and continued for forty years under five different architects. It was financed by private donations from various parishes across France; the names of donors are engraved across the church's walls.

the Angelus bells, the Vesperbells: church bells are rung to mark fixed times of prayer. The Angelus is a devotion commemorating the Incarnation of

Christ, usually recited three times a day. Vespers is the evening prayer service.

362 *years of persecution and strife . . . Mother Church*: from the mid-seventeenth century, the Polish-Lithuanian Commonwealth, founded in 1569, was devastated by a prolonged period of war. A series of invasions and partitions of Polish territory carried out by the Russian Empire, Kingdom of Prussia, and the Habsburg monarchy led to the dissolution of the Commonwealth in 1795. Despite the strength of Polish resistance movements, in which the Polish language and Catholic faith played a vital role, sovereignty was only regained after the First World War with the establishment of the Second Polish Republic in 1918.

363 *fox-trot*: usually danced to big band music, the foxtrot premiered in 1914 and reached the height of its popularity in the 1930s.

364 *Stephen's look of surprise*: RH would later express her disapproval of Souline's drinking habits: 'Thank you, thank you for saying that you will be careful not to drink so many cocktails, that you'll avoid spirits. Wine is good for you, by all means drink wine, but the other things—well I just sit and tremble. Darling love—if I did not fear for your health you should not only drink but have a bath in vodka! Or in cocktails, or in whiskey and brandy, for that matter!' (26 Oct. 1934; Hall–Troubridge Papers, 46.6).

365 *she was prejudiced against Wanda's religion*: Wales has a long tradition of religious nonconformism. Non-Anglican Protestant denominations, including Methodism, offered alternatives to the Church of England (established in Wales from 1534 to 1920) and the self-governing, but still Anglican, Church in Wales (established in 1920). Welsh Nonconformists were also 'critical of what they saw as the "alien" status of the Roman Catholic Church' (Paul Chambers and Andrew Thompson, 'Coming to Terms with the Past: Religion and Identity in Wales', *Social Compass*, 52/3 (Sept. 2005), 275–405 (342)).

statue of the silver Christ: as the name suggests, the Sacré-Cœur is dedicated to the Sacred Heart of Christ, a symbol of boundless divine love. The church features a 1912 silver statue of Christ by French sculptor Eugène Benet (1863–1942).

366 *Our name is legion*: in the New Testament, Jesus addresses a man who is possessed by several demons: 'What *is* thy name? And he answered, saying, My name *is* Legion: for we are many' (Mark 5:9).

monstrance: the vessel in which the consecrated host, which worshippers consume during Holy Communion to be united with Christ, is carried and displayed during religious ceremonies and processions. Wanda and Stephen are separated from the host by the 'lake of fire'. This phrase appears four times in Revelation and is symbolic of eternal pain as punishment for wickedness, e.g. 'And the devil that deceived them was cast into the lake of fire and brimstone, where the beast and the false prophet *are,* and shall be tormented day and night for ever and ever' (Revelation 20:10).

the Lady Chapel: as Catholics believe that Christ's body and blood are present in the consecrated host, it is treated with profound reverence. Stephen and Wanda will observe the ritual during which the host is carried from the Lady Chapel, a side chapel within the Sacré-Cœur dedicated to the Virgin Mary, to the high altar in the main basilica. The Sacré-Cœur has continually displayed the Blessed Sacrament (a consecrated host) since 1885, before its construction was completed.

367 *And even . . . heavy-laden*: in the Middle Ages, people with leprosy had to wear bells to warn others of their presence. The New Testament offers accounts of Jesus healing the afflicted, e.g. 'And there came a leper to him, beseeching him, and kneeling down to him, and saying unto him, If thou wilt, thou canst make me clean. And Jesus, moved with compassion, put forth *his* hand, and touched him, and saith unto him, I will; be thou clean. And as soon as he had spoken, immediately the leprosy departed from him, and he was cleansed' (Mark 1:40–2).

368 *1*: RH adds a note to her handwritten draft: 'Mary 25. 1921' (Hall–Troubridge Papers, 14.2).

369 *like Dead Sea fruit*: 'a fruit [. . .] which, according to legend, appears tempting but dissolves into smoke and ashes when grasped'; here used figuratively to describe 'something which does not live up to expectations' (*OED*).

Brand's jelly: see note to p. 206.

370 *the Ideal Bar*: although the bars in the chapter are fictional, Paris was home to a number of lesbian and queer establishments in the 1920s, including *Le Monocle* in Montparnasse, and *Claire de Lune*, *Chez Ma Cousine*, and *La Petite Chaumière* in Montmartre. Cline observes that RH's 'portrayal of the Paris homosexual community', which was 'wrapped up in self-loathing', 'deeply disturbed many of her friends' (*AWCJ*, 273).

Dickie West the American aviator: possibly modelled on Amelia Earhart, the first female aviator to fly solo across the Atlantic (in 1932). Born in Kansas in 1897, the boyish Earhart fits the description of Dickie as belonging to 'the younger, and therefore more reckless, more aggressive and self-assured generation'. Earhart achieved international celebrity status in June 1928, just a month before *TWoL*'s publication, when she became the first female passenger to cross the Atlantic by plane. She is rumoured to have been romantically involved with feminist Eleanor Roosevelt (1884–1962), American First Lady from 1933 to 1945. Earhart disappeared during an attempt to circumnavigate the world in July 1937 and was declared dead in January 1939.

apache scarf: a necktie inspired by a cowboy's neckerchief and named after a group of Native American tribes in the American Southwest. An apache scarf was a fashionable accessory for a woman in the 1920s. A 1925 American *Vogue* illustration shows a female model wearing a tailored double-breasted jacket together with a flared skirt and apache scarf ('The

Double-Breasted Note is a New Theme with Molyneux', *Vogue*, 66/12 (Dec. 1925), 56).

371 *Like the horseleech's daughter*: 'The horseleach hath two daughters, *crying*, Give, give' (Proverbs 30:15). A horse leech is a predatory worm that infests the mouth and nasal passages of horses.

Camel cigarettes: an American brand of pre-packaged cigarettes, first introduced in 1913 by the R. J. Reynolds Tobacco Company. In contrast to Brockett's 'strong, rough tobacco' (p. 225), Camel cigarettes originally featured a blend of Turkish and American leaves and were marketed as milder than competing brands.

Enfin: literally 'finally', but often used in speech to mean 'well' (similar to 'Eh bien', p. 286).

372 *bibelots*: small ornaments or decorative objects; trinkets.

en secondes noces: in a second marriage.

Yet nothing escaped . . . notebook: gathering case histories of his clients without their knowledge or consent, Monsieur Pujol takes on the sinister role of an amateur sexologist. Pujol's collection of visual evidence is reminiscent of Hirschfeld's *Zwischenstufenwand* (Wall of Sexual Intermediaries), an image tableau featuring photographs of gender and sexually nonconforming individuals, first shown at an international medical congress in London in 1913 (Hirschfeld, *Von Einst bis Jetzt: Geschichte einer homosexuellen Bewegung* (Berlin: Rosa Winkel, 1986), 181).

a petit verre: literally 'a little glass'; a drink.

absinthe: a highly alcoholic anise-flavoured drink originating in late eighteenth-century Switzerland. On account of its green colour and fabled hallucinogenic properties, it is often described as *la fée verte* or the green fairy. By 1915, the drink had been banned in several countries, including France, owing to concerns about its harmful effects and its potential role in violent crimes.

Crénom!: a contraction of 'Sacré Nom!' (p. 317); an oath.

just a common whore: Ellis comments on 'the frequency of homosexuality among prostitutes'. A note by an unnamed friend included in *Sexual Inversion* reads: 'From my experience of the Parisian prostitute, I gather that Lesbianism in Paris is extremely prevalent; indeed, one might almost say normal' (*SI*, 211).

373 *ces invertis*: 'these inverts'.

'Le salaud!': 'The bastard!'

374 *Le Narcisse*: 'The Narcissus'. Narcissus is a genus of spring-flowering perennial plants of the amaryllis family. In Greek mythology, Narcissus is a beautiful young man who falls in love with his own reflection and dies when he falls into a pool; the flower bearing his name springs up in his place. Freud associates male homosexuality with narcissism: 'In all the cases examined we have ascertained that the later inverts go through in their childhood a phase of very intense but short-lived fixation on the

woman (usually on the mother) and after overcoming it they identify themselves with the woman and take themselves as the sexual object; that is, proceeding on a narcissistic basis, they look for young men resembling themselves in persons whom they wish to love as their mother has loved them.' See 'Three Essays on the Theory of Sexuality', in *The Standard Edition of the Complete Psychological Works of Sigmund Freud*, vii, trans. James Strachey (London: Hogarth Press, 1953), 123–246 (n. 145).

belotte: or 'belote', a thirty-two-card game played in France since 1900. The rules of the game were published in French in 1921.

vendeuse: saleswoman.

375 *Elgin marble*: the Elgin Marbles (also known as the Parthenon Sculptures) are a collection of architectural decorations from the temple of Athena (the Parthenon) on the Acropolis in Athens. Most of the sculptures were created under the direction of sculptor and architect Phidias (*c.*480–430 BC). Thomas Bruce, 7th Earl of Elgin (1766–1841), who served as the British Ambassador to the Ottoman Empire, ordered for the sculptures to be removed from Ottoman Greece and transported to Britain where they are still held in the British Museum. Many of the sculptures depict scenes of conflict and war, including the battle between Centaurs and Lapiths at the marriage-feast of Pirithous and Hippodamia.

376 *boites:* short for *boîtes de nuit*, nightclubs.

fœtid: 'Having an offensive smell; stinking' (*OED*).

377 *Of all ages . . . Dance of Death to Stephen*: the Dance of Death, or the *Danse Macabre*, is an artistic genre of allegory of the late Middle Ages on the universality of death, functioning as a form of memento mori to invite reflection on mortality. The inverts of 'all grades of mental and physical ill-being' stand in stark contrast to the ideal of the respectable and intellectually gifted sexual invert that Stephen represents.

'Et voilà, mes filles!': 'There you go, my girls!'

chaplet: a string of prayer beads.

378 *one-step*: a popular social dance with basic steps.

'Ma sœur': 'My sister'. Stephen responds with 'Mon frère' ('My brother').

'It's looking for God who made it': Stephen is reminded of the hunted fox in Chapter 15 (p. 124).

379 *'Do you comprehend? There is no destruction'*: in UT's words, RH wanted to write 'a novel [about sexual inversion] that would be accessible to the general public who did not have access to technical treatises' (*LaD*, 81). Ellis's Commentary highlights the special 'psychological and sociological significance' of RH's literary treatment of sexual inversion. For Douglas, the theme of sexual inversion 'is utterly inadmissible in the novel, because the novel is read by people of all ages [. . .]. Therefore, many things that are discussed in scientific textbooks cannot decently be discussed in a work of fiction offered to the general reader' (in *PP*, 37).

381 *Notre-Dame-des-Victoires:* a Catholic basilica in the second arrondissement, constructed between 1629 and 1740 in the French classical style.

déjeuner de noces: wedding breakfast.

Palais Royal: a former French royal palace originally built in 1639 opposite the Louvre in the first arrondissement. The complex was partially commercialized in 1784 and redesigned as a new style of shopping arcade, selling luxury goods to the elite.

'Va donc! Tu ne peux pas m'aider, mon chou, veux tu te taire, alors!': 'Go then! You cannot help me, my dear, do you want to shut up, then!'

eyes like those of a blackbird: Lady Anna 'loved the songs of blackbirds' (p. 33).

382 *Missals:* liturgical books containing instructions and texts for the celebration of Mass.

The Mass . . . third and fourth generation: see p. 104 with note.

383 *'Quel type! . . . ce n'est pas celle-là qui trouvera un mari!' . . . 'Mais oui . . . bizarre'*: 'What a one! Looks more like a man; it is not she who will find a husband!' The guests respond: 'Well yes, she is really strange.'

'Faut dépêcher vous . . . chemin de fer . . . Guard de Lions': 'You have to hurry, 'urry, if you're going to catch that railway'. 'Guard de Lions' is a mispronunciation of the Gare de Lyon, one of the six large railway stations in Paris, located in the twelfth arrondissement.

384 *the last of the Gordons*: *The Last of the Mohicans: A Narrative of 1757* (1826) is a popular historical romance novel by American author James Fenimore Cooper (1789–1851). The novel engages with the genocide of Native American tribes as a result of settler colonialism. 'Mohicans' was Cooper's composite name, which he derived from two different Algonquin tribes, the Mahicans and Mohegans.

385 *Houlgate*: a seaside resort in the Normandy region of northern France.

386 *sex-frustration*: Krafft-Ebing, among others, maintained that sexual abstinence could contribute to psychological and physical ill health. To quote from his section on 'Homosexual Feeling as a Congenital Pathological Manifestation': 'Neuroses (hysteria, neurasthenia, epileptoid states, etc.) co-exist. Almost always the existence of temporary or lasting neurasthenia may be proved. As a rule, this is constitutional, having its root in congenital conditions. It is awakened and maintained by masturbation or enforced abstinence' (*PS*, 227). The presumably 'normal' wife of Krafft-Ebing's Case 113, a neurasthenic man with an 'abnormal sexual instinct for his own sex', became 'hysteropathic and anæmic, and the patient attributed this to sexual abstinence' (*PS*, 263, 266).

388 *bairn*: a Scottish term for a child.

389 *double pneumonia*: inflammation of the tissue in both lungs (hence 'double'), caused by an infection in the air sacs.

Calvary: the site of Jesus' crucifixion ('And when they were come to the place, which is called Calvary, there they crucified him', Luke 23:33).

392 *And so Jamie . . . home before her*: the high rate of suicide among homosexual people is noted in a number of sexological works. Hirschfeld compiled a list of over 100 cases, stressing that he knew more than half of the affected individuals personally (*Die Homosexualität*, 903). Although the suicide risk was deemed higher for men, Ellis notes that 'Homosexual relationships are also a cause of suicide among women' (*SI*, 202).

395 *like a poisonous asp pressed against their bosoms*: according to legend, Cleopatra died by suicide at the age of 39 after allowing an asp, a poisonous Egyptian cobra, to bite her. She is often depicted holding the snake to her chest.

canker in our midst: used figuratively, a canker is 'A malignant or destructive influence that corrodes or corrupts, and is difficult to eradicate' (*OED*). 'The Canker in Our Midst' is the title of Edgar Wallace's controversial *London Mail* article on sexual perversion in the theatre world, published 1926.

that curious craving for religion . . . hand in hand with inversion: Ellis remarks that 'it is undoubtedly true, beyond possibility of doubt, that they [persons of homosexual temperament] have been prominent in religion' (*SI*, 28). Carpenter discusses the 'connection of homosexuality with divination and religion' at length in *Intermediate Types Among Primitive Folks* (London: George Allen and Co., 1914, 12).

396 *Nature . . . increasing numbers*: *The Intermediate Sex* opens thus: 'The subject dealt with in this book is one of great, and one may say growing, importance. Whether it is that the present period is one of large increase in the numbers of men and women of an intermediate or mixed temperament, or whether it merely is that it is a period in which more than usual attention happens to be accorded to them, the fact certainly remains that the subject has great actuality and is pressing upon us from all sides' (*TIS*, 9).

'Plus je connais les hommes, plus j'aime les chiens': 'The more I know of men, the more I love dogs.'

397 *le revers de la médaille*: the other side of the coin.

when you come into your kingdom: one of the two men being crucified next to Christ converses with him: 'Jesus, Lord, remember me when thou comest into thy kingdom. And Jesus said unto him, Verily I say unto thee, To day shalt thou be with me in paradise' (Luke 23:42–3).

398 *young cherry-tree*: in Chapter 11, blossoming cherry trees herald Martin's proposal (p. 96).

400 *scyllas*: or scillas (sometimes called squills), bulbous perennial plants that produce bell- or star-shaped flowers in the spring. In Greek mythology, Scylla and Charybdis were dangerous sea monsters; in idiomatic English, to be 'between Scylla and Charybdis' is to be forced to choose between two risky or unpleasant situations.

403 *Faubourg St. Germain*: one of the most exclusive districts of Paris, historically home to high nobility and the centre of upper-class social life.

ancien régime: the 'old order', the social and political system of France from the late Middle Ages until the French Revolution.

406 *Claridge's . . . Ciro's*: Le Claridge Champs-Elysées was a luxury hotel (1914–76). '[O]ne of the first in Europe to offer a cocktail', it was 'filled with the famous and the wealthy' in the 1920s ('Paris Claridge's Last Day', *Globe and Mail*, 29 Dec. 1976, 10). Ciro's was a fashionable restaurant chain with establishments in cities including Monte Carlo, Deauville, and London. The Paris branch was opened in 1912 on the ground floor of the Hotel Daunou at the corner of the Rue de la Paix and the Rue Daunou. It was advertised as 'the leading restaurant from the point of view of *cuisine*, but also the most sumptuous', attracting 'all the best-known actresses and leaders of society' ('Ciro's', *The Bystander*, 14 Jan. 1914, 104).

407 *Barbizon*: a small town and *commune* on the edge of the forest of Fontainebleau, around 37 miles south of Paris.

408 *Rip Van Winkle*: the eponymous hero of Washington Irving's popular short story, published in 1819, who imbibes a magic potion and sleeps for twenty years, waking up to find that he has aged (hence 'growing hoary like Rip Van Winkle') and the American Revolution has taken place.

412 *Pontresina*: a mountain village and popular starting point for walks through the Val Roseg (Roseg Valley) towards the 'wide slope of the Roseg Glacier' (p. 413) in the Eastern Swiss Alps.

a double cure: the thermal springs at the French spa resorts of Vichy, in the Auvergne-Rhône-Alpes region, and Bagnoles de l'Orne, in the Orne department of Normandy, are known for their healing properties. The Comtesse would have been among thousands of annual visitors taking a cure. RH and UT took the waters at Bagnoles de l'Orne 'at irregular intervals, for John the humanitarian was reaping the harvest sown by John the sportsman' (*LaD*, 85); RH would meet Souline there in 1934.

413 *for as great . . . Stephen*: in a letter to Souline written on 27 July 1934 at the Pont Royal Hotel in Paris, RH expressed a similarly passionate urge: 'For you are not a woman of ice and this I well know, my little virgin, and I agonized to take your virginity and to bind you to me with the chains of the flesh because I had and have so vast a need that my wretched body has become my torment—but through it all my spirit cries out to you Souline' (Hall–Troubridge Papers, 46.5).

416 *marry you from my house*: traditionally, a woman would marry 'from the house' of her parents or guardian. Stephen is clearly being sarcastic here.

420 *mendicant*: 'a person who lives by begging' (*OED*), often used figuratively as is the case here. A mendicant is also a member of a Roman Catholic religious order who has assumed a vow of poverty and committed themselves to work and charity.

422 *Auberge du Vieux Logis*: a restaurant at 33 rue Lepic, Montmartre, now Le Basilic.

'En voilà une originale—et quelle cicatrice, bon Dieu!': 'There's an original—and what a scar, good Lord!'

423 *Moulin de la Galette*: a seventeenth-century windmill that opened as a cabaret in 1830. Pierre-Auguste Renoir (1841–1919) painted *Bal du moulin de la Galette* (*Danse at Le Moulin de la Galette*) in 1876. Roe explains that 'the old windmill-turned-dance-hall was nowhere near as decadent as the Moulin Rouge. In fact, by the standards of Montmartre, the Moulin de la Galette was really quite proper' (*In Montmartre*, 66).

temple of faith: the Basilica of Sacré-Cœur (see pp. 362 and 365).

'Sainte Marie . . . notre morte': 'Holy Mary, Mother of God, pray for us, poor sinners, now and at the hour of our death.' These lines end the 'Hail Mary', a traditional Catholic prayer.

426 *To give light to them that sit in darkness . . .*: 'To give light to them that sit in darkness and *in* the shadow of death, to guide our feet into the way of peace' (Luke 1:79).

427 *our name is legion*: see p. 366 with note.

'We have asked for bread . . . will you give us a stone?': 'Or what man is there of you, whom if his son ask bread, will he give him a stone?' (Matthew 7:9). We are reminded here of Wanda's prayers in Chapter 47 (p. 366) and of Adolphe Blanc's words in Chapter 48: 'Many [inverts] die, many kill their bodies and souls, but they cannot kill the justice of God, even they cannot kill the eternal spirit. From their very degradation that spirit will rise up to demand of the world compassion and justice' (p. 379). The closing paragraphs build on philosophical traditions that present intellectual and creative labour as a form of spiritual childbirth (see note to p. 333).

MORE ABOUT **OXFORD WORLD'S CLASSICS**

American Literature

British and Irish Literature

Children's Literature

Classics and Ancient Literature

Colonial Literature

Eastern Literature

European Literature

Gothic Literature

History

Medieval Literature

Oxford English Drama

Philosophy

Poetry

Politics

Religion

The Oxford Shakespeare
